LIFE

A NOVEL BY

LINES

Joseph Viertel

SIMON AND SCHUSTER · NEW YORK

COPYRIGHT © 1982 BY JOSEPH VIERTEL
ALL RIGHTS RESERVED
INCLUDING THE RIGHT OF REPRODUCTION
IN WHOLE OR IN PART IN ANY FORM
PUBLISHED BY SIMON AND SCHUSTER
A DIVISION OF GULF & WESTERN CORPORATION
SIMON & SCHUSTER BUILDING
ROCKEFELLER CENTER
1230 AVENUE OF THE AMERICAS
NEW YORK, NEW YORK 10020
SIMON AND SCHUSTER AND COLOPHON ARE
TRADEMARKS OF SIMON & SCHUSTER

MANUFACTURED IN THE UNITED STATES OF AMERICA

Acknowledgments

I dare not yet name those in the Soviet Union who helped me—at risk to themselves. They were a courageous and determined band of men and women.

Outside the Soviet Union many other people helped, among them:

In New York: Sarah Frankel, Moshe Decter, Schlomo Noble, Sheila Kessler, Ernest Leibov, Mark Garrison.

In Vienna: David Gavisch.

In Jerusalem: Catriel and Ora Katz, Anatoly and Karni (Jabotinsky) Rubin, Yakov Schultz.

In Tel Aviv: Ernst and Assia Levin, Naum and Klara Alshansky.

In Migdal Haemek: Nikolai and Lisa Dulets.

Eliahu Valk, writer and editor for *Kol Yisroel* (*Voice of Israel*), who now lives in Jerusalem, enabled me to meet many activists inside the USSR. A native of Riga, he had studied for two years in Minsk, and was also uniquely qualified to comb through the early manuscripts for technical errors, which he did with dedication and creativity.

Dorothy Feeney orchestrated the typing of successive versions, proofread, and assumed all the burdens of getting the manuscripts to the publisher.

My son Jack, screenwriter and drama critic, gave me much valuable advice and useful criticism. Other members of my family, from my grandparents to my children, contributed in a thousand objective and subjective ways, and over several decades.

Owen Laster provided the enthusiasm and encouragement I needed.

Michael Korda, with the insightful help of Leon King, edited passion-

ately, imaginatively, and ruthlessly. I doubt that many books these hurried days are so carefully combed.

Finally Janet. Wherever I went—to Minsk, Moscow, Vienna, Jerusalem, Sharm el Sheikh, Los Angeles, New York, St. Croix—she was with me, often putting her own ventures aside. With love and care she kept me—and this book—on the track for the years it took to learn about, gestate, and write.

Few writers are satisfied with their finished work, and I'm no exception. The shortcomings, however, are entirely my own, and cannot be attributed to any of those whose help I was so unstintingly given.

Postscript: Elena Hess, my most dedicated informant and guide inside the Soviet Union (Minsk), has just been given permission to leave the USSR with her husband Gregor after nine years of having been refused. The Hesses and their two daughters are now in the U.S. Igor Reichlin, a Refusenik in Leningrad for two years, has also just been given permission to emigrate and is now in Rome. I'm glad to be able to thank them by name. The others still languish in the USSR, waiting.

New York
August 7, 1981.

PART
ONE
Yuri

1

YURI WAS NOT EXACTLY AFRAID to call on little Yascha Moskovich, but he was not happy about it as he ducked into the entry to escape the drizzle. The janitor's wife's eyes narrowed into slits. "You're going upstairs to visit *them*, Professor Karpeyko?" Yuri nodded. "Again?" He hurried up the narrow stairs.

"Someone else is already up there!" she shouted after him. "It's a meeting?" Unauthorized meetings were a conspiracy. And this time she knew his name.

"No, no!" he called back, half in disgust. "The kid's sick!"

In the old days, Julia, Yascha's mother, used to bring the kid to the hospital rather than to her local polyclinic whenever he had an acute asthmatic attack because Yuri was the only doctor in Minsk she trusted; she'd leave him there overnight. But after the family applied to go to Israel, she was unwilling to take him out in that delicate condition and expose him to the bullying of other children. So whenever the boy began to gasp for breath and to turn gray, she'd call Yuri. The fact that he was no ordinary doctor but a professor, indeed an *akademik*, neither awed nor deterred her. And he discovered he could not refuse her—something residual, a turmoil about his own origins. For two years now he'd been responding to her calls.

Julia was only a few years older than Yuri's daughter—perhaps twenty-seven, Yuri guessed. She had once been an attractive brunette, one of Yuri's favorite mothers. Now she was suffering, and not only from malnutrition: her face had become haggard, her hair was tangled and neglected. Resignation had become her trademark. Yes, she sighed, they'd probably get their exit visa sooner or later. Minsk was no place for them, not what it once was. In their parents' day, before the Nazis, it had been a golden time for Jews. They were citizens first class, in positions of power. Her

own father, Moishe Solsky, had been in the KGB—the NKVD in those days. Imagine!

"Now what are we in Minsk?" In the days when she still had her job, people at work used to look at her strangely, as if to say, "Still living? What *chutzpah!*" All their relatives gone. The graves, Yuri thought, all those putrid bodies he'd seen with Pyotr, piled on each other, rotting away.

"I remember it only too well," he wanted to concede, but did not. Every Jew or part-Jew in Minsk was in the same fix.

Yascha was worse than usual today. For three hours he had been gasping for breath like that, Julia said tremulously, as she held the door open. Yuri saw they had a visitor, something rare, a hulk of a man, six foot seven or eight, close to two hundred fifty pounds. The giant was kneeling before the boy, holding a kettle of steaming water, trying to get Yascha, who was sitting on the bed, to inhale the steam. Not a bad idea. Sasha, Julia's husband, sat helplessly in a wooden chair. As Yuri opened his bag and took out the adrenalin and syringe, Julia said hurriedly to the giant, "Don't worry, the doctor won't make trouble." She introduced the giant. Leon Pavlovich Baryshin. Yuri shook hands and wondered where he'd heard the name.

He uncovered Yascha's upper arm, swabbed it with alcohol, gave him the injection quickly. That small arm had grown thinner, he was thinking. "Just a few minutes now, Yascha. It'll be all right." He listened to his wheezings with the stethoscope; the gesture seemed to calm the boy, and his breathing became less labored.

Yuri wrapped the blood-pressure tape around Yascha's arm. "You ever hear about Olga-Volga the Two-Headed Skapoochski?" he asked the boy in a matter-of-fact tone. Yascha shook his head. Yuri pumped the bulb and adjusted the stethoscope. "It was your typical Skapoochski, nothing special you know, with the body of a jackass and the usual two little heads, one at each end, but on this particular collective farm near Gozevna Olga-Volga had a very important job . . ." Laconically he began one of the fables he'd invented to keep children quiet—a few of which were so admired they had been reproduced in *samizdat*.

"D-d-do you know what you can g-get for such a st-story?" asked the stocky giant who had listened, silent and erect, as Yuri treated the patient. "Five years!" He spoke abruptly. Except for the stutter, he asked the question in the tone of a drillmaster, a stern military man. Now Yuri remembered. He was one of the trio of Jewish colonels turned Zionist— Davidovich, Ovsischer, and Baryshin.

"There is nothing illegal about any of my stories," Yuri said quickly,

not intimidated. "They're harmless beast fables which make fun of a few stupid bureaucrats. Do you think I'm an idiot? They merely point out the shortcomings of the bureaucracy. Such shortcomings need exposure. This strengthens the Party. You know that."

Baryshin smiled. "I know it. You know it. But will the procurator know it? I'm glad you have been thinking in advance about your defense! It's good to be prepared!"

Yuri shrugged. "Why should I worry?"

"Why should anyone? Better still, why *shouldn't* everyone?" He leaned back in his armchair. "You are part Jewish, Professor?" Yuri half nodded, with some reluctance, but concentrated on his professional work.

"I hear you have contact with Americans," Yuri said. "In that case I'll give you the names of some American medicines you should get for Yascha. He can take it by mouth. This way he won't have to wait for the doctor. Very effective." He printed in English "Brethene." "Our laboratories don't manufacture it yet, but I'm sure they will soon." Yuri kept up with the latest international literature and wished more of these medical tools were available to Soviet physicians. "Also an inhalant." He wrote "Vanceril." "Get them from your American friends."

"Well, if you ever think about leaving town," the giant stammered, "you can reach me through Shtainberg, the surgeon. You know him?" Yuri nodded. "He knows where to find me."

Lately Yuri had suspected Shtainberg of Zionist leanings. Well, it was nothing to him. He wanted to keep his distance from the issue. However, there was nothing in the law against humanitarianism.

Carefully he took two fresh oranges from his bag and placed them on the table, and bid them all a hurried goodbye. He was late to the hospital.

2

HOLDING A FLAPPING COPY of *Sovetskaya Byelorossiya* over his bare head with one hand, hugging with the other the black bag in which he had his medical things, he shouldered his way into the pelting rain, loping toward the curb on Prospekt Pushkina where his car was parked—a tightrope walker trying to keep dry.

How nice, how luxurious, he exulted, half drenched though he was, that I don't have to wait in the rain for the damned trolley bus, like those representatives of the *narod*, the lowly masses hunched and soaked across the street in that long queue! His eyes searched for the reassurance of the new miracle in his life—the shiny white Zhiguli parked down the way on Pushkina. Six years ago he'd thought applying for a car was a mad extravagance; Cleo had not had to press him too hard to put their names on the list because in those days he had thought, what harm? We'll have private cars when shrimps whistle on the hill. Why not let Cleo dream away?

He would always remember with special vividness, in full color, the glorious day after the notice came. That Thursday morning, only three weeks ago, Cleo seemed to have had a shot of sexual adrenalin. She simply wouldn't let him get out of bed. "Stay, stay!" she had commanded. "Let's make love!" Something Cleo simply didn't often demand so bluntly. Usually she was shyer and slyer. Somehow she had gotten her nightgown up and off before he had wakened, had put on a touch of scent; her lip was at his ear, her tongue sharp, incisive, in all his secret places.

"Cleo! Let me breathe! Give me a chance to open my eyes!"

"No chance!" she sang out in her high but silken voice. "I have you in my power at last!" She jumped out of bed. "*Look* at me, my darling." She swayed slowly in provocative rhythm. "I feel so sexy this morning. Forget everything." She bent and kissed him, a long, insinuating kiss. She *was* a lovely woman, he thought, her full lips now in that secret smile, someone

who knows more than she can ever tell. He loved her gentle, almost plump face, the large overpowering deep-set gray eyes, the tousled short black hair with its tiny flecks of gray, her musical voice, that look of love and lust. He loved her body, the only one he knew with such intimacy—the full behind and her unusual conical, but hospitable, breasts. But, best of all, he loved the spirit that moved her, soaring, as it did now, skyward, as if she were made of air.

It was better lovemaking than they had done in a long time, reminiscent of those secret interludes in the dark days when they had been two children, wild in the swamp. She murmured as she rode him, he was her hero, and he took her ravenously, like an eager boy out for the first time, full of hunger.

Yuri wondered, as he lay exhausted, what had brought Cleo on just this particular day—a day when they should have been dressing to go to work. As they relaxed quietly in bed in their afterglow, Cleo had finally propped herself on one elbow, looking him over like fallen prey, smiling at him with her big fat secret like the cat who'd eaten the canary. She leaned to his ear then and whispered suddenly, in a staccato hiss, "We've got a car!"

"What are you talking about?" he said, almost irritably. She hopped out of bed. "A car! Our own car!" she shouted with glee. "It's coming! Now we'll be free! We can drive anywhere! We're free as birds! Look, Yurochka, look!" She hustled to the bureau, humming and bobbing her head to a gay polka, took her purse, opened it, and, half dancing, hastily pulled out the envelope, her hands moving like light. "See for yourself!" Standing naked at the bureau, trying to ignore the disheveled image of his own head, that flying gray hair and disheveled beard mercilessly reflected in the small mirror, and hers, tousled black with the tint of salt, equally loveblown, still bobbing with merriment, he examined the paper she was showing him. They felt the excitement of children.

It had come in the mail the day before—one of those omnipresent form notices; they were among the very first lucky ones, the chosen few. She held the paper high in triumph. "We've come a long way, Yurochka! I want everything—yes, yes, I don't deny it." She kissed him wildly, repeatedly, almost as if she could begin again. "For you, too, darling, my darling gypsy, because all you ever do is *fantasize* and wait. You're too absent-minded to know *what you want!* Climbing stairs, seeing patients in the middle of the night! Long after you are off duty! Driving yourself into a coronary! We *both* work hard enough. Now we have it—our magic carpet!"

He had to chuckle. Seven thousand rubles! Two years' work for them

both. This would take practically everything they had! But the car struck a responsive chord in him. They had saved all that money so he could spend it on some archaeological artifact. Now it would all go for Cleo's whimsy. Well, she worked hard not only at the hospital, but did the shopping, tended the house, all so conscientiously and uncomplainingly. She asked little enough of him; *she* had earned a third of the money. Why not? What could you do with an amphora but stick it in a cabinet and look at it?

Cleo had turned out to be a wizard, for in the three weeks they'd owned it he had come to love this *thing*. Indeed, taken all in all, their lives were now all one could hope for: they had what most others only dreamed about. If one had to work, as indeed life demanded, the tasks that he and Cleo did were at least satisfying. If their work was not celebrated in Soviet literature, ballet, and art like those of soldiers or cosmonauts, it was surely honorable and, like Father, he had achieved honor in it. They also had this wonderful apartment and all the marvels Cleo knew were necessary for a family to prosper—a first-class kitchen in which she loved to bustle, the carpets and solid furniture Father had given them. Father had once been such a big shot he was able to buy in the very special shops open only to the highest government and Party officials in the Byelorussian Republic—the silver samovar, full settings for twelve in the finest porcelain and silverware, a few small precious sculptings, all kinds of stuff that Father had forced on them over the years, and his own treasured archaeological collection.

Yuri felt grateful. And now, for icing on their cake, they had the Zhiguli. Father, the old Bolshevik warhorse, naturally had been aghast when he first saw the car, but he consented to ride in it notwithstanding. For all Yuri knew, it may have been Father's standing in the Party that had pushed their names to the top of the list. *Svyazi*, the magic key in such matters, was worth vastly more than money.

Although Yuri attended all meetings of the Party units at the hospital and at the Institute, conducting some and putting on a serious mien, he found it impossible to take Party matters seriously in his heart. Nevertheless, the car made him grateful to the Party. From it, he knew, sprang all blessings. He confidently expected to be called in soon—perhaps this week, or surely next—by Igor Soloviev, the Byelorussian Republic's minister of health, to be told that his temporary appointment as acting director of the new Pediatric Hospital had been made permanent, that he was now the director. This would be a fitting climax to his career. He had been acting director long enough. Father had hinted to him that he should expect to be called at any moment.

He scrunched low now through pelting rain, jogging toward his car, which was parked, half-hidden, behind a huge yellow BELAZ truck; as he neared it he heard a grunt, then a hoarse warning shout, and he saw two teenage boys dart from behind the white Zhiguli and take off like maniacs. He recognized them—a pair of no-good hoodlums—the sons of the secretary of the Institute's Party committee and personnel administrator, Mariya Kalnin. Always swaggering around the Institute drinking beer, careening around Lenin Square, the two Kalnin boys were out for trouble, and usually managed to find it. What were they doing in this out-of-the-way part of town?

Yuri noticed something else about his car—was that a smear of black paint on the back fender? Those bastards! Too wet to examine it now. He hurriedly unlocked the car door and ducked in, out of the rain, his tall frame squeezed tightly into the small bucket seat behind the wheel. He mopped his eyes and face, patted his mustache and beard dry with a handkerchief, ran a comb through his straight, thinning gray hair, and put on his distance glasses.

As he inserted the key into the ignition, he looked up and was dismayed to see that the windshield had been struck, cracks extending like spokes from the point of the blow. His eyes darted here and there searching for other damage: the wiper was gone! Damnit! Why hadn't he remembered to take the bloody blade with him when he parked? He always took it, but he'd been in such a hurry to get out of the rain this morning, thinking only of keeping dry. Idiot!

The downpour was torrential now. How was he going to drive without the damned wiper? Fuck their mother! The time and thought he always had to give to these primitive logistics. Oh, yes, and this was Friday, so Father was coming, and he'd promised Cleo to buy some good vodka for the old man. He could ask Natalya at the hospital to go to one of the special shops and fetch it for him, but that was frowned on. Better to go himself. The fewer people who had exposure to the special shops, the better the bosses liked it. Back to standing in line—even at the special shop. Right now he'd better hurry to the hospital. He had two otitic meningitis cases, one a six-year-old girl, a very sick kid. He felt he could pull her through; she was a sweet child with a trusting and hopeful mother, a beauty, too, a sweet blond. He admired that woman. More worrisome was the Sikorsky boy. He'd swear the kid had leukemia. Another terrific mother. His heart went out to her. In fact, his mothers were all a marvelous lot. The plainest of them were beauties to him. They counted on him and, in his way, he needed them, too.

He started the car, keeping his head half out the window, and drove to-

ward Ulitsa Prityckogo, in the direction the two brats had taken. If he could ever lay his hands on them, he'd tear the little hooligan bastards apart! Suddenly that idea seemed ludicrous to him. Here he was, forty-five, his hair going gray and his belly getting softer by the minute. Those two young hooligans could tear *him* apart.

Suddenly he saw them. There! On bicycles now, in no hurry and unmindful of the rain, they pedaled insolently around the circle along Prityckogo toward the Center. The dirty bastards were laughing; their mirth infuriated him.

He noticed a policeman at the taxi stand in the circle, opened the window, and called him over. The young *militsioner*, smugly dry in a great gray raincoat that reached to his feet and a rubber hat with side flaps that left only his eyes, nose, and mouth visible, came slowly, leaned forward, and half inserted his gray rubber-cowled head into the car—a detrunked elephant, Yuri thought. "You know your windshield is broken, comrade?" His tone was sympathetic.

"Yes," Yuri said dryly to the elephant.

"And no wiper? You should not be driving in this weather. It's dangerous. For your sake as well."

"I agree." Yuri suppressed his impatience. "See those two hooligans over there? On the bikes? *They* just took my wiper. I bet if you can catch them, you'll find they still have it. So why not give it a go? They're the ones who smashed my windshield as well." The policeman removed his cowled head from the car window and squinted in their direction. "They also smeared paint on my fender," Yuri called. "A brand new car. How d'you like those bastards?" The policeman glanced at the paint scrawl. Something about it caught his attention. He lumbered slowly around the car, as if he were making a survey. The two kids pedaled on and disappeared, unhurried. Yuri fumed. When the policeman returned and lowered his head to the driver's level, Yuri noticed a change in his demeanor.

"And if I arrest them and they don't have the wiper?" The voice was a challenge, the eyes evasive. "You have proof?"

"Proof? I *saw* them."

"That is not proof, mister. You have witnesses? You must have at least two—" The "Mister" reeked with irony. The kids they made policemen these days!

Yuri shook his head in bewilderment. Ah, well. He had to get to the hospital. He would complain to the right person about this baby elephant when an appropriate occasion presented itself. "Thank you, *tovarisch militsioner*. Next time I'll be sure to carry a witness in each pocket." He shifted into gear and started off.

The young officer stepped back and beeped in his direction, and Yuri stopped. The *militsioner* followed him slowly. "*Grazhdanin,* you are not authorized to drive this vehicle without a wiper," he said quietly. "It is a violation. Your documents, please."

Yuri laughed. The guy sure had no idea who he was. How would he? This was what you could expect. "Comrade *militsioner,* I'm a physician. I'm the director of a hospital. I'm needed there in five minutes. There are sick children, and one of them could be yours. I promise I'll drive carefully and slowly. I'll keep my head out the window. Okay?"

Without awaiting a response, Yuri rolled up the window and drove off. In his mirror he saw the *militsioner* put the whistle to his mouth again, then take a pad from an inside pocket and begin to write in the rain. Imbecile! Couldn't tell the victim from the criminal. Yuri did not stop. Soon he had to open the window to put his head out to see, but by the time he reached Academiceskaya the rain had let up. He drove into the hospital grounds, parked, picked up his bag, and squeezed out of the cramped driver's seat. As he was locking the door, he saw it. The black paint on the rear fender was no mere daub. It was a scrawled word: Зионист ZIONIST.

3

Yuri stared in disbelief. He looked around to determine if anyone else had observed it. So *that* was what the militiaman had seen. "Zionist" was not a good word to be driving around with these days. He walked around to the other side. There was more paint. ПРЕДАТЕЛЬ. Traitor. No better than "Zionist." The word was sloppily written in huge block letters across both doors. Not so funny. Words first, then rocks. In spite of himself, he had a sinking feeling in the pit of his stomach.

Three bodies, or what was left of them, a sight he could never obliterate, swung before his eyes; he could see them as clearly as if they hung there this morning and not almost thirty-three years ago. They could be seen in the square from the window of the toilet in the railway station, where he and Pyotr had been hiding. Each grotesque corpse had pinned to it a sign. Those on the men said BANDIT and, in red letters, DIED SLOWLY. The woman's head, almost bald, was bent crazily, eyes popping, her mouth open, tongue out. Blood covered her dress, to which was pinned a crude sign: KIKE BANDIT. And below: STRANGLED SLOWLY. "That her?" Pyotr had whispered. He had no recollection of how he had responded. Strangled. Fucking bloodthirsty cannibals. He remembered being blind, powerless, feeling suffocation. Oh, God! That was before Pyotr and he had opened the first of the mass graves, but by then he'd seen Nazis shoot people in the streets, the early roundups, had heard the deadly ba-zoom-zoom-zoom from the Yubeleinaya market. But nothing was engraved in his soul like the woman there. *Kike bandit.*

Blinded by the recollection, he ripped his bag open, seized a pair of surgical scissors, and like an idiot started compulsively to scrape the paint off the car. But it was no good; he merely made scratch marks with it. Well, he could not leave the car parked here with those painted scrawls. Everyone knew his new car. He thought of the underground private garage as-

signed to his friend Mitya Orensky, the director general. Mitya was still in Moscow, not due back until later today. He was coming to dinner tonight. Mitya wouldn't mind. He stored the Zhiguli there.

Yuri sent for his first patient. He managed to see two dozen youngsters, to admit most of them, to reassure the new mothers and tell them when they could visit each day. The fretful mothers were astonished they could now come to see their children and were pathetically grateful. Then, making rounds, tending to his sickest patients, satisfied that both of his meningitis girls were responding to the sulfa, he was nevertheless unable to bring himself on this particular day to entertain them. "Tell us a story, Doctor, tell us!" the kids in the *Cheboozashka* ward begged. "'The Two-Headed Skapoochski'!" "No, 'The Flying Hippoloximus'!" But Yuri shook his head. Yuri had instituted the practice of painting one of his whimsical animals on the door of each ward, so ambulatory kids who could not yet read could identify their rooms. When he visited a ward, the kids clustered around, eight or ten eager creatures (those who were sickest merely turning their heads from where they lay), begging for the treat that was to come. Today, however, he was in a hurry and had to leave them disappointed and complaining; instead he passed out candies as a substitute for a story.

When he had finished rounds, he stopped in at the pharmacy to get Father's morphine. Forty-two quarter-grain tablets. This weekly chore, as usual, left him slightly uneasy. As acting director, of course, he was not questioned even about controlled drugs, but, as always, he filled out every form scrupulously. It would never be detected, he knew, so carefully and conscientiously did he account for the stuff in his reports. Still. He stuffed the packet of pills into his bag and hurried back to the car.

He knew he himself had to get that paint off before he drove away again. There was no one he could imagine asking to do it for him, or even to help. He felt a deep shame that he wanted no one else to see those words, not even Cleo. He had read the editorials and heard the lectures and been to the last two Party meetings on the "Zionist Question." He had read the articles in *Sovetskaya Byelorossiya*, attacking Davidovich and Ovsischer. He knew Ovsischer, a colonel in the air force; he had treated his daughter when she broke her leg. What had got into that man? Why had any of these guys become Zionists?

He took a trolley bus to the paint shop, stood in line for ten minutes to purchase a scraper and a bottle of turpentine, and returned directly to the car, where he removed his jacket and sweater and, using surgical gauze as rags, did the job in Mitya's overheated garage. The car looked terrible when he had finished, but the words were gone. The painfully slow task

made him late to the meeting of directors, but the others seemed to have had no trouble getting on without him.

Shtainberg, who was not a director but performed surgery in many of the units, was talking when Yuri finally slipped noiselessly into an empty chair beside Tanya Rodenko, director of the gynecology section—a skinny, blond, frizzy-haired woman with a pinched, pale face, wrinkled eyes, a broad ski-slope Slavic nose, and thin lips. Tanya had become lately renowned as a fighter for special privileges for women. It was she who had suggested to Yuri that mothers should be permitted to visit their children in the wards, and over the muttered objection of every surgeon and most of the medical staff in the pediatric building, Yuri, who thought the idea marvelous, had instituted this change. No one had yet raised formal objections. Now Tanya uttered a rude contralto laugh over Shtainberg's voice and muttered, "What the hell happened to you, Yuri? Did you fall into a barrel of paint? You smell awful!"

The black-bearded Shtainberg looked down at the interruption and paused for a moment. When he had finished, Yuri told them what had happened, without, however, mentioning the words he had erased or that it was the Moskovich boy he'd been visiting when the vandalism took place. "Smeared with paint," was how he described it. "I can't decide what to do about those two hooligans. Mariya has no idea how to handle them." They all knew Mariya, for, like Yuri, they taught at the Institute.

"She needs a man," one of the women, the director of urology, said prissily.

"What she needs is a guillotine," Shtainberg said in his hoarse guttural voice, and laughed alone.

"Your poor new car!" Tanya cooed sympathetically. "What a shitty thing to do. You really must report those kids to the *militsia* or there'll be no stopping them. There's so much hooliganism these days. The young people have gotten out of hand. Really. You must, Yuri. Even Mariya would be grateful." Yuri was touched by Tanya's effusive sympathy; he liked her, although he had little regard for her professionally.

When the meeting was over, he asked Tanya if he and Cleo could give her a lift home. "My, yes," she said, "that would be nice." She hadn't yet been invited to ride in his new car, and had wondered how long it would take him to get around to asking her! How lucky they were! How long had they waited? Only six years? Not bad. Possibly he was one of the first because he was a member of the Academy of Medical Science. He shrugged. They found Cleo on the top floor of the pediatric building outside the operating room, removing gown and mask. Cleo was chief anesthesiologist, and, like Shtainberg, she worked sometimes in one build-

ing, sometimes in another. The last operation had gone well, and she was in one of her typically jolly moods, for which she never needed any special reason, although the rings below her eyes attested to the fact that she'd had a long, hard day. No matter. She was happy as a child.

They drove toward Tanya's place on Krasnoarmeyskaya, Tanya chattering in her usual fashion and Cleo laughing at each of Tanya's wry criticisms of their colleagues.

"You really should have been at the meeting, Cleo. Ask Yuri. That Shtainberg is a pain in the ass. You'd think we were back in elementary anatomy. The way he goes on in that dry, pedantic fashion, with his shitty little jokes, outlining his procedures and reading from his case histories. And I hate that beard of his—he lets it get so matted and filthy. There's something about these Jews, really. I don't know why they're such dirty people—and they're such know-it-alls, too. We could do with fewer of them, don't you agree?"

Yuri glanced quickly at Cleo, whose cheerful, untroubled expression did not change. That's twice in one day, Yuri thought. The Jews. Again the Jews. It did not stop with news articles or television attacks on Zionists; it was something in the air these days.

"—and what would the Civil War have been without the Jews, Tanya, tell me that?" he heard Cleo chirping. "Read your history. They were the brains of the whole Revolution. If not for them, we'd all still be out there sweating our tails off, harvesting wheat for the Tsar's landowners. You especially, Tanya! And during the last war, Jews made the best partisans. I happen to know—I was there." She touched Yuri's hand. Her assertion flew in the face of all Soviet mythology, but Cleo, who *could* claim special knowledge about the partisans, laughed on merrily. "Also, I happen to like Shtainberg. He's a sweet man and a superlative surgeon. You should listen more closely to him. Have you ever seen him work? I have. I've seen them all! Drop into the operating room sometime. What fingers! The best in Minsk. He talks like that all the time he operates, you know; he keeps the entire team relaxed. They all try to do it, Lazarev also. He even tries to be funny, but Shtainberg is just right." Tanya had lapsed into sullen silence. She had given them their opening and had hoped for a different response. When they reached her building, she thanked them coolly for the ride. She had no patience with Jew-lovers.

Yuri drove to the auto repair shop on their way home to buy a new wiper. He was amazed that Cleo had seemed so unconcerned by his account of the vandalism or by the way the car looked. He knew she loved her Zhiguli. "Oh, kids," was all she said. "They haven't enough to do, that's it; they run wild." Yuri could still not bring himself to tell her

about the words he had erased. He was not one to blurt out what was on his troubled mind. He was to be leaned on, not to lean on others, and surely not on Cleo.

The garage on the Parkovaya Magistral had no wiper, of course. The windshield? Yes, the grease-covered mechanic thought it could still be serviceable, "if some *militsiaman* doesn't nab you." Yuri felt suddenly depressed by the man's silly grin. It was not only the car.

Cleo, restless with excess energy, asked him to drop her at the open-air free market, on Komarovka, where she happily joined the throng and surged with them through the gates.

When he reached Father's flat, Yuri found the *starik* in one of his frequent petulant moods, his hawkish face, his shifting, suspecting eyes, and his glistening pate combining to make him positively menacing. His body was now so thin and frail, Yuri wondered how long he could go on. The emaciated old man lived in two modern, brightly-lit, airy rooms on the tenth floor of the glistening white building on Maxim Gorky overlooking all of Minsk. Not many former officials had much better quarters. The only signs of luxury he permitted himself, however, besides his precious carpet, were his shelves of books. He had one of the great libraries in Byelorussia on general surgery. There were also books in a dozen languages dealing with everything from thoracic and plastic surgery to volumes dealing with mastectomies, in which he himself had specialized in the last part of his career. The rest consisted of works on Marxist theory and the problems of its practice, in which he was still enormously interested. The walls were otherwise bare except for his four unframed black-and-white photographs—one of Mama as a girl in one of her fiery poses, speaking to a group of workers in a tannery; the second of himself, Doctor Ivan Borisovich Karpeyko, in full military uniform with six decorations on his chest, a photograph taken after his return from Stalingrad; the third of Yuri in his white coat, stethoscope loose about his neck; and the fourth a signed portrait of Lenin with his name in Lenin's handwriting. All his other remarkable possessons Father had passed on to Yuri and Cleo.

Father had just celebrated his seventy-seventh birthday at a party of old Bolsheviks at the Minsk Hotel; most of the old guests had turned up in even worse shape than Father. He now had crippling arthritis, two old spinal war wounds which made him limp, severe sciatic pains which often kept him in bed, a stomach ulcer which had been blessedly quiescent in recent years. He also had cataracts in both eyes, a disease which seemed to run in the family; in the old days cataracts had meant blindness, and Father often told how, when he was an infant, his grandmother had jumped from a roof to her death only a few hundred yards from here after her cat-

aracts had made her hopelessly blind. Today minor surgery and a pair of heavy lenses made it possible for Father to go on seeing and reading, a big change from the old days. As with everything, Father attributed medical strides to the miracle of the Revolution. "So I don't have to jump from the roof," he chortled grimly, "another of the Revolution's blessings! Look how we liberated research, how we harnessed the talents of the people of so many nationalities!"

Father had not missed a Friday night with them since the day Yuri had come to meet him, summoned as if by some supernatural force, for their reunion. Yuri would never forget the sight of the old man in the rain at the wrecked Minsk railway station, coming toward him—alone, proudly limping, carrying a cane, his chest resplendent with all the medals he had been awarded at Stalingrad, back from the dead but with permanent damage to his spine. By then Yuri, too, was known locally as a hero of the Resistance; and Father had recognized him in the crowd right away, as if he had been looking everywhere for him. Many people at the station had cheered and applauded as they embraced—two great local figures—father and son. There were sad words about Mama—no tears, because neither could cry. That had been a long time ago, before they fully realized they were the only ones of almost thirty brothers, uncles, aunts, and cousins still alive.

On Fridays Father ran out of morphine and needed a fresh week's supply. Cleo, aware of his problem, had studiously not asked Yuri how he managed to keep Father supplied. Yuri, wary of having too large a supply on hand but afraid to run out, always kept some in his bureau drawer, some in his bag. He also picked up a week's supply each week. Father's addiction went back to the fifties, when in an agony of desperation he had begun to take the stuff from the hospital pharmacy; at first he took it by mouth, but later had begun to inject himself to relieve the incessant pain, which prevented his walking. In those days the system of control of narcotics at the hospital was, as compared to now, almost careless. The morphine, taken regularly, had been an effective miracle cure. He was able to work again, faintly euphoric most of the time. Without it the old man could not operate; his hand, he told himself, had to be steady; he owed it to his patients. Within months he was hooked. In sixty-three, a few weeks after Father had retired from the hospital, Yuri had discovered him on the floor of his flat writhing in the throes of withdrawal. He had been lying alone that way for two days and in a few more hours would have died of shock. Yuri was never sure if that indeed was not the old man's intention. Whimpering like an infant, Father had confessed his addiction to his son for the first time. Withdrawal could be torture. Yuri de-

cided then that addiction for his father was the lesser of two evils. Now, every four hours around the clock, day in, day out, the old man, supplied by his son, administered a fresh shot to himself. Over the years the doses had had to be increased, but without the morphine his back pains became spastic torture. Nothing else worked. The old man also desperately missed the hospital, the other doctors, the challenges of performing difficult, demanding surgery. So the quick injections which he now mixed in the kitchen, using the powder crushed from the pills he got, made him feel a new man, if only for a couple of hours at a time. Without a word, Father now took the packet Yuri handed him, as he did every Friday, and retired to his kitchen. After a brief interval he reappeared, his eyes and bald pate glistening; father and son went down the lift and out together.

Father, leaning on his cane and peering with difficulty through his thick lenses, could see that something had defaced the new car. "It does look a bit more proletarian now, my boy," he said, hoarsely as always, as if his vocal cords had been injured from abuse. "But the *militsia* will be after you to have it painted, you can be sure."

In the Zhiguli Yuri told him exactly what had happened. The *starik* was uncharacteristically silent. "You know, this machine," he said at last, "is truly a marvel of Soviet engineering, you realize that? Do you? So quiet. An absolute marvel." Yuri, puzzled by the non sequitur, was about to remind him that Italian engineers had built the Togliatti factory where the Zhigulis were made, and Italians were still teaching Russians how to make the small cars. Better not. Father needed his articles of faith.

As they drove, the old man apparently mulled over Yuri's tale. "The Black Hundreds again," he muttered. "But why you? It's those cocksucking Israelis, fuck their mothers! They will do us all in."

4

IN HIS YOUTH the old man had not been quite sure whether he wanted to remain a surgeon or work for the Cheka, where he knew almost everyone. Even as a surgeon he had been Somebody. Well-connected. A mover, accustomed to having his opinions count. He could still talk up a storm about Khrushchev and his criminal mistakes in Cuba and with the corn. He was not enthusiastic about Khrushchev's revelations about Stalin's crimes at the Twentieth Party Congress. Why turn the country against its greatest teacher and leader? Everyone makes a few mistakes. He became choleric with anyone who said the Hungarian suppression or the Czech occupation was a mistake. The mystique of Bolshevik Partyness, the dream of an impossible future, had always been more important to him than performing a successful anastomosis, Yuri suspected. Mama, too. For hadn't she also sacrificed her private self for her public dream? Had they both been fanatics? Yet, unlike other prominent parents in the Party, they both—but Mama especially—seemed to have had some time for him. Not entirely enough, but always some. As a child he had never felt neglected. Was *that* their Jewishness?

Nowadays the old man could sit motionless before the television, pausing only to inhale his Kazbek, hanging onto every hackneyed word concerning the month's output at the tractor works or the wheat harvest in the Ukraine. "Tremendous," he would murmur. "We're burying the Americans."

He had been doubly honored in his youth: sent twice to Siberia by the Tsarist police. Years later, while still studying at the Medical Institute, he had sent others to the frigid *taiga* and to their graves—first for Lenin, then for Stalin, but always for some impossibly glorious future, the dream he now mistook for reality. He had seen nothing inconsistent in saving some lives and destroying others. Now that his son was a member of the

Academy of Medical Science, his satisfaction, if not often expressed, was deep.

By the time they reached Yuri's flat, Father was glowing with blessed relief from his shot. Cleo, already home, rushed from the kitchen to greet him, triumphant with news of fresh tomatoes, which Father loved, and marvelous mushrooms. She kissed the old man and bustled directly back into the kitchen. To Cleo he represented all four of their parents, all their aunts and uncles, every one of whom, except for him, had been killed by Nazis or had died during the war, even though on her side of the family there were no Jews. For all her noisy jollity, Cleo had an outsized sense of duty, and she lavished it on Father. She loved to cook anyway, and ate with greater relish than she cooked.

Tonight they had invited Yuri's boyhood friend, Anatoly, and his wife, Irina, along with Mitya Orensky, to share their dinner and to share Father, who was rarely willing to talk to younger people. Tolya Markov was writing a fiction piece for *Novy Mir*, set in Minsk in the days of the Revolution, and told Yuri he would give anything to get the old man started on his experiences. One had to go about that carefully, because Father hated to be exploited, but he had agreed "in principle" to talk to Tolya Markov about those days.

The blond, middle-aged, buxom television announcer was now speaking of the Middle East war, and she had Father's full attention. His only movement was to take long drags on his cigarette, held loosely between two long, gnarled, nicotine-stained fingers. The announcer read in a monotone about Egyptian gains and Syrian heroism, Soviet tanks and Soviet messages of solidarity to the Arab nations. She spoke of movements of the U.S.A. fleet in the Mediterranean and, raising her voice in anger at last, she spoke of Zionist intransigence and trickery. "Such shit!" Father said, snapping her off in midsentence, his cigarette ashes spraying everywhere. His mood had suddenly turned foul again.

Cleo sailed in from the kitchen with a platter, humming because her little single-bite pizzas topped with mushrooms in sour cream had turned out so beautifully, but Father waved her appetizing platter away, his mind far from that room.

"Zionists!" Father raged. "They'll be the ruin of all of us."

"Now, stop that!" Cleo scolded. "Ivan Borisovich, I don't want to hear another word about politics! Have some of my little pizzas. I've been saving them specially for you." To satisfy her, he rammed two into his mouth and mashed his gums against them until they crumbled and he was able to swallow, but his mood became stormier.

"We've had enough!" the old man fumed. "*Now*, just when we are try-

ing to win over the Arabs, a few of our supernationalist Jews insist on declaring their solidarity with Israel, a few palpitating hearts will assemble outside the Moscow Synagogue and say they want to go to Israel to live, the idiots. And the people and the Party will be furious at *all* of us. It'll be terrible! I urge you two to watch your steps for the next few months. Be careful what you say. Whom you talk to."

"But, Father, me? A Greek-Ukrainian?" Cleo laughed.

"Never mind!" the old man said dourly. "You're married to a Jew—even if he's only part-Jew—and never forget it. What's written in his passport means nothing. The Party knows. Bosherov knows—I don't have to tell you about Dr. Bosherov. He's from a family of doctors that goes way back. Before the Revolution they were doctors. His father, his mother's father. He wants that job, Yurka. Your job. Never forget it. You're acting director. Mariya Kalnin is a Bosherov sympathizer, you know that? They won't hesitate, that kind. They'll call on the Black Hundreds if they need to, or the devil himself. I've dealt with them. You don't know the element."

"But really, Father!" Cleo pouted. "The Black Hundreds! That's mythology!"

Yuri could not restrain himself; his mind was full of today's vandalism, and he took comfort in Father's presence. He held his *papyroesa* aloft. "Speaking of such matters," he said carefully, "there was something about the car I haven't mentioned." He began to talk, and as he did so Cleo seated herself primly, hands folded, suddenly quiet. He told her, as he had already told Father, of those scrawled, crudely painted words, the icy behavior of the policeman.

"It's nineteen sixty-seven again!" Father half shouted. "I was close to several members of the Central Committee, and I can tell you, when the Israelis ate mustard in Tel Aviv, the Jews of Minsk got heartburn. I'll tell you something else. That Kalnin woman is an anti-Semite," he fumed.

"She's a Latvian; never trust a Latvian. Watch out for her and her sons. She was once married to a Jew in Riga, you know that? A terrible insane bastard who killed his own baby boy by suffocation. *Her* kid. It made her crazy. I hear she's become terribly fat—if you ask me, it's all gas. She also takes, *v lapu*, you know that? She gets as much as a thousand rubles for every student she gets the Institute to accept. A vile woman! I did everything I could to keep her influence in the Party from spreading. But many people on Engelsa Street and on Komsomolskaya, and on Leninsky Prospekt, and above all Chankov himself, think she's worth two regiments!"

"What are you going to do, Yuri?" Cleo asked. Gone was her girlish soprano; the corners of her mouth turned down, her eyes challenged.

"I'll report the matter routinely—a common act of hooliganism. It happens every day. The cops should do something about those hoodlums. *'Moya militsia menya berezhyot!'* My *militsia* will protect me! Get them off the streets." He looked to his father.

Father snorted. "Don't be naïve, Yurka. You think such hooliganism is spontaneous? Nah, nah, nah." His gaze moved elsewhere, far from that room. "First there is Dr. Bosherov. An ambitious careerist and a son of a bitch. Not a very good surgeon, either. Never was and never will be. And the Kalnin woman, with her sons! Then there's our dear minister of health, Professor Soloviev, right under Chankov's thumb. Don't you see?"

"Oh, those two boys are simply hooligans," Yuri said. "I can't see any dark plot. But I'll report it."

Cleo was on her feet. "Some *gazirovka* with your vodka, Father?" She squirted some seltzer.

Father lowered his hoarse voice with effort. "You know what you should do? Forget it."

"My brand new car? *Otyetz!*"

The old man settled back. He took a long, thoughtful drink of the vodka and fizz, and his eyes took on a sudden mischievousness Yuri hadn't seen in years. Holding up his glass as if proposing a toast, he spoke softly, sentimentally. "Whatever happens, my boy, one thing I want you to know. If you get into a real fix, if your back is to the wall . . . don't call me." He roared, slapped his cadaverous thigh, took a large swallow, and began, silently, to chuckle. "Our great teacher, Josef Vissarionovich, once said that to me on the phone," the old man mused. " 'Don't call me!' "

"Maybe I'd better see Pyotr Feodorovich," Yuri thought aloud.

Father's eyes widened behind the thick lenses. "Are you crazy?" he shouted in his customary tone. "Don't call him either!"

They heard the Markovs knocking on the door, Tolya's characteristic rapid three raps. Father held his finger to his lips, idly rose to greet their friends, and, having shaken hands, wandered about the flat as if searching for something, while the others nibbled food and chatted. He poked at the walls, looked behind books, returned them to the shelves, peered behind pictures. He found nothing. Soon Mitya and Klara Orensky arrived, blond Klara with her big kisses for everyone.

On the rare occasions when Father reminisced, one had to distinguish between what part of his farfetched yarn to believe and what to dismiss. On medical subjects he was customarily precise. In his political reminis-

cences his imagination sometimes overcame the facts. This was well known to Tolya, an old family friend, now a short, peppery semi-bald man who ordinarily was a vigorous, loud nonstop talker himself, and Anatoly in turn had long since cautioned his wife not to quarrel with the old man, but just to listen.

After dinner Tolya mentioned Andrei Sakharov, and this soon got Father on the subject of the kulaks, one of his favorites. Yuri and Cleo had heard it all before (Yuri loathed even thinking about it), and they washed dishes while the old man held forth for the benefit of the Markovs and Orenskys. Since Markov was something of a dandy, nattier even than Yuri, with his fancy shoes, his thin black hair slicked down to hide the baldness, the bourgeois vest, and all the rest, Father tried his best to be his most uncouth. Irina held her tongue, as ordered, and Mitya, in awe of the man who had held his job in the old days—even before Professor Schultz—and Klara both sat openmouthed.

Although Father once considered himself a member of the intelligentsia, he had a deep contempt for today's smart-whip, so-called intelligentsia who had never had to do anything hard, pampered children all. *Subbotnik,* the one day a year when they were shamed outdoors to "volunteer" their services for downtown cleanup, was to them a hardship; they threw up their hands, sighing "What can you do?" As if honest labor were degrading and forced on them by the functional Mongolians who ran the Party. Very well, he'd give them an earful.

"So you wonder what is to be done about the dissidents these days, Markov—Sakharov, Solzhenitsyn, Galyich, and the rest? The brains of the opposition? They'd have been no problem to the old man, our leader and teacher—*he* would have known how to handle *them.* Now the kulaks, *they* were a problem! One day we received orders from Moscow to liquidate the kulaks and their lackeys as a class. Just like that!"

Father was off and running. "Back in the late twenties, it was. Simple, clear. 'Liquidate the kulaks as a class!' I personally received the order from Stalin by messenger, and I confirmed it by telephone because I couldn't believe it. At the time, my old friend Orlov was chief of the Minsk Cheka and I was in his office. Or had it by then become the GPU?"

He shook his head impatiently. "Such an order! From Zinoviev or Kamenev or Trotsky, maybe. But from Stalin? Liquidate a tenth of our people? Millions of small farmers. How could it be done? Josef Vissarionovich assured me personally the order was valid. This was no mere pogrom, you understand, beating up a few old Jews. This was a logistical nightmare. We didn't have the scientific advantages of the Nazis, no modern equipment, no gas chambers, terrible roads, primitive railroads, no dis-

cipline in the ranks. Graves had to be dug by hand. Fortunately kulaks died in transport; they froze and starved. Even so, it required planning, believe me. Organization. Ingenuity. Trickery. But *we* were used to hard work. Most of us had no love for the kulaks. After the Civil War they thought they owned Russia. There were even a few Jews among them. We needed bread, and who had all the wheat? Who had all the machinery? After we'd got rid of the landowners, who claimed to "own" the farms? Kulaks! Bourgeois bastards! Who controlled the food? *They* wanted to call the tune. Stalin finally flew into a rage. Very well, we had our orders."

He drew his hand across his throat and made a choking sound. "All dependable Bolsheviks were called in. I took a leave from the hospital without hesitation. Other doctors could attend the sick. This was more important.

"You know what Lenin said? 'A Central Committee to be effective must be made up of gifted writers, able organizers, and intelligent scoundrels.' We had no writers, but Orlov was an intelligent scoundrel, and I turned out to be the able organizer. We were on our own, hundreds of versts from Moscow and Petrograd. We had no Aeroflot. We deployed our men. I had a plan but no one followed it. Chaos like you can't imagine. People went wild. We killed them in their homes with pitchforks, we butchered them at midday on their farms, we arrested them in the shops in small towns, we rounded them up at night and killed any who resisted on the spot, but it wasn't simple.

"And mistakes were made. It took months and months. Many of them fought for their property; others came gentle as mice. Some of our own people were unreliable. They had kulak relatives and insisted on knowing what was to be their fate before they would arrest them. Several times I had to issue orders to shoot some of our men for protecting kulaks, taking bribes to hide their women especially. I hated it. In Osipovichi one day, we collected a crowd of kulaks in the schoolyard, two hundred of them, including their women—we had them penned like sheep, waiting for trains to take them east, and suddenly they began to suspect, and before we knew it, they were coming at us with staves and throwing rocks, breaking down the fences that penned them in, cursing, screaming that we were stealing their farms, and they were right—that was the idea, since they refused to turn their farms into collectives. They called out to each other to fight, and to kill *us*. But we were the government, the only government. Well, what a day *that* was!

"Looking back, I can't believe it. What made us so savage, so bloodthirsty? They came at us like trapped animals, screaming. We shot them,

clubbed them—did you ever club a living thing? I guess not, Comrade Markov, Comrade Orensky, ladies. You must excuse me for asking. A thing as large as a man? Or a woman? With a rifle butt? I visited a slaughterhouse once and saw cattle clubbed like that by butchers running back and forth on platforms above the animals; they wore oilcloth aprons because of all the blood. But we had *people!* Not cattle. Vile, and not quite *human,* but still people. They ran this way, that way, wives calling husbands, trying to climb the fences, but we had them trapped.

"And what now amazes me is that it was no shock to me then. After all, it was in my blood. You know, my grandfather was police chief in Minsk and my father and mother were revolutionaries from the day I was born. That's why I changed my name from Karpovich to Karpeyko. I hated that tsarist name. And while I was at it, I changed Israil to Ivan. After all, I was Russian! I wanted my children to be Russian—and revolutionaries! The *idea* of violence I got with my mother's milk. But the idea and the act are different things. *Today* I am shocked, but then we did it routinely. Terror had become commonplace, and Lenin had ennobled it. Dealing with the kulaks Stalin turned terror into an art. It was nothing for us to kill fifty, sixty persons in a day. It used to take it out of me, I'm telling you! I think that's how I got my ulcers. Yes, we were under instructions, but we were also hypnotized, we believed with such passion, such zeal, almost a madness it was; you know, those screaming people were to me like disease-carrying insects, poisonous. Maggots eating at my own flesh, they were. I couldn't wait until they were all gone. Every last one. They were the carriers of all the diseases that had made Russia a den of thieves and a land of victims. The sooner they could be dispersed, resettled, exterminated, and buried, the sooner we would all have the New Day. Kind ones, cruel ones, they were all shit. Once they were gone, the *moujik* would come into his own. Those who sweated in the factories, the new intelligentsia, the Jews, *all* oppressed nationalities could *live,* after all those centuries!

"I believed that. With each blow I struck I believed it. And so it has proved to be. Only on those dead bodies could we build a new world, a new society. We had no pity. I struck women with the same force as men; that day in Osipovichi, I seized a woman by the hair, she grabbed mine—I had a little hair in those days—and I cut her throat and then personally beheaded her; she had been screaming foul language at me and made the sign of the Cross, a pogromist's sign. It was bloody surgery, the kind you don't do on the operating table, but it felt good. She'd bear no more kulaks to bleed us or to make pogroms against us.

"That beheading was the signal. We killed almost eighty that day. The

rest we shipped off; we had not enough railroad cars, so they were packed in like sardines. Many of my men were sickened. Some disappeared. Others would not talk to me for weeks. One of our young men spat at me. 'You call yourself a doctor? You're a butcher!' Well, he was overwrought. You young people know nothing about such struggle. Today everything is *blat*: you scratch my back, I'll scratch yours, people give each other bribes, swap one thing for another, buy in the special shops—private cars, insurance, savings passbooks. Everyone looks out for himself. Getting ahead. Careerists! There's no purity any more, no zeal."

Cleo and Yuri were exchanging embarrassed glances as Cleo set out afterdinner sweet aperitifs, Yuri's favorites. How Father, who bought everything in special shops, who still vacationed at the most elegant holiday houses, even if only five days at a time, could rail against the new materialism puzzled Yuri. Anatoly Markov, however, was mesmerized. So were the other three—mesmerized and horrified. Such lawlessness! Yuri could almost hear them thinking. Would the story make his friends anti-Semites? What a stupid concern! "My soul lies buried out there deep in Russian soil with those corpses," the old man was intoning hoarsely in a kind of euphoria. "Ten *million* dead, killed, or starved because there was no food—*liquidated as a class*, done! Look how much better we are! The old Georgian, our teacher and leader, as we used to call him, knew what he was doing when he gave that order. We could use some of that spirit now. Corruption, enemies all around us. Everywhere you look. You haven't learned to be afraid, eh? There's plenty to be afraid of, my friend. Be afraid!"

Anatoly Markov, Mitya Orensky, Yuri, and their wives needed no such admonition. They were all afraid, or at least uneasy, but they were also determined, like so many others these days, to live their lives more fully, to permit their minds to work, and, unlike their parents, to consider all possibilities. Nevertheless, they all understood this must be done within Soviet laws. Among nonlawyers, few had made themselves as expert on Soviet law as Markov—an absolute necessity for him, since he refused to be a slavishly docile member of the Writers' Union of Byelorussia. However, Markov's equivocal attitude was something of which Father was unaware, or he never would have talked as he did. What Markov wrote to make a living, of course, featured workers who exceeded their norms, brave frontline soldiers, cosmonauts, honest farmers who exposed the corrupt leader of a farm collective—characters such as had never been seen on land or sea. But on the side, he wrote for *samizdat*, putting his heart into these pieces, a risky business. This work was typed in as many car-

bons as could be made legible, and together with the work of other contributors was eagerly passed from hand to hand.

Despite the risks, the *samizdatchiki* observed little or no secrecy in distributing issues of *Today*, which, for example, might include a short work by Solzhenitsyn, a poem by Yevtushenko, who, like Markov, wrote mainly for official publications, a story by Markov, a report from the Ukraine by Plyushch, and songs by Irina Beresina from Vilna. It was Markov who had contributed a few of Yuri's children's fables, which, with their sly political overtones, and to Yuri's astonishment, had achieved a certain fame. That people in high places, Antonov in Moscow, head of the Soviet security apparatus, and Chankov, his Minsk deputy, knew of the existence of the *samizdat* network, and read the material carefully, there was never any doubt. Those guys knew everything. They tolerated it, and in that tolerance was the hope for better days. Still, one had to be careful.

Cleo brought out a dish of salted fish to go with the liqueurs. As suddenly as he had begun, Father stopped talking. He leaned forward and turned the television back on, not even glancing at the Markovs or Orenskys for their reactions. Irina Markov was visibly upset and her voice came unevenly when she refused Cleo's salted herring; Mitya was staring at Father, trying to decide if the old surgeon were devil or saint.

Yuri was relieved Father had not regaled them with the episode in Drachovka, which was far worse. Oh, those bothersome palpitations were beginning again. A damned trying day. He nibbled the salted fish and savored his sweet liqueur, trying to settle himself and forget Father's ferocious tale. The liqueur was delicious. Maybe if he drank enough, the palpitations would let up.

5

NEXT MORNING, turning off Leningradskaya Street, Yuri parked his defaced Zhiguli at the little students' park, climbed the Medical Institute steps, and walked into Mariya Kalnin's office to tell her, with more calm and tact than he felt, what her sons had been up to. Mariya was now a grotesquely fat woman with a shockingly young and pretty face for her fifty-eight years. Her hair was bright red, her eyes pale blue and restless, her skin dead white and lightly freckled. Yuri was irritated by the perpetual, ingratiating smile she wore, revealing teeth too perfect. Father's comments had made him doubly wary. When she spoke, it was with little-girlish gushes one might have expected from an insecure sixteen-year-old, reflecting astonishment not so much at what she heard as at what she herself was saying.

Mariya was indeed the properly raised daughter of the leading newspaper publisher in Riga during the bourgeois days, a product of the best orthodonture, schooling, and upbringing. Having earned her degree in medicine in Bologna, she returned to Riga a Party member in the days when to be discovered a Communist there had meant ten years of hard labor; during that time she'd married a bizarre Latvian Jew, a film director, whom she soon cast off. After the war she was assigned to Minsk, where Dr. Mikhail Papko chose her to be his administrative aid and bedfellow, but Papko became careless and was arrested by Chankov's predecessor, Anatoly Denisov, a comrade of Father's; they were the MGB in those days. At Denisov's urging and with great reluctance, Father had testified against Papko, and the man was convicted of taking fees, engaging in a highly profitable private medical practice, and other acts of bourgeois criminality.

Mariya had given the most damaging testimony against Papko. In any case, he was sent to the East, and no one had heard of him since. Mariya

had been promoted to the Institute job, which she held to this day. Father's payoff came in 1953, when, in the aftermath of the Doctors' Plot (on Stalin's order half a dozen Jewish doctors were arrested in Moscow) all Jewish medical administrators were systematically removed everywhere, especially in Minsk, but Father was permitted to keep his job.

Mariya soon married a Byelorussian journalist who, after the birth of two sons, promptly moved to Kiev without her, and she was obliged to raise the two boys without a father.

"Oh dear, Doctor, if you only knew how *exasperating* this is to me. Those boys! *Mi despiace molto.* But I assure you I don't doubt you for an instant. I'm devastated. You're *sure* it was they?" Yuri nodded. The way she sprinkled Italian into her conversation kept him off balance.

"What in the *world* could have given them the idea you're a Zionist?"

"I can't imagine."

"Oh, I suppose it's perfectly natural," she said. "Clannishness. Birds of a feather, et cetera. And, after all, why shouldn't they have their own country?"

Yuri was caught off guard. "Oh, I can *understand* Zionism, Doctor," he said, instantly regretting his words. "Not that I condone it. But don't you sometimes have a hankering to go back to Latvia?"

Her eyes flashed in her fat, white, freckled face. "What has that to do with the case? I was *born* in Riga. It's a Soviet city. I love it. How many Jews in Minsk were born in Tel Aviv, Professor? You see what I mean, Yuri Ivanovich?"

"Well, the nationality problem is one of those things," he said lamely.

"If only those boys had a proper father," she said wistfully. "Boys need a stern hand, don't you agree? Otherwise they turn into savage creatures. What should I do? Maybe you could advise me? I'd be ever so indebted to you!" She positively sparkled with insincerity.

Yuri remained silent. Finally he said hesitantly, "Doctor, do you think I should report the episode to the police? Perhaps a talk from a *militsioner* could make them realize—"

"Oh, dear, no, that won't be necessary. I'd be so grateful, Doctor, if you would please *not* do that. Not that I'd blame you. Your brand new car! I can imagine how you must feel!" She smiled icily, her eyes flashed, and she popped two small sugarcoated cakes into her mouth, ingesting them without a bite, almost inhaling them. She pushed the tray of cookies toward him. "These are delicious." Yuri shook his head. "Then some tea? I have a lovely jasmine. My secretary loves to brew it. She adores the aroma."

Yuri shook his head again. "Thank you."

She spoke now as seriously as she could, suppressing her smile. Her sincerity mask was aglow with light. "Believe me, Doctor, nothing like this will happen again, I promise you. And thank you for coming." She lifted her enormous bulk, using both arms to push herself up, and Yuri realized how quickly he had forgotten the enormous fatness of her. She resumed her ingenuous smile, took Yuri's arm, and, wobbling, led him to the door as if he were a small, errant boy. "I will think of *something*, Doctor. *Mille grazie!*"

At the last moment, buoyed by what seemed to him his sudden unexpected advantage, Yuri said on impulse, "Comrade, I assume you know there's a pediatricians' convention in Stockholm in August, eh? I've been invited, of course. Do you think it will be advisable for me to attend?" He had been working himself up to asking for some weeks; how ridiculous, he thought, that a trip to the West should have assumed such importance in his mind. Worse, he could hear the unsteadiness in his own voice.

Although Yuri had twice been a member of the Byelorussian Party Congress in Minsk, a ceremonial job to be sure, and although he invariably represented the hospital at the all-medical Party gatherings, just as Mariya represented the Institute (rather than Dr. Misharev, her nominal superior, who was "director"), and although they were all equals at such Party conclaves, Yuri had the intuition, gained from careful observation of the arcane interplay between leading Party members, that Mariya had more influence than he, that she might be attending informal caucuses and small gatherings at one office or another, behind closed doors, perhaps involving nonmedical Party people, to which he was not invited, and at which his fate might indeed be determined. The appointment as director would surely not be the decision of the minister of health alone. He could not recall a case where an acting this or that had not quite soon become permanent. Yes, two months was a frighteningly long period of time. A debate must be going on, a debate in which he had not yet been asked to participate. But he could not allow himself to become paranoid. Perhaps a request to go abroad might smoke them out.

"Of course you are not yet confirmed as director," Mariya said softly. "Do you think it wise to leave before this confirmation matter is settled?"

The woman was reading his mind. Her words were issued in a friendly tone; he found no menace in her *style*. But he felt a chill of uncertainty. He had never even mentioned Stockholm to Cleo because of the possibility —no, the *likelihood*—that he would be refused. Or that, if he were allowed, she would not be permitted to go with him. People allowed to go for the first time usually had to leave hostages.

She released his arm from her protective hold and spoke more formally,

but barely above a whisper: "You are of course *acting* director, my dearest friend." And then, smiling sociably, as if she had not uttered these words, "Have you ever been abroad, Doctor?"

Yuri felt diminished by his answer, which was more emphatic than he intended. "To Bucharest, Doctor, and Sofia. Not once to the West in all these years."

"Oh, what a shame! You feel deprived then? Discriminated against?"

Yuri shrugged.

"You sound a mite resentful." She beamed.

"On the contrary, I've never asked to go before."

"You know, my dear Professor, there really isn't that much going on in Stockholm. Foreign medical conventions—why, mercy, there're *such* a waste of time. But I'll inquire on your behalf, Doctor, if you wish. I'll let you know." As if the decision were someone else's and not hers alone, the lying battleaxe.

I'm forty-five years old, Yuri thought. My parents were both leading Party functionaries. I'm a Party member, a war veteran, a Liberator of Minsk, with two Orders of the *Slava*, I'm chief of pediatric medicine, acting director of the Pediatric Hospital of the First Clinical Association, professor at the Institute, not to mention a member of the Byelorussian Academy of Medical Science. And still have never been abroad. Is that not remarkable? What he said, however, was, "I'm sure I shall absolutely loathe it, comrade."

She led him gently but firmly to the door. "My advice would be to save your kopeks and stay right here." Yuri felt a sudden sharp stab of resentment. He was accustomed to *giving* commands. Who *was* this woman? Well, he'd see about her! He knew a few people, too.

Two weeks later, at the end of a long day, Yuri remained late at his hospital to supervise a bone marrow test on nine-year-old Stefan Sikorsky. It was not strictly necessary for Yuri to be present; the technicians were capable of handling the procedure without him. But all the facts up to now indicated Stefan had acute leukemia, and during the past two weeks something about the boy had captured Yuri's passion. It was against his wish and surely against his professional principles to become emotionally involved with any patient or his mother (beyond loving them all indiscriminately), but Stefan and his mother, Galina, had got to him. They had become his burden, his responsibility. Stefan, a thin, brown-haired boy with enormous trusting eyes, had a poodle at home, a present from his father, a man of some status, who, Yuri was informed, worked at KGB headquarters. Stefan had trained the poodle and dreamed of being a dog

trainer in the circus. The boy, whose father must have been very busy, for he never appeared, was attached more strongly than most kids to his worried, pretty mother, who, like Yuri, affected a frenetic gaiety but who never left his side in the intensive care unit put at the child's disposal.

When Yuri had first assumed the Directorship of the hospital on the sudden death of Kamenev, its first director, it was unheard of to permit mothers to visit their children even briefly. In those days, between admission and discharge, a mother was permitted to come to the hospital once a day only to hear from a doctor of the progress of her child's recovery.

Dr. Vladimir Bosherov had privately told other doctors, especially the surgeons, that while he made no formal objection, he felt Yuri's new policy of permitting parents into the wards was destroying the moral fiber of the young, who were unfortunate to be exposed to this decadent bourgeois pattern of excessive sympathy, concern, and pity from mothers. Instead, children should be taught self-reliance, bravery, and acceptance of what they could not change. It was also demoralizing to children whose mothers could not come because they had to work. And it was not an antiseptic practice. Mothers carried infections from outside. Yuri had cut short the doctors who objected, including Bosherov, preferring to make his statement simple: "I am a doctor. I am a humanist. And mothers and fathers are a fact in the lives of children."

'At the last Party meeting, at which the head nurse, Olga Petrovna, was also present, she had brought up the subject, and Dr. Bosherov had been plainly disturbed, but had contented himself with stuttering, "You are a doctor. So am I. You are a humanist, but you are also a . . ." He hesitated. "Never mind." And he had sat down grimly, remaining silent thereafter. Yuri, however, had no doubt that most of the other doctors at the Pediatric Hospital supported his own views, particularly the women, who were in the majority.

Yuri now instructed Olga Petrovna, the dark-skinned head nurse, whom everyone at the hospital called "The Terror," that he wanted Stefan's mother to be present in the operating room during the bone marrow test so that she could provide whatever comfort a mother might for a boy who was probably dying, during what might be a frightening procedure. Considering the status of the boy's father, he expected no objections.

"But, Doctor," the head nurse said severely, "you know the patient and staff are the only ones permitted in the operating room."

Yuri became brusque. "Just do as I say." Was he not, after all, the director?

"I'm sorry," Olga insisted self-righteously. "It's my ass, too. I won't

break Association rules, even for you, Professor." From her tone, she might have been saying "*Especially* for you."

Yuri knew the rule; it had been promulgated long before his time; it applied to all the services in the Association and as acting director of the Pediatric Service he had confirmed it. "You are correct," he said evenly. "Instead of performing the procedure in the operating room, we'll do it right here in intensive care. In the patient's bed. Okay? Bring everything. All the equipment."

"Are you serious, Doctor?"

"I was never more serious. You know the new rules permitting mothers to be present in the intensive care unit, is that correct?" Yuri smiled as sweetly as he could. Olga stalked away.

When the procedure was completed, Yuri bent and hugged his patient for having been brave, not even whimpering. The boy looked at him through ageless eyes. "I'll never get better, will I?" Yuri held him like a pet bear cub, as close as he dared, brushing his soft gray whiskers across the boy's face, and promised the boy he would soon learn to hop great distances like Katya Kangaroo. It was only a matter of practice. Yuri lied and added, of course he would get better, but it required patience. He turned and gave the falsely radiant, moist-eyed mother a quick parting handshake (he could no longer look into her eyes) and dashed from this place of grief to seek the safety of his own flat, a quick vodka, and the comfort of Cleo.

It had been an exhausting day. Galina Sikorsky hurried after him murmuring "*spasiba,*" and tried to press twenty-five rubles into his hand. Many doctors took "presents" for special treatment, Yuri knew, and under rare circumstances, with prominent patients like Stefan, children of Party functionaries, if the child was not really sick and he'd been called unnecessarily, he, too, succumbed—usually not for money, but for tickets to the ballet or opera, a bottle of cognac, or a gift of caviar.

But not this time. He shook Galina Sikorsky off. "No, no, no. Please. Please!" He patted her shoulder. It was almost ten o'clock. Hugging his bag, he loped into the chill dark November night toward his now refurbished Zhiguli in the drive in front of the hospital, fishing simultaneously into his instrument bag for his new windshield wiper blade, which these days he no longer forgot to remove whenever he parked the car.

6

IN THE DARK he had difficulty realizing what had happened. In the dim borrowed light from the hospital windows and a slim new moon, as his eyes slowly grew accustomed to the dark, he saw it all: every window shattered, only fragments in each frame, small shards scattered over the pavement; the seats pulled out of the car, dumped on the cobblestones, slashed many times, stuffing pulled out and strewn about; three tires flat; the car's body bashed repeatedly with a sledgehammer, doors and fenders smashed, hood wrecked, roof crushed. Water from the cracked radiator had emptied onto the pavement. Across the back of his car, this time in red letters two feet high visible in the moonlight, was one word: ZHID. Kike.

He rushed on foot along Akademiceskaya to Leninsky Prospekt to catch a trolley bus to the *militsia* station located in the small, squat, battleship-gray building between the commuter and the long-distance stations in Privoksalnaya Square. There had to be a closer *militsia* station, but he was so undone this was the only one he remembered. On the bus, he tried to calm himself, but could barely see or hear. He stepped on a passenger's foot and almost knocked over an elderly woman in his haste to get off. His mind was in turmoil.

He stormed into the *militsia* station to be greeted by a sleepy information elder who directed him to "Room Eleven in the basement," where he found a florid police captain sitting behind a desk in a bleak windowless room. The desk was illuminated by a single bulb hanging from the ceiling. The officer did not look up as he continued to flip through papers. Yuri cleared his throat. "I'd like to report a crime." He tried to keep his voice steady.

"Yes?" The paper shuffling continued; the officer did not look up, infuriating Yuri.

"And also to make a complaint about a policeman to whom I reported a similar crime some weeks ago. This could have been prevented if he had done his duty. I would like to press charges against him for dereliction." Even as he said it he knew he had made a mistake—his fury was getting the better of his judgment.

"Your name?"

"I am Professor Yuri Ivanovich Karpeyko of the Medical Institute and acting director of the Pediatric Hospital of the First Medical Association."

"Your name, I said, not a list of your achievements, comrade." The officer smiled thinly.

"My car has been wrecked. By the new *stilyagi*—the 1973 version."

"A privately owned vehicle?" Yuri nodded. "Your papers, comrade doctor." Yuri, curbing his rage by regarding this desk official as one of Minsk's typical idiocies, fished out his wallet and handed over his passport. The policeman examined it solemnly. From it, Yuri was aware, he was learning that Yuri Karpeyko was described as a Russian born on October 10, 1928. The officer seemed in no rush.

"Karpeyko? Haven't I seen this name someplace?" He thumbed the papers before him, riffling through them slowly. His question was an opening for Yuri.

"My father is Ivan Borisovich Karpeyko. Formerly chief of the entire First Clinical Association. A leading Bolshevik in his time."

The policeman's eyes grew wary.

"And *his* grandfather was Chief of Police in Minsk in the old days." That ought to keep this dolt off balance.

"Ah, under the Tsar. Your father must be a very old man."

"Seventy-seven. But quite frisky. He still knows all the right people." His frustration led him on. "You may also have seen my mother's name someplace. Maybe you've seen the famous photograph of the triple execution—Orlovsky, Bonov, and the Unknown Heroine, the one in the Museum of the Great Patriotic War? They call her the Unknown Heroine. Nevertheless, she was my mother, Rebekah Karpeyko. Surely you've heard of her?" He felt a surge of mortification as he spoke.

The policeman shook his head. "I was born in nineteen forty-six. In Kiev. Rebekah, did you say?"

What was he trying to tell this idiot? That he was *Somebody*? It was humiliating to use Mama in such a trivial pursuit. All the guy heard was the Rebekah. The *militsioner* yawned expansively and handed back Yuri's card. "You say you have a complaint to make about a *militsioner*? Are you serious, comrade?" His hauteur was intended to be intimidating.

Yuri heard his own anger in the higher-than-natural pitch of his voice.

Calm, Yuri, calm. Such officials are slightly ridiculous, as you know. No mere *militsioner* captain would dare to use this tone to someone like you. But Yuri could no longer help himself. The words tumbled out, close to falsetto. He was surprised himself at his long-suppressed fury. "I pointed out the culprits to this idiot. I knew *exactly* who they were. They were scooting off on bicycles, the two of them. All that fool was concerned with was that I shouldn't drive without a wiper, which they stole. Can you believe it? He deliberately let them get away."

"Aha!" The desk man glowed with sudden triumph. "Here we are!" He selected one *raport* from the sheaf before him and, separating it from the others like a documentary treasure, he read from it. " 'Karpeyko, Yuri Ivanovich.' That's you, correct? 'Disobeying a policeman. Driving without a wiper in a heavy rain. Eluding arrest. Leaving the scene when summoned to stop by uniformed *militsioner.*' That's all you, correct? 'Ulitsa Oktyabr'skaya 28'? Serious offenses."

"That's the blockhead!" Yuri cried, pointing at the report. "He saw *exactly* what those kids had done. And he let them go! What kind of fools are you taking on the force these days?"

"To drive in a heavy rain without a wiper is extremely dangerous, doctor or no doctor. No matter who took it. Having an automobile is a privilege, *grazhdanin.* It involves responsibilities to mere pedestrians like myself. You must know this."

"Goddamnit, you listen to me! That *militsioner* didn't do his job. Because *now*, officer, it may interest you to know, now those same kids, encouraged by him, came back this very night and smashed all my car windows, smacked the car in twenty places, slashed my tires, ripped out the seats, and smeared paint all over the car! A complete wreck! And all because that dumb bastard— I just *got* the damn thing! And you know how long we waited? Six years! You know what it cost? Seven thousand—"

The officer's face reddened and he stood up abruptly. "Come with me," he said softly. "Come." He led Yuri down a narrow hall to the doorway of a small office with one chair and a bare table. "Ilya!" he called, "hey, Ilya!" A short man in plainclothes shuffled toward them from the other end of the corridor. "Ilya, take charge of this citizen. I want to make a call!" He pushed Yuri gently toward the chair. "Sit, *grazhdanin.* What do you think, Ilya? Some kids painted the word 'Zionist' on his car and now he wishes to bring charges against a policeman for not catching them!"

Ilya eyed Yuri cautiously. "Go make the call," he muttered. The door closed. He and Ilya were alone. Yuri had never told the desk man that "Zionist" was painted on the car. Had it been in the policeman's report? A

word to the wise, was it? And now the desk man had passed the word to Ilya.

He and Ilya sat in a silence that grew in intensity. "A call to whom?" Yuri said, as much to break the deliberate silence as to learn anything.

Ilya's reply was barely audible. He was a stocky man in his early forties, with a pocked face and yellow pallor. Liver deficiency. The steel-rimmed glasses gave him the appearance of a petty clerk. His nose was bulbous and he had a bad body odor. "He has a friend. In the Republic *Tseka*," he murmured.

Someone on the Central Committee. Good, Yuri thought. Now they will find out who is who.

The desk man opened the door and re-entered. He leaned toward Ilya and muttered something so low that Yuri could not catch it. Ilya asked a hushed question behind a concealing hand, and the desk man said, "*Da, da*," and smiled enigmatically. Then, without a glance at Yuri, he withdrew.

"Empty your pockets, Doctor, and put everything on the table," Ilya said, his voice barely more than a whisper. Yuri stared at him in disbelief.

"You can go to hell," Yuri said. "Do you know what you're letting yourself in for?" These people should be saluting and yessing him. *Svyazi* was written all over him. They should be terrified to act this way. What had they heard?

"I'm not a prisoner. I came to report a crime and to *make* a complaint. And if you don't stop this nonsense—" He had to gain control of himself.

"Comrade Karpeyko, Captain Grigorenko out there is a strange man, but he is my superior. He said to search you. I must search you. If you will empty your pockets and hand me everything on your person, it would be best." He made a fist and caressed it with his open palm; he had come so close that his body stink engulfed Yuri.

Yuri felt the surge of adrenalin. He heard his own voice, now an octave too high, almost falsetto. "I'm afraid you will have to use force, comrade!" It was happening, all right.

The little man put both hands on Yuri's shoulders and turned him, fingers of steel.

"Turn around and stand with your back to me, mister, hands on the wall over your head!" Ilya was quite calm. Yuri peered at the man; his sober, sickly, pitted face was unmarked by any emotion. Yuri let himself be turned and faced the wall, uncertain, hesitating to expose his back to this creature. He raised his arms, put his hands against the wall, but kept his head turned back toward Ilya. The plainclothesman searched his trouser pockets.

The humiliation was abrupt and unexpected. This oaf, treating him like some common—

He turned back into the room and dropped his hands. To hell with it. His voice was back in its natural range.

"What the hell do you think you're doing?"

The sallow man was going through his effects. His thoughts seemed suddenly clearer. *Why are they doing this to me?* Why are they trying to provoke me? What did they learn from that phone call? His mind was groping toward dark, gloomy places where his thoughts longed not to enter. Father was wrong; he *had* to be wrong. He was letting himself be searched—very well. If there were hidden meanings to what was happening, he'd learn it from Pyotr very soon. If it was merely the stupid bureaucracy—one report leading to another, one typically idiotic act leading to another—he'd have their hides.

"Sit," Ilya said. He separated from the other papers all the Zhiguli documents, one by one, carefully placing them in a small stack on the table.

"So you defied a *militsioner,* Grigorenko informs me," Ilya said soothingly. "Was that wise?"

Yuri, on the defensive, launched into his version of what had occurred that day. "I merely asked the officer to apprehend the two hoodlums who stole my wiper and smashed my windshield. There they were, laughing. Is that too much to ask? He said I needed more proof, other witnesses; he did nothing. Instead of arresting the hooligans, he walked round my car and saw what they'd painted there. 'Zionist' on one side. 'Traitor' on the other. In fact, I am neither. I'm a physician, a professor, director of the Pediatric Hospital."

Was that a faintly encouraging smile he now saw on Ilya's pockmarked face? Smallpox or chicken pox? he wondered vaguely, or the aftermath of acne? It dawned on Yuri that Ilya himself might be a Jew; he might also doubt whatever it was Grigorenko had told him. Encouraged, he hurried on. "These words they painted are political, not words used by hooligan kids. On their own they'd have written 'zhid'—it's more their style, am I right? When the *militsioner* saw these scrawled words, I must say his attitude toward me changed. He became evasive. I explained to him that if he was going to do nothing about the hoodlums, I had to see two very sick children, and I drove off. I contemplated bringing charges against him, but changed my mind."

"That was wise," Ilya said, not unkindly. "So you are neither a Zionist nor a traitor. And your nationality . . ." he glanced at Yuri's passport. "Russian."

"My mother was a Jew," Yuri said. "She's the Unknown Heroine!"

"Ah, yes. I have seen the photograph at the museum."

It seemed to Yuri that Ilya was suddenly anxious to get him back to Grigorenko, that he was growing nervous. Good.

Yuri could hear the sound of his own labored inhalations and exhalations, echoing as if in a tunnel. He sat. Ilya emptied the wallet, examined each card: Party membership, passport, driver's license, hospital card, Institute membership, Medical Academy membership. He returned them to the wallet one by one, keeping the driver's license, which he added to the small pile on the table, and handed Yuri his keys, his comb, his handkerchief, his other papers, and finally, almost reluctantly, the wallet. He counted Yuri's money. "Two hundred ten rubles," he said. "Tickets to the Bolshoi. Excellent location. I've heard about doctors. Patients can never be too grateful, eh?" He handed Yuri the money and the tickets, which he had been given by Arkady Malensky, the theater manager, whose children he looked after. Now Ilya began to repack the medical bag. He opened the blue packet and glanced at the white pills.

"What's this?"

"Something for pain."

"The envelope says 'morphine.'"

"Yes."

"I once thought of studying medicine. Couldn't afford it. You always carry such stuff?"

"Usually. You never know when you'll need it." His heart raced. He hoped he wouldn't be plagued by those damn palpitations. What would this idiot know about controlled drugs?

"I see." Ilya refolded the packet of morphine and dropped it into the bag, snapped the clip shut, and pushed it toward Yuri.

"I regret that I had to nudge you, comrade. You left me no choice. You may go back to Grigorenko." He pointed to the door.

"What about that?" Yuri pointed to his driver's license.

"You will ask Captain Grigorenko."

Grigorenko was at his desk as if nothing had happened. Ilya, who had followed Yuri, stood for perhaps a minute, whispering to Grigorenko, and then shuffled back out into the hallway.

"So, Comrade Karpeyko, as you were saying when you came in, you wish to report some event? A case of vandalism?" There was no trace of apology in Grigorenko's voice or demeanor, only a touch of irony. The phone call seemed to have eliminated whatever caution he had. He was all business.

"Two kids," Yuri said. "Fifteen, sixteen. They're brothers."

"You know who they are? You say you saw them? And they wrecked your car? You are a lucky man to own a Zhiguli. You got it *po blatu?* How much over the list price did you have to pay?" Yuri peered at the man, stared him down. "Did you have it locked?" Grigorenko asked, looking away.

"Of course."

"We try not to create high crime rates in downtown Minsk artificially. Since you seem to know who these boys are, I will ask you, is there bad blood between you and them? Between members of your families? We don't become involved in private feuds and personal quarrels. Those are civil matters."

"These are wild animals, Comrade Captain. Hooligans. They travel in packs, like wolves. Dangerous, drunk on beer most of the time. They threaten ordinary citizens. There are more and more of them roaming the streets. Occasionally they murder someone. You've heard of the Tunick kid? I happen to know who these two are."

"And what makes you certain it's they?"

"The first time it happened, I saw them."

"But not the second time?"

"No."

"You would be prepared to appear in court and testify against them?"

"Yes."

"You wish to send them to the workhouse, where they'll learn to be expert criminals?"

"Let the judges decide that question. I'm a doctor, not a judge."

The sergeant handed Yuri a *zayavlenie.* "Fill this out and return it to us," he said carefully. "You still wish to press a complaint against *Militsioner* Asimovich?"

Yuri closed his eyes. "I don't think that's necessary," he murmured. Captain Grigorenko smiled for the second time, a thin, cool smile, and continued studying the papers before him.

"I came here to make a citizen's complaint about the behavior of two hooligans," Yuri said grimly. "It seems absurd that I should be abused for it. What was the sense to that?"

Grigorenko was his most laconic. "Some people have a way of stirring up trouble, Doctor. Some people are just . . . uh . . . provocative. I see you are a Party member."

"Among other things," Yuri said. Perhaps the apology was coming now.

"War veteran, too," Grigorenko said glumly. "Medals, et cetera. But

ings change, old-timer. These are not the old days. Like football. New
players each year. Trotsky used to have a lot to say. Now he's silent.
Abramovich, Ravich, Kaganovich . . . Litvinov . . . the lot of them." He
was listing prominent Jews of bygone days. "All changed. They are no
longer with us." Said with satisfaction. And Yuri was certain he was not
imagining.

"You will be notified by the procurator's office when you are needed for
preparation for the trial of these two so-called hooligans, Doctor. Assum-
ing they are hooligans."

"Thank you," Yuri said. Why should he be thanking this imbecile who
had twice humiliated him? But he could not unsay it. "Now, what about
my car papers? My license?"

"Comrade Karpeyko!" Grigorenko's voice was sharper. "Driving in the
rain without a wiper. Disregarding a policeman's order to stop. Serious
offenses. Your right to drive has been suspended."

"What? For how long?"

"You will be notified. We must forward this to GAI for action. With
our report."

"What about my wife?"

"Her license is all right." Grigorenko shrugged.

"Goddamnit! Who the hell do you think you are?"

Grigorenko's voice was utterly calm. "I am Stanislav Leonidovich
Grigorenko, Captain of the Minsk *Militsia*. Perhaps you should decide
who *you* are, Professor."

Yuri stormed out, blinded by fury and frustration. He could destroy
Grigorenko with a phone call. But he hesitated to make it. Not just yet.

This time he did not bother to remove the word on the back of the car.
Let the world see it. He arranged for the garage to haul it off and asked
the mechanic to give him an estimate for repairs and repainting. He
notified the insurance agency. Well, he had managed for more than forty
years without a car; the hospital had three Volgas; he could ask Natalya
to drive him when he had to make house calls; it was not exactly a
hardship, and Cleo, in her blithe way, was sure they would collect the insurance, and took it as a mere inconvenience. Of course, he did not tell
Cleo everything, trying to protect her from anxiety.

The garageman gave Yuri a written estimate: the repairs were nineteen
hundred rubles. The insurance agency after a week offered twelve hundred. Yuri hesitated. The seven-hundred-ruble shortfall was a month's salary for both Cleo and himself. Well, they'd manage somehow. They'd
forego their vacation on the Black Sea, and he could put off buying the

new tan suit he'd promised himself. He asked the mechanic how long he might have to make up his mind, and the man shrugged. "Two weeks? Will that be sufficient?" Yuri asked for a month. The mechanic shrugged. "There's a storage charge. Ninety kopeks a day." He lowered his voice. "And, comrade, I can get you eight thousand rubles for the car as is." Yuri would have to think about that, too.

7

THE FOLLOWING FRIDAY, Father came to dinner sick with fear and spewing venom. The cause of his disorder was a long article on page three that day in *Sovetskaya Byelorossiya* which neither Cleo nor Yuri had yet read. But Father kept up, never missed a word, especially of trouble. The article by V. Adolnikov was headed A BASE ACTION! Father, peering carefully through his heavy lenses, put in his teeth to read aloud to them. "Sit down, both of you. Listen to this, my boy."

He read to them with a certain malicious glee, with which Yuri felt he camouflaged a senile terror, the "authoritative" account of the divorce trial of a certain F. B. Cherniavsky, an engineer of considerable distinction. The man had decided to emigrate to Israel—a decision which his wife had bitterly opposed, and which the newspaper attributed to the machinations and influence of "the rabid Zionist, Leon Pavlovich Baryshin."

The tale of the Cherniavskys' domestic woes was told in great detail, mostly from the indignant wife's point of view, and ended on a hysterical and threatening note.

The Zionists threatened her by telephone, with intimidations, blackmail, and direct bribes in the form of parcels from Israel. Cherniavskaya, however, was adamant. Finally, Baryshin suggested to the husband that he should pull out all the stops, really frighten her with a divorce! Desperate, she came to court in a last effort to save her son and husband from taking this fatal step, after which he would lose his most precious possession—his Homeland. This was why she asked the court to give Cherniavsky time to think things over: maybe his confusion would pass.

As a Soviet person and citizen, Evgenia Ilyinichna has understood the true baseness of the agitation of the Baryshin clique: the Zionist propaganda for emigration to Israel is nothing but an invitation to betray one's Homeland, a political, civil and everyday vile deed.

Father stopped reading, removed his teeth, and pushed the newspaper toward Yuri's face. "Eh? Eh? What do you think?"

Yuri was thinking of the hulk of a man he had met at the Moskoviches, the subject of this journalistic attack—an air force colonel, with more decorations than Father and he combined.

Father was more agitated than Yuri had seen him in years. He put off taking his morphine shot. "That son of a bitch, Baryshin. *And* Ovsischer, and Davidovich—all of them. You know what this means?" he said, slurring his toothless words, his eyes beady behind the thick lenses. "It's the signal. Open season on Jews. If they insist on gathering at their stupid monument in the Yubeleinaya, the Black Hundreds will be out in force. Even a pogrom wouldn't surprise me." He rubbed his hand over his hairless pate, a gesture of misery.

Father brushed away the plate of grapes Cleo offered, his mood fouler than they realized. "It's the professional Jews; fuck their mothers! Baryshin and his coconspirators must be denounced! It's up to *us* to denounce them! Otherwise there'll be no end to it."

Yuri slipped Father his little blue packet, which he snatched and, trembling, he took up his cane and lurched off, limping on his spindly legs to the kitchen, still muttering.

They all knew about the killings of Jews that had taken place in the last few months in Minsk—Professor Mikhelson, the Kantors, brother and sister, and the Tunik boy, killed by his classmates. Beer-drinking teenage groups and others were running wild everywhere. Parents, even the police, couldn't control them. The murderers were called madmen by the authorities—and yet . . . Were they returning to the dark days when Stalin had had the great Yiddish actor Mikhoels and half the Yiddish theater murdered? All the wild ones needed was the signal to know that every Jew was under an official cloud. That every Jew was fair game. But hadn't Comrade Ustinov denounced these crimes and called the murderers insane? At least the rash of newspaper anti-Semitism had finally stopped.

The press had been ordered by someone at the top, surely Yuri's old friend Pyotr Feodorovich Ustinov himself, not to stir things up. Until today. Now here it was again, written between the lines of this story, ostensibly about a divorce, that Minskers, and particularly Jews, would be *expected* to denounce all the unexposed Zionists they might know, including husbands and wives, as Cherniavskaya had done.

How far was one expected to carry this? Obscurity was a patented weapon of the Party, and Yuri, in a hurry, often missed the nuances, but Party members, especially of his rank, were expected to understand the

code. The message was clear. Were the same ones—those whose masks had fallen away to reveal the cancer concealed for a generation when the Nazis came—now back in the saddle?

Father returned from the kitchen. In the few moments it took for the morphine to ease his pain and bring on the euphoria, he sat in silence, his always-lit Kazbek hanging from his lips, his half-white eyebrows arched, ignoring the spiraling smoke, the growing cigarette ash, staring at the news article, mesmerized. Suddenly he was agitating again, as if he were at a Party meeting, inspired, snorting, and, only he imagined, spellbinding.

"Why do we need these sentimental Jews? Making appeals to go settle in Israel!" He spat, "*Pfui* on Israel!" His own name, Yuri thought, imposed on him by Grandma Feygele in defiance of Grandpa Boris, never dreaming Father himself would, in the spirit of the Revolution, change the Israil to Ivan. Irony everywhere. "*Pfui* on our renegade Jews! Are they decent Bolsheviks? They are shit! With their bourgeois 'chosenness,' their Bible, their God! We know who they depend on! That great Nazi-in-Jew's-clothing, Kissinger, with his U.S.A. trading rights. I say, to hell with the Americans. We'll manage without them. We're not stupid. Lyonya is following the correct path."

"Who is 'we,' Father?" Yuri asked softly.

The old man stared as if he scarcely recognized Yuri; maybe it was the opium; or was it merely contempt? No, something more. Mama's stare that day.

" 'We' is who it always was!" the old man snapped, and turned away.

Of them all, Cleo was the one who stood up to Father. She had come under the influence of Shtainberg at the hospital, she often lunched with him, and, as Yuri now guessed, Shtainberg was probably an out-and-out Zionist. Why was it that Cleo, even from the earliest days, was drawn to Jews, when she had not a single drop of Jewish blood? Perhaps it was the Greek grandmother for whom she was named; the outcast Greek making common cause with the outcast Jew. When he had asked her many years ago why she was so drawn to Jews, she had said, "I can't tell you *exactly* why. But you're right. I'm drawn."

It was she who took the old man on. "If I were a Jew, to tell the truth, I would want to go to Israel," she said cheerily, "and believe me, I'd get there somehow. Why not? Listen to the way you talk! Isn't it plain it's not safe here anymore? It's not *nice* here. They are making you all criminals. You admit it, old man!"

Father got up suddenly, unsteadily, and started hobbling toward the door to leave.

46

Yuri rose quickly to restrain him. "Father! Don't be a child!"

"I'm not hungry!" the old man shouted. "Not for any food I get in this house!" He pulled himself loose from Yuri's embrace, opened the door and stumbled noisily down the steps to the street.

"Go with him!" Cleo commanded Yuri. "Go, go!"

Yuri chased after the old man and took his arm, but his father twisted free and would not respond as Yuri tried to talk sense to him. Finally they walked in silence together in the darkening city, along brightly lit Leninsky Prospekt, to Janki Kupaly Street, until they reached Father's place.

"I'll pick you up next Friday, the usual time. You'll need your shots." His father seemed crushed by the offer and the necessity, unable to speak. Yuri tried to embrace him lightly and kiss him, a gesture he had not made since they had met at the railroad station after the war, but his father pulled away, went indoors toward the tiny elevator cage, and left Yuri standing in the dark, empty street.

Father was given to melodramatic gestures, but even so, Yuri was unsettled. Cleo should not have talked to him that way. But he could not control Cleo's openness. He decided to write to *Sovetskaya Byelorossiya*, then to go on about his business and try to think as little about the damned article as possible. It would be risky, more risky than he could admit to himself, but come what may, a man had to live with himself.

After Cleo went to bed, he read a piece in a recently received journal from California; his English was improving. Physicians in America sent him journals because he was held in high esteem in certain western medical circles as well as in the Soviet Union as a result of his work in anemia; indeed, the "Karpeyko Syndrome" had led to an invitation to join the Academy of Medical Science in Byelorussia. When he had finished reading the monograph, he sat quietly and carefully composed his letter.

To THE EDITOR:

A BASE ACTION! rightly points out that no nationality can have the luxury of split loyalties which, in extreme cases, can destroy marriages and families. We should not demand of any citizens—of Soviet Jews, for example—that they run to the authorities or to the newspaper office (as did Cherniavskaya) to condemn other citizens —their *husbands!*—advocating emigration. We are citizens of our great country because we want to be. This makes us strong. The handful who mistakenly abandon their homes harm only themselves. Why should our mighty Motherland in all her majesty

threaten a few miserable runaways? Of course, Jews can be *terrorized* into spying on each other. As is known, during the war the *Judenrat* organized the murder of their fellow Jews every day. They did so under threat of torture and death, and, even so, many refused, preferring to give up life. But surely the Soviet Union today does not aspire to the brutalizations of Nazi Germany! Where would the Soviet Union be today had it not been for many great Jews—beginning first and foremost with Karl Heinrich Marx? The list of persons of Jewish nationality who have made giant contributions to the USSR is so long there is not space enough in your newspaper; not the least of these were my mother and my grandmother, not to mention my honored and revered father, a Russian who is half Jewish. To be blunt, they provided much of the brains and most of the inspiration for the Revolution and Resistance, especially in Minsk. During the war, *almost half the Jews in the Soviet Union were destroyed* by a barbaric enemy—among them my mother, six uncles, three aunts, and twenty cousins. Only two persons in my family remain: my father, because he was a colonel in Stalingrad, and I, who performed my duty as a partisan in the forests of Poland and Byelorussia under Comrade Ustinov. People have forgotten: before the war *half* our population in Minsk was Jewish, loyal Soviet citizens. After the deadly work of the Nazis, combined with the explosion in our city's population from other areas, today less than five percent of the people in Minsk are Jewish. Under the circumstances, do the authorities now expect me, for example, a Russian with some Jewish blood, to spy on the pitiful remnants of Minsk Jewry to report which miserable Jewish survivor, however misguided, wishes to emigrate to the land of his ancestors? To a nation, by the way, created by a Soviet vote at the United Nations, and supported by all the People's Democracies! Why this new madness? The USSR is no prison! To live here is the greatest privilege any human being can have today! Articles like A BASE ACTION! only give encouragement to the Black Hundreds element, to the beer-guzzling young hooligans who roam our parks, hallways, and streets looking for Jewish victims at night. Do we want to turn these hoodlums loose and set ourselves back thirty years? The undersigned is a member of the Party, the acting director of a hospital, a professor of medicine at the Institute, an *Akademik*, and the recipient of three awards and medals earned during the war.

Yuri Ivanovich Karpeyko

Yuri did not want to be talked out of sending the letter. Both Father and Cleo had very different but compelling reasons and ways to stop him, and if self-preservation were his only concern, that too would have

stopped him, but he decided to send it and not to show it to either Father or Cleo. What kind of community were they? Were they already doomed? Was he? He felt a terrible need to know, and the answer could come from neither Father nor Cleo. The letter would not be published, he knew. But there would be a reaction. Perhaps if those who made the decisions agreed with him, people like Baryshin, who for years had been refused the right to leave, would be allowed to go at last. That would be answer enough. Perhaps his appointment would be confirmed and made permanent. Those in positions of power would understand that he could not be intimidated, that he understood tactics, and that he spoke common sense. Otherwise? He refused to think about otherwise.

He sealed the envelope, found a stamp, went downstairs, and mailed the letter.

8

NEXT DAY HE RECEIVED A NOTICE to appear on December fifteenth at the office of the procurator as complainant and witness against the Kalnin brothers. He was determined to see that matter through. If those kids weren't stopped, one day soon they'd kill somebody.

That night, an hour after midnight, the phone must have rung for several minutes before Yuri finally awakened fully. He went out to the kitchen to answer it. "Yes? Yes?"

After the static, he heard a man's deep voice—a basso. The man sounded drunk or drugged. "Karpeyko? Izziss Karpeyko?" the voice said over the crackling wire.

"Who is this?"

"You have daughter Yelena at th' Second Medical Institute 'n Moscow?" The man spoke in a slurred Muscovite Russian.

"Yes?"

"I have a message from 'er, you *zhid*. Leave the Kalnin boys alone. Keep your big Jewish nose outa their lives."

"Who is this?" His own voice was scarcely more than a sigh.

"Your wife works at th' Firs' Clinical 'ssociation? She takes th' bus, right? Buses 'r' dangerous. Accidents happen."

"Listen—whoever you are—"

"Too bad about your nice new car, you cocksucker Jew." There was a basso laugh, mirthless but prolonged. Click. The line was dead.

By now Cleo was standing beside him, huddling half bare in her nightgown. "Something serious?" she said. "The meningitis case?" Yuri had suddenly become cold, on the point of shivering.

"Come back to bed," he said.

As they embraced under covers, Yuri's mind whirling, he could feel her soft comforting body trying, without her knowing what had hap-

pened, to offer solace for something unknown, an unvoiced fear, trying to keep him from harm. But he was not worried about himself. Yelena, now, was another matter. He hadn't thought until then about Yelena. Or the woman in his arms. The bastards were capable of anything.

"Tell me," Cleo coaxed. "What was it? It's no time for secrets."

"An obscene call," Yuri said. "Some man. A drunk."

"My God, I thought it was serious. If you could see yourself!"

He decided to tell her. "He threatened Yelena in some vague way. You, too. If I insist on pressing charges against the Kalnin hoodlums."

She sat up and turned on the light. Her face was whiter than he had ever seen it—his normally cheery, pink-cheeked Cleo. Her black, flecked hair was tousled, her upper teeth bared, clamped over her lower lip, as if she were in pain.

"What will you do?" she repeated ominously.

"I'll sleep on it," Yuri said.

"You will not!" She swung her feet to the floor, put on slippers, reached for a robe, and huddled into it. The room was chilled, the heat not yet turned on. "How can you sleep? How can I sleep?"

Yuri knew, had known immediately when he'd heard that low, illiterate voice on the phone, although the threat was preposterous, that he was defeated. How could he endanger them? Even if it were all bluff. "All right, then, I'll drop it."

Yuri lay still, his mind trying to pierce the mists of memory and omen. He said, "Father's right, Cleo, you know. First, unimportant things. Slashed tires. Broken glass. You never saw *Doctor Mamlock*, the movie. I did." Yuri had seen it when he was thirteen and had never forgotten it—a Soviet film depicting the destruction of a German-Jewish doctor in Berlin in the early days of the Nazi regime. An entire nation against one man.

"It's nothing like that. This anti-Semitism is an aberration. It's not sanctioned by the authorities. Otherwise how could you have been made director?"

Yuri chuckled. "Yes? After all we saw during the war, you believe it's an aberration?"

"Oh, Yuri. The war, the war! It's not the war! You're becoming like Father!"

"I'm going to see Pyotr Feodorovich tomorrow."

"Yes. Please! He'll tell you what's what. I know he'll reassure you."

He sighed, but she continued earnestly.

"Yurochka, my darling, we can't let anything happen to Lenochka. You hear me? Nothing! She is *our* responsibility." Her fear filaments were out. "*My*" responsibility, she was really saying. The whole world could go up

in smoke but Yelena was sacred, Yelena, her gossamer overachiever, her female replica of Yuri—in her own unique way, one of the wonders of the world. Yuri, of course, felt no differently. A pure innocent marvel of a child. How could they dare take a chance with her? Yuri was thankful she'd be coming home soon for the winter-session break. He suddenly wanted her safe in her room again.

He turned out the light. "I have to be at the Institute early," he mumbled.

They lay separated this time, sorting their separate thoughts.

"Good night."

"Sleep well."

First she dozed and woke, then he did—short restless naps and wakefulness again. Both went to work in the morning exhausted.

At the Institute he found a handwritten note in his box. "Dr. Karpeyko, I would *so* appreciate it if I could call on you and Cleo at home tonight. About 8:30? For a quiet chat? Please let me know if that's all right. Mariya Kalnin." He did not look forward to her visit with any expectant glow; however, they had no choice but to see her. He left word with her secretary that Dr. Kalnin would be welcome.

Pyotr Feodorovich Ustinov's office phone was busy the first three times he tried to reach him. But on the fourth attempt he got a woman receptionist whom he knew slightly. First Secretary Ustinov was not in the office at the moment. Would he leave his name? Yuri said he was an associate of Comrade Ustinov from the war days, an old friend, and he wished to consult him on a personal matter, which was also a Party matter. Oh, Professor Karpeyko—of course! Comrade Ustinov would have half an hour for Comrade Karpeyko next Wednesday at two. Would he call back tomorrow morning to confirm? Well, Pyotr was after all an important man; his days were booked well in advance, no different from those of a busy physician.

At lunchtime, instead of having his meal brought to his luxurious office, Yuri walked to the Association cafeteria building. He saw Shtainberg there, eating alone—the very man he was looking for—and sat down opposite him. Shtainberg, the surgeon with perhaps the best professional reputation in Minsk, was a broad, bearded man with a bent Jewish nose, a rasp in his throat like Father's, and a peculiar toss to his head whenever he spoke. While he specialized in thoracic work, he did general surgery as well. Cleo, who saw them all in action from her anesthesiologist's chair, told Yuri he had no equal in Minsk. The only reasons he was not chief of surgery were that his name was Shtainberg and he tended to be rather rustic in manner. He smiled at Yuri across the table and barked a bellow-

ing greeting. Cleo liked him, but Yuri had always found him too aggressive and, to be frank, he was not overjoyed at the intimacies Shtainberg took publicly with Cleo, embracing her quite openly and on occasion greeting her by kissing her, however mockingly, on both cheeks in the old style, and calling her "darling." But of course he meant no harm; he was just sentimental. In ways he did not yet understand, Yuri envied Shtainberg's ability to be so demonstrative. Shtainberg brought his own lunch, Yuri had heard, and people gossiped about what occult, "Oriental" reason he might have.

Yuri looked carefully at Shtainberg's supply of food. Two hard-boiled eggs, a large, soft, whitish cheese, a sandwich on soft white bread of pink, heavily spiced salami, a pickled cucumber, and a bunch of grapes. The Thermos contained buttermilk. "Want some?" Yuri demurred. "Look, I eat this stuff every day." Shtainberg uttered his guttural laugh. "You, of course, are very fancy now, with that gorgeous office! And a lovely assistant to bring you the best!"

"I'll try some of your sandwich, if I may," Yuri said, if only to establish contact. He nodded his approval with his mouth full. It wasn't bad.

"Here, have one of the eggs, too, and try the cheese. Anya gets it from a little lady at the market who makes it just for her on her farm." In his boisterous way, Shtainberg could exude enthusiasm even for cheese.

"Could we take a little walk outside?" Yuri said tentatively.

"Why not?" Shtainberg boomed. "Little fresh air never hurt anyone." What fool would want to talk indoors? They took their coats, went to the door, and walked briskly together in silence out to the snow-covered grounds, between the yellowish, aging two- and three-story stucco buildings, two preoccupied professional men.

As they neared his new, towering, nine-story Pediatric Hospital that now dominated the complex, Yuri said, "The Melikov boy, you did him last Wednesday?" It had been a simple appendectomy.

"Yeah," Shtainberg said. "He's doing fine. No problems."

"If anyone sees us together and asks what we talked about, we talked about the Melikov boy's appendectomy, agreed?"

Shtainberg looked at him with renewed interest. "Sure," he said. "What else do we have to talk about?" They walked a little further, slowing their pace, while Yuri tried to frame his question.

"You know a man named Baryshin?" he said at last.

"Leon Pavlovich Baryshin? The midget colonel?" he laughed. "Yeah, sure. Terrific guy. Don't believe all that shit in the papers." They turned at the gate and walked to the left, keeping always within the Association grounds. "Say, aren't you Jewish, or half Jewish?" He spoke as if the

thought had just entered his head instead of having been harbored there for years.

"Partly," Yuri said.

"And Cleo?" Shtainberg boomed. "Not my beloved *Cleo?*"

"No. She's Ukrainian with a Greek grandmother thrown in for confusion."

"I couldn't imagine! She is *such* a *shiksa!* Oh, how I love that woman, Yuri. Do you know how lucky you are? She's *such* a pro in the operating room, too. We're goddamn lucky to have her."

Yuri had not sought Shtainberg out to sing Cleo's praises. "Where can I meet him?"

"Who? Baryshin? What the hell for? You don't want to leave Minsk, do you? Hang around, Yuri. You're no Zionist. The Zionist thing will go away, believe me." He sounded evasive. "The anti-Semitism will taper off."

"I'd like to see him. Very much."

"Everything passes. Didn't Stalin pass? He took a hell of a long time about it, that's all. Hunker down. Why should *you* worry? You don't have a real Jewish heart. And you have a great job. You would *hate* Israel. It's not for you, believe me. Now, I'm a different story." He lowered his voice. "Did you know I was actually bar mitzvah? A misspent youth! That's me! They're after me already. They tell me I'm on too many committees, they think I should give up my position as deputy chief surgeon here, not enough Partyness in my attitude—all kinds of shit. I pay no attention to it; I'm used to it. But I'll tell you the truth, right now this is no place for a Jew. Luckily I'm a tolerant man."

"I believe my heart may be more Jewish than I thought." Yuri could not imagine what had made him say that. He hadn't meant to.

Shtainberg peered at him sideways, as if trying to get his measure. "Some poor bastards have been waiting for five years, y'know. The creeps at OVIR won't let 'em go. One stupid excuse or another. If you applied to go, you wouldn't be allowed to bandage a finger! Goodbye job; overnight you become a parasite. Others apply and get out in three months. Who knows why? If some supreme intelligence in the Kremlin is working on a master plan for the Jews, we schnooks down here don't get it."

"I've never dreamed of going. What for? But I seem to have attracted animosities in some circles. I'm not sure why," Yuri said.

"Why? Have you asked Dr. Vladimir Bosherov? Pure Slav, that Volodya, would never stoop to anything underhanded, y'know." He paused to reflect. "Yeah, maybe you *better* meet Baryshin. It could take a few days to arrange." Shtainberg had become subdued, suspicious, on

guard. Yuri couldn't blame him. "Listen, I'll let you know." Shtainberg spoke in a lower register, now anxious to get away. As they walked, the surgeon was scarcely his usual cocksure self. He was wondering about Yuri, quite naturally. Who had sent him? The Party? The Security people? Yuri wondered how he could reassure Shtainberg that he had not been sent to entrap. To do it he reached far down into himself.

"I think I may be looking for my Jewish side," he said as they reached the door.

"Oh, shit, now I've heard everything!" Shtainberg laughed, neither impressed nor relieved. "I'll be in touch."

9

MARIYA KALNIN CAME to the flat that evening as sweet and unctuous as Yuri had ever seen her. She brought a box of German chocolates as a gift for Cleo and a small packet of six excellent Havana cigars for Yuri. She settled into Father's armchair, but sank so deeply Yuri was afraid she'd never be able to get up.

"I've come to make peace, peace," she said. "Could I trouble you for a glass of water, Cleo, my dear? Those stairs. No, no, water will do. Thank you, my sweet. Well, as you can guess, my sons are not my greatest asset." She bobbed her round, pretty head. "Not that they're such bad boys underneath it all. But why should that be your problem? What I'd like to do is make amends—in simple language, to pay for the damage they've done. There, I've said it, and then . . . then, I hope we could pretend . . . well, we could agree, couldn't we, that it never happened? Would that be satisfactory?"

Cleo and Yuri exchanged glances. "Those words they painted—" Yuri started.

"Yes, exactly. Perfectly disgraceful. I don't know where they get such . . . such perfectly dreadful . . . well, I'm afraid they pick it up in the streets. There's a terrible element about nowadays. They're influenced by such awful . . . I sometimes don't know what . . ." She twisted her pudgy pink hands in what certainly could have passed for anguish. Yuri suspected she was ambivalent toward him. And perhaps the ambivalence extended to Party discussions when he was not present. He decided to court her.

"Do you have some idea of how much the damage to your car was, Yuri?"

"Well, we have an estimate from the garage. It's quite high, I'm afraid.

Nineteen hundred fifty rubles. They must have used sledgehammers, those boys!"

"Oh, dear, Yuri Ivanovich, there must be some misunderstanding. I'm not talking about the second episode. My boys had nothing to do with that at all, you *know* that. They were in Kiev with their father, the little shit, that day. No, no. It was another—" She stopped as if catching herself in time. "But the first time when you actually saw them," she went on smoothly, "would you say a hundred rubles?"

Yuri had never bargained about anything this way. It confused him to be expected to. "Let me see. They took my wiper. They broke my windshield. That alone—"

"Two hundred rubles, then. I don't want to dicker. Two hundred. Agreed?"

Yuri reminded himself who this woman was and of his resolve. "Agreed," he said, trying to force enthusiasm into the word.

"Agreed and *forgotten?*"

"Agreed and forgotten," he repeated. Cleo looked vastly relieved. She let her breath out slowly.

Bustling unnecessarily, Mariya Kalnin opened her purse, took out a wad of bills, and counted out two hundred rubles. Her smile was back as she handed the money carelessly to Yuri. "I don't believe a mother's position is enhanced any if she has convicted children, do you?" The smile.

She closed her purse with unnecessary flourish, and with enormous effort lifted herself from the armchair into which she had sunk too low. "It's so nice to have a chance to chat with you both again. What a perfectly lovely flat you have. So much *room*. And you've done so *much* with it!" She fluttered toward the glassed cabinet with Yuri's archaeological artifacts. The dish from Egypt; a spearhead from Greece; two bowls and a knife from Syria; the spoon from ancient Troy; a set of Persian beads, presumed to have been worn by either a prostitute or a woman of great esteem; a pre-Columbian vase; and a tablet, with Hebrew letters, found in a *tel* not far from Haifa. Mariya looked at them all, oohed dutifully. They were Yuri's secret pride and fortune.

"I had no idea you . . . From Syria you say? Ancient Troy? Isn't that marvelous? And South America? Doesn't it make you feel, all of *us*, too, some day . . . will be . . . how shall I say . . . 'buried'? What language is this?"

"Hebrew."

"You don't say! Can you read it?"

Yuri laughed. "No. Probably it says 'No Smoking.'"

"Or 'Women's WC.'" Mariya snickered.

He led Mariya to his books and showed her his shelf on archaeology. "The Minsk library has practically nothing, so I am obliged to read in foreign languages." The books were in English, German, and Hebrew. She selected one of the Hebrew books and opened it.

"Lovely pictures."

"That's the only thing in them I understand. My patients bring me books and artifacts," Yuri said, "those who can go abroad. I give them the money and ask them to bring back anything—anything at all, as long as it's genuine. They sometimes become interested in archaeology themselves."

But Mariya shifted her attention to the P.P.D. automatic on their wall.

"That, dear Mariya, is a memento of my days in the woods as a partisan, when our dear friend Hitler came to Minsk. You were in Riga then, if I'm correctly informed? Cleo and I were together during those days. This old gun and I were inseparable lovers. Like Cleo and me."

Mariya's face lit up. "Oh, I'm glad you reminded me. I don't know why this gun made me think of it. Your request—to go to Stockholm?"

"Yes?"

"To *Stockholm*?" Cleo exploded. "When? What for?"

"A pediatricians' convention," Yuri said. "In August. I've been meaning to tell you."

"Yurka! How could you *keep* such a thing from me?"

"I wasn't sure—" Yuri started.

"I am the bearer of good tidings, my dear Doctors Karpeyko," Mariya smiled. "Everything is arranged." Yuri stared, unbelieving. He was sure it was a trick, he was sure she had turned him down when last they spoke. Second thoughts. Hers and his.

"Well, I want to go too," Cleo sang like a petulant child. "It's not fair. If he goes, I want—"

Mariya turned the full glare of her smile on Cleo. "You know what, my dear? It's been arranged."

"Oh, my God!" Cleo exulted, her voice running to her high register. She threw her arms around Mariya's great hulk. "You *are* a fairy godmother! Stockholm! Perhaps we can see Copenhagen as well!"

"Perhaps. You may like it so well, you may decide not to come back!" They all laughed. "Of course, Yelena will be here with us, you understand." Her last words were spoken almost grimly into Cleo's ear. Then, more lightly, as if a load were off her back: "I vouched for you both."

Mariya untangled herself from Cleo's embrace. "Well, this fairy godmother is exhausted from waving her magic wand, and she really must be going—so if you'll excuse me. . . ."

58

Yuri and Cleo saw her to the door. Then suddenly she was breathless again, her happy teeth were back. "It's been *such* a nice visit. We have our little agreement now, don't we? You'll be sure to call the *militsia*? And the procurator's office? *There must be no trial.*" Yuri nodded, and she continued, still breathless. "Our accounts are in order, then. I can't tell you how glad I am. There's one more matter, but another day, perhaps." The fixed smile never left her face.

As if with an afterthought, she turned back. "Oh, have you heard about your appointment?"

"Not a word." She had asked the question so breathlessly, he expected her to give him additional good news.

"Isn't that *exasperating!*" Mariya Kalnin said. "Ah, well. *Nichevo.* You will, Yuri, you will. It's the clumsy bureaucracy." She brushed Cleo's cheek quickly, ignoring Yuri, and waddled her way laboriously down the stairs.

10

AT HER SUGGESTION, which he secretly welcomed, Cleo accompanied Yuri next morning to the *militsia* station to withdraw the charges against the Kalnin boys. Grigorenko was not on duty; instead they found a sandy-haired young Ukrainian, who listened sympathetically as Yuri told him that the boys' family had paid for the damages. To withdraw the charges was not entirely simple, of course, but the young man made it as painless as possible: more forms to be filled out with explanations.

That night Cleo had planned for them to go to dinner at the Zhoravinka, the last word in elegance in Minsk, a place where foreigners could be found having entire meals of caviar. The restaurant served all the foods Cleo loved. After that they had tickets for the visiting Bolshoi at the Opera House, given to Yuri by the theater director after Yuri made two house visits to his ailing daughter to encourage her through her measles and to immunize the other two children against it. Yuri put on his gray suit to match hair, mustache, and beard, and the gray tie with tiny red dots. He also pinned his Liberator of Minsk ribbon carefully to his lapel. He called the hospital and checked on the two meningitis cases. They were both stable, responding to the medication. Stefan Sikorsky's condition was also stable. The boy seemed to be in remission, and his mother might be able to take him home tomorrow.

Cleo put on lip rouge, her palest—she loved to be modern. Yuri applied a touch of breoline, combed his hair tight to his head to put a trace of iron into the gray, and brushed his mustache and beard. They put on their heaviest coats; Cleo set her gray caracul hat at a rakish angle before the mirror, and Yuri put on his gray Homburg, straight and square. They had barely stepped out of the apartment when they heard the phone ring.

Yuri darted back to the kitchen and took the call. "Moscow calling," a woman operator's voice said over the crackling. "Is this 267-578?"

"Yes." He motioned through the open door for Cleo to return. He had heard an abrupt loss in power transmission at the caller's first words, a tiny click, and he was infuriated. How dare they! On *his* phone! Then he recognized Yelena's voice.

"Daddy? Can you hear me? How are you? How's Mama?"

Yelena called dutifully each week or two; they were a closely knit family. This time, however, she sounded as if she were flying, elated with good news.

"Guess what? Professor Kozhinskaya has made me her first lab assistant!"

"Lenochka, what an honor!"

"You really have to meet her, Daddy—she's brilliant! She's having two more of my papers published over her name and this time *mine*, too."

"Be careful you don't become conceited."

"*Me*, Daddy? I don't dare. I have six other students working under *me!* Imagine your little Lenochka, trying to boss these six monsters! One of the guys is six foot six! I'm so humble when I talk to him!" Yuri laughed. "We're working with woodchucks now. . . . Yes, of course, still the Australian antigen. And they all get hepatitis. Isn't that sad?"

"They're only woodchucks, Lenka. Be sensible!"

"Kozhinskaya thinks something I mentioned has given her a sudden clue to an antibody. Daddy, if we can come up with a cure for hepatitis— or better still, a vaccine! Imagine! Half the world catches it now, do you realize that? Eighty percent of the Africans and Asians! I'm so excited! Even sour old Kozhinskaya smiles now and then!"

When she had finished bubbling to Yuri, Yelena talked to her mother. Cleo laughed and ooohed and aaahed, "How wonderful, Lenochka! How marvelous!" and told Yelena they were just fine. "Dearest, thanks for calling. I hate to rush you, but we're just on our way out. Well, darling, we're going to the Zhoravinka. . . . Yes, where the foreigners eat! . . . Now, don't be so chauvinistic! The food is superb! And then to the Bolshoi. All right? We're so happy for you, Lenka!" She made a little kiss into the phone and hung up. She turned to Yuri, staring, and without warning her face crumpled. For one instant she looked like an old woman, but she covered her face quickly with both hands, took out a handkerchief, patted her eyes, and said briskly, "Come on, Yurka, at least *she* has no problems. Let's go. For God's sake, let's have some fun." Yes, Cleo, too, had begun to worry.

11

AT THE GRAY Byelorussian Central Committee headquarters on Engelsa Street, Yuri had to wait in the second story anteroom only a few minutes before the receptionist escorted him through a maze of halls into a more intimate waiting room, where Pyotr's secretary greeted him with a smile and asked him to have a seat. In a few moments Pyotr himself, the first secretary of the Byelorussian Communist Party, an alternate member of the Politburo in Moscow, lumbered out, embraced him, and called him *synok*, sonny, and with considerable ceremony escorted him to his inner sanctum.

Once, long ago, Pyotr had been a mighty skeleton with enormous strength; now his cheek scar was faded but still visible. Yuri detected a more pronounced ponderousness in his words and movement than when he had seen him last—only four months ago. Pyotr walked slowly, holding an arm possessively about Yuri's shoulders, as one would guide a beloved, if somewhat incapable, child; and he had a hacking cough, which had become worse since they had last met.

His old friend had certainly come a long way, Yuri observed, examining this huge, sumptuously furnished, ornate office. Nowadays one could scarcely imagine this slow-moving man lying on his belly as lithe, lean, and comfortable as a snake, behind a low line of shrubs along that deserted stretch of railway track, every inch of it familiar to him—waiting, waiting, the automatic held loosely, almost carelessly, in one hand, listening for the sound of the approaching locomotive, casually asking fourteen-year-old Yuri to check the grenades again and the fifteen-year-old Pavel to check the ammunition, as if the three "men" were lolling about some vegetable garden hunting for rabbits. Pyotr, who before the Germans came had supervised railway-bed maintenance crews, claimed to know every centimeter of track between Minsk and Brest.

Those were hair-raising times—days and nights of deadly common pur-

pose, which one almost missed these days. That eternal wait long after dark, the almost welcome sound of the antiquated steam locomotive, laboring, puffing, and suddenly *K-BAAM! ZOOM!* The sudden, deafening roar, the world crashing and thumping, the enormous flashes of light, the trembling ground, as if the earth itself had exploded, the air full of sound and debris, and before these had even stopped echoing, other smaller crashing explosions, until finally the shapes of dazed, wobbling figures—their prey—in helmets, silhouetted against the blazing sky, emerged like drunks into the night through train doors and windows. Yuri could still feel the surge of gladness, the thrill of exhilaration that had filled him when he saw them stagger and fall. Like Father, he had been planning to be a medical man, to spend his life healing, but also like Father he could not deny the excitement, however abhorrent.

Only a month before that, they had come upon a small ravine in the marsh, and had seen the earth freshly dug. Pyotr had ordered them to dig into it; perhaps something valuable had been hidden there—arms, supplies, ammunition. Instead they discovered the first of the mass graves—an area half the size of a football field, hastily backfilled trenches full of decaying, stinking corpses. Pyotr had estimated there were three thousand bodies—men, women, children—rotting there, decomposing, still in awkward postures, as if they had been buried alive. Pyotr had stared, then muttered, "Cover them up. They stink."

"Who do you think they are?" Yuri had asked, but Pyotr's face had remained clouded over. "Who did it?" No reply. They had all heard about the five thousand in the Yubeleinaya market, machine-gunned in two grim hours and buried by bulldozers. Including Mama's three sisters and their eight boys and girls.

These staggering shapes, *they* were the murderers of those women and children. His women. How easily, how exultantly, they had mowed them down, shadows scythed by Pyotr's chattering gun and his own grenades. Difficult to think of their victims then or even now as human. Those shapes were the beasts sweeping over the land, a plague, killers of old men, of children, Jews especially; that was all he knew then. The black shapes had begun firing, and Pyotr had somehow been hit. It had turned out later to be an ugly wound, half his left cheek torn away, blood, so much blood it covered his face, and Yuri and Pavel had had to drag him, almost unconscious, the last four hundred yards. Afterward they had stopped running, and the three of them had finally made it to the forest camp where Cleo was waiting.

"Yurka was all right," Pyotr had muttered to Cleo. He always gave credit to others. "Pashka as well. Two fine men." Cleo was fourteen her-

self then. Pyotr was the "old man"—twenty-three. It was he, the old man, who knew the safe houses in the countryside, the families that would take them in, including Cleo's. It was he who knew the other bands of partisans hiding in the marshes and woods. It was he who took over from Kuznetsov, he who kept in touch with Zorin, the leader of the Jewish partisans, and Ponomorenko, the commander of all the partisans, the man whose staff planned their strategy and gave them their targets.

"You saved the old man, sonny," he had muttered despite the ghastly wound which Yuri could not bring himself to look at, even though only a month earlier he had been quite able to look at all those rotting corpses. Cleo had run to pump fresh cold water and had cleaned the wound; *she* could bear to look at it with compassion. Cleo was unbelievable. With Pyotr's jawbone exposed, she and Yuri had contrived to bandage and rebandage his cheek with wet packs as if they had been doing it all their lives. "If only we had a doctor," she had said.

Gystarazh, a woman doctor with the Jewish partisans, was Cleo's idol. She made her way like some holy saint from camp to camp, tending the wounded and sick. She heard about Pyotr somehow and one day showed up to treat his wounds. "I'd love to be a doctor, like Gystarazh," Cleo said after her idol left.

Pyotr's pain must have been almost unbearable for days, but he continued to walk, fight, talk. "Your father would be proud of you," he had said to Yuri, "as both a fighter and as a doctor. If it's ever over, *synok*, I will recommend you for a Hero award. Pasha, you as well. And Cleo shall be a doctor. I promise. You all, of course, must do the same for me. Hero of the Soviet Union. That's the least I deserve, don't you think? You get it for saving my life and I for providing the life to save!" He had started to laugh at his grisly joke but had fainted. Extravagant days. Extravagant gestures. Today, of the original small group who had found their calling in the woods, there were only Cleo and he and Pyotr. Many others, too, but they had come later. They had all been to the celebration at the Yubeleinaya. Of course, so high an award as Hero was bound to be denied a mere boy. Today each of the two men wore a ribbon in his lapel, Pyotr had the Hero ribbon he had longed for, and Yuri his Liberator ribbon, and two Orders of the Slava, shadowy proof that it had all happened. Cleo was their undecorated heroine, the child nurse.

"So tell me, sonny, to what do I owe this pleasure? Hey, how d'you like my new office? It's fantastic, don't you think? Ha, it was a nice party, wasn't it?" The old fatherly warmth, even though Pyotr was not that much older than he. The office was lordly in appointment. Hard, stately chairs, each almost a throne.

Yuri said softly, "You know I wouldn't bother you unnecessarily, Pyotr Feodorovich. I know how busy you must be."

"Beautiful hotel, the Yubeleinaya, you agree? Kuznetsov and I must've put away three *pollitri* of vodka in fifteen minutes. Once we got started on old times! Believe me, I was *blind* that night. He, too! Kuznetsov's not the man he was, you know. I remember nothing! What a party! Those were great days we celebrated, Yurka. Right? Not like nowadays. Nobody believes in anything nowadays. Eat and run, drink and run, fuck and run. Minsk is a barnyard!" He had another small coughing spasm but recovered quickly. "Hey, you've heard my daughter Katerina has a son? Almost two now, my little Grisha! Calls me De-da! So I'm a grandfather —how d'you like that?—and no effort at all! In those old days I thought I'd never live to be a *father!*"

"Who expected to live?" Yuri said. "Who expected miracles?"

He noticed Pyotr's ashtray full of extinguished butts. Pyotr reached to his inner pocket, took out a fresh cigarette, and lit it. Pyotr's skin was gray. He offered a smoke to Yuri but Yuri shook his head. He had the impression that for all the reminiscing Pyotr was not comfortable with the old days.

"How's your old man?"

"Still going. He misses practicing. He reads, keeps up, but it isn't the same. Cleo's trying to fatten him up."

"Ah, Cleo! How is our lovely Cleo?"

"The same. Conscientious as a schoolgirl, our best anesthesiologist. She wants every surgical procedure to go perfectly. I don't know how she does so much. Keeps our house immaculately, she cooks, shops, and works a full day. Never a complaint. She's also anxious to live better, always better . . . a woman born for luxury. You wouldn't expect our little girl from that primitive farm to dream of dachas, but she does. An insanely optimistic woman. But she keeps me going! No different from the old days!" Both men laughed with pleasure at the memory.

It had not been easy to join that band of tough and unruly men in those bleak subzero January days in forty-two, but what choice did he have? He could have stayed in Minsk to be machine-gunned to death with all the others that March. Still, until he met them, he never realized how suspicious the partisans in the woods were of any strangers, and most of all Jews. Most such groups refused flatly to accept Jews or gypsies. Gypsies were unreliable enough, but everyone knew the Nazis were sending Jews out of Minsk as spies, holding their parents or children hostage in the Minsk ghetto to insure their treason. Anatoly Bratine ordered that any

Jew seeking to join his band was to be shot on sight, and "Slavek" Kozinets did the same. Any number were killed.

Yuri had been unaware of this, and when, after they had repaved downtown Minsk, their twenty-man work crew had been taken by a Nazi overseer, drunk on beer, to repair rail lines west of town, on the first evening he and Andrei Khess scrambled up the frozen road embankment and escaped into the woods. They fumbled through the brush for several hours, terrified Andrei chattering away, until they reached a barn, where they spent the rest of the night hidden among underfed cattle, warming their hands over fresh manure and huddling their bodies alternately against each other and a bleating calf.

Andrei was a Jew, but Yuri felt his own bloodline was superior, representing the perfect, natural Soviet alliance of nationalities. His father and mother had often assured him so. When the Nazis came, Mama, of course, had warned him against telling anyone he was partly Jewish, but Yuri had never felt more Soviet. His heart was full of murder. They would join the partisans and kill "Fritzes." His mind flowed with plans for revenge.

In the morning they took to the woods and made their way steadily westward toward Brest, until late in the clear cold night, drawn by the faint smell of smoke, exhausted and frozen with cold and fear, Yuri, whose pains seemed to originate in his knees, stumbled first into a clearing in which a small, unattended fire was burning itself out. Andrei followed.

As Yuri moved forward, holding his hands toward the flickering, dying coals, he felt something push him suddenly from the back, and, turning, found himself staring into the barrel of a Mauser, held with careless bale by a gap-toothed boy no older than himself. As Yuri raised his arms, he saw Andrei do the same. Yuri felt a new pain in his armpits and tried to control the trembling which seemed to seize him. A black-bearded man, exhaling vapor, stood behind the boy with the Mauser, his eyes glistening with the reflection of the still-flickering firelight.

Yuri could see no one else, but he sensed the presence of others in the dark. The bearded man was reassuring. His face was calm. But Yuri had heard there were Lithuanian guard units fighting at the side of the Germans, anti-Russian Lithuanians who had infiltrated down into Byelorussia, and it was even said they had fought as fiercely as the Nazis themselves, helping to rout the Soviet army at Orsha, halfway to Smolensk. Who could be sure who was who? They must be careful. He would say nothing until he knew more.

The bearded man spoke, very low. "Name?"

"Andrei Khess."

Damn that guy! They'd agreed Yuri was to do the talking! You couldn't shut Andrei up and you couldn't trust him to use his head.

"Khess!" The guy with the gun cried "Oy-oy!" and began to mimic what he conceived of as a Jewish intonation. "So how did you find us? With your big nose, you smelled us?"

Andrei was intimidated and shut up.

"Blindfold! Both of them!" It was the soft-spoken bearded man. From somewhere behind him Yuri felt a rough cloth thrown over his eyes. Total blackness.

"You? *Your* name?"

"Yuri Ivanovich Karpeyko."

"Ukrainian, eh?" Ukrainians were nowadays generally considered as unreliable as Lithuanians. They might be this or they might be that. The German radio was daily exhorting Ukrainians to seek their "freedom," and the German radio, which, of course, told nothing but lies, said many Ukrainians were joining the Nazis.

"No!" Yuri cried out. "No, no. I'm Russian!" His damned name, with its Ukrainian suffix! Suddenly he abandoned the stupid-boy role—it would not work. "My father changed his name from Karpovich during the Revolution. He hated Karpovich. It was the name of his grandfather, who was the police chief in Minsk under the Tsar. He became Ivan Karpeyko. This was how my father felt."

The silence encouraged him. "My father's an old Bolshevik, one of the oldest. I swear it, a friend to the whole *Tseka* in Minsk. He's a colonel in the army, serving now under Lelyushenko! I'll show you! I have a letter from him."

Another voice, a high screech. "Fucking liar! What branch of service?"

"A medical man. A surgeon."

"Ah—so he's a Jew, then, right?" The voice spit out the word with venomous belligerence. Now he was addressing the unseen others: "This guy *sounds* like a Jew. I know the accent. They can't hide it. That R in 'Russian.' You hear how he says it? Gargled in the back of his throat. Say 'On Ararat are great grapes,' you little bastard!"

"*Na gore Ararat rastyot krupnyi vinograd,*" Yuri repeated, hearing his own voice tremble, and doing his best to move the *r*'s forward in his throat, while his mind rocked at the notion that to be a Jew in the Soviet Union had for some reason suddenly become dishonorable. The Nazis, sure, anything was possible from them, but this from his fellow Soviets!

Until the day the Germans had swept through the city last summer,

Jews in Minsk had been respected by everyone in town, and why not? They were the big shots, even after the terror of thirty-seven. A man like father, part Jew, all Russian, a man of medicine, was especially beloved. To voice anti-Semitic sentiment, as these inquisitors were boldly doing now, had only six months ago been considered not merely illegal, but a symptom of reactionariness, a bourgeois crime. It could lead to long sentences, having to "sit" for years. In a few aggravated cases, it had meant the firing squad. The judges, many of them Jews, would not stand for it.

Then what devil had got into these same good people? Yes, he had seen it in town. Why had they been turning against their own Jews? Pointing them out to Nazis? What had turned them inside out? Was it merely to save themselves? Or was it something too appalling to face? Could his old friends have been such hypocrites all his life? It was as if his friends, friends of his parents, were tearing away their most private, blank masks and proudly exposing a secret ugliness. Boys he had known since babyhood, girls from Komsomol whom he had kissed and whose breasts he had fondled, refusing to recognize him. Had the souls of his countrymen been poisoned by the Nazis? That must be it, and like mindless children they were suddenly free to behave like ferocious beasts. Would they get over it?

Neither he nor Andrei Khess voiced what both were thinking. His countrymen would come to their senses, of that he was sure. Their souls would return. It could not be otherwise. As close to death as he was at that moment, Yuri's brain still ground out his strategy for survival.

"It is quite true that on my mother's side—"

"Aha! So then your mother's a Jew! Fuck your mother! Where's she? At the front driving a tank, defending Moscow?" A demonic laugh, echoing in the trees. The same high-pitched, semi-hysterical voice. Yuri began to long for one word from the bearded one again, the soft voice which had seemed in command and not unfriendly.

"I can't say." It was true. Even in his extreme peril he could not confess how two days ago he had seen her taken away. He could not talk of it. "But she's with the Resistance, believe me. Want to see the letter from my father?"

Finally he heard the soft voice of the bearded one: "Where is this sacred letter?"

Hand trembling, he reached inside his clothes and found Father's letter from Kiev, where the old man had been stationed last spring before the storm of the Nazis. Yuri blessed himself for holding onto it. He blessed Father for having written it. He took it out with frozen fingers, held it,

felt it snatched from his hand. There was a moment of silence; and the bearded man's voice, slowly and carelessly: "Throw the damn thing into the fire." Then, somberly, "Lie down, my young friend."

Yuri knelt, stumbling to do it, and stretched out in pain on the uneven frozen earth. He could hear the sounds of Andrei doing the same. He tried to dig his fingernails into the ground, but his fingers were numb and the dirt was as hard as a diamond and his hands hurt.

Suddenly Andrei was screaming. "Why do I have to lie here? Aren't you Russians? The Nazis killed my mother, my sister! I want to kill Nazis! What do you want?"

"I'm sorry, boy." The gentle voice paused. Then, two soft words: "Shoot them."

A single shot sounded, echoing through the trees, and the earth trembled. Yuri was knocked breathless by the body of what seemed to be an animal plunging onto his back and covering him like a blanket. Somewhere inches above his ears he heard a girl's voice. "You have to shoot me first!" And there followed a great mixture of voices, men's urging, the girl screaming. Yuri felt someone tugging; the girl's voice had become a piercing shriek as the others tried to pull her off. "You cannot do it!" she screamed over and over. "You cannot, you cannot!" The girl wriggled as if more completely to cover him, his face ground into the earth, and for a moment Yuri thought he would suffocate as the result of his rescuer's efforts.

A voice he had not heard previously spoke, the voice of command, the voice that was Pyotr's. "Cleo, stop acting like a child. Get off that kid. What's going on here? You, too, kid. Get up. Both of you. Take that foolish damn thing off your face." Yuri stood, hurriedly removed the blindfold, and for the first time saw Pyotr and Cleo. Andrei lay still. Pyotr was a bony, slim, raw man in those days, and Cleo was a plump child. The young man with the Mauser turned Andrei over, ripped the bloody blindfold off: half of Andrei's face was gone, a mass of blood, and one eye remained.

Pyotr glanced, looked away. He spoke to the others simply: "I know who *this* kid is. Put down the goddamn gun. His father took out my appendix; did a marvelous job, too. Stop acting like idiots." And before them all, he stepped toward Yuri and gave him the first of his bear hugs. Yuri liked the strong smell of the man. "Get that one buried." And to Yuri, "I'm sorry about your friend. Mistakes are made. It's war." Cleo stepped back, looking unbelieving at Andrei's body.

"Crazies!" she shouted with the lung power of a banshee. "Murdering our own people! He's a child! He could have helped us! Karil, you're in-

sane! You're an animal!" She began to sob hysterically. Two men appeared out of the darkness and dragged Andrei off like the remnants of a sheep who had been attacked by wolves.

Yuri's head spun. He looked to the man who had embraced him and to the screaming, sobbing girl, and thought of Andrei, alive a moment ago. Finally the man put his arm around Cleo, and slowly her sobs subsided, but she could not seem to stop shaking her head. Embarrassed, Yuri peered at her curiously, his head tilted forward, regarding her from under knitted, puzzled brows. "*Spasiba*," he murmured, but the girl looked at him wide-eyed for an instant and began to sob again, and turned and ran into the darkness. She's crying, Yuri thought, and he was *my* friend. Why do I feel nothing? Why do I always feel nothing? He turned to Pyotr, who for a long time looked into the darkness that had swallowed the girl, then turned abruptly back to face Yuri.

"Her name is Cleo?" Yuri asked, and Pyotr nodded. "Cleo," repeated Yuri softly, speaking the odd, unfamiliar, un-Russian name.

The older man took hold of him clumsily again, one shoulder in each giant claw. "*Tovarisch*," he said, as if to a long-lost friend. Yuri was sure that until now he had never set eyes on the man, but the man surely knew Father.

A voice spoke somberly from an unseen mouth in the darkness. "All right, he's your creature now, Pyotr Feodorovich. We'll have to find him a gun. And you teach him to use it." Later Yuri realized it was the voice of Kuznetsov, their supreme commander in the forest. And so it had been.

He was aware that Pyotr was talking, repeating himself. "I say, you're enjoying your new Zhiguli, sonny?"

"Oh, yes! And Cleo is in heaven. At least she *was*. We were amazed to be among the first."

"Why not? You're a Liberator of Minsk. A medical man. With a medical wife. A car is needed in your profession, is it not? Who needs a car more?" Ah! So it had been Pyotr. That explained it. Should he mention that his right to drive it had been suspended?

"I hear you've been appointed director of the new Pediatric Hospital. What a beautiful facility! I'm sorry I missed the dedication. Well, you pushed hard for it, that much I remember. How you used to plague us! So I hope now you're satisfied. And who could deserve the post more? I'm sure you'll make an absolutely first-rate director."

"*Acting* director, Pyotr Feodorovich. For nine weeks I have been acting director. Don't you find that a bit strange?"

Pyotr reflected for only a moment. "Well, you know how it is, *synok*.

These things go more slowly every year. To tell the truth, I haven't been in the best of health, so I'm not up to date. I thought the matter was settled." He appeared suddenly to become meditative. "So tell me, you have any other problem? I'll see what I can find out about the appointment."

"I'm not sure, Pyotr Feodorovich. Something is going on. It started with the Zhiguli."

"Yes? The car made problems?"

Yuri told him the fate of his car. Pyotr coughed as he listened. When Yuri started to describe his treatment at the police station at the hands of Grigorenko, Pyotr quickly held up his hand and put a finger to his lips. Yuri stopped talking. Pyotr seized his pen, wrote briskly, and handed the note to Yuri: "Ears."

Pyotr flicked the cigarette lighter, lit the paper on which he had written the word, set it in his glass ashtray, and watched it burn to ash. He emptied the ashes into his trash basket neatly, almost delicately, as if he had done it often. Looking up, he said with a forced brightness, "Why don't we get a cup of coffee and you can tell me the rest?"

They did not go for coffee. Instead, they entered Pyotr's sleek, specially built Volga in the courtyard below. He introduced Yuri to the driver, Ashot Toumasyan, who solemnly shook Yuri's hand. The glass partition between the driver and the back seat was half open. Pyotr cranked it shut. "To the airport, Ashot," he shouted to the driver. "And take it easy. No hurry." He closed his curtain and the one behind him over the rear window, then leaned across Yuri and pulled that curtain closed. They had only the borrowed light from the front. "Now," he said, "you were saying."

Yuri told his story from the Kalnin vandalisms to Grigorenko's lifting of the Zhiguli documents, and mentioned Father's instinctive concern that there had been too much for coincidence.

Pyotr listened carefully throughout. When Yuri had finished, Pyotr reached for a phone concealed in the corner of the car behind his left shoulder and dialed a number.

"Gregori? I'm calling about a physician at the Pediatric Hospital at the First Clinical Association. Yuri Ivanovich Karpeyko. . . . Yes. . . . Yes, that's the one, the professor at the Institute. Haha! What've you got against professors? You have material on him? . . . Sure, I'll hold."

They rode in silence for almost three minutes, Pyotr holding the instrument to his ear, not willing to look at Yuri. Gregori Chankov was the man who today held the top Security position in Minsk. He ran all the

organs in the enormous block-long yellow KGB building on Leninsky Prospekt.

Yuri could see that Pyotr was listening intently now; he could hear the metallic voice. Chankov spoke uninterruptedly for perhaps three or four minutes, almost a recital. Pyotr's expression did not change. From time to time he made responsive sounds. "I'm surprised. I thought it was all settled." Chankov went on and on, and finally wound down. "I see," Pyotr said. "Yes. I understand. . . . No. Nothing." He placed the phone carefully back in its concealed nook in the corner of the car, and they rode in silence for several moments.

"Yuri Ivanovich," he said at last with a new formality, and he seemed slightly bewildered. "I am amazed. Chankov's people are putting together a very detailed dossier on you. I don't like the sound of it. Not a bit. Chankov seems to be interested in you personally. There is considerable material." They were both silent again.

"I can't understand it," Yuri said at last.

"Nine weeks, you say. You should have come to me sooner. But how could you? I've been on my back, out of things. At least three complaints he says against you. You have been seeing fairly often several known Zionists. People who have applied to emigrate, is this right? One— Moskovich?" His tone put new distance between them.

Yuri was impatient. "His kid suffers from acute asthmatic attacks."

"Another complaint by the head nurse at your own hospital. You did not treat her in a fraternal manner, yes?"

"Ah, nonsense. I called her down. I'm the doctor. I have every right. A mean woman. Very unpleasant—she lacks simple human kindness."

"She's a Party member. You apparently degraded her before ordinary Soviet citizens. I know your temper, Yuri Ivanovich, but that is not the behavior of a Party member."

"I am also a physician, Pyotr Feodorovich. I have patients. Children. I have my medical duties, which include plain everyday human—"

Pyotr glanced across at him with a certain puzzlement. "Ah," he said sadly, "a serious transgression. Above all, you are a Party member. Everything else is subordinate. Have you forgotten? First things have probably slipped your mind. First the Party. Yes?"

Yuri bowed his head.

"You also wrote a strange letter to the editor of *Sovetskaya Byelorossiya*. That was unwise."

"Tell me, Pyotr, why the hell did we bother to kill all those Germans?"

"What is that supposed to mean? The Party, my boy. The Party comes first, no matter what."

Yuri nodded, mute, depressed. Of course.

Pyotr lit a cigarette, his hand unsteady, and inhaled quickly, eyeing Yuri out of the corner of his eye. He seemed ready to take a new, more positive tack.

"I understand from Chankov you have changed the policy of the hospital so that mothers may now come into the wards and visit their children."

Yuri was delighted that Pyotr had at least heard about the good things, an innovation in which he took pride. "Yes, yes. Don't you agree that's a great improvement over the old rigid ways? So much more humane! The separation of parents from sick children is really obsolete."

Pyotr took a long drag on his cigarette. "This is not good for the children. Not for *our* children."

For a moment Yuri felt unnerved, as if he had not understood his friend. "These kids are sick and scared, Pyotr. We're talking about children one, two, three years old—some aren't even talking yet. Oh, at the hospital, the staff people always do what they can to reassure them, of course—we've always done that—but Pyotr, there's nothing like a mother. What's so progressive about separating hospitalized children from their mothers? Why should an acutely sick baby have yet another trauma piled on? In America, in France, they don't—" He stopped abruptly, sorry for having uttered those words.

Pyotr smoked in silence, further poisoning his already half-destroyed lungs. "You're a sentimentalist. It is un-Soviet to make such decisions, except collectively. Many on your staff opposed this policy. Collectiveness—you know it quite well. This is a Soviet reality. We cannot change it. Chankov says there have been frequent complaints by doctors—"

"Complaints?" Yuri asked, shaken. "Many, you say?"

"Quite a few."

"Must even medicine be so goddamn political?" Yuri muttered, shaking his head.

"Everything is political."

"Okay, then, I'll tell you the truth, Pyotr Feodorovich. To most of the doctors, mothers are a pain in the ass. The more a mother sees, the more questions she asks—they're an abomination, they interfere with their practice! That's the long and the short of it, Pyotr, believe me!"

Pyotr listened carefully and leaned back in his seat, putting out his cigarette and making a tent of the tips of his fingers, as if trying to decide how much to tell his old friend. "You have a competitor, I'm sure you're aware. Vladimir Bosherov. Volodya wants that nice office, the perquisites. It seems he just won't give up. He dug around, and now he has hit gold. Ambitious, a good Party man, excellent surgeon, fine administrator, from

a great Minsk medical family, going far back. *And,* unfortunately for you, our Volodya is a pure Russian—mother, father, not an ounce of blood of any other nationality."

"No Jewish blood for sure." Yuri spoke with quiet irony, the first thin vapors of defeat seeping into his pores. "No doubt his r's are perfect."

The irony was lost on Pyotr, who continued, "Ethnically he is in the mainstream, Yurka, and you know Russification has become the new byword. And it makes sense, after all. We move with the times. Volodya understands these mothers better than you, with your foreign and—forgive me—your somewhat mawkish emotionality. It takes a Russian to know a Russian. These are the facts that Soloviev and Bosherov naturally keep pressing on Chankov and now Chankov presses on me." He paused. "I am going to tell you something, Yurka. And why?" He shrugged. "If I were in good health I would open the door and ask you to leave the car. So I tell you this much because I feel a cold hand on my back and because of what I owe you: that I am here at all. That I'm a father and a grandfather, still alive, I owe to you. My entire self." He waved aside Yuri's protest. "Just as you owe me yourself. So listen carefully.

"Never for one moment do *I* forget the importance of the Party. It comes before everything—for me, of course, more than for most. Everything must run. People must be fed, educated, clothed. They must have work. So I tolerate corruption, if that helps—moral corruption. By now I scarcely mind it. I'm used to it. Do I shock you?"

"Not much," Yuri said; he was shocked only that Pyotr would speak of it.

"Do you know, Yurka, that Mariya Kalnin collected a hundred thousand rubles from the families of young people who were admitted to the Institute last year alone? She gets gifts—things money cannot buy. Food, furs, trips abroad. Still, she will take only capable students, I'll say that. She invariably does whatever I ask her to do, and so, in spite of everything, I support her. Chankov in many things needs my cooperation; I need Chankov's. There's only one Chankov in Minsk. He reports only to Andropov in Moscow—before he reports to me. I cannot roll over him. Well, your father will tell you, he knows. Karpeyko in those days not only ran that complex where you work, he was much more. He had power. Ask him. Your subordinates must want you where you are, and I, I must make *sure* they want me, every day. I tend my crop. Wherever possible they must have their way.

"Perhaps it *was* your new car. I thought we were doing you a kindness. But jealousy can be a terrible spur. Do people know your mother was a Jew, your father partly so? Who knows how such things get started? Per-

haps it was letting the mothers visit. Perhaps it was no single act on your part. I hear quite ordinary folk going about saying, 'The Jews have everything. We have nothing.' That girl Nonna in my office—she comes all the way from Nizhni Novgorod—she announced to me recently that seventy percent of the best jobs in Minsk are held by Jews. Can you believe it? Where does she hear such nonsense? Oh, maybe once, before the Nazis killed most of you. But now? The entire Jewish population's under five percent. We saw the graves, you and I, but does it do to tell her a hundred thousand Jews of Minsk, maybe more, were massacred by the Nazis? What the hell does *she* care?

"Then suddenly a policy pronouncement from Moscow: a collective decision, and I'm an alternate member of the Politburo. Zionism *is* a national danger, a Party danger. A menace. High state policy. Expose all Zionists; find one who is respected. A big one. Show all those Jews toying with Zionist ideas *no* one is too big for us, too popular for us, that we don't care a damn for America's opinion. So your name comes up in a conversation Chankov has. Perhaps with Bosherov. Well, Chankov is tempted. To make an example, a medical man may be even better than air force colonels. Better still, why not all of you? You, Davidovich, Baryshin, Ovsischer. A doctor. Yes. He toys with the idea. It intrigues him for several reasons. And at the same time he can get his old friend Volodya Bosherov a top post, and Dr. Bosherov will be forever his. Yes, I'm beginning to put it all together now. Chankov couldn't be happier if they made him a full member of the Politburo.

"Chankov. Your father never did trust him, did he? Twenty years ago Rosovsky tried to have Chankov expelled from the Party—ah, you didn't know about that?—on the grounds that he was mistakenly arresting members of the intelligentsia, especially Jews, on trumped-up charges of spreading anti-Soviet sentiments. In fifty-three, during the Doctors' Plot, he was planning to arrest your father, and Rosovsky got furious. He charged that Chankov could not distinguish between constructive ideas and anti-Party agitation. Your father charged this was because Chankov's primitive brain couldn't distinguish between mere complexity of thought and anti-Soviet thought. Your father was right. If Chankov can't make out what's said to him, it's subversive.

"I'll never forget the Party meeting when Rosovsky leveled his charges as if he were a machine gun. I've never witnessed a stormier session. Chankov lost his temper but kept his Party membership. He received an innocuous reprimand. Your father was not arrested. Since that night Chankov has never considered your father his boon companion. In a few years he had Rosovsky's job, so why bother himself over a mere doctor, a

professor of surgery? But he never entirely forgot him. Then your name came up. Karpeyko! Aha! Get the son and the father suffers! If he can have you sent away for this anti-Soviet and Zionist business, your father ends his days in ashes. How will your father take care of himself? He's an old man. Sick. Tired. And dependent on drugs." He paused to let that bit of Party knowledge hang for a moment. "Chankov's not dumb."

It is too much for me, Yuri thought.

"Tell me frankly, Yurka, you are developing Zionist leanings?"

"Pyotr Feodorovich! You are talking to an old friend! Have you lost your mind?"

"Maybe you haven't yet realized it, Yurka, my boy. Sometimes our minds take a while to catch up with our hearts. Let me tell you something: you *are* a Zionist. That is a new fact. Certified. You write a letter to *Sovetskaya Byelorossiya*, and it is made brilliantly clear to all. Zionist, defender of Zionists! If you don't take rapid action, you'll be charged and convicted. They're already seeing to Davidovich and they're looking hard at Ovsischer and Baryshin. And now you. Do you know these other three Zionists?"

Yuri shook his head. "I've never met Davidovich or Ovsischer. I saw Baryshin once for a few minutes at the home of a patient I was treating."

"I can't do anything for such people, of course. I can't stand them. Now, you are a special case." He drummed his fingers nervously against his palm. "You see, they don't mind nowadays, men like Chankov; their consciences don't bother them because these are not the Stalin days. Neither you nor Baryshin nor Davidovich have to be shot. You will simply have a hard time living here. You will merely be sent away to sit for a few years, unless you move quickly. Difficult questions. Your little *samizdat* stories, your father's drugs, that letter you wrote, the new hospital policy, the way you humiliated the head nurse. How you respond will make no difference. Moscow has set the line: make an example. A way will be found. All very legal. Or at least so it will be said. What else?"

He shrugged expressively. "Who knows? Some of your patients may have given you presents? Perhaps you have saved a child or made a midnight call and someone was grateful, gave you an envelope? Or a bottle of cognac or an archaeological piece? It will be used against you."

Yuri held up his hand as if to protest. But Pyotr shook his head impatiently. "Some mother will testify to it, *believe* me. The procurator will seduce her, tell her she must say this to save the Motherland, and she will state that you are a wonderful man, a savior, she felt the least she could do was give you a small token—ten rubles, or a precious recording, or an imported scarf for Cleo—and she will seal your doom. Especially a mother

with high connections, the kind of patient you have. You won't even remember the occasion. This is how it can be, Yuri, my son." The pit of Yuri's stomach churned; both men heard the rumble.

Pyotr took three quick, impatient drags on the cigarette and inhaled deeply, "I'm killing myself with this goddamn poison, but I can't stop," he said ruefully.

They had reached the airport. Pyotr rolled the separating glass partition down. "Drive out to the runway," he said to Ashot. At the tarmac he stepped out of the car, looked about briskly, glanced toward the three parked Aeroflot Ilyushins, said sharply to the driver, "Excellent," and stepped back into the car. The "inspection" trip was over. He gave Ashot an address, ground out his cigarette, and closed the window and curtains again.

As they rode, Pyotr seemed newly preoccupied. Yuri was having trouble absorbing all this. What would he tell Cleo? Father? Yelena? "I remember, Yuri Ivanovich," Pyotr was saying, in a voice tinged with exhaustion, "your father gave you a certain letter after the war, a very old letter—it was received by your grandmother? You were always a great one for carrying letters, but this one was very old. Am I correct? It came from some relative in America. Is that right? You still have it?"

"I have it, yes. It's falling apart now. To my grandmother from her brother in New York, and you know something? He had a son, this American, who, I am told, became a very important man in America. I think more important there than even you are here. He was a judge, on the highest court in America."

"So. Chankov says you have relatives also in Israel."

"None that I ever heard of. Father never mentioned any. Really, I find that difficult to believe."

"For your sake I hope you have. Listen to me carefully, because after today, I can no longer tell you anything. No more advice. Don't trust me. Never again. Never visit me, no matter what happens. I will not help you. I cannot see you. I am going to do one thing, because I owe you that. I am going to give you one big advice. Do not take it lightly. After that, nothing. You understand?" What was left of the old kindness had evaporated, as if by sheer force of will, as if Pyotr had now steeled himself for this moment. Yuri merely stared at his old companion, feeling betrayed. "You are a Zionist, Yurka. An ingrate to your Motherland. Emigrate. Find your relatives in Israel. Let them ask for you. And go. Before you are charged with crimes. Otherwise . . ." He shrugged.

Yuri's mind could not keep up with Pyotr. "Give up my position in the hospital? At the Institute? Leave Minsk?"

"Not Minsk. The Soviet Union!" Yuri felt outraged. This was his old friend?

"But I am no Zionist, Pyotr Feodorovich! I swear to you." Feebly spoken. No heart.

Pyotr said, "I promise you, you will be. It is less dangerous to be a Zionist activist than a dissident, a troublemaker, a reactionary. People like Sakharov and Kopelev want to turn us upside down. They threaten us. No matter how desperate you get, avoid them at all costs."

The driver was opening the door and Yuri became aware that the car had parked somewhere in the outskirts of town. He recognized Gorky Street two blocks away. "This is the place you wanted, Pyotr Feodorovich?" the driver said.

Pyotr nodded and closed the door quietly. Ashot got back in. Pyotr pulled the curtain half aside and said to Yuri, "You see behind that fence, the small wooden shack? It looks like the others, except for the green trim." Yuri could see it—one side facing a diagonal, narrow side street, the other on Ulitsa Tsnyanska, where the car was parked—one of half a dozen one-story old wood cottages, anomalies, out just beyond the Gorky Street high-rise apartments which were the new Minsk.

"Do you recognize it?"

Yuri shook his head, feeling his throat constricting.

"The *Zhidi* use it as a synagogue. Chankov once pointed it out to me. The only one still left in Minsk. The old Jews go there to pray. The young ones are the scum who come not to pray but to make Zionist plots and propaganda. Perhaps a hundred, perhaps two hundred of them. A few will be arrested. In America they'll make a little fuss over it, not much. Others will be permitted to go. They'll get their exit visas. Take my advice. Join the scum. Go to their synagogue. Let them advise you. It's your only chance." He dropped the curtain, tapped on the divider. "Okay, Ashot," he shouted. "Let's go!

"When we get back to the office," Pyotr said with quiet authority, "I want you to come up with me. I will give you a form I have in my desk. In a few cases they pass them on to me. You will be given the same form by OVIR. It takes time to fulfill the requirements. I want you to study it, get all the necessary documents quickly. Time will be your adversary. Right away you must get in touch with your relatives in Israel. Find a way. You understand? No one will take a blood test to see if your type is the same as theirs. Ask them to send you a *vyzov*. When it comes, take it to the OVIR office, and they'll give you this application to emigrate, the form I'm going to give you, and you must follow their instructions to the letter. They will not be pleasant, but do not allow yourself to be pro-

voked. You must do it. You and your family. This is all I can give you in exchange for my life. I should tell you nothing, but what can they do to me in my condition? In Stalin's day I couldn't have done this much. Maybe in fifty years we won't have such problems. My heart weeps, and for Cleo, but I cannot see you anymore, you understand? Come, we are here." Yuri followed in a daze.

Back in his office, Pyotr opened a drawer of his desk and pulled out a four-page form. He handed it to Yuri, who glanced at it quickly: QUESTIONNAIRE FOR APPLICANT FOR EMIGRATION. Yuri folded it with distaste and put it into his pocket.

Suddenly Pyotr's arms were about him in his great bear hug. He still smelled good to Yuri, but more strongly of tobacco. "*Synok!*" Pyotr put his face to Yuri's, first one side, then the other. Yuri felt the scratch of the older man's scarred, rougher face. "Sonny," the older man repeated. "*Nichevo.* Never mind, it'll work out somehow."

"This is the best you can do for me, Pyotr Feodorovich?" Yuri's voice was uneven. Pyotr closed his eyes, returned to his desk. Gone was any trace of the effusiveness with which he had greeted Yuri an hour earlier. Yuri peered at his old comrade and commander, trying to pierce the puzzle. The man had the pallor of death. How else to explain his candor? "*Spasiba*," was all he was able to say, almost in a whisper. "Thanks." An idiotic response. For what?

"*Proshchay.*" Pyotr's voice was sepulchral, as Yuri backed out of the door. He walked blindly past Nonna and was alone at the top of the long flight of steps.

When he pushed open the outer door to Engelsa Street, the gray daylight had the effect on his eyes of blinding sun. A bus passed, a truck loaded with concrete blocks rumbled by. No one knew anything.

His thoughts turned to mothers he had been obliged to tell shocking bad news: Your child has chronic leukemia. Paralysis. Damage to the brain. Malignant tumor. You never told a mother the case was hopeless. But facts were facts. You knew where you stood with Pyotr. His precision was a kindness. How many mothers had cried out the agonized question to him? Why *my* child? Why *us?* Why *me?*

Something was missing in his own reaction. Where was the anger he should feel? The passion? Defiance? Why did he feel only numb? Less than numb—nothing at all. Where was his bitterness at the injustice? God, the stairs he'd climbed, the distances he'd trekked! His coronary was long overdue! Had he ever complained? Oh, *Cleo* had complained for *him:* he had to take care of himself, he had to remember he was getting

on toward fifty. Well, he had felt all along it was a privilege to serve. For the greater good. He'd drunk that with his mother's milk. His fables may have made fun of everything in sight, but only for fun, to get a laugh from the kids; when it came to action, by God, extraordinary! And this was his reward?

Suddenly his breath was coming short. For no reason he started to trot along Engelsa Street toward Leninsky Prospekt, slowly at first, then faster. Dimly at first, he became aware that someone was running behind him. As he ran faster, so did his pursuer. Already? His breath was coming in short gasps now, his heart pounding irregularly. The runner following had drawn alongside. "Hey, Yuri! Have a heart! I'm too goddamn old for this!"

It was Shtainberg. Yuri wanted to cry out, to laugh with relief, but he was too short of breath. He slowed down and they walked together in silence. The palpitations had stopped suddenly. When they had regained their breath Shtainberg spoke. "Cleo said you had an appointment with god. So I hung around god's office and waited for you."

"Pyotr Feodorovich is an old friend—from the war days," Yuri said defensively.

"How is the old bastard?"

Yuri shrugged.

"The word is he's got a touch of carcinoma. He's coming in next Monday for surgery." Yuri was astonished and shaken, although he had realized Pyotr was not well. No wonder he had said they would not see each other again. The man and his words took on a new dimension. His frankness was unique. He could be soon out of action. "Right lung," Shtainberg said. "The boys at the top want him to go to a special hospital in Moscow. But he's a funny old bastard. Born in Minsk and I guess he's got it in his head to die here. They've asked me to do the job. Then when he dies, Chankov can blame it all on me and say it was a Jewish plot. Stage a cozy little pogrom. Keep the natives happy." Shtainberg chuckled like a man gone quite mad.

They turned a corner and headed toward the bus stop. "Look, Yuri, I got hold of the guy you asked about. The big man. He'll be at the synagogue at ten on Saturday. You know where the synagogue is?" Yuri nodded. Strange, it was pointed out to me today for the first time, he thought. "Saturday at ten." Before Yuri could say anything, Shtainberg hurried toward the approaching Number 23 trolley bus. He hopped on and disappeared into the crowd of passengers, and the bus lumbered off.

12

YELENA KARPEYKO WAS PACKING her things in a black stupor. Still no call from Hans. Kozhinskaya refused to see her. A fourth-year molecular biology student at the Second Medical Institute in Moscow, with a special interest in immunology, she had lived these last two years in esoteric realms that even her physician parents found surreal: in pursuit of an antidote for the Au antigen, in her world of mice, dogs, monkeys, and now woodchucks, she had outrun their imaginations, limited as they were to their workaday medical practices.

Why had everything gone wrong lately? Whom could she count on? Mama? Mama would go up in smoke. Daddy? She was really afraid of him. Daddy could be a pixie, telling all his gawking little patients those silly cautionary fables about furry little bears, making fun of everything and everyone, but she'd never forget the terrifying, unjust whipping he'd given her—his open palm to her bare bottom when she was a second-grader, not yet eight, simply because, quite innocently, she had called her teacher a *"zhid parkhatyi"*—a mangy kike. It was an expression she'd heard a friend use, and although she'd known it was somehow derogatory, she'd had no idea what it meant. And when she'd tried to explain that to Daddy, he just wouldn't *listen!*

Sweet, quixotic Daddy that day a ferocious beast, in the grip of some uncontrollable rage.

Next day, Mama, in tears, had tried to explain, had told her about the Minsk massacres and about Daddy's mother. So it was, for the first time, she had discovered that she herself—and Daddy—and Grandpoppa were all Jews, at least partly Jews and, therefore, in some secret peril, which could not be discussed with others. Nevertheless, Daddy was not to be trusted to deal with the unexpected. And she had a big unexpected surprise for him right now. Tipsy on Stanya's wine as she'd been when

the call finally came through, she had tried to resist his suggestion that she come home right away; she wanted desperately to talk to Kozhinskaya. Maybe Zhitnikov would reconsider. But no, Daddy was compulsive, and he insisted. Come home. And considering realistically what Zhitnikov had told her, what choice had she?

Only three months ago everything had been so perfect. So much in three short months!

She worked each day in the second story of the laboratory in the long yellow stucco building on Piragovskaya Street under the benevolent eye of Marta Kozhinskaya, the microbiology professor, who let her do pretty much as she pleased in their all-consuming project—one step in their search for a hepatitis vaccine. Kozhinskaya, an idiosyncratic curmudgeon and a near-genius in immunology, had made clear to Yelena on several occasions that she expected her to go far in this field. The older woman's praise was grudging as she reviewed Yelena's findings and notes; she found fault with Yelena's jumping to premature conclusions (which were oftener right than wrong), and occasionally Yelena wondered if this scientific giantess was secretly jealous—of her youth, her face, her body, for Kozhinskaya, now in her late fifties, was and had always been dowdy, squat, a mannish woman with large, owlish eyes; broad features; flat nose; unkempt hair, now graying, which she wore in a loose bun; and large, square, efficient fingers.

Yelena's work with viral cells taken from hepatitis-infected woodchucks invariably got her Kozhinskaya's highest rating, accompanied by her most scathing wrath which drove the young woman often to tears. On one such occasion the professor told Yelena angrily that she must be prepared to give up everything else, as she, Marta Kozhinskaya, had done herself—to eat, drink, dream of viruses! The State Prize committee was standing award in hand, waiting for her (and of course for Kozhinskaya herself) to complete the work. They were in a rarefied competition with a U.S.A. team headed by Blumberg. This was heady stuff for a twenty-one-year-old undergraduate. She was prepared to work hard, even to be humiliated. Kozhinskaya touched Yelena's cheek with her hard fingertips. There, there.

Ah, but perhaps she was too pretty for her own good, the older woman continued, since young men were bound to pursue her and turn her head, and this might deflect her from her great gift. Men, of course, could be useful. They made good colleagues. In general, they were more dedicated to their work than women. Romance, on the other hand, was available to every second-rater, a consolation prize to all but a handful of women with her special spark. Geniuses married their work.

It was not surprising that she would attract young men. Wraithlike, her posture was erect and forbidding, and her eyes, though a brilliant blue, seemed somehow to be looking always inward. Merely getting her attention in any way but professionally was, for most boys, a triumph.

Her skin was clear and white, pale as a blond's, but her cropped hair was curly and startlingly jet black. She had her mother's high cheekbones (but none of her stylish fleshiness) and her father's cleft chin. Like her father she was tall. Had she been American or French, she would have been taken for a fashion model—not quite cadaverous, but thinner than was good for her.

Stanya, her robust roommate from Tashkent, tried to "bring her out," interest her in good times. She introduced Yelena to every Stasyk, Tolik and Vanya, all the terrific guys at the Institute or across the river at the university, but none of them interested her.

Yet meeting Hans Erich in September (without benefit of Stanya) had been the discovery of the microscope again, another magic door opening. She had met him in the Institute cafeteria. If there were gods, she thought, and God or Zeus looked like anybody, he must look like this man across the table.

When Hans first spoke to her, it was in a voice and accent like none she had ever heard, the voice of a deity. His correct Russian had an alternately clipped and liquid quality. The students eating at her right and left disappeared, as did those beside Hans. They were alone on an island.

"You are Roumanian?" she asked. He smiled and shook his head. "Lithuanian?" He laughed with pure pleasure.

"German," he said finally. "From Dresden."

She answered his questions and asked him questions merely to hear him speak again, but she was troubled, because she had never heard anything good about a German. She had never met one before. Well, she would have to tell her family that she'd met one who seemed quite nice indeed. Why did everyone say such terrible things about them? Were they to blame for their parents? Look at the things said of Jews, and Grandpoppa, whom she knew firsthand, was, although grouchy, really a dear. Was it her Jewish portion, small though it was, that gave her a natural empathy for Hans—the hated German, the despised Jew? She said nothing of this.

Hans, a young physician from Dresden, was doing postgraduate work at the hospital here in plastic surgery. He expected to remain in Moscow for three more years, as did Yelena. His specialty was cosmetic rather than traumatic surgery—a strange specialty, Yelena thought, for a good Communist, but there are all kinds. German women, especially those of the

new ruling class, were propelled through life by vanity, he told her. They all wanted to look like Rhine maidens, to be desired not so much by their husbands as by their husbands' bosses. Yelena found Hans's jocular iconoclasm enchantingly diverting. In that way he reminded her of Daddy.

He told her something of Dresden, where he lived with his father and stepmother. His mother had fled to "the other" Germany, in the West—was now "with" an American colonel in Frankfurt. He preferred to remember her as she used to be.

He spoke as if his mother scarcely mattered to him any more; yet he seemed deeply unhappy. Yelena felt sorry for him and wondered if somehow she could make him happier. A stranger in a foreign land, he must be dreadfully lonely.

She talked about her own family. How Daddy and Mama had met when they were little more than children and—more to stay alive and eat than to fight—had joined the guerrilla forces, living off the land and killing Nazis. Strangely, Hans didn't seem to mind when she mentioned this. "They don't speak much about it," she added.

What she found impossibly difficult was to take her eyes off that marvelous, chiseled face. So young, it seemed, and yet with a gentleness and understanding that only age should properly bring. He was sandy-haired, if you could call that fleece, so fine and straight, ordinary hair. He was outdoors a great deal and skiing was his favorite sport. His bronzed face was darker than his hair, a long lock of which occasionally fell over one eye. His hands moved slowly when he spoke, graceful as a pair of ballerinas. How superb a surgeon he must be! In a low voice she was telling him something about herself now, which is to say her work, for there was little else to tell. Neither of them had touched their sandwiches.

"What else do you do?" He asked the question in several different ways.

"Nothing," she repeated. "Really." Smiling uncomfortably. "What should I be doing?"

"Ah, you must have many men chasing after you," he ventured.

"No." Softly. "Oh, boys! *You* know! I was never interested." She made a grimace, turning the corners of her mouth down.

He thought about that, smiling.

"May I tell you something?" He rose to leave, having eaten nothing. "Yours is the first face I have seen which plastic surgery could not improve. In every face there's always *something* to make better. But in your case—nothing. I've been trying all through lunch to find *something*."

She laughed and, looking down, grew very red. She wanted to tell him

that his face could not be improved either, but was much too shy. Instead she said "You haven't touched your lunch!"

He laughed and sat down again. "Neither have you." She reddened again.

"Do you ever go dancing?" She shook her head, ashamed of her answer. "I never learned." No doubt she should have. There were so many things she should have learned—to be ready with a million graces for this man. He was asking for her address! She gave it to him in a low voice, as if it were illicit.

"Suppose I come for you at nine tomorrow night, and I'll show you a place where we can have quite a pleasant evening. Not a crazy place. Just very nice. Don't dress up. As you are now."

She was unable to reply. She was accustomed to turning boys away with a laugh, but she had no experience at saying yes. She merely nodded and squeezed her eyes shut very hard. Of one thing she was sure. He would never come. He took a final bite of his sandwich and left.

He came for her, indeed; they walked to a small, dimly lit place off a narrow alley, between Little and Great Piragovskaya Streets, a place with bare, unpainted tables and chairs where students could drink beer and vodka and entertain each other. Many brought their own musical instruments. Hans had brought a guitar. They both wore American jeans, the elite student costume. When his turn came, Hans played and sang German songs. Then, hesitantly, a romantic Russian ballad. The other students laughed and applauded, the girls wildly.

He took her to museums, old cathedrals, palaces, the Kremlin, told her about the fabled tsars and tsarinas who had briefly graced them, described the palaces of Leningrad, which he had visited but she had not. She wondered briefly, while reproaching herself for her own elitism (I'm like Mama, she thought) as she traveled about the city with him, about the meager lives of the huddled women she saw everywhere (almost for the first time really *saw* them), women of the *narod*, often wretched and glum, many prematurely old, jostling their packages, hurrying, dull, worn. She saw, as if for the first time, no-nonsense women driving buses, sweeping Red Square, queuing up, or handing out towels and slippers at the museums. In bustling Moscow, outside the cloistered Institute, she was forcibly obliged to consider these women she had seen many times before but never noticed, women whose lives seemed to Yelena a terrible threat. Why was *she* so lucky? What had *she* done to deserve her life? These women, unaware of their plight, hunkered down, followed instructions, plodded confused through their joyless days.

She yearned for him to embrace her, but he never did. She wanted him

to kiss her, to assert their bond, yet he did not. She felt helpless in his magnetic field. Nothing had prepared her for the whirlwind of feeling Hans stirred, singing softly into her ear, telling her about lovers kept apart, kissing her eyes with butterfly-light lips. ("Your eyes—why do you look always inward with them instead of out? Look *out*, Yelena, otherwise how can you *see* me?" Softly, her whisper in a low, inward register, "I see *you*.") And finally, finally, one late October afternoon alone in his tiny room, where she had gone trembling with anticipation and fear (both his roommates being on holiday in Leningrad)—the goal she had sought and been terrified of, the act that was to bind them forever.

When she recovered from her initial shock of seeing him naked, she found him more beautiful than when clothed, his arms and hands and lips taking her to the next plateau of love. She helped him remove her things. Oh, if only he would find her as beautiful as she found him! His wonderful surgeon's hands *made* her feel newly beautiful. The back of her neck crawled deliciously. God's hands and lips were welcome everywhere. Welcome, welcome.

"Please, Hans . . . Hans, please . . . *take* me. *Take* me," she pleaded. She spoke in a melodramatic tone words she had read somewhere, words which did not sound like herself at all. He would know what to do.

"Ah, you are so young," he said, "so very young." He placed her in position, kissing her the while, bent her knees, and unexpectedly she felt terribly awkward, and suddenly, passionately, did not like lying so, with her legs spread, knees up, like a common sow. She felt neither romantic nor desirable this way. In one sudden gesture he had spoiled it all. But she was unable to move, because he was pressing upon her. Ah, now . . . so that was it! She felt sudden, sharp pain, and against her will she uttered a piercing cry, and yet embraced him entirely with her legs, forced herself to do so. As he moved in and out of her, slowly, but with urgency, in a little while the sharpness of the pain subsided and became an ache, a chafing, and she felt the wet warmth which, when she stole a peep down, she saw was her own blood. Well, it was to be expected! Although her yearning had evaporated and all her wonderful sensations had disappeared in that fraction of a second, she was glad anyhow as he pressed on. This is how it is, then. He was taking his pleasure with *her*. Slowly, deliberately, she tried to relax. Slowly. Gently, now. Perhaps that was all there was for her. Next time she would do better.

He was appalled to discover she was a virgin. She was shocked that he hadn't believed her. "I will never lie to you," she said. "Don't you know that?" And laughed with pleasure at his discomfort.

With the repetition of their encounters, each grew more sensitive to the

needs and desires of the other, even to their growing fantasies, which they confided to each other in post-orgasmic relaxation. They became prone dancers in a sea of feeling, to some classical rhythm.

During these weeks Kozhinskaya did not mention Yelena's absences from the lab, her careless omissions, her hurried work. She observed her protégé with curiosity, but kept her own counsel.

Yelena was naïve but not stupid. After she had gone to Hans's room for perhaps the tenth time, she applied, in misery and with racing heart, to the hospital's gynecological department for a birth control device. But too late.

They were swinging along their favorite walk in the snow-covered university mall on a subfreezing night, in the shadow of the great structure with its cake-top starlit Stalinist tower when she got up the courage to tell him. She spoke in such a low voice that he was unable to hear her, so he leaned toward her and asked her to say it again. This time she shouted, as if in anger. How could he not *know?*

He was instantly enraptured, exultant, proprietary. "We are going to have a baby? How about *that?*" He lifted her and swung her around as if she were a ballerina. "Wonderful, Yelena! Fantastic! We'll get married tomorrow!" She knew perfectly well he was only saying it. "You'll love Dresden. Now, see here, you must take care of yourself! No more standing around the laboratory all day! I simply forbid it! I want four kids, you know, two boys for you, two girls for me. Each of them perfect, like you! Thank God my children won't have a mother like mine!" She became quiet and let him carry on. His reaction was all she could expect, but it left her with a sense of depression, a malaise almost as great as if she had been told she had an incurable disease and her life would soon be over. She smiled at Hans bravely and did not say, as she had been prepared to, that perhaps the sensible thing was to abort, that she was not ready for all this joy. Instead they went to his room and made love, he rapturously, she with a reticence which he appeared not to notice.

Oh, how she longed for someone to ask about all this. Perhaps she should go home and spend a week with her parents. But she dismissed the notion. Neither of them would be happy or helpful. They still thought of her as a preadolescent child! And so, on a cold December evening after classes, she chose Marta Kozhinskaya. For hard decisions a curmudgeon was preferable to a marshmallow.

Kozhinskaya, alone in her darkened laboratory, pored over the notes for a new article by the light of a small desk lamp, deep in concentration. She heard the door open and a student enter on tiptoe. "I'm busy,"

Kozhinskaya called into the gloom. "Come back later!" The student ignored her, kept advancing. Kozhinskaya removed her glasses in a gesture of impatience.

The Karpeyko girl. Well.

"Please," Yelena whispered barely audibly. "May I?"

"What is it, Yelena? What's the trouble?"

"Professor Kozhinskaya, I have no right. Only I—"

"Come, child, please. Spit it out, whatever it is. What's on your mind?"

Several seconds passed before Yelena could finally get the miserable words out.

"Pregnant?" Marta Kozhinskaya stood abruptly, almost as if she'd been catapulted from her seat. "Don't you know you could become useless to the laboratory for months?"

"Oh, but Professor, I could—"

"Do you expect this laboratory to compete with a baby?"

Yelena had never thought of such a thing, but the words struck terror into her. Before she could utter a word, Kozhinskaya took another track. "Why do you come to me with this news? Why me, eh? Have you told your parents?"

Yelena shook her head.

That seemed to sober Kozhinskaya. "All right," she said, turning businesslike. "And who is the father?"

She told her. "A German, eh? Could I meet him?"

"Why, I—uh, I—"

"How can I help you if I have no idea what you are up against?" Her square fingers touched Yelena's shoulder gently, a new familiarity in her fingertips. "Or *whom* you are up against?" She half smiled, a suddenly daring woman. "If I may be forgiven that indiscreet phrase. Bring your young doctor around to my place—shall we say tomorrow night?"

"Yes, Professor. Oh, yes!" What would Hans have to say to this?

"About five; it's very nice then."

Hans, when Yelena told him, was amused. "Of course, why not? I'd love to meet her. Although I can't imagine what she expects of me."

"I think she wants to see for herself why I love you."

Professor Kozhinskaya had a spectacular tenth-floor flat in the Lenin Hills, overlooking the Moskva River and Luzhniki with a striking view of both the ski jump on her bank and the great stadium on the Luzhniki side. They could see the illuminated hydrofoil ply its way up the black river. The spacious apartment and the view befitted a renowned Soviet scientist.

Her Radiola was softly playing something of Tchaikovsky's. The living

room contained an upright Bechstein—*German*, Yelena noted—and the rest of the furniture was more cosmopolitan than her own apartment in Minsk, so lovingly assembled by Mama; there were freshly cut flowers everywhere. The place seemed entirely out of keeping with Yelena's picture of Kozhinskaya. The square, squat woman had removed her everyday glasses and was wearing butterfly-shaped decorative ones. She was dressed in a caftan of blue silk brocaded in gold, and her hair, usually kept in that square, loose bun, now hung in two neat braids, each bound with a small red-ribbon bow.

On the coffee table Kozhinskaya had set three large bottles, each with a different kind of wine, and with the wine two enormous platters of *hors d'oeuvres*, caviar, smoked salmon, exotic cheeses, salamis, mushrooms and tomatoes, a bunch of grapes, and plums. Yelena had never seen such a spread; even Cleo, the irrepressible housewife of Minsk, never put out anything like it.

Hans remained unusually silent, and answered Kozhinskaya's questions about his work, his home, and his family pleasantly but with uncharacteristic brevity. Kozhinskaya poured the red liquid into large glasses, the kind one might use for tea or water, and filled hers and Hans's again and again. Yelena, pleading her condition, only sipped hers, while Kozhinskaya described the area or the country from which each wine had come. By the time the first hour had passed, all three bottles of wine had been emptied, and Kozhinskaya darted to the kitchen, returned with two others, and uncorked them expertly. "They mus' breathe," she sighed happily. "Jus' like us." Her eyes glinted, pupils darting from Hans to Yelena and back.

"So you want t' marry my mos' talented student?" She spoke airily, introducing the subject as if it could scarcely be a serious one, honoring Hans with a smile that was a grimace thinly disguised. "C'n you give me one good reason why?"

Yelena had the feeling that controls were being abandoned. They were suddenly all freewheeling.

"What can I say?"

"Oh, shouldn' be difficult! People marrying every day, f'r one reason 'r another—social advantage, necessity, loneliness, desperation, even political advantage—but duzzn' always work, duzz't? Divorces, quarrels. *You* know. I see 'em every day. I'm not an *idiot*, young man. But I'd like to hear from *you*, the promising young doctor from Breslau—izzit Breslau?"

"Dresden," he murmured, unsettled.

"Ah, 'scuse *me*. Because, you see, we are, you see, a triangle. Y'mind 'f I'm blunt? You 'n I're struggling for the shame woman. Shame woman! I

know why *I* want 'er." Her hand fell over Yelena's, who, though she wanted to withdraw it, was afraid to. "Mos' original mind in the laboratory, bes' I've observe in long pr'fessional life." She removed her hand, slowly, insinuatingly. Yelena found it even gentler than Hans's caress. "She's prodigy; she has pershistensh, shkill. She can become a leading Soviet microbiologis', 's a leading figure in the worl'! A Madame Curie, p'rapsh. Incredible skills f' one so young. Wha' happensh if she marries you? Be a tragedy! Can't be microbiologis' in 'er spare time! No, no! Mind on 'r husban', home, social life, shildren . . . strange country, new language . . ." She shook her head and her two ridiculous braids wiggled. "Terrible waste! You still wish t' marry her?"

Hans looked miserable, Yelena thought, even in his winey haze.

"You do know she's going to have a baby?" he asked uncertainly.

" 'f *course* I know. I know everything but the answer to my queshion." There was something smug about Kozhinskaya now. She took Yelena's hand protectively and spoke with increasing vigor. "Whosh ever heard of a German, 'specially *doctor,* who doesn' expect 'is wife to stay *home,* bring up 'is shildren, care for 'is housh, entertain colleagues for the poor 'zhausted man, go where he goesh, do what he wansh? 'm I right?"

"And what's so terribly wrong with that?" Hans spoke sternly. "If a woman loves her man—"

Kozhinskaya stared hard at Yelena, who, astonished as she was at her professor's attack, had not expected to hear such a response from Hans.

"My dear young doctor, you're from 'nother culshure, you so blind you can't see it? Maybe's no importance to you, but do you realizhe, thish girl's *Jewish?* Oh, not 'ntirely. Mother's Ukrainian, but from her father, Jewish blood. T' Adolf Hitler jus' 'nother Jew. Into gas schamber! Pfft! In Dresden, how d'you think? All your neo-Nazis 'n' anti-Semites. I hear Dresden *prides* itself on being assolutely *pure* of Jews. Izzat the place f'r Lenochka? And your child, that child, *her* child—you unnerstan', that child's g'nna be a Jewish child! Zat occur' to you?" Kozhinskaya's tone was triumphant, sadistic.

Hans could conceal everything but his change of color. The blood left his face. He was aghast, silent, for a fraction of a second too long. He bit his beautiful thin lip. "Professor, you're inventing this *slander* for your own purposes!" His words were a growl. As he stared at Yelena, his color returned, he half recovered, but when he spoke there was tension in his voice. "If it's true, what difference does it make? Who needs to know? Anyhow, those days in Germany are long over, done with. I tell you this: Dresden has less anti-Semitism today than Moscow."

"Go, children, go. I've shaid all 'm gonna shay!" Kozhinskaya had done her work; she was in full command again, drunk or sober.

"Yelena, in the morning, yes? Come to my office before classes." She led the way to the wardrobe, "Here are your coats. Bundle up. It's chilly these nights."

Hans was too exhausted and cold or too disturbed to talk as they made their way to the trolley stop. Yelena found herself shivering. Each wore gloves and kept gloved hands in pockets. The trolley bus, when they boarded it, was so crowded with fans from the hockey game they had to stand, neither daring to say anything. Yelena's mind was a potpourri of elusive thoughts. She had to decide. A life was growing within her. How did the old woman discover about Daddy's being partly Jewish? Hans's reaction she buried from herself. When they reached her stop, she said, "Hans, let me go home myself. It's only two blocks; I won't get lost." She tried to smile, more to reassure herself than him. "You go on home. It's too cold to be out."

Hans looked stunned, and before he could protest, she stepped off the trolley bus and the door closed behind her. Hans waved, forlornly, she thought. Always in the past he had accompanied her back to her room. She tried to smile at him as the trolley lurched away, but the smile would not come. He could easily have insisted.

13

IN THE MORNING Yelena approached the yellowish three-story administration building with misgivings. Damn, why had *she* not told Hans Daddy was Jewish on that first day? Perhaps he was afraid it would affect his career in Dresden or maybe, for all she knew, his standing in the Party there—God alone knew how the German Party stood on this question. She sought frantically for excuses for him.

As she climbed the stone stairs slowly to Kozhinskaya's office, her mind was beginning to clear.

"Come, come!" That authoritative voice gave no sign that the speaker had changed in any way. If anything, her voice was more demanding than ever. Yelena slithered in, holding two texts and a notebook to her chest, as if to shield herself. "Lock the door." Meekly Yelena obeyed.

"Sit down where I can see you."

Primly she sat, back as straight as always, head high, knees together; never had she been more self-conscious. Today she was wearing her long bell-bottom jeans and white blouse.

"Well, so I have met Prince Charming," Kozhinskaya said gruffly. "I apologize if in any way I humiliated you. I didn't mean to. But it's as I said, you are too attractive for your own good. You were especially beautiful last night. I can't say the same about your Hans!" Her lips quivered with fury. "And you want to quit and get married and have babies and live in Dresden and change diapers and mop floors and entertain his doctor friends. . . ."

Yelena was confused. Her memory of Hans's reaction, an incomplete knowledge of herself, fear of Kozhinskaya's bullying, headiness at her extravagant praise last night combined to silence her. To her own surprise she spoke at last in a small voice. "I'd like to go on with my work. If I may. I'm not ready to get married yet. I'll see."

Kozhinskaya stood abruptly, took a quick step toward her, leaned forward, put her hands on the young woman's shoulders, and in a gesture so swift Yelena was not sure she had done it, brushed the top of her head with her lips. "Thank God," she said in her customary rough, mannish voice. "Thank God for that."

"Do you think I should abort the baby?" Yelena asked, timorously.

"That's what *you* want?"

"My father will kill me!"

"Leave your father to me! Do you want the baby?"

This was another thing Yelena had been trying to decide since the moment Dr. Spenskaya had confirmed her suspicion. She took a deep breath. "Yes." She was astonished that she had made a decision, and made it alone. "I'd like to have it."

"Then why not? Have your baby! What lab is lucky enough to have its own baby? My first godchild! You can go on with your work in the lab—in a week or two after she's born you'll be perfectly able to come back. The students and I will look after her. That way we save you for science."

Suddenly Kozhinskaya had a strong arm about Yelena's shoulders, a protective, possessive gesture. She kissed Yelena's cheek. "I have been thinking anyway of asking you to be my full-time assistant in the Au antigen work—to supervise the other six people in the lab. This will be a great responsibility, you see. And we'll have an opportunity to work more closely together. Would you like that?"

Yelena was too stunned for a moment to notice how the hard protective embrace had grown subtly gentler, how the hard hand opened and closed on her shoulder. Some of the others were fifth- and sixth-year students; one was a graduate student over six feet tall, a football player who intimidated her. She was now to give him orders!

Thus the unexpected curmudgeon. Yelena blessed herself. In looking for advice she had chosen wisely. Hans—well, Hans talked romantically, but she had learned a thing or two about romance. He'd wait if he really loved her.

"You'll do it?" Kozhinskaya seemed peculiarly anxious.

"Oh, yes, yes. Thank you!"

"There are no hours, you know. You are always on call."

"Yes, Professor, I know. I realize."

"Lenochka—" It was the second time she had used the intimate form of her name. Once last night. "Lenochka, as we are going to work in greater intimacy, I think it will be all right if you address me as Marta Ilyinichna. Yes, even when others are present. I won't mind. I prefer it."

"All right, Marta Ilyinichna. As you wish."

"Now tell your parents. At once." Kozhinskaya leaned toward Yelena as if she were about to attack. "*At once!*"

Euphoric, her future beckoning, Yelena called home that night, not to follow Kozhinskaya's advice but only to tell them breathlessly of her new appointment. Daddy and Mama were both understandably proud of her, but for all their enthusiasm she sensed a kind of holding back, especially from Daddy, a kind of strange reserve, new and unfamiliar. Was something wrong? She decided not to speak of Hans or the baby. Why spoil their evening? She'd find a way later.

She went about her work, her classes, supervising the lab work. They were working now with human livers infected with hepatitis B or with cancer following hepatitis, and although the work might be considered grisly by others, she worked happily. Her tact and good cheer with the others, her mood of high purpose, her commitment to and delight with the most insignificant discovery by one of her colleagues gave the lab a new spirit. Unlike Kozhinskaya, she knew how to give credit unstintingly. It worked wonders, and even Kozhinskaya mentioned it approvingly.

Yelena was, in spite of herself, distressed by Hans's neglect. Almost a week and no call. Ah, but she missed him! Could *his* feelings be switched off like that? The nights were bad. But during the day she thought, well, it's not easy for him either—to get used to the idea of a wife with concerns of her own, ideas of her own, a life of her own. But of course he would grow accustomed to that! Or perhaps she had *not* made the right choice. She was unprepared for this dilemma. Hans would call soon, and everything would be perfect. Call, Hans, call! Everyone had problems of one kind or another. She'd work them out—somehow. Another week passed.

When she returned to her apartment from the lab at three one afternoon, she found a cryptic message directing her to appear immediately at the office of Igor Zhitnikov, dean of student affairs. Puzzled, she hurried off to comply.

Zhitnikov, who was not only dean of student affairs, but also secretary of the Party unit at the Second Medical Institute, the Party's principal faculty advisor (assisted by Professor Kozhinskaya) to its Komsomol unit, now sat behind his desk, and without prelude addressed Yelena.

He did not ask her to be seated. Attendance at institutions of higher learning, he began, was a privilege. Komsomol membership was also a privilege. Both entailed responsibilities. Openings at medical institutes were scarce throughout the Soviet Union, as she must be fully aware. She

must also be aware of her father's vicious Zionist activities. Why had she not long ago denounced them? How could she expect to continue here if it was her father's intention to emigrate with the family? He paused and an ominous silence filled the room. Emigration? Yelena was stunned into incoherence. She closed her eyes and shook her head. "What? My father?" Of course, if she was prepared to disassociate herself from such plans and above all to denounce her father's behavior to the Komsomol's Executive Committee . . . well, this fact would be taken into consideration. He understood from Comrade Kozhinskaya that Yelena herself was an intelligent woman; she could understand that the Soviet Union was not educating microbiologists at enormous state expense for the benefit of Israel.

Yelena's head swam. "Israel? But Comrade Zhitnikov, what are you *talking* about? My father has never so much as—"

"Denials? Ah, my dear young woman, that is not the way. It's quite clear. He has written a letter full of anti-Soviet statements to the newspaper, slanders, accusations of official anti-Semitism, and so forth. He's defending the most vicious Zionist propagandist in Minsk in this letter. Certain people in authority in Minsk expect him to apply at any moment to emigrate to Israel. You're not aware of this? You've heard nothing at all? Well, perhaps you can bring him to his senses! Get him over this raving. You see the effect his actions would have on you! You could no longer remain—"

"Does Professor Kozhinskaya know—"

"Certainly. What I'm telling you is a collective decision. You will be expelled unless you denounce—"

Yelena's dilemmas about Hans and the baby had left her mind. Her future—the man was talking about the rest of her life! She could see herself in ten years, bent, trudging the street on her way to a job as a shop clerk.

"I must talk to him. I can't believe it! Really, it sounds like a witch's brew."

"Very well, talk to him. Be prepared to tell us what you intend to do. The Komsomol Executive Committee can meet with you—" he scanned his calendar—"here. Friday evening at five o'clock. In this office."

He jotted a note in his calendar and stood abruptly. She was dismissed.

14

On Saturday the sun shone brightly in a clear cold sky—an unusual morning for December. Last night's snow had already melted by the time Yuri bought his ticket and boarded a tram on Ulyanovskaya. He was distracted; Cleo had been weeping all morning. She could not stand being pushed. And they were being pushed.

On Wednesday, their old friend Mitya, his familiar, thin, almost ascetic face the picture of pain (Yuri thought Mitya should have been an eleventh-century monk), had invited him to his elegant office. As they sat opposite each other, Yuri could not help but think of Mitya's slim, blond wife, Klara, who was forever flirting with him as if she were a young girl. How many times had the two couples been in each other's homes or off together on vacation, frolicking together like kids! And now this. Mitya had a habit of separating his words with a short unmusical hum, almost the sound of a bee. "My dear Yuri," he had commenced without ceremony, in his low, thin voice, "I have some very bad news. Mmmm. I hope you can be philosophical. Hmm. Dr. Bosherov has been given the permanent appointment as director of the Pediatric Hospital." He hummed on for several seconds. The formality of his speech was something entirely new between them.

So, the first shoe had fallen. Yuri regarded with mournful eyes his friend of so many years. Finally he said, "It wasn't your idea, Mitya, I know. And it's not exactly a surprise. Am I to remain on the staff of the hospital?"

Mitya lowered his head and stared at the top of his desk, unable to look at him. "Hmm. Volodya Bosherov thinks that would be inadvisable. Well, you can see *that*. Hmm. You're to be transferred to the Second Polyclinic,

where you will take over as chief of pediatrics. Your salary, I'm sorry to say, must be slightly reduced." The Second Polyclinic was a run-down miserable building serving outpatients only. Its director was Nadezhda Leonidovna Topelova, reputed to be a bitch on wheels.

"I see." Yuri refused to ask the size of the reduction. He cleared his throat, which seemed suddenly to have become restricted or congested. "Tell me, Mitya, what other good news do you have for me?"

"Nothing else," Mitya said, and for the benefit of any hidden microphone, "You may go," motioning Yuri to accompany him. They both put on their greatcoats and hats, Mitya wrapped a muffler about his throat, and they walked out on the grounds to talk. Now Mitya's tone changed; he spoke plaintively. "I don't know what's happening, Yurka. Mmm. But it's not good. They are not telling me everything because they know how close we are. But I must warn you the phrase 'for the time being' was used several times. You're being transferred to the Second Polyclinic 'for the time being.' You see? It does not sound promising. Mmm. There were complaints of all kinds leveled against you by Soloviev himself. Bosherov is like that with Chankov." He put two fingers together. He shrugged like a man in misery. "Mmm. Bosherov's a careerist who'll stop at nothing."

Yuri thought Mitya was on the point of tears, and he felt sorry for his friend. "Tell me what they said." He spoke softly. "It's better if I know exactly what to expect."

Mitya walked slowly, his head down, watching for slippery spots, concentrating his gaze on the snow, which covered all the grounds but the walkways. "Mmmm. First, you are too individualistic. They of course accuse *you* of being a careerist and opportunist. Not collective enough. The decision about mothers visiting was not simply a bad decision, you see. Not merely nonantiseptic; not merely upsetting to the ward matrons, the nurses, and some of the doctors; the big sin—it was not made *collectively*. And made you popular with patients! Another sin. You did not consult. You lack Partyness. That kind of nonsense."

"Yes, a serious error, Mitya. My lapse into bourgeois humanism. What else?"

"Dangerous stuff. Those stories of yours. Mmm. Not so bad *telling* them to kids. But they never should have been put into a typewriter!"

"That was Tolya's idea—"

"They're anti-Soviet, Yurka. You understand what that means? Subverting the minds of impressionable, sick children? Bosherov started Chankov digging, originally just to discredit you so he could get your *job*, but now

they have dug up stuff—God, Yuri, you—and Tolya—should have *known* better!"

"Well, you read the stories, Mitya! You and Klara thought they were rather funny!"

"Mmmmmm. We should all have known better. Listen, Yurka, I'd appreciate it if you would keep me out of it, eh? For old times' sake? Is it too much to expect? Soloviev asked me if I'd ever seen your stories and I told him, no, I hadn't. I said . . . mmm . . . I was surprised. So . . . mmmm . . . now you know the worst about me. Do I disgust you?"

"No, no, Mitya. It's all right." Yuri had no difficulty seeing how it was.

"Mmmmm. Then, to make things worse, Mariya Kalnin reported seeing Hebrew books and artifacts from Israel in your house."

"You've seen them, too. Do I hide them?"

"You are known to be treating Zionists, known parasites, families that have been refused permission to emigrate. People on whom the KGB keeps tabs. You walk into places like that? You go to their homes? *This* you never told me. You have been seen with a man named Baryshin, the infamous Zionist activist. There was a long attack about him in the papers just a few weeks ago. You saw it?" Yuri nodded. "They're saying you're a Zionist agitator, too. You could be arrested. They want a big trial. A Minsk version of the Moscow trials."

As his old friend kept murmuring softly, what Yuri wanted to do was to lie down in the snow, lie there till he froze. What was the use of everything? Of anything? But he forced himself to walk on and talked in normal tones. "You and I have been friends for how long, Mitya? Since our medical school days, right? We have always talked frankly. What is behind it all?"

"You don't know?" Mitya asked incredulously.

"I hate to believe it."

"It was written on your car."

"By hoodlums. We have hoodlums running things now?"

"Mmmm. A collective decision, Yurka. Not mine. It's not personal, believe me. It's just—ethnically, you are not in the mainstream. Those are Soloviev's precise words."

"The new catchphrase," Yuri muttered. "Pyotr Feodorovich used it also." He bit his lip. "So now I am to become a kike. And my Cleo? And Lenochka? What of them? Are they also to become victims? What are we coming to?"

They returned to Mitya's office in silence, and stood awkwardly after Mitya had hung his overcoat, muffler, and hat in the wardrobe.

"So . . ." Yuri said. Solemnly they shook hands. "I'd better take my things out of my office before Volodya gets there."

When he told Cleo and finally had confessed to her everything that Pyotr Feodorovich had told him, she simply refused to believe him for a long time. Later, after absorbing the facts, she asked, "And what will you do?"

What he had told her had driven her to despair. "To Israel? Of course I like many Jews. But to live *only* among Jews?"

"Not so bad; I hear there are also a few friendly Arabs," Yuri said smiling, trying to lighten her mood.

"Ah," she cried. "Very funny!" She sat on the ottoman next to the table with the fresh fruit. "I have my work, I have my hospital. I work with thirty surgeons. They respect me." She bit furiously into a peach, ignoring the juice that trickled down her chin, fighting back tears. "Yurochka, we have *everything* here. Look, Algerian peaches! And what's to become of Lenka? She's making a brilliant career! Her professor adores her! You think she'll come with us? Why should she? We'll never see her again! *Think*, Yurka. Think what you're doing!"

Yuri spoke metallically: "Yelena will come with us."

"She's twenty-one, Yurka."

"She'll come. She's our daughter."

She gulped the rest of the peach and threw the pit angrily into the basket. "A dozen doctors came to my office after work today," she said hesitantly. "A committee. Led by the world's greatest gynecologist, our old friend Tanya Rodenko."

"Yes?"

"They said I must divorce you. You're corrupt, you take money, you've poisoned the minds of children, and now you're trying to betray the Motherland by running away."

"Pigs."

"They shouted, they really frightened me. You wouldn't believe they were professionals. I've never heard anything like it."

"What did you tell them?"

"What could I do? I cried. I begged them to leave me alone." She took another peach, bit into it, rose and stepped toward him, burying her head in his shoulder. "They won't. I hate to go back there! What's to become of us, Yurochka? We were so satisfied! Everything was so lovely!"

He curled his arms about her and held her protectively. "Listen, Cleo, we survived in the forest. So we'll survive this. You've always wanted to visit the West. Think of it as an adventure. A new life, marvelous new

friends. I have powerful connections not only in Israel, but also in America. We could go there. After all, Stalin's daughter went there!"

The thought of America, for some reason, seemed to pacify her slightly. "The food is marvelous, and I hear all anesthesiologists are rich." He'd gone too far in fantasy, she was in tears again, and this time there was no comforting her. This is what drove Yuri up a wall, that the bastards could do this to Cleo.

Gently he said, "Cleo, listen to me, my pet, what will we have if we don't have each other? We'll go wherever you want! Would you rather wait for me here five or ten years, while I sit in some camp in the north if I'm lucky, or if I'm not, in a psychiatric hospital being drugged to death?" She closed her eyes and shook her head.

He had more bad news after Wednesday. On Thursday Mariya Kalnin summoned him. By now he knew what to expect. At her side was Joseph Misharev, the Institute's director. Yuri was faced with the power of both the administration and the Party, side by side. There could be no misunderstanding. Neither of them bothered to rise or greet him when he entered. It was the unhappy duty of Mariya Kalnin to inform him, after so many years of working as colleagues, et cetera (she almost drooled with pleasure during this breathless, apologetic peroration), that it would no longer be possible for him or Cleo to visit Sweden this summer.

Her reasons were so vague and transparently false he did not bother to listen to her. He diverted himself by studying Misharev, the perfect bureaucrat. Although educated to be an ear, nose, and throat specialist, Misharev had not practiced in recent years. He wore a bushy black beard, but had almost no hair upon his scalp. What you noticed were the eyes squinting out of the wrinkled face of a rhesus monkey. Now the monkey spoke almost as if Yuri were not present. "Dr. Karpeyko will be pleased to know that we have appointed a new assistant for him for the instruction of pediatrics. Doctor Serafima Gavrilovna Morzhevskaya, a talented and dedicated woman. She has been promoted to assistant professor."

Yuri did not respond. "Comrade Karpeyko has been overworking lately; we've all noticed it. The quality of his work has suffered. Therefore, we would prefer him to permit her to instruct half his classes and seminars, and he will confine himself to the other half. The two professionals may work out their scheduling between themselves. Dr. Karpeyko's wages will remain unchanged for the time being. That is all." The second shoe had dropped, and Yuri knew there would be a barrage of shoes before long. He turned and left without thanking them for his new assistant—indeed, without a word.

Yesterday, Friday, the dreadful call had come from Yelena. He tried not to think about her. Somehow he could manage whatever awful things befell him, but Yelena! Her news had really put Cleo in a state. They moved so fast! It was mind-boggling to think that she could be praised to the skies, called a genius by her professor, and less than two weeks later . . . He was determined not to think about it. The mind, the spirit, could stand only so much.

It was a relief at last on Saturday to be on his way to the synagogue. To *do* something. He hoped Shtainberg had not misled him, and that Baryshin would be there. When it came to a subject like emigrating, Yuri was a babe in the woods. He knew only what Pyotr had told him, and he hated the thought with all the bitterness and the limited passion of which he was then capable.

His bus was approaching Gorky Street. Only a woman and a small boy got off with him. He walked rapidly toward the fenced wooden shack with green trim on Tsnyanska Street. The small yard, which contained two bare apple trees, was littered with junk, old boards, a rough table, and a bench in disrepair, with one leg dangerously askew. A dozen men stood about in the yard, stamping their feet to keep warm, and talked desultorily, their breaths frosting. Standing a head taller than all the others was Baryshin, wearing a *kepka* that tried in vain to give him a true proletarian air; it could not conceal that he was a member of the military elite. The other men wore headgear of other kinds—wool hats pulled over ears, a housepainter's white cap flecked with paint, fedoras, round skull-caps of variegated wool, merely symbolic, not worn for warmth. As they turned to look at him, he noted fear in some eyes and welcome in others. He walked quickly toward the group and, as if to reassure the worried ones, addressed the tall, heavy Baryshin. "Comrade Baryshin. Remember me?"

"*Shalom!*" Baryshin cried, as if greeting a long-lost brother, and embraced Yuri. While he had not heard the Hebrew word used before, Yuri understood the warmth of the greeting. Without indicating it, he responded inwardly. Baryshin, his stuttering under control, introduced the others, men whose names Yuri thought he would never remember: Ogush, Georgi Shapiro, Yarmolinsky, Mark Ouspensky, Valentin Kagan —half a dozen more. He shook each one's hand solemnly. "Have you s-seen our gorgeous *shul?*" Baryshin asked. Yuri shook his head. He had no idea what Baryshin meant. From his German he assumed he must be referring to a school of some sort. What school?

"C-c-come. Let me show you true opulence." They stepped into the cottage, little more than a hut. A cramped anteroom perhaps two meters

square was surrounded on three sides: on the left by a tiny room, scarcely more than a closet, where overcoats, men's and women's, each more threadbare than the next, hung in hurried disarray; directly ahead by a small windowless room with four benches occupied exclusively by huddled, praying women, perhaps two dozen, most of them bent and old, mumbling words which Yuri presumed to be Yiddish; and on the right by the main room of the *shul* with five rows of benches, enough to seat as many as seventy. The walls were bare unpainted wood and in the main room, through each one of two windows, the morning sun shone brightly. No women here. Some thirty men were scattered among the benches reading from prayer books, mumbling a singsong aloud, their heads bobbing in a vertical swaying rhythm, each independent of the other, each reading from a different part of the prayer book.

Most of the men were in their sixties or older, some bearded, all wearing hats of one kind or another, mostly black fedoras; several wore black yarmulkas, and seven or eight wore *tallises* as well. Yuri had never before seen these white tasseled prayer shawls with thin black stripes. No one seemed to be in charge or conducting the service. Not only did Yuri find the scene untidy, primitive, and foreign, but the sight presented by these men and the strange sounds they made somehow deeply offended him. For all his wide acquaintance in Minsk, he did not recognize one soul in the place.

Baryshin reached into his back pocket, pulled out a white yarmulka, and placed it on the back of Yuri's head. "Go on in, doctor. Have a l-l-look around." Yuri stepped into the main room for a moment and noticed, at the front of the room in a small cupboard with glass doors, the unpretentious scroll, covered by a discolored once-purple velvet cloth. A few heads turned toward him as he entered, but for the most part the others continued their devotions unabated. The place was adequately heated by a potbellied coal stove. As quickly as he could decently do so, Yuri withdrew to the outer yard and took off the yarmulka, with Baryshin following him. Yuri had to keep moving his arms and stamping his feet to keep warm despite the morning sun.

"Who are those people?"

Baryshin shrugged. "Jews. What else? *Observant* J-Jews. They believe in the Lord, they study and pray, and argue with each other, and await the coming of the M-Messiah. They are content to live here in Minsk, and if you ask me, they are all crazy. Some are cowards, some fanatics. They can't see what's happening in Minsk. How they ever escaped the Nazi shootings who can say? They were surely ideal candidates. Dreamers. People who like to be pushed around. And how they hate the

men out here in the yard! We out here, who have ap-p-plied to emigrate to *Eretz Yisroel*, the land of Israel . . . we who've been turned down by OVIR. We're a threat to them. They fear our Zionism. And we wait for the b-bastards at OVIR to change their minds. I'm waiting almost f-four years. Sometimes they do. Remember the Moskoviches? Where we first met? The kid with the asthma? Gone! Got their permission last week, and tonight they're in Vienna! For them it's next year in Jerusalem! So. How do you like that?"

"Well, I'm glad for them." His voice lacked enthusiasm; he did not convince even himself. "Shtainberg said you could help me. You would tell me what to do."

"It's so cold out here. You mind if we go in where we can at least be comfortable?" Yuri put his yarmulka on again and followed the giant back into the *shul*. They hung up their coats on hooks in the cloakroom. Baryshin led him to the corner by the window where there were no *doveners*; there were several deserted benches brightened by the slanted rays of the morning sun, shunned by the faithful, who preferred the secrecy of dark places. The two men sat in isolated sunny splendor. Baryshin had picked up two prayer books as they passed the back wall and now handed one to Yuri, indicating he should open his. And so they sat, two praying Jews on the eastern wall of the only *shul* in Minsk.

"So at last you understand, Doctor. *Bist a Yid*, eh?" Yuri shrugged, not immediately understanding the Yiddish, then, calling on his scanty knowledge of German, nodded, resigned. So everyone was now saying, he thought; I *am* a Yid. I am a Yid.

The prayer book was undecipherable Hebrew. Baryshin, his book open in his lap, began to move his head and shoulders forward and back, bending at the waist, bobbing in the strange back-and-forth rhythm of the faithful. He accompanied these movements with a singsong gibberish, in a cadence synchronized with his body movements, a parody of the others. And then, in the same cadence, singing in strangely accented Russian, Baryshin's words began to make sense. His voice was in a high alto which Yuri now recognized as the singsong of the ghetto, the Yiddish rhythm he had heard in early childhood in unassimilated Jewish neighbors. He now understood Baryshin's first full sentence.

"To start with, Doctor, my name is Leon Pavlovich. But call me Leon. We're informal."

Yuri, responding to Baryshin's gentle tugging, began to move his own shoulders and head as much like his mentor's as he could bring himself to. Talk about droll! "Okay, Leon, I'm Yuri Ivanovich."

"So tell me, Yuri, and how is the family?"

"Leon, my friend, is that what I came here to talk about? My family's health?"

"So what else? That's what it's all about, the family. Keeping families together. What else? My friends, the Americans, have a nice expression: 'Which do you want f-first, the b-b-bad news or the g-good news?'"

Yuri smiled. This was always the way. Clowns against the system. Air force pilot or not, he liked the stuttering fat giant. "Why not the good news?" he said.

Baryshin grinned, too, not quite a sinister grin, as he bobbed back and forth, swaying to some inner drummer. "The good news you wouldn't believe! In America," he sang, "In Am-merica d-doctors are paid, who knows, three, four thousand rubles a month! And those are the rotten doctors! This is no fable, my friend! I know how you like fables! Fancy specialists like you, they make half a million a year! Why should I lie?" He rolled his eyes upward. "With two doctors, you could have *two* dachas . . . you've heard of Cadillacs? You could live in Florida or California. I personally do not recommend California because of earthquakes. Oh, what a life!"

He paused for breath. "So that's the good news." He pursed his lips mischievously like a comic performer, still swaying. "And now for the bad news. Very simple! You can't become an American doctor from here! Examinations! Exclusions! They wouldn't welcome you, believe me. In *Israel* they want you. But in Israel the bad news is, *everyone* is a doctor."

Yuri stopped his swaying and bobbing when he heard footsteps. Four more men entered together. They all wore *kepki*. Baryshin tugged at Yuri to resume his unfamiliar chanting and praying. The newcomers sat on the other side of the room, nodding briefly to acquaintances and shaking hands as they donned prayer shawls. Two of them, Yuri noticed, wore Soviet civilian decorations in their lapels. They made Baryshin uncomfortable.

"I have been advised," Yuri sang in a low voice, "by a wise man . . . to go abroad. And this advice has been reinforced and further reinforced. I have been advised to go very quickly. Before the security *sotrudniki* become too interested in me. I have to get out with my wife and daughter. And I have heard you are the one who can help us."

"Yuri! Not so fast! One little drop more of bad news," Baryshin said. "One *doppel*. Maybe you don't want to hear it? Those fables of yours! V-v-ver—ee funnee! But, ay, are they no good for emigration! Trouble, my friend! They are troub-ble! And then you go put them in *samizdat!* Doub-ble troub-ble! So it's going to be an interesting race. Will you be arrested or will you get out of the country first? Ordinarily I'd bet on the organs.

You must learn the laws, my friend! Certain things, yes; others, no. So in your case we'll make you a number-one special with our friends in New York and Jerusalem. What's your telephone number?"

Yuri gave it to him in singsong. Other men now entered singly or in pairs. The place was filling up. All took up praying in the same fashion.

"You have r-relatives in Israel?" Baryshin sang.

"No. But look here," Yuri said. "I have this letter from America." He reached into his breast pocket and brought it out. Baryshin took the paper, which was decaying at the creases, unfolded it like silk, and placed it where he could read it on the open page of his prayer book. He mumbled and hummed as he read and rocked. "My Yiddish is only so-so," he said, deciphering slowly. When he had finished, he turned the paper upside down and shook it.

"Th-this is one of your fables?" he asked. "This letter is dated in 1889! It's falling apart. This relative of yours m-must be over a hundred and t-t-ten years old! *Mazel tov!*"

"This letter," sang Yuri, beginning almost to enjoy the silliness of the singsong, "this letter was written to my grandma Feygele. From her brother Moishe in America."

"From the letter it looks to me like they weren't crazy about each other," Baryshin sang.

"Does that matter? Leon, this is very important now. Listen. The man who wrote this letter, this man was the father to Yakov Singer in America. And Yakov Singer, Leon, was a very big man in America!"

He could see that Baryshin was excited by this news. For several moments he rocked without replying, singing gibberish as if to the Lord. Then, "Yakov Singer, the big judge? From the Supreme Court of America? He's your relative?" His enormous head bobbed and swayed, and his eyes rolled back in his head as he looked at the ceiling. "Double *mazel tov!* Now—about this great relative, you want the bad news first or the good?"

"Stick with the good, my friend Leon. I need good news."

"An advisor to President Wilson he was. Practically in the same bed with the great Roosevelt he slept. I remember when he was appointed judge of the Supreme Court just before the war. A giant of a man. A Moses. If America had *tzaddiks!* Not since the Baal Shem Tov!"

Yuri had no idea whose image Baryshin was summoning, but he got the idea. "And the bad news, Leon?"

"He's dead. For many years. You knew that, yes? So the even worse news is you'll have to deal with his children, he should only *have* children! Which I'm not sure. And the children of great men, Yuri, speaking

from my own experience, are not this and not that. One way or the other, you can't count on them."

"Maybe you could find out for me. My father also doesn't know if he had children. Everyone else who might know is gone."

"Come," Baryshin said suddenly. He rose, replaced the prayer books, fetched their greatcoats, and led the way out through the courtyard into the street. He took Yuri's yarmulka and put it into his back pocket. They walked half a block in silence.

"I don't trust Ginsberg," he said. "The last g-guy to come in. Now, listen, I have to tell you a couple more things: when you get your *vyzov*, you go to OVIR, you know all about that?" Yuri nodded. "You'll soon lose your job, your wife hers, too. You're prepared for that? Save your kopeks, you'll need them all. Sell everything except what you want to take with you. Your friends you can forget. A few will stick with you but be prepared for the worst. After you become social lepers, you'll receive the names of other social lepers. You'll keep each other company. Then we have to hope Chankov is sloppy. That's our big hope. And worry.

"It's better if you know all this ahead of time. Also, they may come and tear your house apart. They may call you down for interrogation. Ah, those fucking fables of yours! What an excuse you've given 'em!" He peered down and smiled at Yuri's forlorn Chaplinesque expression. "Cheer up! It could be worse. In the old days you'd have been shot. Now, who knows? We have to move fast! Come, here's our bus, I have the tickets." As they rode back toward the Center, he said, "While you're waiting, you must come to our seminars, Tuesday and Fridays, learn Hebrew, get a head start, prepare for your new life. Your family as well. From what I hear, you don't know anything about being a Jew. Don't come if you're being followed." He slipped an address into Yuri's pocket.

Yuri was unnerved by the suddenness, by the organization of it all. He suspected operatives of any kind, including Zionists.

The mere thought of telling Cleo she would have to learn Hebrew! She and Yelena would think him completely mad. English, *maybe*—it was cultural—but Hebrew?

They rode in silence until they reached Lenin Square, where they got off. They stood together at the bus stop for a moment. "My friend, you go right, I'll go left. A week from next Tuesday a woman named Friedkin will come to your polyclinic to see you. She has a little boy, Yossele, suffers from migraine headaches. N-n-never mind the k-kid's headaches. She will tell you what we're able to find out about your relatives in America. I'm expecting a phone call from America on Wednesday."

They had reached the corner and the two men separated, turning in opposite directions. *"Shalom,"* Baryshin called.

When the Friedkin woman came to his clinic with her son, she slipped him a piece of paper on which a message was written: "The only surviving son of Jacob Singer is Martin Singer. Very rich. Has homes in New York, Florida, and Maine. Probably now in New York." He read the message and in a pure reflex action examined the boy's throat, his nose, his ears.

PART TWO
Martin

1

Hᴜɴᴄʜᴇᴅ ᴀᴛ ᴛʜᴇ ᴡɪɴᴅᴏᴡ in his exquisitely furnished, walnut-paneled office, dominated by Schattenstein's three full-length oils—of his grandfather, father, and Uncle Nate—Martin Singer, his black beard flecked with new gray, squinted down at the bustling Fifth Avenue shoppers nine floors below. He did not feel at all well. He might *not* be recovering, he ruminated gloomily. Perhaps he should take Jenny's advice and go see Sam Rose.

It was eerie, this sense that he might not be around much longer, and instinctively, with his cast of mind, he sought support in the past. Turning from the window, he examined his father, somber and gaunt in his judicial robes, staring down like some lanky, graying, beardless Jewish Abe Lincoln, shaggy-maned, head forward, slightly off balance because of the shortness of that left leg, his clever blue eyes accusing Martin, with that sharp intellectual arrogance of his, of being a grave disappointment. Well, perhaps he was, at that. What, after all, was he? A mere merchant. One who had made a not inconsiderable mark, but was it enough? Father, up on that wall, signaled eternally that it was not. Well, why not? He had pursued happiness, after all, like a good American. What was it Father had expected him to pursue?

Uncle Nate's portrait, bright and flashy where Father's was somber, reassured him. Nate, a full foot shorter than Father and Grandfather, wore an unpressed seersucker, a bright red tie, and a jauntily tilted Panama. A jolly dwarf flanked by two giants, his oversized head and thick lips were unlike those of his father or brother. Uncle Nate, the only survivor of the three, was at seventy-five a rather absent-minded gnome, hiding away these days in his flower-smothered castle on the De Lido Island off the Venetian Causeway, tending his orchids. It was this little man who had long ago taken Martin to his bosom and ultimately had given him control

of Singer's, the store they both loved, and had allowed him to buy him out over the past ten years. Uncle Nate, he often said to Jenny, was more of a father to him than Father. Now Martin was beginning to think the unthinkable—had the time come to sell the store out of the family? Both his sons had made it clear that they wanted no part of it. He thought briefly of discussing his thoughts on selling with Jenny. No, better not.

Martin's gaze wandered briefly to his grandfather and back to his real father. That goddamn sense of inadequacy! Why did he let it get to him?

Not long ago Martin had pressed his mother, but she had shed no light. "Nonsense. I never heard your father utter a single word of criticism about you"—which, of course, signified nothing—"even when you married Jenny."

Recently he had begun to bug Jenny, too, about this sense of having somehow failed, seeking, he knew very well, *her* reassurance. Not only had he failed his father, he complained, but how about Josh? To be a failure to both a father *and* son, that was *something*, he said lugubriously. At which Jenny had sighed, saying (as he knew she would), "Oh, Marty, what a crock of shit. You're a big success! Don't *you* know that? You never failed your father. You never failed Josh. You never failed anyone. Everyone should be such a failure! What is *with* you? A gorgeous guy like you!" A few days later, though, Jenny had Clara bring down out of the attic one of the cartons in which they had stuffed all the old letters, news clippings, photograph albums, theater programs, and God knows what, they had found in Martin's father's Washington apartment after his last stroke. "You know, this junk has been cluttering the place up ever since your father died. Should we throw it out? Maybe you should give it all to Harvard. Better in their attic." Most of the letters were old and in Yiddish, a language he could not decipher. The photographs were faded snapshots of people in old-fashioned clothes, unidentified relatives and their friends long dead. There were old theater programs in Yiddish, invitations to weddings, brisses, bar mitzvahs, clippings from the *World*, the *Herald*, the *Times* and the *Vorwarts*. Next day at the store he asked Myra to put together a transfile of all those letters Rachel Aronowitz, his Israeli cousin (she called herself Rachel Aron now), had given *him* when he visited her in Savyon ten years ago and those sent north by Jim Singer from Atlanta after *his* father died. Martin had never looked seriously at any of the stuff. He had Fred, the chauffeur, bring it all home and deposit the transfile on the library floor. None of this stuff had ever been looked at by Owen Stokes, Father's biographer. Too ancient and irrelevant to the life of one of America's great justices.

He felt the gnawing pain in his lower abdomen. Yes, he, Martin, was

interested, and he thought, yes, he'd have to get to it soon. Once he'd satisfied his curiosity, he *could* give all this *khozerei* to Harvard. He rather looked forward to beginning. After all, it would be a sedentary undertaking—and one that would be entirely different from merchandising or the Board of Overseers, the Harvard Club, or indeed anything in *his* own life—a task he could pursue whether well or ill, right to death's door, if necessary. Pain could not stop him. He could hole up in the library he loved so well and search out what was there about his father and his father's father, about Grandmother Sheyna Rasel, Uncle Nate, and the rest of those old boys and girls while he still had the strength to be curious. It could keep him going, keep his mind off his health. He'd had enough of doctors to last the rest of his life, whatever was left of it. He had seen friends go down slowly, agonizingly, kept in a state of half-aliveness by a medical world gone mad with misused power; it was not for him.

In fact, his psyche had still not recovered from the shock, the despair that had engulfed him when he learned what the surgeon had actually done to him. Not a single hint of warning before the surgery. The sneaky son of a bitch, giving him the word when he was lying there helpless and heavily sedated. The surgeon must have been shouting, Martin realized later.

Sam Rose, silent, stood beside him, the helpless family friend and doctor. "Can you hear me, Martin? I said we got it all! I'm afraid the tumor had spread a bit further from the prostate than we thought, so we really had no choice. You know what I mean? It was your testicles or your life. Can you hear me? You understand what I'm telling you, old man? You're a lucky boy, you're clean as a whistle now. You should be up and around in a few weeks."

Heaven knows how he could have managed without Jenny. From the day of the operation she had been unbelievable, which is to say that while he cherished her spirit, he did not believe a word she said. What she had *said*, smiling and trying not to cry at the same time, after a week when all Martin knew was agony and drugged sleep, was, "It won't make a particle of difference, Marty, it really won't, I *swear* to you. You must *believe* me." Well, how could he? Two weeks later, when he was able to be rolled to a half-sitting position and the pain was almost endurable, she said, "All that matters to me is that you'll be well again, I found *that* much out about *myself*, buster—I need you more than I ever thought, because while you were up in that operating room I had to think about what it would be to lose you. Oh, brother, I can't lose you."

"You'd really miss me, eh?" he kidded.

"You bet. I'd be in pieces." And she kissed him sweetly, tears in her

eyes and in her voice, as she said in the softest, most loving tone he'd ever heard her use, "Fuckin' ain't everything, man." Then, drying her eyes with her bare knuckles like a small girl, she sniffed, "It only seems like it at the time."

"And who can tell?" she added cheerily. "The way things are going, maybe they'll be transplanting balls pretty soon." He doubled over, laughing but in pain. "I sure hope they're working on it," she said. Then, grimly, "They better be."

She told him again how lucky they were, as she had done for twenty-nine years. Jenny was a confirmed blessing-counter. "Three wonderful kids, Marty, even if you don't approve of every last thing they do . . . the Board of Overseers—my God, what would *they* do without you up there? Harvard without a Singer—it's unthinkable! And your mother! You're all she has left. You're so *needed*. I should only be so needed." He started to tell her how much he needed her, but she rode right over his courtly compliments. "And the store, my great rival! What can I say?"

Later that same morning in the hospital, just before she left his room, she said, "One more thing, Marty. Let's not tell anyone about the operation—the private parts, I mean." She squinted hard, simulating pain at her own pun. "Not even the children, you know? People might feel differently about you, and I don't want them to. Oh, me, I won't, but other people, you know, might."

"If you say so. You're my P.R. lady."

"Sufficient unto the hour, bubbala," she said, kissing him.

And so it had been decided. Nurses and doctors were instructed. No one was to know, and indeed it remained a well-kept secret to this day.

Except for the only person whom Jenny felt she had to tell, a doctor also sworn to secrecy.

Martin turned away from the portraits and sat at his desk, utterly fatigued. If I've borrowed the time, he thought, what's to be done with it? If he were to sell the store—and he was being pushed into making up his mind to do it—what then? No women, no travel, no store. No golf, no skiing, no tennis, no flying the Beechcraft, no camaraderie with friends. It would be he and Jenny locked in a box. Waiting. That would be very major surgery: amputation of the ego.

In fact, he mused, he still could not resist trying to charm a woman now and then—from Dior reps to restless fashion designers. Men could still be conquered, too, with his Eisenhower grin and his warmth. But to what end? If you couldn't fuck the women or sell something to the men, why bother?

His mind returned to the cartons in his library. They were long gone,

those old letter-writers, those long-gone snapshot-subjects, and one day, perhaps soon, he, too, would be flung into those cartons. Well, Harvard must have someone in Semitic Studies who could translate Yiddish. And he could pump Mother and Uncle Nate for whatever was not written down. They might have a yarn or two. To his own surprise, he was actually anxious to begin!

Myra Verrett interrupted his reverie. Myra had served him in every way for twenty-two years. At forty-eight she was still neat and trim and, as always, anticipated his needs with her own brand of ESP. Fred, the chauffeur, loved him in much the same way; he expected it from those who served him.

"A Mr. Schulman's calling," Myra said. "He says it's personal. *Very* personal. Something about a man named Karpeyko? He refuses to tell me a thing. He says he *must* talk to you right away, and only to you."

His feeling of weakness intensified. He was not up to the unexpected today. "Schulman? Karpeyko?" He shook his head, puzzled. "Just find out what it's about, and I'll get back to him." Myra smiled an apology and left.

2

MARTIN WONDERED if the call had anything to do with Josh, God forbid. The boy had not been home in more than five years, not even during Martin's illness, when it had been touch and go. The other two had been reasonably attentive, visiting occasionally, helping Jenny over the rough spots, but Josh remained a continent away doing God-knows-what somewhere in the Pacific Ocean. Funny kid, out living under water in one of those habitats or riding around the ocean bottom in a submersible, obsessed with sharks and whales and porpoises. His conspicuous absence at the time of the surgery had been a blow to Jenny, who, though she'd never been much of a mother, believed in the *idea* of family—indeed, of the extended family—and that when push came to shove, her darling Josh really loved his father as she did—as they were all supposed to. Nothing in Jenny's life distressed her so much as the hostility between her husband and younger son.

Martin dismissed the subject whenever she raised it. He could not bear to talk of it, to reveal that flaw in his own psyche, even to Jenny. Oh, once he had told her with a somber tension that merely hinted at his passion, "He's the only person in the world who ever publicly humiliated me."

Myra popped back in. "A *woman's* calling—this time all the way from La Paz in Baja, California," she said, half taunt, half in anger. Myra secretly hated any call he got from a woman, including those from Jenny. "This one won't even give me her name. All she'll say is it's *very* personal and *very* important. She sounds hysterical and a little cuckoo to *me*."

"It's a goddamn epidemic," Martin said, trying his wan and winning smile. "What did that last guy have to say for himself?"

"Not a thing. I'm sure he wants to hit you for a donation. He's from some organization. The National something-or-other for Soviet Jewry.

Something about Russian Jews. He left a number, but he was extremely rude." Martin shrugged. Causes.

"*This* one says it's about Josh." Myra's sniff filled the room like a fog. "She's calling collect, no less."

"Oh, Christ. Put her on."

The woman on the phone was crying. She sounded like a child, talking fast and hysterically. "Oh, Mr. Singer? Mr. Singer . . . this is Tammy Glop-glop. We're in La Paz in Baja, California. . . ." He could barely make her out. "It's Joshua. You see, we came down here on this, like, pre-honeymoon?—I guess Joshua told you we're engaged?"

"Engaged, did you say? Well, what delightful news, Miss—?"

"Glop-stone." It might have been Gladstone or Farnsworth, but it was smothered by the wail and muffled words. ". . . the whole camera crew?" More tears and a sniffle. "And he brought a little—you know—*stuff* with us."

"Stuff?"

"You know, to smoke. Just a little grass, Mr. Singer. Nothing big. La Paz is a small town, Mr. Singer. There's not a lot to do. And the police, glop, the hotel lobby! In the middle of the night!" Small wails. "And marched right on up to our room . . . no warrants, no papers, just barged right in, and there it was! In the medicine cabinet. In a bottle marked 'Vitamin C.' They just took him away! Isn't that awful? Yes! He's in jail, Mr. Singer, in a perfectly terrible place! And my own lawyer's away in London, and I'm half out of my mind! They won't even let me in to *talk* to him in that filthy place! I was hoping *you* could do *something*. These Mexican prisons are so awful, nothing like the jails in L.A. Oh, they're *in*famous. They're traps! They've got perverts, and murderers, and just *terrible* bums. God knows how he'll . . . glop . . . glop . . . and you have to bribe the guards . . . and I don't know *how* and—" Tears, followed quickly by coughing and wild, forlorn, hysterical giggling.

"How long has he been there?"

"Ooh-ah. Lemme see. Three days? Since Saturday."

"Three days? You've been hysterical for three days? Calm down. Why didn't you call me earlier?"

"Josh said . . . I mustn't. He doesn't know I'm doing it. You mustn't tell him." The hysteria had stopped abruptly. An act.

"Well, I'm glad you did. I really am. You did the right thing, Miss . . . uh . . . Farnsworth."

"Barnstone," she corrected.

"Yes." He finally got her name, which turned out to be Tammy Barnstone, properly spelled, and the hotel phone number, and promised to get

back to her tomorrow morning with instructions. He was relieved to hang up.

He wondered what Josh was doing in La Paz. "Camera crew"—something to do with making a movie. He recalled Jenny's saying something about Josh's trying to get backing for a feature on whales in the wild. With Josh no venture was too far out. Who the hell would pay to see whales in the wild?

He asked Myra to get Art Michaels at the Paul-Weiss firm—his Birmingham-speaking lawyer of many years and an old friend. Art listened to his story patiently.

"Well, naow, Mah-tin, ah doan' happen to have connections raht in the great metropolis of La Paz," he drawled, "but ah reckon ah kin call mah ol' friend Pete Gonzales in Mayhico City. He'll know the best li'l ol' lawyer in La Paz. Whah doan' ah git back to you in a coupla hours?"

Martin asked Myra to call Roger. The kid was resourceful, he had his head on straight, and he'd do anything for his brother—Martin couldn't imagine why. Roger was at Covington and Burling when, like now, he wasn't on loan to the Treasury Department. He specialized in all the tax matters he had drafted the legislation for. Next year, if he didn't go permanently to Treasury, he was expecting to be made a partner. His voice as commanding as ever, Roger was a Washington Wise Man.

Roger's reaction was low key, reassuring. "Bringing pot *into* Mexico? You're supposed to get the stuff *out*, Dad." Martin told him about his talk with Art Michaels. It was decided that Art would tend to the legal end and Roger would mosey over to State and take a crack at the government. "I'll get back to you, Dad."

As Martin hung up, he was thinking, okay, Josh, my lost son, the goddamn marines are on the way. Never did a kid deserve the marines less.

He'd heard about those Mexican jails. A guy like Josh, who didn't know when to cringe or even how, could get himself hurt in a place like that. Suddenly he caught himself. My God, here he was thinking about Josh with a splash of guilt and sympathy. Like a goddamn *father*. To hell with it.

"Myra!" he called. "Be a nice girl and ask Dan Roselli and Mike Shapiro to come up here." Old Dan and Mike, legacies from Uncle Nate's day, and men he could trust, would have to get something done about the Christmas display windows; the lighting wasn't at all right at night. No detail too small, that's what the staff said about Martin Singer. A small click in his mind, and Joshua was out and away in the memory bank. By the time he left the store, all he longed for was getting home and that first stiff vodka Gibson.

3

A COCKY LITTLE JEW with no respect, a bushy mustache, and a bushier head of black curly hair, which he tried to cover with a child's pointed red woolen hat stretched to its capacity, waited in the subfreezing December evening in what had finally become a swirling snowstorm, to accost Martin Singer as he was being helped out of his white Mercedes 600 by Fred the chauffeur in front of his Gramercy Park town house.

"You Mr. Singer?" The man was holding up an envelope in a hand clad in a child's red mitten. "Martin Singer?"

Ah, a process server, Martin thought instinctively. If you live in a house like this, someone's bound to sue you for something; there's no such thing as enough insurance.

"What can I do for you, my dear man?" He flashed his famous grin which, with the help of the faint glow of the streetlamp, fully illuminated his bearded face, deathly pale beneath the whiskers. Martin was especially courtly to strangers.

The little man, encouraged now by Martin's warming smile and his gallant greeting, said, "I got an important letter for you."

"Ah! A letter. Yes. And hand-delivered at that! I thank you so much. May I have it?"

"I gotta talk to you about it. Could we go inside? It's cold as a witch's tit out here."

Enterprising little fellow, Martin thought, pushing some bizarre product, no doubt. The ingenuity of salesmen today! They circumvented the store's buyers and somehow got right to *him*; it seemed to be the name of the game.

"If it's a business matter, perhaps you could see me at the store. My secretary will be glad to—"

"Oy, I had it already with your secretary this afternoon!" The man stood now, half blocking his path. Fred moved forward, faintly menacing, hand in pocket, but to Martin there was something harmless about this little guy, and he waved Fred back. Standing made him tired.

"Would you mind telling me what this is all about?"

The small man's teeth chattered. "Right here? In the snow? On the sidewalk? I gotta tell you what it's *all* about? Look, it's personal. It could take a few minutes. Could we go inside? I dunno about you, but I'm freezing my balls—"

Martin smiled inwardly; he had learned to treat his secret with irony, but one that still had much pain. What would this little guy say if Martin mentioned that in cold like this he was lucky—he had no balls to freeze off? "My dear fellow—"

"Do you know you're actually *worse* than your secretary?" The man was belligerent now. "Okay, if you gotta know, I'm in the Jew business. How's that? Okay? Take a look at this." He shoved the envelope toward Martin, who took it with deep suspicion. He was a sizable contributor to UJA, Brandeis, and the Federation of Jewish Philanthropies, and he mistrusted pushy people. He did not relish inviting this creature into his home. He fished out his reading glasses and read the stamped envelope's peculiar foreign scrawl:

Martin Singer,
Son of Supreme Court Justice Jacob Singer, Deceased
Somewhere, USA
Probably New York
c/o National Conference on Soviet Jewry
10 West 42 Street,
New York City

The return address was undecipherable to Martin because it was in the Cyrillic alphabet. Martin ducked back into the car and beckoned the stranger to join him. Fred hurried to turn on the rear seat light and shut the door. In the envelope were two sheets of paper—one relatively fresh, with Yuri's difficult but manageable English, and the other old and yellowed, a sheet which had been refolded so often it was falling apart at the creases. It had script of a kind Martin had seen before. Of course! The letters in the cartons. Yiddish. And although Martin did not yet know it, this old letter had been written by his father's father.

He started to decipher Yuri's letter while the small man sat beside him gnawing his red mitten.

December 2, 1973

To Mr. Martin Singer:

Excuse me, sir cousin, the intrusion. I am Yuri Ivanovich Karpeyko, member of the Byelorussian Academy of Science, pediatrician, holder of title Liberator of Minsk, twice awarded Order of the Slava, and author of fables for children. I reside together with my wife Cleo and our daughter Yelena, for how much longer I can't be sure, at Ulitsa Oktyabr'skaya 28, Apt. 14, Minsk, 220085, Byelorussian Soviet Socialist Republic. Telephone 267-578. My grandmother Feygele Karpovich was sister to your grandfather. . . .

"You gonna read that *whole* thing out here?" the little man whined. "Parked in a goddamn blizzard? Bad for your eyes, Mr. Singer. You couldn't take it in the house, there's maybe a brighter light?"

Martin folded the letter and got out of the car. Fred was out even faster, holding the door. "It's okay, Fred. Will you pick me up tomorrow at nine?" Fred tipped his hat.

As the chauffeur drove the Mercedes off, Martin winced, leading the way across the wide sidewalk as grandly as he could, up the two granite steps; he touched the brass lion's-head door knocker as if it were a talisman, carefully, and gently stamped his feet free of snow, reached for his key, turned the gold-leafed handle of the eighteenth-century Florentine door, and walked through the narrow hall into the great foyer. The little man mimicked the same stamping gesture and followed. It is conceivable that the uninhibited fellow following Martin had somewhere seen another foyer like this, but not likely. Surely there was no other like it in New York, nor any other town house like it. He stepped onto the thick Persian rug, took in the great winding white-marble balustraded stairway, the enormous brass English chandelier, the Italian sculpture, the portraits of people past in their gilded ornate frames.

"Oh, wow!" he said. He stared at the Cezanne, then turned to the Rembrandt, with unbelieving eyes.

From somewhere, Clara, a stout, yellow-haired woman wearing her black-and-white maid's pinafore costume, appeared and silently took their things, hanging the little man's threadbare cloth coat, the childish red mittens poking out of its pockets, and Martin's alpaca with equal reverence. After smiling nicely, she disappeared without having spoken a word.

"Can I get you a drink?" Martin asked, leading the way to the library, more impatient than ever for his own.

"A scotch and water on rocks, if it's not too much trouble," the cold man said, his teeth chattering. Martin first made his own double Stolichnaya Gibson in the cut-glass shaker, putting in three drops of vermouth from a dropper, then carefully slipping two onions into the iced drink, stirring, and pouring it into a glass. Only after he had surreptitiously taken one quick but heavy swallow did he pour a generous three ounces of Teacher's for the guy. A roaring fire was in full blaze and the stranger stood, his teeth still chattering, with his hands toward the black marble fireplace, examining all the crystalware, onyx, ivory, jade, and brass Martin had collected so assiduously around the world.

Presenting the guy with his drink in cut crystal with a ceremonial gesture, Martin sat at the oversized eighteenth-century desk his father had used in his chambers on the Court. "Your health, sir." And they both sipped. When the vodka had at last stirred his own system, Martin turned on the antique ship's lamp he had found in Shanghai, took out his glasses again, and resumed reading Yuri's letter:

My grandmother Feygele Karpovich was sister to your grandfather Moishe Singer. Before recently anti-Semite campaign here, she is revered as local organizer of revolt, heroine of 1905 uprising. I give into your hand letter of 1889 which your grandfather in America write to my grandmother in Minsk. Is in Yiddish, I cannot read. If you also will not understand Yiddish, we are already having something in common.

Since end of October 1973 my wife Cleo and I encounter certain personal difficulties. I am accused of doing Zionist activity, which is ridiculous, but against my wishes I am being driven to become more Zionist. My wife is not Jew, but she will suffer also if I am arrested. She is physician like me, chief of anesthesiology of First Clinical Association of Minsk. Our daughter Yelena is brilliant girl, molecular biologist of high talent, studying and working at Second Medical Institute, Moscow, making research on hepatitis and certain consequent liver cancers. With heavy heart we wish to emigrate from our native home before is too late. The organs of Security have me under active investigation. I have a high friend, he say they can accuse me under criminal law for my fables even though fables are for children and harmless. However, he inform me I am target of Security organs for internal political reasons, not connected with security or with anything I did or did not do. Is clear to me Minsk is

no longer a city where Jewish citizen have decency or personal safety.

Is not much time. I need now *vyzov* or invitation from relatives in Israel if such relatives exist. Please, are such relatives existing? Without invitation, nothing can happen. Once arrested will be too late for me, but still time for my wife and daughter. Separated from me, will be no life here for them. If we will have invitation from Israel we can apply immediately to go out in strict conformity with Soviet law.

Influential friends here, even fellow Party members, cannot help us. My father, once prominent official here, tries to discredit me, and when I inform him of my plans, he calls me traitor. I am not. He is almost seventy-eight, living in past, and refuses to face new facts. Therefore, I turn to you, my own flesh and blood in far-off America. You are my lifeline. America has big influence here. I put my family and myself in your powerful hands. Please to let our Soviet authorities know we have strengthy friends in America. In this event we maybe can go out. This is our best chance.

Respectful and fraternal greeting to you.

Karpeyko, Yuri Ivanovich, MD, *Akademik*
Professor Pediatrics
Institute of Medicine,
Minsk

Pensive, Martin refolded the letter and replaced it in the strange envelope along with the unintelligible relic from Grandfather Moses. He finished his Gibson and mixed a second double. What did this person in Minsk expect him to do? Merely to give this little guy warming his hands at the fireplace Rachel's name and address? Was it possible he—the Singers—still had relatives in Minsk? Martin was no fool. People were not only always suing you, but they were constantly devising ingenious little extra-legal schemes to do you out of all you had. He studied the bushy-haired man at the fireplace; he had the appearance, the voice, the intonation of those 1930s Bolsheviks from City College.

He again took out of the envelope the accompanying ancient letter and, opening it carefully, laid the fragile, flaking paper on his desk. Somewhere in those cartons were other letters with the same peculiar lettering. It was Yiddish, all right.

"Now, then," he said to the stranger, "what in creation is this all about? I never heard of this man. Tell me, who the devil is he?"

"Like he says, Mr. Singer, he's your cousin. That's all I know. Maybe a

second cousin once removed, whatever that means. I like that touch—'sir cousin.' Isn't that nice? A Yiddish Mark Twain."

"What do you know about him?"

"Only what's in the letter. Someone came out of Minsk with it and had it delivered to our office. You don't trust me, Mr. Singer, right? I don't blame you. Such a house. You must have *schnorrers* on your neck day and night. Here, maybe you should read this. I had your grandfather's letter translated."

Martin took the typewritten pages.

"Do *you* read Yiddish?"

The stranger shook his head. "Not I. No, I have a friend, an old man, works up at Yivo, the Yiddish Scientific Institute, on Fifth Avenue. Schmuel Rosenzweig, a brilliant Yiddish scholar."

Martin opened the folded fresh sheets neatly typed. His eye fell upon the date 1 December 1889.

My fiery sister Feygele!

How shall I answer you? If you wish to hear from me no further, you shall not. Your letter, of course, made me sad and sick. No one likes to be cast out or declared dead. To me you are still my little sister, the headstrong, willful girl I remember rolling noodles with Mama; I will say with complete frankness you are far braver than I. I am as natural a coward as you proved to be a natural heroine. Believe me, I have not forgiven myself that moment, but if I were to have the same choices again, can I say I would do different? I doubt it. One never knows until the moment is gone, and there is no second chance. For you I have nothing but admiration. More than that —awe.

I was most grieved to read about the assassination of Boris's father. But to be police chief in these troubled times in any Russian city is a dangerous job. I really liked the man; we did several important pieces of business together. He also saved our lives. I like Boris, too, very much, and hope you will make a good life with him, although Papa surely must have cast you out for marrying a *goy*, even the son of our family's savior. If you can bring yourself to carry messages from me, a man you consider dead, to Boris and his mother, tell them how sorry I am.

You are wrong: I am interested in more than gold. Also, gold does not lie in the streets here. However, although you have called me terrible things, I would like you to know that except for my sad feelings at getting your letter, I am otherwise content with my decision to come here. I do not *feel* guilty. You call it running away. To

me it is the opportunity for a life. After you have been in the Movement as long as I was, you too will come to realize the futility of it. Then America may beckon to you also. You and Boris will always be welcome in my house here, even if to you at the moment it is nothing but a mausoleum.

Your "dead" brother,
Moishe

P.S. Whether you and Boris believe me or not, I had nothing to do with what happened to our old comrades. In the Movement we all knew the high risks.

Martin refolded the translation and placed it on the desk beside the letter from Yuri Karpeyko.

"I'm damned. And who are you? If you don't mind my asking."

"Oh, I work for an outfit with headquarters in Jerusalem. My card—" he handed it to Martin. It said "National Conference on Soviet Jewry, 10 West Forty-Second Street." "We're actually a multinational corporation, but we don't like to draw attention to ourselves. Our leader, the old man who inspired me, believes in the 'anonymous' syndrome."

"How full of mystery, young man."

"Nah. No mystery. We get Jews out of the Soviet Union and transport 'em to Israel. Actually, the parent company has no name at all. I personally am not anonymous, however. My name is Yoshke Schulman. I'm a New Yorker. Born and bred."

Martin decided not to mention that his daughter Nettie was on her way to Haifa at that moment. The less he told this guy the better.

"And you do this sort of work for money? Is it a full-time job for you?"

Yoshke Schulman shrugged. "If you wanna call it money, I draw exactly two fifty a week," he said, "and that's exactly about a third of what I used to make, and, yeah, it's more than full time, only they don't pay overtime. I used to write a column for the *Voice*. Five years ago I went to Israel and did my first interview with Aaron Weisbrot. He wouldn't tell me anything for publication, swore me to secrecy. Then off the record he told me what was going on. I don't know why. We just got along." He shrugged expressively. "I kept coming back for more. What a man! Maybe half a dozen times. Well, I was having problems with my wife, and one day I decided I had it for Aaron Weisbrot more than I had it for my wife. After that . . ." He spread his hands. "It's my job to bring out the Karpeykos before they throw the guy in the cooler or some loony bin. Simple? I have to rescue them. By legal means."

Yoshke Schulman had consumed his three ounces of scotch and had

begun feeling an intimacy with Martin and his surroundings which was entirely one-sided. "Got quite a place here, Mr. Singer. I hear this house is a regular museum. Full of stuff from far and near. Rare and marvelous and very expensive. Looks it. At your table nothing is served but the great wines, great vineyards, great years—"

"Where'd you hear that?"

"Oh, the Harmonie crowd. I meet all kinds of big Jews."

Martin could scarcely imagine this creature getting by the front door of the Harmonie.

"Manny Loebman, he's a dear friend of yours, right? Manny's one of our biggest contributors."

Martin had to hand it to Manny. He'd never said a word, and they'd been intimate friends for thirty years—since their undergraduate days in Eliot House.

Schulman was still wound up and going. "The big difference I see between you and Loebman is he's a 'big Hebe.' That's what he calls himself. Whereas you're hardly a Hebe at all. From what I hear, you give all your money to Harvard. Don't you have any feeling of affinity?"

If ever Martin had felt no affinity it was to the uncouth man before him.

Yoshke was talking overdeliberately, now determined to sidestep every question by six feet—a result of the Teacher's. Martin himself was feeling a bit lighter and was, finally, warmed quite through. The pain was faint, almost gone. "So tell me, Mr. Singer, *do* you have relatives in Israel? Who might also happen to be relatives of our man in Minsk—our Doctor Karpeyko? Yes or no?"

"As a matter of fact, yes. I have a cousin there. She lives in a place called Savyon. Rachel *was* a Singer. So she must be related to this Russian, too. If indeed the man is who he says he is."

"You don't have to concern yourself further. This Rachel—you'll give me her full name, and I'll take it from there."

The temptation was enormous to do exactly what the man asked—and to send the guy packing. Still. "Once arrested will be too late for me," the guy had written from Minsk. What a bleak little sentence!

"Maybe I could be of *some* use," he said. "I know a few people, you know, who might be able to help. Jack Javits, Hubert Humphrey, Henry Kissinger, Henry Jackson . . ."

"Yeah? Yeah, I suppose you do know all those guys, a man in your position. I'll tell you the truth, Mr. Singer, they couldn't hurt. Might not help, but couldn't hurt. Sometimes when they really want something, the Russkis actually listen to those guys. But not always. Don't get me wrong.

Henry Kissinger and a subway token still takes you all the way to New Lots Avenue." He drank a long eager slug of Teacher's. "But it's early. The guy hasn't even applied yet. Later, if he has trouble, if he's arrested, we'll have to go to the big shots for help. Meanwhile, would you mind putting me down the name and address of this Rachel? Kindly print." Martin could see the guy wanted to get out of there.

Martin found Jenny's address book in the desk, and there it was. He copied, carefully printing "RACHEL SINGER ARON, HERZL WAY N 11, SAVYON, ISRAEL."

Martin gave him the paper. Yoshke stared at it as if in awe. "Rachel Aronowitz is *your* cousin?"

Martin was puzzled. He liked Rachel, but this awe seemed misplaced. "She calls herself Aron now."

"Such a family!" Yoshke shouted, clapping his forehead like a child. "In Russia a *shlusselful* of doctors—not to mention a molecular biologist, whatever the hell that is. In America, the son of the great Jacob Singer, holy of holies, and the King of Fifth Avenue to boot. And in Israel Goldie Meyerson's protégé! Christ, it's a regular Jewish mafia!"

Martin laughed. "Rachel would love to hear she's Golda's protégé! To her, Golda's a Goldie-come-lately, born in a ghetto. Rachel's a *sabra*, born near Petaq Tikvah."

If the cocky little Jew had become suddenly a bit less cocky, it was also making him slightly less unlikeable. "I've seen Madam Aron only twice, you understand," Martin said, "once here, once on a UJA junket to Israel. We did discuss the possibility that we might have some Russian relatives, and she gave me a load of letters she had, which she'd never read herself. . . ." He indicated the five cartons on the floor. "They're part of that stuff. But we both agreed that the likelihood of any of our relatives in Minsk being still alive was pretty slim. We were certain they'd been wiped out in the Holocaust. I'm sure you know Minsk was totally destroyed in forty-one and -two and, of course, all the Jews . . ." Yoshke nodded, but he was scarcely listening. His head seemed to be buzzing with its own challenge.

"Finally, *finally*," he cried, "I'm dealing with beatuiful people! Up to now, who gets the Panovs, who gets Voronel, who gets Levich? Not yours truly, no, all too big for *me!* But this, the Karpeykos, will be a challenge. And once Rachel hears about it, you'll see action. Wait! You know where I met her? Would you believe in Aaron Weisbrot's office? She takes a big interest in the Movement. You know her grandson Gideon?"

"My dear fellow," Martin said, barely listening, "I wonder if you could

do something for me? Would you mind giving me the name of the gentleman who translated this letter of my grandfather's? You say the man works in a Yiddish institute?"

"Schmuel?" He hesitated. He looked toward the cartons. "You got Yiddish needs translation? He's a terrific scholar." Almost reluctantly he took up the translation of the letter and on the back of it wrote "SCHMUEL ROSENZWEIG, YIVO INSTITUTE, 1048 FIFTH AVENUE." "You understand, he's a learned man. He doesn't fool around."

"I understand perfectly," Martin said. "I will approach him with all due respect."

Yoshke Schulman nodded skeptically, not entirely satisfied, took a final impatient slug, and drained the last of the scotch, as if preparing to leave. "Would you like to read a couple of the doctor's fables? His stories are a collector's item in Minsk. Not exactly Solzhenitsyn, but very nice. A little too cutesy-pie for me, but what the hell, it's for kiddies." He reached into his breast pocket and removed several folded typewritten pages. "Brought from Minsk by the same lady who brought the letters. You'll have to get them translated." He jutted his chin toward the cartons. "So you'll add 'em to your collection." He placed the pages on one of the cartons, and as he started for the foyer, they heard the front door open and the sound of women's voices, one a quick, quiet greeting, the other an almost raucous shout.

4

BEFORE HE COULD WARN THE LITTLE MAN what to expect, into the library sailed Jenny Singer like a tall ship, in high boots and a dashing dashiki, all purple and gold, her full lips lush and red, snow still melting on her full face framed by the Sassoon bangs, boisterously calling her husband's name. She kissed him wetly, putting a lipstick smear on his mouth, which she then rubbed off affectionately with a forefinger inside her St. Laurent silk scarf, giggling like a girl as she did so. "You both have drinks? Good. Mind if I join you?" She poured a gin and tonic. "How about some cheese and hors d'oeuvres? Clara!"

She hadn't changed in thirty years, Martin was thinking. Even as a student at Hunter, when he'd first met her at a U.S.O. dance in forty-two, she had been what she was to this day—tall, noisy, generous, dirty-mouthed and direct, boisterous about everything. Her regular features were generous, particularly her mouth, and her eyes were extra large. Some, like Martin, found her a riot. And she'd turned out to be a terrific hostess, which this house and he both needed. Thirty years ago Martin had thought time and his mother might smooth Jenny's rough edges; but Deborah Singer, his mother, had decided it wasn't worth the trouble, they would soon enough be divorced. Both wrong. Jenny was still a working girl, not your typical country-club woman. She put up with the women at Golden Oaks only so that Martin could enjoy his tennis and golf. Her father was a Roumanian who, until his death, cooked for Lindy's restaurant, and her mother was one loud Litvak Jewish mother. Everybody in her family shouted; their Bronx apartment had been a boiler factory of shrieks and howls, the antithesis of his own homes in Washington and Cambridge, which had always been peopled by great men and bright women saying profound and witty things in sedate, carefully modulated tones.

Martin was sure Yoshke Schulman, smashed as he was, would notice

that one of Jenny's eyes was brown, the other blue, giving her face a faintly comic cast. She also had one slightly crooked eyetooth—revealed only when she smiled broadly—a tooth she refused on principle to have straightened. She had steadfastly turned aside her friend Liz Eagleman's kindly-intended suggestion to have that tooth straightened, her nose narrowed, and her tits made smaller. Who else, she asked Martin, but Liz would have the *chutzpah* to make such suggestions? Liz maybe thought she had the right because she had once been Miss New York and runner-up for Miss America, long, long ago. Now she and Jenny shared many of the same clients—Liz for P.R. and Jenny for advertising. They were entirely uninhibited with each other. They even shared the same analyst, Dr. Adelsheim. Well, Jenny needed all the help she could get to deal with Marty's "problem," which was also hers. . . .

Jenny, after her usual long day at H.P. and B., the ad agency where she was creative director, had, before coming home, put in a trying hour with her shrink.

When Martin introduced his mercurial wife, fresh from the shrink's couch, to the cocky little man in the library and described the man's mission to her, Jenny had not quite thrown off her well-disguised wretched mood, but she was soon genuinely captivated, as Martin started to tell her the man's mission.

"That's a real name, Yoshke Schulman? It sounds too Jewish to be true. And you're in the Jew business? How terrific! Isn't that marvelous, Marty? So tell me, Yoshkeleh, how's business?" Clara entered, silent as a ghost, with a tray of caviar, sturgeon, cheese, and crackers, and Jenny insisted Yoshke have some.

"Business this year?" he crowed, catching her spirit and gulping down a caviar canapé. "Business has been totally fantastic! Would you believe forty percent ahead of last year in volume? And volume, that's what our business is about. Volume is the bottom line. More than twenty-seven thousand souls brought out in the last eight months—how's that? Souls! Yes, ma'am. Compared to seventeen thousand in all of seventy-two."

"Sounds better than A.T. and T."

Jenny took the two letters that Martin now handed her, delved into her enormous bag for her glasses, and read each letter carefully, the two men sitting silent until she had finished.

In spite of herself Jenny was startled by these two unexpected pieces of paper from the great beyond. All those letters and junk she'd dumped on Marty, mostly in Yiddish. Marty's family, his heritage from way back. And now these. It was enough to bend your eyes back. Was this something Marty needed? With all his *tsouris*? God, who knows, maybe it *was!*

She studied the letter from Minsk again. This poor guy, whoever he was —thousands of miles away, crying help. Help—why not? Who *was* in a better position to give it than she and Marty? *Together*. Something real again. Something Adelsheim had not-so-subtly been suggesting they try to find. The idea excited her. Still, she knew Marty. He'd tell her she was always getting worked up. Marty was filled with dark suspicions, worried about being taken. She'd watch her step.

She turned to Martin, rattling the letters as if she were shaking the dust off. "You know, Marty, we have to do something about this guy. What's really going on over there with these Jews? You been over there, Yoshke?"

"They won't let me in," Yoshke said. "They have a file on me."

"Well, we've been once, but everything is all so *arranged* for you, it's a drag. They won't let you change one comma in your itinerary. Marty wanted to come home ahead of schedule and they wouldn't let us! Can you imagine? I suppose maybe on one of those group things, but that's not for me—getting up at six in the morning. Jesus! So what did we see? Palaces and museums, Leningrad and Moscow. Period. Marty really *hated* it. Even so, Marty, maybe we should go over and meet this man."

"If there's one place I have no desire to go back to—" Martin started. He was sure he was not going anywhere, ever again.

"Listen, no kidding, Marty, I have to get away. If I do one more peanut butter commercial, I'll get hives."

"I can only repeat," Martin said patiently, "if there's one place I have no desire whatever to—"

Jenny turned to him, radiating encouragement. "Then what *are* we going to do, Marty? He's your cousin. Can you believe such versatility? He *has* to be related . . . to *you*, Marty, not me. You have the brains in this family."

"What the devil can *we* do?" Sometimes Jenny's sentimentalism drove him up a wall.

"How do *I* know? *You* know everybody. In desperation the poor *schlemiel* has turned to you. We have to get him out. That's all there is to it. Somehow. The man is absolutely right. Like the letter says, it's our bounden duty. He's not only our *landsman*, he's got *your* blood in *his* veins!"

"Look, my overblown sentimentalist, read what the man says in his letter." Martin, with supreme effort, assumed a phoney, not very good Russian accent, skimming the letter. " 'I am Yuri Ivanovich Karpeyko,' hmmm . . . hmmm . . . yes, 'even fellow Party members cannot help . . .' He's not Hans Christian Andersen or the Man of La Mancha, you understand.

He's a member of the *Communist* Party! That means he joined of his own free will, you see? Ninety-five percent of the Russians do *not* belong to the party."

"Is that true?" Jenny spoke in wide-eyed disbelief to Schulman, who nodded vague confirmation through what had become for him a drunken haze. For a moment Jenny seemed rattled, then recovered her aplomb. "Well, it shows he's ambitious, right? He wanted to get ahead. He's your typical old-fashioned American. When in Rome, man. He doesn't belong in Minsk. He belongs *here*. Horatio Alger, doctor of medicine. That's our Yuri! You bet!"

Martin stood up, ignoring the recurring pains which seemed to have shifted now to his lower back, to face her, and his voice was as quiet as hers had been boisterous.

"Don't get carried *away*, Jen." So Marty thought he had her number. She was being carried away as she always was, eh? Not this time! "This gentleman here, Mr. . . . ah . . . Schulman?" Martin said, with his charming smile. "Yes, after all, Mr. Schulman's entire business is to—"

But Jenny was too wound up to pay Martin any heed.

"Ah, so! We're just gonna sit on our *tochases* and get fatter and fatter? Yoshke, you have hardly *touched* that caviar! Go *on*. Isn't it delicious? Marty, his glass is empty." Yoshke shook his head, put his hand over his glass. "God, if I don't lose five pounds next week I'm really going to a fat farm, so help me, Marty. Lookit that!" She put her hand on her trim belly. "Hey, Marty, you heard about this new Atkins diet? Supposed to be foolproof." Then sharply shrill: "And what about the Holocaust, Marty? If there could be *one*, what's to stop another? What makes you so sure the Commies won't pick up where the Nazis left off? Gas is cheap. These people are your flesh and blood, Marty! We should be doing *something!*"

The two men sat silent, Martin slightly bemused, the stranger amazed, thinking, this is the way rich women carry on?

"This isn't the Holocaust," Martin said placatingly.

"Who says it couldn't become one?" she cried. "Who's to *stop* them? Did anyone believe Hitler would make a Holocaust? Not your papa, man! Not Mr. Roosevelt! Not the Pope! I'm serious! Am I right, Yoshke?"

"If you'll excuse me, Mrs. Singer," Yoshke Schulman said, trying to bring them back to Gramercy Park, "nobody is suggesting you should go personally to Minsk and—"

"Who needs suggestions? If we *want* to go to Minsk, why can't we go? Who guarantees it *won't* be another Holocaust?"

"That's not the point, Mrs. Singer. I appreciate your sentiment; it's admirable. But right now what the doctor needs, I mean Doctor Karpeyko

and his wife and daughter, what they *need* as a practical matter is a *vyzov* from their relatives in Israel. An affidavit, an invitation, guaranteeing that they will be reunited with their family and that they will be taken care of. Without that, nothing can happen."

"Then what are we waiting for?"

Martin said quietly, grimly, "Mr. Schulman has Rachel's name, Jen, and he'll get all the necessary papers from her. Now, perhaps Mr. Schulman has business elsewhere? I don't think we should keep him. Why don't we just let him—"

"No!" Jenny cried with a touch of desperation, and turning to Yoshke, "Can't we give you some dinner?" Yoshke gobbled another caviar canapé, licked his finger, put down his cut crystal glass, and started firmly toward the foyer. "Could I have a rain check, Mrs. Singer?"

"Call me Jenny," she said, trailing him. "My name is Jenny. Sure you can."

"I gotta go see my little boy. It's my night to visit. Or as they say in the divorce trade, tonight I exercise my visitation right. Also I'm wearing his mittens and his hat, which he needs in this weather."

Jenny thought Yoshke was cute, but too small, bushy, and furry for her. She hated the way she noticed men nowadays.

As they followed Yoshke to the coat closet, Jenny kept talking. "Look, can't we write this guy ourselves? He seems to speak some English. Couldn't we send him money? Wouldn't he like a little cheering up? We ought to be able to do something!" To Martin it was remarkable that Jenny could picture this Russian so vividly, feel for him, believe in him. The man had no more reality to Martin than King Tut.

From somewhere out of sight Clara reappeared and while she helped him on with his threadbare coat, Yoshke said, "Sure. But remember, your letters will be read by others, so don't write anything he'll be sorry for. You can't send money. It's against the law to have foreign currency. You can call him up. The phone service isn't bad. Do it. Encourage him. But keep in mind, Big Brother is listening. Be careful. And while you're on the phone, talk to Big Brother. You know what I mean?"

"Call him up?" Jenny said. "You mean it? We can do that? So we'll do it, and thank you for coming! Yoshke, I admire you." Yoshke looked at her hopefully. Well, why not? Amazons did it, too. It'd be like trying to drive a nail into an earthquake.

As they headed through the narrow hall to the front door, Jenny said, "It's okay if we keep his letters and his little stories?"

"Of course. He wrote the letter to Mr. Singer. And that golden oldie was written by Mr. Singer's grandfather. Mr. Singer says he's gonna have

the rest of those letters translated. That should be very nice. Maybe you'll find out who you are." He opened the door and started out, then hesitated. "Here's my card if you want me." He fished a scruffy card from his overcoat pocket and handed it to her.

He put on his pointy woolen hat, pulled a scarf over his ears, and tied it under his chin like a child. Martin held the door open, watched him walk down the two steps into the wildly swirling snow, closed the heavy door slowly, and turned back to Jenny. He did not much look forward to telling her about Josh. At dinner.

5

FIRST, HOWEVER, HE DECIDED TO CALL cousin Jim in Atlanta; Jim might know whether they had a cousin still in Russia. Jim, whose father, Lewis Singer, had left him the largest millwork and lumber operation in Atlanta, a city which seemed to be growing faster than the state of Florida, had sold that business and bought himself a bank. Jim was so gentile now, he'd been admitted to the City Club. Still, he might know.

Jim didn't.

Martin's mother was equally noninformative. She wanted to talk about her symptoms. "My ears have been ringing all day, Martin. I'm simply going out of my mind. Do you think I'll ever get well?" As for relatives in Russia, she had not heard of any. "Why do you ask?"

Martin told her. "How dreadful!" his mother said. "You must do everything you can to save him, Martin; you must overlook that he's Russian."

Uncle Nate was more informative, if a bit grumpy because he had been tending to his orchids and did not relish being interrupted. "Oh, sure. Pop had a sister in Minsk. I can't remember her name. . . . What? . . . Feygele? Yes, that's it! How did you know? . . . Yes, Yes! I don't think Feygele and my Pop had much use for each other, though. Pop also had a brother Herschel, the one in Palestine, and Ma's sister was Herschel's wife. Two brothers married to two sisters. When I was a kid I remember the women used to write back and forth."

He was interested in the new cousin, and he hoped everything would be done to rescue the man, so long as he personally was not required to set foot out of Miami Beach. Martin could hear his impatience to get back to his orchids.

Clara was serving the New England chowder when Martin launched into his tale about Josh.

Jenny poured herself a slug of Beefeater, her staple beverage for emer-

gencies, and peered at him through squinting, accusing eyes. "Marty, I'm
going out there. I'll get the first plane to L.A. They are not gonna push
Joshie around!" Half weeping, half fuming, "Goddamnit, Martin, that kid
has been kicked around and told to get lost all his life! Oh, I'm not
blameless, but Marty, don't think you've helped any!"

He'd known she would react badly, but in a way it wasn't a total disaster: his Russian relative had been lost in the shuffle. And she wasn't going
to L.A. or anywhere else.

In the morning Martin decided to stay home. He told himself it was to be
with her and soothe her, more than for any practical or logistical purpose,
but the fact was he wasn't up to going to the store. The upper abdomen
this time. As for Jenny, she wouldn't dream of going to work. "How can I
think about Adirondack Dog Food? I'm a wreck. Can't you see I'm a
wreck?" She hated Martin when he was this way, trying to calm her. She
thought she could read his mind: serves the kid right. Didn't he realize
they could *kill* him down there? *Her* Josh? Six lousy ounces! She'd heard
of kids. . . . Martin could see her looking through him. He saw the flash
of resentment, of fury. His grief was heavy, and confusion reigned in his
own heart. So many strings pulling this way and that.

The phone rang; it was Art Michaels. He was now warning Martin,
who informed Jenny, that the situation was grandiosely corrupt; these
prisons were a trap for Americans. A family as illustrious as the Singers
must be prepared to pay what amounted to a ransom if the boy was to be
released and the matter remain confidential. The exact amount demanded
was still unclear because there were so many fingers in the pie, but between eighty and a hundred thousand dollars. Great caution was necessary. There were eerie cases where the money and the prisoner had both
disappeared. Art was doing all he could to find out exactly how much was
needed. It might take a week.

"A week?" Jenny screamed. She didn't give a damn about the money.
She took her third Miltown.

At noon Roger finally called from Washington. "Dad, the guy over at
Foggy Bottom surprised me. He was sure not sanguine." The message
was that there would have to be some quid pro quo, but the State Department was doubtful it could persuade the police chief and the city prosecutor in Houston to give up a certain Pedro Matanzas, accused of raping
and strangling six nurses, or to get the authorities in San Diego to free
one Julio Ortiz, who had totally blinded two young women bank-tellers
with acid—just to spring Josh, who, after all, did seem to have had six
ounces of marijuana in his room at the time of his arrest in La Paz. State

would have to talk to Justice. Roger's only acquaintance there was Hugo Sears, an assistant to the new acting attorney general, and Hugo didn't know which way was up.

Jenny was beside herself. She was going and that was that. Martin pleaded with her not to run off half-cocked. She might make things worse. They finally settled on Roger's going, and Roger agreed to leave that night. He promised to leave no stone in La Paz unturned. "As a matter of fact," Martin reminded Jenny, "we're having Hugo Sears for dinner on Friday—that's only three days. He's Max and Jean's houseguest, and they're bringing him. So let's see what light he has to shed. I've met Sears only once, but we have many mutual friends. He's one of Barry Goldwater's boys. Maybe he can do something."

Three days! Martin was always so goddamn patient, always talking her out of rash, foolish acts. She felt mean toward him for those three days.

So preoccupied was she that she barely noticed that while she managed to go to her office, Martin stayed home all three days; dimly she was aware that he closed himself into the library with an elderly stranger, both men on their knees like kids, examining the material in the cartons on the floor. Martin introduced her to Schmuel Rosenzweig. On the third morning, Martin told her Rosenzweig was sending a young man, some graduate student from Yeshiva, who would be working in the house; he'd be using the movie room; it would be helpful if Clara would bring the young man lunch each day, and the meals had to be kosher. He hoped it wouldn't be too much trouble. Jenny was grumpy, not at the request but at Martin. How could he be thinking about anyone but Josh? How could he be so frivolous! Yeshiva boy!

"He's going to be sleeping here, is he?"

"No. He'll be working from nine to five. He'll go home to Brooklyn."

"Thank God. And how long are we to have the intense pleasure of his company?"

Martin shrugged, and gestured toward the cartons. "Until he's finished."

On Friday Martin napped all afternoon to conserve his strength for the party. Jenny was so nervous about Josh she could scarcely dress herself. Martin had to zip her up and hook her up and pin her brooch on, and she felt nothing was right; her eye shadow was too green, the lipstick too red. The diamond pendant did not satisfy her and so she switched to the emerald brooch. She fumbled for minutes with her pearl earrings. Her black hair was too short, it looked almost like a boy's crew cut, it was ugly, wouldn't stay put. Her bangs were too long, seemed uneven. Wearing an unbecoming Dior black velvet original—a portrait dress with huge

net sleeves—that she had bought in Paris two years ago for twenty-nine hundred bucks (including letting it out and the hooks), she felt like a klutzy Raggedy Ann. A total waste on her, this *schmatta*, and she promised herself never to buy one again.

The first to arrive with their houseguest, Hugo Sears, were Max and Jean Kahane. Max, at seventy, was the undisputed monarch of the public relations business. His clients ranged from minor princes learning the common touch to movie producers—men he instructed in sex, murder, sci-fi, and outer space. He worked with mayors, governors, and occasionally presidents, all striving to be well-liked and re-elected. Max's houseguest, a heavy-set, red-headed and red-bearded bachelor in his late forties, was the assistant to the new acting U.S. attorney general. Jenny smiled at him hopefully. Maybe he *could* do something for Josh.

Max's wife Jean, withered, dry as an ash, was his party-giving partner; they complemented each other almost as if theirs were a purely business arrangement.

Tonight the guest list was not only almost exclusively Jewish but satisfyingly distinguished. She had, for example, invited, not one but *two* Nobel laureates: Eliot Krieger, a skinny professor from Ann Arbor, as gigantic an authority in economics as he was short in stature and bald of bean. The other was the playwright, Elmer Lehrman, in two of whose shows she and Martin had invested after meeting him three years ago, a towering literary figure with a pug nose and a head of lush, wavy, brown hair that made a mockery of his sixty-two years. Elmer's wife, a former Broadway actress, was an alcoholic and out of circulation. Elmer, sweeter than ever, actually gave Jenny the eye tonight, and she felt herself responding involuntarily. Well, couldn't hurt to flirt—she needed *something* to take her mind off Josh.

On the other side of her enormous living room Jenny put pudgy Herbert Selzman, a federal judge of the Appeals Court, who dutifully smiled his dimpled kewpie smile at his wife, Gerda, squatting on the ottoman at his feet; like a handmaiden, she almost never left his side. The people one was obliged to invite into one's living room just to keep up! Soon the room was buzzing with guests.

Standing at the huge Steinway grand, arms akimbo, Liz Davidson was having a go at Eliot Krieger, whose eyes seemed glazed; he appeared to be drinking hard in self-defense. Liz, stunning in her wine-colored Halston pants suit, looked every inch the former beauty queen, but she could also talk a blue streak. Why not? P.R. was her business. The two investment bankers and their wives, members of Century, the German-Jewish club, were all old friends of the Singers—Bunny and Trudy Gottlieb, a staid,

respectable couple who prated tirelessly about their grandchildren, and Manny Loebman and his wife Jeanette. Manny, affable, thin, with prominently high cheekbones and an egghead, had always loved Jenny, but he was Martin's closest friend, and she had responded to his advances only playfully, as old friends do. Manny and Martin had been Eliot House roommates, for God's sake!

Manny had eyes she thought of as black, and his speech was staccato. He was a decisive mover and shaker, and not only on Wall Street. She loved Manny's *involvement* in everything. Presidents were always calling on him for advice. He was out there punching all the time. He cared! He always gave her a big hug and kiss and cried, "Juicy Jenny, my sweet peach!" She could probably go for Manny if she let herself. But it was unthinkable. The Gottliebs and Loebmans, like the Kahanes, were also members of Harmonie. Both men were taking turns pumping Marshall Gordon, the tall, rotund member of the Federal Reserve Board, up from Washington to find out what the Fed was up to.

Sonny Dembitz was holding forth blurrily on Watergate. Sonny, a trim but dissipated cosmetic prince, thought he was Frank Sinatra. His yacht, the *Sonny*, except for Ari Onassis's, was the longest in the world. Sonny was supporting four ex-wives and had brought number three along tonight—Ada Danescu, the blond Roumanian beauty, a luscious actress everyone wanted to get his hands on, but who was nobody's fool. Every hand that landed on her had to come bearing fruit—Cartier peaches or Tiffany grapes. Sonny had not entirely recovered from a minor stroke— his brother Max was running Demonde Cosmetics these days—and his speech defect caused by the stroke camouflaged his natural incoherence.

Noah Pulvermacher (called Jiggs by his family because his older sister Margaret had been called Maggie), a cheerful and athletic young newspaper publisher, and his sprightly wife Judy provided a touch of light relief from all the ponderous, ailing people in their fifties, sixties, and seventies. Judy Pulvermacher was talking animatedly to Martin's mother, the white-haired woman sitting in a high-back wing chair. Debbie Singer sat in all her radiant, gracefully Sephardic splendor. She had high color tonight, her sharp, blue eyes alight in the face of a pretty good old fairy with blue-white hair. Martin, who had been talking to Herbert when she arrived, hurried to kiss her. "Ma, you're looking positively radiant tonight! You're a knockout!" Leave it to Martin, ailing as he was.

Four others filled out the guest list—the Goldens, like the Loebmans and Gottliebs, were from Century—the country club of the old German crowd, which would not take Martin because of his Russian father— Supreme Court or no—Jews were the greatest bigots, Jenny said. (Others

whispered that Martin, with his Sephardic mother, a distant cousin of Emma Lazarus, no less, would have been welcome, but oh, that Jenny!) Harry Golden, suave, with a baby-smooth chin and cherubic face, was the retired chief of one of America's three great national networks. His much younger, Anglo-Catholic wife, Faith, was one of America's Ten Best Dressed, a svelte woman who had been incubated in the upper reaches of Philadelphia's Main Line, and was sweet and gracious to everyone.

The guest in whom everyone was most interested tonight was the acting attorney general's assistant, Hugo Sears, for his boss was the survivor and beneficiary of the Saturday Night Massacre. Hugo's red hair and red beard bristled with nervousness.

And finally, pacing restlessly, was the Man Who Was Always There—Graham Butler, who served a very special purpose for Jenny, for while she took her private pleasure in rubbing American Jews together to see the sparks fly, this unadulterated Irish *goy* was there to be certain that everyone behaved and no blood flowed. From the time he started writing the highly disciplined monthly letter, "Inside New York," for the *Manhattanite*, Graham had discovered that much of what he learned about New York (as well as about Washington and Hollywood) he heard first in Martin and Jenny Singer's living room. As for his propositions, every woman under fifty was eligible. Jenny suspected he got a surprisingly high proportion of yesses; he was reputed to have had carnal knowledge of at least a dozen respectable and safe Jewish princesses, married to men too old or too busy, and this rumour alone provided as much titillation as these evenings could afford.

At dinner, the talk wandered to Watergate briefly, as all talk these days did. Liquor had loosened a few tongues, and if Mr. Nixon's ears ever burned, they burned that night. But although Mr. Sears was polite, he concentrated on his oysters Rockefeller, methodically masticated his beef Bourguignon. Watergate, he announced finally, was a national pity, and he resumed chewing. Jenny was doing her best to display a lively interest in Graham Butler's new biography of Kit Cornell. But as she listened to Graham, she became aware that all conversations elsewhere around the table had stopped; a silence had taken hold, and everyone was staring toward the dining room archway.

She turned. Framed in the arch like Banquo's ghost was her son Joshua. He hadn't shaved for a week and wore dirty jeans, dirtier sneakers, and, under a stained lumber jacket, a red-and-black-plaid wool shirt. His hair was in its usually woolly, wild, and matted state. But he was smiling calmly. He did have his father's radiant smile, Jenny thought.

"Josh! Oh God!" She was up and at him, absolutely unaware of all the

others, her arms around her son in a possessive, protecting embrace. "Ain't chu somethin'!" She clung to him briefly, then held him away to examine him. "How in God's name did you *get* here? Wow, you look good to me! You bet! Decided to grow some whiskers like your daddy's, eh?"

At the mention of his father Josh emitted a quick, unpleasant snort. "I haven't had time to shave, Ma." She buried her head in his shoulder to hide her relief, and also to hide the sharp flash of pain caused by his ugly response. That fucking stupid feud! In front of all their friends. How Martin must feel! Josh glanced over her head, which he cradled indifferently in one hand, looking over the curious stares around the long table. His eyes were glittering as if he had a fever. "Hi, all."

Some there had known him since he was a child; to the others he was an apparition—not, Elmer Lehrman mused, unlike the Ancient Mariner. Perhaps he, too, brought some fevered tale.

"Isn't Roger with you?" Jenny said. "For God's sake, he went out there to *get* you."

"No, Ma. You know Roger. He was right there when I got sprung, but he went back to Washington to his hot-blooded black wife." He quick-kissed Jenny's cheek and disengaged himself from her maternal clutch.

Suddenly Josh saw his grandmother and he stepped around to her swiftly, his eyes alight with surprise and delight. " 'Ey, Debbie!"

Deborah Singer had been watching him raptly. Josh was her favorite grandchild, if secrets were told. For four years they had talked once or twice each month. He called collect regularly, except on her birthdays, when he generally sprang for the charges. " 'Ey, you want to guess where I've *been*, Debbie?"

His grandmother pulled his untidy, bristly face down to her own. "I don't give a *damn*," she said. "You're back home, and it's about time. I was hoping I'd last long enough to see you at least once more."

They kissed—the prim, blue-white-haired septuagenarian, classically neat, powdered and immaculate, and this refugee from the lower depths.

"I hope I don't, like, stink," Josh said.

"I've smelled better. Last we talked, you were going to La Paz, weren't you? To make a movie about whales?"

"Yeah, a movie, maybe a TV special. We got some whales, and guess what? Where do you think I ended up?" Now, as if by accident, he noticed his father, and notice could not be put off any longer. "Dad." Toneless. He waved as if to a faintly familiar acquaintance. He did not move an inch away from his grandmother's chair.

Martin nodded curtly. "Josh."

"You mean you didn't tell 'em, Dad? Didn't even give the folks a hint?

Well, okay, where I've been, folks, and why I stink, folks, is in the pokey, folks. For having six ounces of marijuana—can you believe? A nice little old Mexican cooler—in fact the only one to be found in La Paz, Baja California."

That kid! Jenny thought. Just like that. Now that he'd said it, she didn't care. The way he'd done it, it seemed like nothing. Nothing to be ashamed of.

Turning to the table as a whole, as if he were giving a theatrical performance, Josh said, "And now, ladies and gents, how would all you nice people like to meet my fiancée? Oh, why should I kid you? I've married the girl. Oh, I know what you're thinking. No, no, this is a white girl. A real Wasp. And not pregnant. Direct from Baja California via Aeromexico and United Airlines. She's right up there in the movie room."

Jenny was too stunned to say anything. She glanced across at Martin.

"Call her, for heaven's sake," Jean Kahane commanded in her dust-dry voice.

Looking upward toward the movie room, Josh sang out, " 'Ey, Tammy! They *want* you! C'mon! You're on!"

They heard the sound of quick, light footsteps on the marble steps and a small, thin girl with straight, shoulder-length red hair and freckles appeared in the archway, head down, peering up under her brows at the gathering of her elders in mock terror. She looked almost like Little Orphan Annie or a fourteen-year-old farm girl, wise for her age, the corners of her mouth drawn tightly down, wearing jeans and a tight white jersey blouse over delicate unbrassiered breasts whose nipples attracted every eye. She wore absolutely no makeup. Her shift to a suddenly shy smile cast up under the brows, eyes glistening, was one she had perfected before huge audiences undreamed of by most of those in this dinner group. Without a wasted motion, hers constituted the theatrical entrance of a star. Jenny had all she could do to keep from applauding; this was one fiancée she had not met before. Even Martin for a blessed moment felt faintly less hostile, although more than ever he longed for bed. His upper abdomen again.

It was Judy Pulvermacher who cried, "My God, it's Tammy Barnstone!" As if everyone would, of course, know who that was, while in fact the name meant nothing to anyone in the room except Graham Butler, who had reviewed two of her performances, one in Central Park and one at Fillmore East. Tammy Barnstone's folk and soft-rock albums had been sold and were selling to millions of children under twenty, but of all those at the table, only Judy Pulvermacher and Graham Butler kept up with

the music of the kids. Jenny felt left out. She tried so hard to keep young, but it was so damn difficult!

After introductions all around, the customary minuet, Jean Kahane suggested to Jenny that the young couple join the diners. Josh took the place next to his grandmother, and Tammy sat beside him. All through the rest of dinner Josh kept one hand on Tammy—on her shoulder, her head, her neck. And she touched him as often as she could. They held hands and rubbed knees under the table.

Between mouthfuls of beef Bourguignon and strawberries Cardinale, Jenny's specialty, Josh, still not letting go of Tammy's hand, began his monologue, and all side conversations stopped. He launched into a laconic account of his arrest in the Miramar Hotel in La Paz. Fortunately, Roger arrived from Washington and Tammy's lawyer, Oscar Kunst, returned to Los Angeles. They conferred, and, after a few well-placed phone calls by Oscar, Josh was suddenly sprung just as things were turning hairy. "They wanted to keep my marijuana," Josh said, "and I wasn't about to go without it. It was damn good grass." He reached into his breast pocket. Tammy took a paper and rolled one, and Josh lighted it for her. She took two short drags and handed it back to Josh, who did the same and offered it to his grandmother. She eyed it with some suspicion.

"If you don't mind, I'd prefer one of my own," she said. Josh rolled and lighted a fresh one and handed it to his grandmother, who took a tentative puff. "My very first," she said. "Will I be arrested? Herbert? Hugo? I must say it makes me feel like one of those Freedom Riders."

Liz Davidson broke the uneasy silence. "I could use a spot of brandy," she said to Jenny, "which shows *my* generation." Martin would want his sweet liqueur—he always did, sick or well. Jenny rose abruptly and the others followed into the music room.

By the time Jenny asked Tammy to sing, the word about her had been passed, and everyone in the room knew she was a young Somebody. Nor did Tammy have to be coaxed. She could do folk and lullabies, blues and soft rock, and the success her voice had brought her had led to a great sobering, for not long ago this prepubescent-looking girl had been on hard drugs and into kinky sex. Now all that was behind her, and she took her music, but not her popularity, seriously.

Tonight, as she glanced around the room, taking in the white hair, the bald heads, the wrinkled eyes, she knew it was a night for cooing. Having no guitar, she sat at the Steinway grand, played a few accompanying chords, and sang two short ballads she had composed herself. When she finished the first number the guests wanted more. "This one," Tammy

said, "is an old Yiddish poem by a man named Rosenfeld; maybe someone here knows him?" No one did. "You should," she said. "Really." She played a chord softly, and began, singing a verse in Yiddish, which no Jew present understood. The second verse she sang in English.

> *I raised my eyes to see the sky,*
> *The clouds were weeping . . . so was I.*
> *Today I lift my head up high,*
> *The sun is smiling, so am I.*
> *Why do I smile? Why did I weep?*
> *I don't know why . . . it lies too deep.*
> *I don't know why . . . it lies too deep.*

A lullaby tempo. There they sat, as she went on to the next verse, listening to the voice from their own pasts in that minor key, some undistinguished words from the *shtetl*. By the time Tammy had finished and returned to curl up in Josh's lap like an infant rescued, good and generous feelings permeated the warm nineteenth-century room. Jenny bent to kiss the girl. They wanted still more, but Tammy remained curled, huddling in Josh's arms as if for protection.

It cannot therefore be said that anyone at the Singers' was stone-cold sober at the moment when Jenny decided to mention to the assemblage the plight of Yuri Ivanovich Karpeyko, nor can any explanation be given as to her purpose in doing so; perhaps it was merely the liquor. Or the Jewish music and words. Or old Debbie smoking pot. But she spoke out of a clear blue sky.

"Listen, everybody," she cried in her high musical voice, at the first lull, "I really can't keep this to myself. We have still another problem. May I?" People did tend to listen to Jenny; her voice was so firm and clear. "We have this cousin—what's his name, Marty? Ivan? No, Yuri. Yuri Ivanovich Karpeyko. Yeah. It's no joke. Martin's second cousin, I guess. Until a few days ago we'd never heard of him, but he's there, all right."

"He's where?" Jean asked.

"Minsk." Her guest stared at her.

"You don't believe me? Ask Marty. Minsk, so help me. Right, Marty?" As well as she was able, barely coherent, she tried to tell them about Schulman's visit and Yuri's letter. "Can you imagine? It turns out Martin has a relative who's a member of the Communist Party, Soviet Union, yet! How do you like that? The guy sounds like a knockout to me. Now

he wants to leave Russia with his family, but they're giving them such *tsouris!* He's afraid he's gonna be arrested. So the question is, what can *we* do?"

Manny Loebman confirmed that he knew Yoshke Schulman very well. "Remarkable man," Manny said. "Did he tell you he was involved in the capture of Eichmann?"

Jenny shook her head in disbelief. "That little guy?"

"He was a kid then. He and two Israelis kept the guy at gunpoint in a hotel room in Buenos Aires for two hours until the rest of the Israeli agents arrived. Tough little hombre."

"I wish he'd go to Minsk and kidnap this Yuri Karpeyko," Jenny said. "It would save us all a lot of trouble."

Manny laughed. "The Soviet Union's not Argentina. And it may not be necessary."

"How *do* people get out?" Jenny said.

"There's no mystery about it, Jenny, m' love." Manny never made any bones about the soft spot he had for her. "I can tell you exactly what needs to be done." Manny loved to do things for people in trouble, she thought drunkenly. Just too bad he and Marty were such *damn* good friends. "They need a *vyzov* from Israel—an invitation from a relative. And I suspect if there is no relative, they find one in Israel. But you do have cousins in Israel, Martin, don't you? Rachel Aronowitz, isn't she . . . ?" Martin nodded. "You know all about that, do you? Well, after the *vyzov* comes, they have to go through a hell of a lot of truly nonsensical stuff. Every person in the family leaving, for example, must produce the approval of his parents, even if the applicant's seventy and the parents are ninety. The application becomes an encyclopedia about the entire family, the births, the deaths, schooling, all their activities, their awards, Party membership, if kicked out, what for, and God knows what all. Then each one has to get a certificate from the place of work saying he has no obligations there, a certificate from the management of the house they live in that the place is being left in apple-pie order, their photographs, birth certificates. I think I've remembered most of it."

"Emigration made easy," Martin said.

"That's only the beginning," Manny continued in his rapid-fire delivery. "Then you have to quit your job—they usually can you anyway—and pay for repairs to your house, which suddenly become very high—fork over five or six hundred dollars a person—and mosey on over to the OVIR office *hoping* you'll get your exit visa. And then you *start* to wait. And wait. You become a charity case. That's when we come in. We send them things these people can sell to eat. Once you get your visa, if you

do, the die is cast. They grab your passport, you're obliged to renounce your Soviet citizenship, and you'd better git. Vienna is thataway."

"Sounds a bit tricky, but not all that bad," Martin said.

"Well," Manny said, "they get you with the small print. No sooner do you apply than they start checking records. They do their damndest to get something on you, all full of Soviet legalities. If you have no job, how the devil do you live? You must be a parasite! That's a crime. Have you done your time in the army? If not, what better time than now? Are you a Party member? Have you ever had a sensitive job? Jobs you wouldn't believe are classified as sensitive—translator, for instance. God knows what secrets you might know. Can't let you out with state secrets. Big no-no. Are there, God forbid, any criminal charges against you? And the crimes? Something you may have said, et cetera, et cetera."

"There are!" Jenny cried. "Criminal charges. That's why our poor Yuri's so worried."

"What kind of criminal charges?"

"Oh, he wrote some stories for children about made-up animals. They say they're anti-Soviet."

"Oh, hell, for that, if they want to, they could send the poor bastard away for five, seven, ten years. Maybe longer. He might never make it."

"Jesus," Jenny said. "For writing little fables?" She was having trouble following Manny. Too many drinks, too fast. She couldn't remember how many gins she'd had. "How do *you* know so much about it, Manny?"

Manny Loebman smiled. "Don't you know, sweetie? I'm a big Hebe."

"How long do they have to wait for a visa?" Hugo Sears asked.

"Varies," Manny said. "Theoretically, a few months. Actually, who knows? A year, sometimes up to five, six years. There's no way to predict. It seems entirely arbitrary, and there's no explaining it. Whatever the reasons, they're pretty opaque. That's the tough time, the waiting, not knowing if permission will ever come. Then, when they do get out, some of 'em prefer to come here instead of to Israel. So between Joint and HIAS and NYANA we get 'em in, house 'em, feed 'em and find 'em jobs."

"Yuri and his family can come live with *us*," Jenny said.

Martin laughed. "Oh, Jenny! You know you and houseguests! Like fish after three days."

She glared at Martin. He knew she did not care to be reminded of anything she had said in the past. "In our *house*," Jenny persisted, belligerent. "In our *houssse!*"

Jiggs Pulvermacher began to pace to and fro in front of the great window as if he had become suddenly upset by a clear and present danger.

"And what happens if the Soviets suddenly *do* decide tomorrow to open their gates and let *all* the Jews go? Pull a Pharaoh on us? It's a possibility. Does anyone seriously think we're ready to take in another two or three million Jews?"

"Not *all* in *our* house!" Josh said with mock defiance. "The most the Singers can take is . . . lemme see, besides the doctor—oh, Ma, I'm with you on the doctor—well, maybe two hundred. After all, we have only thirty-two rooms." He drew happily on his joint.

Cherubic Herbert Selzman, who had been his usual smiling but silent self, now spoke. "I'm sure you understand, Jenny, these people may be dangerous. They could become an enormous Fifth Column. Just because they're Jews, that doesn't alter their views. Fundamentally they're still Communists; they're dedicated to 'burying' us. And, Martin, you say this cousin of yours is a Party member. So much the worse. We've got to be awfully careful."

Jenny squinted at the judge, trying to decide how forthright she dared to be. To hell with it. "Herbie, you're still the same old lovable hangman, aren't you? These are two doctors and an immunologist, for God's sake!" Herbert reddened and glowered, nursing his drink.

"This is utterly delightful nonsense," Elmer Lehrman said, shaking his leonine head. "I have news for you. Two million Jews aren't coming. No way. Don't you realize most of them love Mother Russia? It's nothing like the old tsarist days. No way! *Their* blood is there now. No matter how bastardly the system is to them. It was *Jews* who made the Revolution. Karl Marx is God. Trotsky was one of the first prophets, and Litvinov was their foreign minister. Mrs. Molotov was a Jew. Kaganovich was a Jew. They helped create the Soviet Union, and out of all proportion to their numbers. They fought the Nazis. They don't even think of themselves as Jews any more, most of 'em."

Marshall Gordon puffed his pipe and spoke sagely. "I wish I could agree, but I wouldn't depend on it. The Russians, the Byelorussians, the Ukrainians aren't about to give up their anti-Semitism. They could still drive their Jews out, whether they want to go or not. The point is that no matter how great the pressure—and this goes for Hungarians and Czechs and all the rest, Jew and gentile—it's important for us to watch our absorption rate. Within narrow limits we can take in *some*. But we have a delicately balanced society in this country nowadays, and a precarious economy. Dislocations like the influx of Cubans, the Puerto Ricans, the Mexicans, the black migrations northward, they upset the balance. We end up with unemployment, cheap labor, riots, strikes, recessions. Is that what *we* want? You have to be extremely careful."

Eliot Krieger nodded. "Marshall's absolutely right," he said in his bombastic, didactic, but down-home style. "The United States has come a long way since old Miss Liberty was set up in the harbor and Deborah's cousin Emma wrote those marvelous words. I for one would welcome unlimited immigration except for one thing: we're a welfare state now. We just couldn't afford it. Oh, but what a treasure the immigrants were when we could." He smiled with a boyish charm that denied his bald dome and thick glasses. "If it hadn't been for that rabble, I wouldn't be here myself. Most of us wouldn't, I daresay. But that's over. We're a different country now, with an enormous deficit and worldwide responsibilities."

Herbert Selzman spoke judiciously. "Above all, we have Israel now. That makes a tremendous difference. These emigrants have a place that not only will take them in, but that actively wants them and needs them —the way we needed people to settle our West. That should relieve the pressure on us. If they want these Communists, let them take the bodies and we'll pay the cost. A not inconsiderable cost, by the way, as I'm sure everyone in this room is aware."

Jenny's voice, loud and clear: "I'm so *sorry*. Poor *us*." She was feeling queasy, as though her stomach seemed suddenly to have left her.

Graham Butler, who had not insulted anyone all evening, was on his feet. "I can't believe my ears! What in the name of God has gotten into the heads of you people? I'm ashamed! Is there anyone who's *not* an immigrant? You people in this room, have you forgotten the teeming slums of the Lower East Side? What honor there was in those slums! Shame on you! Tell me—I'm your *shabbos goy*, you can level with me—is it anti-Semitism you're terrified of? That if we take in too many Jews, your fellow Americans are going to rise up against you? Despite your eminence and distinction? Is that it? Shame! Trust us! Trust us! You should be fighting tooth and nail for your two million, or two and a half million, locked into a repressive society over there. Who says we can't take 'em? We're more than two hundred million here; we'd never notice 'em. We've lost all our zip, all our purpose. One big closed shop! Why, we could support a billion! Welcome one, welcome all. No handouts! Work or perish! The fittest shall prosper! How d'you think we grew to be what we are? People coming, coming, starting at the bottom. Well, I don't have to tell any of *you*, we're running out of bottom people."

Marshall Gordon, his fixed, sphinxlike smile unruffled, emptied his pipe into Jenny's delicate Royal Doulton ashtray. "Politics, Graham, my dear boy, is the art of the possible. America's not with you. Tell me, would you take in every black, every Chinese, every East Indian, every Hottentot who wanted to come?"

For a moment Graham hesitated. His eyes widened as if he were trapped. He glanced from face to face. All gazes were upon him. His delicate Irish face was open with amazement at the opposition, and he grinned. "Absolutely! As long as they came willing to work. I happen to be in a profession that doesn't deal with the art of the possible. I can be a superlative advocate. Oh, they'd have to pay their own fares and get their own jobs. But if it were up to me, I'd reopen Ellis Island, yessir. I'd take 'em *all* in. Palestinians and Jews, Irish and Vietnamese! We get the best of the huddled masses—the get-up-and-goers. What amazes me is that you don't agree with me. What the devil are you afraid of? What I suspect, I repeat, is that deep down you'd *like* to take those Russian Jews in, but you're terrified of your fellow Americans, that they'll turn on you at the first sign of recession and cry, 'All right, now yez'll all have to git!' Tell me, from the gut, now isn't that it?"

"All *riiight!*" Josh cried with sudden enthusiasm, and took a long drag, which he held in his lungs, as if for relief. Then, as he blew out the smoke slowly, he added, "Right on, man." But Graham said no more.

Tammy's hesitant voice filled the embarrassed silence. "I'm due to go to the Soviet Union—I think in about six weeks. I'm supposed to do three concerts there—one in Kiev and two in Moscow. It's been arranged for months. I guess they asked me because of those Vietnam protest concerts. And they've offered a disgraceful lot of money. Josh is coming, too. I was just thinking—why couldn't we all . . . Is Minsk near either of those cities? Maybe we could go visit your relatives."

"Oh, how great!" Jenny cried. "Marty and I could go, too. Marty! How about it?"

Marty shook his head. His Jenny!

"Sure, why not, Ma?" Josh said. "C'mon!"

But Jenny, feeling the drinks, had vaguely observed Marty's big no-no, and was drifting in and out with the tide. She looked from face to face, peering as through smoke, while the silence grew uncomfortable. She felt angry and helpless. That's what she ought to do—go there!

"*Look* at you," Jenny cried. "My God, the cream of America! A judge, Nobel prizers, big publisher, king of the television business, a gorgeous sexpot, Sonny, the man who gave America its eyelashes, the assistant attorney general of the whole United States of America, the best-dressed woman in the *world*, a woman who was almost *Miss* America . . . and the man, for Christ's sake, in charge of all the money in the country! So lemme ask you, my friends—tell me, *anyone, anyone* o' you fancy Jews— how do we save our poor *schlemiel?*" Their faces were now weaving before her eyes, and the wooziness was getting worse. She blinked hard and

repeatedly, trying to erase the blurring. Why was she weeping? It only made her feel sicker. "Oh, Marty, please escuse me, I think I'm gonna be a little sick. Oh boy! Manny, I love ya!" She walked to Manny unsteadily and managed to kiss him. "No won'er we had the goddamn Holocaust. We deserved it." She stumbled over to Graham Butler, put her arms around him, supporting herself on him, and kissed him. "Any time, kid," she said drunkenly.

He grinned, leaned to her ear. "Give me a ring for lunch, Jen," he whispered.

She stared at him for an instant, kissed him lightly again, and turned to Josh. "Come on, Joshie, le's go upstairs." She sniffed. "An' bring Cinderella. She sings like a goddamn angel."

She lurched toward the stairs with Josh trailing her, followed by Tammy. Martin edged painfully behind. "Better look after her, Martin," his mother urged quietly. "I'll take care of your guests."

Martin, longing for someone who would take care of *him*, wandered alone to the movie room and stared at the five accusing cartons of letters and papers; he fingered Yuri's letter, which still lay on his desk. He looked at the old letter from his grandfather Moses. He felt guilty about Jenny. He felt guilty about Josh. He was tired almost to death, and rested his head on the hard desk surface. He would get at those letters first thing in the morning, he thought. Find out who the devil this guy in Russia was. Get down to beginnings.

Josh had unsettled him. Damn Bolshevik cousin springing up out of nowhere! What *were* his duties? His life, which had been orderly for so long, seemed in the last few years to be coming suddenly apart: Roger marrying a black lady lawyer, however sophisticated and charming; Nettie off to Israel chasing her El Al pilot, no matter how dashing; and Josh—Christ, he was immersed in chaos. If only he had his health. If only he had his balls. If only he were going to live. Those shoulder pains. The sharp clawing at his gut, at his sternum, as if a crab were in there pinching his vitals. Cancer the crab, he thought.

The telephone only inches from his ear clanged suddenly, a fire alarm, and frightened him enough so that he could hear his own heart pounding.

"This is the overseas operator," a woman's voice said. "I have a call for Martin Singer."

He nodded, eyes closed, and waited. "Hello," the operator repeated, "this is the overseas—"

"Yes," he said finally.

"I have a call for Martin Singer."

"Yes. Yes. I'm Martin Singer."

"All right, Jerusalem." He heard a man's voice speaking Hebrew, then static, then a woman's clear voice somewhat accented: "Martin?"

"Yes?"

"This is Rachel Aron. How are you?"

"Fine, fine." This was no time to tell her how he was. Rachel Aron, formerly Aronowitz, his cousin. She inquired about Jenny and the children. He tried to remember the names of her three daughters. Zilch. Even his memory was failing. He used to have a fantastic memory for names, another lost ambassadorial skill. He inquired after Boris. Boris had died six years ago. Idiot. He remembered now—a jeep accident. She didn't seem to mind his asking. He wanted desperately to sink through the floor. It was not like him to be gauche. He was aware only that Rachel kept talking. The Yom Kippur War had kept everyone busy, they were rethinking all the past assumptions, Rachel was saying. There were conferences and meetings all day, every day. He didn't know what the hell Rachel was chattering about.

Then, "Martin, what do you think of the new addition to the family?"

"You have a new grandchild?" He was about to offer congratulations.

"No, no, our new *cousins*, Martin. Three of them. In Minsk."

Jesus, his mind was going to ruin. "Oh. Yes, I know about them. Are they really our cousins?"

"How can I be sure? But I think so. Whether yes or no, did you know their daughter was just expelled from her medical school? They accused her of immorality."

"When was this?"

"The day before yesterday." By God, Martin thought, they do have a network. That Yoshke—what's his name—Schulman. "I think he's in great danger. I spoke to Mr. Schulman at the National Conference a few hours ago. He and I have been talking all week. They haven't bothered the wife yet, probably because she's not Jewish. No one knows what's going to happen."

The tension and tightness of Rachel's voice was somewhat different from Jenny's. Jenny was all alarums and fanfare. Rachel was terse.

"I'm sorry to hear it," Martin said. "Do you know these people?"

"Mr. Schulman is sure they're our cousins, Martin. I've never met them."

"Well, what are we supposed to do about them?"

"We've sent them the *vyzovs*," Rachel said. "One for each, which is unusual, but that's how he wanted it. I don't think we have all the time in the world. I'm coming to New York. I'll tell you then what we can do. I

have to go to Denver and Columbus and Montreal, and then to Dallas and Los Angeles—to make speeches. Also I must go to Washington to see our ambassador for Golda."

"You'll be pretty busy, Rachel. When are you coming?"

"Tomorrow. Can you put me up? The plane fare is so high. And hotels are too expensive in New York—for Israelis, anyway. Your place makes me feel so rich and luxurious."

"We'll be absolutely delighted to have you. It'll be a privilege, Rachel, dear. Dress warmly, though. We have snow and it's bitter cold."

"Thank you, Martin. I'm taking El Al flight 003." He jotted it down. "I arrive at eight P.M. tomorrow, your time."

"I'll have Fred meet you. He'll be wearing a light blue chauffeur's uniform and he has a large button in his lapel which says I'M FRED. If I possibly can, I'll do my damndest to get there, too. I haven't been too well." He hadn't the slightest intention of going.

6

Indeed, the next day was far busier than Martin had expected, or than he was up to. Manny Loebman came unannounced to the house before eight-thirty in the morning, and got Marty out of the bath he loved to lounge in. He found quiet comfort floating in warm water, and interruption made him rather testy. Manny brought with him Carter-Hale's long-delayed offer for the store. The boys on the West Coast, Manny said, had called last night after he returned home (Manny did not otherwise refer to last night, he was so busy with his message) with an offer of a combination of stock and cash—thirty-one million, subject to conditions which Manny felt would not be difficult for Martin to meet. Carter-Hale's registration was still green, so it could be done relatively quickly— say three months. Martin could either sell their stock or keep it. They offered Martin a five-year contract at a quarter of a million a year.

Martin had Manny sit there while he called Andy Steiner at his home in Cincinnati and told him he was now under pressure to "do something." He had a firm offer, and if Amalgamated was ever serious about making a bid for the store, now was the time. Andy told him that his calling was a coincidence, because the accountants had on Monday completed their analysis of the Singer figures; the executive committee had been studying it for the last three days, and they had just authorized Andy to make Martin an offer. So here it was: a million one hundred thousand shares of a thirty-three-dollar Amalgamated convertible preferred with a two-dollar dividend, in a tax-free exchange. It would give Martin an income of two million two hundred thousand a year.

Martin responded slowly. "You understand, Andy, I don't go with the sale. You'll have to find someone else to run the operation." The way he felt, he could barely run to the bathroom.

Andy demurred at first. But eventually, reluctantly, he said, "Well,

Martin, if that's the way it has to be, we'll just have to find the right man. Not that anyone could ever replace you. I'll try like hell to sell that to my guys."

Martin emphasized the same thing to Manny. It was too early in the morning to call California, but Manny thought Carter-Hale might buy the condition, although it was a rough one. They liked smooth transitions and of course they, too, thought Martin was a genius. Martin took a deep breath. "Okay, Manny, here it is: the price is thirty-eight million, all cash —without me. Now go get it. I don't want the Amalgamated deal, but they're at thirty-six three, and theirs is tax free."

Manny, exuding confidence, said he'd get back to Martin as soon as he could raise the boys in San Francisco.

Martin felt a bit put down; he was dismayed that both Manny and Andy felt the store *could* be run just fine without him. Amputations, he thought, are not all done on the operating table. Oh, they had both protested politely, but Martin got the message. He knew now in his gut as well as his head that he was actually going to sell the store; the deal would be made today.

"What's all that junk on the floor?" Manny asked as he was getting ready to leave.

"Oh, ancestral mail," Martin said. "What Jenny calls a shitload of heirlooms. Letters written by my father and grandfather, and *his* father. From my grandmother, too; she could write, you know? Unusual for those women.

"What the hell, I figure I may as well find out whether this Russian joker is actually related to me or not. I'm not going off half-cocked to break my ass over some guy who *claims* he's my cousin. The name Karpeyko—where the hell does *that* come from? Some guy in trouble over there might have somehow found that old letter from Grandfather, if it *is* my grandfather, and decided to put it to use. I just want to be sure of what we're getting into, especially with Jenny in her savior mood. Rachel's coming and she sounds more gung ho than Jenny. Hell, if Jenny had her way, she'd sashay over there, go right to the KGB office, and sweet-talk them into letting this guy go home with her. A true realist, my Jenny. She's my Heroine addict, if you'll excuse the expression. She lives in a world, but it's not ours. She sees herself as saving everybody—me, Josh, the poor Negroes, and now this guy from Minsk. Come to think of it, you're a little like that yourself, Manny."

"Is that bad?" Manny said, laughing.

"I'm not sure. The saviors of this world are not my dish of tea, you and Jenny excepted."

"Oh, you're still sore because your own father was one," Manny laughed. "You've been raised on the anti-hero. Marty, you've got to get over all that. You've gotta come to terms with your old man, and Jenny, and your son—he's one, too, you know—and me."

"Maybe so. Anyhow, this professor from the Yiddish Scientific Institute is going to have these letters translated for me. I was planning to ask Wolfson up in Cambridge to get someone, but your friend, Yoshke Schulman, put me onto this guy, and he's more convenient, right here in New York. The professor's already translated a few himself and the regular translator's starting this morning. Can you believe it, a Yeshiva student in this house? Old man Whitney who built the place eighty years ago must be committing suicide in his grave. I expect the Yeshiva lad any minute."

Manny went to the foyer and got his coat. "I hate to mention this, Marty, after your diatribe against saviors, but I'm an old hand at this Soviet Jew business, so if I can be of any help with your cousin—even if he's not your cousin—"

"Sure, sure," Martin said impatiently, all but pushing Manny to the door. "Go get my thirty-eight million, will you?"

At a quarter to eleven, Schmuel Rosenzweig arrived with his goggle-eyed Yeshiva student, a redheaded young man named Isaac something who wore a skullcap indoors and stared at everything in the house with disbelief. Myra, who had come from the store to help, showed him where he was to work, and Rosenzweig remained with the young man, going over some of the material and giving him instructions and suggestions. The kid seemed bright and faintly amused.

Rosenzweig came down to see Martin in the library with a report on the contents of the cartons, the first of which he had taken home with him. The letters he had looked at, the bony man told Martin in his pedantic schoolmarmish style, were from his grandfather Moishe Singer to one Uncle Yankele Singer in Atlanta; there were replies from the uncle; more recent letters were from people in the old country to Moishe —or Moses, as he later was called—from his parents, his wife-to-be, an Aunt Leah, and his sister Feygele. Ah, so Feygele was confirmed. Two witnesses now.

There was also correspondence between Moishe's wife, Sheyna Rasel, and *her* sister Freda in Palestine. Later letters, the next generation's, after the turn of the century, were in English and could be read in the original. Translation being a tricky business, he had instructed the young man that if words or phrases were, for a more accurate rendition, better left in the original Yiddish and could be generally understood, to leave them so, and that is what he himself had done with the first ones. The earliest letter

they had been able to find was dated April 16, 1873, a hundred years ago. If Mr. Singer would care to have a look . . .

Martin took up the typed translation not knowing what to expect. Well, let's see.

LETTER FROM MOISHE SINGER (AGE 11) TO HIS UNCLE IN ATLANTA, GEORGIA, U.S.A.

Minsk, Northwestern Region
4 April 1873
(16 April 1873 C.E. New Style)
19 Nissan 5633

Uncle Yankele!

Yesterday arrived from you the first letter I ever received, though I love to read the ones you send Papa. I felt important. Well, why not? In a few months I'll be having my twelfth birthday. We are all well, except my brother Yussel. He died last month; he wasn't even four. Mama keeps crying over him. I feel sorry for her, but Yussel was very cranky, kept us all awake, and no pleasure. Papa won't talk about Yussel at all, as if dying were a disgrace to the family.

Luckily, I am not home much. I'm finally in the government school. A month ago, after such a long wait, I was admitted to the gymnasium. How I worked to pass that examination! I failed twice already. I like it there in spite of Papa, who took one look at my silver buttons and spit. I've met many agreeable gentiles in school, especially one boy, Alexei Rosnikov. He seems no different from me. He is he and I am I by accident, right? He is clever, laughs a lot, and thinks I'm a comic. His father is a doctor, a widower, with a very low opinion of the officials of the government. I used to think gentiles all *loved* the Tsar. I couldn't tell one *goy* from another. So live and learn. While I like Alexei, we're still pretty cautious with each other.

You remember, Uncle, how hysterical Grandpa always was, worried they're coming to get him for the army? At the age of seventy? My lovely brother Herschel's always jumping up yelling "Hide, *Zayde*, they're coming!"

But last week was not so comic. A real soldier came to our courtyard on *shabbos* and grabbed me—one of those square fellows, polished boots, huge straight white teeth, with a wide blond mustache. If I could ever look like him! Anyway, he holds me by the collar and says he wants Uncle Efram, he has a notice for him: "Report for a physical examination for the army!" I told him, who? Uncle Efram? Gone away—to Orsha to visit a friend for at least a month! He half believed me! Why not? I was wearing my school

uniform! He gave me the paper and said I should give it to Uncle Efram the minute he got back. If he didn't report in three weeks, he'd be arrested! I found Efram hiding in the big cupboard behind the bed where Herschel and I sleep, shaking worse than *Zayde*. He shrunk from the paper as if it were a live snake. So I translated it for him. Oy! Such misery!

You know what? I heard from the girl who lives over us, Freda Rubenstein—she's about my age, but she knows everybody's secrets —"we" have captured a young Jew from Vilna traveling through Minsk on his way to Odessa. They caught him on the Svisloch dock when he got off the riverboat and made the mistake of asking directions to Jew Street. Now he's in Belinsky's cellar—tied up, under lock and key, and you know what? Freda says her papa and mine, Reb Horowitz of the Benevolent Societies, and Reb Kogan, the head of the Burial Society, are going to turn this gink over to the army—instead of Uncle Efram! Can you believe? Mama takes the gink good food to keep him strong, stuffing him like a chicken we're going to eat! If I bring up the subject, Mama says she feels sorry for him, but this way Efram won't have to go. It's him or Efram! Who asked the clumsy loafer to leave Vilna in the first place?

Efram meanwhile snaps at everyone, even Mama, he's so out of his head. He screams "Yetta, you drive me crazy, you're so bossy!" In his great fright his voice is louder than hers. Papa refuses to talk about it, working silently at his lathe, and on the rare occasions when he gives up his nightly trip to the great rebbe's and does the family the great honor to stay home for supper, he says half as a joke Efram should save his cursing and yelling for the Turks. No chance Efram will ever meet a Turk. He'll soon be far away from here, as you are, right? He'll surely never become a Cossack, swinging a *nagaiki*. Can you imagine Uncle Efram on a horse? Oy, he'd die of fright!

I will give this letter to Uncle Efram to deliver, so no one else reads it but you. Will you keep it for me? I'll keep yours.

One secret for last—at night lately I don't sleep. I listen to Isaac and Herschel, to Papa and Mama and Feygele breathing, to *Zayde* snoring, to the chickens clucking around us, and I have this dream. I'm in chains. I can't move. Then I realize I'm the one they are holding in Belinsky's cellar. They don't know I'm really the Tsarevitch! They think I'm a Jew! A sack is over my head, and I wake up suffocating. So who's worse, us or the Tsar? I make a *tummel* about this, but I'm speaking to the wall. The grownups shush me, this guy's a no-good loafer, they say, and who do I think I am? Even good-natured Reb Rubenstein upstairs glares at me for daring to ask where is the justice of what they are doing. This is truth? These Hassidim? Drunken bums! The women shush me, too.

Mama asks me the worst question! "You want Uncle Efram should go? For twenty-five years? This is what you want?" So, Uncle Yankele, what about this stranger? Isn't he also a man? He hasn't a family also? I hear, every night he falls on his belly, crawling, begging Reb Belinsky to let him go! A grown man crying! Tears streaming! I hate the people I see around me. Especially my own father! That is my confession and secret.

Your nephew,
Moishe

Martin stared at the letter. He tried to picture the home his grandfather had described so elliptically. Seven people sleeping in the same room. With chickens. For a kid, Moishe was a garrulous letter writer, if there could be such a thing. Even as an old man, until his stroke, he'd been a nonstop talker, a real charmer, especially of the old ladies.

"Uncle" Efram must be the Efram Singer who, like Martin's grandmother, died before Martin was born in the flu epidemic of 1918. Efram in Atlanta. Here he was about to flee from Russia just like this Karpeyko fellow was looking to do now. So what's new in the world? A dreadful country, then, now, and always.

He glanced at the next sheet. The original post card was stapled to the "archivist's" translation. The printed-in-ink Hebrew letters were carefully and neatly wrought, and under them was a Yiddish scrawl.

28 July 1874

AN INVITATION
REB ISRAIL SINGER HAS THE HONOR TO INVITE HIS BROTHER REB YANKELE SINGER TO THE BAR MITZVAH OF HIS OLDEST SON MOISHE THE REBEL, MAYBE, GOD FORBID, A FREETHINKER. MAY THIS SON LIVE TO SEE HIS OWN SON BAR MITZVAH. MINSK, 14 Av, 5634
[The scrawl:] *Papa made you this invitation, Uncle Yankele. By the time it arrives, it will be too late to send a present. Please don't. I'll never do as well as Papa expects with the [reading of the] Torah, so I won't deserve one. I'm a rebel? Ha ha! Moishe.*

LETTER FROM MOISHE SINGER (AGE 20) TO HIS UNCLE IN ATLANTA
Minsk, Northwestern Region
16 January 1881

Uncle Yankele!

After six months without a letter, such a reward! Two arrive on the same day—each with money! I don't care about the money, but Papa treasures it, and not for the sentiment, but for what it can

buy! What *I* wait for are your words, your wisdom. To hear that your enterprise is so successful, how you do exactly as you please, and without exploiting people. How different here! We have a few rich people, too, including Jews, but not men of soul like you. While our rich line their pockets with rubles, most of our Jews are fools like Papa, with "religious" souls, incapable of revolt, working like animals all week for scraps. And running to God on *shabbos* for a pat on the cheek, which in reality they give themselves, since God is *their* creation. Papa is so long bending over his lathe, he walks like a pretzel. We have rags for everyday clothes; we freeze because we have no money for firewood; our furniture is falling apart; chickens live in the house with us, shitting everywhere; two families plus David the shoemaker crowded in the small cellar; with *shabbos*, always the marvelous *shabbos*, to look forward to! Some life! No wonder Papa prefers Rebbe Schmulkowitz's place, where they all get free *l'chaims*, wine, or vodka, and can sing and forget their troubles, telling one another they are chosen by the Lord! Papa's in ecstasy! Prayers to the Unmentionable Name, blessed be He, all the joys of the Book! I say it's garbage. Hassidim actually disgust me. They live in a make-believe world.

I remember years ago when I had just performed miserably with my bar mitzvah reading, stumbling, having to be constantly cued by Reb Horowitz. Papa really came down on me by yelling at Mama. He knows I can't stand that.

"Yetta, listen!" Papa cried out, scratching his beard like a great philosopher, a *shtickel rebbe* in his *streimel* and *bekecher*. "Our Moishe has to come to terms with the world he lives in. All right, so he's too good to go to *cheder!* All right, so he has to go to the government school! That disgusting uniform I wouldn't even mention! Nu, so now he'll have to study *harder,* go nights to *midrash,* become a wizard at Pilpul, get to memorize his Talmud-Chumesh forwards and back. To be practical, he has to take his place as a *learned* Jew, *enjoying* the pleasures of the *shabbos* and the Holy Days. Otherwise who'll marry him? Some *grubbe* girl? Some *prosteh zakh?* Let him give up all this impractical nonsense about working hard, about becoming a millionaire! Turning into a Russian! What future is there in that?"

"Can he help it," Mama said, drawing her thin self to her full colonel's height, with eyes closed for my lost soul, but a soul loved as few are loved, "if my impractical son has his eyes on the stars?" I love Mama's face, it's like no other—strong, long, thin, with her straight long nose and deep brown eyes.

Now I have graduated from the Teacher's Training School, I speak perfect Russian, read Russian literature, plus some German and French, and am a teacher myself. My subject is mathematics. I

regularly visit my *goyish* comrades' homes, especially Alexei Rosnikov. I'm as close to Alexei as I am to Abramele Shapiro, my lifelong friend from Jew Street, who is studying to be a physician. The two are such a contrast: Alexei with his narrow face, smooth voice, aristocratic bearing, tall and precise, and Abramele, short, with that large strong head, hypnotic eyes, craggy features, bushy eyebrows, and that shock of black hair, whose laugh is like a roar. Abramele lives in a filthy hovel, but will soon go to Vilna to complete his medical studies. Alexei, on the other hand, lives in a mansion on Hospital Street—not far from the railroad station, half an hour's hike from the Lower Market. He teaches Russian history. Nevertheless, the three of us have no secrets from each other, and together we have organized a small forbidden group. Nowadays nothing honest or useful is "legal." We believe in the rights of *all* the people.

Uncle, have you heard of the famous Sophia Perovskaya? She's a school friend of Alexei's sister, Dora. A young woman, not much older than I, twenty-six, of a family far more aristocratic than Alexei's. Seven years ago Perovskaya was picked up by the police in Moscow for going to the people with her socialism, making speeches, writing pamphlets. She is considered crazy by her family, but quite a number of young aristocrats are active with her. Dora Rosnikov is among them. After they were arrested, Perovskaya and several others (not Dora) were kept in prison for four years! Then there was a big trial in Moscow—maybe you read about it in America? They were freed! The Tsar's henchmen could not control their own judges! Can we be entering a new day when angry young aristocrats like Perovskaya and Dora, Alexei, and others of their class will join workers, students, peasants, intellectuals, and young Jews to struggle together for socialism? Something better for the oppressed! A Jew and a genius, Karl Marx is the foremost exponent of this theoretical socialism (not that his Jewishness is relevant).

Well, to get back to Mlle. Perovskaya, last week she came by coach all the way from Petersburg to visit the Rosnikovs. Alexei invited not only me to dinner that evening, but also several other young people, including Abramele Shapiro and a young woman, Natasha Perkovina, both in our group. I asked if I could bring my sister Feygele, because though she's still no more than a child, she has fire in her somewhere, waiting to burst into flame.

She came. What a night! Beautiful Perovskaya has short hair, a strong mouth, and serious eyes. Without making a big to-do about it, she is ready to kill and ready to die. She makes a lot more sense than Papa's Rebbe Schmulkowitz. She talks so quietly, but her will is iron. She travels about the country, talking in homes and out-of-

the-way *traktirs* to small groups like ours, the intelligentsia, inspiring us, teaching us to organize, the importance of replacing the entire social and economic order—not improve it a bit here and there. We must bring in the millions of "little" people. We need institutions, and these must be created now by all the Jews, workers, and peasants side by side—with the intelligentsia to direct the struggle with force. The French bourgeoisie did it only ninety years ago—so it *can* be done. Assassinations are necessary. Disruptions must be the order of the day. Never having done a murder, I can't say whether I would *like* it, but I think I'd do it if necessary.

As a result of Perovskaya's visit, we have just enlarged our group to ten now, taking in three women (among them our Feygele). We tried to get Alexei's sister Dora, too, but she is not willing to take the risk. She's in love with a young local doctor, Akim Bosherov, and means to marry him. Her spirit and that of Bosherov is with us, but even after the Revolution, she says, doctors will be needed. Abramele, on the other hand, wants to do both—be a doctor and make the world over. He is in the group. Also Pyotr Ruminatsev, a minor railway official, and, of all people, Boris Karpovich. Have I mentioned Boris before? It's a bit comic, because Boris's father is none other than Inspector Sergei Nicholayevich Karpovich, who is most of the time on duty right on Jew Street—a gruff man, short, fat, and bald, with a red, jolly face and heavy gray sideburns. When I was a boy, for some reason he took a liking to me, possibly because of my *gymnasium* uniform, and treated me like his favorite toy. He was always after me to cut off my *peyas* to look like a *goy*, and one day he personally escorted me to his own barber and ordered it done. You should have heard Papa! The crime of the century! *Now* the inspector wants me to shave off my beard, too! He regularly looks in on our family, always speaks to Mama gently, as if she were a duchess. Mama's all smiles with him. She usually gives him a fresh-baked *challa* to take home, and treats him better than the house-to-house beggars, to whom she sometimes gives the family's last bite. It seems Inspector Karpovich's wife loves Mama's *challa*. This good, dull-witted woman came to visit Mama, to learn how to make it, and Mama taught her. It wasn't easy, Mama says. This woman has a hard, gray-limestone face which grows mixed gray and brown hair, cut as if chopped short with an axe. When she smiles, it's like watching a block of ice cracking and splitting into a thousand hairline wrinkles. Next to her, Mama is a raving beauty, even in a *sheitel*. So Boris's mother and my Mama are now buddies. Who'd believe it? A strange sentimental attachment has developed between the Singers and the Karpoviches, but I don't have any illusions about it. It couldn't withstand much of a strain.

At the same time Boris is part of our little outlaw band! If his father ever knew, he would bleed from the ears. That's true of *all* our fathers except Alexei's—we deceive and defy our parents, something which brings us closer to each other. I'm sure Papa would rather have me working nights with Smulka the gorilla, robbing people in their beds, than doing what I am, if he ever knew what I'm doing.

Alexei is our leader. No one ever said so, but we all recognize the fact. *His* father approves of what he is doing, but remains hidden in the background. Because of his aristocratic blood and the fact that the governor's wife is his patient, suffering with intractable rheumatism, Dr. Rosnikov is never molested by the authorities. We are trying meanwhile to convert ordinary people—tobacco workers, railroad employees, and some of our less pious Jews. Some answer us by trying to get us interested in going to Palestine. We talk to these Jews, Abramele and I, and Feygele, too, usually on *shabbos* outside the synagogues or down by the riverbank. We say, why *should* we Jews have to run to America? Or to Palestine? Who's the Tsar? A not very bright man! Outside the synagogues people scurry off in fear when we talk like that, but now and then a few young people listen and agree. So we make progress by centimeters. (Not that I don't think it also takes courage to go to America, Uncle, don't get me wrong.) Uncle Efram writes from New York he'll be going to Atlanta to work for you at last. On such a journey, isn't there danger from thieves? I'm beginning to worry as much about the family in America as in Russia.

For us who remain in Minsk, we have a new worry. We hear tales again of crowds of *moujiks*—Ukrainians, White Russians—running through Jewish *shtetls* or streets in some cities, burning homes, smashing furniture, robbing, raping, killing. They bring back horrible memories of Chmielnicki. Who do you think encourages dumb peasants to such acts? Is it not to take their minds off their real troubles? Things must be changed, and we'll change them! I haven't told Papa or Mama, but I tell you, because you are so far away, and you understand me. All power to the people!

Your affectionate nephew,
Moishe

Martin had been named after his Grandfather Moses while the old man was very much alive, and in defiance of a Jewish tradition observed by even nonobservant Jews. Was that an angry act of sheer mockery? Martin wondered. Father and his father, he had always known, were certainly estranged for some reason. If Father had intended to offend old man Moishe by naming his baby for him, cleverly honoring him personally

while defying his tradition, he appears to have botched the job. These
two letters certainly indicated the old man gave not a damn for any traditions of Judaism, no matter how sacred.

Martin had really known his Grandfather Moses only as an elderly man.
The old geezer had been sixty-one when Martin was born, talked with
the slightest accent, had dandled Martin on his knee and given him expensive presents—elaborate electric trains, Erector Sets, chemistry sets,
books in leather bindings, a Cartier watch when he entered prep school,
and a Chrysler convertible when he entered college. To Martin he had
been a rich, eccentric, faintly foreign old man, rather elegant in style and
dress, interested primarily in all nice things and in the money which
bought them. A bit like Uncle Nate, but much more courtly, more charming. He was always escorting attractive widows and divorcees to the theater, opera, and expensive restaurants—all during his sixties and seventies,
right up until he had his major stroke at eighty-four. Was he *shtupping*
all those powdered women? Who could be sure?

Martin remembered with special intensity how the old man had once
taken him and his brother Sylvan on an all-day tour of the store—Martin
was twelve; the two boys came up from Washington for two days (Father
had just been appointed to the Court, and Mother was in the throes of
moving down from Cambridge and probably wanted him and Sylvan out
of the way); he had been amazed at how much the old man knew about
everything the store sold—from women's evening gowns to games and
sporting goods. He seemed especially proud of the furniture floor, and lingered over "great pieces," pointing out to his grandsons what was fine
about them. Everyone working in the store knew him; they all but knelt
as he passed. The store then was nothing like it was today.

The old man had spent his dotage in Palm Beach and died in a fancy
Jewish nursing home in Miami, a home which bore his name—the Moses
Singer Pavilion—at the age of ninety-two; by then he'd been a vegetable
for eight years. Martin remembered taking Josh to see him for the first
and only time, when Josh was five. It proved to be a big mistake. The old
man was wizened, scary-looking to a kid, a kind of male witch, and incon-
tinent as well, so that the room stank. Josh had started to cry, had wet his
own pants, and had had to be carried out in a hurry.

It was almost too difficult a feat of mental gymnastics to connect the
image of that skeletal, bedded old man (very tall even in his nineties) or
the overgenerous, lanky old foreigner of Martin's boyhood days, to the
firebrand who wrote these letters. Martin had an impulse to show them to
Josh—the kid should know he wasn't the first nutty zealot in the family.
Let him see for himself, too, how views change with age. Who would

have suspected the founder of the great Singer store of having been a raving, bomb-rattling, bloodthirsty Red in his youth? Not Martin, certainly. What would Josh be like in forty years? Would he remember his part in the Harvard Yard bust a bit ruefully, as old Moses must have rued his bomb-throwing—or at least bombastic—days? Hadn't Grandfather, too, in his youth, been contemptuous of *his* father? That was another thing. Was each generation doomed to repeat the idiocies of earlier ones? A continuous performance of sons rejecting fathers. Martin found the letters more illuminating than he'd expected. They had diverted him from his pain for a little while.

So, yes, Virginia, there *was* a Feygele. And she *was* Grandfather's sister. That made her Martin's great aunt. Unknown and far away. And what had become of her and hers?

7

MARTIN WONDERED WHY he had waited until he was on his last legs to find out, when the letters had been in those cartons all these years.

If this guy *is* our cousin, he wondered, why is he in Minsk and we here? What kept Feygele from coming? What forces moved Moses? What was the cause of their rift? He took another Darvocet and read on.

The next letter on his desk was from Jacob Singer in Atlanta, Georgia, to Moishe Singer in Minsk. It was dated August 9, 1881. Jesus, the Singers have been in Atlanta almost a hundred years. No wonder they've become so southern and so gentile. Almost inevitable. We Singers are chameleons, but who knows what we are beneath the surface? Certainly not we! The Uncle Jacob in Atlanta must have been Jim's granddaddy. Jim was probably named for *him*—James for Jacob. It figured.

Jacob's letter was gently scolding in tone, but full of appreciation for the carved swan Moishe had sent him. No doubt influenced by his grow- ing prosperity in the millwork business, he sang unrestrained praises of Atlanta and America—with the merest grace note of homesickness. "Here's a photograph of my wonderful Sadie, myself, and Efram. I'm proud to say, you can't tell us from 'Rebels,' or even Yanks!" Martin was amazed that almost a hundred years ago the feud between the German Jews and those from the Pale was already going strong. "In Atlanta we also have some high and mighty Jews—families who came here thirty years ago from German states, peddlers they were back then, but you should see them now! They own big shops, and a bank yet!" So this yearning to own a bank was in Jim's genes. "They won't acknowledge us Litvaks and Galizianers on the streets. Many of their boys fought for the Confederacy in the War Between the States; this makes them feel abso- lutely gentile. They eat shellfish and pork! In their *shul* they don't wear hats. Southern Christian gentlemen and ladies, you'd think, direct from

their plantations! They have a rabbi who lives like a king, King David Hirsch. If you think the Tsar is high, let me tell you it's much further up to Rabbi Hirsch!"

Uncle Jacob also offered Moishe some career advice, urging that he get out of the revolutionary game and into something to support himself, not teaching, which he considered too hazardous a profession in a Russia which periodically and unceremoniously threw Jews out of such jobs. And finally there was the inevitable family invitation: his brother Efram, the tsarist draft dodger, had already become a great asset to Jacob in Atlanta. "He gets a kick out of dealing with the rough lumbermen living in the backwoods far from Atlanta, who never saw a Jew before. So we've changed the name of our mill and lumberyard to 'The Singer Brothers.' See how fast things move in America? The city is growing and if ever your father wishes to come with the family, God should only be willing, we could go into furniture also. There are plenty of *schwarzes* here to do the heavy work. It's a good life."

And a kind of peroration to support the invitation: "We don't need special passes to go anywhere. We don't have pogroms or persecutions. Oh, once in a while someone may make a remark, but this is a wonderful country, Moishe!" Uncle Jacob was apparently not much impressed by the Klan, which he failed to mention. The letter was signed "Your Uncle Yankele. In English my name is pronounced *Jacob*."

What letters! There was a long reply from Minsk, and Martin could not resist. Merely because he had known the people, he found himself fascinated. The length of Grandfather's next letter intrigued him. Who in the world wrote monstrous long letters like this any more? As a kid he had asked Uncle Yankele to *save* his letters. Was he consciously writing a kind of memoir? Grandfather Moses was surely a long-winded revolutionary sonofabitch. Well—

LETTER FROM MOISHE TO HIS UNCLE

Minsk
20 December 1881

Uncle "Jacob"!

I write your American name because you seem to want it, although it makes you a stranger. New land, and changed dress, customs, and now the names! Why not? What's so sacred? But does something inside us also change? Why not? You say I should enter a new profession. I should have been a professional clown, a wedding jester, a good-for-nothing loafer. I'm also a good listener. People tell me their troubles. But is listening a profession?

Nu, I have followed your advice and given up teaching. I have not become a lawyer as you suggested, but I *have* become apprenticed full time to Papa, and I hope now you will be satisfied that I will not be a complete *nudnik*. To be a lawyer I'd have had to attach myself to Nadler, that *gonif!* The funny thing is this: now that I became apprenticed to Papa, Herschel has donned an apron and taken up the tools beside us, and even our littlest shaver, Isaac, refuses to be left out altogether, and sands the finished pieces smooth as glass. So Papa together with *all* his sons makes more furniture than ever before. I apply my carvings to Papa's furniture. They become a part of the chair or the bed or the chest. This gives each piece character, no? I am also great with finishes—if I say so myself, I have a certain touch with stains, varnishes, and shellacs. All this has had a strange effect on Papa. He used to loathe his work and lived only for *shabbos*. Not now. I can't imagine why, but he now hums at his work, all kinds of rhapsodic singsongs—he sways, he nods, he does everything but get up and dance as he sits with his skullcap tilted, cross-legged at his workbench, singing and hammering on his chisel. He peers from one of his sons to the other under his heavy brows, examining the quality of our work, which each one brings to show him—he gives a quick suggestion for improvement and goes back to his own labors. For a change, Papa is happy on weekdays. Well, why not? We sell more pieces. Four pairs of hands!

One day I took Papa to Hospital Street on the Upper Market to see my friend's father—the dapper doctor, a tall, thin, proper man with a bushy blond mustache between muttonchop sideburns, always a friendly smile on his thin lips. He had mentioned to me he was looking for a new desk for his office. Immediately, my heart pounding, I told him my father was the finest cabinet maker in Minsk, which may have been a slight exaggeration—but how do you get across the absolute truth without exaggerating? I went into raptures, describing the handsome lion motif we could give his new desk—something his patients could really admire—a desk with realistic paws, and the two side drawers, one large and one smaller, each with the face of an open-mouthed lion.

Papa began shaking his head slowly—"Yi, yi, yi—" and raising his eyes to appeal to heaven for help. "Strength! Almighty! I am blessed with such a master salesman, a tongue like oil! *Schlemiel!* What do I know about lions? I'm a cabinet maker, not a zoo master! Where have I ever *seen* a lion?"

"Neither has the doctor!" I said. "So don't worry!"

Papa put on his *shabbos* suit to make the visit. He was so impressed with the doctor's house I thought he was going to *doven*

to it. Hesitating, he told the doctor a price, as high as he dared think of. The doctor said, "Fine." So far, so good.

Oh, the care we took with that desk! We worked for two weeks, all of us. We bought a special clear birch. The drawers must slide like glass! We bought expensive tooled leather for the top. I had to buy a special chisel to work the hard wood for my own intricate carvings on the legs, the claws, and each drawer I had to make with the face of a lion—the work seemed endless. As I carved the face for the first drawer, tiny chip by chip, I can't explain why, I felt the shaggy beast come alive under my knife, and as I sharpened the first great eyetooth, I could hear the animal roar! Everyone in the family —Feygele especially—took it for a marvel. (Feygele and I have our own secret reasons for feeling close, as you know!) I said nothing, merely began to work on the lower and larger drawer—a male head.

The desk, if I say so myself, was a masterpiece, although Papa attributed this result not to his efforts or to mine, but only to the Almighty. Who else? We carried the desk in Papa's cart, protected from dust and dirt with several old blankets. I was so keyed up by the time we arrived, so anxious the doctor should like it, I couldn't sit still.

After maneuvering the massive desk into the doctor's waiting room, we sat—Papa, Herschel, Isaac, and I—obliged to wait almost an hour.

The doctor was with his last patient, the governor's wife, the Countess Olga Zhukova. She was finally ushered out by the doctor himself. The two of them were exchanging farewells, and they both turned to look at the new desk. The countess, a woman whose face comes in rolls and layers, heavily powdered and rouged, suppressed a shriek. "Heavens!" she said. "That lion gave me quite a start!" Then, when she had fully recovered, she examined the desk carefully, touching it here and there, but she said no more, and after eyeing Papa and us three boys as if we were guinea pigs in a laboratory, hobbled through the foyer to her waiting carriage. I couldn't help thinking *she* was the perfect candidate for us to assassinate. We could make our political statement, and who would miss her? Surely not the governor!

The doctor walked around the desk eyeing it suspiciously. He opened and closed the drawers, inserting his forefinger into the mouths of the beasts I had carved. He ran his fingers over the scarred edges of the lion's mane. He squinted, he ogled, but I had no way of telling whether he was pleased or offended. Before he could say anything, I blurted, "My papa considers this his masterpiece, and he wants you to have it as a gift from our family."

The doctor looked to Papa, most of whose expression, luckily, was

hidden by his beard. Papa's Russian is weak, and he hoped he hadn't heard me right. From the wideness and pop of his eyes, I was afraid he might be on the edge of a heart attack, but he remained speechless. My brothers stared at me in horror.

"That is damned kind," said the doctor, as if I had offered him a cigarette or a chocolate. "It's a fine piece, I daresay. I shall treasure it all the more for your generosity." The doctor, you see, was afraid of insulting us by refusing my offer. I had completely miscalculated, thinking he would surely insist on paying.

We trudged home, the four of us, in total silence, except once when I said, "I think he really liked it." Papa did not utter a word to me for four days. On the fourth day, the Countess and her footman appeared at the door of our cellar workroom. Papa and I jumped to our feet. The Countess was there, she said, to order an exact replica, and gave Papa a handful of money. "Take this on account," she said. It was a hundred rubles.

So that's how it started. Like a miracle, which was what Papa named it, and he gave *me* twenty rubles, all mine. And two to Herschel and a few kopeks to Isaac. Well, do I have to tell you how it feels to make your first twenty rubles with your own hands? Better than wages for teaching! Now we are like you, my uncles—a success! Right here in Minsk! We have more orders than we can fill.

Beilis Machinovsky, for example, that contractor bastard, who goes to Doctor Rosnikov for his gout, comes to us now for pieces!

Papa and I are learning to combine talents, and so while I was feeling closer to him, I did try to talk to him, an honest talk—at least a *try*—about the ideas of Karl Marx and also the fact that Jews are not the only people on earth, or even in Minsk! This great man, I told him, who by sheer coincidence (is it coincidence, do you think?) happened to be of German Jewish stock, though an apostate, was showing a new way to mankind, a way that had to be struggled for by everyone, suffered for, sacrificed for. And you know what he said? My Papa: "You sound like the *goyim* with their Jesus. We have been plagued by false messiahs for generations. The Christ, Shabtai Zvi, Frank! And now this crazy *meshumed!* They've all led us into one quagmire after another, generation after generation! We can't afford more! Enough!" So I stopped talking to Papa entirely. I won't try again! False messiah! The less we try to be honest with each other, the better. He sticks to his lathes, I to my carving chisel.

What worries me is that I don't feel *enough* zeal for the Movement! With our newfound personal prosperity, will I lose my fervor, as Feygele says I am doing, turn into another Machinovsky, become

a traitor not so much to the Jews but to my socialist comrades and to the cause of *Narodnaya Volya*?

To guard against the evils of this, the money I make from my furniture sculpting does not go to the family. It goes to the Movement. Not for some mythical god—or to one of Reb Horowitz's benevolent societies—but for the salvation of the working people. Papa asks me, what do I do with my money? And I tell him I buy books. I am a freethinker, Papa knows, and since he cannot read a word of Russian, I even showed him a few such books—if he only knew what was in them! I have written several of these pamphlets myself. He may suspect, but doesn't know for sure, that they call on the people, the workers and peasants, to rise up at the proper time; they call for the bloody death of the new tsar and his henchmen— that scourge of "holy men."

So far, all I have done is talk, read, write, organize, as Perovskaya taught us we must do. Feygele is fantastic. She inspires strong men like the railroad workers, with her thick curly hair flying wildly as she speaks. I hope I will have the courage to act when the time comes and that some daring mission will be entrusted to me. I hope I can be brave in the face of danger and even of death. Why do I do it? Is it possible we Jews are made of some special stuff? Why do we feel all the troubles of humanity on our own skins?

Is it any wonder that boys like my brother Herschel—yes, even good Talmudists like Herschel—talk of stupid things like going to Palestine? In this he is encouraged by Freda Rubenstein upstairs. Such foolish idealists! The lunatic idea these marvelous fools like Herschel and Freda nourish is that they should go there and somehow become "true Jews." Jewish *moujiks!* The sand and swamps there are worse than the marshy mosquito-infested banks of the Svisloch, if possible. What will grow? How will they live? Do you suppose poor Herschel secretly envies our Russian *moujiks*—those "thick-skulled idiots" whom he says are stupid, illiterate, unimaginative donkeys, a lower form of life than their own animals? Is my brother's ambition to go to malaria-land merely a "cover," an unaware rejection of *all* intellect—of everything, as you yourself have correctly said, that we Jews—even we who are socialist—hold to be of value? A *rejection* of true Jewishness? Can the sight of the ruin of the great Temple, the presence of the Wailing Wall, make up for an active life of the heart and mind? For seeking further, as you've said, to find justice? Can this be better than joining all humanity in the great task of liberation? My brother is no mystic, he does not run around dancing and singing like some of those wild-eyed drunks and crazies, including that girl *meshugina* upstairs, who wants to become a *farmer*, a *moujichka!* Both she and Herschel

turn their backs on me when I question them; perhaps they hear the taunt and scoffing in my voice. They clam up, become secretive, so holy! I do not understand them at all.

Poor Mama is in despair over all of us. She lives in fear that one day all her children will suddenly disappear. What then? I wish I could comfort her! But these are not times for mothers! Young people vanish from Jew Street and indeed from all the streets of Minsk every week, to America, to Palestine, anywhere but here!

I send this by the "Jewish Post"—a friend who is emigrating—what else?—who will mail it from another city. To be safe—nothing is *safe* safe—I leave it unsigned. My great affection goes to you and Aunt Sadie and your firstborn son, Leib, or, as you write, "Lewis."

With affection

Ah, Martin thought as he put down the last page, the first appearance of Rachel's parents! The merest breath of Herschel and Freda. Those were their names, all right, he recalled. Rachel, when she got here, might enjoy reading these, too, and she'd be able to read them in the original Yiddish. Martin pushed the letters aside. Clara had come to tell him luncheon was being served.

8

WHILE JOSH, TAMMY, AND MARTIN were having lunch, Jenny slowly balanced her way down to breakfast, her head several sizes larger than usual. Always the amateur actress even *in extremis*, she carried her head carefully in both palms to keep it on. "Got a toothache, Ma?" Josh asked over a bagel. His voice reverberated as if her brain were an amplifier.

"Shh!" She hated these damn dinner parties more and more. Why did she give them?

"So, Mom, you gonna go to Russia with us?" Jenny wondered why Joshua was shouting.

"Ssh! Not so loud. Russia? What for?" It hurt too much to argue.

"To rescue our Communist cousin, right?"

"Who? Oh, Joshie, you are a *meshugina!* Why are *you* going? Please keep your voice down."

"We told you last night. Tam's going over to give three concerts. They've made her an offer she couldn't refuse. We'll be going in about six weeks. They're firming up the date."

"Yes? That's lovely. I can't remember a thing—isn't that awful?"

"Well, are you coming, Ma?"

"Do I look like the Marines?"

"You look absolutely gorgeous, Ma," Joshua said, holding his voice to a near whisper. "Right, old Dad?"

Martin forced a smile. "Your mother is always the cat's meow as far as I'm concerned."

He stared from his son to his wife, his eyes watering with pain. His gut at the sternum bothered him again. He'd give half of what he was getting for the store to be comfortable for a while. To live a bit longer.

"Isn't she terrific, Tam?" Josh was saying. "Can you believe this woman's over thirty? How'd you like the way she told off all those creeps?

Damnit, I trust her lately even if I never did before." Tammy had gripped Josh's shoulder, as if to restrain *him.*

Jenny took her palms from her own cheeks—an act of daring—long enough to seize Josh's face, to hold him steady in order to kiss him quickly, and, before it was too late, she restored her hands to her own cheeks again. Holding herself so, she tiptoed to the head of the table where Martin sat, and she bent like a woman with restricted vision to find his lips, amid all the whiskers, with her own. "Good morning, Marty. The cat is here to meow." She was disturbed by all that hair on his face, something that did not ordinarily bother her. Quite the contrary. Now she had a momentary, distressing recollection of that beard vainly scratching her breasts, her thighs—not an edifying image at this hour and in this circumstance. She turned to Tammy. "Kid, you were terrific last night. Saved the whole goddamn party. Without you I'd've been bored out of my skull. Aren't all those fancy old Jews a drag? You sing like a diabolical angel. Joshie, I hope you showed your appreciation."

She reached for a glass of clam juice, took aim at it with one eye shut, and drank it in three gulps. "Jesus, this stuff is poisonous."

She was thinking of Graham Butler—indeed, she'd been thinking of beautiful, clever Graham since the moment last night when he'd leaned forward, grinning as if imparting a piece of Manhattanite cleverness, and whispered to her. *Give me a ring for lunch, Jen.* Well, why *not?* Jenny had quite forgotten what she'd said that brought the unexpected invitation on. All she knew was that if she was going to stray, Graham was certainly safe, gentle, bright—sometimes even witty, especially when he was panning a movie. *Give me a ring for lunch, Jen.* Jesus, wouldn't *that* be something? A *thing* with Graham. Do that to Marty? She never had, never would. Temptation! Could she? Pick up the phone, actually dial his number? Not in a million years! But why not?

In her head a melancholy tune, an old line, buzzed, half remembered. Where had she heard it? "I don't know why . . . it lies too deep."

PART
THREE
Rachel

1

It was twenty-three below, centigrade, when El Al's flight 003 set down at Kennedy. Martin, despite recurrent pain in his shoulder and abdomen, did go to the airport to meet Rachel—not that he was up to it, but Grandfather Moishe's letters somehow made him feel he ought to. Jenny insisted on going to the airport, too, to look after Martin.

The International Arrivals Building was in evening turmoil; Fred slipped the airport cop five bucks to let him keep the Mercedes where Martin had told him to, motor running and heater on full blast, so Rachel could enjoy some American warmth on arrival.

Rachel was not difficult to identify when she sailed into the huge customs hall in the wake of a group of Hassidic Jews off the El Al flight. Her entrance was that of a minor cinema personality. Two men with cameras, fellow passengers apparently, tried to take Rachel's picture, but she shielded her face with her purse. She was wearing large dark glasses. Three other young men, escorts it seemed, talked animatedly to her and to each other, ignoring the photographers, and ran interference for her through the crowd. Rachel had a sprightly walk, that of a much younger woman.

Her companions rushed her through customs, armed as she was with a diplomatic passport. She *was,* in fact, on several missions for her government. She carried three urgent messages from her friend Golda Meir, the prime minister of her embattled country: Golda's secret letter to Dinitz, ambassador to the U.S., warned that the truce with Egypt was fragile, and listed all of the equipment lost in the Sinai. She implored Dinitz, as she had done by cable, to turn the screw at State and Defense another notch: replacements quickly—more tanks, F-2s and parts, parts, parts—everything on the list; replacements were short in everything, but here was a priority list; the commanders in the field were nervous; the situation was explosive, and nobody trusted the Egyptians.

Rachel carried a personal letter to Kissinger to the same effect: please hurry! We need help *now*. And to the leaders of Jewish organizations in the United States a third letter: please appeal to Kissinger, Nixon, and Schlesinger, firmly, with plenty of heat, but nicely. We are eternally grateful; we are also desperate.

In addition, Rachel had come to address UJA meetings in Los Angeles, Cleveland, Columbus, Montreal, and New York, as well as in several smaller cities, to beg for financial support from her American brothers and sisters. This year the goal was to raise five hundred million from the Jews of the United States and Canada.

All these entreaties, those made by Golda and those she would make herself in the days ahead, had highly personal connotations to Rachel: her grandson Gideon—Catriel and Lili's son—was flying a delta-wing fighter, from the airbase in the Sinai; he had flown sixty missions in the three weeks after Yom Kippur, and she prayed for his life every night. Not to God, but to whoever could hear; mostly, she knew, to herself.

Gideon was her special love—was it because of her son Catriel's death, or Lili's abdication as a mother? Nowadays Gideon was doing reconnaissance, still dangerous work because of the SAM missiles Egypt and the Russians were putting into place. At the same time, her reckless—perhaps foolish would be a better word—granddaughter Michal, because her Arabic was flawless, was serving as an interpreter in the interrogation of Syrian prisoners of war taken on the Golan. Everyone in the family was serving in some way—young or old—for they were part of the unacknowledged establishment, part of the highly visible circle which included not only the Dayans, Allons, Avigur, Narkisses, Weizmanns, and Golombs, but Golda herself. After all, Rachel's parents had been among the earliest *chalutizim*. Rachel worried about all her children and grandchildren, but about Gideon most.

Martin and Jenny watched as Rachel's young male companions, security men employed to keep the plane safe and to look after her, converged to kiss her on both cheeks (you could almost see them blessing her). Waving a skycap aside, she took up her large canvas valises, one in each hand, and strode toward the exit. She was on another mission, too—not for her government but for herself. She was determined to go to Minsk and bring out her cousin Yuri Karpeyko, a man of whose existence she had just learned. What else would Boris have expected of her?

She carried in her unopened luggage sensitive and extra-legal paraphernalia which had been carefully prepared (without Golda's knowledge or the consent of Avigur, Weisbrot's superior) by certain specialists who

worked for her friend Aaron Weisbrot—men she could trust, who were truly artists in their field. Oh, they had done what they could to talk her out of her rash plans, of course, for they did not at all approve, and they suspected Weisbrot's boss (but not Weisbrot) would go up the wall if he knew. However, Rachel wielded considerable influence herself and so, reluctantly, they had done what she asked and kept silent. Perhaps, they reasoned, if Weisbrot knew, so did Avigur. She had pleaded with Aaron not to make things complicated for her.

"A pro I'm not," she had reminded Weisbrot. "I'll *never* remember everything unless you keep it very simple. Use my maiden name—Singer, okay? I'll get nervous and frightened if I'm questioned in English, and if anyone shouts at me I'll be lost. Who knows, I might forget myself and say something in Russian—oy, what a disaster! Or worse still, Hebrew." She laughed. "Bear in mind, Aaron, I am seventy-three" (she always lied about her age, but never by more than a year or two), "my nerves are weak, and my memory is like mercury—very slithery. So be nice, be helpful."

Aaron Weisbrot put both forefingers together to form an A-frame. They were artist's fingers, Rachel thought. Aaron's was the face of abstinence, a face seized by the spirit. No priest, rabbi, or other cleric was so single-minded. His life (all of it—he had no wife, no children, no other thought) was to bring the exiles home.

"Does Golda know what you're planning, Rachel?" Aaron asked softly.

"But of course," she lied. "It's simply not to be discussed—with anyone."

Golda would kill her, Rachel thought.

"I'll get the photographs back to you by El Al—to your home, Aaron, all right? And you'll send the passports, the visas, everything we talked about, in the diplomatic pouch. Seal them. I'll get them from Dinitz in Washington, but I don't want Dinitz upsetting himself."

Weisbrot nodded dourly.

"Have you thought of taking someone with you, Rachel?"

"Who? It's a one-woman job."

"Never. Your grandson. Gideon."

"He's a little boy. And right now he's flying a jet in the desert."

"I could send for him. He at least is a professional."

"He's a child."

"No, Rachel. *You're* a child. One woman against the Soviet Union. Please."

She dismissed his suggestion with a wave. But in the back of her mind

she wondered. Aaron might be right. Still, what could this cousin possibly mean to Gideon? She should jeopardize her own grandchild, with his whole life before him? Whole life? Flying that jet? Everything was relative.

2

RACHEL MARCHED THROUGH the customs door, a valise in each hand. Two men from the New York Consulate in heavy overcoats and black fedoras welcomed her. She waved them off, speaking quickly but gently to them; relatives were meeting her, she explained, thank you for coming; she would be in touch. They bowed, shook her hand, and departed.

She was five foot two (once she had been an inch taller, but had shrunk with age). Her face had not been touched by cosmetics in years. No one believed Rachel was seventy-five. It was not just the way she carried herself; her skin, though touched by age discolorations, was so weathered from sailing, by the sun, wind, and sea, it had a patina that made it ageless, and the tiny weather lines in the bronzed skin, crevices around her eyes, were all smile lines. Yet the large eyes themselves told a different story. They were sometimes blazing blue, like Martin's or the sky; at other times they took on a faraway look, shifting focus, a darkened sea, and sometimes they became thoughtful and watery. Jenny wondered, when Rachel had that faraway look, if she were seeing sights too terrible to be kept in focus. Was it mere memory sadness? No, Jenny decided, those were frightened eyes, darting here and there, the way an animal's eyes shift in the wild as it looks about before it will eat. Then the eyes might lighten again, or burn unexpectedly as if refueled. Rachel, hatless, wore her hair in a short bob, as she had done since she was a girl; its color was a "light black," as she called it; some Israeli friends suspected she tinted it, to keep from going gray, but where would she have found such drab, dull dye? It surely wasn't Clairol, Jenny thought. One could see Rachel had once been a pretty woman—the Slavic upturned nose, full mouth; indeed, except for her height she had a remarkable resemblance to Martin, Jenny thought, but what you always came back to were the large blue eyes. She moved with the grace of a cat.

Her hands, however, gave her away: thickly veined, competent, and square, they were too large for a woman as slight as she. Her handclasp was gentle, however, a simple grip, no shaking. She was not satisfied until she had hugged Jenny and Martin in turn and brushed them each on both cheeks with her lightly furrowed lips. Her unadorned face was lit, a hostess's welcoming smile. For a moment Martin, overcoming his discomfort, had the feeling that he and Jenny were the ones arriving and that Rachel was welcoming *them*. Jenny, who felt twice Rachel's size, reached for both suitcases, lifted them a few inches, and groaned.

"Hey, skycap!" Jenny called to a passing porter. "Have I got a treat for you!" Rachel laughed.

The moment they entered the Gramercy Park house, Jenny asked Clara sweetly to set out the snack she had prepared, and, switching suddenly to the voice of a longshoreman, she called up to Joshua to come on down here and meet his Israeli cousin.

Joshua reminded Rachel of her Gideon. Yes, this boy was surely a member of the family, even if at first he seemed so alien. He made a career living in the open sea? She was unable to picture *him* in anyone's air force. But diving in the open sea, was that less dangerous? Family, the *idea* of family, was almost sacred to Rachel. Cells (the DNA, was it called?) that were in this youngster's makeup were in hers—they had, if not the same fingerprints, transcendent ties, though they lived continents and oceans apart, spoke different native languages, were separated by fifty years. I am of him, she thought, and he is of me.

The redheaded girl, Tammy Barnstone, Jenny confided while taking Rachel aside to show her the new kitchen, was a famous youth personality—a heroine among the anti-Vietnam War set, a successful singing star. Rachel noted how the girl casually mentioned "her" agent and "her" lawyer. What a tiny, very young woman to be in business! A child! A nice *shiksa*, nervous on meeting Rachel, she was becomingly self-effacing, but clearly devoted to Joshua. The fact of this *shiksa* troubled Rachel. Young American Jews, especially the elite ones, scarcely recognized they *were* Jews any more. Oh, a few gentile golf clubs, yacht clubs, and city clubs still did their best to remind them, but without much success. They married gentiles like Tammy or turned apostate and got in anyhow. Even in the U.S. government. Look at Jim Schlesinger. Or Kissinger, about to marry a woman whose name started with "Mac." Her cousin Jim Singer, in Atlanta, was a banker now, a millionaire, and half gentile. Or maybe by now all gentile.

Why should this distress her? Why did she care? She could not say. These *goyish* Jews or half Jews or Jews who married Christians lost all

trace of their origins, but when a Hitler arrived on the scene, they trudged into the oven with the rest. In Israel it was quite the other way. Survivors built Holocaust museums, monuments, made speeches, wrote books, songs, plays, so their children's children's children would never forget. Never. The Eichmann trial replayed it. That *they* were Jews was in the front of every Israeli mind, as Englishness was in the British mind during the days of Victoria.

But Israeli Jews had added an element to go with their pride. Jews, yes, proudly, fiercely, but with a bucket of fear on each shoulder. And why not? Her tiny country stood exposed to numberless enemies, betrayed by old friends, including those whose Communist leaders—Jews among them —it had once felt closest to—Russians, Poles, Roumanians—for the leaders of Israel had come from these very lands and, with the Bolsheviks, had shared certain ideals of socialism and a hatred for the tsars. Now, instead, Israelis were completely dependent on America, their last and only hope.

How tempted Rachel herself had once been to abandon the Jewish experiment and join her American cousins, Jacob and Nathan Singer, and her Uncle Moses, to have an easy American life, too! A girl's fancy, before she had met Boris. The thought had passed fleetingly through her mind again in forty-seven, when she had wanted to leave Boris.

Had we been living in America, she thought, Boris and I would have been divorced in no time. Yet in America would Boris have lived such a double life? As a lawyer representing Histadrut, but underground working for Etzel? Awful people, the Etzelniks, killing British soldiers, blowing up the King David, defying Ben Gurion. She hated them. And Boris one of them? Had she married never truly knowing him? In a weeping fit she once called him a murderer, and he was. But divorce? During the siege of Jerusalem when each day might be their last? Oh, they had shouted, she had threatened to leave (and where to?). She'd been forced to provide a safe house in Jerusalem for Boris and his friends—friends she hated. Cold-blooded cutthroats. Until Deir Yassin, when Boris himself had at last been revolted by the wholesale massacre of Arabs and quit, denouncing his former friends publicly in letters to the newspapers. So the impossible happened: she and Boris found each other again. Oh, how she missed him now! Friends had told her that after a year or two the pain would go away. How wrong they were! What she would give to have him with her on this journey among strangers, kind as they tried to be.

At ten o'clock, while Clara was serving a cold supper of smoked sturgeon, fresh tomatoes, black olives, and cream cheese, Martin told Rachel,

while Jenny, Joshua, and Tammy listened attentively, about the old letters, Jenny interrupting to bubble over the Yiddish-laced translations.

Rachel nibbled at her food, listened, but with effort, and began to show the first signs of fatigue; she nevertheless said she was fascinated. "You know, Martin, so much has been written *about* the Russian Pale, but all the sources are oral, or they're professional stories—by Sholem Aleichem and others, *recollections,* you see. Sentimentalization of the *shtetls*—mostly after the fact. Recollections tend to be rosy—don't you think? Like our Israeli memories of forty-eight. We think of those days so romantically, but it was really awful—grimy and filthy. The letters you describe, written *then* by people who were *there,* as far back as the eighteen-seventies or eighties, they are rare. Most of the letters we have from then are short and don't tell us much. May I see them tomorrow? Right now, I'm ashamed to say, Martin . . . Jenny, my gracious hostess . . . Joshua . . . Tammy . . . and Clara—thank you very much for the supper, it was delicious—but if it's all right, I'd love to go to bed, please. For me, it's four o'clock tomorrow. I've been traveling for fourteen hours and I'm not as young as I thought I was. You wouldn't mind?"

Martin smiled, shook his head.

"You see, tomorrow, early, I have to go to Washington, so I'll read the letters on the plane, okay? But I tell you, no matter what those letters say, I know two things: one, Yuri Karpeyko is our cousin. No question. Two, we must get him out. That's our duty. We'll talk about it tomorrow night, all right?"

Jenny was up at dawn next day to have breakfast with her at six-thirty. She had arranged for Clara to make breakfast before the sun rose. She asked that Martin be excused, "because, you know, the poor guy's not feeling himself." All that, and to boot, the breakfast was Israeli: hard-boiled eggs, olives, cucumbers, tomatoes, buttermilk, herring, and salami. Black coffee. It amused Rachel; such thoughtfulness! Why? She dared not confess to Jenny she had looked forward to an *American* breakfast. Orange juice, scrambled eggs, bacon, and coffee.

In fact she could scarcely tell Jenny anything, because the younger woman simply chattered on. Wasn't it *fantastic* discovering this cousin in Minsk? A famous doctor! How her mother had been after her from the time she was six to marry a doctor or a lawyer! She'd heard in Russia most of the doctors were women; was that true? Rachel nodded, her mouth full of buttermilk. "So how do we go about saving our doctor, Rachel?"

Rachel merely studied her as one would a curious child. Before she could answer Jenny asked about Yoshke Schulman from the National

Conference on Soviet Jewry. "Can *they* really do anything to help get him out?"

"Well, they got in touch with me right away. Your Yoshke Schulman," Rachel said, "he called me. So we sent off the *vyzovs*. Yes, the National Conference is useful. I met this Yussel Schulman once in Israel. But the *vyzov*'s only the first step. Now our Yuri must do for himself. Whether the authorities will let him go or not, you never know. Me, I don't think they will. He's too important in Minsk, too big a figure. A member of the Academy of Medical Science, director of a hospital, et cetera. They can't stand that. They'd rather have a show trial and make him a villain. His daughter and wife, maybe yes, they'll be able to go, if they're willing to leave him and take the chance that he may never be allowed to join them. But he himself, I doubt. More likely they'll send him to prison. Or to Siberia."

Jenny, swallowing the last bit of hard-boiled egg, cried, "How awful! But Rachel, how can we *let* them? They're like the goddamn Nazis! *Why* do they want to put him on trial? For writing fables for children? Isn't that silly? Can you believe such stupidity? Stories like Lewis Carroll's, or Dr. Seuss's—you know Doctor Seuss?" Rachel didn't, but she held up her hand like a traffic policeman.

"Jenny, for heaven's sake, calm down. Are you always like this? So excited? You're worse than an Israeli! Listen to me. Many Jews in Russia want to leave now, hundreds of thousands—maybe half a million. No one knows how many. And we *need* them in Israel. So we invent relatives for them if they don't exist. After all, aren't we *all* somehow related? We send a *vyzov* to anyone who asks, but very quietly. A few misuse our *vyzovs*, and after they get out they go to America, and it makes me furious. We don't *want* them to go to America. Anyhow, Golda says in Russia everything must be by the Russian book. We warn each applicant not to break any Soviet laws. *We* certainly don't break them. No criticism of the Soviet government. No agitation inside Russia for more freedom. None of that. One simple thing: let us go. We want to be united with our families, in the land of our people. This is not against Soviet law. So these are still the rules. Well, such rules won't do Yuri Karpeyko the least bit of good. He's in too much trouble! So in this case for our Yuri I'm taking a big chance. With the help of one old man in Israel I'm going to have to do something Golda would kill me for." She smiled grimly, "If she knew."

"What?"

"That I can't tell you."

"Listen, Rachel, why don't *I* go to Russia to see this guy? It's all boobalabaabala to me until I *meet* the man. Maybe he *should* come to America, not Israel. Who knows what he wants? For all we know, maybe he's a *spy*, God forbid! I'll have to see him for myself. What's the big deal? Hell, we've *been*, Marty and I."

"Of course. What a marvelous idea." Rachel smiled. This might work out better than she'd planned. She had already eaten too much and said too much and it was time to start to La Guardia. "You're American, you see. You can go without trouble. For an Israeli like me to get into Russia, however, it's really impossible. But not absolutely." Her eyes flashed and she grinned.

"*You're* going?" Jenny cried.

"Shh!" Rachel leaned close to Jenny and lowered her voice. "A small bit of my secret: I'm going. Yes. So why shouldn't we go together?"

Jenny began to backwater. "Last time I went, you know, I went with Marty. He took care of everything. But he's just not well enough now— you can see how he is for yourself. . . ."

Rachel looked down. "I am sorry about Martin. I hope he'll be feeling better soon." She would never ask a question about Martin's health; they'd tell her when and what they wanted. But to bring this brassy American along would be a godsend. And better without Martin than with him. A dim plan was turning in her mind.

"Trust me, Jenny. *Come,* and *I'll* arrange everything. Tonight we'll talk about it, shall we? And we'll call our relations in Minsk."

"Yeah, Yoshke said we could do that."

"Oh, yes, we do it all the time. Why else would he write you his telephone number? You and Martin can talk to him yourself. I think it will help his spirits. From his letter he seems to know English. Also, I speak some Russian."

"They won't bug what we say?"

Rachel shrugged. "Maybe, but it's a big country. They have millions of phones."

"Jesus," Jenny murmured, "ain't you somethin'? You got grit, lady."

Rachel laughed. "To make such a call, all you need is a telephone." She rose, took up the thick briefcase she had brought down from her room, walked briefly to the foyer to get her worn overcoat. "May I have those old letters Martin was talking about?"

Jenny hurried to the elevator, went up to the movie room, and brought down the original Yiddish letters, which Rachel stuffed into her bag. "I must make the eight o'clock—what do you call it—'shuttle'? There's enough time?" Jenny was seeing her to the door. A brilliant sun was ris-

ing; that was one nice thing about the house on Gramercy Park. You could see the sky and the sun. A lovely day to fly. *Fly me, I'm Jenny!* She thought of Graham Butler. Why wait? She'd call him from the office today. Or would she? The thought made her dizzy with guilt and fright. Would she be caught?

"Oh, lots of time," she heard herself say. "There's Fred now. See, he has the car all warmed up for you." Fred took Rachel's briefcase, which she surrendered reluctantly. "He'll meet you when you come back, too. What plane are you catching?" No, she wouldn't hear of Rachel's using a taxi. Neither would Fred. It would be his pleasure, Fred said.

3

ON THE PLANE, she peered out the window during takeoff, and as the 727 overflew Philadelphia she opened her briefcase and began to read the letters in the original Yiddish. They only confirmed what she knew—the references to her parents, to Aunt Feygele, about whom her parents had told her many times. There was no doubt about Yuri's authenticity. His daughter's name—Yelena—must be a Russification of their common grandmother, Yetta, just as Martin's was an Americanization of Moishe. And her own name was originally Rasel, after her American aunt, Sheyna Rasel, until under the influence of Ben Yehuda's Hebrew it had become Rachel, as David Green had become Ben Gurion; Aubrey Epstein, Abba Eban; and Goldie Meyerson, Golda Meir. Yes, Rasel Aronowitz had become Rachel Aron. Palestine had become Israel.

But it was not only their names that made Israelis different from American Jews, she thought as she read the letters, not only the geography and the geology; there was something more *intrinsic, essential.* Yes, some in their family had come to the Holy Land, others to America, and others had stayed in Minsk. But hadn't those who went to America *sought* something subtly or entirely different from those who had gone to Palestine? Were Moishe and Sheyna Rasel Singer braver than they were wise? To go from one *goyish* country to another? Or was it *her* parents, Herschel and Freda, determined to build a *homeland* for Jews with their own hands, who were the brave but foolish ones? They came to a land in which there would be no one *but* Jews.

Ah, there was the rub! They dreamed of a place where they would never have to live side by side with *goyim* again, only to learn in the most painful way that Arabs, Moslems, and a few Christians, far stranger to them than Byelorussians or Russians, more primitive, yet more polite, were already *there.* Why, heads in the desert sand for fifty years, had the

newcomer Jews pretended the Arabs were *not* there? Until today, when here she had in her own hand this bloody lethal list—more tanks needed, more planes, more guns, more bazookas—to repel the biggest pogrom in history. How insane! The exclusivists, the Chosen People, *had* to mix with the world after all. Exactly what they had run away to avoid. Herzl must be twirling in his grave. So must Mama! Nevertheless, was there any turning back?

Like other Israelis, Rachel was determined, but she was also discouraged. How could they have been so wrong? The national schizophrenia led to a shuttle of indecisive "seekers for something more," back and forth, from Israel to America and vice versa, people with changing minds, who in their own or in later generations decided they or their parents or grandparents had come to the wrong place. This traffic was persistent. True, most people stuck with their original decisions. But beyond responding to different perceptions, after coming to the two countries following such different stars, they had by now each given their blood, their sons and daughters, to their respective chosen lands; much blood had been shed in both places; their *dreams* were now different. Women like Lauren Bacall and Jenny Singer, two Jewish girls born in the Bronx, had hopes and lives so dissimilar from those of Rachel's daughters—Judy, Aviva, or Eva—three Jewish girls born in Rehavia, that they could scarcely be compared. Men like Martin Singer, his father Jacob, his uncle Nathan, and all their descendants would have lives, attitudes, aspirations, and fears entirely unlike those of her Boris or of their son Catriel. Yet there was something—they were still a family!

If these differences separated American and Israeli relations, she hated to contemplate what a chasm there must be between them and their Russian cousins! Yelena Karpeyko, the touted youthful microbiologist near-genius, great-granddaughter of Feygele Singer Karpovich—wasn't she, too, a Jew, at least partly one? What would she be like? The people who had been coming to Israel from Russia in the past few years—at least those she'd met—were an odd lot, often not quite stable, she ruminated. As the blue and white 727 wheeled and started its final descent into National Airport, she thought, here we are, the last three multimillion-soul communities of Jews—most of those still alive after the Holocaust—two and a half million of us in Israel, six million in America, and two and a half million more in the Soviet Union; we tell each other and ourselves we have everything in common, that we're dependent on each other in a thousand ways—and yet, how different we are! In the last hundred years, a speck of time, in so many ways we've become strangers.

Oh, we try to reach each other across continents and oceans; we make

speeches and say we are closer now than at any time since the destruction of Jerusalem. But what is the truth? We are three cultures, have three *Weltanschauungen,* three languages, three alphabets, indeed three primary loyalties (for no matter what she said to others, Rachel believed in her heart that just as Jews in America were Americans first, so the elite Jews of the Soviet Union were more Soviet than Jewish in their hearts). Yes, she thought, we must cross more than continents and oceans to reach each other nowadays.

So what binds, then, for I believe we *are* bound? Religion? To more Jews than not, religion was myth and ritual. Not language. What then? If we're so different, how are we the same? She smiled as she reflected that she was not the first, nor would she be the last, to ask the question. Well, whatever the common denominator, at least we have it all in the Singer family. The cream of each society: the Karpeykos of Ulitsa Oktyabr'skaya, Minsk; the Singers of Gramercy Park, New York, and the Arons of Herzl Way, Savyon. All direct descendants of Israil and Yetta Singer of Jew Street. The same blood ran in their veins. Did these strangers in America and Russia mean more to her than, say, Amira Moumahd, the Arab woman who had brought up all her children, had helped nurse Boris and her when they were ill, had lived in their house for thirty-five years? She loved Amira, yes, and yet—would she risk her neck for her as she was about to for a man she'd never met? Never! Was this bond, this knot that no man could untie, some form of self-hypnosis? Or mass hysteria of togetherness brought on by men like Pharaoh, Haman, Torquemada, Chmielnicki, Streicher, and Hitler? Ah, what a sad riddle!

Rachel Aron was a pragmatic woman, and since these ruminations were neither practical nor useful, she put them out of her mind. She heard the stewardess's "Welcome to Washington's National Airport," tucked the letters, the spur to her thoughts, into her briefcase, and followed her fellow passengers down the aisle. She had not finished the letters, but she would read the rest on the return flight.

At the end of the ramp, waiting for her hat in hand, was Shimon Gold, from the embassy, Ambassador Dinitz's emissary, to bow and greet her with a warm *shalom.* Shimon took her directly to the ambassador's office, where she and Simcha Dinitz talked. The ambassador was a friend of her son-in-law Eli and knew her whole family, as she knew his, and they each asked about relatives and friends.

She reached into her briefcase and took out the twenty-page list of spare parts for planes, tanks, anti-aircraft, and dozens of different kinds of am-

munition, a list prepared by Dayan's office. Here was the letter for Dinitz. Another for Kissinger, and this last one for President Nixon, Golda's "good friend."

Dinitz read all three. "Exactly what I've been telling them. But with this Watergate scandal, you can't imagine how preoccupied the President is! Luckily Kissinger is a *mensch*. I expected you were bringing these, so I made a date with him after lunch. You wish to join me?"

Yes, she would very much like to meet the new American secretary of state. Since she was no diplomat, should she leave all the talking to Dinitz? Simcha Dinitz laughed. "Rachel, Rachel, that will be the day! Be yourself! When have you left all the talking to anyone, even when Boris was alive?"

Rachel laughed with some pain, thinking of their fierce fights; the old sinking feeling.

At lunch in the embassy dining room, they were joined by Shimon Gold again and by Chaim Perl, the information officer, an English Jew who spoke like Abba Eban but, unlike Abba, was an emaciated fellow with a bushy mustache, about forty. These young men, too solicitous for her, always made her uncomfortable, like a woman made of spun glass. She told them about the discovery of her newly-surfaced cousin in Minsk. The reactions of Dinitz and Gold were sympathetic, but Perl thought it only amusing.

"D'you know, Rachel," he said deliberately in his most clipped Oxford English, although until then they had all been talking Hebrew, "there's a theory—well-documented, I daresay—that if one were to draw a circle on the map three hundred miles in diameter, with Minsk at the center, you would include within that circle the birthplace of every family in the Israeli Establishment. You, for instance, madam. And you, too, Mr. Ambassador. Minsk, you see, is what's at the heart of Israel—not Jerusalem at all. So this Yuri chap more than most would really be coming home. See what I mean? In five years he'll be running Hadassah!" He chuckled. "D'you think they'll let him go, actually?"

Rachel smiled. "Oh, maybe I'll go and fetch him." She spoke airily.

"I wish you'd see Manisch, our New York consul general," Dinitz said. "That's all he does now—works on Russian emigration. It's becoming a serious *aliyah*."

"We certainly need all those people," Shimon Gold said, "if we're to keep a balanced population. The Yemenites, Moroccans, Iraqis, and the rest, they multiply, while we Ashkenazis keep subtracting. *We're* using condoms, IUDs, diaphragms, and the Pill, and they're not. Five hundred

thousand Russians! They can save us for two generations. It's not MIGs and Russian tanks or ground-to-air SAMs I'm afraid of, Rachel. I worry about our poor, our uneducated, our unmotivated. Their secret weapon— well, you know what it is. Ten, twelve, fifteen in a family! Something like that is happening here in America also. The cleverest, the brightest have the fewest children. The most ignorant, the most lawless, the poorest have the most. It's happening world wide. You've seen the statistics. Where will it end?"

Rachel was amused at Shimon's deadly earnestness, and turned to Dinitz. "So what's to worry, my dear Ambassador? In two centuries we'll all be Chinese."

Tied up in Washington traffic, Simcha Dinitz was saying something, but he soon realized she was not listening; she was too caught up in her own thoughts. It was those damned letters—they'd set off a chain of memories. Father as a young boy; Freda, the "girl who lives upstairs," was *her* mama! She had never before thought of Mama as a girl, a sexy tease. Well, Papa had been no match for her, was finally unwilling to struggle against her—Herschel the fatalist.

Rachel had heard from Papa those same stories about his grandfather, hiding under his daughter's skirt in his old age to avoid service in the Tsar's army. Papa himself used to laugh as he told it, but had Papa turned out much better? She remembered his discouraged smile, his terrible-smelling pipe which she hated, while he told her his little secrets about how to grow good lemon trees or date palms. Papa worked not to build a new land, but merely to have something for himself, to stay alive. It was Mama who had all the vitality and bustle; it was *her* death Rachel had found impossible to accept—a vibrant woman wasted to an exhausted skeleton, going down in pain and nausea.

And then, on the same date Mama died, eleven years later, Boris— killed, mercifully, in seconds, by a stupid wartime accident, an overturned jeep, crushed like a beetle. Boris, a supply brigade commander, a hundred miles from the front in the Sinai. Crazy, a man of sixty-six becoming a soldier again! She preferred to think of Boris when she had helped him off the sinking freighter—the awful ships they used in those days to bring in newcomers!—on a foggy night in twenty-three.

Boat owners like Rachel were always on call in an emergency, and a sinking ship from Odessa, unseaworthy from the outset, bearing newcomers, was a first-class emergency—especially, as in this case, at night in a dense fog. Rachel knew the waters of Haifa bay as intimately as she knew the

furniture in her home, and she soon had her twenty-four-footer under way, handling her lovely, graceful craft alone, using hands and feet, without help. Standing to, with no motor aboard, she was able to lift the most helpless immigrant aboard. In those days her arms and legs were an athlete's. On this night, Boris was the first of her passengers, emerging from an impenetrable mist. She got a kick out of how he pulled himself aboard, hand over hand on the lifeline, and immediately took over, helped her throw out more lifelines and pull the others into the boat, told them where to sit and when to shift. In the dark in that boat he was little more than a shadow and a voice to her. Features were indistinguishable. He made no mention of the fact that she was a woman—something she had tired of hearing from amazed new immigrants, most of them half crazed with fear. Boris, from his voice, was as relaxed as if he were on a pleasure cruise, and throughout the short trip to shore he spoke to the others wryly; his attitude seemed to keep their spirits from flagging. He comforted those sick from the motion of the boat. He complimented her. "I like the way you handle her—it's a privilege to observe someone who's so good in the dark. You have supernatural powers?" She laughed. "A night like this is terrific for practicing navigation by instinct, eh? Steady as you go, lady." And addressing the others again in his cultured Yiddish: "I've always said, nothing like a sea cruise to revive the spirits, eh? You know where you're going, lady?"

Before they landed, he had become a partner in the enterprise, for he, too, had sailed many small craft in Odessa and was undaunted by the sea. But he won her stiff-necked heart when he admired her boat, on which she had spent so much love, effort, and antifouling paint. "Wonderful lines, lady," he said. "Do you ever race her? When you're not sailing, what do you do?"

"Can't you see? I'm in the import business. I import people!"

He laughed with open admiration, and she could tell he didn't laugh often. Well, she'd never picked up anyone like him before, so she decided to take him home.

Boris Aronowitz, it turned out, was no settler either. His hands were soft; they had never done hard work. He did not pretend to understand Zionism; he was not interested in Palestine as a home for Jews. He had come, he said, because he wanted to get away from all the *goyim* of the world. And in Palestine there were Jews. Rachel assured him he had the *makings* of a Zionist. Those eyes. He said to Mama, all he believed in was the law, in the courts, in justice. Well, they needed men like that, too, didn't they? Did everyone in the country have to be a farmer? She felt her job must be to teach him Hebrew and English.

In three months she knew he was her man. As soon as he had mastered enough Hebrew and English to get along, she told him, they must go to Jerusalem so he could study further. He must do what was necessary to become a licensed lawyer. Between Hebrew and English lessons, she showed him how to harvest the grapes, and they talked. Some days the lessons went on all day, for fifteen, sixteen hours, from the time they awoke until bedtime. They spoke as they ate, as they worked, and on Saturdays as they hiked about the *moshav* from one farm to another.

The Bedouins, she told him, poached on what little they succeeded in growing in the early days. They had to establish guard units. People killed Arab poachers, took the law into their own hands. He was depressed by that news. She began to feel possessive about him. One day she took him to a *kibbutz* not far from the *moshav;* they rode there together on a camel, a comic ride. Each could feel the other jostling, and they felt physically close, a good sensation, the two of them astride the camel, comrades. He gestured and asked about the watchtowers, so menacing, and she told him the *kibbutz* had to be protected from marauders. *Kibbutzniks* took turns. Some Arabs behaved like crazy men, and they had modern guns. Not most, but many more than the first settlers had imagined. Those stupid pioneers had believed the land was unpopulated. Mama and Papa expected a deserted place, with perhaps a handful of roaming friendly Bedouins, a few camels and goats.

Illusions die hard. The Arabs had entire cities—Jaffa, Acre, Nazareth, Ramallah. More Arabs lived in Jerusalem, *their* city, than Jews! They also had farms—however primitive their tools. Many were diseased, backward, uneducated, superstitious, restless, sometimes violent. But there were so many of them! And in turn the Arabs had never dreamed so *many* Jews were coming. Jews had somehow seeped onto their land. They had not heard of Zionism until it was there in their midst, thousands of Jews surrounding them. They tried not to see Jews and the Jews tried not to see Arabs. Mutual blindness, but it was not possible for long. Soon every settlement became a frontier to be defended. Passionate Arabs hated them, not as the Russian peasants had, but for being interlopers, invaders. Envy played a part. Arabs in their exasperation robbed, slaughtered, pillaged. Rachel's two brothers spent half their time working on the *moshav*, the other half carrying guns and serving in the guard units "taking care" of crazy Arabs. One brother, David, she told Boris, had been ambushed by three Arabs on horses; that's how he had lost his eye. . . .

Rachel shook herself from her reverie. The limousine had stopped. She was in Washington, D.C. This was Foggy Bottom. Dinitz showed his cre-

dentials to several men and they were escorted to the Dog Run on the seventh floor, into a large, stately office, with a young, plump, curly-headed, bespectacled Jew behind a great desk, and the flag of the United States behind him.

4

After rising to greet his guests, Secretary Kissinger sat back, adjusted his glasses professorially, and read Golda's letter in silence, then passed it to a tall, balding, thin aide, a man he kept calling Joe (had she heard Dinitz introduce him as Mr. Sisco?), who read it also.

Kissinger spoke softly then, encouragingly, but his words were noncommittal. He knew from his experiences in 1970 that when the bureaucracy favored a presidential directive, they could implement it overnight, but if they were inherently opposed, months could be consumed in detailed memoranda and study. And, unfortunately, he explained, our bureaucracy in this specific matter "is difficult to hurry."

He would see what could be done to speed up parts deliveries. He would talk again to Schlesinger. Jim, too, had his own bureaucracy to contend with.

American Jews, she thought—at the very top, ministers of foreign affairs and defense; still they held back. What did he mean by the "bureaucracies"? Anti-Israeli *goyim*? What else? They were afraid of the *goyim*. Not merely American *goyim*, but those of the entire world. Were there not still American clubs that these eminent officials could not join—and right here in Washington? In their "own" country?

Kissinger was gallant to her personally, in his slow, studious, obscure way, speaking his ponderous Germanic English. When he learned that she was a first cousin of the late Justice Singer his interest grew noticeably more intense; even the "general"—was it "Hague" or "Haig"?—and the other gentleman—Joe Sisco?—seemed interested.

When they had finished their state business, and Ambassador Dinitz nodded to her as if signaling her it was time to leave, Rachel took courage and asked the secretary if she might have one moment for a personal mat-

ter. He glanced at his watch, caught the eye of his assistants, nodded. He was quiet, listening, his head cocked while she spoke.

She told him about her cousin in Minsk. He would understand this, she said, for he had known what it meant to be trapped in a country where you were threatened each day. He had been fortunate to get out in time. It should also be kept in mind that this cousin of hers in Minsk was, like her, a cousin of the late justice of the Supreme Court, Jacob Singer. The justice's son Martin was today one of America's leading merchants, the owner of Singer's on Fifth Avenue. So there was a very important American connection. Was there not something the United States government could do for this man and his family to get him out? It was a small family. There was only a wife and one daughter. Three people. They were threatening the poor man with arrest and trial—if you can believe it, Mr. Secretary—for writing subversive stories for children! Fables!

Mr. Kissinger smiled sympathetically, made a comment she felt to be reassuring.

Yes, of course, she realized Soviet Jews were not being massacred wholesale any longer; the Soviets of today were not Hitler's demons, or Stalin's. She understood. But how sure could anyone be of the future of these people? How many foresaw the Holocaust in 1939? The secretary must be aware that something new and strange, beginning with the Six-Day War six years ago, had been happening among Jews in the Soviet Union. They had a new awareness of themselves and of their origin, these Soviet Jews. Applications to leave were multiplying rapidly. Some the Soviets were permitting to go; others they harassed; a few they imprisoned or committed to special psychiatric hospitals. Anti-Semitism was on the march there. The Soviet press and television was using "Zionism" as a code word, like Stalin's "Cosmopolitanism." Everyone knew what it meant. It was open season on Jews.

Kissinger nodded; he knew it, too, but his tone was placating. "As you know, Madam Aron, for three or four years we have been making quiet appeals to the Soviets to ease Jewish emigration. We have been pleasantly surprised to see the degree of their cooperation. I think your cousin should have an excellent chance to get out through regular channels, with a little added push from us. Has he applied for his exit visa?"

"Mr. Secretary, my cousin is threatened with arrest. How can he expect a visa? He's in trouble—I'm not sure what kind, and I'm worried about him."

Mr. Kissinger asked his secretary to take Yuri's name, address, position, and those of the members of his family. "We often find the opportunity to

give our Soviet counterparts lists of persons who are being harassed and in whom we have some special interest. We certainly have a special interest in the cousin of one of our great Supreme Court justices. Dobrynin is not happy about these lists, but he takes them. Many are then allowed to leave, more than half—including some who were in deep trouble. I'd like to suggest that your cousin Martin should go see the senators he knows— Jack Javits, Scoop Jackson, Jim Buckley, Abe Ribicoff, perhaps others. I've met Martin myself several times at Manny Loebman's in New York. And his wife, what's her name—Jenny? She's an original, isn't she? Our senators make trips to Russia, some see Gromyko, and they also drop in on Dobrynin here. The more of us who show an interest in his case, the better. The Soviets are mercurial on this issue. Sometimes they're responsive, sometimes not. We do not ask them for a reply, and we never know what other purposes they have to serve.

"When you get home, madam, I hope you'll reassure your prime minister we are prepared to do whatever needs doing. We understand the need not only for more armaments for Israel, but also possibilities, new openings, accommodations for progress toward a peace. The president is very firm about the deliveries. So don't worry. They're coming. Everything should be there by the end of the month. And please convey my warmest personal wishes to Golda. Tell her America is determined never to abandon Israel, not President Nixon, not any other American president. And your cousin's name will go to the head of our list, waiting for the propitious moment. That I promise you. Before you return, I hope to give Ambassador Dinitz a written reply for you to deliver to your prime minister from the president. Okay?"

It was the first time Rachel had been to Foggy Bottom, and she had certainly started at the top. She wondered with an inward smile what Henry Kissinger would have become if his parents, fleeing Hitler, had chosen to settle in Jerusalem instead of New York. Would he have been anything more than a distinguished professor at the Hebrew University? Could he ever have forged his way into the inner circles of the government of a state with fewer people than Chicago? She thought of the establishment of which she was a member. Where were the Germans among them? She had serious doubts that despite all his abilities he could have made his way into that arcane, tightly knit, exclusive group as easily as he had made his way into white Christian America's governing circle. And on the other side of the coin, what if Goldie Meyerson had been willing to settle in Wisconsin? What would *she* be in America today? The principal of a junior high school?

What drove some Jews in one direction, others in another? Was it merely the books one happened to read, companions one happened to have, where an uncle happened to live? What caused some to dream of a homeland while others had headed for the *goldene medina?* Today, yes, when people arrived from the Soviet Union at Vienna's South Station they were asked there on the platform, "All going to Israel? Over here, please. Going elsewhere? Please stand over there."

People *knew* where they wanted to go; they'd spent months deciding. Was there some common essential, identifiable element in their choice? Some strain of character? Something inward that, in the final analysis, distinguished Jews who chose America from Jews who chose *Eretz Yisroel?* Or who chose to stay in the Soviet Union? Had these impulses changed in the last hundred years? Henry Kissinger had married a woman named MacGinnis; Schlesinger was a Lutheran. Joshua Singer was married to Tammy Barnstone, a *shiksa* from California. And the Jews who had remained in Russia—then and now? Were they lazy, too frightened to do *anything?*

No, too simple! It was something more complex. They, too, were taking on protective coloration, marrying and becoming Russians in greater and greater numbers. Yuri Karpeyko was married to a *shiksa,* but could anyone assert that he or Aunt Feygele, who ninety years ago had joined both the *Bund* and *Narodnaya Volya* as a girl (something rare indeed, according to Mama), *and* married a *shaygetz,* a woman who had killed two minor tsarist officials and instigated riots in Minsk and Petersburg, who had hidden from the Cossacks for five years, was less brave than her two brothers, who had chosen to leave—each to a different land? Maybe the letters she had not yet read would reveal something more. Maybe not. No matter. She had work to do. She had to call Golda tonight and tell her of her talk with Kissinger.

About Yuri, she had little or no faith in the American effort. If Kissinger was going to wait for the "propitious moment," it could easily be too late. Once the Soviets imprisoned Yuri, they would never let him go. Those "lists"—such a naïve, *American* idea!

On the return flight to New York, she allowed herself to drift, for a few moments, to thoughts of Boris again, as she did so often when she was troubled. But the still unread letters in her briefcase called, and she took them out reluctantly and forced herself to read them during the rest of the flight.

5

LIKE MOST ISRAELI YOUNG MEN, Gideon Aron had two full-time jobs and in his case a dangerous hobby as well. Flying F-2s from the Etzion Air Base in the Sinai was one job, but he was anxious to get back to the other, writing his column for *Haaretz*. Since the "end" of the Yom Kippur war, during this so-called truce, he had grown increasingly restless flying surveillance over the desert. (No one, he hoped, would ever again call on him to engage in his hobby, which he hated.) Why was this bloody state of emergency lasting these many weeks? What was taking the bleeding politicians so long? During a *truce*, no less, an agreed cease-fire, his previously unscathed squadron had in one month lost five planes and three pilots to those illegally emplaced, uncannily accurate SAM missiles. So much for "war" and "peace."

He stood, hunching his tall, powerful frame at the memorial service being conducted in the blast-furnace heat of a desert sandstorm by a young rabbi muttering *kaddish* for Reuven Zucker, the squadron's most unscrupulous poker player and most militant atheist, who had got it yesterday. The whole week had been a downer, Zucker's death coming on the heels of Shimon Galit's. Everyone looked dazed. The excitement of sudden death, he decided, was not the best antidote to boredom.

Gideon's buddy, Dulech Nezer, a young Groucho Marx, muttered after the service, "Another goddamn week like this, and I submit my goddamn resignation." He spit the sand out of his teeth.

Gideon laughed. "To whom?"

"I'll go bananas. When I go bananas, they'll *beg* me to go home. Tell me, is this a way to make a living?" Dulech had been contaminated by American slang when he took his refresher course in Texas.

Gideon didn't need these new fears either. He was having enough trouble handling his load of guilt.

It had been one thing, back in sixty-seven, to destroy unmanned planes on the ground, sitting ducks on runways or in hangars, in surprise low-level forays—only machinery; actually, it had been exhilarating, seeing all that steel and aluminum go up. But this time around, strafing endless columns of fleeing, cowering, terrified men as you raced over them at the speed of sound—so what if they were Egyptian?—watching bodies fly into bloody fragments, always started a churning in his gut. After the first mission he threw up all over the cockpit. After later missions he *forced* himself to, by ramming a finger down his throat. Did he do it for Grandma Rachel? He needed to reassure himself about his own humanity, and vomiting helped. But not much.

What kind of men *were* they? He could scarcely ask Dulech this question, so he unburdened himself to Danielle Mendes, the only woman in the control tower, who, without his knowing exactly how, had become his woman. Danielle, out of uniform and away from this barren and fiery desert, would have been a dark-eyed beauty, a sex object if Gideon ever saw one, with the high forehead, topped by her full, soft, raven-black, straight hair, wisps brushing into her large, widely spaced eyes from time to time; her brows were carefully trimmed to make them arch when she wrinkled her forehead, as she had a habit of doing. The narrow nose, with the smallest suggestion of a ridge attesting her Jewishness, was set in a slim, smooth, lovely face.

What one noticed about Danielle, however, was her skin—smooth, clear, and bronzed. If you were a man you felt tempted to touch it, to pet it. Her body, like her face, was slim, but her femaleness, while small and neat, oozed; and despite the constrictions imposed by her uniform, she bobbed as she moved, both fore and aft so that even women watching her could not ignore her femaleness. Danielle, as it happened, needed comforting of a different kind herself. The man in her life, she told him one night, Noach Cohen, a marvelous musician, had died in a tank on Yom Kippur on the first day of the war, on the Golan Heights. A gentle boy—an oboist with the Haifa Symphony Orchestra.

Noach Cohen must have been more than a good musician, Gideon decided, considering the artistry he had passed on to Danielle in the care and tending of men in combat. She brought real enthusiasm and inventiveness to lovemaking, reminding him of his fantasies when he was sixteen.

Danielle, he thought, was physicially the Algerian prototype. She had been taken to Marseilles as a child, when her parents decided free Algeria was no place for Jews, and there she'd become more French than Algerian. She had worked in the traffic control tower in Marseilles, but

when both her parents were killed in an auto crash, she and her aunt decided the place to come was Israel. She learned Hebrew quickly and got a job in the control tower at the small airport in Haifa. When she was called for her army service, she volunteered to work in the control tower here.

Gideon wondered how she and the four other women at the base had managed to get assigned here, for ordinarily women weren't permitted so near the front. "It wasn't easy, *mon amour*," she cried in her strangely accented Hebrew (not quite a French accent, he decided). "I had to fight the whole bureaucracy. Those old rabbis! Telling us what the Holy Book says about the place of women! Well, it's not holy to me, *mon cher*. It's no more enlightened than the Koran. First a beady-eyed captain, then a major, and finally a brigadier—can you imagine? *Vraiment! Merde,* how I hate those Russian and Polish know-it-alls running things in Jerusalem! Well, I found a way. Here I am!"

Danielle's supply of Rishon le Zion wine seemed to be limitless, and a good thing it was. She also had a supply of grass, and liked to get high.

Gideon decided Danielle was much more like the others of their generation than he was—into themselves, so far from sacrificing *anything*, he sometimes wondered if his grandmother wasn't right. How was the country to survive? The Arabs from Gaza and the West Bank were already doing all the heavy work, the work the old *chalutzim* used to do for themselves. "What the devil made *you* come to Israel?" he asked Danielle.

She thought a moment before she answered. "Perhaps I was bored?" She popped her lips. "My aunt wanted to come. Who knows?"

"You prefer Haifa to Marseilles, then?"

"I'm not sure. Haifa's rather boring, too. Everything so hard to get, not much of a flat I have, one little room—where's the fun of it? I rather expected more excitement, you know? Jews are a real drag. But of course not Noach. Or you."

Since she worked in the tower she was knowledgeable about the activities of the squadron. She seemed to enjoy hearing from Gideon about his experiences in the air, the foul-ups, the near misses, the hairsbreadth escapes. When Galit went down, she had to hear every detail, why he hadn't used his chute, what the SAMs were like, and the same when Reuven had got it, as if she were widow to them all. Before each mission she'd seek Gideon out to wish him good luck like a nervous mother, ask him where he was heading, how high they'd be, could SAMs reach him at that height, how many of them were going out this time. She said ritually he should take care. She wished she could be with him, she said.

She'd leave him a bit of nonsense as a souvenir, the cork from their last bottle of wine, or the empty bottle itself, a handkerchief, a lipstick; she'd press her body against him, as if she were trying to stamp herself into him permanently. Her good-luck kiss. Any day it might be the kiss of farewell. But except on these occasions, she was not usually this serious.

She not only enjoyed their lovemaking, she liked to speculate about it. Was sex better hidden or in the open? Forbidden or encouraged? Had Gideon read those ads in the papers—well, they carried them in *Haaretz*, didn't they?—couples advertising for other couples, swingers? That might be fun, mightn't it? Like bees tasting different flowers. Two boys, two girls—he might want to think about it. She and Noach had answered one of those ads, but before anything could come of it Noach had to go to *milium*, into the reserve, and the war came. Gideon thought about it, but he was too old-fashioned, living in the generation of his grandmother. Danielle laughed when he demurred. "Ah, Gideon, if it's decadence it's also pleasure, *n'est-ce pas?*" The way she talked, her swinging style, lent credence to rumors that had begun to irritate him.

Rumor: Dulech himself claimed to know for a fact that Danielle had been providing her brand of comfort to Reuven Zucker whenever Gideon was off base or asleep. Reuven was not the first. Gideon tried to tell himself that Dulech was eaten with jealousy and therefore trying to make trouble.

However, he asked her one night why she had been particularly attracted to him, with so many others around. She told him blandly, it was his columns in *Haaretz*. His marvelous wit. She had bought *Haaretz* every day just to read his latest. How lucky for her he had turned out to be tall and good-looking, too! In that jagged way. "I love the way you look. That dark beard—you must have to shave twice a day! And the black hair on your fair body, your chest, I love to feel it with my face. Your eyes are so gentle, too. And how is it you're so muscular? A newspaper man with such strength!" No one had ever flattered Gideon so nicely. "A *sabra*, too, descended from a founding family, so gorgeous, probably rich, *n'est-ce pas?*" How lucky could she get? She felt very "upper class" with him; now, was that frank enough? "Even before Noach was killed, you were my ideal. You were *his* ideal, too. We used to read you every day."

"Doesn't what we do make you feel a bit guilty? How long is Noach gone now—two, three months?"

"Can anything bring Noach back? Well, you see, here *you* are! Risking your neck every day. Where do you fly tomorrow? Ah, yes, *that* one. So.

You see how brave you are! You turn me on, that's all. What can I say? Ah, you're fishing for compliments, eh? Come, lie back. Yes. Just so. You like that?"

In the last war, everything was over so fast that Gideon had never had a chance to think of girls. Danielle was still living in Marseilles then. Everything had been different then, he told Danielle. After one hectic week he was back finishing his final year at the university in Jerusalem, one of the nation's youngest heroes. But when would they wind it up this time? The trouble was, he was six years older and a hundred years wiser now. Those who were optimists today simply didn't understand the situation, he told her. As part of his work in the years since sixty-seven, he had cultivated a number of Arab friends in Old Jerusalem, including a few athletes, and today he understood better than he wanted to what lay beneath their elaborate hospitality, their whiskery kisses of greeting and farewell. Gideon could speak Arabic like a Palestinian, and he often passed for Palestinian. They were honest friends, and that's why he finally understood their two-level lives—one accommodatingly human, the other narrowly, passionately Arab. ("I guess every day you guys pray that we would leave," he had suggested to one of his Arab football player friends.

"No, Gideon," his friend replied solemnly, "we pray you will leave *five times* a day.")

As he talked of the Arabs, Danielle nodded gravely. She knew. She had been in Algeria. The Arabs would never give up.

Gideon never mentioned his secret work—his "hobby," as he preferred to think of it. What would she have thought of his three weeks in Beirut, where a year ago he had prepared a house-by-house map, learned the hour-by-hour habits of his prey, in preparation for the commando attack on PLO headquarters and the gunning down of the man who had planned most of the PLO raids on northern Israel? Although he hated doing it (fear was at the foundation of the hate), about this work, at least, he had no sense of guilt. Men like that bastard they had wasted were no innocents.

A most unlikely hobby for him, particularly since all through school he had avoided every conceivable form of contact sport—he couldn't stand the violence of soccer, football, even basketball. He liked to *watch*. The sports he preferred were sailing, especially with his grandmother, who'd taught him all he knew about it, and swimming. He'd chosen to become a pilot primarily because there wasn't all the pummeling of infantry training, and tanks were too bloody hot.

Now, however, flying these stupid missions, he could not avoid a growing sense of futility. Couldn't U.S. satellites handle surveillance? Was

there any sense to Reuven Zucker's death? Or Shimon Galit's? Gideon sure as hell objected strenuously to dying senselessly.

He wanted to get back to Jerusalem to talk things over with Rachel—maybe *she* could cheer him up; he wanted to get back to work, to push those sluggish politicians toward making *peace*. But Dov Litani, his commanding general, would not hear of releasing him. No way, Dov said, when he went to his hut and asked him for the tenth time, the day after the Zucker service. Air surveillance must continue, Dov explained, as to a backward student. How could they depend on America? Couldn't Gideon see the Americans were wooing the Egyptians? Why else would the Americans let the Russians install SAMs where Egypt had agreed not to? Each day Gideon had seen with his own eyes the new concrete work the Russian crews were emplacing in the sand, hadn't he?

"Not only that," Gideon half agreed, "Russian crews must be manning those SAMs. They're no Egyptians. They really know what they're doing. You should see how they can trace our flight pattern, our altitude. Well, you've been at the debriefings. You've heard it all. Those guys are hair-raising."

Dov Litani sipped his iced tea. Even with the air-conditioning in his hut, it was hot. "You've noticed that?"

"Makes me goddamn nervous," Gideon said. "I've got to get back to Jerusalem. Who wants to get killed taking photographs?"

"Look," Dov said, "I have a thought. If you have to unwind, why not take an overnight in Eilat or Sharm? Bathe in the sea. Relax. You'll feel better."

It wasn't much, but it was the best offer Gideon had. He decided to press his luck. "Okay if I take Danielle Mendes?"

Dov seemed surprised; his dark eyes glittered, his right forefinger plunged into his curly black hair and began to twist a lock of it. "You know Danielle Mendes? This intimately?"

Shows how much a general knows about what's going on at his base!

"Yes, Dov. Do you mind?"

"No, no. Sure, why not? So, take her, we'll find someone to cover for her. You can go tomorrow. But come and see me tonight. It's important. Okay?"

"Okay, Dov, sir." Gideon saluted, a faint gesture of mockery observing one of the formalities of military life that no one observed. He wanted Dov to know he was put off.

He went to find Danielle at the control tower; she was having her tea break below, sitting alone, her straight black hair astray, wisps falling into her eyes; faint patches of sweat under her arms. He invited her to Sharm.

The idea delighted her. "A holiday! Why couldn't we take Dulech? I rather like him, you know? And Yetta Gold, isn't she his girl?" Yetta was the small, dark girl—her parents were Iraqi and Polish—who worked in the mess hall. "She'd love to come. I think she's sexy, don't you? And, oh, what she'd give to go to Sharm! She's a scuba diver, you know, and that's the best diving in the world. She told me the divers' slogan: 'Divers do it deeper.' Isn't that cute?" Danielle uttered her low, contralto laugh. "Lucky Dulech! Lucky Yetta!"

Gideon was not sure what Danielle had in her head or why she wanted company, but he agreed it might be more festive if four of them went. Dulech, of course, was delighted, and so was Yetta, her dark face aglow.

When Danielle went to ask Dov Litani about Dulech and Yetta, the commander said he had no objection, and it was arranged.

When Gideon returned in the evening to see General Dov Litani, he met two men he knew but whom he had never seen at the base before, men in civilian clothes who said they'd come from Jerusalem. Dov asked him to sit down. The men were serious, behaving with exaggerated correctness; they were men connected to his hobby. They were there, they said, concerning Danielle Mendes. Gideon was surprised but not astonished by what they told him. Too much about Danielle had been not quite authentic. Yes, come to think of it, she reminded him of himself in Beirut, an outsider playing a risky role. Her accent? No, not French at all. It was Arabic, Syrian Arabic, with French as a second language. She claimed to understand not a word of Arabic, although she had told him she'd lived in Algiers. In fact, Damascus, the men told him, would have been more accurate. No, not a Jew. The men had intercepted telegraphic messages in a code they had broken, specifying the squadron's flight plan, day after day. They showed him the intercepted messages that had preceded Reuven Zucker's fatal mission. No question about it.

They had also carefully checked her cover story: there was a Noach Cohen who played the oboe in the Haifa orchestra, all right, but he had been on the Golan and was believed to be a prisoner of the Syrians. So far as was known, he was not dead. No other member of the orchestra had ever heard him talk of a Danielle Mendes. She had never been in Algiers or Marseilles. She had been given Israeli citizenship and issued a passport on forged information a year ago. One of the men showed Gideon a photograph from a Damascus paper. There she was . . . a triumphantly smiling young woman in Syrian uniform, a submachine gun loose in her hands, in Damascus, describing a successful hijacking. It was she. The caption identified her as Rashaa Mausili of Damascus and re-

ported that her male companion of many months had been killed in the hijacking operation. Her shortwave transmitter, the men said, could reach Eilat, and someone had another, more powerful transmitter there.

The men told Gideon what he was expected to do; Gideon flatly refused. They pressed him; he protested, argued, sweated. He couldn't, absolutely not. He suggested every conceivable alternate solution—arrest, trial, exchange, interrogating her for further information. Getting someone else to do it. Not he.

But the men were unmoved, insistent. Tel Aviv had considered every alternative, at the highest level; it had gone right to Lekhitov. The war was still being fought under a different name. No one wanted Israelis captured simply to exchange for her. That she should go without a trace was essential. Those few who had to know would be told or given a cover story. It must look like an accident.

Now they realized the loss of all five planes and three pilots was her doing. Weiss, Zucker, and Galit. The same old story. Her parents had fled from Jaffa in forty-eight. She was one of those passionate Palestinians, born in Damascus. Her lover had been killed during the hijacking. She'd become unstable. Maybe she'd always been unstable. That did not make her less dedicated—she worked for Habash's Popular Front. The maniacs.

Gideon argued passionately far into the night, but the other three closed in; they brought an order directly from Jerusalem. Everything had been carefully analyzed and dissected there. At dawn Gideon went to bed, dizzy, grim, battered. He doubted he could do it. For a long time he did not sleep. What would his grandmother think of him? Danielle was a *woman*.

When finally he fell into a light, fitful sleep, he dreamed. SAM missiles, silent, puffed around him in a deep blue sky, to a Strauss waltz, and his grandmother Rachel, sitting in the plane beside him, seized the controls and took them up, up, higher than he had ever been—he was amazed the plane could make it—the altimeter was at half a million meters, they could see the curvature of the earth; still the missiles followed. He had difficulty breathing. Suddenly they began to fall, to roll and fall like a stone, and he was able to save himself only by waking up. He had never dreamed about flying before.

6

NEXT MORNING THEY WERE OFF, with Gideon at the controls. Danielle told Yetta to sit up front with him. She and Dulech would sit in the back.

Dulech was a tour guide in civilian life. He'd once taken a group to Sharm el Sheikh, so he knew it as well as Yetta. "We're building a nice hotel there," Dulech said, "with good plumbing, so I guess it was worth defending." He thinks it's a joke, Gideon thought, but is it? Other nations defend their way of life. We defend a hotel. Is that our way of life? Are we forever transients? Or can we manage to stay a bit longer in Israel? He might try a column on it when he got back. If ever.

Glancing over his shoulder, he thought, who could be more westernized than Danielle? Except that she was darker, she reminded him of Bardot. Was it possible those two men had made a terrible mistake? Turning back, he said quickly in Arabic, "There's a plane at ten o'clock." Her eyes swung to ten o'clock; she recovered, leaned forward and shouted, "What did you say, Gideon?"

"I thought I saw a plane," he called back in Hebrew. "It must have been a sunspot."

Gideon had expected a bit of cactus so near the sea, but there was not a weed or a plant in the endless flat desert, only occasional hills and sudden far-off mountains; only camels and goatskin tents of Bedouins here and there as their bus drove to the beach from the airdrome. No wonder his luxury-loving mother Lili dreamed of the French Riviera!

At the beach, the concrete skeleton of the hotel under construction rose out of the sand behind a row of completed beehive-shaped rooms, perhaps twenty of them, igloos painted a bright yellow. At the end of the row, a one-story flat-roofed metal structure served as a dining room. On the beach itself across a road, three small, widely separated wood shacks offered food

and drink, while closer to the water's edge had been erected three enormous umbrella-type structures, providing cover for shade-seekers.

By the time they arrived, late in the morning, the relentless sun, reflected by the almost flat surface of the blue and aquamarine water, almost blinded them, even with their sunglasses. Merely to be able to see the clear water so close, rather than from six miles in the air, would have refreshed Gideon, had he not been so preoccupied.

All four made directly for the beach from the bus, and Danielle selected a spot some distance beyond the last of the umbrellalike structures, where they pitched their tent, working up a great sweat. They put on their brief swimsuits, tiny patches of convention, and Yetta, as soon as she was in hers, ran down the beach toward the Red Sea Divers' station, where a dive boat left for scuba sites. Yetta called that she'd try to catch the first afternoon boat; she'd be back before dark. In a short while the other three saw the dirty, white twin-screw heavy-duty tub racing along the coast toward the first drop-off.

Danielle, Dulech, and Gideon, long since bronzed by the desert, lay blissfully coiled in the soft, tepid water, swimming, floating, or surface diving, examining the tan and purple shallow reefs teeming with brilliantly colored smaller fish flitting in and out of holes, munching coral—butterflies and parrots, and a few shy lobsters hiding in crevices with protecting sea urchins. Half a dozen Israeli servicemen lay on the beach. The rest were American tourists from the hotel, perhaps thirty of them.

Strange people, Gideon thought, desperate to visit the Sinai and somehow to get a "piece of the action," most of them Jews, reeking with pride and sentimentality. They wanted to touch an Israeli, these middle-aged men and women, and rush home to Cleveland or New York to brag to their friends.

Dulech drifted off alone at about five and strolled down the beach toward the Red Sea Divers' dock, half a kilometer away, until they lost sight of him. Gideon and Danielle romped in the water. Playfully, Gideon ducked Danielle's head beneath the surface while she thrashed in protest; he allowed her to surface. She was not a strong swimmer, and in the water she was no match for him. It would be easy. "You mustn't *do* that, Gideon. You scare me!" He laughed and pushed her under again, and let her surface. She sulked, but he insisted on cavorting about her like a dolphin, surface diving, swimming great distances from her and returning, carrying her screaming on his back and dumping her, noticing her feeble breast stroke. She looked at him strangely; had he noticed that quick dart of her eyes in the plane? No, he only wanted to play.

Dulech returned in an unusually bleak mood. He spoke in monosyllabic grunts in response to their questions. It was as if he had been wounded into silence. No one mentioned Yetta. Danielle suggested they take supper at the hotel. All three put on their uniforms and walked across to the dining room. They had soggy fried fish and tomatoes and drank too much white wine, as if it were soda water; soon, unsteadily, they retired to the tent, where a modest breeze cooled them only slightly in a darkness relieved by a bright full moon seeping through open flaps. Silence enveloped them like a mist, and each lay in his separate circle, curled or spread, wearing their bikinis, now dry.

At about nine they heard a rustle and Yetta ducked in through the flap. She found her own circle of space and lay down in the sand, speaking no word.

"Have you had supper?" Gideon asked.

"Yes."

They lay for a short spell longer. Dulech's voice, sepulchral: "I saw you on the beach. I saw that skinny kid, too."

"Ah."

"Oh, terrific, man! That's all you have to say?"

"We went together on this dive. You can't imagine! We went down almost two hundred feet. Fantastic. You become euphoric, it's so damn beautiful. Another world. We came off the boat and took our wet suits off on the beach. I think we both wanted that magic feeling to last. So you *saw* us?"

"I saw."

"Something happened to my tank down there. I lost my air. I panicked; I don't usually, but I did this time. I expected to die, but he calmed me down. He shared his air at two hundred feet. It's something quite special. I can't explain. You're just there, the two of you, alone there. Really alone. He saved my life, you know? So later, on the beach, he said we should take our swimsuits off. He's English, only eighteen. So that's something daring for a repressed English boy, isn't it? For a change I didn't argue. He had the whitest skin I ever saw."

"Spare me the details."

Yetta spoke calmly, as if still in her reverie. "Twice in less than an hour. You never did that."

"Cunt."

Dulech curled up as if poisoned, about to die. Gideon half expected him to groan with pain or spit with anger, but there was only silence.

A sudden movement made Gideon turn his head. He saw Danielle

crawling across the tent on all fours toward Dulech; the whiteness of her hands in the moonlight flashed swiftly about Dulech's brief trunks, pulling, pulling. She began to kiss him, without encouragement, to lick him, as if licking a wound, a consolation. *Don't cry, Dulech.*

Gideon heard her wordless murmuring, like a mother's to a sick child, a nurse's to a dying patient, as she went busily about her quiet task. Dulech lay, straightening himself, upon his back; Yetta turned then, with lassitude, looking toward the action, languorous, yawning. Gideon could see the increase of intensity in Danielle's black hair, shaking into loose, wanton strands, the methodic bobbing of her head, short locks flowing like dark water; Dulech's breath became labored, shorter, harder, as if he were climbing a mountain growing steeper and steeper, having difficulty with his footing at each step, but determined to climb on, perhaps for ten minutes, until after a sudden gust, his breath stopped.

Gideon could tell only by the resumption of Dulech's more normal, steady breathing after a bit that it was over, he had reached the top of the mountain, but Danielle did not tarry for a moment over Dulech. She left him like a fallen prey, and crawled to where Yetta lay, an iguana's crawl now, slimy, heavy-lidded; she seized Yetta's face in both hands, bent as if to kiss her on the lips, opened her own mouth, and let the viscous stuff drip out. Then she spat the last of it in her friend's face. Yetta made no effort to avoid her, as if she deserved it.

Danielle crawled, now majestically, Gideon thought, like some half-gutted forest beast, half-satisfied but still restless. She came toward him, and spoke in a low voice. "Gideon? Do me, please." To Gideon she seemed to be breathing shallowly herself, and rapidly, as if having the same difficulty Dulech had suffered from earlier. Gideon half pitied her now; she seemed defenseless as she lowered her head and raised her buttocks. Well, she *tried* to be French, a Syrian interpretation of French, anyhow, he supposed. Reduction seduction, he thought. We are the flesh, nothing more. Mind, spirit, soul, whatever you choose to call it—eliminated. A girl of the Koran, utterly corrupted. A sacrifice to a dumb cause—no less than the mindless sacrifice of Athenian maidens to the Minotaur. If only he could reach her, save her!

As he hesitated, she whispered, "Please, Gideon, don't be mean."

She meant him to play a part, a charade they had played before, back at the base.

"Beg," he said flatly, offended by the role she gave him.

In quick gestures she stood, pulled off the two small pieces of cloth she wore, holding them out to him, as one might hold burnt offerings to a

god, then as he took them and tossed them aside, she turned back to him, sank to her knees, elbows in the sand, buttocks presented. "I'm on my knees," she whispered over her shoulder. "What more do you want?"

"Beg," he repeated dully. By nature he would, even now, have preferred a word of sentiment, a *human* word, but it wasn't in her nature, and it would have changed nothing. He was too old-fashioned, even sentimental, for this woman. He marveled at her cold sexuality. No doubt she could kill a man as coldly as fuck him. Had, indeed.

"Please," she said in a voice now hoarse, and slowly wriggled her buttocks, a triangle of flesh still white and unbronzed. "Hurry. I'm in a bad way."

Gideon wondered what had inflamed her. Was it her foreknowledge? He knew the passion for martyrdom among unstable Palestinians.

He knelt behind her and, supporting his full weight on his elbows, reached up with fingertips to touch only her erect nipples with a tenderness exceeding anything she was entitled to feel, the merest whisper of a touch, but technically perfect. He felt nothing for her any more, was surprised her excitement scarcely touched him. His limp penis spoke eloquently for him and to him.

"Gideon," she whispered to the dark. "Please."

He stood abruptly and hurried from the tent. He ran toward the sea, plunged into the soft, gently cooling water, and swam, swam fiercely toward some impossible shore, trying to swim away from himself and his task. After a time, he lay on his back and let the small surge of the sea raise and lower him like a gentle mother.

By the time he returned, the other three were asleep, or pretending to be. Danielle and Dulech had put on their swimsuits again, and lay in the sand curled in prenatal balls. Yetta lay stretched out, arms over her head.

At the first faint sign of light, before anyone else on the beach was awake, the four of them rose and, led by a silent Danielle, ran for a long swim; they watched the sun come up with awe-inspiring splendor. As Dulech and Yetta headed back toward the tent, traipsing clumsily through knee-deep water, Gideon cried, "Come on, Danielle, let's make it up. Let's go for a swim!"

She grinned at him impishly. "You are such a bastard," she said. "I'll never forget what you did. To leave a lady in that condition."

They were swimming out, Gideon easily, she with more effort. "I was embarrassed," he said, to comfort her. "The others were watching us, you know."

"Bastard," she gasped, trying to keep up.

"Never again," he said. "Here, let me help you."

He surrounded her waist with one arm and, kicking, using his free arm, he moved them out into deeper water. They swam for almost twenty-five minutes. At one point, she suggested going back. He nodded but kept swimming, saying it was so lovely, so peaceful. He estimated it was five o'clock. He took a sighting on their location. As good a place as any—coral, overgrown bottom, two hundred feet—they were far enough. The sluggish action of this water would not wash anything waterlogged up to the beach for several days—perhaps weeks.

"Listen, Rashaa—" Her eyes opened wider than he had ever seen them, but she said nothing. He could have sworn she gasped in terror, and nodded, almost with relief.

He pushed her head quickly beneath the surface, bracing himself for her struggle.

7

AT SIX FIFTEEN, Gideon came dashing from the sea to his comrades in the tent, gasping news of the disaster, the "accident," and pointing to the location where he had last seen Danielle swimming out foolishly, against his advice—pointing twenty-five degrees off from where they had been.

The search went on for several hours. Other Israelis were enlisted; young men from the Red Sea Divers, including the eighteen-year-old English visitor, went down in shifts over sandy bottoms and reefs that were more than a kilometer from the site of the drowning. No body was ever found. Sharks roam those waters.

The local military police became involved. A captain demanded to know the identity of the drowned woman, but Gideon took him aside, showed him certain identification; a telephone call was made, and the questions stopped. No record was made of the incident.

Gideon told them only what he absolutely had to on the flight home. There'd be no public announcement at the base. Just that Danielle had gone off for a few days. As few people were to know as possible. It was a security matter. Did they understand? It was serious. Yetta and Dulech were both shocked, incredulous, but both knew the importance to every Israeli of security.

When he had returned to the base and reported to Dov Litani, Gideon learned that Dov also had news for *him*. As soon as they had disposed of the Danielle Mendes (or, as Dov preferred to call it, the Rashaa Masili) affair, Dov told him that Aaron Weisbrot had called to ask that Gideon return at once to Jerusalem. "Something to do with your grandmother. No, she's all right. You're not to worry. He wants you up there no later than tomorrow. I told him I thought we could spare you—for a day or two. So go."

Dov knew of Weisbrot, naturally. It was, after all, a small country, and

men in Dov Litani's position knew Weisbrot had for years worked directly under Avigur. What Dov did not know was that Gideon had once worked with Weisbrot, as an advance man on the Beirut raid. The original idea of that raid had been to rescue certain Lebanese Jews; but this had become impractical, and the objective of the mission had changed from rescue to assassination. What did the old man want this time? Weisbrot's specialty was bringing Diaspora Jews home. Rachel used to do that, too. Weisbrot was dealing heavily in Soviet Jews this year. Had Rachel been somehow pressed into that service? Many Soviet Jews were arriving these days; maybe it was a debriefing job? Ah, no, there were many people more fluent in Russian. Tel Aviv had thousands. What kind of future was there in intelligence work? Or in bringing in more exiles? He thought of Danielle Mendes being consumed by sharks and smaller fish. He wished he'd never met Weisbrot.

In one of Rehavia's narrowest streets, on a steep hill down which children still rode on their homemade scooters, in a nondescript three-story building that had once held apartments, Weisbrot had his office. One new feature Gideon noticed: window air-conditioning units—unnecessary in these December days, but it was nice to know that when summer came, the work of ingathering could go on in comfort. Otherwise the place was the same Spartan office.

Weisbrot hadn't changed, either. The same wispy white hair stood in the same electric fashion atop that still cadaverous face. The old man reminded Gideon of Grandfather Boris—Rachel herself had mentioned the remarkable resemblance. And they were alike, as she said, in more ways than simply appearance. They were of the same school. Was that what made Gideon unconsciously willing to do the old man's bidding?

What Weisbrot told him in his spare office in Rehavia took him completely by surprise. Nobody in the family thought any of their relatives were still alive in Minsk. So the Nazis must have missed a few! The entire harebrained scheme hatched by Rachel was typical of her. What the hell did she care? Well, thank God for men like Weisbrot, more cautious, who had enough sense to send for Gideon to watch over that crazy old woman! Talk about *chutzpah!* Still out sailing her damn little boat with her bare toes and square fingers! Skipper Rachel Aron to the rescue!

Weisbrot explained ruefully what he had agreed to do. Why? Because Rachel had asked him to! But if Avigur ever learned of it, that would be the end of his career. "He'll go to Golda and she'll drop me in the nearest *tel* and close it up!" High policy! Weisbrot did not agree with Avigur, or with Golda, not by a long shot, and that must have entered into it. Big

power politics was all very well, he said, but in his opinion, within limits, whether you broke a Russian law or not was not the big thing Golda thought it was. The Soviets would do what was good for the Soviet Union. It made no difference what Israelis did or did not do. There were others who agreed with this view, including most of the recent newcomers from the Soviet Union. Still, one could not be reckless. Rachel seemed suddenly much younger to Gideon.

Weisbrot, on the other hand, seemed to be getting old. They all were, these Jew-savers, from the semi-active Avigur down. The very business they were in—saving Jews—had gone out of style; not many young people were going into the business these days. Too busy playing tennis, going to discos, watching TV, spilling their guts to shrinks, or making money.

Was this a particularly Israeli thing, Gideon wondered, this dependence on the elders? Wasn't it one of the things that got Jesus of Nazareth so riled up? When today's old men were young themselves, had they, too, had the same problem with their elders? Or did they not ignore the words of caution, the hesitations? When they were young, they abandoned their universities; built, bought, and manned the boats; defied the blockade; brought in weapons from Czechoslovakia, America, France; they defied the world. Nobody had to draft them. They had not been awed by Turks, British, or Arabs. They defied policemen, cruisers, tommy guns; outwitted bureaucrats. People like Rachel.

Gideon dared not overlook their histories in dealing with these old men. Avigur, Rachel, Weisbrot, and Company had been bringing in boatloads of Jews before Gideon was born. He could not sell them short. But perspectives had changed. Now they were like rich old misers, no longer interested in making new fortunes or taking big risks. They wanted to keep the fortune they had made. Play it safe. Except Rachel.

Weisbrot tried to make an impatient Gideon understand why he had tried so hard to talk Rachel out of her scheme. Antagonizing the old men in the Kremlin, Weisbrot explained with patient emphasis, was not in Israel's interest. Indeed, many secretly believed those men in the Kremlin were, in many ways, Israel's unacknowledged friends and allies. For all their anti-Zionist propaganda at home and at the U.N., they had never wavered from the principle that Israel's existence must be insured—they said it lightly, but they always said it. They wanted a radicalized Israel, but an Israel. Every Russian official had had Jewish comrades in their early days. They were no angels, these men, but who was an angel?

The old men in Moscow felt Israel should exist and *be as Russian as possible*. The Israeli elite were Russian. And how else to explain this new

flood of educated Russians? All having been nurtured on the Communist dream! Even the Politburo took a few small chances. The men in the Kremlin surely envisioned the day when Israel could be made a Communist state, a loyal ally of the Soviet Union. They knew better than anyone of subliminal longings in the Jewish soul for socialism and egalitarianism. Wasn't there in the Israeli air a new contempt, even malice, toward millionaires, toward successful entrepreneurs, men who were perceived by hundreds of thousands of Israelis as enemies of the people?

So if the Kremlin bosses wanted to dream, why shouldn't the wiser old men of Israel make use of such dreams?

"We will have forty thousand more from the Soviet Union this year alone! Yom Kippur War or not, you see? We all take chances, don't we? *We* know the people who are coming are more Jewish than Soviet. Not every one of them, of course, so that's *our* gamble. But we think nine out of ten. So why should we antagonize those boys in the Kremlin? Forty thousand this year, forty thousand next year—it adds up! It keeps us Russian, it keeps us European." Weisbrot's wise old eyes narrowed, the wisps of white hair giving him the air of an Einstein, a Ben Gurion, as he leaned toward Gideon now, "So let me be frank. I would rather have forty thousand Jews arriving in Vienna next year and *no* Yuri Karpeyko, than we should get Yuri Karpeyko alone and no forty thousand. You understand?"

"Of course," Gideon said.

Rachel, Weisbrot said, was an amateur. She needed a more experienced person at her side. Weisbrot arranged Gideon's release from active duty in the Sinai and Gideon never did get to say a proper goodbye to Dulech or Dov Litani. The old man set up briefings for Gideon. He would meet newcomers from Vilna, Moscow, and especially Minsk. By the time he reached Minsk he must know more about it than the people who lived there. He needed thorough briefing.

Between his visits to Weisbrot and briefings, Gideon tried several times to call his grandmother, who was staying with her cousin, Martin Singer, in New York. He finally reached Martin. But Rachel was not in New York, Martin told him. She was in California raising American money for Israel.

Next day Rachel called from San Francisco, full of a new American euphoria, bubbling with the successes of her trip, to say how nicely the American cousins were treating her—and, in fact, how nice were all the Americans she had met. Gideon would love Martin's wife, Jenny, a "big woman" with whom she had spent a little time—"A very nice *meshugina*.

She comes like a hurricane, Gideon, with a joke for everything. Just your type. Listen, their daughter is in Israel right now. Yes, she's seeing an El Al pilot—a man named Avram Yevorakh. . . . You *know* him? You flew with him? Good! He lives in Haifa somewhere? . . . Yes? So why don't you look them up? . . . No, they're not married! They're living together, what else? You young people today! It's disgraceful! Well, be nice to the girl, Gideon, because her parents are being *very* nice to me. And she's *your* cousin, too. Her name's Nettie. . . . That's too American for you? Well, but if she marries this Avram, maybe she'll change it to something better."

Gideon was finally able to get a few words in, to tell his grandmother why he'd called. Weisbrot had told him everything. She needed a guardian, Weisbrot thought, someone to carry the heavy bags. She chuckled. That Weisbrot—he clucked over her so! Besides, Gideon said, he wouldn't miss it for anything. Gideon would bring everything Weisbrot had promised her. The old man, however, was still waiting for the photographs from Minsk. Rachel promised, yes, she'd send them, as soon as they arrived in America and she'd had them processed. How wonderful that Gideon would be coming! She couldn't think of better company. The American woman, this Jenny, might be coming, too; it looked that way now. Jenny wanted to deliver a few pairs of blue jeans and some Seiko watches so their Russian family could sell them on the black market to have what to eat, and she wanted also to buck them up, raise their spirits, to say keep their chins up, she and her husband were doing everything they could. They shouldn't lose hope! So American! So useless!

"Listen, I'll be frank, I hope she doesn't come," Gideon said. "She could mean *tsarah*."

"At least she's a real American," Rachel said. "That could be of *some* help."

"Well, there's that, of course," Gideon conceded. He would be in New York as soon as the photos came and the things were ready. In the abrupt Israeli way they said goodbye and hung up.

He decided to call Avram Yevorakh in Haifa. It might indeed be a good idea to meet this Nettie Singer. Maybe from the daughter he could learn something about the mother with whom he would have to cope. Gideon believed in knowing as much as he could, to leave as little as possible to chance.

Before he left for New York, he went to Haifa and spent two days and evenings with Nettie and Avram. Nettie wondered why her cousin was so interested in her mother. But she answered his questions and let it pass,

because she was too bewitched by her Avram to think of anything else, and she found Gideon charming. Another new relative. Already a friend of Avram's. She was so lucky!

On the day of his departure she drove him to Ben Gurion Airport (Avram would be flying the plane). Gideon would be staying with her mother and father. "Tell them not to worry about me. I love it here in Haifa, I love Israel, I'm so happy here with Avram. *Tell* 'em, will you Gideon? I'm so glad I have an Israeli cousin! You know something else? I've gone and bought an apartment here in Haifa—with my own money. For Avram and me. But don't tell 'em *that*. They'll die."

Gideon eyed the still willowy, dark-blond Nettie, so open and careless and in love, but unable to keep even one little secret. "You love Israel? Is very nice. I am glad. And you are very happy?" He laughed. "But, of course, you realize you are the only one in the whole country?"

It was her turn to laugh. "Everyone doesn't have my Avram!" Or your money, he thought. Or your passport. She turned to him intently. "Now, don't let my mother intimidate you, Gideon, okay? She'll try. She's done it to me all my life." And she kissed him goodbye, an open, friendly American kiss, a kind Gideon was not used to.

"I'm glad also I have an American cousin," he called to her as she drove off.

8

FRED, THE CHAUFFEUR, wore a long face when he greeted Rachel at La Guardia on her return from Washington. Mr. Singer had had a bad morning, and his doctor had ordered him back to the hospital for tests. He and Mrs. Singer were there now. "Take me there," Rachel said.

Memorial was the most sympathetic hospital Rachel had ever seen—the staff treating visitors as if they were patients. She found Martin's large cheerful corner room on the sixth floor; in silk pajamas, he was half sitting in an electrically operated bed, looking almost comfortable, certainly better than he had last night. Jenny sprang from a corner chair in the shadows and threw her arms about Rachel, as if Rachel were her mother. What an overpowering, demonstrative woman!

"Will you just look at *him?*" Jenny cried. "I *know* it's something he ate, but these doctors! They love to use those big goddamn machines. X-ray, cardiogram, myelogram, angiogram, brain scan, bone scan, and now they got this monster, the cat scanner. Well, Marty wants his doctors to make a living."

Rachel thought Martin's smile a bit wan. "They agreed to give me the room next door," Jenny was running on hysterically, "just in case—so in the middle of the night, if he gets sexy and feels like—you know what!" Jenny's hysteria was suppressed with enormous effort. Thank God she hadn't called Graham!

Fred, the chauffeur, had explained to Rachel on the way from the airport that this was a hospital exclusively for cancer patients. Hearing it, Rachel wondered if Mama's fate was what awaited Martin Singer—she knew *that* war.

"We haven't told Marty's mother he's in the hospital," Jenny was saying. "Why worry her, when I'm sure it's *nothing.*"

Over the loudspeaker in the hall a woman's voice was saying gently, "Visiting hours are over, please. Visiting hours are over."

At that moment, as if to defy the announcement, Joshua and Tammy burst into the room, both dressed like street urchins, Rachel observed, but this was true everywhere now. Jeans, pulled-out shirts, running shoes. They'd just jogged up from Gramercy Park. Martin appeared to be touched by their visit. Rachel could see his eyes filling. Jenny kissed her son with more than her usual emotionalism. "I'm so *glad* you've come," she exulted. "You have no idea!"

Josh grinned. "Better late than never, right? How late am I? Five years?" He turned to his father. "How's it goin', Dad?"

Martin nodded. "I'm managing, kid." He took Josh's proffered hand. "For a reactionary bullshitter, a liar, a supporter of the white rich upper class, a traitor to my origins, of which I've been accused of being secretly ashamed, I'm not doin' too badly."

"Ah, Dad, cut it out." He put his hand gently on his father's forehead.

Jenny came on like a referee at a wrestling match. "Break it up, break it up, you two! This is a hospital, for God's sake!" She turned angrily and hugged Tammy Barnstone. "I bet it was *your* idea to bring him up here, right?" She said this in a voice so low that only Rachel and Tammy could hear. Tammy was silent for a long moment, then said softly, lying in her teeth for all their sakes, "No, I think Josh really *wanted* to come."

Jenny continued to hug her. "You're gonna be good for that kid of mine, *shiksa* or no *shiksa,* and that's no bullshit." She let her go, tenderly, reluctantly. "He needs someone like you." Turning back to Martin, for no good reason she leaned toward him and kissed him. Would she ever feel guiltless? This plague was the pits. A nurse peered into the room, watched them from the door for a moment, and left. Jenny said, "C'mon, everyone. That's the signal. Closing time. Let's give Marty a break. Get some rest, hon."

She tried to herd the others out, but instead of going, Josh bent and kissed his father on the lips, and Martin reached up and embraced his son. Tammy, a stranger to Martin, came to give him a cool, daughterly kiss. And Rachel, after kissing him goodnight, too, said, in her low contralto, "We're kissing cousins, at last, Martin." Surrounded by Americans, she could hear her own slightly Hebrew-accented English and wondered if that accent would become a problem for her in the Soviet Union.

Before Jenny could get to the door, the phone on the bedside table rang, and Jenny reached for it. "Danny? . . . Yes, we don't know. I happen to think it's something he ate, but I'll let you talk to him yourself." She handed Martin the phone. "Danny Roselli."

Martin listened to Danny, half sitting, his attention wandering. "Danny, listen. . . . Yes, well, you heard a rumor and it happens to be a true rumor. . . . Yes. I had planned to come in and tell you today, but I just never made it. I had to check in at this bloody hospital instead. . . . Yes, it's true. I've made a deal. Now, stop fretting, Dan. You'll be taken care of. You of all people. . . . Sure I know how far back we go! I've already talked to Art Michaels about it. You have to trust me, that's all. I'm sure Carter-Hale will want you to stay on. What would Singer's be without at least one Roselli? Danny, listen, why don't you come in and see me here tomorrow? Room six twelve. . . . *Sure* I'm well enough. . . . Well, of course I know how you must feel. See you tomorrow." He handed the phone back to Jenny, who put it on its cradle. The conversation seemed to have exhausted him.

"What was *that* all about, Marty?"

"I've sold the store. Now please don't *you* hassle me."

"You *what?*"

"To Carter-Hale. They're the right people for it."

"Jesus!" she hissed, barely above a whisper.

"It's the right time," Martin said faintly. "And we had to keep it confidential."

"From your *wife?* What a *guy!* I—I'm speechless!" But of course she wasn't. "So what'll you do yourself, Marty?" she cried. "The store! My God!"

Martin closed his eyes and lay back in silence. He did not answer and Jenny grew frantic.

"Listen, Marty, you can't *act* like this! You're behaving like someone who's getting *organized* to *die!* Now, listen to me! You're feeling better, aren't you?" He nodded, exhausted. "Right! Better! It's *nothing*, I tell you. Get it through your head! It's that lousy can of tuna you had for lunch; Clara keeps the stuff for so long, it just went bad. Aren't I always right? I got X-ray eyes, don't I? *You'll* see. After they've taken all their goddamn tests, it'll turn out to be nothing. Nothing! Now, listen, I'll be back later, Marty. I'll be sleeping right in the next room, you understand? Is there anything I can bring you?"

Martin closed his eyes, as if he were trying to concentrate on a single simple thought. "I'd like those letters," he said with some effort. "Whatever that Yeshiva kid's been able to get translated."

His speech was slow, a bit labored, a bit slurred. He seemed tired. It was probably the Percocet. Jenny tiptoed out and joined the others in the hall.

As they walked through the corridor, Rachel, turning toward Jenny, re-

alized her stately, striking American cousin was weeping in silence, like a child. Tears streamed down her lovely full cheeks. "Jesus, please, God," she muttered at the elevator, and Rachel reached up to put her arm about the younger woman, who seemed twice her size. "Oh, Rachel, he's a *nice* man," Jenny wailed. "And there are so many shits walking around healthy. How can *anyone* be *religious?*"

"Hey, Ma, you really think he's got it again?" Josh said. "Couldn't it be hepatitis? He looks jaundiced."

Jenny's tears kept rolling. "How the hell do *I* know? What's he doing in *this* hospital? God, how I hate this place! Sold the *store!* Jesus! His *life* he sold!"

"Ma, don't be such a pessimist. He's gonna be okay! And he'll find plenty to do. He was a slave to the bloody store. Let's go get a bite. How are you for Maxwell's Plum? I know the head *shamus* there."

Jenny nodded, sniffling. "Whatever you say, Joshie." She got almost enough comfort out of her son's new presence to shift her mood.

The youthful maître d' at Maxwell's Plum was a friend of Josh's from California, a guy he used to take diving off Catalina, and they hugged and kissed each other, and then the young man hugged Tammy, too, because Tammy had status, and even people with status were glad to get a hug from the maître d'. They got a table by the window while those still waiting grumbled. Two young girls came over to ask for Tammy's autograph.

Taking advantage of the privacy afforded by the crowded New York restaurant and to lighten the bleak mood of the moment, Rachel told them about her trip to Washington, how Dinitz had simply ignored her when she said she might be going to the Soviet Union. "He didn't think I was serious."

Jenny, still shaken by Martin's sudden setback, found the elderly Israeli woman's talk hard to bear. "For God's sake, Rachel, how *can* you go? You know they're not letting Israelis in."

"But on this occasion, Jenny, I plan to be an American, you see. For six marvelous days!"

"How can you? *You* don't have dual citizenship."

"Shh!" Rachel's mouth was fixed in a Mona Lisa smile. "Maybe you should go with your children," Rachel said. "Tammy and Josh're going—when did you say?"

"The date's set now," Tammy said. "February twenty-eighth."

"Oh, yes?" Rachel was immediately interested, and asked questions about their itinerary and who was going. She felt suddenly lucky. Her mind was filled with possibilities.

"You'll come with me, Jenny, then, won't you? If the children are going—"

"Jesus, I'd love to, but everything depends on Marty's condition, right? It's not exactly what I'd call *epess* at the moment. Would you?"

She stared at Rachel and spoke almost rudely. "I might just decide to go, but not if you're planning to do something crazy."

Rachel seemed not to hear. February twenty-eighth might be ideal for her. She had speeches to make, people to see, in the next few weeks. Long before then Martin's tests should be definitive, and maybe the news would be good. Maybe he wasn't as sick as Jenny feared. In any case, the formalities would take time. They'd have to apply right away for tourist visas and who knows, Martin might be recovered by then. So she'd apply for him, too. If when the time came, Martin wasn't well enough, Rachel went on, it was simple enough to cancel. Rachel would go to see Simiro, the Intourist representative in New York, tomorrow, and attend to it all, if Jenny would simply give her their passports. How were Tammy and Josh going?

Josh said they were flying to Helsinki, where Tammy would have a warm-up concert, staying only overnight. Then on to Kiev and Moscow. Rachel thought that was perfect. "We can all go on the same flight."

"If you can get tickets," Josh said. "We have sixteen of us going. I think we've got all the first-class seats."

Rachel laughed. "Israelis don't travel first class. However, maybe on this occasion we'll make an exception." She got the name and Los Angeles address of Tammy's manager, who had made all the arrangements, and said she'd consult him about the details when she went out there. Six days in the Soviet Union was perfect. While Tammy was giving her concerts, she and Jenny and Martin, if he was able, would be sightseers, nothing more. Typical Americans, taking advantage of détente.

They would avoid group tours. They could visit Moscow, Vilna, and Minsk—a somewhat different itinerary—and see their relatives, but they could go and come back together. "Naturally we will go deluxe class, Jenny. That will make us not only rich but also gullible. This is not difficult for them to believe. The KGB is sure American tourists are *all* gullible."

Joshua slapped his open palm on the table, rattling wineglasses, dishware, and silver, and eliciting stares. "All *right!* Ma, Rachel's pierced your veil! Gullible American number one! That's why I love my mama so! Listen, you guys, I wanna go to Minsk, too. Just a one-day side-trip. You don't mind do you, Tam? I'm *entitled.* This guy's my relative, too, isn't

he? Now, look me over, ladies. If you were the KGB, tell me, would I look dangerous?"

"Perfect!" Rachel cried. Her agile mind raced. This could work. "So we'll have youth *and* gullibility! Jenny, you *must* come. Tammy will sing while *we're* being gulled."

Rachel's amusement was tainted with fear. Here were three American innocents, none of whom had the slightest idea of what she intended to do. If she chose to, which she did not, she could safely tell them her plans right here, whereas in Israel they'd have to use a secret government office like Weisbrot's at the end of a dizzying maze of corridors, each person having been through two or three security checks and scrutinized on a closed-circuit television screen. A wild, open place, this America, while an equally wild paranoia gripped the soul of Israel. Tonight, for example, she knew that when she called, Golda would, first of all, be preoccupied with whether the line was secure.

By the time Fred returned to pick them up, Jenny had decided that if Rachel was going to Gramercy Park to call Minsk, she wanted to talk to their cousin in Minsk, too.

In Martin's library Rachel removed her overcoat, sat at Martin's desk as if it had been hers all her life, studied her watch, and said, "It's six-thirty tomorrow morning in Minsk. A rather awkward hour. It's five-thirty in Israel. So would you mind if I try Golda first?"

She spoke to the overseas operator, and her voice carried new authority: "Operator, I'd like to call Jerusalem in Israel. The number is 32141. It's a person-to-person call to Prime Minister Golda Meir. My name is Rachel Aron." She gave Martin's number and hung up.

The four sat expectantly for a few moments until the operator rang back. Rachel answered and lapsed into her natural Hebrew, her voice quickly rising to a half shout. "*Ken, ken!*" Sure enough, Golda was worried about the security of the line. "Don't worry. It's secure *enough*, Golda. Don't start with that, because what I'm going to tell you will be published in all the morning papers."

"Beautiful," Joshua sang out.

"Listen to me, Golda, everything will be delivered by the end of the month. Kissinger promised. Every item on the list, if they can possibly do it. I saw him myself. . . . *With* Dinitz, yes, of course. . . . Oh, I agree he's a nice young man but, as you say, he works for *America*. . . . No, not Dinitz—Henry!"

She talked for five minutes to the woman who headed her government. It was all gibberish to the Americans, but they heard her cheerful tone,

her encouraging, reassuring, "*Ken, ken, ken.*" And, finally, "*B'seder, Golda! Shalom, shalom. Laila tov.*" She hung up, turned to the others, and said, "It's five-thirty and the woman's already had breakfast. With such a woman, who needs men?"

Without pausing, she lifted the phone again and gave the overseas operator Yuri's number. "No, Operator, that's Minsk. M-i-n-s-k. You have to go through Moscow." While they waited for the operator to call back, she muttered, "Poor man, we may be waking him out of a sound sleep! *If he's able to sleep any more.*"

This time they had to wait fifteen minutes. Tammy and Josh held hands while Jenny tried to read the translation of the letters she would deliver to Martin later tonight, but she was unable to concentrate.

When the phone rang, Jenny and Rachel took separate extensions. They heard a sleepy, perplexed, high-pitched male voice saying, "*Da? Da?*" The voice asked uncertainly who was calling.

"You speak some English, Yuri Ivanovich?" Rachel asked, although she could have answered him in Russian.

Yuri was slow adjusting. "Vaht you vahnt?"

Rachel repeated the question. "Yes. I understand. So who is spicking?"

Rachel spoke carefully—more carefully, it turned out, than necessary. Yuri's English was not bad. "I am . . . your cousin . . . Rachel . . . calling from New York. We are thinking about you. I want to come to see you. I don't know if Martin Singer can come. . . . He is not feeling well. Sick. . . . Yes, I realize you are a doctor. . . . We don't know. . . . In the abdomen. I want you to talk to Martin's wife, Jenny Singer. You understand me, yes? Jenny Singer. Here she is."

"Yes! Yes!" The sound of a man desperate and afraid. And moved. His voice high, almost shrill.

Rachel motioned to Jenny to speak. Jenny's hand was unsteady.

"Yuri?" she shouted. "Are you all right?"

"Up to now. All right."

"We have been thinking of you. Rachel saw Mr. Kissinger today. . . . Yes! Kissinger, that's right. He promised to help. He will ask your authorities to let you go. I'm going to see American senators, Yuri, friends of ours." She talked slowly, trying to visualize the man she was talking to. "We are doing everything we can, Yuri."

Rachel spoke again. "Will you send us pictures of you and your wife and daughter?"

"Pictures? Vaht minns 'pictures'?"

"Photographs."

"Ah, photograph. Yes. Of course. My English is bad. No practice. Is early morning khirr. Vee yet slipping."

"We're doing everything we can," Jenny cried.

"Yes. Thank you. I send! Yes."

"You got the *vyzovs?*"

"Yes, yes! Thank you. Vee khov! Yes! Vee go now to OVIR. Vee make application."

Jenny, tensed by the effort of understanding the accented English and by the strain of talking so carefully, gave the conversation to Rachel with a sense of relief. Rachel talked to Yuri now in Russian, no doubt to Yuri's relief. She spoke quickly, decisively, like a general in a situation room. Her conversation was laced with the names of cities Jenny recognized: Minsk, Vilna, Moscow. Rachel paused to listen from time to time while Yuri spoke. The conversation lasted for almost ten minutes. To Jenny the call had elements of an awkwardly surreal dream.

9

AT THE HOSPITAL, Sam Rose looked in late in the evening to find Martin watching the midget Sony TV over his bed. Dick Cavett and Bill Buckley. Sam turned it off. A wave of depression swept over Martin, seeing Sam again. Was it to be instant replay? The cancer game? But Sam would have none of that. He wore his customary air of optimism, which always took a bit of doing when he came to Memorial.

In Martin's case, however, he was genuinely hopeful tonight. His avuncular manner was reinforced by his Lionel Barrymore-ish voice and face, his reassuring, gentle eyes. "I don't believe it's a recurrence, Marty," he said abruptly. "Everything we've seen so far, which of course isn't absolutely conclusive, tells me it's something entirely different. I may be going out on a limb, but if we were back in the days of diagnosis by hunch, I'd have to say gall bladder. Yep. Stones and all. Wait, you'll see. You have typical gall bladder symptoms. Trouble is, once you get into a place like this, with your history, you've got to take the full treatment. So don't panic, my boy. It's *not* what you're afraid of, and I'll bet on it. How're you feeling?"

Marty's Ike grin flashed for the first time in several days. "Better already. If only I could believe you, you goddamn professional optimist."

"Was I optimistic about your prostate?"

"No."

Sam had never tried to kid him, that was true. "This may be serious," was what he'd told Marty after that finger wave deep in the rectum. "I'd like you to see a surgeon." Well, this time he seemed positively cheerful; so maybe, just maybe, it wasn't the end of the world after all.

"You guys've got me so doped up I wouldn't feel pain if I had any, Sam. But I was in bad shape when I came in this morning."

Sam touched Martin's shoulder reassuringly. "What the hell is this I hear about Jenny's taking the room next door? That's so goddamn alarmist. And, if I may say so, ostentatious. Now, you're not going to die. So look, you want to take an old friend's advice? Tell her to sleep at home. Too much flair for dramatics, your Jenny. You know what a private room here costs?"

Martin laughed. "It's a lucky thing I sold the store today."

"You sold the *store*? Why'd you do that?"

"Ahh, tired, I guess. I made my own diagnosis, Sam, and it wasn't gall bladder. Also, I happen to be getting thirty-eight million in cash, so just in case it *is* gall bladder, I'll have a future."

"Martin, my boy! And they complain about the money doctors make! You ought to be ashamed! Now, listen, *you're not that sick*. Can you get that simple message through your thick head?"

While he would never have admitted it, Martin was feeling the first faint glow of elation by the time Sam left. Maybe he was going to live a while. It was a thought he'd have to get used to. He'd have to decide soon what he wanted to do to take the place of the store. Maybe he could accept Bok's offer to head the development committee of the Board. So many new buildings going up there. And maybe, just for the hell of it, he could also teach a course at the business school. Merchandising. A professor. Follow in his old man's footsteps.

What the devil was holding up Jenny? He had to share Sam's marvelous news. He also wanted to read those letters—more now than ever. Not because he was going to die, but maybe because he was going to live. He'd become intrigued by old Moishe the terrorist, bomb in hand. It *did* give him a different perspective about Josh. *You need some perspective, Martin.* Difficult to achieve, whether you're dropping bombs on Hamburg or having your son shit all over you.

He had wondered at the time why one of the members had suggested that he, of the entire Board of Overseers, meet with the committee of the Students for a Democratic Society on that spring day in 1969. He had only recently been elected, and the other overseers scarcely knew him. Now, of course, he thought he understood why, only too well. They were all so uptight over Vietnam. In that room you could feel the hate for every kid in the SDS. *Demands*, from *kids*? Of course, they never actually *said* it was Jewish kids who were in the vanguard, but hadn't these riots in the East started at Columbia? A Jew school in a Jew city? Led by a Jew kid? And after all we've done for *these* kids, giving them the Har-

vard seal of approval! *This* is the thanks we get! No one said anything of the kind aloud, of course, but the grim faces around the table said it only too eloquently.

He had known that Josh was somehow involved with the revolt movement, because he and Josh had had furious quarrels, which Jenny always broke up. It had never occurred to him, however, that Joshua was one of their *leaders*. The grandson of the great American lawgiver, a prince of the lawless! In the name of higher law! A Tom Paine? Hah! A hoodlum! But before the confrontation, the other members of the Board had been embarrassingly flattering to Martin. Yes, *he* was the one to deal with "these kids," the only one. He was so rational, so forthcoming, so full of goodwill and charm, so courteous. Yes, unanimously elected. The kids had asked for a meeting at Massachusetts Hall. Martin would speak for the Board. He'd been sucked in.

The president's office, which was not of enormous size, was jammed before the kids arrived, overseers and the five members of the corporation standing or sitting, a few leaning with their backs against windowsills. Finally, the kids were summoned and came swaggering in, six of them. They *looked* like hoodlums. Was this the cream of American youth? Young men with high IQs and seven or eight hundred SAT scores? Were these our future Ph.D.s, American scientists, economists, bankers, Nobel winners, senators, presidents? To begin with, the shock of seeing Josh among them set him back. What was the kid doing here? They stood there, slouching, hands in pockets, wearing plaid shirts or T-shirts, jeans or corduroys. One T-shirt said NO ROTC. NO EXPANSION.

Martin, in his custom-made tweed suit, vest, narrow lapels, the button-down collar, was in the uniform of *his* class, 1943. He greeted them gently. "Gentlemen," he said, "we've assembled here because we are anxious to hear your views. You have in this room all the members of the corporation, the president and fellows, and all the members of the Board of Overseers who could be present. You also have three deans, whom many of you know. You see, we make no bones about our concerns. We would all be appalled if the disgraceful episodes which have taken place at Columbia and on other campuses were to happen here. We've decided the only way to avoid that is to hear what *you* want, and try to work things out. We understand only too well your underlying concern. Many of us have sons of draft age. I have one, myself." He looked toward Josh, whose face remained impassive. "Some of us have misgivings about the war in Indochina. There's agonizing disagreement in this room, as I'm sure there is at the highest levels of our government. Men who were once Harvard students like you are in Washington today trying to end this war. They—

and we—are human, not divine. Well. We're ready to listen. At this moment you have the undivided attention of the Harvard Establishment."

Hardly had Martin finished than their leader, a round-shouldered, bearded boy with horn-rimmed glasses who said his name was Gordon, reached into the back pocket of his corduroys and pulled out a folded yellow paper, which he unfolded sullenly. Joshua kept his arms across his chest. The round-shouldered young man started to speak—in tones of insolent understatement. People held their breaths to be able to hear him. Josh stared at Martin as his leader spoke. "You want me to list all six of our demands or should we discuss them one by one?" The leader was Jewish, too, Martin decided.

Something bizarre, Martin thought—a Jewish elder and a Jewish youth, going at it before all these Wasps and Irishmen. *Goyim,* Grandfather Moses would have called them all. But the bearded kid—and Josh—were not concerned about that. They believed they had larger concerns. Had it not, Martin wondered, even entered their heads? They were Jewish troublemakers, couldn't they see it?

"Let's take 'em one at a time, then."

"'Kay. Number one: we want ROTC disaffiliated from Harvard College. Harvard shouldn't be training officers for an unjust war. ROTC is an arm of the very military-industrial complex that General Eisenhower warned against. No more ROTC. Beginning now. Today. Okay?"

"I understand how you feel," Martin said. Why wouldn't he, after all the battles he'd had with Josh? "But consider this, you men." He addressed them respectfully with sweet reasonableness, and thought he was making headway. After a brief lesson in civics ("Only Congress can end this war, Harvard can't"), he made his final point. "You fellows whose families can afford to pay your tuition, and you others who are so bright that you can get scholarships, have you thought about the men who are in neither category—but whose tuition is paid for by the government *because* they're willing to become reserve officers? They're not your rich, they're not your big brains. But they *are* worthy people. There are only about a hundred of them. Are you prepared to do them out of a Harvard education by abruptly terminating ROTC? Think about it. . . . Now, I've tried to give you a reasoned answer. I'd appreciate if it you'd do me the same courtesy."

Josh lowered his head and peered up at him as if at a dragon, and suddenly spoke, out of turn. "You have a son who's subject to the draft?"

"I have."

"Well, we're not worried about *us* being drafted, see? About your son being drafted. Every goddamn one of *us* can wriggle outa the draft. I

have a doctor all lined up. *You* lined him up, he'll give me any letter I need. He'll swear I've got ulcers, flat feet, cancer, whatever. *You* know who we're drafting. Not us. Black kids, poor kids, illiterate kids, and we're sending them out there to the boondocks in Vietnam to get killed for us rich smart guys, for Martin Singer and McGeorge Bundy and the Rostows, for Nate Pusey and David Rockefeller and Henry Kissinger, and the rest of you selfish heroic bastards. And who's elected to lead this dumb rabble out into the jungles to get their balls cut off by the Viet Cong? The fucking officers being trained right here in Cambridge, Massachusetts! We say *no! Hell, no!*" The other five now joined the show. "*Hell, no! We won't go!*" Martin was astonished that six voices could create such bedlam. Without pause, Josh continued, still shrill, "You've only heard demand number one, and all you've given us is *bullshit*. What we want to know is, yes or no?"

"Joshua—that's what you said your name was, didn't you?" Martin had no idea what made him engage in *that* charade, but he needed time to calm their voices and to put some distance between this kid and himself (for the benefit of the Wasps?).

"I never said, but, yeah, that's my name all right. Class of sixty-nine. Son of a Harvard man, grandson of a Harvard man. 'Kay?" His voice was imitative, mocking.

"Well, Josh, your eloquence is commendable, but let me say this," and he gave them his broadest Ike grin, "trying to keep within the bounds of the possible. 'Kay? We could give some thought to *phasing* ROTC out. Here's one formula we've been discussing, 'kay? We can let those who are enrolled finish up. We'd take on no new students for ROTC training beginning with the next freshman class. That way you don't hurt the hundred boys who are already in the program. It's orderly. It's reasonable. You make your point, which is essentially symbolic, isn't it? 'Kay?"

Suddenly Joshua was snarling, his words came like an animal bark, and they struck Martin as if his son had aimed a torpedo at him. "'Kay? It's not! We say BULLSHIT! BULLSHIT, BULLSHIT, BULLSHIT!" The other kids again filled the small room with a chorus of bullshits. "You know who the man is?" He turned to the other five boys, whose faces wore sneers, impassivity, or hideous mocking grins. "My own fuckin' father! And they put you up to it, right, Pop? You let 'em do it to you! 'Ho-ho-ho, LBJ, how many kids you kill today?' Phase out? Hell no! Cut bait, man! Pick up the phone and call your old fucking friend Bob McNamara and tell him, 'Bobby, boy, beginning tomorrow, *today*, Rotsee is out of Harvard. O-U-T!" A dull silence, and Gordon's gloomy echoing voice—

"It's nonnegotiable."

The older men stared in silence.

In the office of Harvard's president, before a Pusey, a Rockefeller, a Bundy, and a Saltonstall, Martin felt unmanned, his stomach pitched, he wanted to sink through the floor.

Josh talked on, words spiked with venom, but couched in a soft, gentle tone. "You gentlemen are all *for* this war, right? Please let me finish, now! Any war can be rationalized, and I've heard this one at the breakfast table. We have to stop these commies! We have to stop 'em everywhere, or they're gonna take away our store, right? That would be a re-e-e-el calamity! An institution as sacred as St. Patrick's, and right on the same avenue! And our house on Gramercy Park, a place that's truly obscene! Thirty-two rooms for a family of four with thirty million dollars worth of art! And the place in Kennebunkport, and the one in Palm Beach! That's what you're afraid of, gentlemen. Isn't that what you're *all* afraid of? Well, we the undergraduates of Harvard aren't having any. We call it BULLSHIT!"

He used that shouted word each time as if he'd invented it.

Abe Lincoln said it first: he was too old to cry, but it hurt too much to laugh. Martin was silent in his humiliation, in the presence of his peers. His son had turned him into a horse's ass. The Jew who failed.

The bearded boy, still mumbling, motioned to the other five, and they marched out in ragged single file. They could have been Viet Cong or followers of Che Guevara.

Martin looked about the room. Some of the men eyed him sympathetically, others contemptuously, but all were visibly angry. For a few moments Martin could not talk. Finally, with a superhuman effort at a smile, he said softly, "I'm sorry, gentlemen. I've let you down." And, too old or not, tears glistened in his eyes as he walked, numb, out of the president's office to seek the security of the Mercedes, in which Fred sat waiting for him on Massachusetts Avenue.

He had never since been able to talk about that humiliation rationally. Jenny never understood what the trouble was. So Joshie was a little fresh to his father. So what? Two weeks later the SDS "occupied" University Hall. Pusey sent for the cops and the bust followed. Heads were banged, students were arrested, and Joshua Singer was suspended from Harvard College three weeks before he was to receive his degree, summa cum laude. He already had his Phi Beta Kappa key, because he was one of the Junior Eight. And somehow, Martin, consigning his wounds to subconsciousness, had continued to serve on the Board and was re-elected by the

alumni who never heard about the episode and which was never mentioned again by any of the forty-odd men who had observed it. It was too goddamn painful even for *them* to talk about.

More than four years had gone by, and Martin, doing his best to rationalize forgiveness, began to think of Josh's action in political terms. Hadn't the boy had *his* constituency, after all? He had *his* act to perform. And it had been just as unfair of his followers to have seduced him into the position of one of the student spokesmen as it had been for the Board of Overseers to do so with Martin. They were both, he tried to tell himself, with new insight and with the need to rationalize and forgive, *victimized, used* by non-Jewish America. In a way he hoped that was it. He had not wanted to lose Josh for those years now gone. What good is the world, or thirty-eight million dollars, if you lose your own son? But tonight, by God, Joshua had bent and kissed him. On the lips, as grown men, even father and son, rarely kiss. Of course, Josh had the impression his father was dying, and there was still a possibility he was, but he had the kiss. He hoped he would live to savor it.

10

WHAT THE DEVIL WAS KEEPING JENNY? He dozed, but her footsteps in the hall wakened him. Visiting hours or no, that woman could get into any hospital at any time, or into Fort Knox or a Russian nuclear launching silo if she had to. She was carrying a manila envelope with the letters.

Jenny would not go home to sleep, even though Martin, trying to control a new sense of elation, told her all the encouraging things Sam had said. Martin hedged the news. Medical hunches weren't much. Only the machines would tell the story. Sam had been foolish to opine at all—it may even have been unethical these days—but he did it because a good friend needed reassurance.

Jenny, on the other hand, after a day of recurrent depression, was wildly elated. "See, Marty? What'd I tell you? You just aren't dying every time you get a little bellyache. Gall bladder! Jesus, what a relief! You know what you're turning into? A goddamn hypochondriac! Like your sweet mother, God bless her. Don't *get* like that, Marty!"

"Sam says you're to go home to sleep, Jen. There's no reason to take a room in the hospital."

"Oh, what does Sam know? Maybe I'll just crawl into bed with you right now and we can cuddle up. Christ, we can make love *some* kinda way, so why don't we do it here? Hey, wouldn't that be a riot? The nurse walks in and finds you kissing my you-know-what! On an inclined bed! The mind reels!"

Martin was always tickled by Jenny's dirty talk. Emasculated he was, castrated, but not by *her*. Never by his Jenny. What would he do without this woman? She made him feel more man than most men with balls. She was always telling him how *good* he was, even when his efforts at lovemaking were so clearly a failure it made her weep. She wept, he knew, for *him*.

She tossed the fat envelope with the translations at him, and took a

lightly scolding tone, as she so often did, kidding her own outrage. "So tell me something: how come you never mentioned you were selling the store? I'm hurt, I really am. Am I your wife, or some kinda glorified housekeeper and hostess with the mostest, who happens to work her ass off for Heller, Poor, and Black? What made you decide to do such a crazy wild thing? And not even discuss it with me?"

"It's my store, isn't it?" Martin said, in no shape to argue.

"You'll be home every day for *lunch!* Clara'll hit the ceiling!"

"Jenny, my dear love, one minute you go bawling down the hall, figuring I've got a couple of months to go; and at the first hint that I may not be in such bad shape you're all over me like a tiger! It's that shrink of yours!"

"Yeah? So tell me, my prince, let's talk about money. How much are we getting for the store?"

"Thirty-eight million."

Jenny sat in silence, trying to picture the amount. She saw bills stacked higher than the World Trade Center. Finally she said, "Christ, that's only half of Buick's ad budget for this year!" Then she stood and clasped her hands over her head like a fighter who has just knocked out an opponent, and began to laugh. "Jesus, Marty, what are we gonna *do* with all that *money?*"

"Who knows? We'll invest it, I guess. Should give us an income of two million a year, give or take a hundred thou."

"Oh, this is so crass, talking about *money* this way, Marty. But I like it, I like it, it's *nice.* Make me one promise, though?"

"Yeah?"

"Don't you dare give it to Harvard! And we're not buying any more art or brass or ivory or crockery or any of *that khozerei.* We got *enough* crap around the house!"

"Hey, Harvard's not a bad idea. I'm glad you suggested that."

"So help me Hannah, *I'll* kill you!"

"What's *your* idea?"

"Don't worry, I'll think of *somethin'!* You bet! Thirty-eight million! Leave it to me, bubbala. Hey, tell me, will they hear about it at Golden Oaks? The price and everything?"

"I'm afraid so. Carter-Hale's a public company, and they'll have to make a public announcement. It'll probably be in tomorrow's financial section of the *Times* and the *Wall Street Journal.*"

"Goody! I can hardly wait not to talk about it in polite society! Not only the most marvelous Russian-Jewish family in America, Marty—spirit, brains, heart, American tradition—but also as rich as—I dunno—the

Shah of Iran, maybe? Christ, what'll we tell Josh? He'll never talk to us again."

"Let me tell you something, Jenny, m'dear. I have a terrible, melancholy sense that Josh won't mind. Not any more. He kissed me tonight. You notice?"

"Whaddaya think made me bawl, you klutz? I was so . . . that girl Tammy is somethin'! You know, she's the first one I've ever liked. Thank God she's the one he married. Only don't tell Josh we like her, for God's sake. It'll ruin everything. Just play it cool, okay?"

"Do you mind if I read these letters now, Jen?" He tore open the manila envelope.

She would have to read them, too, she thought. She wouldn't think about going with Rachel to Russia just yet. Sufficient unto the hour. Maybe Marty *would* be able to come. The main thing now was to get him on the road to recovery, *alevai!*

"Go ahead and read, Marty me lad!" Martin took up the first page of the letters, relieved to have something he could give all his concentration to.

LETTER FROM MOISHE TO HIS UNCLE

Minsk, Northwestern Region
10 March 1883

Uncle Yankele!

"Practically twenty-two—old enough to be married," you wrote me. (I do keep all your letters on hand, you see!) I tell you the truth, I have not seen a girl in Jew Street who has made me *want* to get married. Most of them are so—so *fromm*. A few have mustaches, yet! Others weak eyes. The first girl I ever noticed was the girl upstairs, Freda Rubenstein, when she was fat and red-cheeked. She always seemed to know when everyone but *Zayde* and I were out. She used to come down to our cellar to torment me, sticking her tongue out at me, and one day I noticed she had begun to swell up at the chest. If I was studying, she would come down calling my name singsong. I would tell her to go away, and she would poke at me, scratch me, stick her tongue out, until in a frenzy I would get up and chase her around the courtyard, up the stairs, back down into the cellar, until I would catch her and throw her to the floor, both of us panting. I hated her. . . . So one time I kissed her to shut her up, and she screamed, "Oy, he *kissed* me! He's a *sinner* —*Zayde*, did you see that?" I never did *that* again.

But there is someone.

Our group in the Movement meets twice a week. We used to

meet in one of those *traktirs* at Railroad Terminal Square, but we noticed plainclothesmen listening, so now we gather in someone's home, each time at a different place. In our group there's a young woman, Natasha Perkovina, a year older than I and a friend of the Rosnikovs—Andrei asked her in—a convinced socialist, restless, with bright green eyes and a fierce spirit. Something is gnawing at her from within to make her bitter and sardonic. At first I kept my distance. Natasha wears her gold hair piled very high, polishes her nails, and wears tight dresses over a thin—some might say emaciated—body. She holds herself aloof, but at the same time makes no bones about despising both her parents, who, she tells us with disgust, openly take lovers as the mood seizes, because neither has anything better to do. They have never shown the slightest interest in her. Her deep hatred for them puts me to shame, because while I am furious at Papa I cannot quite hate him with the passion of a true revolutionary. You see, revolutionaries, too, have their weaknesses!

In our little cell of ten there is another, Ivan Tarkowsky, whom I may never have mentioned, a lisping French instructor, and for a while he seemed interested in Natasha. Oh, we all jockey among ourselves challenging (never openly) Alexei Andreyev, pretending to be equal in rank, and yet, aren't we human? Are we socialists or dabblers? Who can tell? Recently we decided to rob a small bank for funds. Our first "action." We fight endlessly among ourselves over this "action," often merely for the sake of seeing who can prevail. How shall the stolen funds be used? Who will be the cock of the walk for this night? On one occasion before the robbery, simply to get the upper hand over me, Feygele, and Abramele, "Professor" Ivan Tarkowsky, the above-mentioned French instructor, who manicures his nails, accused the Jews of lacking solidarity with the Russian masses. "*Your* brother," he railed at me and Feygele, his voice dripping malice, "I hear your brother ith planning on emigrating to Palethtine!" Is that a new low in dialectics?

Finally, for the sake of the robbery we put aside our petty arguments. Not that any of us had the slightest idea of how to go about such a mission! I therefore volunteered to plan the entire event. (Was this *my* supreme bid for power?) No sooner was it agreed that I was to plan everything than I was besieged with volunteers. Tarkowsky locates two revolvers of his father. Lyudmila Butonova wishes to carry the money. Abramele Shapiro, the short, strong, and craggy one, volunteers to drive the decoy getaway wagon and to procure a team of horses for this purpose. Andrei also wishes to act as a decoy. Boris and Feygele talk idly to the bank clerks, learn their procedures, the location of the safe where the money is kept. Natasha will appropriate her parents' troika for the main escape vehi-

cle, and also sews masks for each of us. Igor Petrovsky gets the dynamite and a detonator. Peter Rumiantsev gets the tools—a drill, an axe, and a hammer.

I take Smulka aside one day and ask him how difficult it would be to rob this bank. At heart he's a braggart. For *him*, he says, easier than taking a nap. For an amateur, impossible. With Smulka's help everything is carefully prepared for weeks in advance, and something new happens at our meetings—everyone is looking to *me*, because I seem to know what I am doing! (Why not? I have Smulka's daily advice!)

The robbery comes off! With almost split-second timing. A small bank, but a bank! Boris and Feygele, working in tandem, do a magnificent job of infiltration and detection, so that we know exactly where the money is and how much (9,200 rubles!). The pistols are effective threats, the masks fit, the drill, hammer, axe, and dynamite work perfectly on the safe, and almost before we know it, we all head toward Abramele's getaway cart together. A magnificent job! We hear the police arriving sooner than expected and Abramele's fat gray nags take off like racehorses. Lyudmila and Feygele, with the money, meanwhile move quietly into Natasha's troika around a corner with Natasha and me. The others, appearing to be bank customers, cry "Stop thief, stop him," and run after Abramele, who drives off like a madman, that thick hair of his flying, with the police in quick pursuit on horseback. Meanwhile, Natasha's three horses parade in stately fashion to Governor Street and into the traffic, with four of us and the 9,200 rubles, to Andrei's place. The amusing thing is that we are now the envy of gangs of thieves as far away as Odessa! Heros to revolutionaries, anarchists, and common gangsters! The police arrested Abramele. They found no money, of course. A crowd gathered, including many Jews. Abramele is no shrinking violet, so, standing on his toes, he denounced police tyranny to the crowd, his hypnotic eyes boring into them, his irregular features handsome in anger. Nevertheless, we hear from Boris he has been taken in and beaten to learn the names of his confederates. We are nervous.

Boris, of course, has spoken to his father, trying to get Abramele released. Andrei's father likewise has some influence—and Natasha says she will see some of her aristocratic friends who know the governor, as she does herself. She and I have worked closely together on the matter of Abramele's release. But that's not all. One thing leads to another.

Why deny it, Natasha has opened her spirit to me. For a long time I was simultaneously attracted and repelled by her person, for she seemed both inspired and conceited, and since she is not brilliant, her only cause for conceit could be her appearance and sta-

tion. She is cultured (possibly overcultured), a spoiled child, a carefully-brought-up aristocrat educated at the Marinska *Gymnasia* for certain elegant young women. She has been to all the proper balls and dances in Minsk, a life I scarcely knew existed until she described its terrible decadence and boredom to me—everyone wears white *gloves* at these functions so as to be sure not to *touch* each other, and says scarcely anything but what a wonderful event it is, what lovely music, etc., etc. She drinks wine at every meal and smokes cigarettes like a man. Originally I took these as signs of refinement, of nobility! At our group's meetings I noticed first how this noodle-waisted child took up my arguments, supported them with a certain quiet inner fierceness, with an authority to which she seemed completely accustomed.

She wears a perfume that makes me unstable, a little watery in the knees, you know? More refinement, yes? Her lips are reddened —just slightly—by something artificial and very sweet to taste. (Aha! How do I know?) She wears soft clothes which make her womanly qualities clear, but she is, as the French say, *très petite*, so there is always a childlike element to her, too. You didn't know I also learned French? It is the language of culture throughout Russia, Natasha says; she speaks it like a Frenchwoman. How disconcerting to realize that whereas I had felt all doors would open once I learned Russian, the real aristocracy considers Russian itself a language of boors.

When she asked me to accompany her to her home in Governor Street, I writhed. What would her parents say and do? I admitted nothing. The drawing room, which turned out to be larger than our entire courtyard, is filled with spectacular furnishings from France, paintings from Italy, draperies from Spain, and rugs from Persia. Alexei's father's place looks like a small annex to this palace. In one corner of the drawing room—really a ballroom—barely noticeable, is a huge mahogany grand piano. I had no idea what it was at first —I'd never seen such a large one. Her parents were nowhere to be seen, only a manservant in blue uniform who let us in. She asked me to make myself comfortable, gave me a glass of delicious wine, and when I asked if she could play this enormous musical instrument, with its glistening black and white teeth, she admitted she could, that in fact she had spent countless wasteful hours practicing the pianoforte since she was a child, and when I pleaded with her to play, she asked, how could I demand anything so frivolous of her? She had not touched the instrument since she gave her soul to the Movement. Well, what could I do? I demanded that she play for me. The Cause, I bellowed, does not exclude beauty. Beauty must be brought *into* the Movement. Meekly she sat, utterly erect, her neck like a swan's; she began to play with magic fingers, weav-

ing a wondrous sound! What acrobatic fingers! Chopin nocturnes, she said they were. I was more impressed with her dexterity than the music. Nevertheless, there I sat, the essence of decadence, my legs and arms dangling, the wine tingling in my blood, listening to the sound, an arousing sound, its effect on me no different from Freda's shrieks of laughter when I had chased her into the basement. I was under a spell. *This* was the higher life! If this life were mine would *I* be in the Movement? What was *she* doing robbing banks, plotting much darker deeds which I cannot reveal? Merely to liberate *me*?

Her parents, she murmured, were in Petersburg for a fortnight; they go there often; Minsk is too provincial for them. How could I tell anyone else of this, except you, Uncle, six thousand miles away, whom I will not have to face? Since I have trusted you with so much, I trust you with this also. Or do I have some inner need to tell *someone on our side*? Am I bragging? It's always a possibility. With everything at hand, why couldn't they even love each other? Why couldn't they ever think of *her*? She had been left to governesses, a ma'mselle, a *Fraulein*, tutors. She touched my arm and looked at me sadly, almost with a yearning, then as if distraught, picked up her father's riding crop which was on the table and tapped it impatiently into her open palm in great distress, as she continued to ramble on. I don't think she meant for me to reply to her, but I felt called upon. I answered as a man of the world, which I am not. I answered as a sophisticate, while I am of course entirely naïve in these matters. I was pompous. A poseur, I little realized the impression I was making. "Romance," I said, sententiously, "that is easily within reach, that is at home, between people of the same class like your parents, approved by their families, that can be satisfied like a common thirst or hunger, cannot be a romance of great sentiment or passion of the soul. . . ." I continued with this line of *dreck* until she gave a small high cry, the sudden meow of a cat, and without warning began to beat my face with her father's riding crop with all her might. The first unexpected whiplash struck me across the cheek like a bolt of lightning. And she kept striking. A high color filled her cheeks, her cat's-eyes blazed, she looked like a madwoman, and finally I put my hands up to protect my face, stung and burning, and then began, in spite of myself, of the intense pain, to laugh. I caught her hands, ripped the crop from her fingers, seized her by the shoulders, and began to shake her. As I did, I realized she was weeping, and so I drew her to me to offer comfort, although I was the one who smarted! We remained so for several moments, then I held her away briefly and tried to kiss her, but gently. I was not expecting the response I got.

One must draw the curtain here. We met! And what a meeting it was! There was neither refinement nor grossness about it—only intensity! I had never dreamed! This was the first serious experience for me, and absolutely the first of any kind for her, she said. I was awkward, she a bit less so, but during these two weeks, just as practice had made her dexterity at the piano a thing of beauty—and has made me a respectable sculptor—so did we perfect ourselves in the most vulgar yet delicate of arts. Nagging in the corner of my brain was the possibility that she was less of a neophyte than she claimed, but I did not mention it. However, on the third night she did a strange thing. She insisted we bring into her bedroom and hang the paintings of both her parents on two walls facing the bed. I am still shocked at her peculiar pleasure in this, especially as she insisted we keep the chandelier jets blazing just when one normally would extinguish them!

Now I have difficulty looking at her at our group meetings! Nevertheless, I wallow, Uncle. We missed one group meeting, but we tell ourselves the Revolution can wait, at least until Natasha's parents return from Petersburg. We laugh a great deal, mocking ourselves; she plays the piano; she tells me about the lives of Mozart and Bach and Chopin and Beethoven; we talk, often nonsense; she brings me strange, delicious things to eat; I order her about, and she bows and meekly obeys, calling me "Your Hebrew Majesty"—as if we were children. We also fight. We struggle, even physically. I spank her. She pouts. She runs her fingers through my beard. Is it the forbiddenness, the defiance, that pleases Natasha most? Why must I be so skeptical? Half mocking, for fear of letting myself go? Is that my nature? Her parents will never dare say anything to her about me, she says in her remote authoritative way, because if it comes to that, she has seen sights and can name names. As a child, she discovered her mother half undressed on a divan with her uncle—her father's own brother. Imagine! Her parents and their friends, by their behavior, she says, have driven her like whips to the Movement. Would *her* experiences have done that to *me*? I'd have joined the fun, I fear. Do I shock you, Uncle?

Natasha *envies* me my Jewishness, Uncle, something new. "*Your families!*" she says. "You have so much warmth, so much trust!" I hadn't noticed, but perhaps she is right. I certainly feel this between Mama and me, if not with anyone else.

Natasha's fearless soul is eager to possess *my* soul and, through me, the souls of all the suffering and the persecuted! At the same time I'm afraid she has a touch of treachery in her, and I do not dare trust her with my soul. So we belong to each other, but elusively, feeding each other's fantasies! Could we ever marry? How

bourgeois of me! Soon I intend to ask her about other men she has known. Doubts nag at me.

Your nephew,
Moishe

LETTER FROM MOISHE TO HIS UNCLE

Minsk, Northwestern Region
4 April 1883

Uncle Yankele!

As if my life were not sufficiently complicated, Papa last week—all smiles and a bit coy—comes home from the great *rebbe's* house after a two-day visit, and says he has invited for *shabbos* dinner our upstairs neighbor Reb Rubenstein and his wife, and, more important, their daughter Freda—the same, yes, the same: "You sinned!" Not the younger Rubenstein girl, you see, only the older one, Freda,—as if it were the most natural thing in the world. Mama doesn't have enough to do on *shabbos*; a family of seven to clean and sew for, prepare a *shabbos* dinner—chicken soup, *gefilte* fish, *cholent*, a *tsimmis* with *challa*, *schmaltz*, necks, gizzards, a noodle pudding, and strudel and jam—lighting her candles, saying her prayers, dressing in her finest, polishing her jewelry, ironing her best embroidered blouse. *That's* not enough, we also have to have in the neighbors? So I'm not supposed to wonder what's afoot? Freda, whom I've known all my life, is now a serious, determined girl, nothing of the old fatness or of the spiteful creature who once tormented and aroused me, but we've had little to do with each other, she and I; she and Herschel I see together a great deal, talking, reading together, Herschel looking at her in that special way. They are both interested in the Promised Land, Jerusalem, a place that for me has no reality and merely perpetuates the superstitions of our people. Now, however, she did not address herself to Herschel at all. But of course she is Herschel's. What is the problem? I am the eldest! Can you imagine? So I began to understand what was afoot. How could I be so stupid? How could Papa? Herschel is looking at Freda. Freda is looking at me. The time came for the Rubensteins to go. As they were leaving, Reb Rubenstein went out of his way to inquire if I would do *him* the honor next *shabbos* with Mama and Papa to come for supper. But no invitation for Herschel! This was no good. Herschel looked as if he had lost his best friend.

Saturday I couldn't, because I have to make the rounds of the synagogues, propagandizing the young ones, handing out leaflets. So first thing Sunday morning I went upstairs and asked Freda to come out with me. Jew Street was crowded with the usual beggars,

shoppers haggling with the rags-and-old-clothes-man, neighbors bringing in buckets of water from the pump, boys just out of *cheder* running this way and that, two of them shooting toy pistols left over from last *Purim,* a couple of younger Hassidim arguing cheerfully and exaggeratedly rolling their eyes away from Freda to avoid sin. We had to dodge to avoid the crowds—a regular *Simchas Torah,* it was so busy—and we reached finally the shops on Petropavlos, the bookstore of Reb Gruber—and, pretending to be looking over the books in Gruber's stall, we spoke.

She kept putting her fingertips in her mouth as she talked. Out of a blue sky she confessed that marrying me was *her* idea, not her father's! How do you like that? She liked Herschel, but she was drawn more to me! Well, it was not exactly *her,* but only someone *within* her. "Another," whom she could not quiet, something quite frightening to her, this "Other," who had been drawn to me since childhood—and *I,* except for a few childhood episodes, I could hardly remember saying ten words to her! The way she looked at me! I was completely unprepared. It was heady, but unlike our en- counter as children, she did not stir my desire at all. She said, "I'm not old-fashioned, Moishe. I hate my life here. But we could go to the Holy Land, the land of our fathers, where we would not suffer as we do here!"

This was a shock. I wondered if I should not bring her into our group, but I dismissed the idea. Three Jews were enough. Three women were enough. Instead I smiled at her unrealistic suggestion. "Freda, it's a desert there, a wasteland. There's nothing there to go to. Camels and nomads!"

She was crazy!

"We will not be in Minsk forever," she said quietly. "Why waste your time with those *goyim* railway workers and professors? It maybe gives you some thrill to talk of assassinations, robberies? For what? It will be hundreds of years before things here can change! Meanwhile we'll grow old and die! This is no place for us, Moishe!"

I was astonished. Freda had always seemed to me a girl who wanted only to be left in peace in the kitchen. "There are quite a few of us," I said quietly. "Soon there'll be thousands, then millions. And you, you want to run to the Holy Land, or to America, maybe?"

She turned the corners of her mouth down disapprovingly. "America? And live where the *goyim* can *still* burn my home down? You never heard of the Ku Klux Klan?" Total foolishness. America at least *I* could understand. *You* are there, Uncle. But she talked on, almost exultantly, as if lifted and sustained by some inner spirit, her eyes brilliant. "I am going to the Holy Land," she stated,

"where we belong. A few are there already." She told me more about her group of young people—some twenty. They meet twice or three times each week, to exchange books and pamphlets about life in the Holy Land, letters from those already there. People come to teach and train them. The French Baron, Rothschild, has been giving money for settlements. The land is empty, except for a few Arabs. "Come to our next meeting, Moishe! Tomorrow night! I'll take you. You can hear me make my first speech!"

"But, Freda, a holy land. Who's holy? I hate religion with all my strength!"

"Nu, what does that matter?" she said. "You're hard. You're tough in the soul. Like me. *With* religion, *without* religion, we're going to build a place where our Jewish children can grow up in peace. No more pogroms, no ghettos, no rocks thrown at us, no insults, a place where we will be the *only* ones, where we can be ourselves every day. Every minute."

If she had told me she wanted to go live on the moon I'd have believed her better. I was vaguely under the impression that the Holy Land had disappeared altogether, that it was a mythical place, like Hades or Olympus.

"Herschel comes to the meetings all the time," she continued. "He's enthusiastic, but I'm not sure about him—he's too soft and gentle. It's a hard place to live, the Holy Land. How would he manage?"

To put an end to what I knew to be foolish talk, I consented to go to her meeting. It was easier to do that than deal with the prospect of getting married to my brother's girl.

Next night I did go to her meeting, together with Herschel, who looked angrily at me throughout the meeting. They held it in one of those ramshackle, crooked, falling-down huts down by the river. I was afraid the roof would crash around our heads. Freda presented me to her comrades as if I were a jewel she had captured for their cause; several had heard of me. For my part, I found them an unprepossessing lot; short, ugly, wearing heavy glasses, intense, and doctrinaire. What a doctrine—built on sands and swamps. The evening was spent arguing violently how much they should depend on financial support from home (the children run around with tin cans asking every Jew they meet to "support the colonies in the Holy Land") and how much they should be self-sufficient once they arrive. The evening confirmed everything I feared for them. A sorry-looking band of amateur adventurers.

I excused myself long before the meeting was to disband. Freda looked at me, heartbroken. Tears were in her eyes. "You *must* leave, Moishe?"

"Yes. Herschel will see you home."

She lowered her head. There was no other way. I had a duty to think of Herschel, and my soul thought of Natasha. The break had to be clear, clean, and public. I left.

The following week, I went with Mama and Papa to have supper at the Rubensteins. Open defiance of Papa is not my strong point. All but one member of the Rubenstein family acted as if my presence made it a holy day, but the younger sister, Sheyna Rasel, a twelve-year-old, even plumper and sturdier than Freda had been at the same age, turned out to be a thorny little rose, not a beautiful rose as her name says. Yes, Sheyna Rasel spilled her chicken soup, tore her dress (deliberately, if you ask me), and marched in anger from the table, giving me a look—I can't describe it. Terrible manners. Hate and love together, as if I had committed treachery. I won't forget that cold, accusing stare. From a child! Later they forced her to come back to the table, but she sulked and otherwise misbehaved all evening, casting darts at me with her black eyes. Did she think I was treating her sister shabbily? Or what? Before supper was over I asked Freda to come outside with me. In the courtyard I took both her hands, as if to hold her attention better. I said I was not ready to marry anyone. Moishe Singer was not what he seemed; he was a strange one, *also* possessed by someone within him, a quite obstinate Other, with many unpleasant facts about him, and under no circumstances was I going to any Holy Land. Would she please go tell her father she had changed her mind? "Herschel!" I said. "Why not Herschel? Perhaps he *would* go with you. You underrate Herschel." He was not so soft as he seemed. (I lied, telling her this, but I wanted to destroy any lingering hope of me.) She listened, and stood a long time, no longer shivering; she withdrew her hands from mine, and I saw her set her jaw firmly. Again she bit her nails, which were down to the skin by now anyway. Both she and her little sister have this nervous habit. For a time she seemed unable to speak, but when she could, she said, "What's the hurry? A man who can carve things of beauty, who is himself beautiful inside and out, is a whole man. We *will* go to the Holy Land together. We will make a life. So when you are ready, you'll say. My Other One advises me she will be patient." How do you like that?

I seized her cold hands again, both of them, rudely, and raised my voice in anger. "Don't wait for anything!" I shouted. "Enough nonsense about your Other. You'll only waste yourself! Have a good look at Herschel! See how he longs for you. How can you be so cruel? I *don't* long for you! There is someone else I long for! You understand?" And tugged her roughly back upstairs along the bal-

cony to her house, not looking at her. I can't stand to see a girl crying. If they want to go to Palestine, so let them!

A kiss through my now-flourishing whiskers for little Lewis.

Your nephew,
Moishe

LETTER FROM MOISHE TO HIS FAMILY IN ATLANTA

Minsk, Northwest Region
14 November 1883

Uncle Yankele, Aunt Sadie, Uncle Efram, and my brand new Aunt
Fanny!

Mazel tov to the newlyweds! May you both be happy forever—
Aunt Fanny, you are beautiful in the picture. You know how lucky
you are to have Uncle Efram for a husband? Within a hair he was
of becoming a Cossack for the Tsar—did he ever tell you that?
They were ready to put a horse under him, hand him a whip, and
have him gallop up Jew Street and smash everyone in sight!

As you know, Uncle Yankele, my friend Boris Karpovich has
long been with us in the Movement. I have also become friendlier
than before with his father. The old man used to be a mere inspector, but now! He was just appointed *chief* inspector for not merely
Jew Street but the entire Lower Market, forty thousand souls, and
ten thousand tons of mud, including Komarovka Square and all the
mosquitos in it. For what reason he takes to me I can't imagine, but
we continue to be fast friends. His treachery, however, would never
surprise me. He continues to ask all kinds of questions about my
family, about you, my American relatives, our *gutte Yiden*, the *tzaddik*, the rabbis, the Hassidim, our customs, traditions, etc. He knows
nothing about my work in the Movement, although he claims to be
a devoted student of political matters! I am likewise curious about
him, and so we have long talks about the deadening hand of the
civil service, how best to climb the ladder to bureaucratic success,
and his old-age pension. He's curious about Jewish life, he says, for
professional reasons: the more he knows, the better he'll be able to
manage the area, and thus he will be in line for further promotions.
I am to be his tutor. He's astonished, for instance, that *any* Jews are
thieves. If they are so holy, if they cherish family life, he asks, why
do they steal? If they have such a strong community life, from
where come Jewish whores? What are the rabbis and wise men
doing while this is going on? I explain that we have our *grubbe
Yiden*; like other people, we're all types. I should really introduce
him to Smulka to give him the real lowdown on our criminal life.
Well, if the thieves are *smart*, he tells me with a wink, they'll go
outside his sector to do their dirty work, to the Upper Market, to

Governor Street, to Priobrazhenskaya, to Zaharovskaya, where the banks are. Why steal from the poor if you can steal from the rich? It makes sense. And it would make *his* work easier, which is all *he* cares about. *Zhids*, he says, have to be crazy to steal from each other. I pass his word along to whom it may concern, and have been thanked by the *gonovim* (the same old bunch, Uncle), who never dreamed they would be invited by a chief inspector to go on to richer pastures. They have never done so well as now, climbing into the second stories of the homes of merchants and aristocrats in the Upper Market. They owe it all to me, they admit it. (I have come to really *know* many of Smulka's buddies, since the bank. In fact, Smulka has promised me to spring Abramele from the jug. How, he hasn't said.) As for Inspector Sergei Karpovich, what thieves do in other parts of the city, does he care? The chief inspector in the Upper Market is his rival for promotion, and he is looking worse and worse, and this delights my friend. Through me he has exported crime from Jew Street to the *goyim* and given his career a boost. He keeps showing me the statistics, also to his supervisor. Meanwhile the fancy bourgeoisie and the aristocrats are close to hysteria. Sergei is my ever-grateful friend. To seal it further I carved him a fat little monkey. It resembles him, but I didn't point this out. If there is ever anything I need, he says to me, winking his slitted eye, just ask, my boy. If he knew about *my* activities! Or his son's! Maybe *he* can help us get Abramele out of the clink. But how to approach him?

Well, when Papa learns how thick I am with Inspector Sergei Karpovich, that I have even been to his home and eaten his *treyf* food, that the inspector has taken a gift from me and a fancy to me, his tongue begins to wag to his old buddies.

It's not long before such talk has astonishing consequences. A delegation of rebs comes to call on me one evening, as I finish sanding a dressing table. Reb Horowitz, the *nogid* of Minsk, gray whiskers almost to his knees, comes leading the pack; in single file follow Mordecai Kogen, the weight-uplifter muscle-nut, then Schmulkowitz the holy man in his fanciest robes, Reb Rubenstein, my almost-father-in-law, Rabbi Levitzsky himself, and Meyrovitz, a Hassid convert like Papa—at Schmulkowitz's, they say, after a couple of *l'chaims*, Meyrovitz and Kogen do a brilliant toe dance, holding their delicate hands out, fingertips high as they twirl, singing and approaching the Almighty on tiptoe! I'm overwhelmed—traditionalists and Hassidim, together in the same room! What can it mean? They haven't come to see Papa, they've come to see *me!* Papa squats, humming, hammering tacks, moaning about the ache in his back, but exquisitely satisfied. Little Isaac is polishing a new

table, Herschel is planing. The *altes* have arrived just as I am preparing to leave for our weekly meeting; I can't wait to see Natasha again. Instead I have to go back into the house; Mama *must* heat up five glasses of tea while Reb Horowitz begins intoning his business. What a long-winded *kocher!* The others are not slouches either, each embellishing and re-embellishing. They ask questions. Exactly *how* friendly am I also with *Gospodin* Dr. Andrei Feodorovich Rosnikov? Do I realize he is the doctor for the Minsk army-induction center? How did I come to be acquainted with Chief Inspector Sergei Nicholayevich Karpovich? I tell them I'm in a rush (I really am!), and they are filled with delight. What if I'd mentioned my *very personal* friendship with the female aristocrat, Natasha Perkovina, an acquaintance of the governor himself? And how intimate am I with her? Fits of delirium, I guarantee. But I didn't.

To be brief, the result is this: because of my unique relationship with so many influential *goyim* (two), because of some mystique they sense in me, I am this night being formally inducted as the recognized connection between Minsk officialdom and all the *Yiden* of Jew Street, from the Svisloch to Komarovka Square, from Ratamsk Street to Saslaki, including all the alleys, containing perhaps fourteen thousand souls (there had already been a secret meeting and a vote!). At my tender age! Unprecedented! Reb Horowitz, who until now has performed this selfless and dangerous function (I could barely *imagine* his having a rational discussion with Inspector Karpovich), hereby relinquishes the scepter to my sturdy hands. New faces are necessary, he says, especially since last year's May laws, which make life for Jews a more ticklish proposition than ever. I am in a terrible hurry to get to my meeting. Yes, I say, with impatience. Thank you, I say, for the honor. (I haven't the faintest idea what obligations the honor imposes on me!) I am late. I hold out my hand and cry, *"Gospoda!"*—"Gentlemen!"

Horowitz chortles, "You see, he is more Russian than a Russian!" And he kisses me on the mouth with his whisker-covered face, one eye closed tightly. That is an experience I hope never to have again. "You'll get Abramele Shapiro released!" Reb Schmulkowitz thunders. "Save Reb Shapiro's Abramele!"

"Gentlemen, I'll do my best. I *must* go! Please excuse me." But they *hold* me, leathery hands gripping me like talons. And Reb Horowitz, between wheezes and coughs and winks, interrupted and prompted by the others, embarks on a lesson. I listen. I'm trying to understand why they've selected me. Is it because I can humanize us to the others, who see us as antihuman, as we see them? While all the time we are—alike? Is it because I am *them?*

11

MARTIN WONDERED, as he set the letter aside, exactly what *were* the qualities that made one person a representative of Jew Street and excluded others. Whatever it was, he, too, was carrying on in Moishe's path, a family tradition of sorts. And so had Father—on the Court, at Harvard. There were simply different ways of doing it.

Horowitz, acting the schoolmaster, describes to me the approved technique for dealing with officials—one of the techniques handed down from generation to generation. This was the method, he says, employed to get me into the government school when I was eleven years old, and he points to himself mischievously as the man who did it. He looks over to Papa! Papa nods in confirmation Yes! For me, this revelation is a thunderclap! I am so stunned my legs suddenly feel a bit unsteady, and I *sit* and *listen*. So I hadn't done it on my own? It wasn't my Solomonlike examination? The schoolmaster who told me I had done brilliantly was a liar? Brilliant, schmilliant! Brilliant boys fail all the time. No, no, Reb Horowitz had pulled strings! He was neither bragging nor seeking thanks, merely stating the fact. I was trying with new respect to see this ugly bearded savior who asked no acknowledgment from me—who hurried on, ignoring his own respiratory infirmity. There is a right way and a wrong. Ritual, traditional on both sides, absolutely rigid; rites to be ignored at the peril of the entire Jewish community. At times lives would be at stake. I was all attention. Power. New power. Within my grasp. Number one: meet the official in question—a headmaster, a police inspector, a judge—at exactly eight o'clock or exactly some other prescribed, agreed-upon time, in a private dining room of a small, little-used inn or restaurant. Usually one near the railway station.

Share *schnapps*, a bite of food, talk of this and that. Then explain what is needed by our people. So-and-so, for instance, wishes to become a doctor and go to medical school; the people badly need, for instance, a doctor, since there is much disease. "Abramele?" I asked. They shrugged. "How else?" And Reb Schmulkowitz, reminded, instantly set up a new wailing for my friend languishing in the clink. The others joined him like a Greek chorus. Or so-and-so wishes not to have to go into the army, as he is the sole support of his aged parents and nine brothers and sisters. Or so-and-so, caught stealing, is not really a bad boy, but nevertheless will be severely beaten by his own parents, who beg that he not be put away. Or if there were to be, God forbid, a threatened pogrom: Does Your Grace think Jew Street could be spared? The police could always direct the rioters somewhere else. The official, friendly but always correct, responds that the request can under no circumstances be granted. Out of the question. Others are involved, higher up. Petersburg is invoked. At this point one is expected to press the bribe—money never folded carefully, but crumpled like trash—as if recklessly, impetuously, into the official's hands, expressing the hope that some way can be found. The official may simply take the money, or he may withdraw from it as from a bouquet of poison ivy, pretending astonishment, affronted that an old friend could think him capable of such venality. He, a man of honor! When this happens, it is necessary to use mock force, to rise and, putting one's friendly arm firmly around the official's shoulder, to engage in a mock wrestling match, during which the official, seeming to be breathing heavily, is to be pressed against a wall, or backward against a table, always a remarkably feeble opponent. When the official is thus held helpless, the crumpled bribe is quickly stuffed into the official's tunic, while he continues to grunt that nothing, absolutely nothing can be done, and the Jew's effrontery will be no help! The Jew is presuming to trade on an old friendship! If the money is offered back, withdraw in horror. Say, "It's not meant for you! Use it where it will do the most good!" Depart promptly, leaving the official panting there *with* the money. He will know there are more crushed rubles where these came from. A few days later, he explains that it is not for him—*none* of it is for him—but there are *others*, *much* higher up. He will make the approximate or even the exact price clear, cursing those who are greedy enough to exploit helpless people. And after he gets *that* money there is perhaps one chance in five, but always a chance, something will be done.

I listened to Reb Horowitz's lesson as carefully as I could under the circumstances, wondering how I could apply it to Abramele. Heady with my new political power, to be utilized only in secret, I

thanked the rebs for the honor, and rushed off to my meeting to discuss how to overthrow, and perhaps kill, all of the officials I had just been instructed to corrupt, as well as the corrupters themselves. At the meeting I did not reveal to my comrades-in-arms my new role in Jew Street. Why should I? Our subject was religion as the opiate of the masses. We agreed to redouble our efforts to proselytize at the doors of the churches and synagogues and among the workers. We agreed that as soon as the Revolution succeeds, formal religion is to be outlawed, and the practice of it shall be punishable by death. These false, man-invented gods, are the idols which keep hundreds of millions in the chains of ignorance and superstition. Uncles: "There is no other god before *men*" is the only correct First Commandment for men. We must learn to support *each other*. Our world must be cleansed of the curse of this opium, these myths, the burden of the ages.

Your nephew,
Moishe

LETTER FROM MOISHE TO HIS UNCLE

Minsk, Northwestern Region
1 December 1883

Uncle Yankele:

Almost nine months since the bank, and Abramele still locked up! I am beside myself! Boris can't do anything with his father. Neither can Alexei. Natasha's friends at the governor's mansion have been useless. Smulka asks for more time, grinning impishly.

I have been to one official after another and everyone keeps saying, "Yes, yes, don't worry, as soon as the investigation is over, he'll be released." I've hired a *goy* lawyer, given him over fifty rubles! Reb Shapiro, Abramele's father, keeps stumbling over to me despite his customary vodka poisoning, wailing in my face, "His mother you'll send to the grave! He'll fall behind in his work, he'll be thrown out of the medical school. His life will be a nothing. And where will be our old age? You're a *macher* now? So *do* something."

Little does he suspect I have my own reasons for wanting Abramele out. If they should ever break Abram's spirit and he named names! Nerve-wracking. All right, my lawyer said, there's a certain Judge Pazhnev, his honor, Feodor Pazhnev, the only one who has the authority to dismiss the charge. Supposed to be the meanest living thing left in Minsk, a bigger anti-Semite than Haman. His wife is worse, fatter than he, uglier than a witch, and has a glass eye. Our luck, *he's* the one who must sign the paper. It's reported that he also smells terrible because he has stomach trouble

and cannot control his gas. But I'm a man of affairs, entrusted with the community's welfare—it's up to me, right? I can't pick my judges or go running to the rabbis! I made inquiries, and to my surprise (and not *such* a surprise!) I discovered from Sarah the Salt-seller, who do you think is one of her regular visitors? (He'll take either jewel; he's not discriminating, although he prefers Stephanie to Anka.) I interview Stephanie, and what she tells me could turn a priest's ears to hot peppers. I did some hard thinking. If I am responsible for Jew Street and in addition my comrades and I in the Movement are in great danger, I have to spring Abramele. Enough's enough. My ruminations did not make me happy, for all I could see was the *only* way. And the more certain I became, the more miserable I grew.

I screwed up my courage and took my sweet Natasha to a *traktir* for coffee. I passed on to her reports I had from Boris about Abramele's ordeal. Boris heard it from his father, who would, however, do nothing to stop the questioning (and the beatings). The old man is such a policeman in his heart he still has some curiosity to know who robbed the bank! Even though it's not in his area! Strange! So we are back to Judge Pazhnev. And the only safe, sure path to the judge's judgment is through his hyperactive loins. With that wife, what else? Natasha said she had met the good judge and the wife, too. "I remember the old goat flirted with me once at a dance. He wears a false hairpiece, you know." I kept going into details about Abramele, embellishing. The lash, smashed fingernails, and so on.

I was glad to see Natasha was getting upset, trembling with rage and compassion. I reminded her it was not only a matter of compassion. If they broke Abramele's resistance, she and I would be in big trouble. More lashes, smashed fingernails, etc., only this time *ours*. While she was reacting to that, I had a drink of vodka, because I did not like what I was doing. Sarah the Salt-seller's girls came next in my discourse. I had to be frank. I spoke in my most clinical fashion, describing some, leaving the rest of Stephanie's "specialties" to her imagination. Pazhnev's weakness must become our strength. He gives Stephanie expensive gifts on the side, perfumes and silks as tips, beside the regular fee. Other customers don't give such gifts. Stephanie, God knows, must be over thirty! "Ah," said Natasha, immediately seeing my point. "We must go at once to this prostitute, this Stephanie, and employ her to secure Abramele's release. How clever of you! I shall talk to her myself!"

I joined in her enthusiasm for a little while, to let her think this is what I had in mind. We drank and talked, but suddenly, I fell silent, unresponsive to her chatter.

"What's the matter, Moishe? Losing your nerve?"

"We must be extremely cautious," I said. "Stephanie isn't the most reliable person in the world. A whore with a whore's honor, after all, is always for sale. How can we dare put ourselves in the hands of a whore? *Our* judge is sure to say 'Stephanie, what's Shapiro to you?' And she'll say, 'He's nothing to me, Your Honor, tee hee, but Natasha Perkovina, he must be something or other to *her!* Because she asked me'—etc. Then we are really in the fire."

Natasha considered my point for several moments. "Abram's parents could talk to the prostitute," she said absently, without believing her own suggestion, playing for time. Her mind was working furiously in another direction, the direction I wanted it to go, and hated it to go.

I laughed. "His father's too drunk and his mother wouldn't talk to anyone like Stephanie to save her entire family." Natasha continued to ponder the vexatious problem, biting her lip. I allowed her obsession to work its gruesome way.

"Never fear, my darling. I'll find *someone* reliable. Leave it to me," she said.

"What do you mean?" Oh, how I hated myself!

"Please." I took her hand, protesting, held her tenderly. "Don't be reckless, Natasha. Protect yourself." And added quickly, "Protect us all."

She smiled, steel and silk lace. "Leave it to me." Then abruptly, businesslike, "Tell me, why would any woman, even a prostitute, love our funny little Abram? You know him so much better than I. . . . Stephanie . . . or anyone I choose . . . she must be convincing."

I said, "He *enjoys* helping people. He'll make a marvelous doctor. A guy with a heart. He has emotions—bigger than lifesize. Generous—he'll give you anything he has if you say you like it. If he were less of a shrimp, women would be buzzing like bees buzz lilacs. I'm surprised more don't anyway."

Natasha was looking into the distance. "Helping him will be a challenge." I felt a chill; perhaps she intended me to. She was suddenly unreachable, and a thought crossed my mind: my love may *be* a madwoman.

"Anything for *Narodnaya Volya,* Your Hebrew Majesty." She spoke remotely. We separated, I with a heavy heart but much relief. I suffered for many nights.

Abramele was suddenly freed by order of the Court last week! Judge Pazhnev's signature was on the document. All in proper form. My suffering was worse. Natasha refuses to tell me anything. But at the last meeting of the group, after she had shaken hands

with Abramele, she leaned down to embrace him impulsively, in spite of his slightly repulsive appearance, and murmured, "The things I do for the Movement. My God."

There is something new about her—her mouth looks almost like a scar, somewhat askew and smeared. She has a wild, catlike look these days, closed, ready to resist, as if she has been almost mortally injured—internally—in some unmentionable way. She remains silent at our meetings. Still, I am touched with a kind of madness for her, too. What has she done? What have I done?

Your nephew,
Moishe

LETTER FROM MOISHE (NOW "MOSES") TO HIS ATLANTA RELATIVES
New York
1 February 1888

Uncle Yakov and my whole American Family!

A surprise that I am writing you from New York in America, no? You are not hearing from a man with any joy in his heart.

What started this long chain of happenings for me? Perhaps if I write everything from the beginning I can get the *golem* out of my system. Nu, I'll try! . . .

The translation ended abruptly. Grumpily, Martin turned on the television, asked for his medication, and a late late movie put him to sleep.

12

Despite what Sam had urged, Jenny insisted on sleeping at the hospital for the next few days. She went to her office for most of the working day, dreaming up and discarding slogans, supervising layouts, shooting commercials; she had her hour with Adelsheim, but ordered dinner with Martin and spent her evenings with him in the hospital, and after the eleven o'clock news, went to bed in the next room.

One by one, reports on Martin's tests came back negative. At the end of the week what they could tell him with medical certainty was that he had a few minor arthritic spurs, worn discs he could live with, and a very bad gall bladder indeed, chock-full of stones, and these and his gall bladder itself would have to come out. But that was it—all things feared were eliminated. It would be relatively minor surgery, unconnected with his cancer two years ago; there was no recurrence. None at all. Exactly as Sam had predicted.

"Okay?" Jenny cried triumphantly. *"We're through with that!* You worry me to death, all that gloom, Marty. I got enough trouble with the Demonde account."

While Jenny was at work during that week, Martin did not lack company. When he was not out of his room having tests, he was besieged by visitors. Myra Verrett came every day to make sure there was nothing he wanted and that he was not overtaxed. As Art Michaels worked on the sales agreement with Carter-Hale, Myra would go down to Paul, Weiss for the drafts and bring them to the hospital for Martin's light reading; he made notes, calling Art from time to time, half sitting in his electric bed, to go over ambiguous passages. Art was impressed at how sharp he was. Dan Roselli and Mike Shapiro, who had been with the store since Uncle Nate's day, and other store people came to be reassured by Martin about

their jobs under Carter-Hale management. The Loebmans visited faithfully every day; so did Jean Kahane, the Gottliebs, and the Goldens. Even Elmer Lehrman showed up twice during the week, and Graham Butler took time out from dalliance to visit or call each afternoon. Martin decided that because of the hospital he was in they all probably thought he was dying. Joke on them. By the end of the week, the room was overflowing with flowers, books, candy, and especially vodka, of which there were two cases, all Stolichnaya, and half a dozen bottles of sweet liqueurs. Everyone knew Martin's tuneless characterless ditty which, after two vermouthless Martinis, he took to rendering at the club: "Vodka is good for you, vodka is dandy; don't give the gin to me, and don't give me brandy; Stolichnaya—hey!" And, indeed, daytime vodka and liqueurs late at night sustained him in the hospital when his mood sagged. Better than Demerol, they made cancer and even an infected gall bladder seem remote, and life very good indeed.

One person who attended him regularly, as if he were still a child, was his mother. Sometimes she came in a wheelchair, sometimes on the arm of Bertha, her "companion." She sympathized with Martin's aches and pains and did everything but rock him in her arms. Nice old broad.

On her last visit, before he was operated on, she wanted to talk about the relative who had surfaced in Minsk; Martin wondered whether he ought to take Jenny to Russia to see the guy and his family. But Deborah Singer took a firm, motherly line laced with her Sephardic heritage. "In the first place, I do not trust Russian Jews," she said. "They are liars and lazy and they play on one's natural emotions—your father, bless him, being the exception. So stay right where you are, Martin. You're in no condition, do you hear? I'm your mother and I can tell. What on earth can you do for him in the final analysis? Do you plan to visit Mr. Kosygin and lay down the law to him? You *hated* the Soviet Union when you visited, didn't you? You were a nonperson there. You yourself said even in China they treated you with greater respect. So why torture yourself? If you want to help this man, do it through normal political channels. That's where your strength lies. After all, we know so many people!"

"The way Dad helped the Jews during the Holocaust, Mother?"

"That's terribly unfair, Martin. He did what he could. Mr. Roosevelt simply couldn't—"

"Well, Jenny wants to go even if I don't."

"I don't think you should let her," his mother said. "Women going halfway around the world alone!"

Josh and Tammy visited regularly, too, together and on occasion sepa-

rately. Josh told his father about the film he was making, about the pattern of the gray whale migration south from the polar regions near Alaska in December to Scammon's Lagoon off Baja California, describing how their young were born and nourished briefly by their mothers in tropical waters and how, in March and April, they headed north—an army of whales, pod upon pod, mothers, fathers, children, in their great annual pilgrimage. "No one has the faintest idea how they *know* to come, or *why* they want their children born in the same place where they were born, but they *do*." Martin wondered whether it was the same impulse that brought the Jews, like a tide, back to Israel. Josh went on breathlessly, telling Martin more about whales than Martin really cared to know, but he was glad to be hearing it, glad to sense the enthusiasm beneath the words, glad that Josh was finding *something*, and he feigned fascination. The toughest part of the movie project, Josh admitted sheepishly toward the end of his exposition, had been raising the money for it. He'd had to become an expert on the motion picture as a tax shelter, and he'd never realized how important taxes were in raising capital. "We needed a million bucks, and I found myself dealing not with the people who had the money, but with their accountants and lawyers! We did it, but it took six months of sweat. I had to be a producer, a broker, and a tax wizard. Boy, how I could have used Manny Loebman! That's when I *really* took up smoking pot."

Martin turned in his bed and said mildly, "You could have mentioned it to *me*, Josh, you know. And saved all that bother."

"Ah, Dad! My ego, my ego! Jesus, how can you talk that way?" Jenny all over. Or was it something more fundamental? He, Martin, had bailed out of a B-17 and lived to tell it. Maybe that one thing was what did it for *him*.

Martin changed his tone. "Well, damnit, I think it's goddamn marvelous you were able to do it *without* help. Marvelous, I mean it. No previous professional experience at any of it and absolutely no help from your family, which any other young man would've screamed for. I'm full of admiration for you. Proud of you. And that's no bullshit. I believe you can do anything you want, Josh, do *you* know that?"

"You think so, Dad?" He was remembering, too.

"You're damn right I do."

"No, you're not a bullshitter. Dad, I want you to know something. I find it really hard to talk about this. But I've waked up crying a couple of times thinking of that day. I've been trying to find a way to tell you. I though you ought to know it. Okay. I've said it. It was an awful thing for me to do. Awful."

"It was. In front of all those *goyim*. It was. I'm glad you've told me what you just did, because now that I'm not going to die—not right away, anyway—it's nice to know."

Josh took Martin's hand and simply held it. Neither of them said anything further on the subject. They began to talk about Tammy and why Josh was so taken with her, what a hard life she'd led, and how Josh had brought her back from the edge—a life filled with hard drugs and the hard hearts of hangers-on. Martin began to suspect his son resembled *him* —the way he had wanted to do everything for Jenny (and still did!), his son wanted to save Tammy Barnstone. Were they a clan of saviors? Terrible tradition.

"Well, I know how you feel, Josh. I rescued your mother from a boiler factory in the Bronx."

On the seventh day the gall bladder surgery was performed; the surgeon found many stones and a decayed gall bladder; Martin suffered agonies for two days, and Jenny stayed with him all that time, although he had round-the-clock private-duty nurses to adjust tubes and I.V. bottles, to give medicine and keep charts. By the third day he was feeling better and began to sit up and eat, and the worst was behind him. Sam told him he'd have to take it easy for at least six weeks—no, a trip to the Soviet Union was absolutely out of the question. He must treat himself like a king, and perhaps in two or three months he could go about his business. Whatever business he had left.

Rachel had gone off to Columbus, Ohio, where she was met by assorted Kobackers and Lazaruses, entertained like royalty, and at the Park Sheraton Hotel ballroom addressed three hundred of the richest Jews in Columbus. After she had finished speaking, more than three million dollars were pledged by moist-eyed merchants, bankers, attorneys, restaurateurs, and doctors for 1974's United Jewish Appeal, to help in the defense of Israel and to help Israel settle the new immigrants now coming from the Soviet Union and elsewhere. Later in the week she addressed a similar gathering in Cleveland, provoking another outpouring of money to help a small country seven thousand miles from Ohio. Rachel called Jenny between receptions and speeches to find out about Martin's condition, and when she told Jenny matter-of-factly about her dinner meetings, Jenny wondered how in the world she did it. Jenny was pretty good at the hype business herself. She could sell dog food to cats and vice versa, but this kind of "selling" was beyond her. She had never been to a UJA meeting—Martin had been to them two or three times and hated them, but he invariably gave large sums; Jenny had once asked him why he had

contributed two hundred thousand dollars at a dinner he said he had loathed. Martin shrugged. "I really don't know. You'd have to be there to understand it. Once I've left, I feel as if I've been rolled, taken. And yet, not quite, not quite."

"You're a pushover," Jenny had kidded him. But two hundred grand was a good-sized push, especially back in those early days. And now it had become a yearly thing; it had gone up to three hundred and he didn't even bother to go to the dinners any more. Jenny decided she would have to go and hear Rachel herself. Their paths were due to cross in Los Angeles, where Jenny had to go sometime during the coming weeks to map out the year's print campaign for Demonde Cosmetics and to decide on a TV campaign for the first perfume Demonde had ever introduced.

Martin would be in good hands and she'd be gone only three days. She had told him, yes, when she got back she was going to Russia with Rachel; she definitely thought she wanted to see his cousins. Martin's reaction was simple, querulous, and out of character for him. Over his dead body she'd go to Russia! He was sick, he goddamn-well needed his wife at home. Bad enough she was going to L.A. for three days. What the hell was this Russian cousin to him? He felt no affinity for the man, and God knows what mischief Rachel might have up her sleeve. Two women alone in the Soviet Union? No way!

But she'd more or less promised Rachel. Rachel had made the arrangements so *easy*. One morning she had calmly asked Jenny for their passports, and simply taken over. "You're being unreasonable, Marty. It's not like you."

"No way," he repeated.

Jenny had secretly vacillated about going for two weeks. Should she— or shouldn't she? Sufficient unto the hour, kiddo. Well, now that she'd finally decided, here was Martin deciding otherwise. *For* her.

"Why *not*, Marty? The kids are going, too."

"Terrific!"

"Tammy's doing three concerts there—isn't that marvelous? And you'll have Clara and Myra and Fred and the nurses. What more do you want? This is something I want to do, Marty."

He closed his eyes as if he were in pain. "Please don't, Jen."

Secretly she was half relieved, but she'd never say so, and she ended the quarrel equivocally with her usual, "You're a fine one."

13

THE LARGEST UJA DINNER IN THE WORLD was given yearly in New York and the second-largest in Beverly Hills, but Beverly Hills was usually more spectacular because so many non-Jewish film celebrities were on hand. It was the next best thing to the Academy Awards. This year it was being held at the Mountaintop Country Club, where gentiles were rarely admitted as members. There *was* a gentlemen's offer, that when the L.A. Valley Country Club, or Crowfoot or Rio d'Oro in Palm Springs, took a few more Jews, Mountaintop might open its doors wider to gentiles. It was perhaps the only country club in America which many motion picture stars, directors, and establishment gentiles *wanted* to join and could not. Even for a Jew to join, the initiation fee was forty thousand dollars.

Well, why not? The immaculate Robert Trent Jones eighteen-hole course sat over an ocean of oil. The parking lot tonight was a mass of Continentals, Mercedeses, Cadillacs, and Rolls Royces, with occasional Porsches and Citroens serving as grace notes. Chauffeurs gathered in groups playing cards or talking. The huge glass-and-stone clubhouse, capable of seating a thousand diners, was a Frank Lloyd Wright wonder, and the ladies' locker room was the Taj Mahal of locker rooms. The ladies' room, Jenny observed to Max Dembitz, her table neighbor, was much too fancy to pee in.

While members of the club, some six hundred couples, were not *required* to attend in order to maintain their membership, they more or less needed a note from their doctor in order to be excused. And for this occasion, non-members—activists at UJA, stars, doctors, lawyers, psychiatrists, quacks, agents, singers, musicians, writers, bankers, and, above all, studio executives—dutifully made their appearance, ate their caviar and *foie gras*, pressed duck, or New York cuts, and had their cherries jubilee or chocolate mousse, while an orchestra played "The Anniversary Waltz,"

"Hava Nagila," and every hit tune from *Milk and Honey* and *Fiddler on the Roof*.

Jenny was at a round table reserved for the Demonde Cosmetics organization. Max mentioned to Jenny that he was prepared to pledge a hundred thousand this year, a figure Jenny had thought a little chintzy compared to Martin's three hundred; but after all, on this occasion she was not Martin Singer's wife; she was only a lady from Demonde's New York advertising agency and simply *had* to go to the dinner because, as she explained carefully to the dimwit with whom she had to deal all day, she was a cousin of the principal speaker. And she knew in her secret heart (how she hated to admit it!) she had the clout necessary to be invited merely because she *was* Martin Singer's wife. And because Sonny Dembitz had been her dinner guest in New York only a few weeks ago. Jenny did not bear the Singer name lightly. Connections, bubbala, was the name of the game.

She watched as Rachel entered on the arm of Sidney Schlegelman, the president of Americana Pictures, who had brought her directly from his palace in Bel Air. They walked to the dais, Schlegelman stopping now and then to introduce Rachel to a major contributor. The principals of the theatrical agencies of M.B.M., of the American Music Corporation, and Century-Wolf followed—all the ten-percenters, plus Kahane, Jacobson, and Messerman, the three lawyers who had turned into movie mavins, followed by contingents from Paramount, Universal, and Metro. They were long and short, fat and skinny, gray and bald, young and old, thirty *machers*, and all of them men except for one young woman on the far right who, Jenny assumed, was the token exec, the "industry's" nod to Women's Lib.

Jenny excused herself, went up to the dais, leaned across, and took Rachel's square hand. "I feel so lucky to be here! Wild Indians couldn't keep me away. In my whole life I've never been to a UJA dinner, would you believe? I don't know why. Marty never would take me." She turned to Schlegelman, whom she had never set eyes on before. "Rachel and I are cousins, you know. And, would you believe, we've just discovered we have *another* cousin neither of us even knew about in Russia? In Minsk, no less. Isn't that a riot? By the way, I'm Jenny Singer." Schlegelman took her hand and murmured an inaudible greeting, then asked politely, "Mrs. Singer? What studio are you with?"

Jenny laughed. "I'm in the ad business. We do Paramount."

Schlegelman nodded. "Oh Singer, of course. The shop on Wilshire. I'm pleased to meet you." Jenny realized that at last he knew precisely who she was. Well, she'd never heard of *him*.

She loved these encounters with big egos. "I'm not entirely hopeless, Mr. Schlegelman. Isaac Singer, from the old Selznick days, was our uncle, and his son Louis is our cousin."

"Ah. Of course. Lou's a talented director."

"Also my son Joshua is making a movie—*The Year of the Whale*, Mr. Schlegelman." Schlegelman's brow wrinkled as if in deep concentration. "Oh, yes, I think I've heard something about that project."

My husband's father, she wished she could say, was Justice Singer. Remember? While your old man was peddling sack dresses, kiddo. Instead she leaned forward further, her décolletage in Schlegelman's nose, kissed Rachel on the cheek, and said, "Maybe we can talk later, Rachel, okay? Privately."

Rachel nodded. "Oh, Jenny, I just got a call from Simiro. We've all been cleared. We leave on February twenty-eighth. We're on the same plane as Tammy. Everything's working out."

"Marvelous!" Jenny said, wondering what the old lady wasn't telling her that was "working out."

She started back to her table, stopping only long enough to kiss Cousin Louis, who sat at the head of his table, and to tell him Rachel wanted to see him after dinner. After all, they *were* all family. God, how she hated country clubs. Even this one. So full of shitheads. Rich ones.

The food was delicious, though; Jenny adored good food. Even Max Dembitz couldn't spoil it. She cleaned her plate, trained by her mother to do so in order to help the underfed Polish people and starving children everywhere. She had had two portions of pressed duck and was digging into her chocolate mousse when a series of chords and trumpet blasts brought the diners to a half silence, until even the clinking of glasses and silverware was stilled. Schlegelman, a tall, curly-haired, heavyset man, with thick lips and heavy glasses, stood, and a small microphone was placed around his neck by a girl who was too pretty to be anything but a starlet. Schlegelman said good evening and complimented all the nice people for coming out, the usual palaver. He thanked everyone, including the Board of Governors of the Mountaintop Country Club. He said everyone in this room (Room? It was more like Yankee Stadium!) was deeply concerned by the recent trial by fire to which Israel had been subjected, and was still undergoing since the guns began to explode on Yom Kippur, and he was sure that everyone in this room wanted to do his utmost to help this valiant little country, because to every Jew in America Israel was more than just another beleaguered country; to its fate was tied the fate of Jews throughout the world. It made Jews here in sunny California shud-

der to think what the consequences to them would be if Israel ceased to exist.

Many people in this room had not only been to Israel, but there were those, whom he would not name here, who had actively purchased weapons back in forty-seven and -eight, and others who as youngsters had run ships with illegal refugees back in those days, and others who had helped Israel to fight—men like Mickey Marcus, whom it had been his privilege to know. "Israel has come a long way since. But it has a long, long way to go. And here to speak to us tonight, directly from her home in Savyon, Israel, about what is still needed and why, is a young woman, born in Israel. She has lived there throughout her youth, and now at 'seventy or so' (she refuses to tell me her right age), just when she's beginning to turn from a girl into a mature woman and entering the prime of her life, she's agreed to tell us what she knows. She comes to us with impeccable credentials, a close friend and associate of another young woman, Golda Meir, our own Goldie Meyerson of Milwaukee, who has also 'done the state some service' in these past few years. And, in case this credential is not enough, she happens also to be a first cousin of our own late Supreme Court justice, Jacob Singer, one of America's great and first Zionists. So need I say more? I have the honor to present Her Excellency, the Special Ambassador of the State of Israel, Rachel Singer Aron."

During the applause, the movie starlet helped Schlegelman remove his mike; she placed it carefully about Rachel's neck.

In all that ostentation, Jenny was struck by Rachel's simplicity, by her simple black dress and opal beads, in glaring contrast to her own outfit and to those of the other few women in her audience, the Mainbochers, the Saint Laurents, the Puccis and Guccis, and the Diors; Rachel's simple bobbed hair rebuked all the tinted locks, the curls, the Japanese styles, the Sassoon cuts. She was reminded of Josh's appearance at her black-tie party at Gramercy Park.

"Ladies and gentlemen," Rachel began, "this is my first time at the Mountaintop Country Club. It's very nice. You really have built a gorgeous ghetto here. And this meal! I've eaten all over America, even in Dallas, and I think you have the food problem licked here in California! I hope you're not offended by my reference to a ghetto. After all, didn't we, or our parents, or *their* parents, all come from there? And it's difficult to erase this entirely from our minds. In my own head I picture it this way: around every Jew there's already a small ghetto the minute he or she is born. A small invisible globe, maybe two meters in diameter—that's about six feet, for the benefit of the nonmathematical artists here—and it's also infinite, because there's an opening in the bubble that reaches out all the

way to God himself. I happen to come from the largest ghetto in the world. The biggest, the best, and the fanciest. The only ghetto the world has ever seen with its own air force. It reaches now from Dan on the north to the Suez Canal, and from the shores of the Mediterranean Sea on the west to the River Jordan, the Golan Heights, and the Dead Sea in the east. Some of it is bare desert or rock. Some of it is gorgeous. For those few of you who have never seen it, you must come. Since 1967 we can even offer scuba thrills at Sharm el Sheikh. There we are, three million of us, each in his own private six-foot ghetto, and all combined into one that is ten thousand square miles in area. We have a few *shabbos goyim* with us. For the benefit of the reformed Jews and the gentiles among you, *shabbos goyim* are Christians or Muslims whom we ask to do the things we are not allowed to do on the sabbath. At least our religious parties say we're not. They're small parties but they have great influence. Most of us can't stand them. Well, one young man in Columbus, Ohio, said to me after my talk, 'How can you dare to call Israel a ghetto? *You* don't have any pogroms!' "

She paused while her audience laughed in appreciation and in sadness. "This young man had been to New York and had seen *Fiddler on the Roof*. That was his idea of a pogrom. I said to him, I also saw this show, and when the Cossacks came and told everyone in Anatevka they had to move out, that their village was to be destroyed, everyone around me in the theater was crying. Tears were streaming down every face! What for? Where were these poor people from Anatevka going? To New York, to Chicago, to Hollywood, and to Jerusalem! The best thing that ever happened to them! No more going to the well for water. No more tuberculosis. No more Cossacks. So why was everyone in the audience crying? The grandchildren of these people being kicked out of Anatevka were all sitting right there in the theater in their mink coats; they also paid fifty dollars a seat. What for? To sit there and cry? Maybe they were worried someone might come along and tell them their time was up in New York? Nah, nah! Couldn't be! It was pure sentimentality. I watched the same thing happening in Haifa, where I saw *Fiddler* in Yiddish, and in Jerusalem, where they gave it in Hebrew. Grown soldiers crying their eyes out. Our chief of staff yet! Some soldier!

"I realize there are descendants of German Jews sitting here among you. For your help we are always grateful. In some cases your great-grandfathers came mostly to America in 1848, and then ninety years later some of you yourselves escaped here from Hitler. And you've always been much fancier Americans than those who came from Anatevka. But how many of you sitting out there—I'm just curious—how many of your par-

ents or grandparents came from Anatevka? You know what I mean—from Lodz or Minsk, or Vilna or Odessa? Or one of the little *shtetls*? *You* know what I mean! Let me see who you are."

Scores of hands went up, and a few people laughed self-consciously. Rachel darted her head with satisfaction, and even Jenny, whose hand waved like a kid who had to go to the john, had to smile. "Me, too," Rachel said. "So you see, we're related. Not only was Jacob Singer my cousin, but all of you in this room, all with their hands up, we're all related. So *shalom!* And from Israel I bring greetings to you all, including the Germans and the Sephardic Jews here tonight, from almost three million other relatives, but the time is too short, so I just can't name them all. I don't want to hurt the feelings of the Germans among you, because I realize that *you* are the equivalent in America of our *chalutzim*, our second wave of settlers. Because even before you, the elitest of the American Jews—the Cardozos and the Lazaruses of America, came—the Sephardics. And when the Russians came to America, they brought problems—Gurrah Shapiro, Legs Diamond, gangsters, *goneivim*, all kinds of trash. Well, in Israel, it's my duty to tell you, the social pyramid is exactly reversed. I hope I'm not giving away state secrets, but it's a fact. At the very top, the Ben Gurions, the Sharetts, Ben Yehuda, my friend Golda, the Dayans, the Allons, the Jabotinskys, almost everyone who is anyone—they're all Russians or Poles; the great writers, artists, bankers—Russians and Poles, a few Roumanians—all Litvaks and Galizianers. The Germans and Austrians came later, and because they were so brilliantly educated, they made their way in Israel just fine. But at the bottom of our social ladder are *our* Jews from Africa and Asia. We hope this won't be forever, but that's the way it *is*, and I didn't come ten thousand miles to tell you fairy stories. The Sephardics *we* have taken in from Morocco and Yemen and Iraq, from Egypt and Syria, were mostly poor, mostly struggling, illiterate; they now make up half our country, and contribute eighty percent of our crime, but they're improving: They have *nowhere* to go but up! They also have nowhere to go. And they are also, by the way, very expensive. So you see, Israel is a mirror image of the American Jewish community— everything is the same, only backwards. And like everyone who travels long distances to reach a faraway place, it's always nice to meet someone from your own hometown. My parents' hometown is Minsk. Anybody here from Minsk?" Fifty or more hands went up. "Please come and see me after the meeting and we'll talk about old times."

There was a scattering of laughter and applause.

"So when will we get rid of the ghetto mentality? Some say never. I am

more hopeful. You should also be more hopeful. I believe the ghetto will wither away when there's an end to pogroms. I'm talking about, for example, the pogrom of 1948, when on every side Arab nations came at us with tanks and rifles and killed some of our bravest young men, not to mention women and children, with their mortars. I'm talking about the pogrom of 1967, engineered by Mr. Nasser, when instead of killing us one by one, the way the old-fashioned pogromists did, he decided to blockade us and starve us all to death, wholesale. I mean, if he succeeded, that would've been a *real* pogrom. And I'm talking about the latest pogrom of Yom Kippur, 1973, just a few short months ago, when Russian tanks—thank God, manned by inept Egyptian boys instead of trained Russian peasant-soldiers, tried to overrun us from the other side of the Suez Canal and Syrians tried to do the same on the Golan and we were saved by blood. The blood of our children. Blood, as Goethe said, is a very special juice. I apologize for speaking personally. But in 1947 my only son, Catriel, a young doctor, was killed when his bus, going up to Hadassah Hospital on Mount Scopus under a Red Cross guarantee to help the sick, was ambushed. Many of you know about this episode. A son. Many of you have sons, so I need not dwell on the meaning of that. He was twenty-two and for a doctor a very funny boy. We feel blessed that *he* had a son. So we still *have*, you see. In 1967 my husband lost his life when his command car overturned. An enemy didn't kill him, only a careless driver, but it was during a pogrom when people tended to get reckless. We were married forty-three years. It happens I still loved that man. Maybe here in Hollywood that might have entitled us to an Oscar. So I had two men in my life and they are both gone. And this young man in Columbus, Ohio, was worried only that we weren't having enough pogroms.

"But of course in a way he is right. These are different kinds of pogroms. We pay in blood, but for a change we are *winning* pogroms. That's new. Tel Aviv is not Warsaw. Jerusalem is not Minsk. Haifa is not Kishinev. Why not? Not only because of us, our brave boys. But also because on the outside, beyond the narrow border of our ghetto, we have good friends. Friends with power and friends with resources—money to buy the things we need to defend ourselves and factories to make them in. Yes, friends even against the mighty, pernicious Soviet Union, which would like nothing better than to see us disappear, thrown into the sea— so they could claim credit with a hundred million Arabs and dominate another region of the world! The region with half the world's oil. Just our luck, when God promised us the promised land, there wasn't a drop of oil

under it! Because in those days, God himself didn't realize how important oil would become. Who needed oil as long as you had a good camel? Who knew? Maybe our prophets weren't so prophetic, after all. A lot they didn't see in their crystal balls. And by the way, all this that I'm telling you is absolutely confidential. If Golda ever finds out that I called Israel a ghetto or talked about our wars as pogroms, or that I cast some slight aspersion on the ability of our prophets to see the future—to forecast jet planes, automobiles, and oil-burning electric generators—the religious parties will disown me, they'll call on Golda and I will be ex-Special Ambassador and she won't talk to me for a week. So please. Not a word. In a small gathering like this, I'm sure such an indiscretion will never be leaked. Is Rona Barrett in the room? You especially, Rona, I'm counting on you to keep it quiet."

Laughter. "So now I come to the really funny part. We lost almost three thousand young men in the first three weeks after Yom Kippur. I don't mean they got lost in the desert. We lost them for good. We buried them. Three thousand mothers, three thousand wives and sweethearts, I can't say how many fatherless children. These three thousand young bodies saved the rest of us. You know how many three thousand is to Israel? In America, it would be like two hundred and ten thousand young men in *three weeks*. You lost in Vietnam in ten *years*, fifty-two thousand. And you know the trauma *that* was! In World War Two you lost in four years three hundred forty thousand. No pogrom, leaving out the Holocaust, has ever cost so many Jewish lives. So we survived as a nation. How many more times will we have to do it? This was the fourth time in twenty-five years! How many more?

"But who has time to cry? We pray for peace. We pray for the Arabs to get some sense. And meanwhile we prepare for the next round. More deadly weapons. More sophisticated ways of killing the enemy. That's what makes *me* cry! How many wars can we afford to fight before all our sons and daughters become animals? Professional killers? Where is the Jewishness in all this killing? The boys come home, and you know what gives them nightmares? Not the loss of their companions. No, about that they are saddened. They died bravely. But about the killing of their enemies they have nightmares. *They* are children, too, our enemies' boys, just like ours. Even younger than ours. Egyptian children, Syrian children, sometimes sixteen. This is what gives our boys nightmares. Some of our boys refused to do it. There are many stories I could tell you, but while we are winning these wars, we are building up a terrible guilt in the hearts of our young people, the victors! That, thank God, is *so* Jewish!

Nasser, if they could have got to *him*—ah, well, they might not have felt so guilty, but killing these poor little schnooks! Awful. Well, I don't hear anyone laughing, so I guess this isn't so funny after all.

"And now to the brave part. Here in America we have friends. Not just the six million Jewish citizens of America, but more than two hundred million Americans! Black, white, yellow, and brown. Catholic, Protestant, Jewish, and atheist. They give us planes. My grandson, Gideon, a twenty-seven-year-old *mensch*, the son of my son, the doctor, he flies an American-built Phantom fighter stationed in the Sinai. For him I say a special prayer each night; but also I say a special prayer for the President of the United States of America and his secretaries of state and defense and for the Congress, who, acting for the American people, 'give us the tools so that we can do the job,' to use a phrase that is still appropriate."

Applause.

"People here talk to me about Watergate. In Israel we can't think about Watergate. This is a tragedy for *us*. This I cannot even think about, much less discuss. We love your President not because he is Richard Nixon, but because he is America. After we have been abandoned by all our old friends—Czechoslovakia, France, England, Russia—yes, the Soviets were our friends for a few months, remember?—there is this lighthouse for us—America.

"We will do the job, never fear. *With* all the tears, with the widows, the orphans, the obituary notices. With terrorists dropping bombs into our buses and supermarkets, yes. We are prepared to live with all that in this elusive quest for peace with our neighbors. But is this all?

"No, no, not on your life. We have another job; while we are holding off tanks, we must at the same time take in every Jew who wishes to come. This we cannot put off or delay. A Russian Jew gets a visa to emigrate that is good for twenty days. This is our *raison d'être*; this is what sovereignty, our army, our air force, our flag, 'Hatikvah,' our *kibbutzim*, are all about. This mission is the heart of Israel. Oh, yes, there are voices in Israel, just as you have voices in America, that cry out, 'Slow down.' 'Not so fast.' 'Close the gates!' 'We can't absorb so many!' 'Where can we put them all?' Well, in America you heeded those voices and you slowed down. I am not in a position to comment on your internal affairs. But in Israel we cannot and we will not. Two nights after Sadat's troops attacked us on the Suez front, two nights after Yom Kippur, I was at Ben Gurion Airport to meet a plane coming from Vienna. Out of that plane came one hundred and fifty-two new immigrants—from Kiev and Kharkov, from Minsk and Vilna, from Moscow, Leningrad and Tashkent. And every al-

ternate night, three or four times a week, while the fiercest fighting was going on at the front, these planes kept coming out of the night—bringing us men, women, children, coming home. Israelis—volunteers—came to the airport with their private cars, driving with blue headlights in the blackout, to welcome them and bring them home to their first Israeli bed. Newcomers who had waited sometimes for years for permission to come, and they were coming now because the Soviet Union wanted *something* from the United States, *something*. I really don't care what, but an American Senator said, 'Give us Jews, if you want that, we want Jews'—Mr. Henry Jackson, may God bless him, who is in this room tonight—"

Great applause, stamping and bravos, as if the audience were at an operatic performance.

"Well, he's too shy to stand up, which for a senator is a maximum form of humility, but thank God for him and all those in Congress who voted with him! And so they came to us, these human beings, with *nothing*. The clothes on their backs. Torn suitcases, ersatz handbags. The Pilgrims of 1973. And Israel took them in. They were citizens on the spot, and Israel assumed a new responsibility. To house and feed and clothe thirty-five or forty thousand intelligent, highly-educated human beings, each with a personality, an ambition, a hope, to find them the right kind of work, to help them find fulfilling lives, to make them glad they had decided to be Israelis. With almost all we will succeed. A few have been so traumatized they will never be happy anywhere. But we'll have their children and their children's children.

"So where do *you* come in? Every immigrant of this kind who comes to Israel costs fifteen thousand dollars to absorb into our society. Housing, jobs, language instruction, career training, education, and all the rest. This is for those of you who enjoy statistics. But it is not just a statistic. This is the human face of a human nation where every person counts. Don't misunderstand me. They are not all lovable. They are not all saints. Believe me, some of them could drive you crazy. But you know, Boris, my husband, may his tender soul rest in peace, during the war of forty-eight, as a lawyer he defended a Jew who was accused of treason. Yes, it was a very mixed-up time, people being killed all over, and this particular man was executed, the only Jew ever to be executed by his fellow Jews in Israel for treason. He was an unpopular Jew, he liked Englishmen, he had an English mistress, and in those days the English were our local villains. So it was a case a little bit like Sacco and Vanzetti here. He was *not* guilty of treason. He may have been vain and stupid, a social climber, and nobody liked him, but you don't shoot a man for being vain or stupid, or

playing tennis with unpopular foreign friends. His wife, who loved him, God knows why, started a campaign to clear his name, and my husband, bless him, after all kinds of hesitation, took up her cause. And finally he told Knesset, in those early days when we hardly knew which way was right or wrong, 'We can't be too busy for one man! For one family! Even though this man is dead. We must have justice, even unpopular justice!'

"And Ben Gurion agreed, and the little newborn nation listened, and the colonel who had ordered this man executed was reprimanded and punished, and the man's name was cleared; later his son was awarded a scholarship by the government when he grew to manhood and went to the Hebrew University. Why? Because in Israel, every man, woman, and child is important, is an individual, with individual rights, hopes, dreams, aspirations, whether he is a persecuted day-laborer from Yemen or Morocco, a professor from Heidelberg University, or a doctor from Minsk. And our government was not too proud to admit a tragic mistake. Where else?

"Now, to greet each newcomer with warmth and with love is not an easy task, and a particularly difficult one to institutionalize. We have our own bureaucracy, you know, and bureaucrats in one place are not so different after a while from bureaucrats anywhere. They have stamps and forms and questionnaires. They have buses and maps and they're overworked. Some of you are actors who have been in plays in New York for long runs. You know how difficult it is to keep your part fresh and spontaneous, how hard you have to work at it. Each night you have to fall in love, or make up with someone, or commit suicide, and it must look each night like the first time, right? Well, so with a bureaucrat. The faces swim before their eyes. So we go out to give our bureaucrats pep talks. We remind them of what they are doing and why they're doing it. Be nice. Be warm. Be understanding. We're not always successful, but we're also not doing badly.

"So then we come to America and give our pep talk to you. The same problem. How boring it must be to hear the same thing year in and year out. And how painful to hand your hard-earned money to people seven thousand miles away each year, and to hope they use it wisely. Fifteen thousand dollars each, isn't that an awful lot? And small thanks you get for it, in the bargain. All that happens is we'll be back next year and ask for more. Well, what can I say? We need you. We thank you. We pledge to you our lives, our fortunes, and our sacred honor, but from you we need only money. How much you need us is not for *me* to say.

"Now, I'll tell you another secret—also mustn't get out of this room,

Rona. Three or four weeks ago I just discovered I have a living cousin in Minsk. Yes, my cousin! A physician. How he stayed alive after Hitler's beasts came to Minsk—this I cannot say because I don't know yet myself. Now *he* would like to come to Israel. He and his wife and daughter—his wife is a *shiksa*, by the way, but she wants to keep him company—so those three people I promise you I'll take care of *myself* personally. *I* will be financially responsible. Therefore, for these three people we can already subtract forty-five thousand dollars. I'll explain this to Golda. So that leaves only five hundred and fourteen million nine hundred and fifty-five thousand dollars to go. This cousin, by the way, put my whole message in a few words, I think. He was writing to another cousin in New York, Martin Singer. You all know who Martin is—a very special man. 'I turn to you, my own flesh and blood, in far-off America,' this cousin wrote. 'You are my lifeline.'

"That's what Israel says—we turn to you, in far-off America. You are our lifeline. And who knows, maybe we're yours! That's not for me to say. So maybe we don't *all* have the same grandfather; do I have to tell *you* we're still each other's flesh and blood? Who knows exactly how? But don't *we* know it? The same evils threaten us, some more than others, the same things excite us, even when some of us won't admit it. We're a family. Why else would the marvelous people of New York pledge almost two hundred million? Why from four other cities—Washington, Miami, Philadelphia, Chicago—did we find another hundred and twenty-five million? I ask you. From the smaller cities across America, from Palm Beach to Tacoma, from Montreal to Vancouver, we expect ninety million. This leaves your great unique community, Los Angeles, Beverly Hills, Brentwood, Bel Air, Westwood, Santa Monica, Malibu—you know the places I'm talking about, and the amounts I'm talking about are more than *you* have been thinking about, because this is a special year. This is the third year of a new *aliyah*, the beginning of a new wave of immigrants from the Soviet Union—in three years, eighty thousand have come.

"Will this wave of immigrants swell to two hundred, to five hundred thousand? We don't know. Nobody has solved the puzzle within the riddle within the enigma to this day. What the Soviets will or won't do. So, to this great community I come asking for one hundred million dollars. A round sum. And a fortune. Our experience is that of the entire amount given in a community, seventy percent must come from this Initial Gifts dinner. So who has seventy million dollars to give away? Who in his right mind? Maybe the grandchildren of Anatevka! I hope so. Thousands of frightened, persecuted people in the Soviet Union, threatened with going to the gulag or to insane asylums, who were not lucky enough to get out

at the same time as your grandparents or parents and mine, hope so also. And Golda *prays* so. And Golda is not religious."

She sat down. There was, for a moment, silence. Everyone in that room was a practiced mathematician, the actors, artists, writers, and directors, as well as the bankers among them. They could calculate what they were being asked for, and it was twice what they had been asked for in the past. Then the applause started. It started half-heartedly, gathering momentum and volume until Jenny found herself deafened. People began to stamp their feet as well. As they thought back on what Rachel had said, each had been moved at one point or another. Some began to shout, and bravos came from every corner of the dining hall. Jenny was astonished. It was a goddamn revival meeting. Jenny had found *herself* teary-eyed at various moments during Rachel's talk. She considered herself a smart, jaundiced advertising woman. Rachel's talk had been disorganized, abrupt, at times full of bathos, sentimental, then tough. A real snake oil pitch, but with this snake oil was a genuine product. It *cured*. Cured whom? Cured what? Guilt? Rootlessness? Identification-pressure? Goddamnit, it *was* real. This was a difficult concept for Jenny to grasp; and it was probably just as difficult for many of the motion picture people in that room, some of whom saw the entire enterprise as a Colossal Motion Picture—*Exodus II*. But Colossal Motion Pictures were big hits today. Mr. Schlegelman turned to the Hollywood starlet and said, leaning toward the mike that still hung around Rachel's neck, "Honey, will you please give me the cards?"

A large file case was delivered by two uniformed waiters to the girl, who placed it on the table before her, standing between where Rachel sat and where Schlegelman stood. She handed Schlegelman the first card. "These are in alphabetical order," Schlegelman said solemnly, "and when your name is called, please state your pledge. If I fail to pull anybody's card, please don't be insulted. We'll call on you after the cards are all called. The first card is John Aaronson of Beverly Hills."

From somewhere back in the room an accented voice (was it Russian?) said, "Fifty tausend dollar."

"Thank you very much, Mr. Aaronson. That is exactly twice as much as Mr. Aaronson gave last year." There was a scattering of applause, and Schlegelman, a man accustomed to being heeded, held up his hand for silence. "If we can please dispense with the applause until the reading of the cards is completed. Please. Abbott Productions, Culver City."

A mustached dandy stood up at the table next to Jenny's. He looked like a reincarnated Adolphe Menjou (poor Adolphe would turn over in

his grave, thought Jenny), and spoke with a resonant actor's voice. "We at Abbott, as a result of history's need in this hour, and in response to this brave lady's account of her country's need, and in recognition of our fellow religionists' need in a country that has turned on them, have decided that we, too, will double our contribution this year from seventy-five thousand to one hundred and fifty thousand."

The girl handed Schlegelman another card, but before reading it, Schlegelman said, "We appreciate all the sentiments behind each gift. It does seem ungallant to ask each of you to hold your comments down to the barest minimum, particularly when you are all so generous; but we have almost eight hundred cards to read tonight. So . . ." He smiled at the soft groan. Jenny had never witnessed anything like it. The high point was quickly reached when the American Music Corporation announced its pledge of one million dollars, almost three times its 1973 gift. An elderly gentleman, Lester Messerman, the company chairman, was allowed to make a two-minute speech, softly spoken, to accompany this gift.

All went smoothly for fifteen minutes, when Schlegelman, beginning to be slightly hoarse, called the name of Sam Candell. Jenny watched a lanky man in his early forties, who could have been a cowboy—he was wearing a business suit and a string tie instead of the black tie uniform of everyone else in the room—stand slowly but with some majesty. His face was weatherbeaten, his hair dark blond and wavy, his nose too long and straight. Jenny was struck by how tall and erect he stood. "Ah regret to say," Sam Candell began, "that because of business conditions in mah field, this year ah am able to come up with only twelve thousand five hundred dollars."

Schlegelman looked hard at the card. "*Twelve* thousand, Mr. Candell? But last year you gave forty-five thousand—"

Sam Candell spoke quickly. "Ah was out of my mind last year. Ah'm in the housing business, and you all know what's happened to housing this year. Ah'm in hock up to my eyeballs. God knows where this twelve thousand is gonna come from—"

Schlegelman was relentless. "Sam, do you realize there are boys *dying* out there on the Suez front? Tonight? Giving their *lives?* While we sit here over our chocolate mousse? Where do *you* get the *chutzpah*—"

A man in a different part of the hall was on his feet, calling, "Mr. Schlegelman, sir!" Rachel's expression had turned inward. Her mouth set in a thin line. She clearly hated what was going on. Jenny thought Schlegelman was a shit.

The stranger continued. "My name is Wolper, sir, and I work at the

Bank of America. We do all of Sam Candell's financing, sir. I've known Mr. Candell since he was a youngster. He just can't afford to contribute even twelve thousand five hundred dollars to UJA or to anyone else. Please take my word for it. His house is mortgaged to the hilt. He has land, lots of land, out in the desert, also mortgaged and costing him a fortune each month. And not only that, sir, but to my knowledge he has been an active, dedicated Zionist for all the years I've known him. So much so that right now his daughter is spending a year in a *kibbutz* near Tiberias, her own decision that I *know* was inspired by what she heard at home. You're picking on the wrong man, sir."

Schlegelman renewed the attack as if he had not heard a word. "But *twelve* thousand paltry . . . we have a quota here. Seventy million dollars. If we listen to every hard luck story, how do you expect us—"

Another man rose and without being recognized cried, "This is disgraceful! I happen to be Sam Candell's accountant, and damnit, I don't know where he's gonna find twelve thousand bucks. Stop harassing the poor guy! Now, I happen to be with one of the Big Eight accounting firms, and gentlemen, we expect our word to be taken at face value! Now, cut it out!"

Schlegelman had begun to turn quite red and spoke angrily. "All I know is what I read on this card. And this card—"

Another white-haired and short man was on his feet. He spoke in a resonant, almost melodic voice, with a liturgical rhythm. "Mr. Schlegelman, sir. I am Rabbi Krentzman of Temple Sinai. And this browbeating of Mr. Candell must stop! You're not running American Pictures here. I bar mitzvahed Mr. Candell. He was a good boy. He's a good man, more community-minded than ninety percent of the people in my congregation. Mr. Candell is a *giver,* sir. A *generous* man. If he says that's all he can give, I for one can tell you it is *more* than he can give. You would be doing us all a favor by stopping this disgraceful conduct."

The rabbi sat down. There was applause. Rachel whispered to Schlegelman, who, turning red and without a word of apology, took the next card. "Harold Cohen!"

"Jesus H. Christ," Jenny said to Max Dembitz, "that really does it! No wonder Marty never took me to one of these things! It could make you an anti-Semite!"

The peer pressure could be felt from one end of the room to the other. This dinner would be followed by smaller, less elegant gatherings with less prestigious speakers. Within the next three months volunteers would fan out across America and every Jew in the land would be "cased" by his

Jewish neighbors for his or her ability to give—and would be asked by phone, by mail, or in person to contribute—from a dollar to a million. No Jew, Jenny knew, would be left unturned.

People could be deprived of freedom in more ways than one, she mused. While there might be mistakes of the kind that happened to the luckless Mr. Candell, the cards in Schlegelman's hands, everyone in that room knew, contained a great deal more than their names. They contained data on each person's income, declared and undeclared—his net worth and potential. They indicated what each had contributed in the past five years, and what they contributed to other charities, their club memberships, guild and business association memberships, university and government connections. They even bore marks indicating the number of times the person had visited Israel—all data fastidiously and meticulously collected by an army of volunteers. The web was complete. There were no secrets, not even Swiss bank accounts. These cards contained information about each donor often not known to his psychiatrist or rabbi, his family doctor, his wife, broker, or to the Internal Revenue Service, but all the information was good, kind, and optimistic; there was nothing derogatory on them. And at the bottom of each card was the amount of money the person would be expected to give for 1974. This information had been conveyed, one way or another, subtly or coarsely, to almost every contributor some weeks before the Initial Gifts dinner, and sometimes had been the subject of heated negotiation. The dinner was the climax, where it all came together, and where Rachel's speech was designed to bring in the waverers, and up the ante of the fainthearted.

Jenny saw this at her own table, for when they came to the D's and the moment approached for Max Dembitz to announce the Demonde Cosmetics gift, he called a hurried huddle with the two associates nearest him, and when his name was called, said "Demonde Cosmetics is pleased to pledge one hundred and fifty thousand dollars."

An extra fifty thousand for Rachel, and for how it would look to the neighbors. They wouldn't be outdone by Max Factor, no way.

PART
FOUR
Bloodknots

1

By THE TIME JENNY FLEW OFF to California, Martin was sitting up at home, taking solid food and notice. The contracts for the sale of the store had been reviewed by Carter-Hale's California attorneys. Martin found the arrangements for their taking possession reasonable but boring. He could scarcely wait to be rid of the store. Trying to read the contracts, he found himself dozing from boredom, so he was glad that he had a new stack of letters which had just been translated by the Yeshiva boy.

The letter he had begun at the hospital, written by Grandfather Moishe to his Uncle Yakov, had originated in New York, the first such. He had seen no more than the first few lines the day before his operation. Now he started it again. It was a monster of a letter. My God, how he *wrote*. Nobody did that any more. Today it was postcards and telegrams. And if you had anything important to say, you reached for the phone. Old Moishe must have developed writer's cramp. And he wasn't the only one in the family. They all wrote like demons.

To a degree he had never thought possible, Martin had begun to feel some affinity to old Moishe. His grandfather and he had a few things in common which, while he understood them in himself, rather offended him in the old man. His womanizing, for one. His rather flimsily held "beliefs," which could never successfully contend with narrow self-interest, for another. In pursuit of his self-interest, he was a demon warrior; in that of the common interest, a coward. On the other hand, he had been elected to play a role in Minsk that Martin had played with some degree of awareness all his life: he was the representative of those who lived on Jew Street to the gentile world.

Parallels could, of course, be distorted and stretched too far, but there were elements. Each time Martin attended a meeting of the Board of Overseers, could he deny he was conscious of it? At Porcellian, in his un-

dergraduate days, he'd been conscious of it every day. Even in the air force, after his first twenty-five missions, when it seemed too good to be true that he'd survived and his service was over, and he'd been asked to his dismay if he would volunteer for an additional twenty-five, every instinct, every thought, every muscle cried out for him to excuse himself. Preserve thyself, Martin! Another twenty-five is suicide! If he had been a *goy*, he would have: most did. Why not he? It was not that Hitler was out to get him (no denying *that*) that had turned the trick. No, it was merely how it would look to the other guys, the *goyim*. Why not admit it at long last? Well, what else would he uncover about himself? Reading these goddamn letters had by now become a compulsion.

The Yeshiva translator, under Rosenzweig's guidance, had, during Martin's hospital stay, deciphered, translated, collated, and put in chronological order a hundred and fifty more pages of letters and other material. He took up the top sheet. Neatly typed.

LETTER FROM MOISHE (NOW "MOSES") TO HIS ATLANTA RELATIVES
New York
1 February 1888

Uncle Yakov and my whole American Family!

A surprise that I am writing you from New York in America, no? You are not hearing from a man with any joy in his heart.

What started this long chain of happenings for me? Perhaps if I write everything from the beginning I can get the *golem* out of my system. Nu, I'll try! . . .

It wasn't *my* military service. My trouble began because I represented fourteen thousand people from Jew Street to Komarovka Square. Who needs such a burden?

But when it came to army service, I felt no different from my people: why should some poor *schlemiel* from Minsk have to put on a uniform, leave home, family, bride, or children, and ride on a railroad for weeks through the snow and sleet and forest wastes of unspoiled Siberia for the privilege of standing guard along that lovely, touristic coast, peering through an icicle-dripping spyglass for Japanese (enemy) warships? What "enemy"? Any enemy of the Tsar is a friend of ours! Uncle Efram did the sensible thing. He left.

Also, thank God, Freda, with that weird passion of hers for settling in a "Jewish" wasteland, took shilly-shallying Herschel by the collar, said a surreptitious farewell a few weeks ago, and *went*. A dangerous voyage, true—and to the sands of Palestine, a stupid place, but still better than Russia! So Herschel is safe! (God willing,

if they ever come to their senses, they could always come here to America.)

Feygele remains still in Minsk. She's going to make the place over—and *take* the place over, and, incidentally, Boris, my old friend, looks at her in that certain way, and she looks at him the same, and maybe *this* is what really keeps her in Minsk—who knows? I hope she's lucky and doesn't get sent on a long, cold trip. Or perhaps to the grave. Such a fire-eater, our little Feygele! Her own worst enemy.

But to get back to me. It happened like this: as representative of Jew Street it was my duty to turn over monthly to one Officer Pelstoy the names of four young men from my area, eligible for military service. On the first of each month the names would be drawn by lot—rich and poor treated alike, in the presence of a reb and Ulia from the governor's office, who always shows up in his stupified state.

What was *not* known to Ulia (although the rebs knew it quite well) was that one, two, or sometimes three of those names I also turned over, the same day, to my friend Doctor Rosnikov, because he is the man who examines recruits for the army. If he says "medically unfit," out they go! Just a wave of his finger—one life saved! From the families who can scrape together the money—one, two, or three each month—I collected fifty rubles, which they understood was to go from me to the doctor. There was never any argument about this, because up to now my system had been foolproof. Most families find a way to pay . . . don't ask me how! Some can't . . . too bad! For those who could, it enabled the young men to remain in Minsk instead of leaving their families and running off to America or England. Cheaper, too. A blessing all around. For those who could not pay, I felt terrible! What more could I do?

Uncle, I have a terrible confession. I kept fifteen rubles out of each fifty and gave only thirty-five to the doctor. *He* knew. From him I hid nothing. In fact, he advised it. "My boy, look at the risk you run!"

I know, Uncle! You're saying, "This is *serving* your people, Moishe?" Oh, I had trouble with my conscience, and often I was saying to myself, *what* risk, Moishe? Are you a no-good bastard? These people *trust* you, they give you their sweat and bones. Fifty rubles! A month's living! My conscience bothered me as I put the swindled money aside, together with your letters, in a hollowed-out book among Papa's many volumes. Our house is so full of books, who could ever find it? But Uncle, my conscience no longer troubles me. The doctor was a prophet. There *was* a risk!

Listen. This particular month all *four* families gave me fifty rubles. Never before. Without giving the matter sufficient thought, I *took* from all four. Although the doctor and I both were leery that this might look strange to the military, we took a chance.

The first Thursday each month is the army medical examination. Those fit for service, the *shtarkers*, the doctor sent to the larger room to register. The "unfits" he sent home—the fifty-ruble types—together with one or two real cripples. Anemic. Tubercular. A hunched back, and so forth. Written by the doctor quickly, no trouble made by those who passed, because for each candidate it was *his* first army examination, and how could he know this has been going on month in and month out?

But this time! *One* recruit, a big-mouth lout, about ten feet tall, sees the first three Jews sent home and lets out such a yowl! "The yiddles are rejected, hey, doctor, Your Honor? All dying of this disease and that! Something doesn't smell right, doctor! *We* can get our asses shot off, oh yes! Look!" His fellow recruits also began to mumble and shout in a nasty, threatening way. "*Three* rejected, and who *are* they? Yiddles! Every one!"

Dr. Rosnikov, hiding his worry, shouted them down. So you will understand, I'm sure, how it came to pass that when the *fourth* Jew, unsuspecting Schlomo Kogen, *schlemiel* first class, son of your old neighbor, Mordecai Kogen, head of the burial society, and pinochle friend of Papa's, came before my friend Doctor Rosnikov, he looked into Schlomo's healthy eyes, his clear throat, and, fifty rubles or no fifty rubles, declared the poor boy to be a perfect specimen, fit for service! Schlomo must have been stunned; he told the doctor he felt very sick, but the doctor waved him into the room for *shtarkers*.

The doctor came rushing to me immediately in great distress to explain what had happened, returning to me Kogen's thirty-five rubles as if they were tainted with bubonic plague. Once Schlomo was accepted, he said, the other recruits stopped grumbling, and turned to insulting Schlomo instead. Dr. Rosnikov therefore expected no further trouble (for himself—Schlomo's problem was Schlomo's problem).

The good doctor was not my only visitor that enchanted night. Schlomo's father, Reb Mordecai Kogen—your friend, Papa's friend—came to see me also, together with his empty-headed, frantic wife. He was Samson at the temple, fire steaming from his nostrils. I was surprised his gray beard did not burst into flame. As he snorted flame, I saw an ancient prophet predicting doom, and I knew whose! His wife, a shrill echo, repeated his every word, three octaves higher.

Now, I know all about Reb Kogen and his burial society! From

both Dr. Rosnikov and Abramele Shapiro, I learned that Reb Kogen buries no one; instead, the bodies of paupers he sells to the medical school in Vilna for a fancy kopek, and there they are cut up by Russian boys and Abramele, in anatomy classes. An unthinkable desecration under Jewish superstition, but he has made a fortune larger even than mine. The boxes he buries he fills with dirt. If people knew what he was doing, he would *ooser* be the president of the Benevolent Burial Society!

He refused to take back his fifty rubles. No. No. No. He paid, in trust, on the advice of others wiser than he, the *tzaddik* himself, the mighty Rebbe Schmulkowitz of Minsk, may he be in the earth! May I also be in the earth! Fifty rubles, some "foolproof" method!

He thundered and squeaked. Schlomo could have been hidden by his mother's uncle in Vilna, no? For a *hundred* and fifty rubles he could have gone all the way to America! Mordecai Kogen, even though he is one of the Kohanim and presumptively holier than the rest of us, is a man with no saving graces. Yet who denies that *schlemiel* Schlomo, reverent scholar of Talmud Torah, a Maimonides in the making, according to his father, was the apple of the old man's eye, the jewel in his house, the crown for his head? His feeling for this *schmendrick* son touched me. I felt terrible.

That *his* Schlomo should go in the army was worse than his own death by torture! This he explained slowly with tears streaming into his beard, something I never dreamed to see. His face was a ghostly white. If Schlomo is not returned safe and unharmed by tomorrow morning, he, Mordecai Kogen, goes personally to the *goyishe* authorities and tells everything. No matter what! Yes! Everything! He will pull the pillars of the temple down around himself!

His eyes turned suddenly as wild as his wife's. It always seemed a crime to him, he said, spitting on the floor, to have a crazy young man—an unbeliever, an anarchist, a revolutionist, however handsome and also, he'll admit it, a pretty good woodcarver—it was not right for such a one to represent the people of Jew Street!

This was a job for an elder, someone with a little *chutzpah*, a little *schmeichel*, a real Yiddish *kop*. Because of my so-called "connections," he had gone along on Reb Horowitz's say-so, much to his undying regret, may I soon be in the earth!

He was giving me warning. And stupid me, still not understanding the uses of power, I told him again that all I could do was return his fifty rubles, sorry as I was for him. What could I do, since the doctor had been in great danger when the *posheter goy* exploded? The doctor was a man the whole community must protect, he was needed for the future, for other men's sons. Uncles, he didn't give one damn for other men's sons *or* the community. "Now-

adays," I said, "men *escape* from the army," trying to give the old man a rag of a hope. "Every day they escape."

"Not my Schlomo!" he stormed. "Do fish fly?" Kogen's wife squeaked. "My Schlomo is a good boy! He wouldn't *try* to escape."

That was the moment when I realized why I had been keeping fifteen rubles for each candidate. There *was* an enormous risk. *Dissatisfied customers will not take their money back.*

Desperate, I told Reb Kogen I knew exactly what he had been up to all these years, and that if anything happened to me or the doctor, everyone in Jew Street would know what he did with dead paupers. He turned purple. I left home before he could answer. Mordecai Kogen was in no condition to listen to reason or threats. He was half crazy with grief and his wife was completely crazy.

I hurried to warn Doctor Rosnikov. The doctor was not at home; he'd gone to a patient's house. Not there. Gone to another. I chased after him through the snow-filled streets, clawing my way from house to house for four hours. The last patient said she thought he'd gone to the hospital. Another long hour. By the time I had dragged myself through snow and slush to the hospital, through those dark streets, it was already very late. The excited nurse at the clinic said that the doctor had just a few minutes ago been arrested, taken away by two policemen. Mordecai Kogen had not waited until tomorrow morning. He had been quicker than I.

Home I went! Exhausted, back down Hospital Street, the snow heavier by the minute, my feet sucked by the mud at the riverbank, past a small fire near the tobacco plant, to which curious people were beginning to run. When I finally arrived home, who was at our door to greet me but a big military policeman, taller even than I, and unfortunately with a rifle. "Come along, Jew bastard," he said politely in his Odessa accent, pointing his weapon at me, "we have a distance to walk and it's late. My teeth are freezing waiting for you. My orders are to bring you in . . . on foot, it says in my order, *on foot!* see? In chains, it also says in chains. Right here."

He unfolded a piece of paper. "See, this is a warrant. It says here —'in chains,' and 'on foot'! It's a long way. Come."

Beneath the uniform, the foul way he addressed me, I could see he was a decent, stupid man. "Come on in," I said. "Warm up. With your permission, I'd like to pack a few clothes in a valise and put on a heavier coat. Does that paper say we both have to freeze to death? You could use a heavy muffler yourself." Reluctantly he came in, blustering for me to be quick, but I noticed he had slow reflexes.

Aunt Leah happened to be there—Mama says her presence in-

variably heralds disaster. How a woman can hate her father or her sister as much as Leah does I can't imagine; she visits only to torture them. Mama says it goes back to when they were little girls and *Zayde* had insisted Mama, the bright one, should go to school while Leah, the dull one, had to stay home, get up at five, feed the chickens, and fetch the water from the pump. Leah still feels victimized, but she never got any brighter. She was the *last* one Mama wanted to witness my arrest.

I told Mama she shouldn't worry, I was innocent. However, I was worried, Uncles, can you doubt it?

With my clothes I stowed into the valise the hollow book containing your letters, and my fifteen hundred rubles, five years' accumulation.

Feygele, now quite handsome, arrived, saw what was happening, and began to howl with unrestrained boldness at Odessa, calling him a Cossack, oppressor of the people, while little Isaac sobbed, big tears flowing. Mama, unable to control events, yelled at Feygele, "Stop calling names! *Shah!* A revolution we don't need tonight!"

The racket brought our neighbors out into the courtyard to observe my departure. I gave the policeman my wool scarf and helped wrap it around his throat. Then he locked my wrist to his and put the chains on my feet. My neighbors watched in silence. As far as they were concerned, I was going to my execution. Sheyna Rasel Rubenstein darted after me into the snow and recklessly clung to me. She had to be removed from my waist by the policeman, and still she followed hatless and coatless in the snow, calling "Moishe! Moishe!" until my mother came to fetch her. Sheyna Rasel is a big girl now—nineteen, and handsomer than Freda.

I was locked to my policeman. We're *both* in chains, I thought—mine real, his invisible, setting forth into this blizzard, wrist to wrist.

We walked and talked. I did most of the talking. In the beginning he grunted or was silent, surprised my Russian was so much better than his. He had the accent of a Southern yokel. He had no idea why I was being arrested. He said he was a dockworker's son. His father had also been a thief when things got slow at the docks. Snow kept blowing in our faces in great gusts, unusual for Minsk at this time of the year, while he dreamed about the palm trees of Odessa. Along Saslaki Street, we saw Christmas lights dancing in some windows and doors, and watched carts and an occasional sleigh go by, the smoking horses plodding up the hill. The new horse-car passed us, lit with candles, but *Gospodin* Odessa and I were not part of the Christmas festival *this* year.

I called this to his attention. I spoke also of injustices in Minsk

and elsewhere, of the shameful life stevedores, like his father, are still forced into, of how important it is for one who loads a ship by his sweat to own a part of that ship, just as a *moujik* who works the land should own his land, or a tobacco worker part of his factory. Otherwise, people starve and are driven to a life of crime, while the owners keep everything! My polemics are not bad once I get going. Twice when we came to a cross-street, it was I who indicated the way, because I knew which way I wanted to go and, knowing we were heading *generally* in the right direction, he shrugged and came along. He didn't know Minsk very well. One street was as good as another. Plodding along the gas-lit street, we saw a glow from the tobacco plant. The fire I had passed earlier, now much bigger. Odessa and I quickened our pace to join the throng still rushing to see the excitement. A fire for Christmas! Well, fires in Minsk are certainly not unusual, but this one was huge, the factory gloriously ablaze and very beautiful. Firemen arrived to gossip and watch it burn to the ground. "Come," I said finally to Odessa, who was really enjoying himself, "we haven't got all night." And reluctantly, looking for a long time over his shoulder at the crackling flames, he more or less let me lead the way.

At last I saw the sign I was looking for, the tavern owned by Meyrovitz, Reb Meyrovitz's brother, the one who left Jew Street, married that fat, rich *shiksa*, and set himself up with a little restaurant and inn plus three or four sporting girls. Competing with Sarah the Salt-seller. He calls himself Vladimir Viktorovich Proskurov. My best chance. By now I was no longer "Jew bastard" to Odessa, and I no longer thought of him as "Cossack."

I said, "It's not cold enough for you? A man used to palm trees and warm sea breezes? Too bad we couldn't have carried some of that fire with us. Listen, so if we get to headquarters fifteen minutes late? There's some kind of timetable? We're a railroad? They're staying up for us? I promise you, when we get there, no one will know who *you* are, or who *I* am, or what I was arrested for, with these foolish ridiculous chains! What they'll want to hear about is the fire. You have the wrong man anyway. It's a farce, a mistake. So who will ever know that we stopped to get a spot of vodka? Would it be better if we both froze to death and never arrived at all?" I could hear the slow clanking of his mental machinery.

"We're not dogs, are we? *You*, a loyal soldier of the Tsar! Listen, I have one ruble—my last ruble. Let me buy you a drink!"

In we went. Proskurov (Meyrovitz), greeted us—bald, fat, as tall as I, and pink, powdered and clean-shaven as any Russian—with that round red nose of his, he doesn't look even half a Jew. One glance at the soldier, the chains, my clothes, my black beard, and he

grew panicky. But what can you expect of a *meshumed*? Eight or nine rough drinking pals were at a table having *schnapps*. Before Odessa could say a word, I shouted in Russian with gusto, "Can't you see we are frozen, Proskurov? Have you no heart for a fine soldier like Styopka Aleksandrovich? All the way up from Odessa, cold, hungry, thirsty! Close the fat mouth, Proskurov, and bring us each a *shkalik* of vodka!"

As he passed me, his mouth still hanging open, I whispered in Yiddish, "For me, *water*." He hesitated, and I muttered, "For the sake of your old *cheder* friend, my Uncle Yankele Singer."

At this he became agitated, rolled his eyes, and shuffled off, terrified that I might expose him to his customers. For the next half hour Proskurov poured Styopka Aleksandrovich four full tumblers of vodka, and me four tumblers of water. We toasted the Tsar and Tsaritsa. We toasted Proskurov. I acted drunk, made a few jokes. The other guests were uncomfortable in the presence of a Jew in chains and a soldier, and they left before the third toast.

After the fourth drink, my friend Styopka Aleksandrovich put his head on the table and began to hum gently and mumble the names of his six sisters. Soon he was sleeping the sleep of the innocent, without a care.

As he snored, I struggled through his pockets and found the key that locked us together. I was free. I gave Proskurov five rubles and asked him to lend me a razor. I explained to him that the razor was not to cut this nice guy's throat, but merely to shave off my own beard, which I found inconvenient.

"What will I say when he wakes up?" Proskurov yammered.

"Tell him I went to piss," I said. "That's the last you saw of me. An innkeeper's job is to provide lodgings, drinks, and food. You also have girls, right? *That* might interest him. *His* job is to guard prisoners." Proskurov nodded stupidly—a perfect match for Sleeping Beauty from Odessa. I'd give a ruble and a half to have heard that discussion. But for me, *meshumed* or not, he was a lifesaver.

I could see the wheels turning in his head. He should call the police! His duty! Also it wouldn't look bad for him to have a Jew arrested at his inn. *This is the inn where the owner called the police!* Make him a sharp, proper citizen. But what might *I* say as they were dragging me away? "Fine fellow you are, Proskurov! A Jew yourself, and you do this? Oy, go ahead, deny it!"

Did he need that? One wild shout by me to bring his whole house down? Big wheels have little wheels. Proskurov wanted to fade into the scenery, be one of many, faceless. Why do I understand his yearning so clearly?

I went back, relieved myself, took the razor and strap, and in no

time was beardless. I offered Proskurov forty rubles for his new suit of clothes and a fur-lined coat, a fortune for him, and, dressed like a gentleman in clothes a bit loose-fitting, I was soon in the snow again, with only a few fresh cuts on my face, more Russian than Proskurov. I gave him a note to deliver to Mama, telling her I had safely escaped and would write by the Yiddish post; meanwhile she should say nothing—even to Papa or the neighbors. Trust no one— that commandment I had just learned from Styopka, who, trusting no women, trusted men. Me, for one.

By now the sun was coming up. Sunday. In the gray morning light I saw Yoshke the Peddler driving through the waning storm directly toward me, with a wagonload of pots and pans pulled by his exhausted Jewish horse, straggling toward the Lower Market. For two rubles he took me aboard, turned his horse around, and headed to the railway station. The old horse moved uphill as if each step was his last. I was planning to get a ticket through Warsaw to Hamburg. There I could make my decision: Berlin, London, or New York. I was undecided.

As we approached the station, with its arches, ornamental iron-work and many chimneys, I saw a sight I had never seen before. In the square and all around the station were knots of men who appeared to be mostly thugs, ruffians, drunkards, roughnecks in from the country—completely out of keeping with the elegance of the station—peasants in workclothes jabbering as if preparing for a festive hunt. What would they be hunting? Workers were there, too, in their Sunday best, men from the mills, the tobacco plant, the kilns, construction workers, brewers, railroad employees, men from the forge. Yoshke turned his horse around and fled. I entered the station, which was also filled with men. At six in the morning? They appeared to be organized, for many carried huge staves which inside the terminal they clacked against the benches, making enough racket to rouse a cemetery, and laughed at each other's crude jokes.

I could distinguish the words of one of the men who appeared to be a leader, and I felt the fine chill of a new terror. "Let's kill every goddamn Yiddle! You hear me? Death to the Christ-killers! Drinkers of the blood of Christian children!" And a hoarse screech: "Does Grodno know how to take care of their *zhids* better than we do?" A chorus: "NO!" from a hundred throats. Great cheering. A carnival spirit. There must have been a pogrom in Grodno I hadn't heard about yet.

All plans flew out of my head. Through the windows I could see in the square fifteen or twenty empty peasant carts, each drawn by

two- or three-horse teams, waiting. My knees felt weak and watery. As calmly as I could, I walked through the station exit facing Railway Square, past the line of ten or twelve waiting droshkies for hire, shaking my head to the polite but jolly drivers. And there, just beyond the line of peasant carts, stamping his feet to keep warm, with a few uniformed subordinates, no doubt assigned to "keep order," who did I see but my old friend Sergei Nicholayevich Karpovich, chief inspector, standing beside his handsome white Arabian steed. He did not recognize me even when I addressed him directly. "Your Honor, what is happening? Who are all those people?"

Taking me for precisely the smooth-faced Russian I was impersonating, he gave me a knowing look, squinting craftily. "Oh, just some boys looking for a little Sunday fun. Sunday's slow in the provinces, sir. They're looking for a little action." He did not sound at all concerned. "Nothing to be alarmed about."

I clutched my precious valise, feeling in the pocket of my greatcoat for the twenty ten-ruble notes I had just put there, counting them with my fingers.

"Are you not," I asked, "Inspector Sergei Nicholayevich Karpovich?" He was surprised, but I continued, giving him no chance to reply. "Tell me, sir, are you free for a little Sunday diversion yourself?" His mouth had opened slightly. "The Three Lions, just across the square, will you share a bite with a stranger from—uh—Grodno?" As I saw him still hesitate, "An important word in private?"

The reference to Grodno caught his attention. While not likely, I might just be a plainclothes agent from Petersburg with a message from high up. My face and that I knew his name must also have posed a riddle to him. He narrowed his eyes further, and all I could think of was *pig, pig, pig;* this was my old friend, who, I now realized, intended to betray me before dark.

His curiosity got the better of him; he turned abruptly to one of his subordinates, gave him the reins of his mount, and told him to take charge of the detachment.

The warmth of the inn was welcome, but its coziness contained elements of absurdity. The inn had been opened to accommodate the thugs who were plotting to spill my blood. They were drinking and roaring at every table; the obsequious proprietor of the inn bowed to my imperious manner and to Sergei Nicholayevich's uniform and, leading us through the room full of ruffians, showed us to a small private room. He, like Sergei Nicholayevich, could see I was a prosperous burgher with important things on my mind, so after he had served us glasses of tea and cakes, he closed the door on us, backing out bowing.

Sergei Nicholayevich asked immediately if I knew what had "really" happened in Grodno, but I told him vaguely that I had not been there during the "disturbances." Surprised, he began to wonder about me, but this was the least of his surprises, for, casting off all my cautions and fears, or rather plunging headlong directly toward them, I said, "You don't recognize me, Sergei Nicholayevich? My face is so different without a beard? The boy who has eaten at your table, who brought you *challa*, whose mother welcomed you into our home on Jew Street? Your giant Jew? Moishe! You yourself have been trying to get me to shave off my beard, so how do you like? And how's Boris?"

Inspector Karpovich turned choleric, his face growing more purple than boiled beets; an uncontrollable coughing fit seized him. I stood, hitting him gently on the back to help him control his spasms.

When his coughing subsided, he said, "You are wanted by the military, my lad—there's an order out for your arrest!" He should only know!

"Why worry about me?" I said. "Tell me, what's about to happen on Jew Street today? Those 'boys' out there aren't here to decorate a Christmas tree."

He shook his head grimly. "Bad," he said. "It will be very bad. Most of them are from the outside. They are not to be stopped. Those are my special"—he dropped his voice very low, almost swallowing his last words—"confidential instructions." He squinted, regretting he had said these words. "The governor himself."

I reached into my pocket, crumpled my two hundred precious rubles, and put them on the table next to his coffee. "I do not ask the impossible," I said. "There is one courtyard in Jew Street. You know it well. Fourteen families. You know them well. I would appreciate it if no harm should come to them."

"Impossible!" he cried, and never have I heard a man sound so genuine in his regret and grief, so sincerely sorry. He pushed the money away so that it fell to the floor.

"*My* house," I pleaded. "My mother, my father—my brother, my sister!"

"I cannot interfere! I can do nothing!" Sergei Nicholayevich practically wailed, and he was a good actor, I thought, for his voice was agonized, sincere. I hated the bastard. I wanted to kill him.

As he stood, I stooped, grabbed the crumpled money from the floor, and began the ritual, seizing him from behind around his shoulders and neck. He did not resist.

"There are two hundred rubles here!" I whispered in his ear. "Give them to whomever you must! They are not for you; I know

you wouldn't take them!" Holding him against the door, I stuffed them like so much trash into the breast pocket of his uniform. We were both breathing harder than normally. I released him. "You must *try*, old friend!" I retrieved my valise and opened the door. "For the honor of your son Boris! Our friendship! For your *Christian* honor!"

"I can do nothing!" he repeated glumly as he hurried away. Then he turned and called almost as if it were an afterthought, "If you hurry, you can hide them! No time to lose." He had gone through the main room of the Three Lions, had reached the exit, and I followed.

"Where?" I shouted after him as he hurried out. I saw him shrug, and he half turned toward me.

"My place," I heard him say low into the morning sun, and my heart leaped. His breath frosted into clouds as he plunged toward his waiting detachment.

I paid the bill, bundled in Proskurov's fur-lined coat, and hurried into the open. As I darted from the station and started to run the half verst down to Jew Street, I saw two huddled figures around a building across from the station. I could have sworn they were Reb Horowitz and Reb Rubenstein, but before I could reach them, they had raced away like terrified ghosts.

Taking to the middle of the cobbled, slippery road, I ran as fast as my long legs and my breath could take me through deserted streets between the silent buildings, toward Jew Street. How to get my family out, the best route to reach Inspector Sergei Nicholayevich's house, how to dress them, what to take with us? I kept looking over my shoulder for the carts the murderers would be coming in. All I could hear was the sound of my own panting. Downhill to the river. Then, when I had almost reached Jew Street, not more than five minutes to go, I heard them, galloping horses, racing down on me, ten or more carts, fifteen or twenty screaming roughnecks in each cart. I slowed to a walk.

As the first wagon approached, the horses slowed, and the gross lout who was driving shouted at me, "Oh, gentleman, would you like a lift to the action? Oy-yoy-yoy! Squeally zhidovsky maidens for the asking! Get aboard!"

With my heart between my teeth I clambered aboard, clutching the valise; several of the ruffians helped me on, grinning. It was difficult to look into their cruel faces and smile back, but I did. Many had vodka bottles and were drinking freely. Several sang lustily, patriotic songs. Imagine my feelings when I recognized one of our group, Ivan Tarkowsky! There he was, his thick glasses down on his nose almost brushing his mousy mustache, our lisping profes-

290

sor of French at the university—who at our cell meetings sniped
away at the Jews when he was not seeking me out to bemoan the
latest official iniquities against "your people" to remind me, I suppose, that I was not among *his* people. Still, I had never *entirely*
mistrusted him. He worked hard for the Movement.

Wrong again, Moishe! Here he was, stave in his manicured hand,
sitting among these hoodlums by the drum of kerosene, checking
his pocket for matches! He glanced at me and grinned; he had no
idea who I was. As we started up again, I could smell the kerosene,
and I noticed the wicker of rags. Behind us raced the other wagons,
and trailing far, far back, barely visible, came six stately policemen
on horses, a white steed in the lead, slowly clopping through an otherwise empty street, the rear guard to this courageous "action." How
would Natasha feel if she could see this? Surely she must have
heard by now what was happening—the word must be all over
Minsk. Where was she? Was she frantic with fear for me? What
was she thinking? *Doing?*

Oh, at this moment how I envied Herschel and Freda their
malarial swamp in Palestine, if they ever got there, and Doctor
Rosnikov his cozy concrete prison cell! Abramele, thank God, was
back in Vilna (I thought) at the medical school. Most of all, I
envied *you* the safety of America, and I knew at that moment that
if I should live, somehow I would get to America myself! The
Movement in Minsk had in these last few hours lost its spell.

Jew Street was deserted. Not a cat was to be seen, and I could
swear I heard the hens in the courtyards whimpering. In the distance the squatters' huts huddled on the banks of the Svisloch.
Windows along the street were covered, shutters drawn. Our horse-
and-cart parade slowed, hesitated, the nags exhaling a thick smoke,
the wheels clattering over cobbles, axles squeaking. The lead cart I
was in was still several hundred yards from my house, when I cried
with authority, "Here we are!"

The driver, thinking he had heard the command of a general,
pulled the horses to a sudden halt; without further signal the carts
behind us stopped, and scores of red-faced louts, many by now so
drunk they barely knew which way to go, jumped to the cobblestones, eager for the sport to begin. Some were swinging sloshing
cans of kerosene, others carried staves, sledgehammers, long-handled
axes, all shouting in great disorder. One man handed me an axe.
Some took hurried last swigs of vodka and smashed the empty flasks
on the muddy cobblestones. In chaos they entered the nearest court-
yards, like agents of the devil. I remained behind, unnoticed, in my
cart.

Trying to ignore the screams of my terrified neighbors, men and

women I had grown up with, I started my nervous horses toward the Singer courtyard. "Go! Go!" I flipped the reins, and off they trotted. It was a tougher job to make the old nags stop when I reached my house, but I pulled the reins with all my strength, crying "Enough! Halt! Stop!" in both Russian and Yiddish. By the time I dismounted my right hand was bleeding, cut by the reins; with my frozen left hand I clutched my valise—my holy icon.

After fastening the reins to the post in front of our courtyard, suitcase in one hand, axe in the other, I dashed ahead and slipped on the ice, to fall flat on my face just as I entered our yard. I rose, stumbled forward blindly, tore the *mezuzah* from the doorpost, thinking wildly I could always swear we were the *goyishe* janitors! I smashed open the locked cellar door with the axe. Huddled about our stove were Mama, *Zayde* trying as usual to crawl under her skirts, and for some reason Aunt Leah again, with her fancy feathered hat. Feygele, too, and I had never seen *her* so white and grim, and Sheyna Rasel Rubenstein from upstairs, along with her mother —not only neighbors now, but *mischpochah!* The women were stricken at the sight of me and my axe, but stoical Sheyna Rasel showed faint, hesitant signs of puzzled recognition. Reb Rubenstein was not present, still no doubt scurrying back from the railway station to sound the alarm! But Papa was there, his hand on Isaac's shoulder. Papa had prepared for the worst, as Jews have prepared for centuries. Pack the linen, put up the shutters, bolt the doors, pray, and wait for the storm to come and, with God's help, to pass over. The victims did not want to see their oppressors' faces. What difference did faces make? It was a storm of nature, an explosion.

Papa avoided looking at me, kissed the Book as he read, redoubled the speed of his praying. Forbidding, arrayed in special prayer *tallis* (usually reserved for the High Holy Days), dressed in his fur-trimmed satin caftan with flowered design—suitable for spring wear —and his round Hassidic street hat, *tefillin* straps wrapped around his arm and on his forehead, he stood before his arsenal of books, the guardian of the law—as if the law could save anyone. Isaac was dressed exactly like Papa. They were reading aloud and in unison— much louder after I entered—for some reason that passage in Genesis where Abraham negotiates with God about God's threat to destroy Gomorrah.

Aunt Leah looked at me and suddenly shrieked an unearthly sound, calling upon the name of the greatest of all pogromists, a blood-curdling cawing of a crow, "*Chmielnicki! Aaannhhh!*" Drawing out her shriek to make it heard for ten versts around. And this, naturally, started up Madam Rubenstein. Oh, what a duet! Mama wept quietly, thank God, with some dignity. I wanted to hug

Mama. Among the ladies only Sheyna Rasel (blazingly handsome, supremely confident) was silent, still faintly smiling, puzzled, while Feygele stared at me, still taking me for a pogromist, cold fury in her eyes.

In a glance I could imagine it all—wigs torn off, women stripped, raped on the spot by one brute, then another. All the fears, whispered from generation to generation. Men roaring with vodka, laughing, waiting their turns, forcing our women at the point of a knife. All the stimulating, terrible secrets we used to whisper in *cheder* whenever the subject of pogroms had come up.

That morning, my lucky uncles and aunts, safe in your faraway Atlanta, the scenes I imagined were enacted in grim reality in house after house, women and girls torn, invaded, while our men looked on, held helpless by our oppressors—we shall soon have a harvest of half *goyim*. Fourteen people I know of are dead, including two babies; houses burned out; furniture, clothing, holy books, the ark and the houses of prayer smashed, burned. A rampage. Many Jewish men and women in Minsk can no longer look into each other's eyes. Bravery rewarded with death. Those of us who bent our backs to remain, who can say little enough for us?

First I quieted the women. I set down my valise, put a hand over Leah's mouth, calling quickly in Yiddish, "Don't you recognize your own Moishele? Just because a beard is shaved off?" Suddenly they were gasping with amazement, for when they heard my voice, they recognized me, and Sheyna Rasel said shyly, "I *knew* it. I just *knew*."

"Hurry," I said. "Follow me!" It was not easy to keep Papa from trying to gather some of his most precious silk-covered books, to stop Mama from beginning to pack! "Are you all crazy?" I cried. "Come! Out, out! The cart! Get in the cart!"

As we emerged, posted at the entrance to our courtyard, who did I see—to my astonishment—but Inspector Karpovich, astride his enormous white stallion. One hand was on his holster. I had no idea what he would do or whom he might shoot. So ignoring him I urged the family on. I untied the horses. Everyone scooted out and clambered one by one up into the cart; Aunt Leah and Papa pulled *Zayde* aboard, and the inspector, who followed, nodded to me briefly, as though satisfied, a debt paid, and my heart, which had been hammering, began to fall back to its regular beat.

But where was Mama? I looked back. There! God, she had slipped and fallen on the ice at the entrance, the same slippery spot where I had fallen earlier, a hundred meters back! I hesitated.

"They're getting a bit out of hand," the inspector, not seeing her, announced in that under-the-breath tone, and started back toward

the entrance. We could both hear the screaming, and see with our own eyes what was getting out of hand.

"Mama! Hurry!" I thought she would get up and come to us, but she did not. She lay at the entrance to the courtyard. I did not go back.

Inspector Karpovich, looking about, seemed still not to have noticed Mama. "They'll pay for this," he muttered. Meanwhile, I could see who was paying. "My mother!" I cried to Karpovich, and pointed to her fallen form. Our horses had begun to move slowly. I jumped aboard, the valise under one arm, in my hand the axe. Aunt Leah suddenly screamed Mama's name. Mama was sitting up, dazed, and began weakly to call out. She put an arm out, beseeching. Poor Mama, always so self-reliant, wanted help. And how I wished I could run back for her! But I was driving the horses. Papa, stricken, his eyes bulging, turned inward. He looked away. Papa prayed.

We could hear the screaming. Smoke was pouring out of my old *cheder*. A tiny irrelevant bit of my mind recalled Reb Moskowitz, his stupid wife, and the cat-o'-nine-tails, and I thought, good riddance, *cheder*, may you burn to the ground! Who can control his thoughts? I didn't want to think of Mama, sitting there dazed, needing me as I had needed her so many times! And *she* had always come!

Our horses neighed as they ambled off, tense and nervous from the smoke pouring from buildings and the noise; the figure of Mama was getting further away. She stood up with difficulty and began to limp painfully in our direction. Feygele jumped from our cart calling "Mama! I'm coming!" and ran back toward her. Men, women, children were running from fires now, ruffians chasing them through the streets, some carrying choice pieces of furniture or clothing along with their staves. They struck at fleeing Jews until several of them lay still in the street. I saw Abramele Shapiro's mother lying half naked in the frozen mud, and two friends of Herschele being beaten. But no one had yet bothered Mama, who limped along toward a running Feygele. One of the hellions pointed at us suddenly and shouted, and many more started running toward us, brandishing staves, torches ablaze. I struck the nags to get them moving more quickly.

"You know where to go?" the chief inspector called from atop his horse, as we pulled slowly away.

I pointed back to him, and he nodded. I gestured wildly now to call his attention to Mama; he signaled, and I knew that he had seen her at last. Feygele had reached her by now. Our horses were suddenly reluctant, one pulling one way and a second the other, the

third standing fast, so that our pursuers, who had to cover a few hundred yards, were almost upon us. Uncooperative beasts! Now they decide there's no hurry! In a panic I opened my valise, seized a handful of money, and threw it out behind us; the bills were caught in the cold wind and scattered. One pursuer picked up a three-ruble note and showed it to his cohorts. Losing interest in us—except for a smart one who kept crying, "The valise, get the *zhid* with the valise!" they, too, scattered after the bills, scooping up one here, another there, emitting triumphant cries. I saw Mama, now helped by Feygele, staggering in our direction.

Then a large, dark lout struck Feygele, and seized Mama roughly by the blouse and ripped it. I heard a single shot in the cold December morning, and my eyes followed the sound. Chief Inspector Sergei Karpovich's revolver was still smoking in his hand. The pogromist had released Mama, was holding his open, bleeding belly. Chief Inspector Karpovich watched this man sink slowly to the ground, returned his revolver to its holster, dismounted, and, ignoring the wounded man, reached first toward Mama with both hands, lifted her and placed her upon his horse, then repeated this with Feygele. Our cart turned a corner, we lost sight of them, and I cried out, "They'll be all right, they'll be all right, Papa." He continued to pray like one possessed, and why not? His prayer had done the trick.

If only it were Tarkowsky that Karpovich had shot, but of course, no such luck. It was a *moujik* in his Sunday clothes, some poor ignorant bumpkin, in from the countryside for a bit of harmless sport. Suddenly, for no reason *he* could fathom, he had a gaping, painful, fatal hole in his stomach, and his life was draining off in blood and agony. In a flashing moment I felt almost a vague pity for him, and enormous relief about Mama. I had also a strange feeling I can't describe toward Feygele. Anger? A fury of some kind. Why?

Martin set the huge letter aside. How could something written by his grandfather nearly a century ago trouble him? Old Moishe had not been willing to risk his neck to save his mother. So? Instead, he threw money at the problem. Not too edifying. All those goddamn checks he had written to UJA—what did it mean, rich Jews throwing money? But Feygele had gone back. She had risked her ass and her neck.

One thing sure, however; leaving this Karpeyko guy in Minsk to his fate was not quite the same as abandoning your mother. Mustn't get confused. But somehow, imperceptibly, that cousin had become a hell of a lot more than merely a long-lost cousin. God knows what those Russian

goons might be doing to him. Jenny and Rachel were ready to leave the cart and go back, were they? And he was telling Jenny she *couldn't?* Did he have the right?

Something else troubled him. Moishe—and Feygele—had apparently thrown themselves into the Movement. Both feet, head, and heart. Yet even then in the Movement there were Tarkowskys. He recalled the public furor over Father's confirmation in the Senate, the thinly veiled speeches, the polite venom, obscure code-words, references to "alien" values. And a vote of forty-five to thirty-six. Thirty-six senators of the United States against one brilliant Jew!

In Russia this year they were calling it Zionism. But the name made little difference. Non-Aryans, heretics, Cosmopolitans, Christ-killers, drinkers of Christian children's blood, perpetrators of the Protocols of Zion, Jew radicals—stylish dressing for old stupidities. That day in Pusey's office he had felt it under all his elegant clothes, the familiar cold sweat felt by Jews since the beginning.

Son of an associate justice of the highest American court, a Porcellian, Harvard forty-three, the leading merchant of his day, with friends who were generals, college and bank presidents, senators, chiefs of great American corporations and unions—sweating because, as Lord Beaconsfield and Sigmund Freud and Albert Einstein and Jesus of Nazareth had all learned of themselves, he was a Jew, and heir to special ills. His cousin in Minsk, poor bastard, must have forgotten that, as Martin himself had from time to time. But they reminded you. Sooner or later. Was that what made this poor bastard in Minsk more than a long-lost cousin? Well, if *he* wouldn't leave the cart—*couldn't* leave it, could he? Sam Rose had made that crystal-clear—at least he ought to let Jenny go. After all, what could happen to her?

2

He returned compulsively to his grandfather's letter.

Madam Karpovich took us in as if seven Jews came calling every year the Sunday before Christmas. She was tactful and quiet. Aunt Leah beat her breast and wailed about her lost sister. The rest of us tried to ignore her. Boris was there, too, for which I was grateful, and when he learned the secret of my transformed appearance, he greeted me in comradely fashion, which only the two of us fully appreciated. But where, he asked, was Feygele? Her absence upset him. I told him about Mama, how Feygele had gone back after her and of the marvelous behavior of his father. I sensed that, having assured himself of Feygele's safety, he had only a polite interest in the rest of my family or the desolation being visited on my neighbors. He feigned shock, of course, but a shock only to some assistant brain. Tut, tut. Deplorable. So they were all the same! Tarkowsky was not alone! I wondered bitterly about Alexei and Natasha. Where had *they* been, where had *she* been, while the Jewish ladies of Minsk were being forced to the wall? I was beside myself. Some solidarity!

Good-naturedly, Madam Karpovich prepared food. She consulted Papa, who advised what her guests could eat, since even her plates were not kosher! She took his advice in good spirit and cracked her granite face frequently to smile reassuringly at each of us.

From the window, I saw Karpovich's Arabian mount approaching, the inspector in the saddle, supporting both Mama, who was riding almost in his lap side-saddle, and Feygele, who rode in front of her like a boy. My heart leaped. Mama was talking, nodding. He was supporting her, holding her naked shoulder. They entered the house, Karpovich still clutching Mama's arm, Feygele following, her hair wild, her eyes crazy. Karpovich treated Mama as if she were a

countess; for her part, she was strangely flushed, reminding me of a startled eagle, with her narrow straight nose and its tiny hump, her lightly freckled face, her customary erect soldier's posture.

Suddenly her eyes, which had been fogged over, flashed with scorn, and she pierced Papa with what I can only describe as the original evil eye. "You!" When she turned to me, she wore an entirely different expression—one of grief. I grieved, too, my flaws reflected in that wild, sorrowful stare. I can't describe her expression, Uncles—the crumpled features of one who sees her life's work in ashes. How I wanted to embrace her, to comfort her, to have her comfort me, but I dared not.

Nor did she come to me. I will never forget how she turned instead, slowly and before us all, half unclothed as she was, and put her arms deliberately around the paunchy Karpovich and kissed him on the mouth. An unthinkable act for a pious Jewish woman. No one spoke until Karpovich, who reddened slightly, broke the silence.

"You must all stay the night," he said gruffly, good-naturedly, but quite flustered. These were crazy times, he said. Who could explain them? Something stupid like that.

I could not take my eyes from Mama, the great rip in her blouse, the ugly gash across her throat running to her breast. Her lip was swollen, and I was astonished to realize her wig was gone. Her hair is iron gray, wavy, and long enough to be curled, not shaved as it is supposed to be. The sight of so much of her bare flesh, the bloody lip, the look in her eye, her real hair, and Karpovich's arm around her waist possessively, the way she leaned on him, in full view of Papa, was obscenely disturbing. Suppose she had been killed? I began suddenly to tremble.

Feygele was standing, facing me. She took two steps toward me until we were only inches apart, and spit deliberately in my face. "Go, run to America," she said before I could recover. "Run away." Feygele is not usually given to melodramatic gestures. And before all the others!

The inspector began to talk. I was so stunned by Feygele that for some time I scarcely heard him. But finally, I began to listen. Here was a *man*, I thought, unlike my "friends"—including his son Boris right here—Alexei, Rumiantsev, all of them. Imagine—my comrade-in-arms, Tarkowsky, turns out to be the devil's disciple! I piss on the lot of them.

I know what is in your minds: who am I to complain about *them?*

Speaking of these comrades, Boris, once Feygele arrived, took her under his personal protection, all solicitousness. They were off to-

gether first in one corner, then another, talking earnestly, and once when Boris said something, I saw Feygele smile, then laugh aloud, and she touched him lightly on the cheek. He gave her a comb and she managed to bring her wild hair under control. Immodest for a Jewish maiden as it was, she combed it publicly until all the tangles were gone; then Boris helped her tie it up. In these gestures there was an intimacy I never suspected. When it was time to go to sleep, Boris dragged out his own mattress for her, and held her hand longer than necessary to say good night. They had seen each other at our meetings, of course, but never before had I seen behavior like this.

Next morning, Inspector Karpovich took me aside and said confidentially, "You might be interested to know the governor next week is going to name me the next commissioner of police." There was a certain charm in his shy attempt to conceal his pride. The new police lord of Minsk! "Over the heads of three men senior to me."

He chuckled. "Well, I kept out of trouble, never pried where I wasn't asked. Followed orders, humbled myself, never complained, never did anything unusual until today. I hope today will not change His Excellency's mind. I can't decide what got into me! Don't make sudden moves, that's the sure path to success in the bureaucracy; still, I never really expected it!"

I congratulated him, and said that I hoped saving my mother's life would not destroy his chance for advancement. I told him I would always remember this day, but he waved my sentiment aside as if it were foolishness.

The peasant he had shot died the next day; his name was Ulevich and he had three children; the *Minsky Lystok* reported that he was a rioter who had died of "a police bullet received when a uniformed guardian of Minsk attempted to quell the riots." The paper did not name the "guardian," nor did it list any of the Jewish dead, injured, or raped. Perhaps the names were too difficult to spell!

Before he left for work in the morning, the inspector (soon commissioner) advised me somberly to leave town at once, since a general alarm was now out for my arrest throughout the *gubernias* of Minsk, Vietbsk, and Mogilev. Bidding me goodbye, he winked as he handed me a small package wrapped in newspaper and tied with a string. When I opened it later, it was a wad of two hundred rubles.

I had to decide quickly where I should set out to. Beyond all reason, the magic of America beckoned. Your letters—come, they

said, come, come to our vast land, and meet a new breed of people. Enough for everyone. Even luxury for everyone. Each man his own master. It was too much to resist.

That evening I talked about my intentions to Mama. Sheyna Rasel listened intently. A few meters away stood Boris and Feygele, watching us warily. Mama, still numb, listened as she put the cold supper out on a crate in our wrecked cellar flat, nodding as I spoke. Papa did not respond at all. What surprised me most was Sheyna Rasel. She had been unwilling to leave my side from the moment we all got into the cart yesterday. She took my hand from time to time as if for her own protection, and remained in our cellar to share our supper instead of going up with her own family. She made no effort to hide her feelings. She at least did not blame me for any inattentiveness towards Mama. "Yes, America is the only place, Moishe!" she cried. And with stunning intensity—almost a gasp: "Take me with you, Moishe, take me along!" Mama tried to quiet her foolishness, but a weird desperation seized this determined creature, suddenly dear to me; she called to me, as if to heaven, "I'll be good, you'll never notice me. No trouble, no trouble! Take *me*, take *me*, take *me!*" And to my family, she pleaded, "*Make* him take me!" She twisted my heart, this sturdy, up-to-then self-sufficient girl, whom I had just begun to notice.

From across the room Feygele said sharply, "Go. Go already. Both of you. America is where you belong!"

Ignoring Feygele for the moment, I bent low to Sheyna Rasel and said softly, "I'll send for you—all right? So. It's a promise." What made me say it? Mere kindness? To taunt Feygele, the avenging angel? Something I can't help, I do it all the time. Agreeable Moishe. Saying what others want to hear, even when I don't mean it. She was quiet then, squinching her eyes very tight in a kind of luminous yearning for some future time, a radiant time that could never actually be. She frightened me. Still, I dared not unsay what I had just said.

"You'll send, you'll send, you'll send!" she muttered over and over, seizing my hand and holding it too long, biting her lower lip, engraving my words. She kissed my hands, each of them, solemnly as if in a ritual. She turned to Mama. "He'll send, he'll send!" Papa glowered at me with the menace of an old man who knew more than he could say.

I took hold of little Isaac and kissed him. "Isaac, for you, too, I will send—when you are grown a bit more. This is no place for people like us. In America everything will be possible. You'll see. Will you come?"

Poor Isaac! What could he say? He looked at Mama and Papa. "If they let me," he said. Isaac will be a *mensch* some day.

I turned my entire attention to Feygele. I don't know why. She has this inner fierceness which is missing in me. The trouble with this fierceness is, it could land her in Siberia or on the gallows. I caught her by surprise. I said, "Feygele, why don't you come with me? The two of us in America, they'll never be able to stop us. Two Singers! We'll go right to the top."

She looked at me out of eyes that had turned black with rage, bullets of scorn. "Here I was born! Here I'll die! This land is my right! We have been here for four hundred years! How did I ever get brothers like you and Herschel? Running, to Jerusalem! America! Why are you running? To get away from *yourself*? But you never can, you never can! Who will make the world over? Not you! But it must be done."

Without giving an explanation, I handed Papa half my money to restore his machines and lathes and to fix up the house; I kept what I needed for my passage and to start again in a new land—plenty, I thought, a small fortune. Papa was amazed at the amount I gave him, but he did not thank me, nor offer any blessings for my new life.

I left home, but before leaving Minsk I wanted one last time to see Natasha in spite of everything. Who can say why? I was consumed with feelings stronger than good sense. I wanted to hold her, to feel her flesh quiver on my fingertips, to feel her warmth; perhaps I had mistreated her in my mind, maybe there were reasons she had not come to me. Flesh, Uncles, flesh and the sense of being wanted can undo a man. I was even mad enough to think, if she wants me enough I might entice her to give up everything and come with me! I was willing to take the high risk of a few more hours in Minsk for this.

Natasha herself met me at the great front door. For a moment she failed to recognize me and started to slam the door in my face. She told me she thought I was from the secret police. I merely put one foot in the door and told her who I was; she shook her head in disbelief, and when I attempted to embrace her in my customary way, she still evaded me as if I were a stranger. When I persisted, she said, in a dull, disinterested voice, "Please don't." She laughed artificially, and a bit harshly. "You look like a spoiled, rich merchant now, a greengrocer—no, a butcher, actually. Your *lips* are so big!"

"I thought during our trouble you might have come around," I said mildly. She glowered. How dared I?

"Come," she said. "I'll show you something. Look." She led me into a guest bedroom and I thought, well, we shall soon be in that bed. But she opened a huge carved wardrobe with a gesture of triumph. I saw wooden cases, ten or more, one of which had been opened to reveal four Mauser rifles still in shipping grease. We had been waiting for these for months. "They were delivered Thursday," she said. "From Berlin, to Warsaw, to us. We are asked to get them to Kiev."

I stood openmouthed. Forty guns!

"We could have used them in Jew Street yesterday," I said bitterly.

She rocked back and forth. "You are *so* Jewish," she said, closing the wardrobe door clumsily. She jerked her hand as if toward a pet dog, half snapping her fingers in invitation, and whispered, "Come, come, come, come along. Away from all this—pss, pss, psst . . ."

I followed her back to the drawing room.

"The things I do for the Cause!" she muttered.

We stood measuring each other. Her eyes were dulled, almost dead, but her color was high, as if rouged, her hair half undone. Without a word, listlessly she began to disrobe, like a prostitute. I had the urge for just a moment to sweep her up and carry her into the bedroom, but I did not. She was deliberately vulgar. I merely watched her undress. I watched her coarse gestures. Whatever had to be done, apparently *she* wanted to be the one to initiate it. She flung her clothes from her. Finally she stood naked, her clothes disarrayed on the floor. She held her arms above her head, hands together, as if someone were pointing a gun at *her*, and led the way deliberately to the bedroom, certain I would follow. For a fleeting moment I wondered, was this her penance for having deserted me? I did not care, and I did not follow her into the bedroom. I heard her call my name, insinuatingly, invitingly. I fetched my greatcoat and headed for the door. "You mistake me for Judge Pazhnev!" I called bitterly. "You are confusing me with another customer!"

I heard her scream—a cry of hysterical outrage—but I let myself out the door and slammed it behind me. You can imagine my turmoil as I stood in the street outside her pink mansion in the dark night. My comrades—my own sister—even, in her distorted way, Natasha. Would everyone always turn on me this way? Is no one what he seems at first? Is treachery in every breast? Will there ever be *someone* I can trust?

Natasha long ago accused me of harboring venomous, baseless suspicions—my "nature," she called it. If so, life has confirmed my nature. I have had great expectations of people, but suffer terrible

disappointments. I got Yoshke the peddler to drive me behind his limping beast to Railroad Station Square.

We arrived in New York, all but four of the thousand who set out—three had died (including two infants), and the fourth, a Hungarian girl barely out of her teens, jumped overboard and drowned herself as we were entering New York harbor. They say she was ill with tuberculosis, her lover no longer wanted her, she knew she would be sent back by the authorities, so she leaped into the sea.

It seemed quite the most sensible thing to do. I myself did not know her. The rest you recall—the frantic prayers as we arrived, the ferry rides, the venomous behavior of the American Irishers drunk with power at Castle Garden, the questions, the showers, the medical examinations, the waiting on hard benches for hours. Waiting, waiting. And those few sullen souls, rejected for one reason or another, dry-eyed, hunched, suicidal, discussing their plight with lawyers from Immigrants' Aid, looking for reprieve but knowing in their hearts they would have to go back. Then, once out of Castle Garden, the rounding up of the greenhorns at the docks by the "boardinghouse vultures," the dressmaker bosses looking for cheap clever fingers, the one-time-only joy of families reuniting—a husband and wife, a father and children, often quite shy with each other! Barely remembering each other. Before long I'm sure they'll take each other for granted, perhaps begin to dislike each other. I thought how some day I might be coming down to Castle Garden to greet Sheyna Rasel! This thought surprised me, an acknowledgment to myself of an unwanted obligation; it annoyed me.

When the American Irisher at Castle Garden had finished grilling me, he told me I was free to go, I could go anywhere. This made me intensely uneasy. Anywhere? Where is that?

I hauled my two valises across Battery Park to the El on State Street. Preoccupied faces hurried past me. Signs in English, Yiddish, Russian. On the way to East Broadway, I noticed an unusual man—short, fiery, clean-shaven, heavily freckled, with long, wild, red curly hair, crooked teeth, a thick red mustache, and blue eyes like sapphires. I was aware he had been trailing me since I left Castle Garden, muttering, I couldn't tell whether in my ear or to himself. We came to a dead horse around which flies buzzed.

After a few more steps I turned on him and asked impatiently, "What do you want of me?" My heart went faster, for he was the first person outside Castle Garden I had dared to speak to.

"Moishe?" he responded to me. "Are you Moishe Singer? From Minsk?" He spoke in sneers.

"So? What if I am?"

"So I am the cousin of Abram Shapiro!" He held out his hand, reaching way up to me, and I reached down reluctantly and took it. "The name is Mendel. Also Shapiro. He wrote me you're coming. Heh, you are some giant! So big I was afraid to talk to you!" He laughed. I was glad to meet anyone, even a sneerer. In my mind I said thank you to Abramele. Mendel picked up one of my valises and I took the other and we walked together, back toward the dead horse again.

"A pleasure to find you, Moishe. I was getting tired of meeting the boats. Tell me, what do you do, Moishe?" he asked.

"Hanh?"

"What did you do in the old country? Your trade?"

"Oh," I said, going back to a time that seemed already part of someone else's life. "I made furniture. Hand-carved furnishings. See those hands? They are talented. And in the middle of doing that I was also trying to make a revolution against the Tsar. I guess my heart was not in it, because the Tsar, you notice, is still the Tsar of all the Russias, while I am a greenhorn in America."

"That's a fact?" asked the cousin of Abramele, as if with genuine surprise. "He's still there, the Tsar? I'm sorry to hear that!" And I liked him instantly, my revulsion gone.

"I was supposed to be a socialist," I continued, "but I'm a failure in revolution. Perhaps I'm more of an anarchist." I had reached this conclusion only a moment earlier.

The redhead glanced up and down East Broadway like an exaggerated conspirator, something of a comedian, as if to see if anyone had overheard or understood me.

"You know," he said softly, "a few months ago four anarchists in Chicago were hanged? By the neck? Until dead? The Haymarket Rioters? You see that horse?" A million green flies buzzed over the carcass in the middle of the street. "That horse was an anarchist. You want to start a riot on East Broadway?"

I shrugged. What are riots to me? I have seen the best of them!

"Ah well," he said, inexplicably delighted. "Come along with me." Adding in a voice not much above a whisper, "I, too, Singer, am an anarchist. You are looking at Mendel Shapiro, pain in the tochas and troublemaker first class." He looked capable of at least murder, but how choosy could I be? A friend is a friend.

And so I know my first "American," who had a letter only two days ago from Abramele that I was coming to America. He had cheerfully lied. He'd never been down to meet a boat until today. He showed me the letter. Abram had made up his mind to follow

me to America! He should be here soon. This cheered me enormously.

Always looking to right and left as if still avoiding the secret police, Mendel led me to his home, a house on a place called Rivington Street, where he rents a room; he influenced the landlady to rent me a space also, upstairs from his flat. This landlady, a Roumanian woman, Madam Davidescu, about Mama's age, has five children from seven to seventeen, and her place is littered with clothing which they are all sewing "on contract." The other tenants are Singer sewing machines, which run all day and most of the night. So do I need to make the name Singer famous? It's in every home! One of the most famous names in America! The family sews in the living room, the bedroom, the kitchen. A whole room I don't have. I sleep in a long hall on a hard table with a straw-filled mattress, and worry all night about falling off! I come to a rich land and end up on a table in a narrow hall. To stay balanced on that table through a whole night you have to be an acrobat! Two dollars a week. Is that a reasonable rent? What do I know? I'm a greenhorn.

Mendel took me to a man who changed my remaining rubles to dollars—one hundred precious dollars, which I sewed into my pocket to keep for any emergency, may I never need them! Mendel showed me also how to look for work. You know the Pig Market on the corner of Hester and Essex? There I now go and stand early each morning with my box of carpenter's tools, and those who need repairs, household fixings, they come and hire me to do odd jobs, cabinets, shelves. I fix windows, doors. Landlords pay as little as possible. Women give me work. They pay less.

Through my work I have met more people than I knew in Minsk. Some ask me to supper—women with unmarried daughters in their closet, or socialists. They confess their personal difficulties while I work. One woman gets hives during her "time of the month," especially if she eats herring; how do you like that? The men talk socialist politics with passion and heat, but not much light. (I listen, but do not mention any ideas of my own.) I have been invited to join five synagogues and two socialist organizations. A few say they wish they were back in the old country! Were they expecting maybe to be met at Castle Garden by President Cleveland?

What can I say about New York? Sometimes I'm afraid I'm merely in a different part of the Pale—so many Russian Jews! Galician! Polish! Litvak! Hungarian! Everyone speaks a different Yiddish. Only the *children* learn English. But I've made up my mind to learn it, too. They give free courses at the Educational Alliance, and I go three nights a week.

Instead of Russian peasants, here we have to contend with the Irishers and Italians who live nearby. And the crowds! The push-carts! The hustling! Everyone runs, shouts; who in this country walks or merely talks? The screaming could scare the hood off a *golem*. Not to mention the thieves and murderers walking the streets at night! Smulka would be a little angel here. Still, the days are not so bad. It's the nights.

In my dreams, and worse, when I'm awake and thinking clearly, again and again appears to me that *schleppidich* Schlomo Kogen, suffering tortures in the Imperial Russian Army, trying to cast the evil eye on me! Mrs. Davidescu says I'm always calling in my sleep for *Papa!* Papa, of all people! I can't believe it!

Perhaps, deep down, I am plain homesick. Longing for the family. I've even thought about Sheyna Rasel. Should I send for her? I have the ship ticket money already. But what's the rush? I'm holding off. Maybe it will pass. What a nuisance my conscience is! I must try to get rid of it.

Your American nephew,
Moses

3

LETTER FROM MOSES TO HIS ATLANTA RELATIVES

New York
13 August 1888

Uncle Jacob, Aunt Sadie, Cousin Lewis, Uncle Efram, Aunt Fanny!
Thank you for your letters. It's wonderful to hear from American relatives in America!

Now that I am an old-time New Yorker (six months already), I think I'm accustomed to your real American names: "Uncle Jacob," for example. Does this mean I'm *not* still a greenhorn? Dear Uncles, Aunts, also Cousin, emphatically it does, although I still write in Yiddish. I have new clothes, I've taken my first papers, and I have a Yankee outlook. All I have left from the old life is Abramele Shapiro, the Minsk jailbird, socialist, and medical student, who now lives across from me on Rivington Street.

He, his cousin Mendel, and I all live on the same block. Abram (he does not like to be called "Abramele" any more) sleeps on the kitchen floor next to the stove; his landlady is Mrs. Tessie Rifkin from Warsaw, an intense, chubby creature also about our age. Very pious woman: *shabbos* candles, prayers, the whole thing. She can't afford a mattress for Abram. She has a husband, ten years older, Rifkin the Trimmer, a skinny scarecrow of a man, in the needle trade—you should never be so unlucky as to meet this man, a splitter of hairs, a Talmudist, a Pilpulist.

They have two baby daughters, twins, both sick most of the time. When Tessie Rifkin discovered that Abramele had been studying in the old country to be a doctor, she reduced his rent to a dollar and a half a week. Over this she had some fight with Rifkin the Trimmer! If you want my opinion, Tessie is also much happier since Abram came. Leaving aside her babies altogether. Abram may not be handsome, but he's a charmer in his rough way!

In Atlanta, you heard about our great blizzard in the middle of

March? I should like to ask who arranged I should be at the Educational Alliance just on that occasion? Such snow! Exactly the same snow we have in Minsk, only more of it!

I went back inside, where my English conversation teacher, a young woman from uptown, Miss Weldon—Uncles, I don't have to tell you this is a genuine American name—was bundling herself into her clothes for *her* trip home. Who arranged *this?* I knew she would never be able to get home, since one could scarcely move on the street. The red horse-cars on East Broadway were not running, in fact were not to be seen. Horses are not so dumb! So after we stood side by side looking together out the window at the snow a few minutes in silence, I suggested to her that if she would come home with me, only a few streets away, I was sure my landlady would find her a place to sleep. She was worried about getting word to her parents, but what could we do? The new telephone at the Alliance was already out of order, and all the telegraph wires were out. The whole city was standing absolutely still, except for the cold wind and the swirl of snow.

Before this moment, Miss Weldon and I had never exchanged a private word, although she was always pleasant to me in class. I considered her a well-proportioned, rosy-cheeked, black-haired American goddess, way up there, out of reach; she knew everything I didn't—and suddenly here I heard her muttering under her breath, "Oh, goddamn, damn!" and grinding her teeth. Then she surrendered to fate, sighed, and said to me, "Thank you kindly, Mr. Singer." So we walked out together. I held her arm like a gentleman.

"Oh, dear Jesus!" she gasped. The snow was already half a *sazhen* deep. One step down the stoop and we were in snow above our knees. The wind howled louder. "How will I ever walk through that?" I understood enough English and enough womanly physiology to realize I would have to carry her, so I did. Against such a gale! She thought it was funny, and I laughed merrily to be agreeable, but I can tell you, carrying a healthy full-grown woman (not fat, but no feather either) four blocks through this kind of snow is not *funny*. She was soft, but heavy. I soon had trouble breathing—out was easy, but in was harder. Still, we arrived and, once inside, I let her walk up the four flights on her own legs.

Mrs. Davidescu oozed kindness to her, moved the children in with her so Miss Weldon could have a bedroom all for herself! That's how downtown treats uptown. I think Miss Weldon was a bit worried at our toilet, a separate building down in the yard for all the families in the house. You have to plow your way through the snow and fight the wind to reach it, but she kept her worry to herself. She looked around the flat as if she had stepped on the moon;

for her the experience evidently was a marvelous adventure. Mrs. Davidescu brewed us glasses of tea; Miss Weldon, laughing, learned to drink it through a lump of sugar held between her teeth. The children ran about, crazed with delight not so much by the snow outside as by the fact that stranded here we had a great lady from uptown.

For my part, I found it an unexpected opportunity to practice my English. She complimented me, said I was making excellent progress, but I saw her hold back a smile at the way Mrs. Davidescu and I pronounced certain words. In the morning I did not go down to the Pig Market as usual—who'd look for a carpenter in snow a *sazhen* deep? Instead I offered to take Miss Weldon home on the State Street El. Not a chance! The Els were still not running. You couldn't move an inch! We were stranded together in the house along with Mrs. Davidescu and her children (them I could do without!) for three days and three nights!

Mrs. Davidescu at least had her piecework and could sit and sew on her Singer machine and earn a dollar. Miss Weldon tried to sew on the machine, but was terrible at it. We talked, Miss Weldon and I. I taught her pinochle. She wanted to teach me bridge, but we had the wrong cards. Thus I had continuous private English lessons. I told her how I used to design and carve wood pieces in the old country. I told her about Mama, whom I miss more than ever, and *Zayde*, Herschel, Feygele, and Freda. She told me a few things about herself. She had gone to a snobbish girls' school, she had "come out" at a big dance uptown, where she was "introduced to society" in New York. Like Natasha in Minsk, she went to fancy dances. But she's nothing like Natasha. Finally she grew impatient with this nonsense kind of life and wanted to find work. One day a teacher from her snobbish school brought her down to the Alliance to see the immigrants in an English class. She studied for two years to be a teacher then, but it was not easy to find work in the public school system. However, as long as she did not require pay, the Educational Alliance "permitted" her to teach English to foreigners like me.

I told her I, too, had been a teacher in Minsk—of mathematics— and in my professional opinion she was a brilliant teacher, especially when she read a poem like "The Raven," with great emotion. I asked her how it happened that she was not married, and she grew red in the face. "Oh," she said, "I'm in no hurry! I have time!" But I could see I should never have asked.

On the fourth day, Miss Weldon and I were able to go out, and I took her home. She lives in a part of New York which does not resemble the Lower East Side in any way. It is like Governor Street in Minsk, only bigger. Her home is not Natasha's pink palace, but

is quite a nice building with a brownish stone front. I met her mother and father—he's a banker!—and of course they had been frantic with worry. Over four hundred New Yorkers died in this blizzard! Imagine!

They were both gentle people. Father, a bit pompous, thanked me for bringing their daughter home, but they spoke English so rapidly I could understand scarcely a word. Miss Weldon told them about our days and nights together, and both parents took it with surprising merriment and great relief. She told them I, too, had been a teacher. For a moment I was tempted to tell her bank-president father that actually I was a bank robber. This would give me something in common with him, too—but I restrained myself. Instead, I touched my hat, shook hands, and rode back downtown.

All the way downtown I thought of the Weldons. True, they are not Jews and they are not socialists, but they were not haughty either. They accepted me with more than politeness. And they seemed to really like each other! They have not only money, but taste—I could tell that from the furniture and the paintings. Miss Weldon and I, without pressing a point, got along also. Something in her, which I do not understand at all, drives her toward "less fortunate" people like myself, just as something in me, which I understand much better, drives me toward more fortunate people like her.

After this Miss Weldon took greater interest in my progress. She called on me more often, and after class gave me the names of many books to read, by writers I never heard of—Charles Darwin, Nathaniel Hawthorne, spooky stories by a man called Edgar Allan Poe (the man who wrote "The Raven"), and books about Indians by James Fenimore Cooper. These I found at the Rivington Street branch of the Alliance library.

One day I felt bold enough to ask Miss Weldon if she would do me the honor to have tea with me after class at a café in the neighborhood. She said, "With pleasure, Mr. Singer."

It pleased me to give her such pleasure. I was proud to be her escort, too, for she makes a fine impression on observers: an almost classic face with a cleft in the center of a strong chin, jet-black long hair put up in a bun in the back, with a little straw hat tilted in front. When I walk, I feel important! While her cheekbones are high, her cheeks are full, her nose a bit broad and uptilted, her eyes widely spaced and a deep brown. When she smiles, which is often, there's a dimple in her right cheek, and her teeth are straight and even. She's robust, tall for a woman, taller than everyone else in the class but me. (Of course, except for me, we students are either short Jews or short Italians.) She's also an athlete—rides a horse and plays

tennis—and her voice, with a touch of strange hoarseness, is arresting. If she were a man, what a lawyer she would make!

She has no need for male protection—except for that one *schlepp* through the snowstorm, which she has still not forgotten. She says it still embarrasses her to think of it. Going to a café with me, however, she takes in her stride. I half expect her to march up to the bar, bend an elbow, and order a drink. In fact she did order a gin fizz the first time we went, but only on the understanding that we go "Dutch treat." That's how she wants it, and no argument. It's almost like going out with a gentleman. But not exactly.

Her clothes make her different from most uptown women, who are held together with stays of steel and whalebone, pinched here, pushed out there. Not her. She is entirely soft beneath her clothes; this I assure you, for I have carried her against a demon wind! I know what she feels like, and find it difficult to forget! Her dress on the evening we went to the café was simple, a delightful pinafore. She listens more than she talks (except in class!), and laughs easily, making me feel witty and wise as she responds to my sallies. She also asks me about my life in Minsk. That's a sign of interest in *me*, correct? Not so much the facts, as my feelings.

Why she finds this past life of mine so fascinating I couldn't say, but no detail is too insignificant for her. She has made me describe to her what Karpovich did on Black Sunday several times, and each time she asks about some new detail—about Mama, Papa, Karpovich, even his *horse!* About Sheyna Rasel, *Zayde*, Feygele, Tarkowsky, forcing me to fix in my mind all the things I would like to forget. She asks me to explain. Why, why? Why did I think Feygele urged me so angrily to leave? How do I feel toward Feygele?

However, I don't mind telling her everything, even a little about Natasha (to a point of discretion!). She keeps coming back to Mama, to Feygele and to Freda and Herschel—do I miss them? Do I miss Freda especially? Have they written from Palestine? Yes? What do *they* write? Would I rather be with them? Why did they go there, of all places?

I try to explain, without much success. I tell her that land is held holy by the People of the Book, it is where our ancestors came from, there is a strong historical-religious tug, a tendency for Jews to consider it "home." And she laughs, but in a most polite way. "Why, goodness, the Man we consider the Son of God, our Savior, was born there, died there, and preached there his entire life. His Apostles walked the length and breadth of that land, from the Sea of Galilee to the Mediterranean. Does that mean I want to *live* there? If all Christians ever decided they simply had to go live in *their* holy land, holy Saint Michael! What a crush!"

The way she put it, I was forced to smile myself. Herschel and Freda's decision (Freda's, really) was incomprehensible to me, so how do I explain or defend it?

And what of Freda's younger sister? persists my cross-examiner. The girl called Sheyna Rasel? I tell her I have recently received a letter from her.

"What did the girl have to say?"

"Oh, nothing much. Just writing me the news of the neighborhood."

"Don't you ever read between the lines, Moses?"

You see, suddenly she's calling me Moses, no more Mr. Singer.

"Why on earth would an eighteen-year-old girl write you all the way from Minsk to give you the news of the neighborhood?"

I bought tickets for a Yiddish play on Second Avenue and took Miss Weldon, promising to translate for her. So polished my English isn't, but it's better than nothing. Beforehand we had a fine dinner at Lorber's, the fanciest restaurant on the East Side, with my last dollar. (Except for the secret hundred I still carry sewn in my pants—a magic wad that separates me from all the other greenhorns on the East Side!)

Before the play began, three short, bushy-haired men in the pit— a violinist, a cellist, and a saxophonist—played the "Star Spangled Banner." Such pandemonium! The din, the cheering! I thought a fire had broken out, but people were only screaming, cheering for America! Jews from all over eastern Europe, cheering! They clapped and held their hands over their hearts, as if they had suddenly fallen in love. Moses in the flesh carrying the Commandments in God's personal handwriting couldn't have agitated them more. People sang their hearts out, and I louder than any! What do I feel for America? Who can say? Is it only a place? Or a place in the heart? An idea? A prayer? When the musicians finished, people began to call for an encore: " 'My Country!' 'My Country Tiz'!" they clamored, until they played this song also, and everyone joined in as before—men with beards quivering, women with children in their arms, singing their hearts out in terrible, accented English.

Miss Weldon was looking around. I saw tears fill her eyes, then finally stream down her cheeks. Why was she *crying*? She grew up in America! She smiled up at me reassuringly, her dark eyes glistening.

The play was *Minna*, with David Kessler, a corker of an actor, and Bertha Kalish. Not exactly an "onion" play, either—too unrealistic, about a woman trying to break out of the "enslavement" of her marriage to become "independent," whatever that may mean.

I translated from Yiddish to English for Miss Weldon a bit freely, but the audience was talking so loud, disputing the significance of

this or that with each other, and making remarks to the actors, agreeing with them or insulting them (several very heated arguments took place between members of the audience), that I missed parts of the play altogether. But oh, what a fierce discussion we had afterward, Miss Weldon and I! I said it was unrealistic to expect women to be "independent" like that. For what? What would they be without husbands and children? What would they live on? Miss Weldon exploded. "Have you ever discussed this with a *woman*? Then why not *listen* to *me*?"

"Are you a woman, Miss Weldon? In the full sense?" I tried to pierce her armor deliberately. Her eyes blazed at my impertinence. Her anger enchanted me, and I thought, oh, what a spirited wife this woman would make! Yes, even though she *is* a *shiksa*. Still, I mentioned nothing. Since that moment, an armed truce. We joke with each other, she sulks occasionally, and sometimes she calls me insufferable. Now that she knows me better, she's not quite so polite! She's agreed to come with me to Cooper Union to listen to William Jennings Bryan talk. This shows she is more interested, insults or no.

While I'm busy with Miss Weldon and my work, Abram perseveres in his intention to become a physician. He, too, attends class at the Alliance; he has a Mr. Pomeroy. Beginning at midnight, Abram studies medical books in English. To eat, he works all day for a Yiddish paper, which pays him fifty cents a story. You should see our pugnacious gnome running to every funeral, wedding, fire, and disturbance on the East Side. He covers all the socialist meetings. From our training in Minsk he has no trouble giving his articles exactly the socialist flavor his editors demand. Solidarity! Well, he'll do anything to get through medical school. He takes his entrance examinations this month.

As for socialism in America, who needs it? The police here *laugh* at the socialists. So what makes us think we downtown Jews crowded in one corner of New York should (or could) turn the United States of America inside out? Is Mr. Grover Cleveland the Tsar?

Do Cossacks ride up Rivington Street brandishing whips and chains? Who can believe that the boss of Fashion Frocks is a class enemy? Silverman the *schlemiel*? All the joy, Uncles, has gone out of class warfare, the magic has vanished. Marx sounds merely foolish here.

I've received two letters from Mama, and one from, of all people, Rabbi Levitsky. Nothing from Papa.

After class last night Miss Weldon said she knows a man in the furniture business who would like me to come to his shop. "An op-

portunity," she says. Well, this is the land of opportunity. I'll let you know as soon as I know.

Your nephew and cousin,
Moses

LETTER FROM MOSES'S MOTHER TO MOSES

Minsk
24 August 1888

Moishe, my firstborn:

What sadness of the heart, but don't feel upset, I'm also rejoicing —for the new life of my two precious sons, may blessings fall on you both like rain. What is my life but yours? Bereft I am, yes—first Herschele to the Holy Land, and then you to America. So much I must imagine to find a mother's joy! But don't worry, I can imagine it very well! Your letters help. Be healthy and keep writing.

My prayers for you and Herschele I send to the Uppermost three or four times each day. He'll look after you and protect you, but to be safe, I remind the Nameless One in case He is too busy. As for your leaving Minsk the way you did, what else could you do? I tell Feygele, close the big mouth! Now that we understand the whole story, why you had to leave—Reb Kogen and his wife went all over Minsk with it. What else did they want from my boy? He should be in the earth, Reb Kogen! I told him to his face. You performed only your duty, Moishele. You alone made it possible for many fine Jewish boys, other mothers' sons, to escape the slavery of the army. So—now the terrible price is separation. Terrible, but in this world there's worse. You are alive, a free man, not in prison or sent east. I thank the Blessed One. And that you didn't come to me on that day when I fell, you shouldn't keep writing about this. It's nothing to worry; this, too, I understood. Of course we didn't talk about it; what was there to talk? So for a tiny moment you were only confused. If Feygele hadn't come for me, in another minute you'd have come. This I know. There is nothing to feel guilty about. Also, you knew the inspector would protect me. Didn't all turn out well enough? I'm alive, Papa's alive, my children are alive and safe. This is what counts.

People are leaving Minsk every week, going to Germany, England, America, Palestine. But Papa won't hear of it for us. He will never leave his beloved wonder rabbi! Isaac and Feygele are well. If she marries Boris Karpovich, Papa shouldn't die from a stroke. I owe my life to Boris's father, so can I deny his son my daughter, Jew or no Jew? Poor *Zayde*, may he escape the evil eye! He has still escaped the army! Aunt Leah has a terrible cough, may the Al-

314

mighty spare her; it's no wonder she's sick—her house is always
freezing and filthy.

Be a good boy, Moishele. Keep bundled—all that snow in New
York! I never would have imagined! Papa doesn't mean the things
he says about you, just in case you hear anything.

Sheyna Rasel (such a nice girl!) asked me for your address. I
guess she also writes you.

Our friend, Commissioner Karpovich, is today one of the biggest
men in Minsk—head of all the police in the city. So with a protector like him, I don't have anything to worry. You see? Papa's doing
all right, the customers miss your famous carvings, but our needs are
modest now.

My prayers are for you, my firstborn!

Mama

LETTER FROM MOSES TO HIS UNCLE

New York
14 October 1888

Dear Uncle Jacob,

My first step! Miss Weldon insisted I must meet this student in
her other class, one Dominick Roselli, already an established furniture maker—also a financial success, according to Miss Weldon.
The trouble is, he's slow to learn English. Italians are not very
bookish, Miss Weldon says. They don't put much stock in education, but they are musical, she says, so they have their good points.
This Roselli goes to the Grand Opera, climbs up to the peanut gallery twice a week, knows all the arias by heart. Isn't that marvelous?
Crazy people. So one rainy morning I went to see him on Canal
Street.

Upstairs, in an open loft, I found him with three old men, all
working. Dominick Roselli was singing at the top of his lungs—
every note off key. Otherwise his place reminded me of Papa's shop
—bigger, but quite as dingy and dark. I sniffed with pleasure the
familiar odor of sawdust and shavings, of lacquer and stain. You,
Uncle, must know what I mean. The delicious quality of that air!
Spoiled only by the smell of garlic, which was overpowering, and
Roselli's singing, which was deafening. The quality of the wood-
craft was high. His three workers are humbled, not-quite-broken
men in their sixties, maybe seventies, beaten by life, but proud of
their craftsmanship.

Roselli rose to greet me, showed me the shop, told me the men's
names (unpronounceable), and put me to work for a few minutes;
he observed me, and promptly offered me two dollars a day to start,
twelve dollars a week; then he'd have a look at my finished work,

and if it was good, perhaps two and a half. A tremendous wage. Without hesitation I took the job. I've been with him several weeks already. I'm getting my two and a half. We work long hours, six in the morning to seven at night, but at least I'm finished with the Pig Market, finished wondering do I or don't I have a job for the day. I sweat more than the slaves in the needle trades, but I get paid more.

Roselli is short and powerful, always bare above the waist, sawing or planing; you can see muscles ripple in that compact body. The eyes set in his square face are almost black and very sharp, his cheeks a reddish bronze, his nose has a slight curve, and his black hair is long, loose, and curly. He has the grace of a wildcat, the smile of an angel. I wouldn't put anything past him.

Miss Weldon speaks highly of him, but what does *she* know of the jungle world? A naïve rich girl, a bourgeois child. Roselli's too oily, he oozes compliments. She says he's just very Italian. Perhaps. When he smiles, I smile back at him. I can be just as oily. Do I expect to remain in his workshop all my life? I'll keep my eyes open. Working more than twelve hours in this loft, I should really paint myself black, because I'm like your niggers; my back aches incessantly. What's aggravating, Roselli seems scarcely to strain himself (he's a bull), yet he works harder than any of us. But I suspect his working is an act. Why should a boss labor so hard?

Within a couple of months, I discovered something I never realized: how business in America works. It's not like Minsk. There, Papa and I made the furniture and sold it to those who ordered it. Here, first comes the cabinet maker, then follows a man who makes nothing, but runs instead the whole day from loft to loft, buying everything Mr. Roselli can make, and everything many others make also. A "jobber." He carts the furniture around in his truck and sells to the stores—little stores, big stores, department stores. *Finally*, to the stores come the customers. And, as Marx explains, this is why a piece of furniture which I can make in two days, for which I receive five dollars, is sold to the store customer for eighty dollars.

I learned all this from Aaron Finkelstein, the jobber, who was so delighted to discover in Roselli's loft someone who talks Yiddish that he takes me for beers and talks and talks. He explains everything. More money can be made buying and selling in America in ten minutes than by the sweat of the brow in ten weeks. For Marx, a classic case. However, I should worry about Marx and straightening out mankind! I have other ideas. I want to put on a white shirt, with a fresh collar every week, and have always a few dollars in my pocket, so I can have a serious talk with Miss Weldon. *She* has plenty of time for the downtrodden—for uplift work —teaching immigrants at the Alliance, having supper with such a one as Moishe Singer!

When I can live the way she lives, maybe I, too, will devote myself to uplifting my fellow humans. Meanwhile, I leave the Revolution to Mendel Shapiro, our harmless neighborhood anarchist. Let *him* go listen to Emma Goldman or lie down in front of horse cars, and write fiery words in the Yiddish press!

Myself, I've learned a few hard lessons. Lesson number one: I wouldn't trust a fellow worker more than I would trust the worst capitalist. Who are we all interested in before everything? I, I, I. Correct? Why deny it? That's how we were made—if not by the Lord God, then by whoever is willing to take the blame. So let it be with Moses Singer.

Your nephew,
Moishe

LETTER FROM MOSES TO HIS UNCLE

New York
15 December 1888

Dear Uncle Jacob,

Whom do you think Miss Weldon is going to marry?

Since the sudden success of my new showroom, where I now receive daily more orders than Roselli and the other workshops where I buy can supply me in a week—the most highborn people are beginning to come to us from uptown in fancy carriages, climb two flights to our loft, and are delighted with our "bargains"—I decided on a few changes in my personal life. If I could do all this in a few months, what can I do in a few years? First I made up my mind I should now move uptown myself. I couldn't afford yet the best neighborhood, but on East 98th Street new flats are going up, so I reserved an apartment. I asked Roselli and his Italian crew to make my furniture—rich, not outlandish. Also, I purchased three new suits, each with two pairs of pants—simple, elegant, the kind I see on some of my best customers.

"A fine suit of clothes, Mr. Melrose," I happened to say one day. "And where did you get it? Tillsbury's Men's Furnishings on Fifth Avenue?" Well, up I rushed to Tillsbury's—but only to learn the price. By asking a few questions, I discovered that Tillsbury's buys from Helmstadt's Cloaks and Suits, East Broadway, and who do you think makes these suits for Helmstadt's? Krones, who lives over by Clinton Street, not far from me, and Mrs. Davidescu knows him personally. He makes only the finest garments for the best manufacturers. From Krones, a nice schnook, I bought three Tillsbury suits at a third of Tillsbury's price! So does it pay to know how business goes around in America? Meet the American Moses Singer. I gave

all my old clothes to Abramele. He'll shorten them and wear them to medical school.

In the evening I wore one of these suits to class—I'm still having trouble with my *w*'s, and my vowels need work. Everyone in the class was staring at me with admiration, if not jealousy. Miss Weldon called on me to recite so often everyone began to groan, and twice she complimented me on my accent. "Lovely," she says, "that was just fine, Mr. Singer!" Well, why not? How many students practice the way I do? All day long I repeat my vowels as I go about my business just so Miss Weldon will say, "That was lovely."

I asked Miss Weldon if she would be so kind as to come with me after class to Lorber's for a "bite." They do things right at that place —white tablecloths, big napkins, the waiters in black suits with white aprons—everything just so. We both had filet of sole. Not to walk all around the barn, I plunged right in. I told Miss Weldon I was growing tired of the bachelor's life. I decided a man should settle down, have a family, and she agreed most vigorously.

Miss Weldon, I said right to her face, seemed to me an earnest, sincere woman. Especially now that I was having a successful career in business, I said. After a long day at the showroom, showing customers around, arranging for deliveries, buying merchandise from Roselli and other furniture makers, arguing and bargaining, I needed the right wife to share everything with. "But, Mr. Singer, a man has to be extremely careful whom he chooses," Miss Weldon warned. "And there must be love, of course."

I was taken aback. I regarded her in amazement. To bring up such a subject! Where was her delicacy? A cultured, educated woman, talking like a child. Love! Love! Natasha cured my taste for it! This is a kind of childish madness which I think engulfs America. What makes everyone here believe in love—not for a week or a year, but for life? Passion, yes. Passion for justice, passion for money, for success, for women, too. I couldn't deny to myself a certain passion for her, although this I would never voice! But love? For a moment I began to have second thoughts about her sensibleness. "But I'm sure you'll find the right girl," she went on. "You're a very particular person." I plunged ahead, hardly hearing her.

"Then would you be surprised," I said, "if I told you I have found her? Who would be a better wife than—Miss Susan Weldon?" I held my breath. I could feel my temples beat.

I had expected her to be a bit surprised. Such a thing had never been mentioned between us, but there must be a first time. One must approach the subject. She began to stammer and her color rose. "Why, Moses Singer! Oh, my, oh, my!" She closed her eyes and kept them closed. She shook her head slowly, her eyes still

shut. I could see she was troubled. "You've caught me off balance. It's not fair. Heavens, we scarcely know each other!" I kept going, like a runaway horse, or perhaps more like a phonograph someone has forgotten to turn off.

"I know all I need to know," I said. "I know you lead a life of uplift. And I have a long way to reach the top. So instead of lifting half the world, you'll help me. I've met your family, I like them. What else is there to talk about? As for me, what would you like to know? I have no secrets from you. Ask me anything. Anything at all."

"Oh, Moses, you are really something! We . . . are . . . so entirely different. Oh, you're a devil. A life of *uplift!* Jesus!"

"What's the terrible difference between us?" I said too hastily. "Different worlds? Oh, no, madam, we live in the same world, Miss Weldon." But she kept murmuring, "My, oh, my, oh, my," and "Sweet Jesus," shaking her head in amazement.

"Did I maybe speak too abruptly?" I said. "Should I have beat around the bush? I should have hinted first, right? Given you a chance to get used to it. Would that have been better? I'm even willing to wait."

"Oh, dear Moses, you are a funny, strange man. Don't you see? I'm already engaged. I'm going to be married in a couple of months."

A cold pailful of water over my face.

"Who?" I said, and heard my voice crack.

"What difference does it make?"

"Who?" I demanded.

"If you must know, it's one of my pupils."

She must have seen my disappointment. "It's a man I love," she said with spirit. This outraged me. An immigrant! A greenhorn! If it were a gentleman from uptown I could have stood it better.

"Just because you love him, that's a reason to get married?"

She shook her head. "Oh, Moses, you're a sketch. You're trying to *arrange* a marriage for yourself! You've picked me out, like a dining room table."

"A man has to be very careful. You said so yourself. And so does a woman."

She ignored my irrefutable logic. "What about that nice girl from Russia, the one who writes you the news of the neighborhood?" she said. Can you imagine her saying a thing like that? Like a big sister.

"Who is this man?" I thundered, pounding on the table and startling the people at the next table.

"Why, Dominick Roselli," she said.

I thought of Roselli at work, a beautiful animal, illiterate, all *schmeichel* and catlike grace, smiling so hard all you can see are

those big white teeth flashing for miles around. Miss Weldon was succumbing to these primitive attractions, like a common chambermaid or peasant. "He's someone from *your* world? Your mother and father know about him?"

"Oh, they're heartsick, of course. He's not suitable, they say—not at all, and you wouldn't be either. They don't believe I'll really do it. They're waiting for me to get over it. But I shan't." As stubborn as Aunt Leah and Feygele combined! I don't know, maybe I saved myself some grief in the long run.

I called the waiter and paid. Never again will I be made a fool of. I escorted Miss Weldon to the El and tipped my hat. "Good night, Miss Weldon."

"Dearest Moses," she said patronizingly, as she leaned forward and kissed my cheek, "I hope I'll see you next week in class?"

I tipped my hat once more and turned back to Rivington Street. I've given up the idea of moving uptown just now. Canceled my apartment, sold the new furniture. I don't go to class at the Educational Alliance. From now on I'll teach myself. I have a lot to learn, and it's not my vowels. Dominick Roselli! *Sweet Jesus!*

With affection,
Moses

LETTER FROM SHEYNA RASEL RUBENSTEIN TO MOSES

Minsk, Northwestern Region
15 March 1889

O Moishe, my Moishe!

I always believed in miracles. That if one wishes hard enough, it will happen. Secretly I squirrel your letter under my covers each night, knowing it will bring a quick dream of you. "Ship ticket," is what you may call it, but I have other names for it; I won't tell you any of them because you may get the wrong impression of me, and could take me for a woman unbalanced, God forbid. Only let me tell you. Yesterday when I got up the nerve to read your letter to my mama, she began to cry and cried all day, right through to the borscht at dinner. Each time she looks at me her tears begin to well up again. How can her tears be my joy? Is that sad? I ask you. Of course I'll miss her, but she can follow me, can't she? She could come to America—why not? I asked Mama not to say anything to my father because it was something I wanted to do myself. Before I went to him this morning, I took your letter down to *your* mother, who is so frantic just now about your father she almost couldn't listen. But I made her read it. Even with all her worries she gave me a little melancholy shout of pleasure, threw her arms around me, led me to a secret box, and gave me an amethyst brooch, which she re-

ceived at the time of her marriage from her mother-in-law. It's the only thing she has left after the riots. She really treats me more like a daughter than my own mama does.

She says your papa won't talk about you, because you've turned your back on *Yiddishkeit*. She talked of Herschel, too—she worries over him more than over you. Of course we hear from Freda—their life is hard, but Freda takes it better than Herschel. She showed me Herschel's last letter from Palestine. Think of it, Moishe, your brother's best friend an Arab farmer! We who never expected to go as far as Bobruysk or Lutsk, we're now journeying off to places with magic names like Jerusalem and New York, while our parents shake their heads in wonder. Don't *they* believe in miracles? Moses, should we be weeping for *them*?

What a time I'm having! My father forbids me to go to America. The voyage is full of terrors for a young girl. He admits he and your father would probably have arranged this match themselves if you'd remained here, but what, he says, do we really know of each other? Can you believe that?

Papa demands I send back the ship ticket, and no arguments. First his Freda whisked away to the Holy Land (if you ask me, she whisked Herschel away!) and now me. He talks as if we were pots and pans. And the dangers to a girl in New York! I will "walk the streets"! I will be forced to sell my body! From the way he talks, you'd think Minsk was paradise! You will soon abandon me; you won't like being tied down. I tell him you are only sending a ship ticket, we haven't decided to get married. This makes him only madder. I tell him in America I'll do whatever I can to help you. At first I can sew like everyone else in New York and earn money for you. I practice sewing like mad, making all my own clothes and shirts for Papa. I also cook, and my meals are delicious! But on he rants. What is to become of him and Mama in their old age? Ah, so maybe *that* is it? Mama says nothing, only cries. Be patient with me, it will take a while until I can get their blessing. Be patient, dear Moishe. I'm coming, I'm coming, I'm coming!

Your grateful neighbor,
Sheyna Rasel Rubenstein

Under his grandmother's letter, Martin found a clipping in Russian with the typed translation attached—an article from the *Minsky Lystok* of March 25, 1889 with the headline BOMB PLOTTERS DISCOVERED. It reported that Moishe's comrades in the Movement had been arrested for assassinating Boris Karpovich, District Commissioner of Police. The only members of the group whose names were missing were Pyotr Rumian-

tsev's, Feygele Singer's, and that of Boris Karpovich, the assassinated man's son. The article referred with a note of alarm to the fact that one of the plotters was the daughter of a Colonel Perkovin, a man "admitted to the court of the Tsar."

The prosecutor said he intended to demand the death penalty for all, aristocrats and commoners alike, and, Martin supposed, why doubt that they were all found guilty and hanged? Why, he wondered idly, had that little band of socialists or Communists—whatever the hell they were— knocked off the father of a member of their own group—if they had? Had there been some subliminal resentment about the fat little man's having defended a Jew? And in doing so, having shot a fun-loving anti-Semite peasant in the gut? Who would fathom it? In any case, they'd all ended up martyrs for *Norodnaya Volya*, those young firebrands. Shades of Malcolm X or Ethel and Julius Rosenberg! *Plus ça change, plus c'est la même chose!* Probably no one would ever know what the story was. Martin picked up the next letter.

LETTER FROM ISRAIL SINGER TO MOSES

Minsk
3 April 1889

Moishele, my son:

I write without much hope that I can reach your heart. I have not been successful in the past. We may be at our final crossroad. But I could never forgive myself for not trying.

If any father can be said to have loved his child, Moishe, I was such a father, and you were the child. You were a delicate beauty, and with a spirit like sunshine in spite of being sickly. When you first attended *cheder* you were a brilliant little boy, your teachers could not sing your praises enough, and you filled my heart with pride. I used to say to your mother, "Moishele is our blessing from the Adored One." Until your voice began to change, you were my soul. But then, like your voice, you, too, began to change. You rejected my faith, the faith of our fathers, and soon you mocked me behind my back, you made a joke of your own father. I heard, I heard! Try to imagine a son of yours doing this to you. How would you feel? The careless way in which you read your bar mitzvah, shrugging at your own mistakes! I thought, He must for some reason hate me, or hate what I am, but, I thought, maybe it's only a boy's revolt; it will pass. I prayed it would.

Then you put on that terrible school uniform, symbol of our oppressors. After that you took up revolution. Very well, I thought, he is going a different way; I will keep silent. Maybe still he will be

a great man in a way that is beyond my experience or understanding or imagination.

I raised no objections. You will remember? We may have argued,
but I said nothing against *you*, even if I did not agree with your
way. Because even then I believed in your soul, Moishe. In the
happy boy who used to sit on my lap and ask questions I could not
answer. So maybe he would find these answers now for himself,
and maybe, in a way I could not understand, he would lead the rest
of us forth from the night into the sun. So I recommended that
those in Jew Street should trust you with their lives, and they did.
On my say-so.

I would not try to tell you the pleasure you gave me in those few
years when we worked side by side with the odor of sawdust in our
nostrils, when you inspired your brothers to do likewise. Those were
my happiest hours. In those days we thought you would marry
Freda Rubenstein, daughter of our dearest friends.

Today I beat my breast, for each time I forgave you, or rationalized what you were up to, there would follow some terrible betrayal. You betrayed also yourself. I could not believe that of every
fifty rubles you took from a desperate family to save a son from the
army, you kept for yourself fifteen, that you had slowly robbed our
friends and neighbors, who trusted you, of a fortune. My son!
My son!

The ideals of your own revolution—*yours*, not mine—you tossed
aside, like a fish's head. Not even this belief was for you an article
of faith. It was merely another adventure, no different from those I
had heard about you and the female trash kept by Sarah the Salt-
seller. And then one final incomprehensible betrayal: of our family's
friend, a man who saved the life of your mother! He, who did something you, or perhaps I, *should* have done. You are accused of having conspired to kill this great true friend.

Much as I would like not to believe it, I make to you the terrible
confession that in my heart I find it difficult *not* to believe! Could
anything worse befall a father than to sink so low in his thoughts
about the son who was once his delight? Did you send your revolutionary friends the money to obtain the weapons for this grim deed,
as the police claim? I saw the money you had! And did you want
this man out of the way only because of your guilty soul? They
arrested *me!* The police refused to accept that you had left Minsk
almost two years already, so I had to send home to your mother to
bring your letters, which for some reason she keeps, and at least
they did this much good: I was released from the prison with a
kick, a spit, an insult. They insulted your mother for good measure.
I hope this makes you proud of yourself.

So looking finally into my own heart, I have had to admit with

tears that I have a son to whom trickery, falsehood, and treachery are no strangers.

Please, my Moishele, I ask now that you do this one thing, one thing only, to restore my old belief in you. In desperation I write, and out of another father's desperation and also a mother's. You rejected the virtuous girl we chose for you—may her name be blessed—and we thank the Almighty your brother married her! In your new land you first consorted with a *goyishe* woman, "highborn" though she may have been in America, thus continuing your aimless pattern. This soul of yours is a ship with no rudder, drifting whichever way the winds and tides move it. My lost son. Woe, woe, woe!

Please stop and try to see yourself! An air person. Without belief of *some* kind there are no limits to a man's malignancy. Now you turn the head of a pure, innocent girl, pretty little Sheyna Rasel, asking her to travel ten thousand versts, to abandon her loving parents forever! If she leaves, the apple of their eyes, they will never see her again! Do you know what this means to them, now that Freda is gone? These people are my dearest friends, Moishe! Why are you tearing them to shreds? Merely to satisfy some selfish intention of yours, perhaps nothing more than the wild blood of youth? Have you no pity? I make this prediction: if this misguided girl should defy her parents and go to you, in the end you'll bring misery to her also!

Moishe, listen to me. I speak with the memory of love, to the smiling boy I took each day to *cheder* with all my hopes on your beautiful head! I beg you, give up Sheyna! Give her up!

If you will do this—call it a sacrifice if you like—you will make a blessing for her distraught parents. You will teach me, an old man, to believe in miracles again, and in you.

If you will not, I cannot speak or hear your name again. I remain, my faith as always in the King of Glory, from whom all things come, still your

Papa

Ah, Martin thought ruefully, father versus son. One reason or another. So in this family, what else is new? It needed no issue, it was in the blood somehow.

ADVERTISEMENT IN THE JEWISH DAILY FORWARD (NEW YORK)
5 SEPTEMBER 1889
MR. MOISHE SINGER ANNOUNCES HIS MARRIAGE TO MISS SHEYNA RASEL RUBENSTEIN AT AGUDETH SHALOM SYNAGOGUE, RABBI JUDAH BAKAL PERFORMING THE CEREMONY.

LETTER FROM FEYGELE TO MOSES

Minsk
15 September 1889

To my former brother:

I am writing to say that I want to hear from you no more. To me you are dead, as you are to Papa, but for very different reasons. That day when Mama fell on the ice and you waited in the cart—no, you did worse, you started the cart up so that you were getting further from her every second as the danger to her increased—that day you revealed your true character. I saw you stripped of all your boasting, sophistication, the aura of mystery you promoted about what you were doing in the Movement, your officiousness. Up to that day I really looked up to you. I learned to hate you that day and I hate you still. It takes a mother to forgive, and I'm not your mother.

As you may have heard, Boris's father was assassinated, our best, most secret friend! This was not enough! Now all our comrades have been arrested, and for all we know, they may be hanged for it, since there is no one else to hang, and it would not surprise me if the information leading to their arrest takes a trail that goes to you. They took Papa in for questioning, saying you were a suspect, but I think this was a smoke screen. I cannot prove it was you who betrayed us, but your past character makes this probable. If it was not you, how is it that I am spared and Boris is spared? Maybe at least you could not bring yourself to betray your own sister!

You are a runaway, my former brother. Tarkowsky had your number. Just as you ran away from your mother's danger, so, instead of remaining to work with your comrades to help make Russia a land of justice for all, you fled. To streets of gold, where you yearn to live in comfort and luxury, something you so adore! Instead of working for the people, you work only for yourself, and so you will one day whirl like a *dreydl* alone. Well, have your carriage and troika, have your palace and servants, your easy life. Speak French for all I care! But know all your life the price was betrayal. Betrayal of family, of comrades, of the land of your birth, of justice and right. In exchange for a kilo of gold. I spit on you again.

Boris and I continue, together with other brave men and women, to struggle each day for a new world. We do not want your money, we do not want your good wishes, we do not want to hear from you further. You are dead. I wish to hear news about you only once more, confirming this fact.

Feygele

4

Yes, Martin recalled, I've seen Moishe's reply, kept all these years by
Feygele's grandson, Yuri Karpeyko, to be exhibited like the magic pass-
word—that old letter Yoshke Schulman had brought, beginning "How
shall I answer you?" How, indeed? Dated in December of 1889. Now this
next one was from the Palestine branch of the family.

Letter from Freda Rubenstein Singer to Sheyna Rasel
Rubenstein Singer

Near Petaq Tikvah, Palestine
11 January 1890

Sheyna Rasel, my dear baby sister!

You can imagine my confused feelings at your amazing news.
How rare for anything to take me out of the hectic routine of my
days—something that starts the juices, stirs girlish memories. Little
Sheyna Rasel, my baby sister, married to *my* Moishe? Blessed art
thou! Why do I still think of him as mine? I will make you a
wicked confession: at night after Herschel drops off from sheer
exhaustion—oh, how he hates to work—I pretend that Moishe,
fresh as a rosebud, slips noiselessly into our bed, takes me in his
arms, caresses me, and tells me sweetly, as he never did in real life,
that every night in America he lies and dreams of *me!* Girlish fantasies! Before your letter, he would hold me thus, night after night,
until I fell asleep. Since your letter, he shows up but slips away
quickly, mumbling an apology about having to get back to *you.*
Gone! And I lie forsaken, but are you to blame? On the contrary.
When one is so bone weary, one becomes defenseless against even
the most unwanted thoughts. "Unwanted" is not the right word.
"Unworthy," I mean. Even in daylight, as I go about real life, tending my husband and my two wonderful boys, cooking, trying to forget that I'm pregnant again, cleaning the house, feeding the

chickens, working in the orchards, picking or spraying or fertilizing, I find myself exulting over your news, singing half-remembered songs. Herschel is glad, too. So it's Herschel and I; Moishe and you. Different from the way our papas planned, or even from the way I planned. Only *your* plan has come true.

Will the four of us ever see each other? As our Arab neighbors say, "*Insh' Allah.*" However, we are double-tied now, for good or bad, two Rubenstein women to two Singer men, and these bonds should hold us together forever even at this distance. The only thing is—would we *know* each other if we met? Why is it to *you* I confess my feelings for Moishe—I, a woman whose face is leathery from sun and *hamseen,* whose hands are harder than those of any *moujik?* Well, to whom else? Could I tell this to Herschel? I have enough trouble with him without that. Herschel, it turns out, was not made by the Creator to be a *chalutz,* a settler. Still we're managing. So! The confessions of a *chalutza!*

Please, please tell me about *your* new life and make at least one confession of your own.

I'm glad we came here from Jerusalem. Herschel insisted on going there first, because for him holiness was the thing. But not I; I want to *make* something for us and our children, and I finally had my way. A city of holy Jewish ghosts and real Arab *fellaheen* was not for me. Awful. Minsk I've almost forgotten altogether. We work in a cooperative settlement, a *moshav,* ten homes, ten farms a few versts from the settlement, Petaq Tikvah, which is supported by Baron Rothschild from Paris.

Here are no pious Jews like those we saw in Jerusalem. Here everyone overworks. We are *doing.* Our house, one of ten alike, is a plain square box we built of concrete blocks, neighbors helping neighbors. The land we got from the baron. Together with the other nine families, we own a camel, five donkeys, three cows, and a herd of sheep and goats, and that makes us feel rich. Flowers and palm trees grow in our garden. It's either stifling hot or we have vicious storms. But snow and ice, thank God, never!

One landowner, Hassan-al Mowry, we helped reclaim a large nearby swamp area, and he's become a friend. In his "swamp" now lemon trees bloom. Today men work in those fields and lemons make a good harvest. I have come to know Hassan's three wives— simple, good women. It's funny. They know each other much better than they know their husband! The men have as little as possible to do with women. Arab men even dance alone—like Hassidim! When I dress up in a *djellaba,* I can do a marvelous imitation of an Arab man at his most abandoned! The Jews of our *moshav* come from either Yassi in Roumania or Minsk. We have our own synagogue, about the size of one of our little houses. We all helped

build it and it looks like it! Now you should hear our men disputing over ritual! Shades of the old rebs! Herschel gets involved, but I, never. There's too much work for that nonsense. Would you believe your sister now smokes? Well, I'm a farmer, after all. I work in the open like a man. I need to be covered with trousers and shirt from head to toe to avoid the mosquito bites that can bring malaria! After the rains the mosquitos are worse than in Komarovka Square! The Arab women are mostly kept hidden by their men, and when they come out they hide their faces with veils. I met a few through Hassan's wives, and talk to them when I go to the well or when we do the wash. My Arabic is becoming fairly fluent, and I cultivate these women for a good reason: they warn me of trouble. And troubles we have right now.

South of us live Bedouin tribes, people who travel the country-side like a herd of animals. They pitch their goatskin tents first in one place, then another, roving aimlessly—people, goats, sheep, donkeys. They live in Biblical days; they prey on the unwary, robbing and killing. They grow nothing, but they steal everything and kill what they can't steal. To make matters worse, living in their own shacks nearby are other Arab families who just don't want us here. They say this land is rightly theirs; they were forced to move when the baron bought it from their landlord who lives in Beirut. So, instead of being angry at their Arab landlord, they take it out on us who are here. At night their boys steal our sheep, kill our dogs, poison our chickens. When we came, we had no idea such people were here!

To guard the *moshav* from Bedouins and our Arab neighbors, we had to build two watchtowers, and we all take turns—our husbands, our sons, beginning at twelve, our stronger girls and women (including me)—we watch through the night for marauders. We've had to become also sharpshooters. Daniel, our oldest, almost six, can't wait to shoot a gun. So many of us left the Pale so our sons *shouldn't* have to serve in the Tsar's army! Well, at least there's nothing imperial about *us!* Some army!

Three weeks ago a terrible thing happened. Herschel was in one of the towers and, at two o'clock in the morning, he heard noises in the sheep pen. He found the person on duty in the other tower, David Conescu, a boy of fourteen, and they went together to investigate. There in the moonlight, they saw three Arab boys with knives killing our sheep. They would catch a sheep and cut its throat, and laugh.

Herschel called, "Get out!" But instead of running away, all three came running at them, their knives dripping blood, and screaming. David fired his gun, and one of the boys fell. The others turned and ran. The poor Arab had been shot in the throat, a boy

of sixteen. By this time everyone in our *moshav* was awake. We brought the boy to our house and did everything we knew for him, but the blood was gushing from his mouth, his neck. He was unconscious, and never awoke. In less than an hour he died.

We sent word to Hassan-al Mowry, our friend, that we had the body of this boy, and he sent two men in a donkey cart for it, to return it to the boy's family. A Turkish policeman came the next day to question Herschel and David, then went away.

Now my Arabic women have warned me we must pay with a life! That's their way—retaliation. It will happen, the Arab women say, if not sooner, later. Nothing can be done. Someone in our settlement must die.

We travel now only in threes. No women may leave the settlement. We work in the fields with rifles strapped to us. And we wait. It's a different atmosphere than we dreamed of in Minsk. We take our meals, laugh at each other's jokes, the men play chess and checkers, and we treat our children normally. At night I treasure my fantasies in spite of my fears. I study my son, his babyish face so serious, and listen while he shows me, so grown up, how he's almost strong enough to lift Herschel's rifle. Nobody will have to come to conscript my Daniel! I, however, tremble for him. But who's safe? Herschel, if you ask me, would be willing to pick up and leave this place in one minute. The death of that boy has left him shaken. But I'm determined to stay. This is the land of our fathers, this is where Jews belong! My son is growing up to be a warrior! A *Jewish* warrior. Something a bit different, right?

Here is a photograph of my two boys, taken by a Turkish policeman from Petaq Tikvah. There you see Daniel and my baby, Yussele. The animal on which they are perched is a lady camel named Abu. Could you send us a picture of yourselves? We'd like to see the "new" American Sheyna Rasel and the "new" Moishe. Please don't tell Moishe what I've confessed, Sheyna! I think of you still and always as my sweet little rose. Give an affectionate hello also to Abram Shapiro. To Moishe . . . well, about him I've written plenty. Enough's enough. Back to work.

Freda

LETTER FROM SHEYNA RASEL TO FREDA

192 Essex Street
New York
10 March 1898

Dear Sister,

How you used to tease me about my stubby fingers, but oh, Sister, you ought to see them now. My fat fingers move like whispers over my Singer machine, and I feel like mighty Mozart sewing

a sonata for Mr. Ike Bernstein. So it turns out lucky I always bite my nails down to the skin. Bernstein says to me, "Sheyna, with three like you I could be a millionaire." This makes me wonder—not about our destinies, but is he paying me enough? How do we become mavins in this or that? Who could have guessed the fat little Rubenstein girl will become the mainstay of the Bernstein Shirtwaist Factory on Clinton Street, New York? A mighty forewoman with eight girls to scream at and laugh with? And a top designer, besides. Yes, Bernstein has used two of my designs, and my shirtwaists have outsold all his others. I should be happy, no? I'm not. I try not to be bitter. The loss of our two little ones to scarlet fever shook Moishe and me to our bare souls.

Abram was the children's doctor. How can I tell you so you'll know about Abram? He neglected his job at the hospital where he is a resident, and for days he tended both of the little ones for hours, days and nights without end. First to be taken was Joshua. My poor little boy died on the third day. Just trembled, closed his eyes, and stopped breathing. Tess, the baby, seemed stronger at first, but at the end, after she, too, had stopped breathing, Abram only lifted the stethoscope from his ear, held it out, and gazed at me, a lost man. Abram is not exactly pretty, you know, but I like his strange looks. He stood silent, that big head on the sturdy body, blinking, blinking; several times he tried to talk, gave it up.

Since you knew him, he has begun to look like a wonder-rabbi, with his large head, those deep-set eyes, the black curly hair, his harsh laugh. He sounds so gruff and angry, but how he suffers for others!

When Abram leaves the hospital next October he could live anywhere, even in Harlem or the Bronx, some of our best new districts, but he insists he wants to move back with us. It's because of me—he doesn't have to say so. I take Abram for a Just Man. Are Just Men allowed to slip once in a while? Even the Nameless One Himself is not so perfect. Abram is no Moishe. He lacks Moishe's smoothness, his polished manner, and his insincerity.

Unfortunately, however, Abram and I are not separated like you and your phantom Moishe, by thousands of miles; we eat our meals together; he used to sleep in a room only a few steps down the hall. To make it worse, we are thrown together alone some nights when Moishe works. If I could understand and control my own feelings! I owe Moishe everything, don't I? I threw myself at him. I worshipped him all through my girlhood. He sent me my ship ticket. We had good times, bad times. I have borne his children. We suffered together, terrible losses. But I wonder whether I really knew him or just wanted what my sister wanted. Papa warned me about him. And *his* papa warned me. Were they right? And

Abram? An unprepossessing little man. A nothing. It certainly doesn't have much to do with thinking. It cannot be talked about sensibly. But never fear, Freda, I'll be strong. Besides, who could stand the *mishagoss!*

Not that I wish to complain about Moishe. I have no right to look at him in a detached way, but I have observed him with a very nice Italian man named Roselli, also a furniture maker; before I came to America they were warm friends, inseparable; they did business together and Moishe really liked him. As always, Moishe bewitched the poor man. We saw him and his lovely wife, who was once Moishe's teacher, almost every other night. They would come here, we would go there. The wife, Susan, is from an old American family. Then one day Moishe began to mutter that Roselli was taking advantage of him, interfering with him, cheating him somehow. I'm afraid Moishe will soon get rid of Roselli one way or another. I see it coming, the way it happened with Mendel Shapiro.

We never see Mendel anymore. And now it begins with Abram, his oldest friend. Moishe began to make bitter comments: he didn't quite trust him, Abram was changing lately, he's arrogant, holds his patients in contempt. And lately Moishe doesn't approve the way Abram *looks* at me. Up to now, whatever Moishe says, I'm always on his side. If he says Roselli betrayed him, I agree. He says Mendel cheated him, so I agree. But I *can't* let him do that with Abram; without Abram I'd be afraid. Abram has taught me that an ice cream soda is no crime; we have a laugh together, innocent laughs, while Moishe is at work.

I couldn't tell you anything certain about Moishe and any particular woman. However, Moishe couldn't live without women and for him one is not enough. He complained to me recently so bitterly about Bertha Golden, his bookkeeper (she worked for him a year already), it led me to suspect—could she be at the edge of her cliff? Was he preparing to push her over the edge? Well, he just discharged her! Now he's begun telling me the virtues of some new, marvelous, talented interior decorator, who helps rich women furnish their houses, a German Jew, Carol Kahn. *She* is going to help him build up his business to the largest of its kind in New York. She is a "phenomenon." Well, we'll see how long *she* lasts.

My son Jacob, light of my life, he's my new dream. Not because I'm his mother, but Jacob does scare me a bit. He *looks* too wise to be a child. He started a year and a half ago in the public school, when he was six. His first teacher, Miss Dinsmore, instead of asking me to come to school as teachers usually do, she came to visit Moishe and me in *our* flat—an unusual honor—the first week of school. I gave her a glass of tea and sent Jacob down to play in the

street. She seemed a flighty lady, with a high fluttery voice. But now it's a year and a half later, and she wasn't so dumb!

Was it true, Miss Dinsmore asked, that Jacob was only six years old? Such a question! Her voice was almost a sigh. Could she see his birth certificate? We showed it to her. When did he first begin to read? she asked us. English, Moishe said seriously, or Yiddish, or Hebrew? She laughed her pretty gentile laugh. Any language, she said. We tried to remember. The headlines of the *New York World* he was reading just after his second birthday. The English ABC he recited complete when he was one and a half. He could add and subtract when he was two and a half. At six he was already our Jacob—could play a good game of chess. He could beat both Abram and Moishe! English he did not read *fluently* until he was three. But Hebrew, Moishe said angrily, he doesn't read at all. Yiddish, either. He flatly refuses, says he doesn't want to. He wants, at six years old, to be an American boy! Only American!

Miss Dinsmore opened her mouth, but for a while no words came. Then she asked if we had heard of Mozart. She must have taken us for terrible greenhorns! Little Mozart, she informed us, could play the piano at two and was writing music at four. So? I told her playing the piano must be much harder than plain reading, and anyhow Jacob could never do such a thing, because we don't have a piano in the house. The long and short of it is Miss Dinsmore believes our Jacob is a genius. Why not? I'm a genius also, on the sewing machine—go ask Mr. Bernstein—and his father's a genius at making furniture.

She asked more questions about Jacob. What could I tell her? That just before his fifth birthday he became very ill? After what we had been through with the other two, you can imagine our nightmares when he ran a high fever, wasn't able to move his arms or his legs. His neck hurt, he couldn't turn his head. Abram examined him, but he was not happy and wouldn't look me straight in the eye. They did more tests, but I refused to pray. "It's infantile paralysis," Abram said. When his fever was highest, little Jacob talked nonsense, but not in English, in Yiddish. "No, no," he called. "I don't want to! Get away." The fever dropped. And I realized Who he was chasing away. After two days, he began to move one leg—a miracle. Special exercises for his arms he had to do, and when he's a little older he must swim. That's why he can't run with the others; maybe that's why he's such an old man already.

Abram says one leg will always be shorter than the other, and both will be frail. He's tall for his age, very skinny, with sunken cheeks and large owlish eyes, like his father's. He has now only a little limp. His face I think is beautiful, with blond, wavy hair and

large eyes that are sharp and blue—can you imagine? From Moishe and me, where comes wavy blond hair?

Yes, Miss Dinsmore, his mother knows about Jacob, so what else can I tell you? Why don't the other children tease him about his limp? Something unnatural for children! He must have some strange power over them. In school, he is a "monitor." The teachers love him. He reads books, but Bible stories puzzle him. Moishe insists he wants our family to be a hundred percent American. Nothing Jewish, nothing religious. We're not interested in the Mosaic laws. The boy listens to his father, his eyes wide with interest, looking like a little *tzaddik*, wrinkling his forehead. "But without the laws of Moses, Papa, shouldn't people be scared of each other?"

"In America," Moishe tells him, "Moses doesn't make the laws. God doesn't make the laws. The people make their own laws." For some reason this delights Jacob.

Miss Dinsmore told us then she could not keep Jacob in the first grade; he was making other children feel inferior. She would have to put him ahead to the second. A few weeks later, his new teacher moved him to third; and this kept happening. So three terms have gone by. He's not eight yet, and goes to school with children three years older, in fifth grade, and his teacher has sent a message: they may have to move him to sixth. He can do amazing things: he can multiply large numbers by other large numbers. "Three thousand six hundred forty-seven times nine hundred fifty-one," he sings, then he thinks a few seconds. And out of his mouth comes such a big number, hundreds of thousands, maybe millions—would I know if he's right? His new teacher says he never makes a mistake. He reads the whole newspaper in two minutes, explains the meaning of difficult English words to me and his father in perfect Yiddish. And with all that, his favorite is to recite for us in English, "I pledge allegiance to my flag," which he speaks with all his heart, it is so full of meaning to him, and in his piping voice he sings every word of "Oh, say, can you see."

A patriotic American, and such a brilliant one! He had to be given special cards from the Educational Alliance and the Astor Library, cards that say this little fellow is allowed to take out their most valuable books, books for grownups. It is something to see the skinny boy stooping over, concentrating on one of these fat volumes and shaking his head in wonder as he limps along. An old man, quick to catch on, to see hidden meaning. Moishe is awed. But I think he would have preferred a boy who is strong and could run with the others. More normal. Not this gangling, frail fellow with stooped shoulders and a little limp. I tell him, "Jacob, stand up straight," but he's soon stooped over again.

You ask in your letter so many questions. Yes, Moishe works all day and many nights. What keeps him so busy I couldn't say. He has a showroom and an office, which I visited several times, but I don't feel welcome. He has a woman who works a typing machine, and another, a bookkeeper. He also has in his place a telephone, one of the wonders of this life!

Moishe wants me to give up working for Bernstein and stay home like a fine lady. It sounds like a lovely idea; it's not exactly easy to make a house, care for Jacob, and work a full day at the factory. But to stay home, just to be Moishe's woman—and a woman he's not crazy about—I'd hate that. Even if the factory's not a paradise, it's other people, it's fighting with Bernstein, having a few laughs with our models, mostly empty-headed but kind-hearted *shiksas*, and in any case, I have no *sitzfleisch*.

Moishe, who has not seen this letter, joins me in sending our love to you and Herschel and to our nephews, Daniel and Yussele. And for you, Sister, a kiss from my heart.

Sheyna Rasel

Martin was appalled at the next letters. How prosperous Moishe was becoming—and how *dull*. He wondered if his own sparce correspondence breathed the same preoccupation with money and success. God, he hoped not! What Moses wrote to his Atlanta relatives became a series of business letters, in which he also opined on public affairs—big-dome thinking. A violent anti-labor bias evidenced itself, more and more strongly. Contempt for those who sweated. *Narodnaya Volya!* As Martin recalled, Grandpapa insisted on *calling* himself a Roosevelt Democrat, but, Martin now believed, Moishe would have made a good reactionary. He was two leagues to the right of McKinley. At the same time, Sheyna Rasel divided her zest and talent between the shirtwaist factory and her adored son. Lucky Father, Martin thought, to have a mother who remained passionately devoted to him, although she continued to describe herself to her sister as restless, restless. In one of her letters to Palestine, she also refers to "Moishe's papa of blessed memory," and indicated that the old man in Minsk had died, in an unpleasant fashion and in excruciating pain.

It was clear from the correspondence that Moishe's mother, left in that dank cellar to shift for herself, had only *Zayde* to minister to. Moses sent her money from New York. Her eyes began to go bad—cataracts, apparently; they seemed to run in the family. In those days, however, there was nothing to be done about cataracts except to go slowly blind. Being the woman she was, she attributed her growing affliction in one sad letter

to a supernatural punishment. The guilts seemed to come with the umbilical in this family.

Her simple letters, while riddled with undercurrents of self-deprecation, were otherwise uncomplaining, full of pride, and cheerful. This cheer, Martin could see well in advance, was a transparent falsehood. Why, Martin pondered, didn't Moses bring his desolate mother over? What kind of man was he? Well, he sort of invited her, in a backhand manner of speaking. The exact nature of Moishe's invitation Martin could only deduce from Moishe's mother's response:

. . . you're a good boy, a fine boy, to offer to bring me to America at great expense. I'm proud of you, but, as you say, who knows if I could stand the long rough voyage, especially not being as well as I once was. And you are right about how hard it would be, starting life in a new place at my age among strangers. How could I leave all my old friends? Remarkable people they're not, but I know them. And what would become of *Zayde*? It took me all my life to get used to Minsk, and to tell the truth, I'm not used to it yet. Herschel asked me also to come to him. But a new place—you can imagine! Only that you *asked* me! If you knew what that means to me, my Moishele, and if I ever change my mind, believe me, will you hear from me! God bless you, Moishele, and you, my daughter, Sheyna Rasel, and your son Jacob, my beautiful grandchild. I received the photographs. In my life I never saw such a beautiful boy.

Maybe she'd have come, Martin thought, if she'd been coaxed, but apparently Moses never coaxed. Martin wondered why.

5

LETTER FROM AUNT LEAH TO MOSES

Minsk
4 Tishri 5659
20 September 1898

To my nephew (would it weren't so) Moishe (written by Rabbi Levitsky on behalf of Aunt Leah):

May the Almighty forgive you. If He can, He is mightier than I think. Just a word to let you know about your mother's suicide, and don't suppose you had nothing to do with it, my boy! Also your sister Feygele didn't help. Such a litter of children my poor sister had! Not to mention the grief this has caused me.

It was pouring that day as if Noah together with his ark was again in our midst, and while the Uppermost was soaking the rest of us, she killed herself. It rained yet almost a whole month after, tears from above. Not to mention my own. I'm not asking favors—who ever did me favors? Your poor mother of blessed memory, may the Lord forgive her, threw her life away, and not merely when she leaped off the roof to the wet cobblestones, but every day she threw it away for fifty-nine years. She may have been blind, but she could see through you in the end, Moishe, and her whole brood of ungrateful offspring! At least that much she saw, I'm glad to say. She thought she was smart, but even a stupid sister like me with no education, who has to have Rabbi Levitsky write for her, even such a stupid sister knows enough not to waste my whole life taking care of a someone like *Zayde*. It sucks out your life.

Her father he was, and mine also, once upon a time, but he's a different person now. In fact he's not a person. Why should I let him attach himself to *my* skirts and follow me everywhere like a goat? Well, your mother was a woman many asked for advice and

if, God forbid, you didn't ask, she gave it anyhow, but on the subject of Zayde she couldn't advise herself.

Oh, I feel sorry for old Zayde, poor wretch, but I also have my own life, the only one I was given. What I mean to say, I decided it's not such a terrible place, the insane asylum. It wasn't easy to get Zayde in there. However, I know a few people, I pulled a few strings—Reb Horowitz, of the benevolent societies, may the old man live to be a hundred. So without a whole *megillah*, that's where Zayde is now, better off than in his whole life. I told him, "Zayde, they've finally come to take you for the army, and no escaping this time. But you'll like it. Go with the nice man." So, weeping like a baby, he went.

Happy I didn't feel. Proud I wasn't. But what a relief! Later I went to visit him there—a pigpen the place is—and I had an inspiration. Do you have to be a *yeshiva bocher* to have an inspiration? I bought him an army uniform. Those Cossacks who drill in the Malinovsky Barracks are so poor they're glad to sell the clothes right off their backs for pocket money, even though they could go to prison for doing it. I shortened it; sewed on ribbons, trinkets, whatever I could; and took it to him with my good news! Already he has been promoted to general. After only six weeks in the Army! That's because he behaved himself.

His face shone like a *tzaddik*'s. Do you doubt he belongs in the insane asylum? He stood as tall as he could, a bit under five feet in his shoes. You should see him, in that filthy breeding ground for rats! Reb Horowitz should hide his face to be associated with such a place—bugs, vermin—well, why should I complain? Zayde is happy, that's the main thing. He sleeps in his uniform at night. The director of the asylum, Haimovich, the number-one slob in all Minsk, told me Zayde orders all those crazy old Jews around; he insists they should salute him and call him "Your Honor."

Greenberg, the *gonif*, the giant deaf mute, it turns out he's Zayde's horse, carries him on his back everywhere, and considers it a promotion to be such an honored horse. In with the filth, they're both in heaven, horse and rider. For my inspiration I don't ask credit. Anyhow, I have made Zayde happy for his last days, no? Which is more than he ever did for me.

Your sister Feygele, married to that *shaygetz* Karpovich boy, another poison for your poor mother's soul, so *mit in dirinnen*, between shipping guns and making bombs, Feygele has given birth to a half-*goyish* baby boy. Could anything be worse?

As if this creature of Feygele's could make up for the death of a woman like your mother! They are calling this creature Israil after your papa, so at least with this name he will probably be able to

figure out for himself that some Jewish blood runs in his veins. Nu, you see, even in Minsk nothing goes smooth. Also, if you can take advice from someone who despises you, don't send any gifts or money to Feygele's baby, because I know you, Moishe, always trying to buy your way back. Money wouldn't work with your sister! To her you have been long dead.

I thought you should know all this, Moishe, so you can stop with the money. There's no one to send it for, and it wouldn't do you any good. No one here needs your money, or wants it.

If I could write myself, I'd tell you what I think of you, but it shouldn't be a shame in front of the rabbi who is doing me the favor to write this. Spend your money on yourself, Moishe; live and grow like an onion, with your head in the earth.

Aunt Leah

LETTER FROM SHEYNA RASEL TO FREDA

192 Essex Street
New York
4 October 1898

My dear Freda:

So at last you had your daughter. As they used to say in the old country, she'll be the jewel of your old age. How flattering you're calling her Rasel! What do I care for taboos? Kiss her for me.

In New York in summer it gets too hot to breathe. But do I take pen in hand to write you about the weather? What I have to tell, dear sister, is so intimate, how else to begin except with the weather, which was the cause of it all?

In the heat firemen open the hydrants for the children, but can a grown woman run into the spray in her underwear? New York is near the ocean, but you can't see this ocean from Essex Street. Of course, we can *visit* the ocean, and finally I did last August, and if I never see the ocean again, it'll be soon enough! What happened I wouldn't wish on Moses's Aunt Leah!

An iron steamboat goes twice every Sunday and also there are trains, but no, not good enough for my Moses! He insisted he must hire a carriage and driver, we'd go in style, the family and Abram, and for the whole week we talked about nothing but the Coney Island Sunday that was coming, Moses and I, together with Isaac, who, by the way, fits right into our family as a young brother should. What a grown, powerful man he's become, with his sad face and thin, elegant mustache.

On Saturday, the whole family went to Ridley's, to buy bathing costumes. When I put mine on in the dressing room, I couldn't believe I would ever dare walk around in the open like that, black

bloomers, with my calves all bare. Moses insisted I should buy black stockings, although the saleslady assured him everyone is going barelegged this year on the beaches. But Moses said, "Over my dead body."

Sunday the sun was still not quite up when the carriage arrived at seven. We were not disappointed—shiny, black, and big. The driver, poor *schlepper*, had on a heavy black uniform, a long coat with epaulettes and gold buttons. "Mister," I said to him, "are you crazy? You'll boil alive like that." He looked at me as if I'd asked him to cut off both his ears and feed them to the horses. He didn't unbutton one button. The poor man must have been seventy, and sweating like someone in an oven. All right, so there it was: my husband, my brother-in-law, our friend the doctor, the poor coach driver, my big son, eight, going on nine years old—five men, two horses, and I, your baby sister, Sheyna. Going to Coney Island. Could I have asked for more? Oy.

Who would have thought that our first sight of the ocean would be an anticlimax? Because by the time we reached it, we had seen so many wonders! The Brooklyn Bridge, an incredible lacework of crossed steel and cables, so graceful! A huge building where horses race on Sundays in a great outdoor oval, and crowds come to wager which horse will win.

On Surf Avenue we saw midgets, a woman with a beard, a fat lady dripping folds of flesh. And never did I see on one street so many drunks, soldiers, clowns, and women of no reputation walking along with their sailors as if they were their wives. A live elephant walked by, men dressed in turbans and bloomers waved to us. We passed theaters showing the Floradora Girls; the Wild Man of Borneo; Harry Houdini, the Escape Artist; and a hotel *shaped* like an elephant. Music floated out of the restaurants, and from the Great Iron Pier, where the steamboats land their passengers, came marching music, "Sousa's Band," the driver called in to us, a famous band. Everyone was having a marvelous time and there didn't seem to be laws against anything in particular. I was enchanted. The driver stopped our coach outside a huge, wooden wall with a sign: STEEPLECHASE.

"Take the little boy in," the driver shouted down to us. "It's the new fun palace." Imagine a whole house—a *palace*—for fun! Could only be in this country. Moishe was a little sour, but he bought tickets for everyone.

The first thing that happened—don't laugh—a blast of air from below blew my skirt way up to my ears. People were standing around laughing at me. Oh, my ears were red! Jacob laughed his

high, wonderful laugh—it's not easy to make him laugh, so how could I keep a straight face myself?

Afterward we went to get "red hots," sausages with mustard, at a place called Feltman's. You never saw such a huge restaurant, with I don't know how many enormous rooms, each crowded with people at tables. The others ate their red hots, and I had my ice cream soda —chocolate—it was heaven. You're lucky, Freda, if you've never had one. They destroy character. I don't think I've ever felt so free, so . . . almost wild. We made our way back to where the driver said he would wait for us.

On our way to the beach we passed a photograph gallery and Moses suddenly announced we should have our pictures taken— pictures to remember the day, and to send to you. In this photo- graph place, whom do you think we met? The owner was Motke Schmulkowitz, son of the great *rebbe* of Minsk, no less, an old friend of Isaac! Can you imagine? Well, there was some reunion be- tween the two young men! The upshot was, Isaac announced he was going to spend the day in the gallery, and we should pick him up when we started for home. I'm enclosing one of the pictures they took. But wait.

It must give health, that cool ocean air. But in the ears, above every other sound, you hear the rhythmic never-ceasing roaring of waves crashing against the beach, always one more crasher, then an- other, as if in this place the Almighty is showing His true Power. The beach of fine sand is almost a verst from Surf Avenue down to the ocean, and long—oh, a beach as far as the mind can go.

Sitting along this beach, about every hundred meters, on enor- mous high chairs two stories up on stilts, are strong young men—to climb so high they have to be brave—called "lifesavers." Romantic, no? Little did I know! Looking out over the ocean like captains of great ships, to be sure no one is drowning. Mostly big Irishers. Would you expect to find a sensible Jewish boy sitting up on such a high contraption? Where would he learn to swim? In the Svisloch? Or the Bug?

Many, many people, including women, go rushing into the ocean, tossed up and down by the surf. A few swim but most stand close to the shore and simply bob with the waves, full of pure plea- sure. And the breeze! The first time I have felt cool through and through the whole summer. You must have such beaches, too. Do you feel about the sea the way I do? From where comes that steady, relentless power, driving and pounding against the shore? Again, again, again. It only reminds me of—I can't write it, I'll let your sis- terly intuition tell you.

They have a huge place to change into bathing costumes. Naturally I took Jacob into the ladies'. Well, such a yell from two of the fattest women in the entire world. "What is this young *man* doing in the ladies'?" You would have thought he came with an axe to murder them. Jacob kept a straight face, but he laughed privately to me. When we came out on the beach, Moses and Abram were waiting for us, laughing at each other as if they were enjoying the ocean air on their skins, as if they felt some strange new freedom, not quite allowed! Is this what we came to this land for, so we could feel like this? Abram stared at me with such open admiration when I emerged from the ladies', he didn't have to say anything—it was all in his face. And remember it was he, not a midwife, who assisted in the delivery of Jacob. This shocks you?

We all walked to the edge of the sea and put our feet in the cold, swirling, foaming water. It felt wonderful. Jacob kept saying, "Can I go in, Ma, can I go in?" A ukelele beating in my ears.

"You'll go later," I told him, but he looked up at the waves as if he were gazing at heaven.

We found a place, spread a blanket on the hot sand, and I put out the lunch. We ate slowly, not saying much, listening to the waves and breathing that marvelous air of the ocean, watching a few white clouds and people playing or sleeping all around us. But Jacob couldn't sit still. He ran forth and back like an Indian, with that sweet little limp, waving his skinny arms. He never seems aware of the limp anymore. I said, "Stay close to Mama, Yankele."

After we ate, Moses lay back in the sand with his face, arms, and legs to the sun, like someone starved for warmth—as though we haven't been living in the fire all summer on Essex Street. "Feel," he kept saying, "feel." He lay still, and one, two, three, he was asleep.

Abram and I sat and talked quietly and ran our fingers through the sand, while Jacob built a sand castle and kept pleading, "Ma, can I, oh, can I?" Suddenly—I don't know what got into him—he jumped up impatiently and said, "I'm going in the water, Ma, watch me!"

Before Abram or I could move, his skinny uneven legs were rapidly taking him away from us, and as if to help himself go faster, he also waved his arms like a bird about to take flight, and there he was, in the shallow water, splashing, his head back, his mouth open, as if he were shouting to the Upper One. Although I felt his freedom, the openness of the place, I ran after him to the water's edge, with Abram beside me, and I called to him to come out immediately, but with the waves crashing, how could he hear me? Other children were jumping in the water beside him all delighted.

"Well," Abram said, taking my elbow, "let him enjoy." It appeared he was being careful to stay in the shallows with his new friends. He would be, if I knew my Jacob, loosed from some invisible bond at last; he was behaving the way I was feeling.

"Come," Abram said, "Let's walk a little." He took my hand. A feeling of laziness, of openness and of marvelous relaxation swept through me. Everyone taken care of. Jacob full of glee. Moses sleeping. Isaac with his newfound old friend from Minsk. I was somehow again a girl, walking with Abram, bending my head to him, listening under the roar of the water, a girl maybe for the first time without a care. The ocean water curled under my toes, a lovely sensation. As we walked, I asked Abram what his plans were. His residency in the hospital would soon be over. In two months, Abram said, he was thinking about setting himself up in his own office to practice. But he was worried; where was the money to come from? Furniture, instruments, examining tables to buy, and the rent to pay until patients would come.

I was surprised. "Why don't you speak to Moses?"

He looked out over the sea, uncomfortable with the question. "Moses has done too much for me. I don't want to owe him more than I do already."

"He'd be insulted if he could hear you. You should be ashamed to talk like that. Even I am insulted. What are friends for?"

He held my hand in a much friendlier way, turned me toward him a bit, and smiled his big, wide, crooked smile. "Moses has only one thing I ever wanted," he said. Abram's hands, his face, told me long before his words. My stomach felt weak. And I didn't ask, I swear.

"His wife." He laughed. "I know, I should be ashamed of myself. But I'm not. You compel me, Sheyna. There's a rich something in you that no one has touched. I bet I could reach it."

My legs turned to water, for I knew what he meant and I was afraid of myself. "Abram, you're not serious," I said, and could hear my own voice trembling. "You mustn't be serious. It's not fair." Why are we such liars? Still, I didn't want to change my life. But before we could say anything more, we heard a great commotion behind us and saw people running into the water and heard them shouting frantically. A handsome Irisher from one of the high chairs was clambering down like a monkey. Soon everyone around us was running and pointing. Abram and I rushed to join the crowd.

Naturally I was looking for my Jacob to pick out his face in that crowd.

"You little devil," some man shouted almost into my ear, but looking toward the sea. "Come back here, you damn devil!"

I looked out to where he was shouting and, beyond the breakers, there was my Jacob. His head was all I could see, and barely see, bobbing in the water, struggling, alone, far beyond where he could stand. I knew he was mine. "He's crazy," I cried to Abram. His head was visible one moment, the next it disappeared beneath the surface. I must have screamed. Abram took my elbow in his iron fingers, as if to give me strength for what was coming.

Before I knew what he was doing, Abram, alone of all the fine people gathered there, including the lifesaver—Abram, without hesitating a moment, left me and rushed headlong out, bursting through the cold and violent water like some fierce sea-animal, thrashing his arms. Without thinking, I followed him. Abram can't swim a stroke; neither can I. I had water in my ears, mouth, eyes; in a few seconds I was breathing water. I was blinded, drowning, and drinking salt water, breathing water.

Choking, unable even to breathe my last, up like a cork, down like a stone, looking everywhere for air, I felt suddenly the mighty hand of the Uppermost on my arm, and I was plucked from the water as if I were a splinter and pulled into a deep round-bottom boat by two red Irishers, one freckled from top to bottom. "Arr ye all right, ma'am?" the freckled one said.

"All right, all right," I managed to say, and remembering Jacob and Abram, cried out, "My son! My baby!" The second lifesaver pointed behind me, to two figures in the bottom of our bobbing boat. My Jacob lay on his stomach, his face turned to one side, yellow with death, poor thing. Oozing from his mouth and nose were mucus and water, and from his nose also blood. Sitting astride him was Abram, pushing with both palms down and inward on Jacob's ribs, as if he were trying to crush his skinny body. "Breathe, you little bastard, breathe!" Abram grunted. "Breathe!"

Down, up, down, a great human pump, like the mighty waves themselves, and water kept oozing from my little one's nose and mouth. All I could do was to try to catch my breath. "He's a doctor," one of the Irishers reassured me. I nodded. Heavy spray swept over us all. As I watched through the salt tears, I could almost feel Abram's palms in *my* back, his hands on *my* flesh. *Breathe!* I thought. *Breathe, sweet Yankele! My angel!* I, who had been choking only a few moments before, held my breath. I could see nothing but his little face, lifeless there in the bottom of the boat, in the shadow of Abram. As a matter of will, I put my faith in Abram, a Just Man, a man who had saved Jacob from death once before. And now—again!

My little one stirred. His face grew less yellow. Abram was still

bent, pushing with the backs of his palms, and I could see Abram's hard breathing, the sound of it drowned out by the waves. Suddenly I heard a sound from my son, a squeak, and I saw his eyes twitch. What can I say? Could any woman have been happier?

Abram looked up at me, only a glance, but he was satisfied. And I ended by falling in love, *letting* myself fall in love with this strangely shaped, deliciously ugly man.

"You don't even know how to swim, Abram," I said, laughing like a stupid clod.

He grinned back, still pumping. "Swim? Swim? Who had time to learn?"

Moses had apoplexy with me for letting Jacob out of my sight.

Could I help thinking about that day he had come for us, to save us all from the pogromists, and his mother had slipped on the ice? What did *he* do? He let Feygele go for her. Did I blame him then? Not at all. After all, he had *come* to save us. But why should I be trying to turn *you* against him? Nu. He was *sleeping*, while I nearly drowned. Certainly not his fault, but I hated him. I'm not very nice, or logical. And how about the time Abram was arrested in Minsk, and tortured day after day to confess who his confederates were—Moishe, for one? I had scarcely heard of Abram in those days, never gave him a thought. Now I can't get him out of my mind—he suffered beatings, needles, starvation, freezing, all for his friends' sake. And all that time, what did the great Moishe do to help him? Oh, what we didn't know in those days, Freda!

Jacob, all recovered in no time, was enjoying his experience as a celebrity and told the driver about his adventure and about the newspaper man who had asked for his name and address, and where he went to school. "Papa, will I be in the paper?"

We picked up Isaac, who chattered on about how great was Schmulkowitz's photo gallery, a tremendous business. He was more excited about that than the saving of Jacob. He was coming back to Coney Island tomorrow again; Schmulkowitz had offered him a position, and Moses could do without him for a while, he was sure of that.

After a year and a day, we clip-clopped back to Essex Street. Moishe was glum, and no one spoke a word the last two hours. I was glad to be home! I've had enough ocean to last me a lifetime.

Abram started to say good night. He was still terribly light hearted, almost as if he'd had too much to drink. After Moishe and Isaac had taken Jacob upstairs, he held me back in the street. He laughed. He kissed me. I was exhausted. What should I have done? What I did, I put my tired arms around this wonderful little man.

"Thank you," I said. "For my son's life. I'm glad we didn't all drown." I kissed *him*. And I went upstairs, my knees weak.

Again today it's hot, but I'm staying on Essex Street.

Your weak-willed sister,
Sheyna Rasel

LETTER FROM SHEYNA RASEL TO FREDA

192 Essex Street
New York
9 November 1898

Dear Freda,

Now comes something—it's not easy. Be patient, because I need all the help I can get. And you are thousands of miles away, so why not? Ha, ha!

Moishe and I—how can I say it? There's a glass wall between us. He speaks *at* me. Not even in the dark of our room, not a finger does he try to touch me with. And if I touch him, his flesh is cold. How I loved him once, but how did *he* feel? Oh, he *sent* for me—a ship ticket—because I begged him to. But what did I ever mean to him?

Life after Coney Island pretended to go on as before. I don't know why that day made a difference, but it did. Abram came to dinner twice a week, and *those* nights I waited for like a baby for milk. A few times, Isaac went out and we were alone together, but he never said anything wrong or improper. Of course, Jacob was there, watching his mother like a hawk.

Then Moses stayed out a whole night, then two nights together. I never asked where or why or with whom, but I began to turn myself against him. Isaac would say, "Where in hell were you last night, Moses?" And he would answer "Someone has to make a dollar, don't they? I have four mouths to feed. I slept at the place." Meaning the showroom on East Broadway. He should live so! Isaac would roll his eyes. I tried to behave normally in every way, because of Jacob. Besides being too smart for his age, he's some intuitive kid. You have to watch every step. A son like that can be some headache! After two months I was all nerves.

One day Isaac moved out, went to live with Motke Schmulkowitz, who has taken to calling himself Morton Smulka, to be more American (maybe that's his own little joke—he's modeling himself on Smulka the thief?). Isaac loves the tintype place. Moses goes banging around the house about this, slamming doors. Took this ungrateful brother right off the boat, took him into his house, gave

him a job, and now in the busy season, just when he needs him most! But Isaac doesn't *like* trading. Photography fascinates him. More exotic, and he loves the hustle, joking with the customers, the honky-tonk of Coney Island. I can see why. It's *his* life. Must everyone be a shadow to the mighty Moses? For two whole days Moses would not say a word to me for daring to defend Isaac. Oh, our Moishele could give lessons to the Tsar!

One morning after Moses had gone to work and Jacob was, thank God, back in school, I set up my easel—sometimes, with Bernstein's blessing, I work at home—when who marches in the door but Abram! Can I say I hadn't been expecting him like this some quiet morning? Sooner or later. This day he was exuberant. "Sheyna, I've rented a place for my office!" he cried. "Will you come help me get it ready?"

"Can't you see I'm working? I promised this sketch for tomorrow." I was already on my feet. "What will I tell Bernstein?" I was putting on my coat.

I grabbed the broom, mop, pail, brush, tied on a kerchief. He took the cleaning things from me quietly, and we walked through the drizzle to Clinton Street, up the stoop to a flat on the first floor.

"The waiting room," he said. "Look! The examining room. And here, my private office."

"It could use a scrub," I said.

"What office couldn't? It needs a woman's hand, my Sheyna. That's why I asked you!" He was half shouting with excitement.

"It also needs furniture," I said stupidly.

"The sofa's coming next week."

"You're starting with the sofa? Some doctor! It doesn't sound scientific to me." I turned directly to him. "So you finally worked it out with Moishe? You got him to loosen up with a few shekels?"

"No, no. A patient, an elderly gentleman, a German Jew, he took a liking to me. He insisted on making me a loan."

"Why not?" I was strangely happy. "You're a good man. Anyone can tell—even a German Jew. If I had any money, I'd give you also. Oh, I *have*. I've saved a few hundred dollars from Bernstein's. . . ."

I must have said one word too many. Before I could go on, he was turning me around by the shoulders like Papa used to do when he was angry, and he was looking into my eyes so deeply, I was a bit frightened. But I peered right back at him. What did he want of me? This was not any dream of *mine* coming true. I had never thought about this. I never imagined to have any man look into me like that, especially not this man, as if a fever were consuming him,

some need too great to be spoken. Moses *never* looked at me like that. "Sheyna Rasel," Abram said softly. "My rose. You know, it's not only the petals that attract a man, but from within the flower, from somewhere mysterious, comes this magic fragrance. It fills the air with loveliness. No scientist, no doctor, nobody has yet fathomed where this element comes from. All we know is it's there—within. That's what I feel. From within, this joy, your radiance, fills me up."

We didn't talk. Not a word. What was there to talk about? Like an animal in heat I got slowly to the floor and began to scrub. I scrubbed the bare wood floor to make a clean place for us. Strength! I prayed for strength from the Upper One. We used our clothes to lie on. He lay beside me. To be exact, nothing like it has ever happened to me, and Abram told me nothing like it ever happened to him.

All right, save your breath! Thank the Upper One you're thousands of miles away. Freda, I had to tell you, only you. Your Herschel must *never* hear of it. Promise! However hard on me you are, you couldn't be harder than myself.

We did nothing afterwards but clean and scrub that place. The wonderful kisses, all we had done, hung over us, neither of us saying anything. We felt too much and too clumsy, and when we had cleaned the entire place, we walked in silence back to my house. The sun had meanwhile come out.

Several times a week Abram came to get me. Each time I took the broom, the pail, the kerchief, although there was nothing left to clean. I learned to paint. The walls were easy, but those two windows! I left more paint on the glass than on the wood. It was as if we were children playing, but not quite children. We talked of his work and mine. We talked about Jacob growing up. He told me about his life in the Movement, back in Minsk. He told me about being in prison there. It wasn't nice. The new sofa came, a welcome change for us both from the hard floor. Soon the new examining table came, the chairs, the desk, the instrument cabinets. I took his lovely medical license and diploma to be framed. Soon it was a fine doctor's office. The sofa had pink roses—what else? I had two signs made: ABRAM SHAPIRO, M.D., the most beautiful signs ever made, one English, the other Yiddish. My money.

Are you shocked? How I need him! Shameless, that's what I am. Yes, Freda. And I say this: everything Mama believed and told us was a lie. At least in America!

Moses saw me go prancing about my chores like a gay circus horse; I had all I could do to keep from singing. What could he be thinking, I wondered. One day he said to me, "Rasel, how would

gave off effulgent signals too obvious for Moses to ignore. They had a wild romp.

Her letter equivocates.

> Dear Sister, you might have thought I was a Frenchwoman, a whore, but actually (I blush to write it), it was all rather exciting and entirely legal. At the critical point I simply closed my eyes and told myself he was Abram! What amazed me was that Moses had learned a few tricks—from maybe Carol Kahn, the great—uh— decorator? The experience I won't forget, and he won't either. So for one night I had the Moishe of my girlish dreams! And maybe yours, too!

A month later this woman—my grandmother, Martin thought with some dismay—made crafty by illicit love, solemnly announced her pregnancy—to her husband's delight. Her baby, she wrote, was "premature" (seven and a half months from the date of the romp). Nevertheless, he weighed six pounds, three ounces. They named him Nathan at Moses's insistence. After someone, he said, who had been a close comrade in the Movement back in the old country, and who had, he believed, been hanged. This could only have been Natasha Perkovina, Martin thought, but he bet Moses never told Sheyna it was a woman. Abram, however, could not help but know. And that was the least of it. They all had their skeletons.

6

Somewhere in Cuba
15 December 1899

Dear Moses and Sheyna Rasel,

Only a few days and we'll all be crossing into the twentieth century. I never expected to do so in a base hospital in Cuba.

I'm one of three American doctors in a hospital that was formerly a *finca*, a farmhouse. We treat yellow fever, malaria, and tetanus—about five hundred pretty sick people, not American army men, mostly natives, men, women and children . . . usually Negro or mulatto. Luckily the locals have no idea how little we know. So far the staff has been spared the contagion. In general things are quiet.

I can't tell you how delighted I was to hear about the birth of your Nathan. I feel so close to the newcomer. I'm only sorry I couldn't have helped at the delivery. I hope you didn't suffer, Sheyna, and that you had the best of medical care.

So he resembles you, Moishe! Glad to hear it. And why not? Over six pounds—*um beshreien!*

So I drink to Nathan's health and happiness with Cuban rum. Terrible stuff, but it's become mother's milk. With each sip I understand my old man a lot better.

By the way, I received a commendation and quite a pretty ribbon from Colonel Roosevelt himself. A touching little ceremony. He called me "typical" of the Jewish fighting type he'd seen on the New York police force. It seems that on the day we arrived, I lost my head and completely forgot I was a doctor when a dozen Spaniards launched a mortar attack against the little field hospital. Against a hospital! I took a rifle from a wounded boy and began crawling through the sugarcane until I could see them. I shot through the cane at those bastards, and I was lucky. I hit three of

them before they hit me. Night after night, back in the old country, I used to listen to my father, usually drunk on vodka, telling us all about the terrible days in Spain, Torquemada and all those blood-thirsty Spanish bishops. Well, I got off a few shots for the old man. One bishop, two bishops. Down they went. I was afraid I'd be reprimanded, but instead colonel Teddy gave me a promotion.

Kiss Jacob for me, and Nathan.

Abram

P.S. You can congratulate me also. I'm getting married. She's one of our nurses, a lively Irisher—Mary O'Donnell, from Newark. Great woman. Yes, I *know* . . . I'm marrying a *shiksa*. Do me something.

A.

P.P.S. Don't tell my mother.

Now Martin came upon a different kind of letter—a series, carefully clipped together in a bunch, like a woman's love letters, each from a different woman. The first, from Carol Kahn, began "You bastard," a mixture of threats, endearments, and unrestrained promises of delight. Underlying it was the furiousness of a woman scorned. Moses apparently shrugged, Martin observed. The others were from other women of higher position than Carol Kahn. As he became richer, vainer, tougher, and more preoccupied with his business and status, old Moishe must have grown ever more cautious, caring more for appearances.

Martin had noted that Moses's own letters displayed a certain irritation that Sheyna Rasel never became fully Americanized. He joked about her accent and about the fact that she was not entirely comfortable in the presence of *goyim*. *He* certainly was, especially with *goyish* women.

Well, they were alike in that, for sure. Martin's women, too, from the Wren in England, whom Jenny also belabored him with, to his princess in Milan, no less . . . there were all these common threads, but you couldn't *tell* anyone. *This* he understood about Moishe. His joy in their broken hearts, their sighs, tears, and tantrums, was clear from the tawdry correspondence. And from Martin's own experience. Moishe apparently had met such women, as Martin sometimes did, by spending ever greater amounts of his time and money on "causes" which were often nonsectarian or Christian; such generosity purchased his way into a society which for smaller amounts would never have accepted him. In this, Sheyna Rasel apparently never joined him: Wayward Girls, the New York Infirmary, the Foundling Home of New York, the Metropolitan Museum of Art, the Met, Catholic Charities; all were beneficiaries of Moishe's largesse—and today Martin's.

Moishe met women interested in art, music, interior decorating, and theater, attractive women, often as rich as he, committed to a cause and to themselves. One activity, of course, led to another. If he took delight in winning their favors, it was pale delight compared to the pleasure he took in casting them off. Barely glancing through the letters, Martin knew it all. Well-known socialites, women of accomplishment, all, one way or another, openly or suggestively wheedling, begging to be given another chance, offering specific enticements, or threatening vengeance or suicide. One of the most violent was from Mary O'Donnell, the wife of Abram Shapiro, his former friend and the seducer of his own wife. Moishe had made it his business to seek her out! An eye for an eye—or whatever. Revenge is sweet. Moishe had collected women, but once they were in the collection, he took not one of the ladies back for so much as a day,

Martin was suddenly appalled. Not at his grandfather's faithlessness, but at his own. To have his transgressions forecast before he was born! Predestined life! Not exemplary, either—not exemplary at all. Well, at least *his* women hadn't written him. Hysterical phone calls, yes. Suicide threats, yes. From Paris, Milan, London. Well, as things had turned out, thank God for the memories.

And the funny thing, and the big difference between old Moishe and him, was that through all those episodes he *thought* only about Jenny, was compelled only by Jenny. Funnier still, Jenny had been the best of them all in the hay. She really knew her way around *him*, while the others were . . . well, a chore. Experimenters. At least so they seemed at this remove. Jenny was the one and only—why kid himself? After all he had hidden from her, could he deny her anything now? If she insisted on making this trip, as she was now doing, who the hell was he to stop her?

Keeping his affairs under cover seemed no more difficult for Moses than they had been for him. Each summer, Father had often told him, Sheyna Rasel and her two sons were parked in the fancy Flagler Hotel in the town of Tannersville, and each Friday night Moses would take the "husband train" to the Catskills and spend two days with his wife and boys. On Sunday the husband train would take him back to town. All week for the rat to play and/or make his next million. Moses's letters grew more and more monotonous. He seemed to be increasingly concerned with money, money, money—making it or giving it away. There were good times and bad, and his mood changed with the size of his bank account. From the time he was thirty, Moses never again made mention of his revolutionist past; his had become a world of success—first and foremost,

Singer's, then located on Fourteenth Street, his charities, his women, and his family, in that order.

In the summer of 1903 when the family was in Tannersville, he must have remained in the city for three weekends running; how else to explain this letter to him from his son, Jacob, age thirteen? Yes, Father *had* been a senior in high school at that age! Clearly his misspelling, his handwritten correspondence for which he was renowned when he was on the Supreme Court (a failing he considered of no importance), had its roots early in life. In all things (but not in spelling), Father was born with an outside arrogance, seen even in this early letter to *his* father.

LETTER FROM JACOB SINGER (AGE 13) TO HIS FATHER MOSES
Hotel Flagler
Tannersville, N.Y.

16 August 1903

Dear Pop,

We sympathize with you, stuck in the hot city. Ma calls attention to your sacrifice a dozen times a day.

First the cheerful news. Who do you think showed up here out of the blue? None other than Dr. Abram! He calls his wife "Miss Mary," very pretty, and she talks with a brogue. Ma thinks she's "kinda dumb" (I don't). Dr. Abram certainly has improved. He's full of good cheer and considerably less homeley than I remember him. He and Ma fell all over each other! Ma's so emoshunal! I think she's always had a soft spot for him. Dr. Abram seems to be crazy about Nate, too, pays much more attention to him than to me. Not that I mind, really. He holds Nate on his lap and tells him tall stories about Cuba.

Now to the painful news. Ma has been after me to be bar mitzvah this fall. I hate the idea! Ma sicked old Rabbi Kirschner, who conducts Friday night services here, on me. He came up and grabed my hand while I was immersed in the seige of San Jacinto in Beard's *American History*, and without ado he started hocking me on the necessity of being confirmed in the Jewish religion. I was amazed by his rudeness but replied politely that I came from a nonreligious family. I didn't want to offend him, but my father all his life hated organized religion. I said this is what I, too, happen to believe, and if there were a ceremony to conferm me in that belief, I would be glad to partisipate.

The good rabbi had a conniption fit, and became nasty. I soon realized my error. I had attacked the poor man where he was most vulnerable—in his busness. I tried to apologize, truly I did, Pop, but he wouldn't listen and flounced away. I must never be so tactless

again. He went to Ma and gave her an earful. She scolded me, although her heart wasn't in it, but she still believes I should be bar mitzvah. She says *you* were. I can hardly believe that. Were you? Ma thinks it's important to observe the traditions of "my" people. *My* people?!

I don't even feel Jewish. I can't say why. I have no desire to *be* Jewish. I'm American. I devour whatever I can find by or about Hamilton, Washington, Burr, Marshall, Jay, Madison, Jefferson, etc. When I read them, or about them, I'm *moved*. This great country moves me as very little else does. The ethic of this country is Christian, not Jewish. The great men who built it were Christian.

Although I know full well no ancester of mine fought at Bull Run or crossed the Delaware or marched on Atlanta (at least Dr. Abram *was* at San Juan Hill!), I feel, for reasons I can't explain, *I* am part of it all.

What has being bar mitzvah to do with *that*? Such a ceremony would be a travesty; I'd be false to myself. My own fourbears are alien to me, Pop. Not you and Ma, of course, but I find those old Jews foreign and unrecognizable, while Hawthorne, Cooper, Poe, Twain, the stories of the taming of the West, of Lewis and Clark, of Indians—these are *mine*. What makes me want to erase my past and to embrace my future I can't say. But that's how I am.

When I graduate from Townsend Harris in June I'll go to City College, I suppose. I'd have preferred West Point, but, of course, not with my bum leg. If I can't be a general, I'll settle for President. In no event, however, do I want to be bar mitzvah. Please support me, Pop. Come up and see us soon. We miss you!

Your loving son Jake

Letter from Jacob Singer to his father Moses
Manpower Mobilization Board
1270 Avenue J Southwest
Washington, D.C.
Office of Jacob Singer, Chairman

2 July 1917

Dear Pop:

This is not easy for me to write. How can I properly respond to your request with frankness and honesty and still not have you feel that I have in some way let you down, or worse, that I have betrayed my family? How I wish we could both pretend you had never written me!

You say I must consider the "powerful" feelings of my "little mother," that she is worried to death night and day about Nathan's

having to go overseas with the A.E.F. Pop, if my "little mother" had meant to ask me to "exercise" my so-called "influence" to intervene, to keep him safely on our side of the Atlantic, could not Ma have doped out a way to approach me directly?

If Nate himself wanted me to intercede with the military authorities on his behalf, he also knows how to reach me. We are brothers, after all. But Mama and Nate have been noticeably silent.

I cannot say I resent your request, because in a family like ours we are beyond such petty feelings. However, you do evidence a certain insensitivity to my position. In case you don't appreciate it, my Hebrew extraction—which I do my best to neutralize—makes me hypersensitive to any possible charges of wrongdoing. I may be chairman of the President's Manpower Mobilization Board, but how long do you think I could survive in this "exalted" position, as you call it, if it were known—as it would surely be—that I did the kind of thing that you requested? And what would the Ku Klux Klan and other anti-Semites make of it?

If anything untoward should befall Nate overseas, I would be as sorely grieved as you or Ma. However, these are difficult times— many Americans, even though we are at war, do not yet realize our peril, the peril to the entire civilized world, the peril of falling victim to Prussian despots. If I did not believe *that* with all my heart, I would never have left Cambridge and my "safe" professorship at the Law School to do this important job for President Wilson and our country. We are fighting this war to defend and preserve a relaxed way of life that permits us as individuals to do whatever odd things we choose and not to do with our lives only what some governor or dictator mobilizes us to do. I'm afraid, Pop, you are still suffering from the drastic effects of your days in Minsk, when young men were forced into the Tsar's Imperial Army, obliged to risk their lives in causes which were not their own. In those days, as you have recounted to me, you used your connections to get boys off. However, democratic America, Pop, is not Imperial Russia.

Americans—including Hebrews—have unlimited rights to own property, to speak their minds, to make millions, to join the Workmen's Circle, or to achieve high status—as you have done, Pop. Well, the time comes when real, painful sacrifice is required to defend all those "rights."

You write of my "duty" to the family. Pop, as I see it, my duty is far greater. I am in the service of our great country, in a supreme effort that will determine if we can achieve dominance over a wicked world and can spread our benign influence. We are led by a man of great vision, who reached out to Harvard to get me, and affords me the privilege of doing this work. Do you really believe I

could be unfaithful to Woodrow Wilson and to all that I believe? Do you know me so little?

Nate will go, he will do himself proud, just as Abram Shapiro served in Cuba under Teddy Roosevelt years ago. I share the anguish and concern this will cause Ma and you, because I feel it, too. I wish I could help him, but I can't.

I hope you will not mind, Pop, that I have discussed your letter and my reply briefly with the President of the United States, who says he understands your anguish and asks that I convey to you that he thinks of each of the boys who must go and fight this war as his own son. Also, on his suggestion I have destroyed your letter, so that it can never be seen by unfriendly eyes.

I will write to Nate and Ma in separate letters. I know how accustomed to getting your way you are in all things. I hate to disappoint you in this, and I hope you will understand my position.

With affection,
Your loving son,
Jacob

LETTER FROM MOSES SINGER TO HIS SON JACOB

New York
6 July 1917

Dear Jacob:

You may be very important in Washington—I can see that by the newspapers; I also know you are brilliant and have an illustrious career ahead of you, but I cannot understand my own son. You are willing to risk your brother's being *killed*, his *life*, in a war in which he, you, your mother, and I have no interest whatsoever? It is maddening, incomprehensible to me. Say all you want about Prussian despots, but for your information, when I was a young man in Minsk, Germany was to us a land of enlightenment. For a short time I seriously thought of going there instead of here. All you can think to say of the Germans, who have given our people the greatest of opportunities, is to call them "despots"? You write to your father as if he were an idiot, ignorant of politics, ignorant of all history, but this is not the point.

The point is, you were our last hope. You have left your little mother and your father in despair.

Your little mother is reduced to *praying* that Nathan will come to no harm, while I, who cannot pray, join her in this hope with all my heart, for the sake of *your* conscience and for our peace of mind. What would be the worth of our entire lives, of all the successes of the store, of all I have built up with the sweat of my brow, of all my charities, if we should lose our dearest Nate? What good is

American "dominance over a wicked world" to parents who lose a son? I do not believe all your "hifalutin'" words and phrases. It gets down to this: you will not take any risk for your own brother! You, who are safe! Your letter boils down to one thing: ambition. Is there nothing you will not sacrifice for it? Give my regards to the President.

Pop

So that was it? Martin Singer lingered over the last sheets, listening to the authentic voice of his grandfather and his father—at thirteen, at not quite twenty-seven—didactic, supremely self-certain. It was curious that someone as anxious to forswear his Jewishness as Father should have become known as "the Jewish Member of the Court," and eventually as a leading Zionist. The firmest of stars twinkles. Whatever his variability, even from the grave, he made Martin feel inadequate. Martin thought of his own sparse letters, hurriedly scrawled half pages he had been obliged by counselors to send home from Camp Kennebec each week—"We got five runs and yours truly scored twice." Or the brief V-mail pieces he had rushed off from England. By the time *he* was twenty-seven, he wrote no letters at all. Just reached for the phone.

He felt suddenly tired. He'd been reading for two hours and he had still not absorbed what he'd learned. What was astonishing was that these letters, neglected for a lifetime, had the *capacity* to astonish him. Think of Uncle Nate, tending his orchids on Lido Island, nearing his seventy-sixth birthday; did he know *yet* that he was the bastard son of Dr. Abram Shapiro? Would he give a damn now if he did know? Martin doubted it. Had Nate always realized that Mike Shapiro, the store's merchandise manager—Abram's son—was his half brother? Father *must* have known all that; must have known that Danny Roselli was the grandson of Moishe's old flame—Susan Weldon. Martin understood now why he'd inherited these two men with the store. Grandma Sheyna Rasel had died during the flu epidemic of 1918, before Martin was born. Martin, though it was none of his business, was glad she'd had her moment with Abram. It would have been a pity if she'd missed it. On the other hand, how would *he* feel if that were Jenny? The immediate stirs passions, the remembered has a sugar-coating, but some passions burn slow and never die.

Was it the clash between father and son back in 1917 that had led Moses Singer in 1935 to turn the store over to Nathan, when he surely knew him to be another man's son? Or had Father simply refused to take the store? In 1935 Father had just been appointed by Roosevelt to the

Court after ten years as dean at Harvard, and what a purist he was! He would surely have avoided the remotest financial tie to any enterprise, lest it color his judiciousness. Vaguely Martin remembered overhearing him say something to this effect to Mother when they were preparing to move from Cambridge. Was that merely sour grapes? Well, no use speculating. That lifelong coolness between Father and Grandfather never ended. Nathan got the store, and what a marvelous gem he'd made of it when he moved it to Fifth Avenue! Martin had only to carry on, establishing branches in Los Angeles, Chicago, Palm Beach, and Westchester—each shop a sparkling gem. Was it enough? Or was *his* a life misspent? Well, someone had to do it. Martin marveled at the irony. In the end old Moishe's malevolence toward his son had been neutralized when he, Martin, son of Jacob, the true grandson of Moishe, fell heir to it all.

Whatever doubts Martin may have nourished that Yuri Karpeyko was his cousin had long since vanished. Feygele's son, Ivan Karpeyko (né Israil Karpovich), the old Bolshevik, still lived—in Minsk. He'd ask Jenny to read this stuff after lunch if she didn't have too big a hangover. Rachel had already read much of it in the original. Rachel puzzled him more than ever. What did the old woman have up her sleeve?

He swallowed the medication his Filipino night nurse was pushing, and finally fell into a drowsy state, reflecting that once there had been another Joshua, who would have been his uncle if he had not died of scarlet fever at the age of two.

At noon he was awakened by a call from Jerusalem. Frances Huggins, his handsome Irish day nurse, was so impressed by the great distance of the call that, against her better judgment, she shook Martin awake. Jews were funny. A call from the Holy Land—for all she knew, to them it might be like a call from the Pope would be to her. A strong young voice: "Mister Singher? This is your cousin Gideon Aron. . . . Yes, yes, I'm the pilot; so how did you know? . . . Rachel told you? . . . Yes, her grandson. Is she there? . . . No? . . . In California? So please to tell her I must talk to her. Tell her I have seen Weisbrot. Yes, Weisbrot call me specially in. She must telephone me immediately. . . . Yes, so how I'm going to explain you what I am talking on the telephone? Sorry, but is impossible, sir. Please ask her to call me. She knows the number. Tell her I am on leave, in my Jerusalem apartment. Today, tomorrow, the next day. . . . All right, sir. Thank you, Cousin Singher." He rang off. Martin called Myra and told her she must get this message to Rachel, who, he believed, was in San Francisco. UJA would know where. Myra could track down anyone.

Martin was almost too tired to wonder what the hell Gideon's call was all about, but he forced himself to consider. Rachel was going to the Soviet Union, and Jenny with her. Two women alone. Rachel and now her grandson were dealing with this man Weisbrot, the man Yoshke Schulman half worshipped for rescuing Jews, no matter where they were. Martin's sense of uneasiness grew.

Was Jenny's trip of the slightest operative use? Hadn't Yoshke Schulman said his outfit could deliver blue jeans and watches for them to sell? Couldn't they cheer the guy up on the phone? Weren't they doing everything that could be done? He hadn't yet written to Bill Cole, his friend and fellow Harvard Overseer, a U.S. senior diplomat now working in Moscow. But hadn't he already called three United States senators, each of whom had promised to leave no stone unturned to shake this guy Yuri loose? Hadn't he just asked Sam Rose to try to find some Soviet-American Medical Association whose American members could put together a petition to their Soviet counterparts and their leaders, as well as to Brezhnev? Hadn't Rachel spoken directly to Kissinger? Wasn't the National Conference on the case? Wasn't Amnesty International? What more could anyone do?

Ah, but he could hear Jenny's boisterous accusation again, as he dozed: "That's your idea of *doing* something? *Bubkes!* You're really something, Marty! It's like thirty-five, when Hitler got loose. What'd we do? Zilch!" Maybe she was right. Talk. Pleadings. Petitions. As she said: *Bubkes!* Back in thirty-five who had expected the Holocaust? And who could guarantee there wouldn't be another by eighty-five? They had to do *more*. If only he felt stronger! If only he could go himself! If only! All arrangements for the trip had already been made. Rachel had coordinated their plans with Tammy's engagements in the Soviet Union, in the works for so many months. Josh, of course, was going with Tammy, and she'd be accompanied by an entire troupe. She was scheduled to give one concert in Kiev and two in Moscow, and her manager had booked her into Helsinki beforehand as well. As long as they were to be in the neighborhood, why not? Rachel had been insistent about the coordination. Was she planning to use the troupe as some form of camouflage?

He worried about Jenny, who had never traveled overseas without him before. Foreign money, foreign languages, panicked her. She was a child about tipping, tickets, reservations, baggage. Another thing: Rachel was using a counterfeit American passport, and that gave him the fidgets. How heavy, he wondered, were the KGB boys on faked documents? If Rachel got herself into a jam, could Jenny avoid becoming entangled? Jenny was *his* responsibility, damnit. He had to protect her. Since he'd

made up his mind not to try to stop her, that wouldn't be easy from Gramercy Park. Maybe he should simply force himself to go. Ah, who was he kidding? He had trouble staying awake two hours at a clip.

Well, he'd call Bill Cole in Moscow and write him a letter. Jenny could deliver it personally. That would at least oblige Jenny to go see him, and if anyone in that Godforsaken land could help Jenny in a pinch it would be a U.S. diplomat like Bill. He called Huggins to ask her for a pen and his personal stationery. He had to get on with it. Tomorrow Jenny and Rachel would be arriving at Kennedy—their flights got in half an hour apart, Jenny from L.A. and Rachel from San Francisco, where she'd made another speech.

"Dear Bill," he started in longhand:

I've asked Jenny to deliver this letter in person. She's in the Soviet Union to visit a cousin of mine, one Doctor Yuri Karpeyko, of Minsk (an authentic cousin we've only just discovered), who is having severe Soviet-type difficulties—he's threatened with imminent arrest on charges that are incomprehensible to me, you, and most Americans. Meanwhile he's trying desperately to emigrate. Official, old-fashioned anti-Semitism, thinly disguised, seems to be at the root of his problem. Our friends in the Senate have spoken with Dobrynin in Washington. At the same time, my Israeli cousin (Rachel Aron) took advantage of a session she had with Kissinger to enlist *his* aid (he says he will do all possible, and perhaps he has already been in touch with Ambassador Toon on the subject). Jenny herself talked with Henry Jackson last night, when she ran into him in Beverly Hills, and he says he'll do everything *he* can. So we have a pretty good team working on the case at a time when the Jackson amendment is being debated in the Senate, and the Soviets are said to be receptive on the emigration question. But in order to leave no stone unturned, I thought I would write you. . . .

Huggins interrupted, bringing him a carton of mail and a glass of orange juice, which she insisted he drink. He set his half-written letter aside and sipped the juice. He flipped two dozen envelopes of junk mail into the trash basket beside his bed, not bothering to open them.

Four real letters in a cartonful of mail. One bearing an Israeli stamp was in Nettie's careful Brearley-learned script—from Haifa, Avram's home town.

As usual, Nettie's was a breezy little note, less than a page. Trip lovely. Avram's entire family wonderful; warm, intelligent, dedicated people.

Brother, sister, both parents. Nettie was indiscriminate with her love. She'd just met her cousin Gideon—old friend of Avram! Small world. Gorgeous man, the cousin. She was in love with everyone in Israel, and they all loved her. Haifa was the most beautiful city in the world. Everyone so straightforward and honest. Everything beautiful, beautiful and "neat." Bye-bye, Nettie, Martin thought. There goes my baby girl. Soon to live in upper Haifa, overlooking the blue, blue sea. And what dandy American-Israeli grandchildren she would produce for him and Jenny—they'd be only six or seven thousand goddamn miles away. Fifty million American young men to choose from, and their Nettie (Brearley, Miss Porter's, and Radcliffe), carefully prepared and carefully exposed to the cream of American youth, Harvard and Yale students all, every one of them more suitable in a thousand ways than this stranger from outer space, had to choose (who else?) the man from outer space. Avram Yevorakh! It was eating Jenny up alive. Well, one precious page from outer space. They didn't write long-winded letters the way they used to, did they?

Two of the envelopes contained more contract documents—exhibits relating to the sale of the store; he'd go over those in due course. The fourth letter was from Minsk. Return address: Oktyabr'skaya 28. Martin opened it with more than customary curiosity. Several glossy photographs tumbled out of the envelope, portraits and full-length shots. So there they were! Not the most professional photos in the world, but clear enough to see what his relatives looked like.

Yuri, despite his neat gray beard and mustache, reminded him a bit of Father. Tall, trim, the Lincolnesque face, thoughtful, scholarly, but with a slight twinkle. There *was* a family resemblance. He wondered vaguely what the doctor might look like without his whiskers. He sometimes was curious about how he'd look himself. It was twenty years since he'd shaved. The round-faced woman called Cleo had a marvelous crinkly smile, her head cocked slightly to one side as if sizing up the photographer. Hair in a short bob, neatly parted in the middle. No resemblance to anyone he knew, but the way she carried herself reminded him faintly of an actress—deviltry in those eyes—a face revealing a glad contented soul. You could feel the warmth even from this second-rate photograph. The daughter, in a head portrait, revealed a thin, quite beautiful, sharp-featured, fragile, not quite emaciated face, with high cheekbones, model-like, with long, light, straight hair, gathered by a ribbon with a small bow atop. Another full-length shot showed her standing next to, and much taller than, her heavier mother; she might be willowy, but she carried her-

self proudly. Her face, though pretty, was almost characterless. How old must she be? Twenty, twenty-one?

The accompanying letter, addressed to Jenny, himself, and Rachel, was brief, and signed "Yuri," as if they were already old friends.

This is the family, together. Yelena, our daughter, comes home from Moscow. I succeed today collecting documents necessary for applications to emigrate, and tomorrow I go to OVIR to present papers. Then we wait. We hope we able to see you when you make visit. Your visit has big importance for us! Time is shrinking short. Speak to our friends at the conference before you leave if you have last things you wish to tell us.

The letter reawakened all Martin's misgivings. He would have to cross-examine Rachel. By God, if he thought the risk too great . . . But he knew Jenny was going. Yes, she ought to go, he thought.

With some effort, he resumed writing. "Bill, because of my health I wasn't able to come, but I'm counting on you to keep an eye on Jenny, and I've told her . . ."

PART
FIVE
The Choice

1

YURI FELT IN OVER HIS DEPTH. Some men, he supposed, were by nature born to resist the established order, demanding reforms—societal perfection. They were self-disciplined, sometimes fanatic men to whom perceived injustices to others constituted outrages demanding defiance, sometimes the risk of their lives, the sacrifice of their children and wives, *everything* subordinated to some elusive but inspiring vision. The Voice of America broadcast stories about such people, and Anatoly Markov celebrated them: men and women, a species apart; they held up signs in Moscow squares, wrote letters to Comrade Brezhnev, sent copies for publication to United States papers; they complained in *samizdat* articles and in letters to the big bosses about KGB violations of Soviet law, insisting on their "rights." They were arrested for their trouble, perhaps for their arrogance, interrogated, tried, exiled, sent to prison or work camp, or worse, to a "psychiatric hospital," and in some cases they merely died for their trouble.

These cases enraged Tolya Markov, made him mutter about "corrective" action, but Yuri saw nothing he could do about it. Fighting with guns as a partisan, side by side with Cleo and Pyotr, when everyone had been fighting, had been one thing. He had suffered for his land. He was young then, angry, and frightened. Resisting his own countrymen in his middle age, however—his own government—was something for which he was psychologically, philosophically, and intellectually unprepared, and Cleo even more so.

To leave Minsk forever—children, hospital, even the seedy Polyclinic, the Institute, the Academy of Medical Science, his friends among the doctors and other scientists, not to mention his hard-won access to the special shops where Cleo could buy whatever her heart desired, the luxurious sanatoria where they took their vacations on the Black Sea or on the Bal-

tic (Cleo called them little honeymoons) when they could bathe in the sea or the pool, make love by moonlight, drink and sing and dance for two entire weeks—was it fair that he must give all that up? And what would take their place? Here he was Somebody—the entire family had an exalted status. They were among the people who counted. And there, wherever he went, what would he be? An immigrant! Faceless, speaking the language with an accent, unwelcome at hospitals, given the worst of jobs, no friends, someone who had to be "absorbed" with the help of an Ulpan, an absorption center! As he had learned only too grimly at the seminars.

What to do? His only protector now lay desperately ill in the hospital. His father, no longer his friend, would not even sign his consent to their leaving. Some father! Cleo was miserable at the prospect of going; Yelena, home now, was in a black stupor—and pregnant into the bargain.

Around and around went his resentments at the illegalities in which he was caught. Yelena, for example—what right had they to expel her from the Second Medical Institute? Other students got pregnant and continued to attend. What right had they to try to turn her against her own parents, and her parents against her? Why did the KGB employ hooligans to do their dirty work? Had they become a nation of gangsters, of outlaws, no better than the drunk peasants and maddened Cossacks the Tsar's men had turned loose against the Jews seventy years ago? Was this outlawry, this hooliganism, this unbridled anti-Semitism, an incurable national characteristic? Unhappy at the realization, he found himself reflecting on thoughts Tolya Markov sometimes had only hinted at obliquely and in hushed tones. Well, what *could* he do, except follow Pyotr's advice? Go.

He was doing that, all right, but his nerves were being numbed in the process. Scurrying miserably and nervously about without his license in the repaired Zhiguli whenever he was off duty at the Polyclinic or not giving a class at the Institute, he was almost grateful that his duties had been reduced so that he could find the time to save himself, to get the documents needed for their applications, to go to Baryshin's "seminars," to prepare himself for a new life, however grim, to read the books Baryshin gave him.

The seminars were held in the early evenings and each participant came only if he was certain he was not being followed. At the beginning Yuri attended with skepticism, with an intellectual contempt for what he might learn at the sessions. Nevertheless, he had made an equally cerebral decision to cooperate with Baryshin and those he worked with, for he would be depending on this man, and he was anxious to meet others in the same boat as he. There might be safety in numbers, after all. Later he

learned that this contempt was anything but intellectual. He uncovered in himself an uneasy *feeling*, the depth of which he had scarcely suspected, for Yuri had always felt his Jewishness was nothing but an infirmity which gave him only trouble. He must have got that from Father.

What utterly amazed him, indeed, was how much he did learn at the seminars, how little he had known! The others, all refuseniks who had been waiting two years or longer to get permission to leave, knew far more about Jewishness, Yiddish history, and lore than he. Occasionally a few of them went on outings—to see Jewish sights; the neglected Yubeleinaya monument; the desecrated Jewish cemetery; the Art Theater, which had once been the main synagogue. They met on rare occasions at "Chaim Park," a mini-park across the street from KGB headquarters, to exchange gossip—who had been given permission to emigrate, who had been questioned. He soon was more intimate with them than with many of his colleagues at the hospital. Georgi, the mathematician; Mark, the electrical engineer; Valentin, the teacher; Lev, the translator for the Trading Office. From them and Baryshin he discovered that Jews as a people had a history as noble as any people in the Soviet Union; that the Old Testament predated all written history, Russian or Western; that the Jews were a dynamic people, who were givers of laws governing relationships among men, sanitation, hygiene, and morality at a time when the rest of the world's men and women ran wild in forests or jungles, or huddled in caves; and that in Minsk, until the war, they had been the movers and shakers while retaining their Jewishness. There had been Yiddish papers, Yiddish theater, Yiddish books.

He learned what "kosher" meant, a term he had until then heard used only derogatorily. Lev read to the seminar from the prophets and *tzaddiks* —men who had provided philosophies and insights still treasured in many lands. Mark lent him a book by Spinoza, one he found difficult going, but stimulating. The works of Marx and Freud were eagerly discussed by the refuseniks as a continuum of Jewish intellectual exploration. Einstein, of course, they all knew, but Yuri had never been aware of the great mathematician's interest in Zionism or of his reactions to being a Jew in a non-Jewish world. He read every word of Kuznetsov's *Einstein: Life, Death, Immortality* and was intrigued with the genius's childishness and his sense of humor, which he found so familiar; he could have been a member of Yuri's family! He was particularly aroused when they discussed the Jews who had become, in the twentieth century, justices of the Supreme Court of the U.S.A.—Brandeis, Cardozo, Frankfurter, Goldberg, Fortas, and, indeed, *his* cousin, Jacob Singer. How much he hadn't known! Had never dreamed!

For the first time, Yuri heard of the men who dreamed of and laid the groundwork for the State of Israel: Weizmann and Herzl; Jabotinsky and Martin Buber; Ben Yehuda and Rothschild, the French Jew who financed the early settlements. He learned about the *moshavim* and the *kibbutzim*, about the War of Independence against the Arab countries in 1948, and the truth about the wars of 1956, 1967, and 1973, not the lies which *Pravda* printed.

Now, for the first time, he was told about the realities of Israel—not the distortion in the Soviet press nor the fictions of the Zionist dreamers. The myths of the land of milk and honey as well as that of the nest of fascists receded before hard facts: what one faced was inflation, the difficulty of finding an apartment, of getting the kind of work one wanted and was trained for. All was not sweetness and light there, Baryshin warned them again and again, but there was work to be done, sacrifices to be made, children to be raised and, God forbid, still more fighting to be done. But the place was *theirs*.

Yuri learned the Hebrew alphabet and a few Hebrew words. Some part of him, he felt in spite of himself, was being forced to be born, to breathe. It had been there, latent, all these years. He found the process painful, surprising, a bit exhilarating—against his will.

While he told Cleo some of what he was learning, he did not reveal everything. Who could say, Israel might *not* be the place for them. The others at the seminars, despite all he learned from them and regardless of the intimacy he felt for them, did not particularly appeal to him. In their presence his instinct was to be more Russian than ever, to separate himself from them; they seemed faintly and distastefully foreign, pushy, arrogant, domineering, abrupt, and he held himself aloof. Yet he felt a primitive oneness with them. He both hated the feeling and could not avoid it. Valentin said he would know a Jew anywhere—and every Jew would know him, without being told. Yuri was not so sure. He gathered there was some way of getting to the United States rather than to Israel, although Baryshin seemed reluctant to speak of this possibility. He would have to find out more about that.

Today at long last he was able to bring all the completed documents to OVIR, to wait his turn to submit his application. He walked erect when his name was called—early and out of order—with his new pride but old misgivings, to the desk of the sallow, pockmarked, brown-eyed young woman who beckoned to him. He held out his papers to her with unsteady hands he could not control. She gestured him to a chair and proceeded deadpan to scan the documents for completeness. Her desk bore a small sign: VERA PETROVNA. She studied the three copies of the *vyzov*

from Rachel Aron (he had asked for a separate one for each rather than a family *vyzov* in case Chankov should catch up with him and spoil the chances of Cleo and Yelena), read each word on the two birth certificates —his and Yelena's—that it had taken him two weeks of steady persistence to obtain. Cleo's birth record had been more trouble—it had been destroyed during the war, and the young man at ZAGS had been reluctant to issue the necessary affidavit stating this simple fact. The stupid son of a bitch seemed to fear that such an admission might be a reflection on the bureau and that he would be held responsible! But after putting up with three weeks of the idiot's hesitation, Yuri had finally prevailed on him to consult his superior, and finally this quintessential bureaucrat was able to sign in his childlike handwriting the "no-record-of-birth" certificate required for Cleo. Talk about underdeveloped peoples! The guy wrote like a chicken and had the brain of one. Yet this, too, had turned out to be one of the easy documents!

Some of the questions on the application itself were troublesome, too, not because they were difficult to answer, but because they made his predicament fully, finally clear to him. Was he a member of the Party? Yes. Expelled? He stated that he had been removed from the Party at a special and stormy meeting at the Institute, and that his certificate of expulsion was attached. He did not mention that many old friends had felt obliged to denounce him, and even worse, that he had sympathized with their betrayals. Honors and awards? Would listing them help or hurt his purpose? He had heard from Baryshin that the more prominent one was, the less chance they'd let him go. That was Baryshin's, Ovsischer's, and Davidovich's problem. Nevertheless, why deny facts? Member of the Academy of Medical Science, BSSR, holder of two Orders of the Slava, Liberator of Minsk, former chief of pediatrics at the First Clinical Association, former acting director of the Pediatric Hospital and now chief of pediatric medicine, Second Polyclinic, professor of pediatrics at Minsk Medical Institute, special citation for research work in anemia. Let OVIR make what they wanted of it.

He had no trouble getting a statement from Mitya that he had no unfulfilled obligations at his work place. Mitya understood everything. He was glad to sign certificates for both Cleo and Yuri, but getting the others was not so easy. Heavyset, gross Nadia Topelova at Second Polyclinic was exasperating. It was not for nothing that she was referred to by her colleagues as "the Bitch Doctor." She let Yuri twist in the wind for three weeks. Each time they would meet she would ask more questions. "Why do you want to emigrate? Where are you going? Why Israel? Don't you realize it's a den of liars and thieves? They kill Arabs merely for amuse-

ment there. Don't you know all the people from Minsk who went there are begging to come back? They loathe the place, the people, everything. Go and talk to them. Who *gave* you this idea? With whom have you been talking? Are you under the influence of our great Jewish military traitors? Ovsischer, perhaps? Davidovich? Or Baryshin?"

Yuri could not decide whether Nadia was a medical woman or a member of one of the Security organs. She seemed to know so much more than he did on the subject of emigration. Why should he think the medical world was immunized from the KGB? He did not argue with the Bitch Doctor, clearly one of Chankov's women.

"No doubt I'm misguided," he said, "but this is what I want to do." Could he possibly tell her he had been advised to do so by the first secretary of the Communist Party of Byelorussia? She would think him a liar and mad.

As it was, she said, "You are more than misguided, Doctor. I think you are unbalanced. You should probably have treatment." Threats of the *psikhushka*.

Eventually, after three weeks of this nonsense, Yuri being always afraid to push her too hard, she had signed the document.

Josef Misharev, at the Institute, had been neither as obliging as Mitya who, after all, was his close friend, nor as difficult as Chankov's creature, the Bitch Doctor. Misharev made no bones about the fact that he would have to consult Mariya Kalnin and, after hearing her views, he had quickly written the note. "Say anything," Mariya had urged him, "but get rid of the Jew troublemaker. If it were up to me, he'd be over the border tomorrow."

When it came to his application, Yuri agonized over how much to leave out. He could make it short and limit himself to bare facts. Instead, he wrote much that had been pent up in him: he omitted the coldblooded shooting of Andrei Khess, and how he himself had avoided the same fate only because of the intervention of Cleo and Pyotr; but he wrote that his mother must have been betrayed by a Russian neighbor, of how he and Pyotr had seen her in a public square. He described the reasons for his letter to the paper; the episodes of the car; the attitude of the *militsioners;* of his growing awareness, in short, that the Black Hundreds were back. Skirting danger, he avoided mentioning what he believed was the *official* campaign of anti-Semitism, of which he had become a victim. Beneath the surface of this flat recitation raged the fury of a man who felt superior in every way to those who had brought him to this pass and for whom he wrote this account. He had been called a hero once; he had a right to tell it as he saw it. He wanted to write much more than he dared.

Finally, the two most difficult aspects of the application were his father and Yelena. His mother and his wife's parents were deceased? Where were the death certificates? They were all killed during the war by the Nazis and buried in mass or unknown graves. The Nazis left no records. She nodded and made a notation on Cleo's application. Only his father was still alive. Ah, then, where, Vera Petrovna asked, was the written statement from his father regarding his attitude toward his son's emigration?

He knew of his vulnerability but tried to pass over it lightly. "My father? He's seventy-seven years old, and a very sick man."

"You are not planning to take him with you? You are abandoning him?"

"No, no, he doesn't wish to go."

"In that case we must have his statement."

"But I have tried to explain: he's a sick man. He's old and senile."

"We must have his statement."

"Please. Permit me to leave our applications as they are. And I will bring you his statement as soon as his physical condition permits. As soon as he is lucid. I promise I will bring it."

"That is not permitted. I cannot accept it. The applications must be complete."

"If you wouldn't mind, then, let us at least see if everything *else* is in order, shall we?" The impassive woman nodded. She had taken him out of order on Major Yevseyev's instruction. The others waiting were probably fuming. Good! It was all the same to her. She was new in the agency and scandalized by the spectacle of these fanatical Jews coming to the office every day, wanting desperately to leave their Motherland. What kind of people could they be? Well, wandering Jews; she had learned this at her mother's knee. As Major Yevseyev had explained to her, they are all shit, these *zhidi* who wanted to emigrate.

She had never liked Jews. So if this doctor, who had some kind of pull with the major (wherever it originated), wished to have her review his documents, she had no objection. If she had said no, it would merely inconvenience him, one person. But if she were to spend the rest of the afternoon slowly going over his documents, it would have the beneficial effect of keeping all those others waiting; this thought tickled her; probably they would sit in those chairs with those hangdog expressions all day and never reach her or anyone else. Talya, the other examiner, was out sick today. She glanced over at the benches where a score of people, the only ones admitted for the day, sat in miserable, sullen silence, looking to-

ward her hopefully. Filth. Let them sit. Let them look. Let them suffer. Let them die. It was her pleasure.

In leisurely fashion she read Yelena's application. Party history: Member of Komsomol in Minsk, then in Moscow. Expelled from Komsomol. Reason: Moral turpitude. What was truly amazing was that the father, the graybearded hypocrite Jew doctor, was still so arrogant. She returned to Yelena's application. Student for three and a half years at the Second Medical Institute in Moscow. All such big brains! It was really infuriating! *Expelled. Reason: Moral turpitude.* Wouldn't you know it! What kind of people were they—to write such things about themselves? Had they no shame? The father sat here and *handed* this sordid material to her as if it were the most commonplace thing in the world. She was growing restless and felt the need for guidance. It was time for her tea break anyway. "I'll be back," she said. "Remain here."

During tea in the back office she managed to convey her puzzlement to Yevseyev about Yuri's continuing membership in the Academy. Yevseyev assured her that nothing was being overlooked. It wouldn't be long. He was a special case; Chankov had called personally on it. Once they accepted his application to emigrate everything would follow. They could do anything to him. Vera Petrovna had acted correctly. She was to continue to behave with complete correctness.

As for the applications, she could accept those of the daughter and the wife, provided the doctor would sign an approval for each. But the doctor's application could not be accepted until he had his father's consent.

Yevseyev, a man of soldierly bearing, with a handsome face somewhat disfigured and flushed by excessive drinking, smiled. "That consent the good doctor will not get. I know his old man." He chuckled. "Before we are through, the good doctor will sit. Or perhaps get a dose of psychiatric treatment."

Petrovna returned to the desk where Yuri was waiting. She slowly completed the examination of the documents, watching the clock. It was nearly closing time; no chance of taking anyone else.

She smiled thinly and spoke as politely as she could force herself to (correctness, Yevseyev had said): "Doctor, I am afraid I cannot accept these applications without your father's statement of consent. That will be necessary."

Yuri pushed the papers toward her. Attached by a paper clip to the top sheet were four slips of paper bearing seat numbers—tickets to the Bolshoi—worth more than gold or money. They were privilege. He still had clout of some kind. How did they do it, these Jews? Vera herself had little interest in ballet or opera, but those tickets could get her a coat with

a fur collar on which she had had her eye for some time. The woman in the commission shop made no bones about her own passion for the ballet and for some weeks had made plain to every one of her customers that she would give anything, *anything*, to see the Bolshoi's *Swan Lake*, a one-night-only performance in Minsk's opera house next week.

Vera's heart fibrillated for only an instant, then resumed its normal beat as she placed her hands over the tickets. "I'll tell you what I can do, Doctor. On my own authority—you see, I am willing to take a chance for you —I can accept the applications for your wife and your daughter. Of course, you must write out your consent, as if you intended to remain here. Which we know you do not intend, true, but for the sake of formality. Have it notarized. You must say you are seeking a divorce also, but of course that is only a formality. Then, as soon as you bring your father's consent, also notarized, for you to go, all will be in order. This I can do."

"Very well." He asked her for a paper and wrote quickly in the approved form which she dictated to him word by word that he had no objections to his wife's and daughter's desire to emigrate and had no material claims against them and was filing for divorce.

He knew a notary nearby and hurried to get his statement notarized. When he returned, she interrupted her next client, a woman, and called him to her desk. She was now very cooperative. Quickly she went through the papers, detaching all the documents dealing with Yuri's application and keeping the rest. She had, of course, slipped the Bolshoi tickets from under the paper clip and put them carefully into her pocket. "You will hear from us when these cases have been processed."

"How long?" Yuri stood and folded the papers she had returned.

"Impossible to say. This must all be checked and cleared. It is my duty to mention that the reflections on your daughter's character may cause some delay in *her* application."

Yuri was able to laugh briefly. She was lying simply to infuriate him. He knew quite well that misbehavior of this sort would, if anything, make it easier for her to get her visa. The shock of Yelena's pregnancy, which he understood was the ostensible cause of her dismissal from both Komsomol and the Medical Institute, he had finally absorbed. This reason given for her dismissal had been, in truth, a favor engineered by Kozhinskaya. Better by far to be immoral than involved in Zionist activity. He and Cleo, who was not as dismayed as he, agreed Yelena's naïveté had been partly their own fault in not preparing her more fully; after all, she was twenty-one, a full-grown woman, in a big city, away from home for three and a half years. And thinking back, he and Cleo themselves, when Cleo was only fifteen and with a war going on . . .

"You know, Vera Petrovna, three other girls in my daughter's class at the Second Medical Institute and who were members of Komsomol also became pregnant. Not one of them was dismissed. Do you think it's only because she was Jewish—less than half Jewish, mind you—" Why was he saying any of this to a clerk? Stupid.

"Are you telling me there is some form of official anti-Semitism at the Institute?"

"Did I say that? I'm merely asking what *you* think. Those, however, are the facts."

Vera Petrovna stood abruptly and, without glancing further in Yuri's direction, called to those huddled on the benches, "The office is closed. Return tomorrow. Nine o'clock." She turned like an archer who had scored a satisfying bull's-eye and marched quickstep toward the back office, humming as she went. Moral turpitude, she thought. No mere pregnancy, she'd wager. A common Jewish whore, probably. Or worse.

The twenty-odd people, defeated again, rose, muttering, each of them doggedly determined to return. One woman, her eleven-year-old daughter in hand, nodded to Yuri, murmuring "Professor!" He did his best to smile and nod back. He touched the little girl. One of his patients. Imagine having to sit like these people, day in and day out!

2

HE TOOK NO PLEASURE in driving the Zhiguli these days. He dreaded having to face Cleo when he got home. He hated what their nights were becoming, what they were doing to each other. Cleo had changed. She was urging a kind of suicide on him—not literally, to be sure, but along a path that would have that result. Cleo's problem was that she was afraid of nothing and nobody. In this instance, such an attitude did not reflect good sense or reality.

Father, for entirely different reasons, was taking the same tack: they must not leave. All right, so he would not be a hospital director. There were worse disappointments. This was no reason to go to Israel. Well, neither Cleo nor Father had been with him on his visit to Pyotr, and he had not been able to persuade them, although he had tried over and over to describe his meeting with Pyotr in the greatest detail. They each, for different reasons, blanked out Pyotr's advice.

Putting off going directly home, he drove to the hospital, although he no longer had official status there, to see how Stefan Sikorsky, who was back in, was doing. Spunky kid; he now wanted to become a football player and be seen by everyone on television. Wanted his father to be proud of him, Galina had said. Yuri had learned yesterday they were again looking for donors of whole blood for the kid. Yuri had the same type and a month ago had given a pint, his fifth since the boy had first been diagnosed. Maybe he could do so again. Stefan and his stoic mother made his own misfortune dwindle. "I'll never get better, will I?" That plaintive question, the kind any kid tired of being sick might ask, haunted him.

Before he could reach the door to the stairhall, Natalya, the careful blond who had once been his secretary but who was now relegated to being the receptionist at the desk, a woman whom he had known well

and had always trusted, was on her feet standing before him. Was she actually blocking his path? "Where do you wish to go, Dr. Karpeyko?"

He told her. "Oh, but I'm terribly sorry, that isn't permitted. You see, Dr. Bosherov has given me specific instructions—" He tried to walk around her, but she held out her arms in a plea. "Please, Professor Karpeyko. You'll only get me in trouble. More trouble." She was an innocent victim of the Karpeyko purge. She looked unhappy. He had no wish to make trouble. He had trouble to spare.

"I see. Can you tell me then, Natalya, how is the Sikorsky boy?"

"I'm afraid I don't know. But I'll find out." She went back to her desk, thumbed through a series of cards, lifted the phone, and dialed. "Can you tell me the condition of Sikorsky, Stefan?" She listened for a brief reply, and turned to Yuri. "Unchanged, Doctor."

"You remember he's a favorite of mine. Wonderful little fellow. Acute leukemia. No chance in the world. I just thought if he needed blood, I happen to have his type."

Natalya looked entirely miserable. "I'm sorry, Professor. I hope you understand."

"Quite well." He wondered whether there were other places in this world where you could be the director of a hospital one day and where on another your former secretary would not permit you to enter to give your own blood. He hyperventilated, as if to restore his sanity. "My wife, however, is still as of this hour permitted to come and go, to do her work here?"

"Oh, yes, Doctor. Absolutely. I think she's in the building now."

Yuri shrugged and shook his head. It was not disbelief. He believed, all right. It was simply so bizarre that believing required special effort.

"Will you send the Sikorsky boy a little gift for me?" He reached into his pocket, found a ballpoint pen. "Give him this. Ask him to write me a poem. He writes good poems. My wife will stop in to see him tomorrow to be sure he knows how to use it."

As he came out the door of the Pediatric Hospital, he could scarcely recognize the usually placid grounds of the First Clinical Association. In the ten or twelve minutes he'd been inside, everything had changed. Black Volgas crawled about the grounds. The entrance to General Surgery was now crowded with uniformed *militsia*, and these were being directed by an officer who was taking orders from a plainclothesman. Revolving lights on several of the cars made the scene eerie amid the great bustling and rushing, people hastening from other buildings and from cars toward General Surgery, cars being stopped at the entrance and

turned away, with the exception of a few whose occupants showed acceptable identification and were rushed inside.

Yuri could scarcely imagine what was going on. He saw, coming out of the surgery building, Shtainberg, with his heavy wool scarf almost covering his beard, pressing his way against the surging crowd and laboriously making progress toward Yuri, waving and calling, "Hey, Yuri, wait a sec! Wait!" Finally he emerged from the crowd and half trotted toward Yuri, by now standing beside his Zhiguli, wondering how he would be able to make his way out to Akademiceskaya again. Shtainberg opened the rear door of Yuri's car and darted furtively into the back seat; Yuri got into the driver's.

"Hey, listen, Karpeyko, from my window I could see you going into your old bailiwick, so I thought I ought to come and tell you. We just lost your old buddy Pyotr Feodorovich. Yeah, about half an hour ago. Kind of a shock, actually. Looks like the death of a king, doesn't it?" He gestured at the general bustle of cars, lights, and people.

"Hell, it was only a matter of time for him, poor bastard, but he was looking good, sitting up and working in his bed—and pfft! Like that. Embolism, or God knows what. Don't know when they'll announce it; you know how they are. Might be a day or two. So I thought you oughtta know, since it might make a hell of a difference for you."

More cars were coming, and additional policemen came to block the entrance to the grounds. Shtainberg kept talking, although Yuri had trouble listening.

"We opened him up—you remember, just about a week after I caught you coming out of his office. One look at those lungs and I knew he'd *had* it. They were pure shit. I removed the right one, but the other was so bad I hated to close the guy up. Well, fuck their mothers, I hope they don't cook up another medical murder plot—a special one for Minsk. With a name like Shtainberg! You can picture Chankov! How I wish the son of a bitch had gone to Moscow to the special hospital those big shots have. His buddies on the Politburo begged him to. But no, he was a local boy. Loyal to Minsk. The chemotherapy made him weak as a fly, and suddenly this afternoon, poof! Out. He didn't suffer all that much. For all I know, maybe he took something we didn't give him. Those big shots can get these cyanide capsules. He had terrific pain, but intermittent. He sure was not happy, though, down to fifty kilos, like a skeleton in five weeks. We did what we could. Oh, we could do an autopsy to see if he took something, but what the hell's the use? I only hope *I* don't end up a murderer in a white coat! Anyway, I thought you ought to know. He was a

terrific guy. I got to respect the son of a bitch. Always in complete control. Got to hand it to him."

Yuri could feel Pyotr's pain almost as if it were his own. He no longer had a powerful friend on Engelsa Street. That would, as Shtainberg had so quaintly put it, "make a hell of a difference." "There been any rumors about who'll be the new first secretary?"

"Aw, how would *I* know a thing like that? I know this much. Old buddy Chankov's in there talking to Moscow and telling everyone exactly what to do. The son of a bitch is using my office as a command post. Set up his headquarters—right here in the hospital, without a by-your-leave. How d'you like that? Looks like Chankov's planning to give him a hell of a funeral. So if that's any sign . . ."

Shtainberg shrugged. "Good luck, Karpeyko. And bon voyage. I'm just wondering how much longer I can stand it around here myself." He opened the car door and started back toward the surgery unit, but Yuri seized his elbow before he was entirely out. He'd have to take his chances with Shtainberg. Strange guy. Instinctively he trusted him; the trouble was he no longer trusted his instinct. Shtainberg was no *stukach*, no KGB stooge, he was certain. But under pressure—give the man six weeks in Lefortovo or Lubyanka, and who could tell? Like himself, Shtainberg was used to his comforts, no more than Yuri any tower of physical or moral strength. Yet who else was there? He tugged Shtainberg back into the car.

"Listen, I have a little problem."

"Yurka, I know your problem."

"No, not me. It's my father. He's a peculiar old man, a real old Bolshevik. He once ran this whole complex, you remember."

"Who could forget? He took me on when I was a kid out of med school."

"Well, he's drug-dependent. Morphine. Long, long time. He's completely addicted."

"No kidding! Oh, that must be tough on the old bastard. Where does he get the stuff?"

"Until now I've been getting it for him at the pharmacy over there." He jutted his chin toward the pediatric building. "It was not much of a problem, a weekly supply for one old man, forty-two quarter-grain tablets a week, and I'd list the users in my requisition, spreading a quarter grain here, a quarter grain there—no sweat, we always had kids with broken legs, traumas, acute post-op pain. But I can't get into the place any more. My access to the stuff is cut off. At Second Polyclinic we have absolutely no use for morphine. And what's more, it's possible I won't be around town much longer. So I thought maybe you—"

"Dangerous as hell!" Shtainberg exploded. "You could sit for five years for that, you realize? And once they bust you, they throw the whole goddamn book at you. I have to think about it, Yuri. I'll give it some thought."

"You have all these people in post-op pain," Yuri persisted, as if Shtainberg had not spoken. He pulled out his first stop. "Cleo tells me you're the only surgeon around who really gives a damn about post-op care. You must prescribe a hell of a lot of morphine."

"Oh, sure. But that's not the point. Maybe if this old guy were *my* father, well maybe then I *might*—" Yuri sensed Shtainberg weakening.

"Forget I asked you," Yuri said. "It was just an idea of Cleo's—"

"Oh, hell, I said I'll *think* about it! You couldn't be setting me up, could you? What for? I've never been involved with addiction cases, but withdrawal is goddamn nasty."

"The old boy couldn't survive for three days. Two weeks ago he used up the last of what I had stashed away, my reserve—just in case I should become ill or something, you know—and for the last two weeks Cleo's managed on some farfetched emergency basis to get a supply, but I can't let her go on doing that. Much too dangerous. How can I let her be put in that position? She hates it, scares her to death." Second stop pulled out. It would be a breeze for Shtainberg.

"Okay, okay. I'll see what I can do." The surgeon was now in a hurry to get out of the car. "Jot your father's address here." He handed Yuri his note pad.

Yuri talked as he wrote. "He needs forty-two quarter-grain pills a week. He mixes the solution himself; he takes it intramuscularly, boils his own syringes so he can give himself the shots. All you have to do is drop the stuff off at his place each Friday."

As he drove home, Yuri had a sense of foreboding. He would find Yelena in her room sulking, her young belly beginning to distend with a German grandchild that Yuri secretly cursed. In an hour Cleo would arrive home, alienated but trying not to admit it even to herself. He recalled the didactic article about Baryshin and the Cherniavskys in *Sovetskaya Byelorossiya*. Could a marriage which had been as good as his own be destroyed by malign outside forces?

His gloomy musings gave way to sudden fear as he approached his apartment building. Two Volgas were parked directly in front of his entry. The young man in a dark brown double-breasted suit standing at the door was not the amiable fellow who had been watching the family

for the past two weeks. This man's identity was unmistakable; he smiled genially as Yuri approached. "Comrade, you are—?"

"Professor Karpeyko."

"Ah, Yuri Ivanovich. We've been expecting you. My colleagues are upstairs." He reached into his breast pocket and withdrew an identification which he held toward Yuri, who studied it as carefully as if it were a child's throat. The man was Josef Mikhailovich Fodorov, a lieutenant of the KGB. Trained dogs, Yuri thought. Trained to torture and humiliate.

"Glad to make your acquaintance."

The young man pocketed his wallet, stepped aside, and with a gesture of mock gallantry, allowed Yuri to enter.

Prepared as he was, Yuri did not expect what he saw in his apartment. Three men—two young fellows led by a chunky, middle-aged man with steel-capped teeth, surely of the soundest peasant stock—were wandering about the place as if they owned it; one was pulling Yuri's books off the shelves, flipping the pages, and placing the books neatly on the floor, one by one; the second had taken the P.P.D. automatic off the wall and had begun to disassemble it as if it were a kind of child's puzzle. Yuri's archaeological pieces had been placed carefully on the floor, removed from their case by Comrade Steelteeth, whose fingers were feeling inside each jar and dish, hunting for something.

Standing, smirking in the corner, was Bella Sorokina, the *dvornik*'s wife, her front tooth still missing from her apologetic, silly smile, as she murmured "Professor." She was dressed in her work clothes and supported herself on a broomhandle.

A twitching Yelena stood in the kitchen doorway, biting her nails, her face streaked and smudged. Yuri was surprised to see Father there, in his favorite chair, staring from face to face, taking long, quick drags on one of his Kazbeks, as if the poor *starik* were not going to be able to get enough of the poisonous stuff into his lungs. What the hell was he doing here? Drawers and cabinets were open and emptied. Yuri's first thought was how lucky Cleo wasn't here! Her beautiful apartment! Well, all could be restored before she came; nothing appeared to be damaged.

The two younger men glanced up briefly at Yuri's entrance and stopped their "work." Comrade Steelteeth stepped toward him, reaching into his breast pocket. "Doctor Karpeyko?"

"What are you doing here? Who authorized this?"

"The search has been authorized by the competent organs. I have a warrant for a personal search as well." Steelteeth produced a piece of paper from his breast pocket, unfolded it, and held it out toward Yuri, who barely glanced at it. "Signed by the procurator. We have brought a

citizen, Comrade Sorokina, to observe that the search is conducted in strict conformity to the norms, that no one is abused, that everything is correct."

"What are you looking for?"

"Ah, perhaps you can help us there. But allow me to introduce myself. I'm Captain Dzyuba. Comrade Selnikov, Comrade Proskurov." Both men dipped their foreheads. Dzyuba brought out a pad with blue backing, placing it deftly on the dining table. "Doctor, will you be so kind as to list for me all articles which you have in the apartment not permitted under law. And sign at the bottom. If you have nothing, write 'Nothing.'"

"What articles?"

"Gold coins. Foreign currency. Drugs. Firearms. Written material of subversive, slanderous, anti-Soviet nature."

"Such as?"

"Anti-Soviet Zionist propaganda. Written material undermining the leading role of the Party. Et cetera."

"We have nothing like that."

"If you will produce such items," Steelteeth continued as if he had not heard, "without our being required to search for them, it goes easier for you at the procurator's. If not . . ." He shrugged. "We'll look. See? Comrade Proskurov has already found firearms, so we're making progress. Hanging right on your wall. An observant lad."

"That's a war relic. I'm a law-abiding citizen." He wrote "*Nothing to declare*" and signed his name in a hasty flourish. He turned to his father.

"*Otyetz*, do *you* understand what's happening here?" Ivan Borisovich tapped his cigarette ash so that it fell to the carpet.

Father spoke sourly. "Beria used to say, 'Don't worry, give us the man, we'll find the crime.'"

"Old man," scolded Captain Dzyuba, as if to a baby, his teeth glinting in the lamplight, "Beria is long dead. You are living in the past."

The *starik* snorted and adjusted his thick cataract lenses that made him look like a staring owl. He must only recently have taken his shot, Yuri thought. He was also wearing all his ribbons, something he usually did only on holidays. For him this must be a special occasion. "Beria, Chankov—what the hell's the difference?" The old man could get away with that, Yuri thought, as his father went on like a stern teacher. "I've known Chankov, my boy, since he was a child. We've had our differences. I grew too old to work. So I'm on a pension, while he . . . he . . ."

"He may soon be the new first secretary for Byelorussia," Yuri ventured. "I regret to report that my old friend Pyotr Feodorovich passed away this afternoon." He turned sternly to his daughter. "Yelena, please

get hold of yourself! Wash your face. Your mother will be home any minute. You want her to see you like that? You're going to be a mother yourself—behave like one!" She went glumly to the kitchen sink. Selnikov stood where he could keep an eye on her as she ran some water and washed her face.

"She's pregnant?" Proskurov said slowly; carefully he arranged the pieces of the automatic on the coffee table, then picked up the heavy upholstered chair beside the sofa as if it were a matchstick and moved it to the kitchen doorway where Yelena was again standing. "Please sit, comrade." His face was totally serious as he regarded her. "Didn't we go to school together?"

Yelena sat, glanced up at him. "Perhaps; I don't think we were in the same class though." Proskurov went back to the parts of his automatic.

"So Pyotr Feodorovich has died," Father said. "It's not surprising. He smoked like a locomotive, more than I." He took two quick drags on his own cigarette. "You hear that, Captain? The first secretary has passed from us. A good man." Father had had little use for Pyotr. "He and Chankov were not exactly close buddies, you know. They put up with each other. Changes will be coming soon to Byelorussia. Who knows, it may be you've even come to the wrong apartment, eh? Who knows, there may be hell to pay for this. Wouldn't that be nice?"

Steelteeth may have been uncomfortable, but he pretended to know more than he did. "On the contrary, old man."

Yuri spoke to Steelteeth with icy detachment. "Captain, you are searching for a strange assortment of things. Please explain what Zionist books have to do with drugs or gold coins."

Dzyuba was accustomed to dealing with suspects of all kinds, particularly politicals. Intelligentsia. They all started out so cocksure of themselves. "Professor, that will be deciphered in good time at headquarters. We have clever investigators who will put the pieces of the plot together. We know all about deviationism and conspiracy. It doesn't happen to be my specialty. I merely search the premises for the evidence they ask for."

Yuri could hear his own voice rising into his giveaway near-falsetto. "And at the same time make a shambles of the place? Look at it! The place looks like a shithouse. Don't you have any sense of Soviet legality?"

"Don't get carried away, Doctor. We *are* Soviet legality. That's why we have Comrade Bella here. That's why we have the warrant, you see? Fully executed. Sit down, have a smoke. See, your father sets a fine example."

Yuri sat on the sofa and lit a *papyroesa* obediently and merely watched, as Father, like a lizard, was doing, while the KGB men continued. Books

were gone through one page at a time. Casual notes and prescription pads were read as if they were the Communist Manifesto. The men punched at the upholstered furniture, felt the walls; Dzyuba took Yuri's camera apart, opened his medical bag, took out everything, emptied his bottle of aspirin pills, examined each one. They rolled back the rug, patiently, unhurriedly. Nothing.

Yuri could see that they had already been through the kitchen. Cleo's dishes and flatware were strewn in the sink, on the countertops. Every drawer and cabinet door was open. A systematic, orderly pogrom, Yuri thought, merely lacking the overt violence of one. Czechoslovakia. Peaceful occupation. Was this Soviet legality, then? Threats, intimidation, but no blow actually struck.

"How long have you been here?" he asked, trying to keep his voice calm.

"They came at four, Daddy. I couldn't get you or Mama, so I asked if I could call Grandpa. They wrote out what I could say to him."

"I came—against my better judgment," the old man said sourly. "I don't walk too easily these days." He struck his cane to the floor several times.

Yuri's head was in a haze. He must think. Somewhere in the house was a *samizdat* with a fable of his. Was there *any* morphine in the place? He worried more about the morphine than all the other nonsense. Surely the old man had sense enough not to bring any with him if Yelena had called to say that KGB men were there. What about Cleo? Would she? No, she wasn't due to get any until Friday; this was only Tuesday.

Comrade Steelteeth reached for the phone and dialed a number. "Captain Dzyuba here. Hey, Maxim, you hear about Pyotr Feodorovich? . . . Yeah! Can you believe it? This afternoon. Well, what do you think? . . . Ah, so things may be looking up, eh? Terrific! Hey, listen, you know where I am? . . . Send a matron. I have two women here, or will have. . . . Yes, fine. Right away, now." He hung up.

By the time Cleo arrived, the search was almost over. Steelteeth was assembling the things he planned to take and had started writing an inventory. Cleo walked in the door carrying her net shopping bag bulging with fresh vegetables and canned goods. She entered apprehensively, having met the young man below, and when she saw the apartment, cried, "My God, what is going on? Who are you all? Look at the mess you've made!" She turned from Dzyuba to Proskurov to Selnikov. "Aren't you *ashamed?*"

"May I have this?" Dzyuba said in a quiet voice, reaching for her filet mesh. He emptied it, one item at a time.

"I have to wash my mushrooms and tomatoes and grapes and the lettuce right away," Cleo said. "Do you mind?"

Dzyuba put the contents neatly on the coffee table, felt each vegetable carefully, as if it might explode, and finally tossed the fresh vegetables and grapes back into the mesh bag, handed it to Cleo, and nodded to Proskurov to go into the kitchen with her. Cleo glanced at Yuri, handed him her purse, bent to kiss her father-in-law and, one arm through the loop of the mesh bag, said "Lenochka, come and help me." Yelena rose and followed her mother into the kitchen; Proskurov trailed after Yelena.

"You eat famously, Comrade," Dzyuba said softly, jutting his chin after the fresh fruit and vegetables.

From the kitchen the men could hear Cleo's moans and groans. "Pigs! Where could these men have been brought up? Look at this place! Come on, let's get this mess cleaned up." They heard water running in the sink, the sound of dishes, glasses, pots, and pans being returned to cabinets or hooks, Proskurov helping meekly. Suddenly the door opened again, this time admitting a mannish woman Yuri had never seen before. She nodded briefly to Selnikov and Dzyuba, closed the door behind her, and at Dzyuba's gesture, the merest jutting of his chin, made her way into the kitchen. The men heard a brief interchange among the women, and then Cleo's voice demanding, "Listen, this is *my* house. What right do you have?" Now she was framed in the kitchen doorway, hands on hips, addressing Father. "Is this house mine or not? This girl wants to search me in my own house! What right does she have?"

Grimly the *starik*, his cigarette dangling from his lips, nodded. She had the right. Cleo spoke to the strange woman. "Okay, let's get it over with, whatever you want! Come, Lenochka! Search." She raised her arms and the woman patted her clothing, manipulated her brassiere, her girdle. She shook her head toward Dzyuba and turned to Yelena. The process was repeated.

"Nothing," the matron said.

Captain Dzyuba, continuing with the writing of the inventory, looked up and said "Thank you, Marina. You may go." The matron left. Dzyuba continued to write, noting each item meticulously; he opened the two suitcases he had brought, and put certain books and the *samizdat* copies, of which he had found three, not one, into the first valise; in the second he placed the parts of the P.P.D. automatic. Selnikov went first to the bedroom where he put clothing back in drawers, asking Bella Sorokina if his work was satisfactory to *her*, then returned to the living room to restore books to shelves. Dzyuba himself replaced the archaeologic pieces as if they were precious metals.

He showed the inventory to Yuri. "Six unauthorized books, you see?

Three unauthorized, privately circulated publications. One unauthorized automatic firearm. Where do you keep the drugs?"

Yuri shrugged with an innocence he hoped was persuasive. "Those books are not unauthorized."

Dzyuba shrugged. "The drugs, Professor."

Yuri pointed to the contents of his medical bag. "It's all right there. See for yourself—aspirin, Argyrol, peroxide, iodine, a vial of adrenalin, charcoal pills, a bottle of sulfanilamide pills. I treat only children, you know."

"No morphine?"

"What for? I treat kids at the Polyclinic. If they're sick enough for such drugs, we send them to the hospital."

"You're sure there's no morphine?"

"Absolutely. In the hospital, yes, I used to use it. But not for outpatients. I treat only outpatients now."

"But when you were director—excuse me, *acting* director—at the hospital?"

"As I say, frequently. Demerol also. For severe pain."

"You never kept any here?"

"No. Oh, well, sometimes I carried a small supply in my bag. For house calls." He was thinking of Igor, the *militsioner*.

"This is your receipt." Yuri tried to concentrate on the list. Six books in Hebrew: four archaeology books and two others that Baryshin had given him—a Russian-to-Hebrew study book and an Old Testament. One P.P.D. automatic, the only memento of his days in the woods. Idiocy. Three copies of *samizdat*—one his story, "The Two-Headed Skapoochski." A second was a Russian translation of a biography of David Ben Gurion, also given to him by Baryshin. Yes, yes, he nodded. Correct.

"Well, do you have everything you want?" Cleo demanded. Yuri was afraid she was about to explode. He motioned slowly for her to try to regain her composure, like motioning a trained dog to lie down. Even as he made the gesture, he realized it was a mistake.

"Almost," Dzyuba said. "Will you raise your arms, Professor? You, too, Grandfather. If you please." He patted Father first, felt his pockets, and seemed satisfied, but as he patted Yuri's coat, Dzyuba reached inside Yuri's breast pockets. "What do you have here? Let me see." He opened Yuri's application to emigrate and all the associated documents. Dzyuba seemed delighted as he read. "Ah, your application to abandon your Motherland. Hmmm." He flipped through the papers, as if he were going to keep them.

"But I will need those! The trouble I had—"

"What's he *talking* about?" Father asked, as if he had been suddenly struck by a new realization. "After all my advice, you are still planning to follow this insane course, Yurka?"

Dzyuba suddenly pushed his hand out and shook the *starik's* hand with vigor. "Wisely said, Grandfather. I like your spirit! Your son has lost his mind. It wouldn't surprise me if our psychiatrists should agree with you. Your words have been recorded by me. 'Insane course.' Very good."

Flinging the application papers to the sofa, Captain Dzyuba sat at the dining room table and handed a paper to Yuri in two copies. "The protocol of the search, Professor. One copy for you, one for us. I have signed it. Please do the same." Yuri signed. "And now the witness. Bella. Right here." Bella Sorokina signed both copies.

Dzyuba pocketed one copy of the protocol, leaving the other on the table.

"Professor, you are to report to Room Nine Hundred tomorrow at ten o'clock. You know the building? Here is your notification. Please sign." Yuri's hand was unsteady. "Be on time, Professor."

"You are through?" Cleo said through clenched teeth.

"For the moment. Failure to report carries heavy penalties."

"All right! Now get out! All of you. *Out,* you hear?" Cleo was strident.

As the man left, her voice went out of control, the sound of a witch gone berserk. Yuri had not heard her make so much noise since the night she'd thrown herself over him to protect him, screaming, "You have to shoot me first!" Now he heard a new, terrible note of hopelessness: "This is *my* house!" Holding the door open to be sure the three men and Bella were well down the stairs, she yelled after them like a fish peddler in the Komarovka Market. "Out of my house! *Out of my house!*" She slammed the door and began to sob, but when Yuri tried to put his arms about her to comfort her, she pushed him away roughly and turned to Yelena, on whose shoulder she cried instead. Father took out another cigarette and tried to light it, but his hand was so unsteady Yuri had to hold it still for him so he could get the damn thing going.

3

YURI INSISTED that Father stay over. Cleo and Yelena served dinner in oppressive silence, washed dishes, put away pots, tidied up the vestiges of police vandalism. Father turned on the television, watching figure skaters.

Cleo poured herself a bit of liqueur, Yuri's favorite, a drink she rarely had, and put on a Chopin record, hoping the pianist's clever fingers might bring her some peace of mind. Yuri, too, had a large slug of the liqueur. Perhaps she should take a tranquilizer as well? She reached for her purse and saw the old man's packet of morphine, which she had got today, earlier in the week than usual. Bitterly she held out the small packet. "Old man!" she called. "Here. Your medicine for next week."

Yuri, who had been staring into space, trying to lose himself in the Chopin, looked over, startled. "Morphine?"

"Of course."

"Where did you have it?"

"In my purse. Where else?"

"They never looked into your purse?" He began to laugh. Cleo's brandy had begun to work, too, and she began to laugh. "That's what they were looking for?" Yuri nodded through his laughter. Even the old man, when he understood what had happened, began to wheeze.

"Three men!" Yuri said, wiping his eyes. "Trained KGB operatives!"

"And a woman," Cleo cried in gleeful triumph, his old Cleo, at least for an instant. "Agh! So *funny!* But whom can we tell?"

The laughter quickly wore thin and their somber mood returned. Yuri went to the phonograph and turned up the volume. Let the neighbors complain. "Now, listen here," he said, in a voice under the music. "You, too, Yelena. You must listen to me carefully."

They sat, Yuri in the middle, Cleo to his left, Yelena to his right, on the sofa. His father continued to watch the skaters on television through

his thick lenses, murmuring, "Fantastic! Look at them!" He could not hear their conversation and did not want to.

"We must be sensible," Yuri said in an undertone. "I may be arrested tomorrow. We must plan." Cleo's eyes were alight for the first time in weeks. She should have liqueur more often, Yuri thought. She was putting herself trustingly into his hands once again. He was thankful for that.

"Listen carefully to your father, Lenka!" A bit tipsy, too, Yuri suspected. Not used to so much.

"I was at OVIR today. They accepted both your applications. Not mine, because I do not have the old man's consent."

Cleo was on a high wave, in spite of everything. She started to laugh again. "That's the *law*? You're forty-five years old! Angh! Idiots!" Even Yelena had to smile. The old man was in another world, now and always. He was watching skaters, and thinking he ought to go home now or his mother would be angry. From time to time Feygele came back into his head this way. His eyes closed. He was six years old . . . skating on wheels. . . .

"Now, listen carefully," Yuri repeated in the most hushed voice he could command, "I see no reason why your permissions should not come through very quickly. I'm sure Pyotr passed the word. They took me out of order at OVIR, for example. About my own I'm not so sure now. If only Pyotr hadn't died—"

"He *died*?" Cleo whispered. "Died? *That's* what all the excitement at the hospital was about? Oh God!" She gnawed her knuckle.

"I don't know what will happen tomorrow. They may hold me for three days; they can do that under the law. We can't be sure when we'll have the chance to speak freely again. If I should not be here to help you, as soon as you get your visas, you must do as they tell you at OVIR. Take all the money you need for visa fees from the bank—whatever you need. Sell the Zhiguli. Sell the furniture, give up the apartment. Go to the Dutch embassy in Moscow; arrange for train tickets to Vienna. Ship my archaeologic things if you can; they're valuable. If they demand too much duty, leave them here. In Vienna you'll be free. The Israelis will meet you at the station."

"But I don't *want* to go to Israel!" Cleo said in a hoarse whisper. "I *won't*!"

"Then go to America! I've talked it over with Baryshin. He hates the idea, but he still gives advice. You must say nothing about America until you reach Vienna, you understand? Israel, always say Israel, you're going to Cousin Rachel. There at the station in Vienna the Israelis will meet

you. *Then* you can say America. To them. Tell them about our relatives in New York. They're big shots. People will put you up in Vienna for two or three days, and they'll send you to Rome. Americans will meet you there—Jews from America. They have an agency. HIAS, it's called. They'll help you. Trust them. You can drink Italian wine until you burst!"

"What about *you?*"

"I'll get to me. Yelena, they're trying to arrange a job for you if you want it at the big hospital in Jerusalem. The Israelis have read your papers, the ones you did with Kozhinskaya. They know your work. I think they want you. They, too, are working on hepatitis B. So. Already you're more famous than your father or mother!"

Yelena's smile was wan. "I've read *their* papers. They're behind us. But Daddy, when will we see each other? Mama in America, me in Israel? And you . . . ?"

"So? Haven't you been away from us, in Moscow, these last three and a half years?"

"Oh, but an hour's flight!" Yelena protested.

"Well, in the West, you can go anywhere; it's not like here. All you need is money. And your mother will soon have money. Do you know how much an anesthesiologist earns in America? Thirty, fifty, eighty thousand *dollars* each year! Two hundred dollars in a *day!* What we make in a month, they make in a day! Cleo will learn the language, pass her exams—leave it to her. It won't be easy, but if I know Cleo . . . ! And to help us out we have rich relatives in New York. The Singers. Capitalists! Shh! Well, I talked to *her* on the phone, you remember!"

"How could I forget?"

"Jenny Singer," Yuri said, trying out the unfamiliar name, "and the Israeli cousin, Rachel Aron. How can she come here on an Israeli passport?" He shrugged. "Well, she *says* she's coming. Now, listen here, if for any reason I'm not here to greet them, if I'm a guest of the State, here's what you must do. . . ."

The two women listened to his instructions like children, Cleo's face uncharacteristically serious, her head shaking in disbelief. Could this be happening to her? She scarcely heard him.

"Now, listen, if I'm lucky enough to get my permission, I'll follow you. Maybe the bureaucracy will succumb to momentum, even with Pyotr gone. We can hope. If not, Cleo, you must ask our American relatives to help. They know Americans with connections—senators, Kissinger, for all I know even President Nixon. Talk to the newspaper people. There's an organization called . . . ah . . . the United States Council for Soviet

Jews—something like that. They agitate for Refuseniks, people like me. They *use* people like you—wives, children of Refuseniks—for propaganda, and you must use *them* to help *me*, you understand? Go to meetings, demonstrations, go to Washington. See everyone you can, yes? Just tell them the truth, tell what has happened to me, to us. According to Baryshin, this can help. Open propaganda and private letters by important Americans to Brezhnev or Kosygin. There are organizations of doctors, men I correspond with. Ask them to sign petitions, to refuse to cooperate on research. They'll help you. So even if I am sent away, it won't be hopeless. Never give up hope—I have to know that somewhere you are making a commotion for me, you see? That you haven't forgotten me. I'll need that."

Cleo's eyes had begun to fill. "You are planning to *sit!*" she cried accusingly. "To *leave* me!"

"I doubt I will be arrested, but just in case . . ."

"Oh, Daddy," Yelena said softly, "what have you actually *done* to be arrested? Nothing!"

Yuri smiled with the special sadness he wore to tell mothers he understood their distress, but it would be all right. He patted Yelena's belly. "What have *you* done?" Yelena put both hands over her face and flushed. Yuri went on calmly. "I understand finally what *I* have done." He pointed to the old man. "I had *him* for a father. And a mother even more Jewish. That's my crime. My real crime is that I've been deliberately blind to what was happening right here in Minsk. The murders. The stories in the papers. All that nonsense about Zionism, which I thought was only political—*only* political!"

At midnight, Yelena finally went to bed, wondering what she would actually do when the time came. She pictured the Vienna station something like the long-distance station in Minsk. She would be on a platform, carrying suitcases, she and Mama, and a little Jew would approach and ask: "To Israel? If not, where?" But long before the question had to be answered on that station platform, it would have to be answered in her soul. It was a nightmare. She wasn't used to making such decisions.

The old man agreed to sleep on the sofa, but he always went to bed late. He crushed one of the pills Cleo had brought, boiled water to mix the solution in the kitchen, and boiled Yuri's hypodermic needle—quite a process if one observed it—and went to the WC to take his shot. By the time Yelena went into her room, the old man was dozing before the television set, indifferent, or maybe oblivious, to the critical days ahead for the only family he had. Yes, the poor man *was* growing senile, Yuri thought. Perhaps now was the time to get his signature.

He peered into the kitchen. The pot for sterilizing the syringe was still on the range, but the packet of morphine, all the unused pills for next week, were no longer on the counter. He went back into the living room, reached into his father's coat pocket, and took out the packet. Father had no other morphine with him. Yuri put the packet into his own pocket. The old man needed his shot every four hours. His next shot would be at two. Two hours to go. Let him sleep.

His father was dozing sitting up, as if frozen before the television. Yuri lit a *papyroesa*, studying the old man by the flickering light of the television screen. How could this man have fallen so far from his Jewishness? How could his mother? *Yiddishkeit*, the quality Baryshin's seminars tried to revive in Jews estranged from their origins, had been something never mentioned in their house. They were a *Soviet* family—something *their* parents had only been able to dream about being. Father had gone to great lengths—had changed the Karpovich of the Tsarist Police Inspector to a Ukrainian Karpeyko, the Israil to a Russian Ivan. If Trotsky could do it, could change from Bronshtain, why not he? Yuri had been seduced by all this *Sovietness*, he felt with growing bitterness. And then the *neighbors*, their *Soviet* neighbors, when the Nazis had come, their perfidy he could never entirely forget. God knows, he had tried! All these years, trying to forgive. For the first time, he allowed himself fully to understand men like Baryshin, Ovsischer, Davidovich, who like him had given everything they had to give—to a mirage, to the idea *they* could be Russians. They had changed into Jews again. It was time to abandon ship, to save themselves, those who could! Yet something so deep held him back. He could not name it.

The old man stirred in his chair. He blinked, rubbed his eyes, turned off the television, and felt in his pockets. He looked over at the dining table and saw his son. He patted his pockets, looked into his breast pocket, stood unsteadily, looked at the chair, knelt, felt into the cracks between arm and seat, lifted himself to his feet, stumbled into the kitchen, was gone for a few moments, and returned. "My medicine?"

"I have it." Father held out his hand, but Yuri made no move.

"Sit down, Father. Here. I have to ask you something."

Father eyed his son for the first time with instinctive suspicion; he had sound instincts.

"Ask." Using the cane, he hobbled painfully to the table and sat slowly.

"I need your consent."

"Yurka, you're not going. Wait until I die, all right? It shouldn't be too long." His voice was filled with contempt.

"Father, there is no life here for me or Cleo or Yelena. You see what they're doing. Times have changed. There are no more Jews with the Cheka. The minister of health tells Mitya there's no room at the top even in medicine for Jews. We're not in their ethnic or national mainstream, you see. *And this is a collective decision.* We are finished. It's not just the Black Hundreds, it's the *nachalstvo* at the top, the *vlasti.* Do I get through to you, *starik?*"

"No need to shout at me, Yurochka, my boy. May I have my morphine now?"

"When you sign a consent."

"Ahhhhh. Ahaaa!"

"This is the last supply Cleo can get you. She puts herself in terrible jeopardy to do it. She could sit if she is discovered. They're strict. Me, I can't get near the stuff any more. But I can make arrangements—with Shtainberg—if you'll cooperate."

The old man was silent.

"You remember when I found you on the floor, after three days without the stuff, lying in your own vomit, your own shit—you remember that? You were in agony, in spasm."

The old man's eyes gleamed, enlarged through glass.

"We can help each other. It's not just this shot. It's your supply from now on."

"Let me have just this one. I'm in great pain. Then I'll write it out."

"I have a pen. Here, write it out now. I'll help you."

Yuri turned on the lamp, reached for the pen, and placed it in his father's arthritic hand. With his free hand the old man adjusted his thick cataract lenses. Helping him, as one would a child learning to write, holding the feeble hand as the old man pushed his face to within centimeters of the paper, Yuri spoke and wrote the words his father had withheld all these weeks:

" 'To the OVIR of the Ministry of Interior. From Citizen Karpeyko, Ivan, residing at 49-11 Gorky Prospekt, Minsk.' Good. You are doing fine. Now: 'I do not have material and other claims against my son Yuri Ivanovich Karpeyko.' Good. 'I do not object to his desire to emigrate to the State of Israel for permanent settlement.' Yes, exactly." Even with help the old man labored, his cramped fingers moving slowly. "And now the date. 'Second February 1974' . . . yes, like that. And now sign your name."

Yuri withdrew his helping hand, while the old man, now unassisted, curled his gnarled knuckles more tightly around the pen. Those knuckles, Yuri mused, had signed God knows how many prescriptions, birth

certificates, death certificates, not to mention orders of execution, death *warrants*. The fingers struggled now to write his name under the hateful words. He finished, handed the pen to Yuri.

"May I have the morphine?"

Yuri handed one pill to him.

"As soon as it's light, Father, we must go and have your signature notarized. I'll call Tolya and see how early we can do it."

Taking the pill the old man tapped his way to the kitchen. He said, "My boy, until you leave . . . or are arrested, I want to see as little of you as possible."

His son had no answer, only a sensation of decay in the pit of his stomach.

After the old man had taken his shot and lay on the sofa without bothering to remove his shoes, his glasses off, sightless, Yuri looked down at him and, duty bound, told him, "Our relatives are coming in a few weeks from America and from Israel. Would you like to meet them?"

His father stared unfocused at the ceiling. "No." The old man's mother, who he again thought was alive, would never permit that. "No." The old lady would thrash him if he did; that Feygele, people said, was a holy terror. He rolled over, his face to the wall, and all Yuri could see was the bald head and the very frail back, racked with the shakes.

Suddenly the telephone was ringing. He looked at his watch. Two-thirty. A patient? An anonymous caller? At this hour and after all he'd been through, he could expect anything. He lifted the instrument as Cleo, awakened by the ringing, came, huddled in her nightgown, through the bedroom door.

"Yes?"

"Karpeyko, Yuri?"

"Yes?"

"New York calling."

Ah! Again! His heart leaped up. He was not forgotten. It was amazing what the mere words "New York calling" did for his spirits! Last time they had awakened him from a sound sleep; this time he was keyed up; adrenalin surged through his system.

He heard their voices—the voices of the two women, across a continent and an ocean, one speaking a pretty fair Russian, the other speaking English, which he could understand and speak quite adequately—voices from another world, the world which only the Voice of America had given him a glimpse of, in many ways a strange and hostile world. Nevertheless, these women's voices filled him with an excitement he would

never admit to. What were they saying? *Yes! They were coming! Confirmed!* Martin Singer himself probably could not come; he was recuperating from surgery, but Martin's son Joshua was coming. It was his wife, who was the entertainer, the girl Tammy, who would be giving three concerts for the young people, the lovers of young music, who filled the halls of universities. The women said they were excited, looking forward to meeting their "Russian relations."

Rachel and Jenny seemed aware that his phone might be tapped and were cautious in all they said. He should get a further message soon, Rachel said, and that was all. By now Yelena had come to the door of her room; in her nightgown she seemed helpless and too pretty for her own good, Yuri thought, still a child, really—too young to be a mother. Since Yelena spoke a fair school English, he asked her to greet her two cousins, Jenny Singer and Rachel Aron, and at the end Yelena said carefully, "I anticipate to see you," with her small vocabulary but perfect British pronunciation, adding "Veddy much, veddy much." Even she was beginning to feel a certain excitement. There was a whole world, apparently, where they were accepted and expected, where they would be loved. Yuri insisted that Cleo, too, speak at least with Rachel. The women exchanged pleasantries. Since Jenny could speak only English to Cleo, and Cleo did not understand a word, she nodded, saying in Russian, "Yes, Yes," which was about half the Russian Jenny understood. The other half came at the end when Jenny, half in panic, cried, "*Da svidanya,* Cleo!" During the call, the old man on the couch did not move; perhaps he did not hear them; perhaps he was asleep, or only half awake, still dreaming of his mother, Feygele Karpovich.

After they had rung off, Yuri forced himself to smile, if for nothing but to reassure his daughter and his wife. "So. You see, we have powerful friends. They have great connections. It will be all right. You'll see."

He embraced Yelena for reassurance, as did Cleo, a shining moment in the midst of gloom, a momentary spray of good feeling, and Cleo and Yelena went back to bed feeling strangely lifted, in an atmosphere of unreality. Though they all were thinking of Yuri's having to go to the KGB office in the morning, they tried somehow, miraculously, to sleep. It was straw-grasping time, but it did not work. Yuri came to lie with Cleo. They huddled on the bed, silent, embracing in the dark, unwilling to voice their frightening thoughts. It was as if one of them had an incurable disease too terrible to name. They could think of nothing they dared say, nor of anything to do. Yuri could feel the tears on Cleo's cheek as he touched her and kissed her cold, dry lips. "Don't worry," he whispered foolishly. "It will be all right. All right."

Her body trembled with cold; her teeth chattered. How is one to say goodbye, she wondered—to love itself, to the man who protected her, thought for her, made so many of her decisions? Warmed her when she was cold, taught her to find pleasure in his flesh and hers? Yes, made her a mother and a first-class doctor. How does one give him up? Just like that! It's like death, but more uncertain, more bewildering.

"What's to become of us? What's to become of Yelena?" she whispered. She knew she was behaving badly and added, "Shh—shh. I know. It'll be all right." He had to leave to urinate again; it must have been the fourth time tonight. He felt as if his insides wanted to leak out.

"Listen," he whispered after a while, "if they let me go, I don't think I'll come back here. I feel too exposed. You must get my application to-morrow from Markov and all these papers and file them with OVIR. There's a woman named Vera Petrovna. She'll remember me. Give them to her. Say I'm busy working. I must go in a little while with Markov to get Father's consent attested. I'll get in touch with you somehow. When I do, I may say my name is Mischa. Will you remember that?"

"Mischa!" She tried to smile, but only a choking sound came from her throat. "Yurochka, Yurochka!" she whispered. "It's not right! How did this happen to us?"

"Shhh! I'll keep in touch. I'll tell you what to do. I'll tell you how I am. Shh! Try to get some sleep. Try." She did, and after a bit she managed to doze fitfully, waking and dozing in starts.

In the gray light, before six, Yuri decided he could take a chance and call Tolya Markov. He apologized profusely for the hour, and Tolya was his usual understanding self. Did Tolya know a notary well enough to get him to come in early? Yes? Where? Good. Oh, he had rather unusual problems this morning, Yuri said. It was anything but normal. Tolya would never know how much he appreciated his help. He'd meet the no-tary at seven-thirty, and right after that he wanted to come and talk to Tolya. He needed some advice. Tolya was always steady and sensible. His writer friend, his boyhood friend, would be glad to see him. Yuri prepared and gave Father his six A.M. injection, retaining the rest of the morphine. The old man scarcely wakened fully even when the needle entered his arm.

Yuri packed a few things. Toothbrush, underwear, razor—just in case. He trimmed his beard, showered, changed his clothes, combed his hair. Cleo prepared a breakfast of yogurt and eggs for him, and he ate in si-lence opposite her, the two of them staring like terrified fools. What was there to say? At seven, before going, he went in to kiss Yelena, waking her from shallow slumber. "Oh, Daddy," she whispered, "I hope it'll be all

right. Oh, how I hope!" Yuri said he would leave the Zhiguli in the northeast corner of Lenin Square. Cleo had a key for the car.

He went to the chair where the old man slept, mouth open, his teeth out. "Okay, Father. Wake up. We have to go." He ignored the KGB man on duty below, whose job was to keep an eye on goings and comings, and half led, half supported the old man by the elbow, taking him out. He helped Father into the Zhiguli, and while the old man muttered protests, slammed the door on him impatiently, went around to the driver's seat, and drove through foggy, empty streets to Leninsky and the office whose address Markov had given him.

The notary was there, a short man with heavy eyebrows and rimless glasses, thin gray hair, ruddy full face. He glanced at the paper Yuri put before him. He was not happy with it, but he was only a notary.

"There's a regular form for this."

"Yes. But this says the same thing. Word for word. I know the form by heart. This is better, written out in longhand. Please."

The notary turned to the old man. "This is your statement? Made of your own free will?"

The old man stared, the personification of defeat.

"He's hard of hearing," Yuri said.

The notary shouted. "This is your sworn statement? You make it freely?"

The old man peered at him, nodded, stared at the ground.

"You must speak, Father," Yuri said.

"Yes." His father muttered the word almost as if spitting it out: "*Da. Da.*"

The notary went to work efficiently. Seal. Date. Signature. He handed the paper back to Yuri. "Fifty kopeks, please." Yuri paid him, thanked him for coming in early, led Father to the car, and drove to Father's place on Gorky. The old man, recognizing where he was, hobbled out and started for his entrance.

"Father. One minute." Yuri was out of the car. "Here." He handed him the box of morphine, which the old man snatched as if rescuing something stolen from him. "It will last you the week. No more than a quarter grain in a shot—be sure! After that, expect Doctor Shtainberg."

Old Ivan Borisovich gave no indication that he had heard his son but silently clacked his way, with the help of the cane, to his entry.

He never looked back.

YURI DROVE THE ZHIGULI to Tolya Markov's place—the house where during the war he had been sent to live for a short time.

Tolya listened carefully to everything Yuri told him. He took Yuri's OVIR application and all the documents, complete now with Father's notarized consent. Yes, he promised to see that Cleo got it. He'd bring it to her later today.

As for advice, he urged Yuri to ignore the invitation to the KGB. "If they want you enough, they'll come looking for you. Penalties? Agh! Empty threats. What can they do to you? Wait them out. Listen, they're so busy down there, they won't notice for days—maybe weeks. They have their hands full. They've just discovered two more wartime collaborators. Imagine, twenty-eight years late!"

Tolya's advice frightened him. It led somewhere he was afraid to enter. Defy a lawful order? Simply not go? "Look, Yurka," Tolya said, "if the bastards invited *me*, do you know what I'd do? I'd go into hiding immediately. I'd disappear. I've told Irina that. The bastards think they're above the law, and they *are*. That's what's wrong. They never observe it, and when that happens, you're better off to lie low. What can they do if they find you? No worse than if they don't."

It occurred to Yuri briefly that Tolya himself might be a *seksot*, provoking him, but he dismissed the dark thought. Too many years. They'd been too close too long. He'd been involved with *samizdat* too long; there were still a few people one had to trust. He couldn't get rid of the feeling he had to urinate. He could not get out of his head his brief encounter with ordinary *militsioners* as a *victim* of vandalism and hooliganism. Swine they were, of course, a lower form of animal than KGB officers. Tolya was talking on; he made Yuri listen in spite of himself, while Irina, in the bedroom, slept on blissfully. Here were the names of people he

could stay with in Leningrad: he would never be found. But it all seemed too pat, too dangerous, to Yuri. The KGB would find him—they always did. They had people in every house.

Tolya Markov waxed passionate, as only intellectuals can. His dialectics were a string of pearls for Yuri's delectation, each argument a lustrous temptation with a glow of its own. Tolya Markov, at last revealed: the full-fledged dissident. Yuri and he were the true heirs of the Revolution. The present regime was hopelessly rotted, and rattled, to boot. "Read Marx and see how far we've come from him! Do we have a dictatorship of the proletariat? Has the State begun to wither away? Can you find freedom of even the most primitive kind? Are *you* free to fulfill your destiny? Is your daughter—or for that matter, your wife? Am I? They're everywhere, spying on us, still controlling everything we do, telling us what we can say, what we can read, see, where we can go, what work we can do! Our parents died, killed, tortured, were tortured, stole, cheated, marched. Why? Because all things were promised, but have the promises been kept? Oh, bread, yes, roofs over our heads, and clothes to wear—but was this the whole promise? Can humans, each with a personality, a separate individuality, accept what might be all right for domesticated animals? It's time for promises to be kept. Lawful procedures must be followed; greater choice must be available; we must have a chance to speak or write our minds." Yuri, he said, had an opportunity to become a spokesman for the suppressed—from underground. His message would get out in *samizdat*. Tolya would see to it.

"You expect me to become a *martyr?*" Yuri said, making no effort to disguise his dismay. "In a hopeless cause?"

"No less than I," Tolya said. "We must support Sakharov, Kopelev, Grigorenko, all the giants of our time. They cry out for us and we must answer to them! They are in our day what Lenin and Trotsky, what your father and mine, were in theirs. Outcasts in their own time—lonely voices calling for justice—but voices which *your* father lived to see triumph. We must do the same."

Yuri's head was shaking no; he could not stop himself. Tolya talked big but always hedged his bets. And yet, in spite of himself, Yuri was tempted. Why not go down fighting?

He memorized the names and addresses of Tolya's people in Leningrad, dissidents, none of them Jews. Yuri quietly put on his greatcoat (he also had worn a *kepka* rather than his fedora so that he would not appear at the KGB without some proletarian gear).

"Kiss Irina goodbye for me." Irina slept on in the next room. Yuri ran down two steps at a time.

He had left himself an hour to see Baryshin before he reported to the KGB. He parked in the northeast corner of Lenin Square and walked through the freezing gray morning to Baryshin's place, where he had gone to one of those seminars, to study Hebrew, *Yiddishkeit,* to learn to be a Jew. He recalled that Georgi, the mathematician, had that time got hold of *Commentary,* the American magazine, and they had read and discussed the article about the "New Exodus," the wave of emigration of Jews from Russia, of which he might soon be a part. Baryshin that night had called his apartment an *ulpan,* the Hebrew word for a school in Israel where newcomers learn the language and the ins and outs of Israeli life before going out on their own. Today, however, what Yuri wanted from Baryshin was advice.

Baryshin was having breakfast with his diminutive Russian wife, Zinaida Aleksandrovna, in their kitchen; he had not yet shaved, and Zina, a skinny, blond, worn-down thing half his size, was still in a robe. Zina reminded Yuri of his army of mothers—a bearer of children who held down a job, took care of the house, and still *worked* creatively at being a mother—all at the same time. Zina was perhaps forty-four and looked sixty.

Baryshin was aglow this morning. Before Yuri could open his mouth to tell him why he had come, the stuttering former air force colonel was exulting that their daughter, who had been given permission last month to emigrate with her husband, had arrived in Israel and was now in a marvelous new absorption center, a *Merkaz Klita* in Israel, near Tel Aviv in a town called Raanana. She had phoned, full of enthusiasm—the people were nice, there were wonderful children everywhere, the place, which was like a luxury apartment house or hotel, was immaculate, flowers growing wherever one looked, a dream place. "But, listen . . . the only thing wrong," Baryshin said with wry irony, "is th-the rabbis there say she's n-not Jewish! B-b-because of her mother, you see—you are what y-your m-m-mother is! C-can you believe it?" He laughed. "She waits three y-years, and now the *rabbis* give her trouble! Iy, yi, yi!"

Zina shook her head in wonderment tinged with disgust, but added without conviction, "But she seems happy, and her husband also."

After congratulating them on their daughter's good fortune, Yuri told them of his summons; in less than an hour he was to report to the somber yellow building on Leninsky Prospekt. "I came to ask what *you* think I should do, Colonel. You have experience in such matters." He told Baryshin about the people in Leningrad whose names Markov had given him.

Baryshin simply whistled. "Trouble!" he said. "Anti-Soviets. Dissidents.

You g-get c-caught with them—" He uttered two short, ominous whistles and drew a finger across his throat. "No! We're not anti-Soviet, Yurka, you see? We have n-no quarrel with them. We merely recognize we're foreigners in th-this land, and we want to go home! We don't th-threaten them. If you're a Zionist in Russia, you dare not be a reformer, a dissident. You see?"

Baryshin pursed his lips, thinking heavily. "I have been interrogated three times. They'll b-be v-very kind. Your close buddies. Especially Sikorsky—watch out for him. Tr-tr-tricky bastard! So *nice*. Trying to help you. Admit n-nothing. Those stories of yours are *not* anti-Soviet, no, no! You have nothing against the Soviets. All you want is to be allowed to leave to join the rest of the f-family in your homeland. Repeat it over and over. N-n-nothing else."

Yuri nodded.

"Th-they may ask about m-me. You have met me. Nothing more. At the Moskoviches, because of the boy. Any b-books they may find, study books, et cetera, you received them from p-patients. Long ago. You can't remember who. Okay?"

Yuri peered at him sadly. "I may not see you again, Colonel."

Baryshin got up. "Come." He led the way to the bedroom. "Don't want Zina to hear. If they question her, she might make a m-mistake." He shrugged apologetically. "S-so listen carefully. To ignore their summons, as your friend suggests, would be a b-big m-mistake. I always g-go when they call me. Not to go, a confession of guilt, see? So go. You'll f-find out what they have on you. Nine chances out of t-ten, they'll release you. After a day, two days, th-three at the most. If what they have on you is d-dangerous, *then* I would go into hiding, yes. But with Markov's friends?" His eyes opened wide and he shrugged to indicate this would be suicide. "I'll give you the name of a Jew in Vilna. He'll put you up. If necessary, he'll give you another n-name. If you get c-caught, it's b-better to be hiding with a Zionist than with a dissident."

"What future is there in hiding?"

Baryshin shrugged. "Better than being in a camp freezing and starving, or in s-some asylum! T-times can change! There's always hope."

Yuri shook his head. His options were narrowing. *If* he were released. Otherwise he had no options at all. He committed the name and address Baryshin gave him to memory. They rejoined Zina.

"*Shalom*," the large man said, patting his back as if to provide a bit of comfort as they stood at the door.

"*Shalom*," Yuri said, his voice hoarse; the word itself sounded foreign coming from his own lips. It was a seminar word, a charade.

"*Da svidanya*," Zina murmured, sensing how he felt about the inappropriateness of the Hebrew, shaking his hand. Her eyes, Yuri noticed, were clouded and uncertain, the eyes of a troubled, beaten woman. They *could* beat you down, beat your wife down. Ah, Cleo. Bastards!

5

HEAD DOWN, a huddled, worried creature hurrying to do as he was told, he started through the cold along Leninsky Prospekt, which was beginning to be busy with the going and coming of workers, students heading toward the Institute, women rushing to get to the shops before the lines grew too long.

When he arrived at KGB headquarters, he used the main entrance on Leninsky Prospekt. The man at the information desk was polite, but told him that Room 900 could be reached only by going outside again and around the corner. He would see a side entrance on Komsomolskaya, just a short way down the street. He should inquire there. This way to the scaffold, Yuri thought. The man might have been giving directions to the nearest tram.

The side entrance led to a narrow staircase with an arrow pointing upward and the number 900. The windowless waiting room into which he came was like any of the countless office waiting rooms he had seen. Four other people sat on wood chairs along two bare walls, each an island of uncertainty or unhappiness. On the wall behind the receptionist were two large photo-posters—one of Brezhnev, the other of Andropov. Yuri thought he recognized one elderly woman, although he could not quite place her. He gave his name to the girl at a desk on the other side of the wood railing, and she asked him to have a seat. In that moment he was transformed into someone he had never been: a cipher, no different from the others—a nonentity sitting along a wall, holding his breath, waiting to learn his fate. The elderly woman, who carried a small package, rose to move next to him. "Professor Karpeyko?" She spoke in a hush, apparently in order not to bother the receptionist.

Yuri nodded.

"You don't remember me? Ida Milshtain? Leon's grandmother? You remember?" She smiled encouragingly.

The image was vague. A tough little Jewish soccer player? Nine or ten, yes. Must have been almost ten years ago. His mother was a teacher, so his grandmother used to bring the boy. A fearless, wiry kid, as he recalled. A fractured leg—or was it an arm? "Yes, yes," he responded absently. "Leon. How is Leon?"

"All grown up now. He's been arrested. I'm trying to deliver him a food package. It's not easy. See how they make you wait? I've been here since eight."

"What's he done?"

"They want him for the army. He won't go." She shrugged. "I don't blame him. So, Professor, what are you doing in such a place? A famous man like you?"

He had to smile. Some fame! "They want to ask me a few questions. I'm a witness." Why should he tell white lies to *this* woman? "They say I'm mixed up with Zionists." She was so Jewish he could see no harm in telling her that much.

"So if you're not, you should be, Professor. It's not a crime."

Yuri had gone as far as he dared. He decided not to become involved. In a place like this, no telling who might overhear, misinterpret.

After half an hour the receptionist summoned Ida Milshtain and spoke in an undertone that Yuri could not make out; the food package was transferred to the receptionist. "You're sure?" he heard Ida Milshtain say. "No mistakes?" The receptionist mumbled something and dismissed her with a jut of the chin.

The old woman sighed with resignation, turned, and, waving only her fingers to Yuri, she made her way to the stairs. "Good luck, Professor!" she whispered as she passed.

At twelve forty-five, almost three hours after he had arrived, the receptionist called his name. She pointed to the door of Room 900. Holding a file folder, a uniformed, florid, puffy-cheeked, middle-aged man with a shock of iron-gray hair cut short and combed back waited for him in the center of an almost empty room. "Please put your hands over your head." Yuri placed his overnight bag on the floor and obeyed. The choleric man frisked him quickly, professionally. He was getting used to it. First Igor, the *militsioner*, then Steelteeth, and now this guy. He had never suspected he was so dangerous.

The guard inspected the contents of the overnight bag and handed it to

him. "Follow me." He led him through the opposite door, through dimly lit corridors that seemed endless mazes, up three flights of stairs, into an office not quite so bare—a room containing a desk, a fading artificial leather chair with wooden arms, a large window looking out on Leninsky Prospekt.

A younger man sat behind the desk, pasty, slightly pockmarked. He rose and introduced himself as Josef Sikorsky. "I am your interrogator, Professor." He did not offer his hand. He was affable, however, even apologetic for the delay, offering Yuri a cigarette from his own pack and motioning for him to take the other chair. Yuri gazed out the window. People were hurrying along going about their business. Buses moved slowly along the broad, tree-lined avenue. Everything normal. Across the boulevard, he could see Chaim Park, the meeting place for Refuseniks, where the latest intelligence was exchanged in the very shadow of the KGB. He could see dark figures huddled in the cold on the benches, talking. Sikorsky asked about Yuri's work at the Institute, at the hospital, at the Polyclinic. He had Yuri explain to him the basis for his admission to the Academy, why his blood work had been significant. For a short while they were two colleagues, professionals. Sikorsky explained that he, too, would have liked to have been a physician, only the money was so bad. "But I'm particularly interested in your blood work, because—well, never mind. We are not here to discuss that."

Something familiar about Sikorsky's face nagged at him. Had this man, too, once been a patient of his? There were so many thousands. Suddenly he knew. How could he be so stupid? Was the pressure draining him of his normal intelligence? Stefan. Of course! Yes, it should make things better. But he said nothing. Sikorsky had the pallor of a man who got little sleep; and he seemed as nervous as Yuri himself. He wanted to know about Yuri's associates; to which doctors was he particularly close? Yuri was cautious in answering; there was always concern about conspiracies. At last he got on the subject of Zionism. The Zionists were well organized, Sikorsky said. They were well financed from abroad, they engaged in propaganda, they had organized an emigration movement in Byelorussia, et cetera. Had there been talk of Zionism among the physicians? The nurses? Did he think the Zionist organization in Minsk had made inroads into the medical establishment? After all, so many doctors were Jews. Yuri said he had not encountered any Zionists among the doctors or nurses he knew. Most of the doctors were women, and the women weren't highly political.

"How about Shtainberg?"

"An excellent surgeon. The best thoracic surgeon in Minsk. No interest in Zionism."

"Shtainberg has no contact with Baryshin?"

"Not that *I* know of." He was beginning to get edgy from having to keep track of his own distortions, to stay consistent.

"In fact, he knows Baryshin extremely well, for your information. They work together. You didn't know that?"

"No."

"How did you meet Baryshin?"

"At the home of a patient." He told him about the Moskoviches, whom he knew were gone.

Sikorsky listened politely. "I run into people with reform manias. They're usually completely crazy and often have to be given psychiatric help. Oh, they sometimes sound logical, but they are anti-socialist nuts who want to turn everything upside down; they mock all we have built up, et cetera. These are crazy people, but they are not well organized like the Zionists. They're not organized at all, in fact, and they do not endanger society. They are simply a danger to themselves. They must be cured. The *psikhushki* do an excellent job of it. There have been many cures."

"A few deaths, too, I understand."

"You must have been listening to lies, Doctor, anti-socialist fabrications, which you are repeating to *me*. I'm surprised—a man of your intelligence!"

"I'm afraid, Comrade Sikorsky, it is you who have been taken in by lies about me. My case is quite a simple one. You want my analysis?" Sikorsky nodded. "I was appointed director of the new Pediatric Hospital of the First Clinical Association—*acting* director, that is. Another man wanted the job. So there followed a conspiracy within the Health Department, and within the Party apparatus. It's a Mafia, not the Italian style, but all our own. Outlaws protecting each other. They don't kill people, but they have ways to get rid of them. If someone is to be accused of conspiracy, it is these gangsters. I prefer not to name all those involved, but this conspiracy led to investigations not of the conspirators, but of me, their victim. These investigations had no purpose except to eliminate me from this job. The Mafia succeeded. However, such investigations, I have learned to my regret, take on lives of their own, and there's no way to stop them. Once you're in disfavor, the wolves descend. You yourself are part of this animal process. Not that I mean you are a wolf. But the wolves use you. You have a part to play, but they don't tell you everything. I have heard all this directly from the lips of the first secretary—sadly the *late* first secre-

tary, I should say—from Pyotr Feodorovich himself. An old friend. And Pyotr Feodorovich advised me, if I did not want to sit for years in the North, I should emigrate right away. Everything else that you have about me is lies."

Sikorsky rolled his eyes upward. "Well, we shall see whose lies are lies soon enough." He extracted from the large folder on his desk a copy of a typed booklet. "Ah, would you like another cigarette? Here, let me light it for you. Your hand. It happens sometimes." Yuri wished he could amputate those damned trembling fingers of his. He took a long drag. "Now be good enough to look at this, Doctor. Have you seen it before?"

"Yes, of course. It's probably my copy of a story for children taken during the search." Yuri flipped the twelve pages. "There's no harm in any of this material. I've read every word of it. Thousands of others have also. As a perfectly competent Party member, I can tell you there is nothing damaging to Party or State interests here." He turned the pages. "A poem by Yevtushenko, see? Not one of his best, I'm afraid, but not bad. About a collective farmer who would like to be a city boy. Here. Here's a description of the *psikhushka* in Dnieperpetrovsk by Vorniev, who spent a year there; he tells how he finally gained his release."

"By lying to the doctors?"

"Well, he was sane enough to know what the doctors wanted to hear. To be sane one need not be entirely honest. Read Marx."

"Vorniev is back there, you know. He *is* crazy. Certifiably."

Yuri was shocked. They had almost killed the brilliant chemist with large doses of sulphur and haloperidol, administered by force against his will, and despite the protests of his family. But Yuri had no time to reflect on Vorniev, for Sikorsky was continuing to ask about the *samizdat*.

"That? Oh, it's a short story by my friend Anatoly Markov—he wrote it for *Novy Mir,* but they didn't think it was good enough. I myself thought it excellent. Have you read it?"

Sikorsky closed his eyes. There was a threat in the very gesture. "You are a *close* friend of Anatoly Markov?" His eyes remained closed.

"Yes, indeed. An excellent writer."

"I see. And your fables?"

"Meaningless," Yuri said sharply. "Light humor for children."

"Children are impressionable, Doctor. They remember these things. It gives them, how shall I say, an unhealthy opinion about authority. Such opinion, derived from such a statement, does not help make good citizens. On the contrary. So it must be considered anti-State, if not anti-Party."

Yuri shrugged. "You have your view. You are perhaps deficient in humor, my dear young man. Your view is not at all objective."

Sikorsky's eyes glazed. "You forget where you are. I have watched my son fade away under your care, Doctor. You have given him funny stories to feed on. But you have not cured him. He's going to die, isn't he?"

Yuri felt the blood rush from his face. For a moment he felt as if he were going to faint. He was being blamed for Stefan Sikorsky's leukemia! "This is not right, comrade. I have tried everything I know for your son. I have given him my own blood many times, as if he were my own son. I've persuaded others to do the same. But all we know in medicine cannot help him. If only we knew how to pray!"

The man at the desk stared out the window. Yuri would not have been surprised to see him burst into tears, but he did not.

"Bosherov," he said in a voice so low that Yuri could scarcely hear him, "Doctor Bosherov says you misdiagnosed the case. Bosherov says you're guilty of malpractice. He says you could have saved him."

Yuri could not believe his ears. "I'm sorry to say Bosherov is lying, if he says that. He knows better. Bosherov, by the way, is an orthopedic surgeon. He knows very little about hematology. I'm sorry—very sorry— about Stefan. It's a tragedy. I wish it were otherwise. With all my heart. I did everything I could. Everything. He's a brave kid, a marvelous kid. And your wife—another brave one. You should be proud of them both."

He could see a glint in Sikorsky's eye. He *knew*. He damn well knew.

"She told me," Sikorsky said in an uneven voice, "everything. I myself don't have much faith in doctors. Can you blame me?" Then, as if disengaging himself from his personal grief, "I don't think we can do more today. Perhaps tomorrow?" He rang a buzzer. "We will have to keep you overnight, Professor. I hope you don't mind."

"This is absolutely necessary? I'm expected at my polyclinic today and I have a class at the Institute first thing tomorrow."

"We will notify them. It cannot be helped."

The broad-faced florid man who had conducted him here had entered the room.

"The professor will be with us, Comrade Lisuyov, at least overnight."

Menacing phrase, "at least."

"Am I under arrest?"

"No, no. We just want to talk to you."

"Why can't I go home? I'll come back tomorrow."

"It's better this way."

Lisuyov gestured to Yuri to come with him. Another long walk, his escort holding him more firmly by the elbow than Yuri felt necessary, through corridors, past closed doors, down five flights this time, and again

through narrower corridors even more dimly lit. They must be in the basement.

Twice during the long walk, when they heard approaching footsteps from a corridor leading to theirs, Yuri's escort told him to face the wall. "Don't look about. It's forbidden." He heard footsteps passing behind him, going in the opposite direction. Once he himself passed a similar couple. The faceless prisoner, a man in prison garb—the sight had its own chilling effect—was facing the wall abjectly, while the two guards nodded to each other rather pleasantly as they passed. All in their day's work, Yuri thought.

Finally they reached a small, windowless office, poorly illuminated by a small overhead fixture. A thin young man with deeply sunken eyes sat at a beaten wood desk on which there was a typewriter. Yuri's escort handed the folder to the desk man, who studied its contents intently for several moments, then placed it alongside the typewriter, into which he rolled a blank form, and said in a monotone, "Empty your pockets."

Methodically Yuri did so, placing the articles on the folder. When he came to his *papyroesi*, he asked, "My cigarettes also?"

"Everything."

The man took his wallet, watch, passport, distance glasses, pen, money, even his handkerchief, typing out each item after he stuffed it into something that looked like a laundry bag. "May I have a look at this?" He took the small overnight bag Yuri had set down, which contained his toilet articles and change of underwear, and unceremoniously emptied its contents onto the top of the desk. He tossed each article into the cloth bag, and typed again, item by item, finally throwing the little valise itself into the cloth bag. "This is your receipt," he said, but the paper remained in the typewriter. He went to a closet, took out a package of clothing, and handed it to Yuri. "Please change your clothes. In there." He indicated another door. The place was no larger than a closet, dimly lit by a weak bulb. Yuri had difficulty absorbing the fact that he was changing into drab gray prison clothes, but he did so, removing coat, tie, shirt, trousers. When he returned, the escort who had brought him to this room was gone. The man at the desk said, "May I see your feet?"

Yuri pulled his prison trousers up six inches. "Your garters, please. They are not allowed." Yuri gave the man his garters. He could feel his socks slip down. "Shoes, too. Not allowed. Use these." He handed Yuri a pair of cloth-soled, unclean, decaying slippers. He stood up, stuffed Yuri's clothing unceremoniously into the bag, tossed in the garters, rammed the shoes in last, and closed with a wire fastener the now well-stuffed bag,

tying a tag to it and tossing it into a corner. Yuri saw his name on the tag.

The man again sat down at the typewriter, and finished the list. Coat, shirt, tie, trousers, belt, shoes, garters. He took the list from the typewriter, an original and carbon. "Your receipt. See that everything is listed. Sign my copy." Yuri signed. It was the desk man who should sign. But why argue?

Yuri tried to read the list but was not able to concentrate on it, and he nodded. His mocking stories of the bureaucracy had barely touched the surface. These people had made a fine art of inanity. As he located his prison trouser pocket and folded the form, the door opened and another uniformed man appeared, this one tall, heavy, and intimidating, a lock of hair rising out of the center of his head like a horn—a rhinoceros, thought Yuri. The guard stood, arms akimbo, while the desk man ran another form through the typewriter and asked Yuri the usual bureaucratic questions as if he were preparing his application for a post at an institute. At last it was done. The desk man nodded to the rhinoceros.

"Come."

"Comrade," Yuri said softly to the desk man, "my *papyroesi?*"

"Not allowed."

"Not one?"

The desk man shook his head impatiently and nodded to the rhinoceros.

"Come."

Again he was led through corridors, past doors, until they reached one identical to all the others, where the rhinoceros stopped, fished for his key, opened the door, and indicated that this was his destination. No window. An overhead light. In the corner of the room was a *parasha*, the small bucket which constituted his toilet. The only piece of furniture was a small wood chair. A straw-filled mattress was on the floor. The room was six feet square, with a low ceiling. Above the door were three louvers which permitted air to come from the hall. His escort locked the door. A maximum of three days, the law said. Apparently solitary confinement. So that he could not contaminate others? Be contaminated? Plot among themselves? He lay on the mattress. It was hard; through it one could feel the coldness of the concrete floor. Well, it would have to do. If only he had a cigarette! He eyed the *parasha* balefully. All the comforts of home. The enormity of what was happening to him had begun to seep through him. His anger was burning slowly, but more brightly by the minute. Everyone correct, proper. Receipts issued. Stalinism was dead. Something else had taken its place. Was it an improvement?

To keep busy, he knelt and urinated into the *parasha*. Good work! You have the hang of it, Yuri.

His second interview with Sikorsky next day started in the same desultory fashion as the first, but soon after they had begun to talk, Sikorsky said, "Comrade Chankov is interested in your case, Doctor."

Yuri wanted to scratch his scalp. His clothes were permeated with the stench of the cell; he stank. His stomach cramps drove him wild. "I have never had the privilege of meeting Comrade Chankov. Perhaps if we could meet, we could clear things up."

"I should tell you that he is not pleased with your interpretation of your case."

"But why not? It's the truth." A good offense sometimes worked. Nothing to lose. "There *is* a conspiracy." Apparently this had disturbed Chankov sufficiently to prompt him to show his hand. A good sign. But right now he must be busy with Moscow, moving to take Pyotr's position in whatever way such men moved.

Yuri heard footsteps; a door opened, and a short, stocky, bald man with jaundiced skin and a fringe of dark hair around the back of his head came bouncing into the sparse, barren office. One could not help noticing the potbelly. The little man's eyes were crinkled. Sikorsky rose suddenly. "Comrade Chankov! Here is Karpeyko."

Chankov did not offer to shake hands. Yuri rose, acutely uncomfortable, distressed at what he knew must be his ghastly appearance after a ghastly night. He surely looked no better than the worst of thugs. Nevertheless, he felt obliged to put himself on an even footing with Chankov. "Welcome, Comrade Chankov, to our parlor of bourgeois comforts."

Chankov took a chair beside Sikorsky's desk and began abruptly to shout: "What's this I hear of accusations? Why don't you answer Captain Sikorsky's questions truthfully? I know your kind! Too clever for your own good. I knew your father. I know your type. What can we expect? *He* engaged in conspiracies. Your old man! You know, I had some experiences with him! Well, we needn't go into that!"

Before Yuri could say a word, he was off on another violent outburst, his voice clattering like a machine gun: "Before we're through, we'll find out all about you! Your father is a dope fiend. This we know. A high Party man and a leading doctor! What filth! And where does he get the stuff now? Ahh? Your wife will be arrested! Your daughter as well! You'll wish you'd never been born. A nest of Zionists! You will tell us what we want to know—everything about their organization, the leaders, who di-

rects activities, where the money comes from. This is your only chance to get a light sentence!"

Yuri knew he would have to take some chances—go with the long shots. "Comrade Chankov, you are through? Listen carefully, I urge you. I speak for your own good and in your interest. I have had cordial relations with Pyotr Feodorovich Ustinov most of my life, as is well known, and I understand everything behind this charade. The great Stalin is no more. We have laws now. How will a court react when it learns of your dealings with Doctor Bosherov? What will happen when the judges realize what a conspiracy you yourself have been involved in, and involving also Doctor Soloviev? At *least* two high officials in the Republic and the Party. And where can this investigation lead? Everyone has enemies. We have cleaned out the stable many times before! Will there be an investigation in which *you* will be the subject? Connections to other connections? Could a man become first secretary if the air is riddled with suspicions of corruption? Not unless the corruption goes all the way to the top! My testimony will not be necessary. I could disappear and it would make no difference. A dozen doctors and *others* know the facts and will testify. Captain Sikorsky has been asking who my friends are. He forgets *I* have Party connections; I have chaired Party meetings at the Pediatric Hospital, I have often chaired the meetings at the Institute. I have hundreds of friends, and *they all know. I am a member of the Academy of Medical Science.* If anything happens to me . . ." He heaved his shoulders expressively.

He had shot his bolt. He had little hope that it would work, but he would wait and see. Yuri could scarcely fathom where his boldness came from. Was he out of his mind to make such accusations? It might be his only chance. Chankov seemed to settle down. He spoke coldly, an icy calm replacing passion now suppressed; to Yuri he seemed more dangerous. His voice was basso and barely audible.

"Comrade Karpeyko, you will live to regret these Jewish fabrications. Nothing will save you. We have the evidence to break the entire Zionist ring in Minsk, and you with it. You will answer for a misuse of narcotic drugs. You will answer for taking gifts from patients, for making charges for your services. You will answer for the anti-State literature you have concocted and distributed to children. You will tell us who supplied you with anti-socialist tracts and books. You will explain to us what you are doing with firearms in your apartment. You are a dangerous person, the more so because you believe you have the right to do these things and to make wild accusations. My recommendation to you is that you now an-

swer truthfully all the questions Captain Sikorsky puts to you, that you cleanse your mind of all the information you are keeping bottled up, and allow us to rehabilitate you, to reeducate you, so that you can be useful once again." He rose and turned to Sikorsky. "I intend to leave everything in the very able hands of Captain Sikorsky. So much for your great conspiracy theory, you see? I take myself off the case, this is how little intimidated I am by your insinuations. Let the investigation take its natural course. We will let Captain Sikorsky decide the charges to file on an objective basis. He will know what to do. I have other duties."

The little man hopped up, as if he were sorry he had bothered to come, and stalked out with short, almost goose-step paces, a little cyclone leaving the scene of the disaster in its wake. Yuri could still not determine whether his gamble had won for him or lost.

While he returned once or twice to the question of drugs, and asked Yuri to analyze dialectically several of his "fables" that had made their way into *samizdat*, the principal thrust of Sikorsky's questions for the rest of this session focused on the Zionist question, and particularly the "antiSoviet" Zionist "organization."

Yuri told him there was no organization he knew of. There were no leaders, there was no chain of command, there was no "propaganda arm," no headquarters. To the best of his knowledge, the movement was spontaneous and resulted from the growing anti-Semitism among officials, from the realization among more and more Jews that the great nationalities of the Soviet Union—the Russians, the Ukrainians, the Byelorussians—were not hospitable to Jews. "We are made to feel like foreigners."

"Since when?"

"Since the war." In the old days Jews could choose—whether to give up their Jewish nationality and identity through intermarriage and absorption, or to remain Jews. At sixteen, if one of their parents was nonJewish, they could get passports that proclaimed them Russian, Ukrainian, Latvian, whatever. For himself, his father, his grandmother, they had all chosen assimilation, intermarriage, but it had not worked. Now they had no real choice. Whatever they *said* they were, people these days looked at faces, not passports. *Assimilated* Jews felt beleaguered, despised. That was why many wanted to leave, to go to Israel. To go "home." The word "home" came like gall to his lips. Minsk was home, damnit! Sikorsky was asking how many wanted to leave. Who could tell? Last year he would have said five percent at most. Now the figure was higher. His experience had shocked him. Now? Perhaps thirty percent, perhaps as many as a million throughout the country.

Sikorsky shook his head in puzzlement. "With everything so marvelous here?"

Yuri stopped himself from laughing by pretending to cough. He couldn't help himself. "You sound like my wife," he gasped.

"All right. Enough for today. I'm going to let you go downstairs," Sikorsky said, as if this were a great privilege. "I would like you to think carefully—honestly, objectively. I must have the names of those persons organizing the emigration. Names, you understand? How is it financed? Who supports the Refuseniks? Who distributes money from overseas here in Minsk, and in other cities? You know them. We must have the names of Zionist contacts in Leningrad and Vilnius and Moscow. Give us those, and you can be released. You can have your visas. You can go. You and your wife and daughter. Is that fair enough?" He pushed the buzzer. "Otherwise you will sit. Think carefully. Until tomorrow." Yuri rose as the rhinoceros entered. "Not yet," Sikorsky motioned to the monster, who ambled out again. Sikorsky got up, came around the desk. He handed Yuri his own pack of cigarettes and a box of matches, which Yuri quickly rammed into his pocket.

"You're a physician," Sikorsky said almost good-naturedly. "You know what smoking does to your lungs, to your intestines, to the circulation. You saw what happened to your friend Ustinov. Even he was not immune."

Yuri had promised himself to stop smoking a thousand times. He'd tried twice. Cleo was always after him: "Your poor lungs! Your poor heart!" None of it made any difference, Habit was habit. And if he chose to poison himself, who were these bastards to stop him? In this filthy place, one had to have something. Sikorsky understood that. At any rate, he would not be forced by *them* to give up anything. Smoking in this place was a necessary act of defiance. He fingered Sikorsky's pack of cigarettes like a talisman.

Worse than the sadistic neglect he had endured in this place was the disorientation he suffered—the unreality—treated by Sikorsky with unfailing courtesy and mutual respect, exchanging views on an equal footing, and moments later—the moment, he feared, had just arrived—being half-dragged, poked, and prodded by a hooligan in uniform muttering "Fuck your mother," shouting as if he were some idiot, "Face the wall!" and being deposited in that barren, putrid cell with his own excrement and a chair to await the next serving of inedible slops.

"Thank you, Comrade Sikorsky," he said meekly. "I appreciate it."

"I hope so," Sikorsky said amiably. "We'll see the next time we meet.

I'm counting on you to cooperate. By the way, I mentioned to my wife that you are here."

Softening up! Yuri hastened to seize the advantage he thought he perceived. "I'm being kept in a cell, Comrade Sikorsky, barely large enough to crawl into. Are you aware of that? Of the appalling conditions here—of the disgusting food? I have a bucket where I must move my bowels a meter from where I'm expected to eat. The air is putrid. It's difficult to respond to your questions with any clarity under such conditions. If this goes on, my answers will become meaningless, no matter what I may say."

As he talked, he could see Sikorsky mentally backing away.

"We'll see. I know how you feel. I have no control of such matters, Professor." He lit a cigarette for himself and rang the buzzer before Yuri could respond, and the rhinoceros was back, holding back his first shout of foul words of abuse until they were safely out of earshot of Sikorsky and well into the world dominated by rhinoceroses.

Whose names could he give them? Baryshin's they already knew. Shtainberg? All he had done was arrange that first meeting with Baryshin. Ovsischer? Well known. *Sovetskaya Byelorossiya* had run three stories attacking him. Davidovich? Also well known. The name of the man who would welcome him in Vilna, Mark Monsky? The woman who had come to his office that day with little Tolchik to tell him about his American cousin? He could no longer even remember her name. He would not, he realized finally, tell Sikorsky anything or mention any names, even those they already knew.

He had the eerie sense that Chankov was backing away, at least for the moment. Chankov had more important things on his mind. For a euphoric second he thought perhaps they all might be glad to see him leave the country. But this was not possible. Chankov had been momentarily worried. He would check his flanks, regroup, and, when he was ready, attack again. Enigma, Pyotr had said. That was their style. Keep them off balance. Once entwined in their clutches, it was not possible to escape. However, the brief comment Sikorsky had made about his wife might be one of those enigmatic signals. He knew how Galina Sikorsky felt about him, but Chankov did not. Not knowing that was careless of Chankov.

Yuri decided to try a bit of enigma himself. Next afternoon, when he was brought to Sikorsky's office, he refused in the politest of terms to add anything to what he had said thus far. He made the speech Baryshin had rehearsed for him. He had no quarrel with the Soviets. All he wanted was to go "home," et cetera. He had not eaten anything for sixty hours. He had developed diarrhea. He felt weak in his joints, was becoming lightheaded, and his own stench, the itching and eruptions in his skin,

bothered him less. No, he said, he knew of no organization. No, not an informal one either. So far as he knew, people were receiving invitations in the mail from relatives to go to live in Israel, as he had, and many were accepting and asking for permission to emigrate. That was all there was to it. It was spontaneous. People heard about it by word of mouth, and through typewritten sheets, handed from person to person. Undoubtedly the KGB had copies of the Zionist *samizdat*. Who wrote them? Where did they get their money? From friends in America, he assumed. How? He had no idea. Where did Jews meet to pass the word? He had no idea. In the street, in their flats, at work, on park benches.

Had he ever heard of Chaim Park? Sikorsky asked. Where was that? Sikorsky led him to the window and pointed. Over there, Sikorsky said with heavy irony, under our noses. Is that effrontery? Had he ever visited the synagogue? Never. He didn't even know where it was. Had he ever been at the gathering of Zionists at the Yubeleinaya monument? Never. He had heard something about this, however. He wondered why the government objected to this little innocuous monument. Sikorsky grew animated. The monument speaks of *Jewish* victims of the Nazis. In Yiddish letters. How could the government permit it? The Kazakhs, the Georgians, the Lithuanians would all be building their own private monuments, each with an inscription in a different language.

"Why not?" Yuri asked. "What harm?" How could this be permitted? It was unthinkable! Didn't the Professor, a man of intelligence, realize the unity of the country was essential? Did he know the government was planning to replace the Yubeleinaya monument soon with a much grander one, dedicated to the "Soviet Citizens" who were murdered by the Nazis? The same people, called by a different name. Wasn't it plain this was much better phrasing? And the inscription would be in Russian. This was Minsk, after all, not Tel Aviv.

Yuri shook his head. "This government must be paranoid," he said. "You will understand why people like me feel like foreigners. Why is my mother referred to as the Unknown Heroine? Everyone knows who she is. But because she's Jewish, she suddenly becomes 'unknown'! The Yubeleinaya monument—also typical! Men like Chankov are paranoid. That's why they form this Mafia. They are the ones who should be sent to a *psikhushka*."

Sikorsky wrote furiously at length in his folder while Yuri sat and watched. He thought he saw Sikorsky nod, as if in agreement. At last he closed the folder. "Doctor, the investigation continues. You are not to leave Minsk. You will sign this protocol, agreeing not to leave. You understand? We will get in touch with you."

Yuri read the document he put before him. The penalties for violating the protocol were prescribed. They were heavy. Unhesitatingly he signed. They were planning to release him from this building. He blessed the day he broke every hospital rule to permit Galina Sikorsky to be present during Stefan's bone marrow test. Chankov had miscalculated more than he knew.

Next morning at eleven o'clock, the rhinoceros came for him. His entire body was crawling; it was as if he had roaches on his arms, his legs, in his groin, and under his armpits. His beard felt caked.

"Come." He followed the guard. A woman clerk was in the small room. She gave him his bundle—his *papyroesi*, watch, wallet, glasses, comb, pen, money, handkerchief. He changed clothes, put on his watch, stuffed everything else back in his pockets. "Where is my passport?" She shrugged. "Retained."

"I must have it."

"It will be delivered. Everything will be put in order."

Yuri decided it did not matter. No license, no passport. He was escorted to the street by a stranger whose face he barely saw. He had been held three days and two hours, had lost nine pounds. Nevertheless, he did not return home. He combed his hair on the street, ran the comb through his whiskers, and purchased a fresh shirt in the department store on Leninsky. Chankov, he knew, would not relent. If he stayed, in twenty-four hours he would have a KGB tail. Probably waiting for him at home right now. Keeping the family's regular watchdog company. If Chankov had his way, he would sit for ten years. No doubt of that. He proceeded to the public washroom in the long distance railroad terminal building, stripped to the waist, washed his hands, face, arms, and armpits, combed himself into respectability, and put on his new shirt. He walked out to purchase a second class ticket to Vilnius on the three o'clock train, bought three magazines and a *Pravda*, in which he buried his face, bought a cheese sandwich and buttermilk, ate slowly in the station restaurant, and when the train arrived, got on.

In Vilnius, where he arrived three hours after he left Minsk, he found the address he was looking for by making repeated inquiries. Most people were able to talk Russian, though a few speaking only Lithuanian could not understand him. On the way he passed a magnificent synagogue closed in by high iron fences. He was tempted to go in, but decided to pass by. He thought, it is mine, built by my people.

When he found the place he sought, he walked around the block twice

and stood across the street for a while, trying to determine if it was being watched. It was one of those gray three-story buildings overlooking the narrow, winding street. Many such structures had already undergone restoration for historical reasons, but this building had not yet been rehabilitated. It was in the old part of town, only a few blocks from Gdeminas Square. These small buildings had neither *dvorniki* nor *dezhurnayii*. At about six P.M. he took a deep breath, entered the building, ran up a single flight of stairs, and knocked at the door.

He heard footsteps. "Yes? Who is there?"

"Karpeyko, from Minsk," he said in a low voice that could be heard only by sharp ears on the other side of the door. "*Shalom.*"

The door opened.

6

CLEO TOOK YURI'S APPLICATION to OVIR and met the charming Petrovna; nothing further happened. Yuri remained missing and the other doctors at the hospital would not give up on her. Who ever heard of wanting to leave one's country? Even under Stalin, when people were unjustly accused, taken away in the middle of the night, sometimes shot, the thought of running away was as remote as flying to another planet. The peasants stayed; the proletariat stayed; intellectuals, scientists, artists all stayed. Did our grandparents have any kind of life? They fought back! They struggled. Only the Jews fled. Old stories that she had heard many times. Stupid stories. Anti-Semites, all of them!

She went to the KGB building on the fourth and fifth days to ask where Yuri was being held, but the people there insisted he had been released, in accordance with the law. She did not believe them. KGB operatives never told the truth about the people they were holding. Still, Yuri had told her he might not return if he were released, that somehow he would get in touch with her. Well, she was waiting.

Yelena was no help, less and less her usual self. She stayed in bed half the day, would not help wash dishes or clean the apartment, spent incredible periods staring out the window at children playing on slides and swings behind the building. She never went out. Once in a while she called Stanya in Moscow to ask about students she knew. Several times she tried to reach Professor Kozhinskaya, but never succeeded. Occasional Moscow calls came for her, but she would hang up as soon as she identified the caller; twice when Cleo answered, a man with a foreign accent who said his name was Hans asked for Yelena, but she refused to speak to him. Yelena was in an almost catatonic state; Cleo was afraid to leave her alone for fear she might do something terrible. When she asked

Yelena questions, her daughter would answer in glum monosyllables, or say, "Don't keep prying so, Mama!"

Tolya Markov came alone to the flat in the evening of the sixth day, greeted Cleo with a kiss, looked carefully into each of the four rooms, nodded to Yelena, and carefully turned up the volume of the two-piano concert on the television so they would be able to hear it in the next building. "I have word from Mischa," he said in a low voice, under the tumult of the television cadenza. How ridiculous, Cleo thought.

"Yes, yes? Is he all right—Mischa?"

"Fine."

"Thank God." She felt the unwelcome tears. "Thank God."

"His visit lasted only three days. He's somewhere out of the city."

"But where?"

"I can't say. You're not to know. I'm not to know. Have you heard anything from OVIR?"

"Not yet. It's much too soon."

"If anyone comes asking for him, you've heard nothing from him. He signed a protocol not to leave the city, but it was too dangerous to remain. He's worried about you now."

"He's worried about *me*? Angh! Yes. Tell him we're fine. Tell me, Tolya, can you help me sell the Zhiguli?"

"Of course," Markov said. "What do you want for it?"

"We paid seven thousand. Can we get that, at least?" He nodded. "We could live on that for two years, if we had to. If they drive me to quit."

Markov said if there was anything she wanted to tell Mischa, she must get in touch with him, Markov, but she must beware of being followed. Mischa had promised to call again but could not say when. Mischa expected—he had reason to expect, he said—that action would be taken promptly on their applications to emigrate, certainly Cleo's and Yelena's. They must be prepared to go. Psychologically. Did Cleo think they would go to Israel or America?

The question made her miserable. "America," she said glumly.

Then she should take English lessons. There was a woman he knew who lived out on Pushkina Prospekt in one of those new high-rise buildings; she taught a small group, people who were planning to emigrate, Jews, of course. She was Baryshin's translator. He gave her the address. "Her name is Hana Manashevich; she and her husband are Refuseniks three years; she teaches English to make ends meet. She used to be an Intourist guide. A charming woman. Go. You'll meet others there. You won't be so isolated; you'll get some preparation for your new life." Cleo

thought she might do it. Perhaps Yelena would come, too. Yelena shrugged. Anything, Cleo thought, to shake her child out of her depression.

Markov left and Cleo turned the television off. The two pianos were driving her crazy!

Two men were now stationed at their building entrance. They worked in three shifts, around the clock, faceless men, offering direct stares and unpleasant smiles to Cleo as she entered or left the building. One of them followed her everywhere. He made no effort to conceal what he was doing. He traveled on the same bus, sometimes holding the door open for her to enter or leave before him. He came to the hospital, skulking through its halls, waiting outside the operating room when she was at work. He ate in the clinical association's cafeteria even though it was supposed to be used only by staff. Sometimes he was replaced by a frozen-faced, thin-lipped, well-dressed young woman who followed the same routine but omitted the unpleasant smile. All of them wore dulled expressions. The other tail stood at the entry and waited endlessly for Yelena, who, until the English lessons started, never left the flat.

They went to Hana Manashevich's for their first English lesson. On the bus, mother and daughter sat in one seat, and opposite them tonight's KGB man and woman sat together, silent. At the Maneshevich entry Yelena and Cleo entered the lift; the KGB couple waited patiently below. "Good evening," Hana said in English, holding out both her hands in greeting. "Tolya Markov has told me about you." Then she added, still in the foreign tongue, "We speak only English here." Soon three others came: a plump young man who was a chemist and a couple in their thirties. All were Jews, all had lost their jobs. All were awaiting emigration permits. They all wanted to go to America.

Cleo soon learned to ignore the KGB people. Let them chase after her if they wanted. They'd learn nothing from her. She and Yelena—and somehow Yuri, too—would get through this terrible time.

Although Markov kept her informed that Yuri was all right, he had no idea where Yuri was. Baryshin alone knew.

One day two unfamiliar men from the KGB came to the hospital to ask her about Yuri. She told them she was convinced he was still being held. They told them no, he had been released. He was wanted for further questioning. He had been told not to leave Minsk. This was very serious. She said she didn't believe them. Everything was done deadpan, as if they were talking about a missing chicken or goose.

Then came the call from OVIR, a woman's voice. "Doctor Karpeyko, Cleo? OVIR speaking. Comrade Dzhervinka here. Please come to the

OVIR office. You've got the permission, and there are certain formalities. Room 104." She was told how much money to bring.

"You have permissions also for my daughter, and my husband?"

The voice of Comrade Dzhervinka was noncommittal. "If you would like to get your visa, please report. Tomorrow will be all right. Between two and four."

On her way to the OVIR office, she passed the state theater. Yuri had told her it had once been the main synagogue. Tonight a sign said they were playing a comedy called *The Danube*. How appropriate, she thought grimly—the river that flows through Vienna, where she'd soon be going.

At the OVIR office they had the approval for her, the interviewer said, although none yet for Yelena. But her application and her daughter's had been submitted together, on the same day, so what was going on? Comrade Dzhervinka was scarcely more than a girl, with a pleasant pink oval face marred only by two small pimples on her chin. She smiled often, revealing good white teeth, and blinked her blue eyes, trying to be cheerful, even helpful. She went to the back office to make inquiry about Yelena's application. When she returned, she reported brightly that Yelena had not been refused. "So you see? It is not bad." It was merely that Yelena's application had not yet been acted upon. Certain technicalities—perhaps in a month or two all would be in order. "So let us talk about your emigration permit, okay? There are certain things you must now do."

Cleo could scarcely hear her, much less understand what she was saying.

". . . necessary to resign from your work. You must bring us your workbook. . . . Now, about your apartment . . . you must call the housing division and ask them to send an expert. . . ."

Cleo thought she must be losing her sanity. "My dear young woman! *Listen* to me. Haven't you understood anything? How can I give up my apartment if my daughter is still there? I have to wait until she gets her permit to emigrate. If we go, we are going together. Don't you see?"

Dzhervinka was determined to be pleasant. "But I have just explained to you that her permit will take at least a month or two longer. I am sure everything will be in order."

"Then I'll have to put off my exit permit for a month or two. I can't go without her."

"Why not?"

"If you don't know, I don't think I can tell you."

There was an abrupt hardening in the OVIR woman. She tried to be

nice to these disgusting people, and all she seemed to get was complaints. She was awfully tired of it. "Doctor, your daughter is twenty-one. I myself am twenty-two. I do this work and earn my living like everyone else. What makes your daughter different? So she's pregnant. She doesn't need a mother. At twenty-one she's a woman. If she is going to remain in your apartment, all you have to do is bring an affidavit from your daughter stating that she is continuing to occupy the family's apartment and will be responsible for the rent. Then you must pay the bank five hundred rubles in order to renounce your Soviet citizenship, and three hundred seventy rubles. . . ."

Cleo wanted to take this pretty girl by the scruff and shake her. Could she confide in this offensive girl that Yelena was taking on morbid suicidal tendencies? Ah, Yurochka, where the devil are you? You're hiding not only from them, but from *me*, too. She stood abruptly, walked out stiffly, and hurried to Markov's flat.

Tolya was at home, but Irina was still at work. She told him what had happened at OVIR. "I must talk to Yuri, I simply must. I don't know what to do. I'm beside myself. Do I dare go to Vienna and take a chance I'll never see Yelena again? How can I leave her here in that condition? You saw yourself, she's a somnambulist in a trance. Tolya, you've got to help me. Please. I must talk with Yuri!"

The arrangements were made when Yuri called Tolya from a public phone ten days later, on the first of March. Yuri had important news. Cleo was to go to the post office at nine tomorrow morning and wait for his call. Cleo had a sleepless night. She would be followed. She might make some terrible mistake. No pills. She must have all her wits. She stared at the ceiling.

"Karpeyko, Cleo!" When her name was called, she rushed to the booth. "Mischa?" She heard his voice. His voice! "Cleo here. How are you, Mischa?" They talked for a moment, reassuring each other by their tones, but not their words, telling in family code how much they had missed each other, worried over each other. Sins were forgiven. Every word had to be careful. "How was your three-day visit to the sanatorium, Mischa?"

"It's not a bad place. The conversation there was interesting. Unusual people. The food could be better, and the beds leave something to be desired, but it's very good for a trim figure. Imagine, in three days I lost four kilos!"

She uttered a small squeal. "*Four,* did you say?" Recovering quickly, "How marvelous! What a spa this must be! You must feel wonderful to be so thin!"

"Is father taking his medicine?"

"Yes. A thoracic surgeon gives it to him."

"Good. I'm glad."

"Listen, Mischa. I went to see our friends, where we applied for those tickets to *The Danube*. You know?"

"Ah? *The Danube*? Oh, yes! I heard you got your ticket."

"You did? But they had only one for me, none for you or Yelena. Can you imagine?"

"They didn't say why?"

"Not really. Something about a technicality. She can have a ticket in a month or two, they say. But you know these box-office people with tickets. How can you trust them? I don't want to go without Yelena! Mischa, what am I to do?"

"Don't worry. Tell me, how is Yelena?"

"Very quiet. I must get her away, Mischa. She needs a vacation."

"Listen, Cleo, whom do you think I ran into yesterday? My cousins. You know, the ones who live so far away?"

"Yes?" She had no idea why this news excited her so, but it did. "Are they nice?"

"Extremely. Now, you must trust me. I'm sure you and Yelena would like to meet them. I'll send my friend—you know, I'll mail him further instructions, when my cousins will be in Minsk. Now, please don't worry. Everything will be all right. You must take your ticket to *The Danube*. You understand? Take it and go. Don't wait. I'm getting tickets for Yelena and me. It's a marvelous show. I'm sure you'll love it. I'll meet you there."

"But you have no ticket!"

"Yes, yes, I have. I'm going. The cousins have arranged tickets for me and Yelena. You understand me?"

"Mischa, I hope you know what you're doing."

"Go."

Either he hung up or the circuit was disconnected.

After the call the KGB man tailing Cleo inquired of the phone supervisor where the call to Karpeyko, Cleo, had originated. The main Moscow post office? He shook his head hopelessly. Moscow was a huge city. But it was something, a lead. At least it should get Chankov off their backs.

ONLY THREE DAYS BEFORE giving Cleo the fateful advice, Yuri himself had been in hiding, hunkered down, terrified each time he heard a door open. When, finally, a nervous and nameless Baryshin agent, after almost two such edgy weeks, had called Mark Monsky's apartment in Vilna, he had told Monsky that "Mischa" was to go to the central post office and telephone from there to the post office in Borisov next day to ask for "Elena Kalmanovich" at exactly one o'clock. The woman would be awaiting the call. She had essential instructions for him.

Yuri placed the call with a clerk. When she called out the name he was using, he stepped to the designated instrument and put the receiver to his ear. The voice was that of a woman he had never heard before. She spoke in a flat monotone. She spoke without interruption for five minutes. She answered his breathless questions calmly as if this were an everyday call.

By the time he left the post office, he had turned quite pale, and his heart was beating irregularly, that old asystolic symptom; he steadied himself, trying to ignore his vertigo. He put his finger to the spot on his neck, and the palpitation stopped suddenly. Still he felt unstable, and it took him time to sort out his impressions.

What he had been told to do was more dangerous than anything he had imagined. He knew of no one who had done it before. It was bad enough to be in hiding. At any moment he expected a heavily overcoated figure with one hand in his pocket to approach him gruffly: "Citizen Karpeyko? Come with me. It is useless to resist!" Uncanny that it hadn't happened days ago. Could it be this easy?

Now if he did what these cousins were asking, his difficulties would only multiply. But his bridges were burned, as the strange woman from Borisov had told him. He had no choice. His cousins, she assured him, would help. He was helpless to resist Baryshin's orders. No, he would do

what Elena Kalmanovich, whoever she was, had told him to do. The Soviet Union was no place for someone in hiding, especially a Jew. *"Zhid,"* those kids had scrawled on his car. Well, they were right.

When he did set out for Moscow on the second day of March, carrying not even a toothbrush, as instructed, he had somehow mastered his fears, or rather suppressed them. This was his normal state, to separate his feelings from the facts. It was important that he act with a clear head. He walked the streets of Vilna again, no doubt for the last time, and looked about for a tail. There was no one. As he walked toward the station, he read, as if for the first time, some of those huge signs in Russian and Lithuanian, signs one saw everywhere, in lights and banners, painted across buildings or bridges; words almost every citizen succeeded in not seeing, messages long since driven out of people's consciousness by boring repetition, slogans which only foreigners now noticed: WORK IS STRENGTH. COMMUNISM IS THE GLORIOUS FUTURE OF MANKIND. HAIL TO THE SOVIET ARMED FORCES. LONG LIVE THE WORKERS OF VILNIUS. Minsk, a Hero City, had the same signs—tired agitprop posted everywhere by bankrupt, corrupted old men, living from fear to fear, even as he was. Over the years fear had become almost a welcome companion. It was a perverse challenge, familiar—life as he knew it. It kept him going.

On the Moscow train he sat in a compartment with two soldiers and their wives. Sitting up, he slept or pretended to sleep most of the time, and read *Novy Mir* occasionally. The trip seemed to take forever.

In Moscow the signs were larger, and he saw more of them. Bigger buildings, bigger nonsense. All so recognizable, yet so comically, perversely dear to him! What a fool he was! From Rizhski Station he walked quickly to the nearest taxi stand and asked the driver to take him to Sheremetyevo Airport.

PART SIX
Arrivals and Departures

1

ON FEBRUARY 28, 1974, two days before Yuri left Vilna for Moscow, two Israelis—Rachel and Gideon—and two Americans—Jenny and Josh—all members of the Singer clan, set forth from Kennedy Airport for the old country.

Not unexpectedly, Martin was unable to make the journey. Although his Soviet visa, reservations, and tickets had come through from Simiro with the others, when the date for departure arrived, he was still having to spend a great deal of time in bed, much of it heavily sedated. Rachel, since she had made all the travel arrangements, promised to take care of canceling for him. She was very firm about taking charge of all matters pertaining to the trip. No, it was no trouble, and no, they needn't bother Myra; *she* would do it. Martin, still fretting about Jenny's going off without him, clucked over her as if he were a Jewish mother. She ought to stay home, he now thought, not for his sake, but for hers. What would she do there?

When she shook her head in that bullheaded way she had, he quickly gave ground. At least she had to promise to be extremely cautious; she was to go see Bill Cole and deliver his letter the moment she arrived in Moscow. If there was any problem, no matter how slight or ridiculous, she should not hesitate to call Bill. He knew his way around there as well as any American. Old Bill, Martin was sure, would go out of his way to be helpful. Martin had called and told him she was coming. But she had to promise.

She promised—okay, okay, she *promised!* She'd go see him. Enough! No, she wouldn't forget to take her just-in-case money, either. Never fear. She'd never take a trip without it. Money never hurt. Wherever they went, Martin gave her fifty crisp one-hundred-dollar bills to stash away, and she had found the safest place in the world for it—in her douche

bag. No use tempting chambermaids, and of course she was afraid to carry five thousand dollars in her purse. The money almost always came in handy. In China Martin had used it to buy some marvelous jade from a "peasant" who just happened to be hoarding it. She'd bought their dining room carpet for the Palm Beach house in Teheran with her just-in-case money. In India they gave it all to fifty beggars. In the Soviet Union last time they had never used a penny of it—they found nothing they wanted and no one to give it to. But this time, who knows? It might be different. And don't forget, Martin reminded her, take toilet paper!

The ungainly task force that took off on Finnair flight 611 on the first leg of the journey—from Kennedy, New York, to Vantaa Airport, Helsinki—appeared, therefore, to be commanded by the two women, who were to sit together in their bulkhead seats in First Class—Jenny at the window and Rachel on the aisle, the latter traveling under her alias, Rachel Singer. While they appeared to be merely two deluxe tourists, they were a study in contrasts. Jenny was bubbling and imperial, words and laughter flowing, a stately, erect, female MacArthur in her long dark sable coat and hood, which a smiling, pretty Finnish flight attendant took and placed on a hanger with respectful fingers, while Jenny gave her the Carol Channing blink several times to signal gratitude. Underneath the sable, she had on a St. Laurent pants suit. She was also wearing heavy eyeshadow, bright red lipstick, and her eyes—one brown, one blue—glistened with Bright-Eye. Her ears glittered with diamond drops which hung from her pierced lobes, while her wrist sported only a severely simple Patek Phillipe watch. In her luggage, she carried nothing more compromising than four pairs of Levi jeans, all cleverly in her own size and prewashed to look used, as Yoshke Schulman had instructed, and in her purse two Seiko watches, all items which she planned to give to Martin's cousins. Yoshke had told her if she said the right words at customs and flashed her dazzling smile, the jeans and watches could pass Soviet scrutiny and later be sold by the Karpeykos in Minsk on the black market to provide them with the money they'd need until they got their exit visas. In all, they could provide the family with enough for almost six months' sustenance in relative comfort.

Rachel, although a small woman by comparison, was relaxed, calm, and quiet. Everything Rachel wore, from the square Joyce shoes to the cheap cloth coat purchased in New York at Korvette's, was excessively American, to go with her passport. Her sinister gray fedora, which she insisted on wearing throughout the eight-day trip, endowed her with a certain irresistible authority. She had had sewn into her luggage by a leather expert recommended to her by the Israeli Security officer in New York,

several documents which she intended to withold from the scrutiny of Soviet customs officials, who, she knew, were the port-of-entry task force of the KGB. She carried Martin Singer's passport and other documents inside her girdle, and in her luggage had extra skirts and blouses that did not fit her.

Gideon, too, was traveling as an American—Gideon Singer of New York. He carried only what he needed—strong nerves, a map and photograph album of Minsk in his brain, and a complete wardrobe for a much older man in his over-the-shoulder carry-on bag. Gideon's mission was twofold: to keep his crazy grandmother from being locked up for the rest of her life, and help her, in whatever ways he could, in her crazy scheme to bring their cousins out—mutually exclusive duties, separated by a line so thin as to be invisible.

Josh, the fourth member of the Singer clan, was traveling as part of Tammy's troupe; he expected to go with Tammy to Kiev and Moscow, but would be leaving the troupe to make a one-day side-trip to Minsk. Josh had brought along his Super 8 with which he expected to take movies of his cousins to show his father; he would also try to get on film young Russians cheering at Tammy's concerts in Kiev and Moscow, as he had been promised they would. He might sell that to a TV network for a news spot. It would be good P.R. for Tammy. Josh, like the others there, appeared to be every inch the tourist.

Tammy, looking like an Economy waif lost in First Class, was recognized instantly by the flight attendants, who clustered about her, chatting and smiling as if she were giving away Arpège.

Her entourage contained sixteen in all, including herself and Josh. The other fourteen—her manager and his wife and the members of her band, technicians, and their women—had come aboard as a group, laughing boisterously and high-strung, most of them in jeans and a variety of shabby coats—lumber jackets, peacoats, threadbare parkas, and bright Scandinavian sweaters; they took up all the seats in First Class not already occupied by Jenny, Rachel, and Gideon, except for one which remained empty, next to Gideon. Nothing was too good for Tammy's troupe.

After ten hours in the air and a stopover in Amsterdam, flight 611 rolled to a standstill at Vantaa Airport, and Jenny led the way shivering down the steps in the dark of a late arctic morning, huddling her sabled path onto the bus. The days were not only short here, she reflected, but wow! Cold as a husky's balls. Jenny's teeth were on edge not only because of the weather; would Gideon's and Rachel's passports get by the immigration people? She was foolish to be concerned. The passports were the work of experts, of whom Gideon was one.

The lobby of the Marki Hotel blessed them with a blast of welcoming, desperately comforting heat. But it was here that Jenny's suspicions began to go into overdrive. The clerk behind the desk counted, looked over his papers several times, and counted again. Then he spoke in a broken English with that peculiarly Finnish lilt that implies puzzlement.

"I have here three *Mister* Singers, on reservation card," he said timidly, as if the American contingent might roll over him en masse.

Jenny turned to Rachel and the old woman looked befuddled. Then, quite suddenly, she blushed.

"My God, Jenny, I never canceled Martin's hotel reservation!"

That blush (what a gift, Jenny recalled later, to be able to do it on command), the fluttering of the hands, the apology uttered with such genuine shame—the old lady must be getting a little soft. It had been all very well to humor her, let her make the arrangements—she wanted so badly to be in charge—but what else might she have fouled up? Christ, to correct an error in travel plans inside the Soviet Union, Kissinger would have to fly over and negotiate! She should never have left it to Rachel. What could be more dangerous than a crafty woman who couldn't keep her facts straight?

Tomorrow, Jenny thought that night after Tammy's concert, as she lay exhausted on the pallet which the hotel insisted on calling her bed. Tomorrow. Moscow. Her eyes, accustomed to the dark, made out the empty bed beside her. Almost out of habit she reached across to it. Wretched, she jumped up, turned on the lamp, reached for the phone, and put a call through.

"New York is on the line."

"Marty, goddamnit!" she wailed across an ocean and a continent. "I just reached over in the dark and you weren't there! I could collapse! Are you okay, Marty? You feeling any better?"

"Sure am."

"Oh, boy, I'm so glad. How I miss you! Tell me, Marty, what the fuck am I doing over here? They ain't even *my* cousins!"

Marty laughed with helplessness. How he'd once begged her not to go! "Beats me. The spirit of holocausts past. The ovens. All that . . . Listen, Jen. Something's happening over there. We may be making some progress. Your friend Yoshke Schulman called me this morning. He's heard from his contact in Minsk by phone. Karpeyko's wife has just received her permission to emigrate. Official. How's that?"

"What about *him?*"

"Not the doctor. Nor the daughter. Not yet. Yoshke's not sure exactly what to make of it."

"His wife? She's not even Jewish. You sure you got the story straight?"

"That's what he said. He says it's odd. Usually the family's treated as a unit. This must be a special case. It could be a good sign. Or, I suppose, the opposite."

"Oy." What was she getting into? "Listen, Marty, I'm getting those goddamn flushes again, and I keep having to go to the john. I'm a little uptight. What should I do?"

Martin laughed again, harder, but sweetly. "Well, c'mon home then, Jen."

She said nothing, and the silence grew. "Ah, see, my sweet? You are so full of it! I can't imagine you uptight. What about? First of all, you're an American citizen, so you're okay—you're okay anywhere. Just remember, you're Somebody. They can't touch you."

"From your mouth to God's ear," she murmured.

"And if worse comes to worst," Martin added, "you've got Bill Cole. So go to Minsk with a free heart, see the poor bastard. Nobody'll bother you. Tell our Doctor Karpeyko we're doing everything humanly possible, okay? We've got permission for his wife now, and we're going to keep the pressure on till we get him. Tell him he's now on every goddamn list anybody gives the Soviets—Kissinger's, Javits's, Jackson's, Ribicoff's, Kennedy's—you know, the whole gang. The Soviets are now thoroughly aware that the United States of America is interested in Yuri Karpeyko. Tell him that. By now Brezhnev must have received a hundred letters from American influentials of one kind or another—I can't count the people I've called. Let our people go! On top of all that, I just spoke to Sam Rose this afternoon again. He's working with a Soviet-American pediatric society—his buddies at Cornell run it—and *they've* agreed to get into the act. They expect to have a few thousand signatures within a few weeks, and *that* ought to shake up the Soviet medical establishment."

"Oh, what the hell, Marty, why not? I may as well go. What would I do with four pairs of jeans and two Seiko watches?" She lowered her voice suddenly, as if she feared being overheard. "There's something funny about Rachel, Marty. She's got something up her sleeve. She's sneaky."

"Ah, Jen, c'mon! She's an old woman, she's Mother's age. Can you picture Mother doing anything rash or sneaky?"

"She's *nothing* like your mother! This woman is an Israeli *sabra*. She scares me a little. Okay, okay, so I'm paranoid. Listen, Marty, you miss me? What're you doing with yourself?"

"Well, for one thing I've been trying to absorb those letters. I never got

a chance to tell you, but at last we know what made Grandpa Moish so sore at Father. After all these years."

"Yeah? What?"

"Oh, I'll tell you when you get home."

"If I ever *get* home!"

"Take a Miltown, Jen; take two. They'll settle you down."

He laughed. Four thousand miles away, but he was *with* her, worrying about her, laughing with her, taking care of her. Such a terrific guy.

"'Night, Marty. I'm not having a wonderful time, but how I wish you were here! Oh, how I wish it!"

In her room, Rachel was examining one last time the extra lining in her purse, the back pockets of two pairs of prewashed blue jeans she had in her valise, the soles of the shoes she intended to wear tomorrow, and the extra passport and papers she would have to carry under her girdle. She carefully compared the Finnish entrance stamp in this passport to the one in her own. They were identical. That little man in New York was a genius! Gideon would need this and the visa tomorrow. It might be a little tricky. She put everything into her purse.

Satisfied with her preparations, but feeling she might be catching a chest cold, she said an early goodnight to Gideon and went off to sleep, while her grandson, with whom she was sharing the room, sat in a chair under a dim lamp and read a murder mystery into the small hours. As Rachel drifted into sleep, her mind drifted to *her* husband, gone now for seven long years. Boris, she prayed, I wouldn't want you to be disappointed in me. Remember that night in Haifa when I *schlepped* you through those heavy seas? And you looked up at me and said, "Can you cook also?" So I'm at it again. Same old business.

2

In the taxi on the way to Vantaa, Gideon said he would take care of the tickets and check-in, so would they both give him their passports, visas, and tickets? Rachel handed hers to him quickly. Jenny, thinking how nice to have *someone* since Marty wasn't here, gave him hers.

When they checked in for their flight to Moscow, the Aeroflot people at Vantaa seemed not to have all their ducks in a row. Gideon and one clerk got into a fierce dispute; Gideon told Jenny it was about seating. Check-in clerks rushed about, made calls; the manifest was rechecked. In the confusion Jenny thought this was not the moment to tell Rachel or Gideon the good news about Cleo's permission. After they boarded, Gideon suddenly remembered he had left his magazine in the terminal and had to rush off the plane and down the steps. He was back again in a short while. Jenny heard Rachel ask Gideon a question in Hebrew. "*Ken,*" he said. Yes. Something.

Half an hour out of Helsinki, the members of the troupe began to move about the plane, changing seats as if they were playing musical chairs; during this gavotte Gideon moved back to talk to Si Goulder, the heavyset, redbearded keyboard man who was traveling with Honey Wright. Jenny watched them with growing interest, almost dismay—she had come to understand that for Gideon, no talk was without a purpose, no contact without a goal. Si and Gideon moved up and down the aisle, keeping to themselves, their talk inaudible. But something on the keyboard man's face registered offense, amazement, excitement—who could tell? They weren't talking about the weather.

When Gideon finally led Goulder back to his seat and to Honey, he turned abruptly, as if the conversation had never taken place, and slid in next to Josh, in the seat Tammy had vacated for a trip to the john. For fifteen minutes the two young men engaged in a quiet talk Jenny would

have given her slightly crooked eyetooth to hear. As Josh listened, he, too, grew animated and intense. After they were through he sat silently for a minute thinking, then rose and marched back up the aisle to where Tammy was now socializing with some of the band members. Without a word of explanation he grasped Tammy's arm and led her off to the front, past Jenny, marching as if his head had been filled with the sound of drums and the blare of trumpets.

It was all Jenny could take. Keeping herself calm—under the circumstances this meant not screaming at the top of her lungs—she unbuckled her seat belt and walked quickly back to where Rachel was perusing a two-day-old copy of the *London Times* with apparent interest. As Jenny sat down in Gideon's empty seat, Rachel looked up from her paper.

"I feel like the woman whose husband is banging every broad on the block," Jenny said. (Not my poor Marty! The thought flashed sickly through her brain—a brief but ridiculous sidetrack.)

Rachel tried to look puzzled.

"Always the last to know," she said impatiently. "Why don't you and I have a nice quiet chat. You start."

Rachel was neither amused nor intimidated by Jenny's sarcasm. "Yes," she said simply, "I was planning to tell you in a few minutes. Please listen carefully." She spoke for ten minutes in a low tone without interruption. At one point Jenny put her hands over both ears.

"I don't want to hear anymore—not another word," Jenny muttered. "You *can't* be serious."

"I am. You must be calm. We need your cooperation."

"But why didn't you *tell* me? What a helluva time to . . . when I can't get out of it! Rachel, I am really outraged. Why didn't you—?"

"Because Gideon thought maybe you wouldn't come."

"Gideon was so right. You bet."

"I don't agree. I don't think you know yourself very well. You *would* have come, Jenny. But it's academic now. You're here."

They sat in silence for the next few minutes. Finally Jenny turned and said in a low voice, "So many things can go wrong. It's such a complicated—"

"For complicated problems you need complicated solutions. Our adversaries are complicated."

"Has it ever been done?"

"I have no idea."

"Listen, Rachel," she said, grasping at straws, "I just talked to Marty last night and he told me that Yuri's wife—Cleo—just got her *permission* to emigrate. Yoshke heard about it only yesterday. So maybe they'll all get

out. Legally. Why don't we have a little patience? Why do we have to—you know—go in like bulls in a china shop? Take all these chances?"

"They'll never let *him* out," Rachel said flatly. "Never. This is what Yoshke hears from Baryshin. And Baryshin is reliable. Now calm yourself, please. We'll be in Moscow in a little while."

Sheremetyevo International Airport was unchanged since last she saw it, the halls, the long walk, the small customs room where the baggage arrived, but there *was* one thing new. Those sour-faced customs and immigration officials were now smiling and pleasant. It was as if some good fairy had sprayed them all with magic dust. The man they drew was friendlier than any had been to her and Marty when they were here before. "Welcome to the Soviet Union," he said. Imagine! Détente, of course, the new era of good feeling. Well, well. Maybe things would be more relaxed. Maybe Rachel's wild scheme had a chance. This customs guy had the body of an athlete, but his sallow complexion reflected the misery of a shut-in Moscow winter. A weightlifter, maybe, Jenny thought. Eyes and hair dark, hands hairy but deft. His competent English was only lightly accented as he advised Rachel and Gideon how to fill out the two currency declarations.

He turned to Jenny and asked her to open one of her bags. As he ran his fingers through the clothing in the bag, Rachel began to fill out Jenny's currency declaration as well as the one for her and Gideon. Absently, Jenny counted out her money and told Rachel how much in currency and travelers' checks she had in her purse, and read off her passport number. Rachel handed Jenny's declaration not to Jenny, but to Gideon, who signed it. Jenny was not sure what was going on, but her attention was divided between the inspector, who had not yet finished fingering her lace underwear like a nervous violinist, and Gideon, who was signing *her* declaration.

"You know pipples in Soviet Union?" the inspector asked as he worked. "You go to visit pipples?" Bland innocence. "No gifts?"

"Nope," Jenny said. "But I'm hoping I get to *meet* some. Just plain folks, know what I mean? My grandmother was born in Vilna."

"Ah, yes, Vilnius," the young man corrected. "So you have relatives khirr?"

She shook her head.

"This is your first visit to Soviet Union?"

"No, no. I've been here once before. I loved it so much I just *hadda* come back, see?" This time she tried to keep the derision out of her voice, but it wasn't easy.

He rummaged meticulously through another of her valises. "So." He regarded her clothing with practiced eye. "You visit for only vun vick?" Jenny felt she might need to urinate standing right there. "No gifts for anyone?"

"You asked me that already."

"So for who all thiz jinns?" He ran his hand over the Levis, still stiff despite the prewash, and regarded Jenny with a detached amusement that infuriated her.

" 'Jinns'? What means 'jinns'?"

"He minns the blue jinns," Gideon said helpfully.

"Oh, they're all mine. My size—see?"

The inspector studied what she was wearing—the sable coat, the snakeskin shoes. "You're wearing jinns? Four pair, all new?"

"They're *not* new. They've all been washed, see? I'm an American, ain't I? I'm not allowed to wear 'jinns'?"

His smile vanished.

"Plizz, I can see your visa, madam?"

She handed it to him.

It was clear he didn't believe a word. Well, tough titty, Weightlifter. I'm from a free country. Belligerence had now replaced terror. "Is against the law to sell jinns here, to make bizness. You understand this, madam? Plizz to kipp in mind."

"I look like I came all the way from New York to Moscow to sell 'jinns'?" Jenny cried, laughing at him. "To make—how did you say— 'bizness'? Oh, Christ!"

Her adversary smiled thinly. "You have books, magazines, ridding materials?" Jenny shook her head. He reached for her purse as if he owned it, took it, opened it. His fingers rummaged through until he came to the Seiko watches, which he removed and held up like dead mice. "This yours? Not gift?"

"I told you, no."

He pointed to her wrist. "You have already votch."

"I've got *three* watches. I always like to know what time it is."

The KGB man—for that was how Jenny now saw him—shrugged. Clumsy Americans. "So okay." He helped her close her valises. What harm could a few pairs of blue jeans or a couple of watches do on the black market? Might make life more tolerable for some Soviet citizen. What was the good of rubles to the average guy, after all? He turned to Gideon's valise and over-the-shoulder bag, rummaging through his stuff as if he were running his fingers through a thick soup. His hand paused as something caught his attention, and he brought out a small rectangular

leather case, no larger than a woman's lipstick. He held it out to Gideon. "Vaht dot?"

"Contact lenses," Gideon said. Jenny had never seen Gideon wear glasses. The inspector opened the leather case, to find two small, shallow, white plastic cylinders, and he began to unscrew the dime-size caps. "Wait!" Gideon cried. "You lose them! Allow me, plizz."

Without objection, the weightlifter handed the case and tiny cylinders back to Gideon, who carefully unscrewed one of the caps. "You see? Lenses. Nothing else." It was a soft lens, in fluid, brown in color; he held it on his fingertip.

"I never see such thing. Vaht is?"

"Put in your eye, instead of wear eyeglasses. You understand?"

The Russian shook his head. "I never see before. You put finger in eye? You don't make yourself blind? How you do it?"

Gideon gave him a short demonstration, gracefully putting the lens into his right eye. The inspector laughed, a child who has discovered something. "You nidding this too see?"

Gideon shrugged. "To ridd."

The inspector admired the camel-hair topcoat in Gideon's over-the-shoulder bag, touched the new suit from Brooks Brothers. But it was when he found a *Playboy* in Gideon's bag that he was truly delighted, flipping the pages to stare at the centerfold playmate for January. He called to another inspector. They leafed through the pages, cares forgotten. Oh, wow, drugstore cowboys like those Jenny used to see at the Bronx pharmacy on Tremont Avenue leafing through *Esquire* to find the Vargas girls. Smiling broadly at Gideon, the guy said, "Is prohibited. I suppose to confiscate." He chuckled. "Americanski vomans," he said with ponderous jocularity. "Spashil." On second thought, he carefully tore out the centerfold. "It's okay? I kipp. Show my vife. For coexistence." Gideon chuckled appreciatively.

Weightlifter turned now to Rachel's two bags. "Open, plizz." Rachel stood, indifferent, eyeing him with what she hoped was American hauteur and contempt. He picked out a bottle of Clairol. "Vaht diss?"

"For my hair," Rachel said. "It keeps me young. Otherwise my hair would be gray, you see? The world would think I'm a *baba*."

"Is American vonity, yes?"

"You could call it that. I *am* vain."

"You say 'baba.' You spik Russian?"

"Few words. *Bolshoi spasiba. Da svidanya. Baba.* Like that." He nodded. American tourists never spoke Russian. A form of arrogance. Those few who did were dangerous.

"Anything to ridd? Books, magazines, newspapers?"

"Nothing. I have a Bible, though. I hope you don't mind. I brought it just in case."

"Let me see." He took the Bible, in Hebrew, flipped the pages, more puzzled than offended, and handed it back. "Only vun?"

Jenny could see that Rachel was under pressure, for she seemed almost angry, and her "American" anger was covering uneasiness. "Yes. Only one."

The Russian noticed her mood, too. Well, too bad. The old woman had evidently not grasped the principle of mutual coexistence. That was the trouble with Americans, they simply did not seem to understand orders from their leaders. Talk about the cult of personality! In America it was every man for himself. They were sick with it. Where was their collective spirit? No wonder their society was doomed.

While he went through Gideon's overcoat pockets, Jenny turned to Rachel. "Don't I have to sign that money declaration?" she asked. Without a word, Rachel handed her the form, and Jenny signed, glancing at the figures Rachel had written. Then she rammed the form into her purse and gave the carbon to Rachel. What she had seen, what Rachel had written, was "Martin and Jennifer Singer." The number of family members in her party had been written as "2." The woman had balls of steel.

The inspector asked to see Rachel's and Gideon's visas, and glanced at the two currency declarations cursorily. So *much* money rich Americans had! Of course, the poor ones stayed home and starved. "Look on this, my fran', you sign both declarations," he said to Gideon good-naturedly.

"Oh, I'm sorry," Gideon said. "Should I cross out my signature on this one?"

But Weightlifter laughed for the first time. "*Nyet*, is not necessary," he said. "Is the amounts important! Must kipp records. You kipp copy. You bring back when you livving—is very important." He took the carbon copy of each, put them on a shelf under a table. "Whenever you change dohlar to ruble, must give this form."

Gideon had a good-natured contretemps with the man to persuade him to let Gideon carry his over-the-shoulder bag with him. "No, no, they vill come," Weightlifter kept repeating. "They vill take baggazh." But Gideon prevailed. The guy had his centerfold; he was entitled to a minor courtesy in return. The women's luggage could be taken to the taxi by a porter but he liked to carry his own.

"*Gott sei dank!*" Jenny mumbled as they emerged at last from the small, dark customs room into the enormous main waiting room, where people

hurried to and fro, all of them carrying their own luggage. Others stood patiently studying huge ever-flipping schedules, while still others stood in lines before counters and bank windows.

Standing in the crowd, close by the door through which they had emerged, poised almost as if ready to take flight, she saw him. The steel-gray mustache and beard of his photos were gone. His hair, also steel gray, was flying wildly as if he had just come in from a storm. Was it he? The way he stood he reminded her of Marty's father! Except for the windblown hair, he could have stepped out of that painting in Marty's office. Rachel approached the man easily, as if she had known him for years. "I'm Rachel," she said in English. "Go with my grandson, please." She embraced Yuri perfunctorily and muttered again, "Go quickly. Please don't ask questions."

Gideon leaned to ask Yuri something in Russian, and Yuri pointed. The two men walked away quickly in that direction.

"Oh, Jesus," Jenny breathed. "I don't believe it." She gazed after them as they hurried through the crowd. "Where are they going?"

Rachel spoke very low. "To the men's lavatory."

"Gee, I could stand a ladies' room myself. I'm nervous as a cat."

"Come," Rachel said. "Let's go."

Because of the attendant they said nothing to each other. Rachel went into a booth and removed the passport and visa she had been carrying under her girdle for this moment. Jenny went into a booth of her own. Oh, for that nice roll of soft toilet paper in her luggage! As they started back, Jenny trailed Martin's Israeli cousin, who kept walking at the same slow pace, turning only to mutter, "Let's find Intourist."

Jenny's mind could not adjust. The guy was here, just as Rachel had said. Why had he shaved his beard off? If only she could summon Marty by some magic telepathy. "Oh, Marty, what I've got myself into! Sure enough, who shows up at the Moscow Airport but Yuri Karpeyko! I was nervous enough in Helsinki, but what's going on now, Marty, it's scaring the shit out of me! If only you were here!"

3

THE YOUNG UNIFORMED WOMAN at the Intourist counter, small, pretty, light-skinned and dark-haired, with broad Slavic features, gave them more of the old détente. Her name, she said, was Liuba. She asked for their visas. Rachel handed her three visas. *Three?* Yes. Yuri's photograph was on one. Beardless. And with dark hair. The special effects processor she'd sent Rachel to. The print Yuri had sent to New York. Beard shaved and hair darkened in a lab. A marvelous job. Jenny could barely hand the girl her own visa; it took her last ounce of concentration.

"We've just arrived from Helsinki," Rachel was saying. "Her husband and my grandson have gone to the lavatory." Jenny's mind floundered. Yes, yes. *Her* husband—oh, boy! "They'll be here in just a moment," Rachel continued in her direct, commanding way. That threatening *hat* of hers. "You will make the arrangements for our luggage, Liuba, my dear?"

Dear Liuba nodded, deadpan. "Everything will be in order. I will show you to the taxi."

"Can you tell us which hotel we'll be in?" Rachel asked.

"You will go to Intourist Hotel. This has a favorable position, overlooking Red Square," Liuba recited. "You will be just beside the Kremlin, only a few meters from Lenin's tomb. I'm sure you will like."

Speaking by rote, Liuba's attention was on the counter before her. She examined a list of names intently, comparing it with a second list. "There are *two* men in your party, you say?"

"My husband and I were at the Rossiya last time," Jenny said. "Very nice."

Her effort at diversion. She was amazed at her own temerity for even trying.

"Here they come now," Rachel said.

In the eight minutes they were gone, Yuri's appearance had been vastly altered. He was wearing, from the appearance of the lapels and trouser bottoms, which was all Jenny could see of his suit, what seemed like a tan Brooks Brothers outfit. His overcoat was camel's-hair, and he wore a gray lambswool, American-made, Russian-style hat and maroon scarf tied in an ascot. His shoes were brown alligators. Yankee Doodle. He was not quite as elegant as Martin, of course, but who was? Tall, aquiline features, with sunken Lincolnesque cheeks, he looked rather *gahtish,* she thought. And handsome.

"We're staying at the Intourist Hotel this time, Marty," Jenny called, playing her part like Lynn Fontanne. Yuri nodded. Liuba, undeflected, now unsmiling, studied the papers before her with knitted brow, blinking in a nervous twitch.

"May I see your currency declarations, please?"

Jenny produced hers, Rachel hers. Across the counter, Jenny could now see clearly that hers bore not only her signature but a second signature that Gideon had written. It said, "M. Singer" in the same square hand as the visa signature she had just seen.

"You will be kind to wait just here a moment," Liuba said, under some strain. Jenny stared at Rachel accusingly, but Rachel, ignoring her, smiled reassuringly at Liuba. "Whatever you say, my dear."

After Liuba left, no one spoke until Rachel whispered something in Yuri's ear. He nodded dutifully as if he were a schoolboy learning a routine. At last Liuba returned half smiling, as if to herself.

"Everything is in order," she said with evident relief. "Aeroflot had also another Singer listed to be going to Kiev." She turned to Gideon, who smiled encouragingly. "But so here you are!"

Gideon said, laughing, "Yes, we are here. Oh, is jost like in America. We get also screwed up the records." From somewhere deep in his memory he called on Dulech's Americanisms from time to time. Jenny was on the verge of saying there *was* a Singer going on to Kiev. Poor Joshie, what they might put *him* through! But she thought better of it. Josh was a big boy now. If he could handle the Mexicans, he could manage anyone.

"Yes, screwed up!" Liuba cried with a delighted squeal. She must make a point of adding this American idiom to her collection.

Except for Jenny's comment about the hotel, Jenny and Yuri had both remained silent throughout, side-glancing at each other and doing their best to look as much like husband and wife as any two people could on short notice, fascinated, alarmed by the mere fact of each other's presence.

She liked his looks. Damnit, he had the face of a man who *could* tell tall tales to children. There was mischief in those features—even if it was cleverly camouflaged by sheer terror at the moment.

Yuri took her arm boldly. "Come, Zhenny," he said in a commanding tone, determined to be observed in his miscast role, although he could not entirely subdue his sense of the absurd. "Vee go at last to khotel. Vee nidd good rest. Maybe liddle slipp." Jenny noticed small beads of sweat above his upper lip. That accent! But Liuba hadn't thought it significant. Americans spoke in so many accents. Jenny liked the neat cleft chin on his gentle face, the intense, concerned expression emanating from brilliantly blue eyes—the eyes of Martin. She saw in him not only bits of Marty but also of all those goddamn television doctors rolled into one— the selfless, dedicated man. Bolsheviks couldn't *stand* the type. No wonder they were hounding him. There I go, she thought. Seeing what I want to see. She did what she could to quiet her own agitation, linked her arm in his, and glided off with him after Liuba, Gideon, and Rachel. Whatever *his* fears, she thought, he was giving a marvelous performance of an eager but tired tourist from New York.

In the cold wind, four typically suspicious Americans watched their bags being loaded into the trunk of a black Volga by an elderly baggage man—counting their pieces despite the repeated urging of Liuba to get into the car, everything would be in order.

"Nine pieces. Okay," Jenny announced.

"Okay, vee go," Yuri echoed, and held the car door for her.

She noticed his fingers—long and thin but, by God, with nails bitten to the quick—that, too, was Marty. It was eerie. Rachel bit hers, too. Incredible! Gideon gave the baggage man three dollars, which he slipped into his pocket like a thieving prestidigitator, and slithered off. Liuba watched while they settled in. "Enjoy," she said, calling upon previously mastered Americanisms. "Have a nice stay. The driver will carry you to hotel. If you wish to take tour tomorrow, ask at Intourist office. You will find in hotel lobby. You are entitled by deluxe rate to six hours touring with guide each day. You must make the arrangement before ten o'clock. So everything will be in order. I promise you, this will be last screwing up." She laughed at her own boldness. "Is all right?"

They nodded and she raised a friendly arm as their taxi sped them off.

"You were very good," Rachel said in a low voice to Jenny as they settled back in the taxi.

"Oh, it was nothin', m'dear," Jenny sang. She was suddenly giggling. Hysterics, she thought, I'm getting hysterical. Get a grip on yourself, kiddo! She stopped as abruptly as she had begun.

As they raced along, Rachel reached into her bag and handed some papers to Yuri. "Here, Martin, you may as well carry your own passport. They'll want it at the hotel. And your hotel coupons. You have your visa now, yes? And Jenny has your currency declaration. Give it to him, Jenny. After all, he's the man of the family, yes?"

"Let me *see* that passport," Jenny muttered. There it was. "Martin Singer" it said—with Marty's birthdate, but the photograph was Yuri—clean-shaven, his hair dark, not gray. "Color of Hair—Brown." "Color of Eyes—Brown." Well, if those eyes were brown, she was Queen Elizabeth.

She gave him back his passport along with hers and "their" declaration. "Keep them all in one safe place, Martin," Rachel continued, as though scolding gently. "I know how careless you can be. But you'll need them handy all the time in this country."

Wide-eyed, Yuri studied the photo in his new passport. He examined the "Martin Singer" written across the photograph in the square, strong, easy-to-copy Roman script. He would need to practice writing his new name that way. The camel hair felt wonderfully soft. He could scarcely wait to see himself in a mirror. If Cleo could see him now! He must reach her as soon as he could. As they drove through the broad boulevards of Moscow, for one fleeting moment he grew heady. So easy! So easy! Could they get away with it? Impossible. It would be only a matter of time until they'd be caught. He'd be tried, he thought gloomily—perhaps one of those spectacle trials—and sent to sit in the tundra for ten years, maybe longer. Still, what choice did he have? He was an outlaw now, a fugitive. No, no turning back.

"Vos very nice flight," he ventured. "You don't agree, Zhenny?"

"Yeah, Marty," Jenny said drily, following his eye signal toward their driver and going along with the absurdity. "Terrific. That was a fantastic hard candy they served for lunch, wasn't it? Didn't you think so, Rachel? Little on the sweet side. Jesus, but I'm hungry! Last time we were here, remember how famished I got? Constantly? Well, it's started, can you believe it? Here less than an hour and I'm starving already!"

"Vee find something to eat at khotel," Yuri said, more to the chauffeur than to Jenny.

Yuri, now silent during the ride into town, studied with unabashed curiosity his fellow passengers, gazing from one unfamiliar face to the other, speculating, trying to convince himself, among other things, of their consanguinity. Did they resemble him? The young man and the old woman, the two Israelis, were related to him, that was clear. There was a faint

family similarity. Yet he felt somehow closer to Jenny, to whom he was not related by blood at all.

More important was to try to discern the character of the three persons into whose hands he had put himself. Little enough hard evidence, but he had his hunches. Instinctively he placed a measure of confidence in Gideon. So thoroughly prepared! And tough. Was he a Security man in his own country? All this American clothing, the visa, the passport, the currency declaration—the hair dye and contact lenses, about which he had spoken in the lavatory, although there had not yet been time to employ either.

Still, however professional, cool, ruthless, and ingenious he might be, how could one man be a match for the KGB on its own territory? How could he cope with all the agents planted at every point—hotel doormen, Intourist guides, hotel chambermaids, drivers, the people at the currency exchanges? It could never work. Coolly he weighed what might be the best moment for him to separate himself from his well-meaning relatives and from this thoroughly harebrained endeavor, for their sake as much as for his. He'd play it by ear, look for the right moment; he could always take off.

In the weatherbeaten grandmother, the one they called Rachel, for all her gentleness and her *baba*ness, he sensed a steel that only experiences of a special kind could have hardened. Gentler, sweeter than Father to the naked eye, he'd wager she was every bit as tough as Father. She and her grandson sat back peering out the window, utterly relaxed. Their coolness amazed and soothed him.

Jenny was something different. Merely married to his relative—Martin —and no blood kin of his, here she was, eight thousand kilometers from home; that said something about her. Cheerfully noisy when she spoke, flamboyant, she was a fire of a woman, terribly Jewish and terribly American. In his present state, he rather welcomed her Jewishness. In some ways she also reminded him of Cleo—that energy and determination. Was there substance to this Amazon? He'd find out soon enough, but he'd better be wary. He was feeling thoroughly demoralized, impotent, as only someone who was once among the mighty can be—stripped of power, privilege, prestige. He trusted neither his strength nor his judgment, however self-confident he might pretend to be. Still, he *had* to pretend.

They were approaching Red Square and their hotel.

"Zhenny," he said, with all the authority he could muster, "I manage all formalities at khotel for your convenience."

She touched his hand. "Sure, Marty." And the moment passed.

They had turned into Gorky Street; the taxi nosed into the curb. Yuri

and Gideon got out and walked together, Jenny at Yuri's side, while Rachel followed with the luggage handler.

"Vee going vid you to New York?" Yuri whispered to Gideon. "My vife and daughter also?"

"Not New York," Gideon said, out of the side of his mouth. "We go first to Vienna. From there is only short flight to Tel Aviv. So you come home! Your true home!"

Yuri did not want to seem ungracious, much less troublesome, but he felt it necessary to speak now, before misunderstandings could occur. "You know, my vife, she is not Jew. She dunt vahnt. I think she prefer America." Gideon was silent. This was not the time or place.

Yuri glared at the squat, uniformed doorman, who gave them each a quick, appraising eye as they entered and walked through the long hall toward the lobby. At the long reception desk a friendly woman, who Yuri suspected must be Jewish, spoke to Gideon. "Welcome to the Intourist," she said in English, smiling. She, too, recognized Jewish faces, but she would never dare expose her Jewishness openly. Only her excessive friendliness spoke of it. "I can have please your passports and hotel coupons?"

As Yuri handed her the papers, fumbling for the proper hotel coupon, he asked Jenny to sign the register for them. She did, amazed to see that her hand had developed a tremor. Yuri glanced apprehensively about the busy lobby. No one for him. He must keep this heavy hat on; his hair was supposed to be brown.

While he found nothing astonishing in the Intourist lobby, Yuri was unprepared for the two deluxe double suites on the twelfth floor to which they were shown by the baggage man. Gideon and Rachel were to occupy one and Jenny and Yuri the other immediately across the hall. As the porter set up Jenny's luggage, Yuri peered from the living room window down at the Kremlin below. A perfect view of Red Square, St. Basil's and the endless queue of tourists before the red marble tomb, waiting to see all that was left of Vladimir Ilyich Ulyanov, the deity of Communism. The scene spread before them like a tourist's postcard. A grand piano and a gold-plated electric samovar surrounded by a dozen glasses in gold-plated holders dominated the living room. The common wisdom was that each ceiling or telephone had its own hidden mini-recorder.

Together Yuri and Jenny went up the narrow stairs of their suite to the bedroom. Each of the two large beds was covered by a quilted comforter. Except for public toilets, Yuri had never, not even in the elegant sanatoria, seen a bathroom the size of the one that adjoined the bedroom. For foreigners, of course—like the Beryozka shops. What surprised him was

that Jenny found nothing remarkable in all this, nor did she seem to share his misgivings about the awkward living arrangements. These could not be altered, he knew, merely to avoid embarrassment; changes reported by the chambermaids could arouse suspicions, and they were not in a position to take the smallest of risks. The sharp young Israeli across the hall would surely point this out if he had to. No chance, for example, that Jenny and Rachel could share one suite and he and Gideon the other. He glanced about the living room—a love seat he could never stretch out on, three chairs, and a piano stool. Well, he could sleep sitting up all night. He had to assume surveillance of foreigners was absolute. They were two adults, and the situation was dangerous. If Jenny could put up with him, why be churlish about the arrangement? He'd try to be considerate. They'd manage somehow.

She led him across the hall to Rachel's suite. Her voice was suddenly unnatural, in a high register. Rachel and Gideon protested. She was going out? But where? Why? They'd just arrived! She was impatient. They were not to worry. She wouldn't be long. She had to go to the embassy. An important letter from Martin to someone there. But for her to go off by herself might raise questions, Gideon said sternly. He would go along. No, she was going alone. "You don't have rubles," Gideon said.

"Never mind. I'll use dollars." She was impatient to get out. "Don't worry about me, I'll be okay. Why don't you go change your money and have lunch?" The delayed jitters had struck her with full force. She clutched the sable about her and sallied through the door, marching past the key woman and into an elevator so fast she almost ran into a passenger getting off. Her companions, standing at the door of the suite, stared down the hall after her, mystified, as the elevator closed on her.

4

FOR THE FIRST MOMENT since she had arrived in Moscow, Jenny breathed easily as the empty lift went down. She felt like uttering a primal scream. What a relief to be free of those Israeli cuckoos. Downstairs she walked quickly, nervously, through the lobby to one of the four women at the Intourist center. "Will you kindly write out for me the address of the United States Embassy, miss," she said in her most imperial voice. The mousy young woman scribbled the Tchaikovsky Street address on a small card and fairly flipped it at her.

Outside the hotel Jenny handed a taxi driver the card, got in, and they sped off.

In Bill Cole's ninth-floor office, the secretary took her coat. "The staff meeting's just breaking up. Mr. Cole should be here any minute. He's been expecting you. Would you like some coffee?"

"Would I? You bet! We just got in from Helsinki, and Aeroflot gave us each a hard candy for lunch. One to a customer."

"How awful!" Would Mrs. Singer care for a bit of fresh caviar with her coffee? *Would* she? Oh, boy! What a blessed place the embassy was! Then why was she still shivering?

Bill Cole had not changed much since the last time she'd seen him at one of those dinners for Overseers and their wives in Cambridge—or was it at the Harvard Club in New York? Must be three, four years ago. He seemed more subdued—his wife Connie had died less than a year ago— but essentially he was the same old boy—tall, reassuring, reminding her of Gary Cooper, with that shy smile and deep-down self-confidence behind the diffident air. And God knows, if you mentioned his name to anyone in the Foreign Service, you got a real hallelujah.

Bill was a stickler for the amenities—there had to be a few moments to sympathize over Martin's illness and to express relief that it was nothing

serious. In turn, she felt obliged to say how much she missed dear Connie, and how the world seemed somehow less without her (she was having trouble conjuring up the faintest image of Connie—was she the little fat bossy one?). Bill responded with a quiver of his upper lip. Poor guy. Finally, just when she felt they might get down to cases, he invited her to lunch with him in his private apartment, within the embassy compound. He led the way down the elevator, past the marine receptionist, down a narrow flight of stairs, through the courtyard, littered with cars parked helter-skelter, the trucks and crates, past a rundown children's playground, and up into his flat. A Russian maid served drinks first. They started with vodkas straight up. Wonderful invention. Her jitters began to fade. The embassy. A safe house.

"Martin made me promise if I had any problems I would lean on you, Bill. And boy, have I got problems!" she said after the second vodka.

Bill held up his large hand to stop her. With a tight little smile, he scrawled "Problems after lunch in the courtyard" on his napkin and held it up to her, then put the napkin in his pocket. She nodded. They lunched on clichés and old times, while Jenny looked around the room trying to find the bug Bill was afraid of. When they were through, Bill took his dark overcoat and black caracul Russian-style hat from the closet, and she retrieved her fur coat. "I'll be back in a bit, Mrs. Gibbons," he said to his secretary over the phone before they left.

Like two prisoners they stalked through the littered courtyard, Jenny's sable hood pulled tightly around her ears; she flung her arms and hugged herself. Bill kept his hands stoically in his pockets. Their breath frosted as they spoke. She told him first about Yuri, what she knew of his trouble with the authorities in Minsk. She told him what little she knew about Cleo and Yelena, about Rachel and the unexpected appearance in New York of Rachel's grandson. She told him then what Rachel had revealed to her during the flight this morning from Helsinki.

"See, Bill, all I ever intended to do—" and she told him of her American do-gooder intentions, which had begun to seem a bit puerile. "I thought it might be a bit hairy, but what the hell, it was an adventure. It was worth a trip, y'know?

"But these Israelis! Oh, boy!" She told him what had happened at Sheremetyevo. "That passport! I really couldn't believe my eyes. He's supposed to be *Marty!* And they've faked two others for his wife and daughter. I mean, this is not for me. I didn't come for *that*. They're planning to take him *out* with that passport. As *my* husband! And they had these even trickier plans for his wife and daughter. But the wife, you see, now has her permission to go. So their plans have to be changed."

Bill Cole nodded into the cold, his breath frosting in white puffs. " 'Miss Sugar,' I think is what Marty would say they are."

"*Meshugga* is right," Jenny cried, feeling some release. Oh, boy, Bill Cole talking Yiddish! Marty'd love that.

Bill Cole shook his head. "Well, now that you've told me this rather sordid and fascinating tale, charming Jenny, what is it exactly you'd like me to do?"

"Tell me, Billy, is there any chance this crazy scheme of theirs can work?"

He shook his head. "Pretty doubtful." Cole took her half-frozen hand. "Still, Jenny, dear girl, it's not that bad. Let's give it a little thought, shall we?"

"I'd like to get out of this country. Today!"

Bill shrugged. "The Soviets are quite rigid in their treatment of western tourists," he continued as they marched between two enormous crates. "Once your travel arrangements have been made, it takes a bloody act of the Politburo to change them. When you do put in for a change, it raises suspicious hackles. And if the embassy does anything to help you, that'll make it worse. They won't let you go; it's as simple as that. They could figure you're on an intelligence mission, start tailing you."

"Damnit, I'm not gonna sleep in the same room with a perfect stranger! No way! I still have my stupid American prejudices, such as they are, and I'm not playing cops and robbers either, not for *nobody*, if you'll pardon my grammar. Certainly not in *this* country. Marty would be furious if he knew what was going on. And how's this guy gonna spend six days with us without being missed? What about his work? Doesn't he have patients? Sick people in hospitals? What about his family—his wife, his daughter? Where are *they*?"

The corners of Bill's fine mouth drooped drolly. There was a challenging glint in his eye, beyond the tight little smile. "I wouldn't sell your Israelis short, my dear."

Bill wore his cool smile. "Let me take you back to your hotel so you can start right in being a bona fide tourist, Jenny. Visit GUM. That should be a postman's holiday for Martin Singer's wife. Take the Kremlin tour. Another treat."

His slightly ironic tone irritated her; she couldn't help feeling victimized and sorry for herself, but Bill patted her sabled back avuncularly. "Listen here, Jenny, you're a big girl. Make up your mind to get through the next six days. I have no doubt you will. Don't try to change plans. Your visa's your visa's your visa. Every hour's accounted for on it. See the sights. If you've seen 'em before, see 'em again. For all we know, your

cousins may get away with their little plot. I don't know of anyone who has, but maybe they have the skills for it. I've had some dealings with those Israeli folks. They're all right, in a hairy kind of way. Of course, *your* cousins happen to be doing something Jerusalem itself wouldn't stand for. If Mr. Avigur or Mrs. Meir in Jerusalem ever finds out what they're up to, it'll be their hides. And if the Soviets get them, well . . ." he shrugged expressively.

"But if *you* get picked up, that's quite a different matter."

"Yeah? Suppose we *are* arrested. What's the worst?"

"The worst? For you? If you want my semi-educated opinion, based on what's been happening around here lately, they'd scare you a little and then they'd release you—after a bit of a hassle. A short bit."

"How short? Five years?"

"No, no. A week at most. Maybe less. Détente's going strong, and like the car people, the Soviets are trying harder, y'see."

"And our cousins?"

Bill drew down the corners of his large mouth. "Depends. If the Politburo decided to make political hay, seven years. Maybe more."

"In Siberia? God!"

"More likely in a prison."

"Jesus! You take seven years pretty lightly, Billy."

"My dear girl, what can I do? I have other duties. These are Israelis, not Americans. Your Russian cousin would come off worst. They'd throw the book at him. These cousins of yours are not children. They know the risks far better than I."

"Boy, what balls!"

Bill Cole closed his eyes. He'd never heard her speak this way at Overseers' dinners. Well, some women were worse than men.

"Be your natural self, Jenny. Be natural."

He ushered her toward one of the embassy's black Chevys. "Our driver is Russian," he said. "We'll talk about sights to see." Once through the embassy tunnel and past the Russian guard their driver raced toward the hotel. Bill Cole recommended a visit to the All-Union Exhibition of Economic Achievement—"more fun than a World's Fair."

The car turned into Gorky Street. Curious pedestrians watched the huge Chevy speed by. "Remember, now, if you have any problems, feel free to call me—any time. You get me? Just tell whoever's hassling you you have to talk to me. If I'm not at the embassy, Mrs. Gibbons will know where to find me. Here's my private number." He handed her a card, which she tossed hastily into her bag. They had arrived at the hotel and walked together toward the entrance.

"What about our Israeli cousins, Billy? If we get caught, isn't there *anything* you can do to help them?"

"I can't promise. I'll do my best to think of them as United States citizens. For Martin's sake. In memory of Mr. Justice Singer, at whose feet I sat in law school. They do have American passports, after all, and I'm scarcely expected to know every peccadillo of everyone's, am I?"

"Billy, you're terrific. Marty said you'd be." She held onto his hand like a child as they reached the Intourist entrance.

"I'd invite you to my place for dinner," Bill Cole was saying, "but it wouldn't be much fun without Connie. Life's gone a bit stale, you know, without her. Anyhow, any visitors of mine are followed, and that wouldn't do under the circumstances, would it?" Sniff, sniff. "By the way, would you like tickets to the Moiseyev tomorrow night? I hear they're as scarce as hens' teeth. And that's a nice, safe, touristy thing to do."

"How great! Can you get four?"

"Four it'll be. I wish I could go with you, but I have nightly duties, listening to two men who make boring, technical speeches at me that I've heard many times before. I'll have the tickets delivered to your room. Or better still, I'll bring them around myself."

"Super. Room twelve-sixteen. Thanks for everything, Billy. You're a great bucker-upper."

He waved her thanks aside impatiently. "Play the string out, Jenny, and while you're doing it, may as well have a good time."

She blinked at him in her special, kidding way. Batting her eyes comically had worked all her life. The bitter cold was beginning to get to her. And now it had begun to snow lightly again. The doorman inside pushed the door open for her.

She found Yuri with Gideon and Rachel in their deluxe suite (all paid for by Martin, she couldn't help ruminating with sudden irritation). They'd had lunch in one of the hotel dining rooms and were only now completing their unpacking. She stood watching them for a few moments, arms akimbo.

"Jenny, you are such fonny lady," Gideon called cheerfully. "Sit a minute. Why you stand like that? Why you watch us? We not going to itt you." His stately cousin reminded Gideon of those "adventurous" Americans he had seen at Sharm—so eager to see it all, to touch adventure and the Jewish Cause—but at the slightest unfamiliar noise, crying in alarm, "What was that?" They "saw the Sinai" and, slightly terrified, hurried home to their plush houses in Cleveland, Chicago, or New York to brag to their neighbors. He decided he'd better turn on the television and turn

up the sound, so they might talk beneath it. A military band was playing heavy marches.

"So who you have seen at the embassy?" Gideon asked in a low voice. He was busy systematically cutting up Yuri's old clothing into tiny strips with a small scissors, and walking in and out of the WC to flush them away; he'd spend half the evening patiently finishing that job.

"Marty and I have a friend there. And I learned something from him, too. You know you could get seven years for this? And what about him?" She pointed at Yuri. "I hate to think."

Rachel said, "So we have to be careful."

Jenny moaned.

"For me, mecks no difference," Yuri said. "I am already—khow you say —an escaper. Refugee from KGB."

"Whattaya mean?"

"He is—how you say in America? 'On the lam'," Gideon explained.

"He's *what*? Oh, boy! Did you guys know that?" They regarded her as if she were a puzzle. "You did, you *did!* But how?"

"Jenny, my dirr cousin," Gideon said, still in that low, below-the-music, surreptitious voice, "we got pipple in Minsk know everything. So they telling Yoshke Schulman, and Yoshke is telling me." Jenny was crushed. Even Yoshke hadn't leveled with *her*.

Gideon did his best to soothe her ravaged ego. "We're trying to do a *mitzvah*, Jenny, no? So for a *mitzvah*, you take a chance."

"Please! I know a *mitzvah* when I see one. A *mitzvah* is when you give to UJA or the Red Cross."

Rachel spoke placatingly. "We're all involved now, Jenny. Nothing we can do about it."

"Why does he have to stay with *us*?" She turned quickly to Yuri. "No offense, you understand. But why can't he just go back wherever he was hiding and meet us at the airport when we're ready to go?"

Gideon shook his head at her simplicity. "He's much safer wid us, Jenny. Is part of plan. They never look for him wid us. And we hov reservation for him—first in Moscow, in Vilna, in Minsk. At hotel, on airline. *Martin* Singer *must* be here, in Soviet Union. You see?"

"Boy, what I would give to be included out!" Jenny sighed.

Rachel beamed her biggest UJA smile at Jenny. "So you'll manage, never fear. There's more to you, Jenny, than meets the eye."

5

RACHEL HAD ARRANGED WITH INTOURIST to take them on the city tour tomorrow and the Kremlin tour the following day. Their evenings were
free. Yuri, she said, had to dye his hair today and tonight he could accus-
tom himself to the contact lenses. They really looked these passports over
when you left. As for tomorrow night, the Moiseyev was performing, but
no tickets were to be had. Rachel's matter-of-factness calmed Jenny somewhat.

"Well, *I* happen to be getting us four tickets, kiddies, courtesy of the
U.S. Embassy. By God, if we're supposed to be tourists, let's at least be
tourists first class."

"Ah," Yuri said under the sound of the military band, his eyes flashing
with the pleasure of recognition, "good connections! *Blat*. So is same
everyverre." Jenny responded with her wide-lipped Peter Pan smile of triumph that beamed "Oh, the cleverness of me!" Such perfect teeth, Yuri
observed, except for the one eyetooth. Poor Cleo, how she would have
loved seeing the Moiseyev. Well, tomorrow he must talk with her. If, as
the Israelis had just told him, she now had her permission to go, he could
not delay. His moves had to be both quick and cautious. Things were
moving more swiftly than he had dreamed possible. He was beginning to
believe he just might, *might* be leaving the country with his relatives after
all. Their departure date: six days from today. Two days in Moscow, two
in Vilna, and two in Minsk. If only he could see Cleo in Minsk! But impossible. So much to say, what to do if plans failed—but no, too risky.
He'd have to depend on go-betweens.

This young Gideon, during their short walk after lunch through Red
Square and into GUM and back, had filled his head with their bold
scheme, their contingency plans, their fall-back positions. One thing made
him feel a bit more hopeful—he was not in the hands of amateurs.

Gideon and Rachel had told him in detail their plans for Yelena; they now had to get word to her, to prepare her. Baryshin, who would be his natural go-between, had warned against calling him.

He'd have to call Markov now and arrange to talk directly to Cleo by phone, whatever the risk. He told Gideon that he had to leave the hotel to place a call from the post office, not far down Gorky Street. Gideon decided to go along. The two women were to stay in the room, he said, to keep an eye on the luggage in both suites. Any maid could be an agent. "Okay, Rachel?" She nodded. "Jenny?"

"Yeah, okay," Jenny said sullenly.

It was clear that now they were here, the commander of this expedition was neither Rachel nor Jenny. They were all in the hands of Gideon Aron, working at his hated hobby.

Fortunately, Yuri's call went right through; Markov was at home. They arranged that Yuri would call Cleo tomorrow at nine. She'd be at the main post office in Minsk. Yes, these days she was being followed. It would be risky, but they had to talk. She said so too. Had Yuri heard that her application had been approved? Yes? Good. Nine tomorrow, then. Yuri and Gideon walked briskly back to the hotel.

Nobody had said anything about their sleeping arrangements, and Jenny pushed the matter out of her head. It wasn't important. Sufficient unto the hour. She unpacked; they went to the bar on the lobby floor for drinks, four tourists, and from there returned to their suites. By the time Yuri had finished bathing and shaving—razor courtesy of Gideon—and dyeing his hair with the Clairol, it was time for dinner. The dark hair made him look ten years younger and rather dashing.

In the next room, visible from where they sat in the public dining room, a private party was in progress, thirty-odd Russians, men in dark suits, women with elaborate wide skirts, some full length. A strolling five-man band in that room was playing what Jenny assumed to be typically Russian dance music, and red-faced excited couples, some young and others middle-aged, were dancing frantically, faster and faster.

No waiter came to take any orders, so they watched. "Is Jewish vedding," Yuri said, finally.

"You're kidding!" Jenny said.

"No, no. True."

As if to prove the point, the orchestra began to play what was unmistakably a hora, and the wedding guests quickly formed a circle. There in a private room just off the main dining room of the Intourist Hotel the hora was being danced. "Is 'Hava Nagila'!" Yuri said triumphantly. Those **seminars had taught him** *something!*

"So how come?" Jenny asked. "I thought all this Jewish stuff was *nyet-nyet.*"

"In Moscow is possible," Yuri said. "In Minsk, not. Is not so clear policy."

Rachel smiled at the dancers, evidently not experienced at this kind of dance, tripping over each other as they whirled, excited and red-faced, in the ever-widening circle.

Jenny found the mood of revelry contagious. "Hey, Marty," she cooed to Yuri abruptly, "let's get it on, okay? Let's get in that circle." She started to pull Yuri to his feet, but Gideon's hand was on her wrist, steel talons pulling her back to her seat.

"What you doing, Jenny? You crazy? Is *private* potty."

Jenny sat back and watched as the music tempo grew faster, and dancers whirled at top speed. "Geezuss!" Jenny whispered, "It's like bein' back at Mountaintop in Beverly Hills, ain't it, Rachel?" Rachel nodded with a strained smile.

"Which one's the bride?" Jenny cast an appraising glance from face to face. Yuri pointed, as a shy girl came close to the door separating the two rooms. Jenny cried, "*Mazel tov,* darling, *mazel tov!*" and waved. The bride smiled to the young man beside her, a handsome curly-haired blond with bright green eyes and a laughing countenance, and pointed to their table. "*Mazel tov!*" Jenny called to him, and the young man bowed. "That's all the way from America, kid," she said to the others at her table. "Why *don't* we dance? C'mon! What could be a more touristy thing to do, Gideon, for God's sake? Dance with your grandmother!"

The orchestra had slipped into an American dance tune, and Yuri stood up and led the way, pulling Jenny after him. They danced on the restaurant dance floor to the same music as the wedding guests in the other room. Other diners, all foreigners, did the same. Rachel danced with her grandson, and to Jenny she looked happy. Gideon's eyes kept darting around the room. In Moscow, yet! Jenny thought. Two Israelis, grandmother and grandson, in each other's arms—that was nice. A Russian dancing with an American. Also nice. A little war was on, but you'd never guess it in this room.

The music slowed and softened and she and Yuri were all but standing still to it; for the first time Jenny became acutely conscious of the man holding her in his arms. Yuri, like Martin, was much taller than she. That was a plus. Small men like Adelsheim or Yoshke Schulman had no appeal for her. He exuded Marty's kindness, too; it fairly oozed out of him. No klutz as a dancer, either. She became aware that he was pressing her toward him, a sudden, unexpected closeness. She could feel his fingers

on her back, and she was sure he was aware of her—her fragrance (the "Y" toilet water after a bath always made her feel fresh) and the sensation of her—as acutely as she was aware of him. Well, why not? They were dancing, weren't they? What harm? He was Marty's cousin, after all. Might as well get something, whatever it was, out of this far-out rescue mission.

As they danced, she saw the somber nonparticipant in the other room, a man standing in a corner, stiff and tall. Not a guest, not a waiter, he was dressed neatly in an ordinary gray suit, watching the wedding guests intently, a visitor to a zoo; his gaze shifted from one to another of the dancers. She nudged Yuri and indicated the guy with her chin, and Yuri nodded. No surprise to him. Around the wedding dancers went, while the uninvited guest, monitoring everything, made certain that the wedding became neither too Jewish nor anti-Soviet. Fat chance, Jenny thought. Well, to hell with him! The music wasn't good, but she swayed with it. She felt ridiculously safe.

She'd better have something to drink. Gin straight up. They did get their drinks eventually; the waiter finally came around more than an hour after they had sat down. By that time the wedding party was fragmenting amid shouts, confessions, tears, kisses, laughter. The Intourist Hotel tonight, she thought, could be the Essex House or the King David Hotel.

Yuri watched in amazement as she put the gin away like a man. Gideon had a vodka, which he chased with beer, and Rachel settled for a glass of tea. Yuri waited until after dinner and ordered a sweet liqueur—just like Marty, Jenny thought. Wasn't it odd? "Ah," Jenny said, "I really love the deluxe service in this proletarian paradise. Dinner in three hours flat. By the time it's over, I'm starving again!"

The four of them went for a walk after dinner. A few drunks careened through the slushy streets, but otherwise people were orderly, and it seemed safer to Jenny than New York. Walking gave them a chance to chat, and Rachel and Gideon were able to lapse into Russian to go over with Yuri for the third time their plans for his and Yelena's departure, now that they knew Cleo had her permission. They switched to English occasionally to bring Jenny into the fold. Rachel told Yuri about the family letters. Jenny added detail to detail, recalling each "family" peculiarity. Wasn't it odd how eye cataracts ran in the family? Martin's father had them, and Moishe's mother. "My father also," Yuri said.

"And mine," Rachel said. "Yuri, have you always bitten your nails? Look at them! To the quick! And look at mine!"

"Marty does that!" Jenny said. "Isn't that weird? Five thousand miles

apart, never met, and yet . . . You like sweet liqueurs, too. I noticed at the restaurant. You bet! So does Marty!"

They began to notice other family resemblances—how much Martin, before he grew his whiskers, resembled Gideon; Yuri was physically so much like Jacob Singer, it was scary. Rachel agreed. Same gaunt figure, same lean face, same cleft chin. "Only vun difference," Yuri ventured. "He vos big zhudge, I am big criminal!" Jenny was the only one who thought that was funny.

Back at the hotel, a wizened maid was just leaving Gideon's and Rachel's suite. Gideon quickly examined his bags and Rachel's. "This one, she open," he announced. "See here?" He showed them how one of the threads he had left for telltale had been broken. Inside the bags, the closets, the drawers, everything had been neatly restored. The maids were experts. Jenny dashed across the hall to look at her things. Nothing was disturbed, but one of the four pairs of blue jeans, which she had hung in the wardrobe, had slipped to the floor. Well, probably slid off the hanger. Gideon laughed. She was naïve. Jenny, on the other hand, didn't believe him. Israelis! They were all paranoid! However, Gideon seemed not unduly alarmed. "Is only standard procedure. Not special against os. They do all the time. They being careful. So we be careful also."

Jenny squinted at him, blinking her Channing blink, you clever devil —making fun of him—but Gideon ignored her.

"Well, we do lenses now," Gideon murmured. He set about teaching Yuri to insert them. Slow work; Yuri found the things uncomfortable. But when they were in, his irises were certainly brown. He practiced inserting and removing them until his eyes were quite bloodshot. Gideon put the lenses back into their cylinders carefully, explaining to Yuri how to care for them. Solemnly he handed Yuri the tiny case and a bottle of saline solution. "When we go to airport, you must be wearing." He went to his bureau and brought pajamas, a fresh shirt, socks, and underwear, all of which he handed to Yuri.

"Well," he said, "better we get some rest, eh? Sightseeing tomorrow." He held his hand out to Yuri. "Sleep well."

Jenny kissed Rachel, and as she started back to their suite, she took Yuri's hand. No harm in making like husband and wife, in case the key lady was watching. Once in their suite, she let him go.

Almost as if they had agreed to the procedure, Jenny went first to the bathroom to change into her nightclothes. Since her gown was much too sheer, she put on her sweeping white-and-yellow Arabian-style hostess gown with its great *keffiyah*-like hood flipped back. When she was ready

to go to bed, Yuri had still not come up from the living room below. She called down softly, "You can use the bathroom now."

He came to the foot of the narrow stairs and peered up at her. "I writing letter. You go now slipp. For you vos long day. I use later."

"Okay." Tentatively.

She tried to sleep, but something prevented her. Well, how could she expect to? Her mind rotated her worries like a carousel of slides: This cops and robbers game was not her dish. Having to share a room with a total stranger, for one thing. Well, she was no kid, and after all, the guy was a doctor. Joshie out there in Kiev somewhere. Marty sick at home. H.P. and B. struggling along without her. Was Heller paying proper attention to the Demonde people? Nettie out there getting banged by that jock from Haifa.

To whom could he be writing down there? Wasn't it dangerous to send letters? Didn't they open mail?

She got up and took a Miltown, and after a bit she fell into a fitful sleep. She dreamed a great deal of nonsense but couldn't remember any of it as she lay awake; she had trouble deciding where she was in the darkened room, peering through blackness toward the other bed. Empty. Ah, yes. Yuri. Downstairs. She put on her hostess gown and stumbled barefoot down the winding steps. He was curled up like a pretzel, miserably uncomfortable on the small love seat, the only thing in the room larger than a chair. His eyes were open wide, glistening like a cat's.

"You'll never sleep on that thing," she said in a stage whisper. "Come on up. There's a perfectly good bed upstairs."

"For sure?"

"Of course. You won't embarrass me. Come on."

"Okay. Khirr is not possible. So I come."

She returned to bed still groggy from the Miltown, and quickly dozed again; this time when she awoke, there he was, covers up to his chin, eyes wide. Would anyone at Golden Oaks, the Harvard Club, or Harmonie believe this?

"Get your letter-writing finished?" she asked, and he bolted up, as if he'd been shocked out of a sound sleep. What had *he* been thinking about?

"Yes."

"Who'd you write to?"

He leaned across the open space between them and whispered: "Cleo." Ah! He pulled back to his own bed.

"You having trouble sleeping?"

"Yes."

"Let me get you something. Stay right where you are." She sprang from bed, her eyes accustomed to the dark now, went to the bathroom and brought him a Miltown and a glass of water. Moscow water, she thought. The trots. Wouldn't *that* be all I'd need? Oh, boy!

"Vaht dis?" he took the pill suspiciously.

"A tranquilizer, that's all. Take it. Can't hurt, I promise."

Yuri grinned. She was giving *him* medical advice. Meprobamate, probably. Americans! He sat up and took the pill. Anything to kill his chilling, concentrated night thoughts.

After morning coffee in the room, she and Yuri set out for the post office, a short walk from the hotel. The camel-hair coat was a bit dandyish, but the Russian-style hat, she thought, saved him. She thought he looked positively spiffy in his new dark hair, his new brown eyes, and the Dior tie. He took her sabled arm protectively; they made a rather smashing couple, she thought. As they neared the post office, he said, "I go now alone. Khirr I can not be foreigner, or be sinn vid foreigner. You understand?"

"But your clothes!"

"In Moscow many Russians verring American clothes—actors, singers, diplomats, big athletes. You vill valk now across stritt, look in vindows. Venn I come out, vee go bock to khotel."

In his consciously authoritative way, Yuri jogged up the steps of the post office, gave his name to the clerk as Solyonov, Mischa, and placed a call to Karpeyko, Cleo at the main post office in Minsk. Yes, an appointment call. Would it take long? No? Yes, she would be there. She was waiting. The call came through in three minutes. It was the first time they had spoken since the morning he had left for the KGB building. "Mischa?" Her cheery voice, so familiar, a dear and treasured voice but with a new tremor; concern for him. "Cleo here. How are you, Mischa? How was your visit to the sanatorium, Mischa?"

In improvised code she told him she had her emigration visa. She alone, not Yelena. Bastards, but of course he had already heard. Oh, he knew the game. Let Cleo go but keep Yelena. Smoke him out. Well, now he had allies. From overseas. "Listen, Cleo, whom do you think I ran into yesterday? My cousins. You know, the ones who live so far away?"

"Yes?" He could hear her excitement. "Are they nice?"

"Extremely. Now you must trust me. . . ."

So, Comrade Chankov, both sides can play.

He told her to go, to go at once to *The Danube*. He was very precise about that. He indicated that he would be joining her. His confidence was deliberately exaggerated. At least *she* could leave without risk, and

that brought him a measure of comfort. He was responsible for her, above all. He and Yelena would take their chances with Jenny and the Israelis and their slippery scheme. He told her he was mailing Markov instructions for Yelena. After the call, he bought a stamp and dropped the letter to Markov into the box.

Ten minutes after he left the post office, a Security organ *sotrudnik* alerted by a Chankov operative in Minsk was questioning the clerk in Moscow who had placed Yuri's call, trying to get her to remember something—anything—about the man who had placed the call to Minsk. The order slip had his name—Mischa Solyonov—but by then fifteen other calls had been placed by a variety of other persons to a variety of other places, and she could not for the life of her recall any of the characteristics of any of the callers with precision, much less the particular person who had called Minsk. The *sotrudnik* regarded her with disgust. Well, he had the name—Solyonov, Mischa—whatever that was worth.

As these inquiries were being made, Yuri Karpeyko, once again Martin Singer, American tourist, was setting out on the city tour with his wife and relatives in an Intourist limousine from the Intourist Hotel, with Sofia, a black-haired, stately woman guide. It was the same tour Jenny and Martin had taken in seventy-one. Little had changed. They took a one-station ride in the subway, appreciated both of the beautifully tiled subway stations, drove through Moscow State University, saw Luzhniki Stadium, sped to the All-Union Exhibition of Economic Achievements, where they visited three of the pavilions—Aviation, Space, and Electronics—went through three museums, and took a look at Lenin's remains. It was an exhausting, unrewarding day, but a day consumed. Sofia, a university graduate in English, was a determined, pleasant young woman who did her job with studied thoroughness, telling them many more cheerful facts than any of them cared to know. Occasionally she would ask questions, but their responses were perfunctory. Jenny noted that Sofia's English was flawless, her pronunciation British. At one point Sofia turned to Gideon. "You speak with such a peculiar accent," she said. "May I ahsk, in what section of the United States do you live?"

"New York," Gideon said. "Ten years ago I come there from Israel." He shrugged expressively, "Because I could not stand. My grandmother also," jutting his chin towards Rachel. "Is terrible country. We don't like."

Miss Intourist Sofia agreed solemnly. "So I've heard. Why do people still want to go there? We have a few Soviet citizens who have this mad idea. Have you heard of them? When everything is so marvelous here! I cahn't understand this! To live in America must be difficult enough, but Israel must be simply ghastly!"

"You said it a mouthful," Gideon said with Israeli spareness, calling on a couple of Dulech's phrases. "Is the pits!" Jenny marveled at him. The American Academy of Dramatic Arts couldn't have turned out a more finished performer.

When they got back to their suite, Jenny went upstairs to shower, and dressed for the ballet in the same crimson crepe de chine gown she'd worn for Tammy's Helsinki concert. Yuri found a radiance in her, an absurdity under the circumstances, but nevertheless *there,* and he was glad enough to have anything to divert him. The scheme in which he was involved was too much for a man in his middle years. He hadn't done anything remotely like it since the war.

Late in the afternoon Bill Cole came by to deliver the Moiseyev tickets. In exchange, Jenny gave him a hug and a big red kiss. "You look ravishing, my dear," Bill said, recovering from the unexpected onslaught.

She motioned toward Yuri and with a grin spoke upward to the mike they all said must be in the ceiling. "Bill! You remember Marty, don't you?" She gave Bill one of her broadly exaggerated winks, twisting her mouth in a parody of Nathan Detroit. The two men exchanged muted greetings, both feeling foolish.

"How was the city tour?" Bill asked in his shy way.

"Splendid!" Jenny said. She held her nose. "*Ooser.*"

"Excellent!" echoed Yuri.

Bill reached to the inside pocket of his overcoat for the tickets. "Best seats in the house. Wouldn't surprise me if you find yourself sitting next to Suslov or Gromyko." He wished them a pleasant evening; they'd surely enjoy the Moiseyev. Indecisively he shook hands with Yuri, regarding him with curious, uneasy eyes from a slightly greater height, and backed out of the room, as if afraid to let either of them out of his sight.

Soon the Israelis were knocking, hungry wolves, ready to go. They decided to try the National Hotel next door.

Waiting for the waiter wasn't as painful because there were a few things still to talk about: what about the jeans, the watches? What was to be done with them? They spoke in low tones.

"You vish give avay?" Yuri said. "So I khov idea. Vee give to Baryshin in Minsk. Vy not? He know khow to sell jinns and votches."

He was thinking of the strained faces at Baryshin's seminars, the desperate laughter. The money those jeans and watches could bring on the black market would be a prize for two or three families. Yuri felt a small surge of new power, as if the money were his. Could money do this? It had something in common with the power of healing, which he knew so well.

"Is too big chance," Gideon said flatly.

"No, no," Jenny said. "They could use the money. Josh will be joining us in Minsk. Why couldn't *he* go see this guy Baryshin and give him the stuff? Yoshke says Americans are always dropping in on Baryshin with things like that."

"Up to *now*," Gideon said sourly. The Israelis were clearly unwilling to expose themselves to *anyone*—except Intourist guides.

Yuri took up Jenny's urging. "Is no risk. Be very usefool also."

"See? Yoshke says the hardest damn thing they have to do is get money in. We're just gonna have to take the gamble, Gideon! You're such a big man for *mitzvahs!*"

"Jenny, Jenny, you making me to laugh! *You* gamble, but what chance *you* take? We get caught, and your husband will call friend Kissinger or Bill Cole, and is okay. For *you!* But for us, so who should we call? Who should Rachel call? No, I can't allow."

"Oh, boy! You got me into this, kiddo. Not a by-your-leave or a pretty please! Who the hell elected you to *allow?*"

Rachel spoke good-naturedly, pouring oil to quiet the waters. "So we'll see. If we find a *safe* way, we can give the stuff to Baryshin. If not, not. Okay?" The voice of reason. The waiter finally arrived, and the subject was dropped.

Jenny was tired of the Chicken Kiev, but it was the only dish she trusted, so she ordered it again. The too-salty gray caviar was no better than the Intourist's. On her last trip, she told her companions, she'd lost seven pounds in six days. Well, so it would be good for her.

The restaurant service was so slow they did not reach the theater until intermission. The fiery folk music was not Jenny's favorite dish, but she was stirred by the urgency of the acrobatic, beautifully costumed dancers. When the lights dimmed, she could have been sitting beside Martin in her season seat at Lincoln Center, lost in the brilliance of the production, the great athletic leaps and pulsing drive of this flawless, talented company. They had seats front and center, as Bill had promised, and the audience was as enthusiastic as the performers, emitting spontaneous hoarse cries of delight, with thunderous and excessive midperformance applause and shouts of "bravo," that, to Jenny, reflected some unseen pressure finding an escape valve.

Yuri, sitting in the dark, found his own pleasure in the dancers. For a moment his danger receded in that darkened theater. The performance was more stunning than anything he and Cleo had ever seen in Minsk. If only she could be here beside him now! Oh, how glad he was that she **was soon to be on her way to Vienna! It amazed him that in his present**

state these dances of the Revolution could still stir him; what reason did he have to feel this surge of feeling for the triumph of the workers? Yet he had all he could do to keep from cheering with the others, not only at the great, almost superhuman leaps and feats of the gymnastic dance, but at the tumultuous cause they celebrated. It *was* a great, a tremendous idea. But what had come of it? He thought of the dekulakization, of the 1937 purges, of the 1953 Doctors' Plot and the millions upon millions of terrible cruelties visited upon the innocent in the name of this vibrant idea. Yet the music pulsed in *his* heart; he knew this *was* his land. These *were* his people. It would never be the same for the Karpeykos anywhere else in the world.

They left the theater after the last curtain call, and waited in line for a taxi at the stand. Back at the hotel, Yuri's thoughts shifted to his call to Cleo. That bastard, Chankov—letting Cleo go, keeping Yelena as bait. They were simply waiting for him to present himself at Oktyabr'skaya Street. Split the family, set the trap, catch the prey. All quite scientific, fuck their mothers.

Before getting into bed he took one of his Inderals for the palpitations and tried to monitor his thoughts, but they were not controllable. His mind ticked from one problem to another. How was Father managing? Cleo had said Shtainberg, "the thoracic surgeon," was supplying him with morphine, but he wondered what the old man was doing for company, for life. Father, for all his reclusiveness, needed a *few* people. Try as he might, he was not able to dismiss Father.

He tried to lie quiet, not to disturb Jenny. At a certain moment, to his great relief, the palpitations stopped as suddenly as they had come. They spent the second night as they had the first, each overconsiderate of the other, tiptoeing to the WC to keep from embarrassing the other, trying not to look across at each other, in that strange intimacy of sleeping a meter apart but otherwise each alone. Except for their regular breathing when either of them dozed off, no other sound was heard in the dark room.

6

The Aeroflot flight to Vilnius—Jenny and the Israelis could never think of it as anything but Vilna—took fifty minutes. Again they were greeted by the invariable Intourist guide with the controlled smile, who led them to their taxi, which took them to their hotel. Although classified as deluxe, the Vilnius Hotel was not in a class with Moscow's Intourist; while each couple had a living room and bedroom, they were little more than dark cubicles, and the furniture was tacky. This sitting room had two chairs with upholstered seats and maple arms, and a maple table; the plumbing pipes were exposed, and the bathroom itself was a Rube Goldberg contraption, with a sunken sump pit in the floor. Trolleys clanged by their windows. Jenny worried about bugs. While they had separate beds, the quarters were closer than Jenny found comfortable. Somehow they'd have to get through the next two days without bumping each other in the night.

They took the city tour on the first day. Veronica, their curly-headed blond guide, gave the prescribed political plug, assured them of the tremendous love and loyalty Lithuanians had for the Soviet Union. They drove about Vilnius's ancient university, visited the city's old quarters with narrow, winding streets, houses which were being renovated—the very neighborhood where Mark Monsky lived—inspected the cathedral and other churches—"Yes, of course this church is used. We have many operating churches in Vilnius"—and museums. Rachel responded to most of the guide's speeches with a hacking cough, which seemed to be growing worse. Jenny was bored out of her skull. Next day in Kaunas, to which they drove in a taxi over the long open stretches of a new highway, past farms and towns, they visited the Devil Museum and more churches, and viewed the undistinguished ruins of forts erected centuries

ago. The person most interested in these sights was Veronica. When they had returned to their hotel, and Veronica and her chatter had left them, Jenny said she'd like to go for a short walk, although Rachel complained of fatigue. Jenny said idly, "You know, if I were really on a tour, what I'd love to do? Visit a family here. Just an everyday family. Would you believe it, Yuri, two trips here and I've never been inside a Soviet home? Isn't that ridiculous?"

"I take you, Zhenny," Yuri said gallantly, but he looked to the others to provide sanity.

Gideon blew up. "Are you crazy? This would be the stupidest thing to do!"

Rachel was appalled at Jenny's inability to understand their precariousness. "They hate foreigners to visit Soviet citizens, Jenny. It will cause questions. You can't do it." Yuri nodded reluctantly. The Israelis had taken him off the hook.

"Well, can't we do something? Go to a movie? I'm going bonkers. I'm *not* gonna simply sit in that little room staring at the walls."

"Take her to a Beryozka," Gideon said. "Special shop, Jenny, for foreigners. Very touristic thing to do. You will like." He was beginning to talk to her as if she were a child.

Rachel was exhausted and wanted to get back to the hotel. Yuri guided Jenny to the Beryozka shop—only a few weeks ago Mark Monsky had pointed the place out to him—a small, anonymous, unmarked shop whose display windows were blanked by white curtains so that the interior could not be seen from the street. Once inside Jenny was delighted by shelves packed with everything she had not seen since arriving in the Soviet Union—cans of fruit juices, French pâtés, high-grade caviars, Swiss chocolates, and shelf upon shelf of foreign liquors, none of it available to ordinary citizens. "My God, they've got Beefeater!" she cried. "My life is saved!" They bought two fifths of the gin and several cans of tomato juice, orange juice, and Schweppes tonic. Yuri exhibited his U.S. passport and their money declaration, and the woman clerk took Jenny's dollars and made change. Feeling an inordinate sense of accomplishment with her acquisitions, Jenny marched with Yuri back toward the hotel at a victory pace.

"You know something, Yuri? My mother was born somewhere in this town. I wonder where."

"In Jevish kvorter, dot for sure. Khirr." He gestured toward the small buildings they were passing along either side of the narrow street. They were not far from Mark Monsky's. "Is zhost khirr, verre vee valking."

"Yeah?" She glanced about. Some of the buildings had central court-yards. Hi, Mama. Here I am. "My mother's sister was still living here when the Nazis came. She simply disappeared. We never heard a word."

"Yes? My mother they hanged. I saw kher there. In skvair. You vill see exact place venn vee come to Minsk."

"Oh, God! How awful! How come *you* escaped? How old were you?"

"Venn Nazis come to Minsk? Thirteen. Khow I escape is long story."

"Tell me."

Slowly he began. He did not tell her everything, certainly not his darkest secret, but as they walked, he contrived with his limited English to make her see the forests in which he had lived like a wild creature. He told her about the murder of Andrei Khess, and how first Cleo, and then Pyotr, had saved him. His broken English made the scenes somehow more vivid to her.

As he continued, she listened carefully. As they walked, she pulled her hood off and let it drop back on her neck. She bent her head toward him and cupped her half-frozen ear so as not to miss a word. She was growing accustomed to the accent. She asked him questions, and as he talked on, she found herself becoming involved as she had never expected to. She was beginning to have feelings for this man; feelings too private to expose. She wondered how much she would tell Marty.

Back at the hotel, the room was icy cold. Gideon was brooding blackly in two heavy sweaters. Rachel, her cold much worse, was bleakly blaming herself for miscalculating about Jenny. The perfect American tourist, gull-ible American number one, as her son had called her, she was not. They could not allow her to jeopardize them with her foolhardiness. Rachel and Gideon were both tight-lipped, suppressing something, when they started down to dinner in the hotel restaurant on the street floor. Jenny snatched up one of her bottles of Beefeater and followed them into the small lift. Something seemed to be wrong with the heat. The entire hotel was chilly, and Jenny was glad to be wearing her sable.

As they reached the freezing restaurant from the cold lobby, an elderly male attendant reached wordlessly for their coats. Gideon, Yuri, and Rachel took theirs off and handed them to him, although Rachel kept her floppy hat. "I think I'll keep mine," Jenny said politely. "I'm chilly. Why doesn't someone turn the heat up?"

She scarcely could have expected the old man's reaction. He began to jabber in Lithuanian or Russian, whichever it was, and reached for the collar of her coat as if it were his and he were going to remove it by force. "He says you must give it to him," Rachel said, in a low voice now seeth-

ing with anger. Jenny's proclivity for making scenes! "Government rules, he says. Give it to him."

"I'm damned if I will!" Even to herself Jenny sounded like a spoiled child, but damnit, she was cold.

Rachel, having given up her coat, turned to her, white-faced. "Give it to him. Or go upstairs. Must you always make a scene? Always be the center of attention?"

Yuri put his arm around Jenny's shoulder. "You must give it, Zhenny. Is rules." His voice, unlike Rachel's, was solicitous.

"I'll be goddamned," she muttered, sweeping the coat from her shoulders. "What a country! Rachel, you've already got a terrible cold. This is crazy. If you get pneumonia, we'll sue the goddamn Politburo." The old attendant took the sable coat and jabbed it onto a hook like a piece of meat.

Gideon said mildly, making an effort to speak with restraint, as they walked toward the table, "Americans really like their comfort, eh?"

He infuriated Jenny. His air of general disapproval bugged her. "You know, you're a pretty fresh kid! You think we're all softies, right? Well, Marty and I have a place in Maine where it's *goddamn* cold. A lot worse than this. But I'm just not about to be told by some fucking hatcheck man what I can wear. It really turns me off, and that's how I was brought up, buster, okay?"

"You so excited!" Gideon said mildly.

"You bet!"

She turned to Rachel to give *her* a piece of her mind, too, but Rachel looked a bit green around the gills to Jenny, so she thought better of it. She noticed the older woman *had* begun to cough more deeply and with worrisome regularity; she was more than simply tired. She *was* ill, Jenny decided. Her own mood was black. She felt suddenly surrounded by antagonists. Her own family, yet! Who *were* these Israelis to be telling her where to go, whom she could see, how she was to behave, what she was to do with *her* jeans, *her* gifts? If Marty were here, he'd know how to handle them.

She never had a chance to voice her complaint. Rachel was speaking, but her voice had a new quality. Gone the schmaltzy UJA speaker, the loving grandmother, the carefree sailor. Between coughs her words came out hard, metallic.

"Jenny, are you a child? You understand we are not playing games? When you call attention to us in *any way*, you put us in terrible danger!"

"Listen, kiddo, I didn't ask for this. I came over here to cheer up my

cousins. I brought some jeans and watches. That was *it*. But before I knew it, you guys—Jesus!"

Rachel, her suppressed anger increasingly evident, continued, "At my age what makes you think I would travel ten thousand miles to deliver a pair of blue jeans? To tell Yuri he should keep his chin up? That we're pulling strings with Brezhnev? Do you think I'm senile?"

"I think you're a *meshugginer!* That's what I think. You and your grandson both."

Yuri, who had been listening with fascination to the sudden clash, turned to Gideon: "Vaht minns *meshugginer?*"

Jenny slapped her forehead. "Oh, Yuri! Some Jew *you* turned out to be!" By now she was sore at everyone.

Gideon twirled his forefinger toward his temple. "Means lunatic. Is Yiddish word." Turning to Jenny, he said, "So while you out buying gin, you had also visitor. You see? When we come to rooms, we find chambermaid in your room. She say she cleaning bath, but she look to us strange. So only before you coming back, arrives a man to ask us question. He want to know, where are you? When you coming back? He say *he* come back. So after that, I'm looking through your room myself. Just to see what is. You know you leave in enema bag something? You see?" He reached into his pocket and pulled out the just-in-case yellow envelope with her fifty one-hundred-dollar bills. "If I can find, maid also can find. That for sure."

"Jesus! The maid went into my douche bag? *You* looked in my douche bag? Is nothing sacred?"

"Not in Soviet Union."

"Boy oh boy! What a place! That's my just-in-case fund. Marty and I always bring that—just in case."

"In case what?"

"Oh, if I see something I like. Impulses. Don't you ever have impulses, Gideon? Who knows? It's always handy."

"So why you don't declare?"

"I just never thought of it. In all that hassle in customs. After what Rachel told me on the plane I was in shock."

"He say he come back ten o'clock. He wish to talk with you. So you will explain to him."

"Okay, okay! Let 'im come!"

"We must have for him answer. Not 'just-in-case.' 'Just-in-case' is no good. Is no crime to bring money in Soviet Union. But is crime to make false declaration. We not taking chance. No time for fooling around. One question lead to others."

The waiter had come to their table and brought them menus in Russian and Lithuanian. Jenny asked for a glass and ice so she could use her Beefeater. The others ordered beers.

"You mind most be clear." Gideon shook his head in disapproval. "Not fill with alcohol."

"Hey, you really are a fresh kid!"

"I'm not kid. Listen here. Rachel and I, we could go to prison ten years —*we*, not you. I'm coming here to look after *her!*" He indicated Rachel, who, though drawn and strained, looked at him with adoration. "The woman I love best in world, okay? Also, t'ink about *him*." He jutted his chin toward Yuri. "So why you put us all in danger? Careless, reckless. So please! No more 'fresh kid.' Okay?"

She was subdued. "Okay, okay."

"So for what is so moch money?"

"For emergencies. In case I see something I want to buy. Or someone I want to give it to. Or I decide to take a side trip to Yalta. Marty and I always carry it—and I *always* hide it in my douche bag. Someplace where nobody's likely to look. People steal everywhere you go."

Gideon was disgusted. "Money so important to you? Can do anything?"

"You trying to make me feel like two cents?" Jenny was feeling suddenly misunderstood and sorry for herself. "What'd I do? Brought a few extra bucks because—because—"

"Money will do anything!" Gideon finished her sentence with deadpan severity. "Is the Marshall Plan for Yuri Karpeyko, Point Four, et cetera. Jenny Singer's colonization program. I know—"

"Oh, shut up, Gideon. Stop insulting my country. You're really beginning to bug me."

"Is not time for argue, Jenny," Gideon said placatingly. "We must be ready for KGB guy when he come. What we will tell him about money? So you must talk, Jenny, because our English not so good. You ready to rehearse? First we put together all American money what we have."

Before dinner was over Rachel complained that she was exhausted and had to get to bed. Yuri went upstairs with her and listened to her chest without benefit of stethoscope. He heard the rasp there, and it worried him. She might have pneumonia. Rachel flatly refused to go to a polyclinic. Soon after, Jenny and Gideon went up to join them; Jenny had brought along, among her twenty-odd drugs, broad-spectrum antibiotic capsules— "just in case," she said dryly to Gideon—and Yuri told Rachel to take one every four hours. If she did not improve by the time they reached Minsk tomorrow, he had a friend there who would take a look at her. Nobody mentioned that Yuri's presence in Minsk would be the greatest secret they

had to keep—that no one, not even a doctor who was a friend, could be trusted. They all hoped Rachel would improve. God knows, with this security guy after them about Jenny's currency, they had trouble enough.

The KGB man did not show up that night, but he came next morning as they were preparing to leave for the airport for the short flight to Minsk. He was a skinny, mild-mannered man with passable English, and spoke affably, unthreateningly. He met them in the lobby and invited Yuri and Jenny to have tea with him.

Jenny glanced at Yuri and accepted with alarm. "Why not?" She put on her burlesque gaiety, grinning grotesquely. "Best offer we had all morning. Right, Marty?"

Yuri nodded agreeably, his heart pounding. The role, the role. Yuri Karpeyko, star performer. He had to keep his mouth shut.

The cold dining room was almost empty, and they took a table by a window, far from the other two couples in the place. While they waited for the lone waiter, the stranger, dressed in a standard Russian double-breasted gray suit hanging loosely on his thin, bony body, fished comfortably into his breast pocket and without a word exhibited something that resembled a driver's license with his photograph. As Jenny eyed the Cyrillic printing blankly, he said, like a friend, "I only trying to help you. There has been a question raised, and I am sure is baseless, so I trying only to put everything in order."

"I see."

"I assure you, madam, this card is authentic, and I am authorized. Now please, may I have a look at your currency declaration?"

"Okay, why not? Let him have a look at it, Marty."

Yuri handed over the currency declaration form, and the man looked it over quickly. "You have declared you brought into the Soviet Union, is written here, one thousand six hundred dollars, five hundred dollars cash, one thousand one hundred dollars travelers' checks. American Express, yes?"

"If that's what it says." Jenny batted her eyes dramatically.

"We have reason to believe you have dollars, much more than five hundred."

"You don't say! How fascinating! Is it possible you have gleaned that priceless bit of information from the little old chambermaid who haunts this charming hotel?"

He regarded her mournfully. "I know nothing about chambermaid."

"Hidden, right. In a yellow envelope in a rubber bag. And that really raised her old eyebrows, didn't it? Wow, you guys are really somethin'.

And what business does a chambermaid have going through my douche bag? Can you tell me that?"

"I am here, madam, on business of Soviet government. I am sure chambermaid is good citizen. You have no cause to denounce her. So you will take me to your room and show me all your currency, please."

"For God's sake, we're supposed to be guests in your country, mister. You wanna know something? We were treated a lot better in China, weren't we, Marty?" Yuri nodded, thinking *Jenny, Jenny, please!* He tried to signal with his eyes, but she was not watching him.

The young man was imperturbable. "You are most welcome in Soviet Union, madam—and sair." He nodded briefly to Yuri, who remained determinedly silent, appalled. "But we have strict laws regarding currency, madam. You and your husband have been notified of these laws, and guests are expected to observe the host country's laws. Is simple courtesy. Is not correct?"

Jenny shook her head.

"Americans don't expect Soviet citizen in New York to observe American laws? Fair?" He looked to Yuri, but Jenny snapped back.

"Sure we do! But we don't *make* ridiculous laws, and we certainly don't go digging into their douche bags! In a so-called deluxe hotel, yet!"

The young man turned to Yuri. "So please, sair, I have here warrant to search for currency." He reached into his breast and withdrew a document which he opened and placed on the table. "You will perhaps ask your wife to be calm? Please explain to her to let me see your currency."

"Keep outa this, Marty," Jenny said, before Yuri could open his mouth. "My husband hasn't been feeling so hot lately; it's the goddamn water. I happen to be handling the family funds at the moment. What it is, I guess there's been some kind of dumb mistake. Not ours, mister. Yours. Maybe your chambermaid has eyesight problems. Okay, here—this is what was in the old douche bag."

She reached into her purse and withdrew the yellow envelope with its package of bills. "Here. Go ahead. Count 'em." The package was now filled with singles, fives and tens, all that she, Gideon, and Rachel had been able to put together. Gideon had found two other American couples in the hotel and they'd provided thirty-odd singles, a five, and two twenties, which now filled out the plump package. A single hundred-dollar bill, at Gideon's insistence, had been placed on top of the wad. All told, there was barely four hundred dollars in more than sixty bills. The visitor counted them patiently, without embarrassment, and for the first time seemed troubled.

"This is everything?"

"You bet! Maybe the maid saw this hundred and decided they were all hundreds, eh? Oh, you wanna see our travelers' checks, too? Maybe the maid's trying to win brownie points—inventing things."

"You keep this in a rubber bag. But why?"

"Why? 'Cause I'm afraid of thieves, that's why! I come from New York, that's why! Poor people want what rich people have, right? I learned that in my cradle."

"No poor people, no thieves in Soviet Union!"

"Oh, brother!"

"Not in hotels."

"So instead you have spies, right? Thieves, spies, whatever. I hide my money. Is that against the law? Is it okay with you?"

"You mind if I have look in your purse, madam?"

She pushed it toward him with such a jerk that an observer, had there been one, would have thought she was striking him with it. He opened it without a word and plowed through it methodically, placing her paraphernalia on the breakfast table. The waiter came, saw the things on the table, and nervously took their order for glasses of tea and tarts.

The young man was thorough. He subjected to the most careful scrutiny every slip they had got wherever they had exchanged dollars for rubles. After they had finished their glasses of tea, he invited himself to their room and asked them to call Gideon and Rachel. Rachel looked haggard; her coughing was worse. When they had gathered in the two-room suite Jenny and Yuri had vacated, he called down and asked to have the luggage of both parties sent back up to the room. From somewhere— Jenny was never sure where—two other men appeared in the hall with the luggage, behind the baggage man. Jenny knew that under Rachel's girdle was what they were looking for. How far would they go?

"Listen," Jenny said with sweet reasonableness, "are you holding us in some way? Is this an interrogation? 'Cause if it is, I want to call our embassy in Moscow." To Yuri she said, "Marty, don't you think we better talk to Bill Cole?"

She started toward the phone, but one of the men beat her to it, lifted the receiver, and said something to the operator in Russian.

"Not now," the skinny young man said, sucking at his luxurious blond mustache with his lower lip.

"Oh, no? Well, when?"

"Later." He wanted to see passports and visas and travel vouchers, and made notes.

The search was similar to the one at Sheremetyevo, but much more thorough. Gideon's wallet, Yuri's wallet, purses, all pockets. As they

opened one bag after the other and examined each piece of clothing with painful slowness, Jenny made a *shtuss*: "We're gonna miss our plane, you guys! You understand we're supposed to leave for Minsk in half an hour? If you change our schedule, Intourist will go up in smoke! They'll go outa their minds!"

The young man with the blond mustache said, "We are almost finished, madam. They are holding the plane for you, so please quiet down."

That did it. If ever there was a time for *tummeling*, this was it. "Quiet down? You son of a bitch! What *are* we, your prisoners? 'Come to the friendly, hospitable Soviet Union! Enjoy detente!' That's what you write in the papers! You know what? You got a really shitty country here. You realize that? Soldiers all over the goddamn streets. Who're you afraid of? Each other? Guys like you? Worried about other guys like you? Jee-zuss! Can't wear your coat in a freezing restaurant! Why not, for God's sake? Nobody'll tell you because everything's a fucking secret. Boy, how I hate this place! Well, I'm leavin' for the airport, shorty. If you don't like it, arrest me. Shoot me, do any goddamn thing you like! C'mon you!" She pointed to the baggage man. "Let's get this show on the road."

The baggage man looked to the thin young man for a signal; he bobbed his head forward in assent. Let her go. The word would be passed to Minsk. This hysterical American did not in any way allay his suspicion. They had that money somewhere, and money meant conspiracy—anti-Soviet activity. She'd lead them to it.

Jenny pirouetted out, and Yuri, doing his best to imitate her, to be as American as he could, marched out behind her, a dignified capitalist in an American-made Russian caracul hat, catching up to her, taking hold of her elbow. The two Israelis followed along sheepishly. Ugly Americans, Gideon was thinking. Typical. A nation of castoffs, so where did they get all *their* arrogance?

The KGB agent followed them into the small lift, hat in hand, and rode down to the street with them. As the elevator door opened, he said, "I hope you will enjoy your visit in the Soviet Union. Where you will go now?"

"Minsk."

"Ah. I am sure you will enjoy. Goodbye, sair. Goodbye, gentleman and Grandmother. Goodbye, madam."

As they drove to the airport, Jenny tried to pacify herself; indeed, she looked to her companions for a word of comfort or sign of approbation for her eloquence, but what she found were faces reflecting varying degrees of hostility. Gideon was so angry he refused to look at her at all. Rachel,

in physical misery, seemed deeply embarrassed. Yuri was perspiring, and so pale she thought he might faint. Finally he spoke in a low, uneven voice.

"Zhenny, vy you meck soch commotion? You know vee are in exposed position. Vy you meck pipple engry, insolt the country?" Was she only imagining it, or did his question carry an extra element of accusation almost as if he was asking, "Who are you to insult *my* country?"

She regarded him with amazement. "You *like* it?"

His head shook and he lowered his voice so that the driver could not hear him. "Like, not like. Vaht difference? Is my country."

SETTLED INTO HIS TINY SINGLE, dingily furnished room at the deluxe Yubeleinaya Hotel in Minsk, Joshua sat gazing down from his window at the ramshackle collection of huts below, cabins in which families were still apparently living. This, he understood, was all that was left of the ghetto the Nazis had delineated when they occupied Minsk during the war. The cluster of wooden shacks was unlike anything Josh had seen on his drive in from the airport. It's a *shtetl*, he ruminated, peering at the enclave of muddied streets, a *shtetl* within a city, lost in a time forgotten, now a living museum. He had walked those streets half an hour before. He had seen only gentile—Russian, Byelorussian, or Polish—faces on the people who entered or left these huts, but back in those days there had been nothing but Jews, not only during the Nazi occupation, but long, long before, a fragment of the Pale of Settlement.

The girl at the Intourist desk in the hotel had been unable or had refused to tell him anything about these huts: "They're only small wooden houses," she said primly, "from the very old days, before the Revolution. Soon they'll be torn down to make room for modern apartments, you see? Oh, I don't know anything about Jews."

But a young Norwegian whom Josh had met at breakfast in the coffee shop had told him all about it and taken him out to see for himself. "Jews, mostly, were living here to start with in forty-one, and this is where the Nazis settled thousands of others from Paris and Danzig and Amsterdam—it was some place where the SS and special detachments could kill them without being troubled by western sentimentalism. The Jews from the West came wearing their yellow stars, while native Jews wore none. After western Jews reached Minsk, no effort was made to send them to extermination camps. It was easier to kill them right where they were. And, of course, the local Jews as well."

Josh looked at his watch. Where the hell was Ma? She, Gideon, and Rachel should've arrived from Vilna two hours ago. He wondered if the wild scheme Gideon had described to him on the plane to Helsinki was actually working. Had the guy shown up at the airport? They were so damn late! Was it possible they'd got themselves into some kind of jam? Well, he'd done his part in the scheme, done the job he'd agreed to. He reached for Honey Wright's passport in his pocket. Getting that thing had taken four days of jawboning, pleading, and bargaining. For a kid from Canton, Ohio, who looked like a brainless fashion model, Honey was a shrewd negotiator. Well, Gideon had said he could promise her anything, and what he'd promised her was money, something he now was sure he could get from Dad. Bill Cole had been reassuring about getting her a duplicate if and when they were sure the original was "lost" and she needed it. It was all part of the Israelis' scheme. Those Israelis could cook up a helluva brew. He'd hate to be up against them.

The ringing phone startled him. "Joshie, you're okay? . . . Yeah, we made it! Wasn't easy! Wait'll I tell you! . . . Yeah, we're right here in the hotel. C'mon up. We're all in Rachel's suite—six eighteen."

The deluxe two-room suites at the Yubeleinaya resembled those at the Vilnius, nothing like the Intourist. Although the furniture was new here, it was sleazy. In the ten-foot-square sitting room, weak electric lamps gave off barely enough light to keep its occupants from bumping into the furniture or each other. As Josh entered, his eye caught Yuri's. So this was the guy!

Josh could not keep himself from staring, until Jenny, giggling an embarrassed high laugh, hurriedly introduced Yuri.

"Terrific to meet you. Did anyone tell him he's the image of Grandpa?"

"Shhh!" Jenny hissed.

"No, no," Yuri chuckled. "In this khotel is okay, can talk. Is not Moscow. No microphones. I know designer, khis daughter vunce my patient. Khee go alvays abrode. So khee tell me, 'Yuri, vun t'ing for sure—vill be no bugs in my khotel. Vill be like New York.' Khirr ve can talk."

Gideon shook his head, put his finger to his lips, and touched the wall with his fingertips. Everyone was silent, watching as he ran his fingers expertly across wall, windowframe, and over the doorframe. At the door between bedroom and sitting room he paused. He reached for a chair, tugged it to the doorway, and stood on it. Over the protruding doorframe, invisible to anyone under seven feet tall, was a recessed box to which he pointed. He reached into his back pocket, withdrew a penknife, opened a small blade, and with a sharp twist of the wrist opened the flush access

door to the recessed box. He reached in and drew forth a mini-recorder. Using his knife as a screwdriver, he disconnected two wires, removed the tiny tape, slipped it into his pocket, and returned everything else to the box. Carefully he closed the access door, dismounted from the chair, and returned it to its place beside the lamp.

"So now," he said. "*Now* is like New York, Yuri."

Josh shook his head slowly, as if in disbelief. His cousin was certainly not new at this business.

"Oh," Jenny said, as if reading his mind, "this is nothing! You see Yuri here? My Russian husband? Turns out he's on the lam. The cops are out searching for him."

"Holy shit!"

"Not to worry, Joshie. They're looking for a completely different guy. One with gray hair and whiskers—well, you saw his picture—and blue eyes. See how his eyes are brown now? Goes with his passport."

"Yeah," Josh murmured admiringly. "Beautiful."

"That's nothing. All new American clothes. From Singer's, no less; wouldn't you know?"

Gideon and Rachel had been silent during this exchange between mother and son, but Rachel began to cough, and her body was so wracked that, shaken, she made her way into the bedroom and sat on the bed.

Josh had been shocked by Rachel's appearance. She sat hunched now and miserable, her face gray; the others followed her solicitously. She dismissed Josh's concern with a wave of her hand. "I'll be all right. I always am. It's just a bit of a cold."

Although not reassured, Josh gave them an account of Tammy's triumphs in Kiev and Moscow—last night's garish torchlight parade in the streets around the university, Tammy borne like some football hero by thousands of disorderly kids in their jeans uniforms, singing her songs as they carried her through the streets and down the steep hill in the park to the hydrofoil that sped them up the Moskva to the reception at the Ukraine Hotel. The police had simply watched. This kind of riot was okay.

"Very touching." Jenny felt a flash of impatience. "Musta been just lovely."

Rachel, trying to listen politely, started to cough again, but controlled herself to mutter, "We have to discuss that girl—what's her name, Gideon?"

"Honey Wright."

Josh said, "Oh yeah, she's all set. Pretty gutsy kid. And the whole

band's clued in. Here." He reached into his pocket for Honey's passport and papers and handed them to Gideon, who examined each document meticulously.

"You had no troubles getting her cooperation?" A touch of surprise.

Rachel started to cough again and this time could speak no more. Her fit had got out of control, wracking her body, and further conversation became impossible. Yuri and Gideon tore off the bedspread, propped her up with pillows, removed her shoes, covered her with the blanket. When she was settled in, Yuri and Jenny stayed to tend her, while Gideon took Josh into the debugged sitting room, where he told him about their difficulty in Vilna and set out their plans for Minsk. There was not much time and there was much to do.

Gideon had weighed each one's suitability for the necessary tasks. Grandmother in her condition could do nothing. Yuri dared not leave the room in his hometown. Jenny was unreliable, if he could speak frankly about Josh's mother. So that left them—Gideon and Josh. Missions had to be performed between sightseeing trips, necessary to keep the Intourist people nonvigilant. He hoped their tasks would not be complicated by Rachel's condition. His grandmother had a strong constitution, and Yuri would be giving her his full medical attention. "Nahthing," he said wryly, "like having a doctor in the family."

Gideon and Josh had seen something of each other during the week Gideon had spent in New York and they'd traveled on the same plane to Helsinki, but although Gideon had recruited Josh to lay the thought on Honey Wright, the two men still scarcely knew each other. They had cooperated warily, supported only by innate family faith. For years they had been dimly aware of each other, as happens with distant cousins, and each had envied in some ways the situation of the other. Here was this guy, Gideon thought, the invincible American in his jeans and cotton batting, who had never heard a shot fired in anger, never been threatened by sudden and violent death, never been obliged to pursue a despicable hobby . . . a rich man's son who had to go *looking* for adventure and danger. Anti-Vietnam riots. A deep-sea diver he said he was now, friend to the gray sperm whale! A maker of noncommercial movies, married to a famous singer of folk, blues, and rock. Well, perhaps a life like that was possible in Israel, too, but not for Gideon. To him Joshua was a lucky guy, committed to nothing in particular.

For Josh's part, he regarded Gideon not only with envy, but with a touch of awe, for like his mother, he was a hero-worshipper at heart. Here was a guy who flew an F-2 jet in combat, worked for Shin-Bet, and wrote Art Buchwald-type columns for the biggest paper in Israel. Josh was flat-

tered to have been invited into the Israelis' rescue scheme, for in his Hollywood-tainted soul, despite the real risks involved, he could not help thinking of it as anything but a "caper." As a party to the caper, he felt entitled to give Gideon a blow-by-blow recital of his dealings with Honey Wright.

"Man, I laid it on that woman—till five o'clock yesterday morning. Never talked so *hard.* Thank God for Tammy, 'cause she really pitched in. You should've heard the two of us. Every cliché we had. How often did a little girl from Canton, Ohio, get a chance to do her thing? A trip she would *remember*, man. Risks? She wants to know if it's absolutely riskless. Of *course.* Would we be asking her to take a *chance?* It was all fixed at the embassy, right? What could go wrong? We finally reached her. She kept blowing on her joint, very nervous, y'know, and got higher and higher until she was, wow, really up. Barbara Fritchie. Betsy Ross. Oh, she told us how she'd marched on the Lincoln Memorial with Martin Luther King when she was a kid, how she chained herself to the White House fence in sixty-eight. This kid *likes* action, man! 'Okay, I'll do it, I'll do it, I'll do it. I feel for this girl—what's her name? Yelena? Whatever. She is my *sister!* "

Gideon was delighted. "You get medal," he said. "I strike it with my own hand."

"That takes care of Yelena," Josh went on, "but what about the man's wife? How does she get out?"

"Cleo? So what we first plan was use your mother's passport. Same way like Honey Wright. She Missus Martin Singher, so would be no problem. Bot locky for us, and more lucky for your *mother*, his wife has Soviet exit visa now. She get the permission. So is not necessary."

"You guys were planning to do something with *my* passport?" Jenny had come back from the bedroom. "*My* passport?"

"Is not longer necessary, Jenny."

"*Jezuss!*"

"So," Gideon smiled up at her. "You off the hook."

"I do appreciate it," Jenny said dryly.

"Don't celebrate," Gideon told her. "For ever'ting is a price. Instead of you, I find way we can use your son."

"Joshie? That's ridiculous. He's already stuck his neck out too far—"

"Is *your* idea we get jinns and money and watches to Baryshin, no? So I'm t'inking, who can do it? Josh can do it. You suggested yourself."

Josh, surging with alternate waves of queasiness and pride, turned to his mother, his confident smile utterly unconvincing.

"Whatever the man says."

Jenny listened attentively to the plan Gideon laid out; Josh nodded by her side. It seemed plausible. Josh sat silent rethinking it in his mind, while Gideon and Jenny began to chat about Nettie, whom Gideon had seen only two weeks earlier in Haifa. Yes, the guy she was marrying was terrific. Gideon had served with him in the Six-Day War. Avram was sometimes a bit serious, iconoclastic, but a steady pilot and a fantastic tennis player—Nettie said he could beat the pants off her, and she'd been women's champion at Golden Oaks. Oh, Avram would lead her a merry chase and a good life—he loved new places, new foods—in fact, he was a terrific specialist in Chinese cooking. And no womanizer. That was important today. Many young Israelis were fast slipping away from the traditions of family, Gideon said.

Although they were talking about her daughter, Jenny found it astonishing that she and Gideon could gossip so calmly. Suppressing tension. She hoped to God Joshie, brooding there in the corner, wouldn't develop ulcers or asthma. She remembered to ask Gideon how Avram was with children. *There's* a nice grandmotherly question, she thought triumphantly.

Gideon smiled. "Who won't like children? They'll have, believe me! So not to worry!"

Ah! she thought. If *that* were my worry!

Yuri, now the family physician, returned to the sitting room. Rachel, he said, was resting easier, but her fever was up and he wasn't sure they had the proper drug. He was concerned. If the correct steps were not taken it could become serious. He intended to get the best medical help in town, whatever the risks. Jenny looked to Gideon. Their experience in Vilna had thoroughly unnerved her. Mildly she asked if other doctors might not recognize him.

"For sure," Yuri said, "bot I only get somevun safe." He spoke with more calm certainty than he felt. Who could tell how much pressure had already been brought on Shtainberg? Still, what choice did he have? Hadn't the old woman from Israel taken enormous risks for him? This was a *medical* matter. He was relieved to be able to devote himself completely to it.

Yuri sent Gideon out to call Shtainberg from the pay phone in the hotel restaurant. The surgeon, he knew, usually operated all morning, and should be back in his office by now. Gideon had enough Russian to manage. "Who is calling?" Shtainberg's secretary asked.

"Mitya Orensky." Gideon gave her the name of the director general, as Yuri had directed.

Shtainberg was on the line quickly. "Yeah, Mitya? What's the occasion?"

"It's not Mitya. It's a friend of Yuri. He's at the Yubeleinaya Hotel."

"You have to be kidding!"

"No. Please don't ask questions. He has a sick old woman here from abroad. He thinks she has bronchial pneumonia. Can you come and have a look at her and bring some sulfanilamide? He would like you to do a sputum on her. Can you come?"

"How old's the woman?"

"Seventy-five."

"I'll be over about five. I have a lung to collapse at two."

Gideon gave him their room number, Shtainberg rang off, and Gideon reported back to Yuri. Thank God, Yuri thought, someone could be relied on. He suggested that the others go down for lunch now. It would be nice if they could bring up some broth and tea for the patient. Rachel, too, urged them to go. She'd be all right, she was stronger than the lot of them, and now she would have *two* doctors, after all. She turned to Yuri, speaking in Russian. "Did you know my son was also a doctor? A neurosurgeon. This boy's papa. You see, it runs in the family."

"Rachel," Gideon commanded, "you'll do what the doctor tell you for a change?"

"I'll be good. Don't worry. You should *know* the diseases I've had! This is nothing."

They had a painfully slow lunch in the dining room. When their food finally came, Gideon took the hot soup and tea upstairs for his grandmother, Jenny carried a thick meat borscht up for Yuri, and Josh brought a pudding. Jenny had noticed Yuri hadn't been eating much lately. Nerves, and why not?

After lunch Jenny, Josh, and Gideon squeezed into a Moskvich for the city tour. Nonna Tarnova, a woman with a sallow face and severely cut straight hair, sporting jeans and dark brown sweater, was their guide. She sat beside the driver. Nonna, like their Moscow guide, spoke a clipped British English, and told them she had just spent three years in Cairo. Gideon would have liked to ask her a few questions about Cairo, but did not trust his English and remained silent. Nonna had the driver take them all over Minsk, spieling as they drove. The city reminded Jenny of Cleveland in the late forties, with its trolley cars, wide streets, and gray buildings. Gideon listened, checking landmarks against his intelligence.

Jenny was soon bored stiff, and remained that way until she was brought up with a jolt late in the afternoon at the Museum of the Great Patriotic War. Yuri had told them what to look for. They wandered past

the captured weapons, tanks, and armored cars of the Nazi war machine and the small guns of the desperate partisans. There were photographs of partisan leaders. Nonna translated some of the notices the Nazis had posted everywhere during the occupation: "Absenteeism will not be tolerated. Those who fail to report for work will be punished by death." She showed them relief maps of the city, which indicated the precise locations where Nazis had machine-gunned people, showing the number murdered in each neighborhood. The area around the Yubeleinaya bore the figure eighty thousand. "Why there?" Jenny inquired with wide-eyed innocence. "Why so many?" Nonna did not reply. "Altogether," she droned on, "over two hundred thousand were killed in this city, many from other areas."

"Many Jews?" Jenny asked, forcing her face muscles into a frightful smile.

"I believe so, but many others as well."

In a corner of the last room in the museum, Nonna pointed to a large photograph of three people hanging in a public square. Signs in Russian were attached to their bodies. This was it. "These people," Nonna said in the placid tones of one reciting the events of the First Punic War, "are three Soviet patriots, murdered by the Nazis and hanged in Railway Station Square, where we visited earlier. On the right is Ivan Bonov and on the left is Dmitri Orlovsky."

As she turned to go, Jenny asked, "What about the woman in the middle?"

"The Unknown Heroine," Nonna said. "No one knows for certain who she is."

Jenny stared at the body of the woman, head askew, feet dangling grotesquely, and she was mesmerized. She could feel her own heartbeat, rapid, pounding. Although Yuri had told them to look for the photograph, he had been singularly detached, as if he were talking about a total stranger.

"What does that sign on her say?" Jenny persisted.

"I cannot read that," Nonna said. "It's not teddibly important. Shall we go on?" Nonna had become oddly impatient.

Jenny held her sleeve. "Please. I'm overcome with curiosity."

The guide glanced back at the photograph with distaste, studied it for a moment as though concentrating on it for the first time in her career as a guide, then spoke each word separately as if she were reading a timetable: "Kike. Bandit. Strangled. Slowly."

8

SHTAINBERG HAD ALREADY TAKEN blood and sputum specimens. He listened to the rasp in her chest with a stethoscope, and invited Yuri to hear for himself. They agreed: bronchial pneumonia in the left lung. He took her temperature—38.4 degrees, a low-grade fever. Both men ruled out lobar, at least for now. Shtainberg would have the specimens analyzed by nightfall. He rather liked the old lady, and spent a few minutes talking with her. Rachel, employing her Russian, told him her parents had come from Minsk to the Holy Land more than ninety years ago. Shtainberg held her hand, nodding, saying wistfully, "If only my grandparents had such good sense!"

Rachel tried to reply, but had to contend with a fit of coughing. Finally with effort she smiled. "But it's never too late, Doctor. Not at all. You seem like a nice boy. So why don't you come?" Shtainberg chuckled and turned away.

"I'm thinking, Grandmother, I'm *thinking*." He ruffled his beard nervously. "Who knows, eh?"

Rachel sat straighter in her bed; the scent of a convert was upon her. "If you come, you'll be my physician," she said cheerfully. "That's a promise. My doctor, God bless him, had to retire. So old. I have also many influential friends, looking for a reliable doctor. So you see, I offer already the beginning of an important practice. And you'll like Hadassah Hospital. What more can I say?"

Shtainberg gave her his most open, black-bearded grin, teeth shining. "You temptress! You are the devil!" He laughed appreciatively.

"Nu, I'll try to be sick as often as possible. At my age it's easy."

He laughed again, patted her hand. As an afterthought, he bent and gave her a whiskery kiss on one cheek.

"*Todah rabah*," she said.

The two doctors went to the sitting room, where Yuri introduced Shtainberg to the others, who had just returned from the tour.

"That's your grandmother?" Shtainberg said to Gideon. "Terrific old girl."

He doubted the pneumonia was virulent, and once they knew whether it was Pneumococcus, Strep, Staph, or whatever, they could stop it in its tracks. He'd call Yuri as soon as he got the pathology report. He'd leave some vials of sulfanilamide and hypodermic needles. "You expect to be in town long?" he asked Yuri as Gideon helped him on with his coat.

"Till tomorrow. It's a long story. Baryshin can tell you all about it."

"They still keep coming to the hospital from the organs asking if I've seen you—if I know where you are."

"I'm sure."

"I haven't seen Cleo lately. How I miss that woman! I do my best work when she's there. But I hear she has her visa to skedaddle. Is that the truth?"

Word spreads fast, Yuri thought. The newsroom at Chaim Park. Still, he did not answer directly. The less said, the better.

"Lucky woman. I hear she leaves tomorrow night," Shtainberg said.

"I'm expecting to join her soon, of course," Yuri said. Shtainberg stared at him as if Yuri had taken leave of his senses. What self-delusion! Surely the poor man must realize there was not the slightest chance he could get an exit visa. Nevertheless, Shtainberg nodded. Why mention unpleasant truths? Poor bastard, more likely within a month he'd be in some prison or a patient in a *psikhushka*. He wondered briefly if there was any way he could help the guy, but he couldn't think of a thing.

"This sick old lady is related to you, Yurka?"

"My father's cousin."

"Ah. Does your old man know she's here in Minsk?"

"No. In any case, he'd never agree to see her. Father is old, but not wise. He has too much blood invested to care for the truth. Blood invested in a fraud."

Shtainberg nodded. "The original believer. I'd better not mention her, then, when I bring him his stuff. He's grouchy enough."

"I can't thank you enough for what you do for him."

Shtainberg waved the thanks aside. "It's a duty. He was once a great physician, head of the complex, wasn't he? But the old man is suffering, Yurka. It's not the drugs. He's got no one any more. He's refused to see

Cleo. Whenever I come, he's sitting glued to the television. His eyes are half closed. Half asleep. Hard to tell what he's thinking."

Yuri shook his head. A hopeless case. The two doctors shook hands, each thinking, for different reasons, it was for the last time.

9

JOSH AND GIDEON WENT DOWN to the coffee shop together; to their surprise they both admitted loving buttermilk.

"You and Tammy must come to Israel for a visit," Gideon said. "I show you Eilat and Sharm el Sheikh. The reefs—fontostic, like naht'ing in the world. Cousteau says also."

"Count on it, man. Whenever I come to visit my little sister, you can damn well count on it."

"Okay! You'll show me how to scuba? I am very nervous under water."

"Why not? If you'll teach me to fly an F-2. I'm nervous in the air."

They were beginning not so much to envy each other as to feel comfortable together.

Before they had finished their *kefir* and cakes, Josh looked at his watch, rose abruptly, walked rapidly through the lobby, and left the hotel alone. The short, fat man waiting at the entrance did not follow him because he was not one of the Americans just in from Vilnius who had been pointed out to him—suspects, he was told, carrying thousands of undeclared American dollars, probably to drop them in Minsk, surely for no good. Unaccounted-for foreign money could only mean anti-Soviet plots.

In addition to Jenny's five thousand dollars in cash, Josh also carried a red-and-white Beryozka shopping bag in which he had her four pairs of jeans and Rachel's two pairs; in his pocket he had both Seiko watches. Leaning against a biting wind that swept up from the river, he walked swiftly along Magistral Parkway. As he passed the Beryozka shop a tipsy young man took his arm, asking if he had "jinns you selling," but he brushed the drunk (or pretended drunk) off and hurried along.

In a red phone booth on Nemiga Street, at one end of the bridge that crosses the Svisloch, he deposited two kopeks and dialed the English teacher, Hana Maneshevich. He spoke to her briefly, walked three blocks

to the taxi stand on Lenin Street just off Leninsky Prospekt, and waited ten minutes for the next cab. He gave the driver Hana Maneshevich's address. She had agreed to take him to see Baryshin and would serve as his interpreter—a task she performed regularly for American, Canadian, or British Jews who showed up to see Baryshin with "resources" for "the cause." Yuri had told Josh not to worry about surveillance at Baryshin's. They never bothered his visitors. While they might attack the colonel in the press, the authorities were reluctant to touch him; he had served with distinction during the war and had enough medals to cover his chest, and this still counted for something. For Yuri, Baryshin was a lifeline. It was through him that he had found someone in Vilna to take him in; it was through him he had got in touch with his American relatives; it was through him that he had been given the word to meet them at Sheremetyevo. In Jerusalem, Gideon confirmed, Weisbrot also gave Baryshin high marks. Baryshin, predicted Gideon, would be delighted with the jeans and watches. But he might be wary about the money. Possession of foreign currency was illegal, and good activists were sticklers for legality. But for five thousand dollars—who could tell?

When Gideon had explained all this, Jenny had cried with delight, "See? Five thousand bucks, just in case! Now that's *my* idea of a *mitzvah!*"

Gideon had grinned shrewdly at her. "Is your money, but my *mitzvah*, Jenny!" From Gideon's viewpoint, it was for old Weisbrot, for Rachel, for Yoshke Schulman, and for the Cause. While it was important to get the cousins out, hundreds of thousands of others were waiting and needed help. Rachel concurred, particularly since the Israelis and Yuri agreed there was almost no risk. Josh, a stranger to such stratagems, only hoped to God they were right.

Hana led Josh to the small lift; they rode up slowly. She knocked on Baryshin's door, and Zinaida Aleksandrovna answered it. The little woman's thin gray hair was disheveled and Josh could see her bare scalp; she was scarcely civil, but her incivility was not directed against them. She seemed to be at her wit's end. She peered around the hall, walked to the lift to see if anyone was in it, hurried them back into her flat, and closed the door quickly; once inside, she leaned against it as if she were trying to hold the world out.

The apartment was in some disarray. Books were in stacks, taken from bookshelves. Pictures were off the walls. Leon Baryshin, Zina said, had been arrested two hours ago. Three times before he had been called in for interrogation, but they had always been polite, never quite like this. Leon had expected it might happen someday, but not so soon. The KGB must

want something quite special. Four men in the search party. They had a warrant. They brought a witness, the *dezhurnaya*, who instead of observing the search to see that it was conducted lawfully, had done a bit of searching herself. One of the men had asked several times about particular people in whom Leon was interested. Had he given money to such and such a Refusenik? Where had the money come from? Did he know anything about the whereabouts of a certain doctor? He, of course, would never tell them anything. So it had come to this. Suddenly she was weeping, muttering through tears. She had no way of knowing what would happen now. She would have to begin to bring food packages to the KGB building now, and hope they would deliver them to Leon—like so many other wives. Hana Manashevich became very upset.

Joshua was out of his league as Hana translated Zina's tearful mutterings. The reference to the "doctor" astonished him. Could that be Yuri? He was afraid to ask. He told Hana to ask Zina if *she* would take the money. Would she know what to do with it? Zina shook her head, exhausted. No, no. Things were bad enough. She was already too deeply involved. Her visitors should please leave—leave her alone. These were not even her people, these Jews. Wasn't that irony? Her family destroyed. Her man had brought her to this. Like a madman, a zealot, a man possessed. Her daughter in Israel now. Of all places! A daughter of hers—a Russian woman of Russian parents! Hana translated faithfully, although she was growing increasingly unsettled herself.

"I think we should go," Hana said to Josh. "Quickly." She held Zina's shoulders protectively for a moment as if to give her strength, and they were soon in the street.

"Give me everything," Hana said. Josh handed her the Beryozka bag, the watches, the yellow envelope. "My turn has come," Hana said with resignation. "I must do the impossible. You must get back to your hotel now. There. There's a taxi stand. I'll take the bus home. Don't make any sign to me. Goodbye. Thank you."

Joshua, glad to be rid of money and gifts, took the first taxi to arrive, and a strange man, who seemed to be a friend of the driver, got into the front seat. They drove off.

Hana walked on to the first rubbish receptacle; she took out the jeans and deposited the empty, telltale Beryozka bag. Carrying the jeans over her arm, she boarded the trolley bus home.

Ten minutes after Josh had left the hotel, Gideon took off on the more delicate of the two missions. Two men, Gideon knew, were keeping a vigil outside the entrance to the house on Oktyabr'skaya Street. If Cleo

and Yelena were to leave the house together, both men would follow them. Gideon suspected a third agent, unrelated, might have been assigned by Vilna to shadow him, following hot dollars.

It was dark but clear outside; the wind was cold and penetrating. Gideon wound his way first through the muddy streets of the old ghetto to see if he was being followed. He heard thin new ice cracking underfoot. No doubt about it, the crackling footsteps behind him echoed his own. He turned. A short, heavy man in a thick overcoat, who made no attempt to camouflage what he was doing, walked twenty meters behind him along the empty street, picking his way, remarkably agile for one so stout. Gideon felt in his breast pocket for Yelena's papers. He was satisfied with the job he'd done substituting Yelena's photo for Honey's on both visa and passport.

Returning to Magistral Parkway, he boarded the Number 29 bus heading for Leninsky Prospekt. The fat guy boarded and sat opposite him. Their eyes met for only an instant. Lidded eyes. Gideon's educated scrutiny told him the man was not only overweight, but slow. Probably a guy they assigned to shadow the middle-aged and elderly, second-rate suspects of doubtful criminality—like Jenny, Rachel, or Yuri. Well, Gideon had been to school on the subject of tails.

At Nemiga, the end of the line, he and the tail changed to the Number 36 bus. They rode for several stops. At the stop where 36 turns into Leninsky Prospekt and heads toward Ploshchad' Pobedy, Gideon rose and shuffled off with half the passengers to change buses. At the curb perhaps twenty people were in a queue at the stop waiting patiently for the general exodus so they could get aboard. The fat tail got off behind Gideon. Gideon started to walk indecisively, as though trying to get his bearings, first in one direction, then another, finally moving hesitantly toward Lenin Square. He looked about vaguely, as if thinking he might possibly be going in the wrong direction, but he kept walking and the tail followed. As the last person in the waiting queue approached the step of the bus to board it, Gideon turned, darted fifty or sixty enormous steps with incredible speed and, as the bus door was closing, leaped aboard, elbowing the closing door, fighting the door, which closed behind him. Aboard, he pushed his way past the passenger in front of him.

The angry driver of the now moving bus scolded, "Stupid man!" and stepped harder on the acclerator. Gideon saw his tail running, mouth open, signaling frantically. Too late. The driver cursed under his breath and raced his vehicle up Leninsky Prospekt. He could have been a bus driver in Jerusalem or New York. Power corrupts, Gideon thought gleefully. He got off at the next stop and walked up Kupaly Street, cir-

cumnavigating Kupaly Park, then along a dimly lit Kuybyseva Street to get to Ploshchad' Pobedy. He was satisfied at last that nobody was following him. At the taxi stand he took the first car in a long line of idle taxis to the corner of Klary Cetkin and Luksemburg. There he bought another bus ticket and stood docilely in the queue until the Number 22 bus arrived. He took this to Maxim Gorky. He was now not quite half a kilometer from the hotel; it had taken him an hour to get there, doubling back on his own track. But he was alone.

Ivan Borisovich Karpeyko was watching television through his thick lenses when Gideon knocked at his door. Adjusting his glasses, the old man picked his way carefully across his carpet (he had fallen twice in the past two days) to the door. Why be afraid? He had nothing to fear. But who could it be? Shtainberg came only on Fridays. No one else came. Who then? He opened the door.

Gideon had to do his best with his primitive Russian. "Ivan Karpeyko?"

The old man mumbled.

"I am your cousin, Gideon Aron. From Jerusalem."

The old man shuffled back to the television set, reached into a glass for his teeth, and put them into his mouth. He snapped his jaws several times to be sure they were in place, then glared at his visitor.

"I don't know you. Get out."

"I can't do that, Cousin. Please. I need your help."

"I have no use for you people. What are you doing here? I will call the *militsia*."

"Listen, I have to talk to Cleo, and to your granddaughter Yelena, but they're under surveillance. It would be too dangerous."

"So?"

"Call them for me. Tell them you're sick. Ask them to come. Say you're afraid it might be a coronary. When they come, we must persuade their tails they've come only because you're very sick. We have to keep them outside, so I can talk with the women."

"You are stupid. Yuri sent you?"

Gideon ignored him. He took the phone, dialed. A woman answered. "Cleo?"

"No, this is Yelena. You want my mother?"

"No, no. You will do. Listen, your grandfather has had an attack. He's in a bad way. I'm with him now. Please come over right away."

"What's happened to him?"

"I think an infarction."

"Who are you?"

"The doctor. Panikov from the Polyclinic. The doctor who usually takes care of him is away. Will you come? Right away, please."

"Wait. I'll talk to my mother."

Gideon held on, while the women discussed the matter. Yelena was back. "Is Grandfather able to talk?"

"I think so." He turned. "All right, old man. It's a matter of their lives. Tell them to come."

Ivan Karpeyko was silent. No one had bothered with him for such a long time.

Gideon said, "He's trying to say something." He put the phone to the mouth of the old man, who grimaced hideously, as if he were being led to the scaffold. "Come," he croaked hoarsely.

A leap into the unknown. Gideon rang off. The two men waited in silence, both watching a television drama about two collective farmers determined to have the same woman—each making long, boring speeches, trying to reach her heart with dialectics and heroism.

10

AFTER BOTH YOUNG MEN HAD LEFT the suite, Yuri and Jenny kept vigil over Rachel; her fever rose; they listened, uncomprehending, as she rambled on in Hebrew to her Boris. Suddenly perspiring, she withdrew from her husband's eerie image in fright, closed her eyes, and dozed. Perhaps she realized she had been hallucinating. Jenny applied cool compresses to the old woman's forehead, trying to keep her comfortable. Within an hour Shtainberg called. "It's Pneumococcus," he said. "Use the stuff I left."

Yuri prepared the sterile syringe Shtainberg had given him and nudged Rachel to roll over so he could administer the injection to her buttock. "Vee know vaht is, Rachel. Vill be all right."

Rachel, wan but composed, replied in Russian. "Who's worried?" Suddenly her face clouded. "Listen, Yurka, you've been in touch with your wife and daughter? Your daughter must be instructed."

"Shh. Gideon's gone. As we planned."

Rachel closed her eyes, satisfied. Yes, she remembered now. Gideon. They must have that girl. If Yuri was stubborn, let him try America, but the girl must come to them. They said she was a genius. And on Yuri she wasn't giving up either, not so easily. She tried to explain this, but only agitated sounds emerged.

After a bit she slept fitfully. Jenny and Yuri watched her, and from time to time glanced at each other. Jenny tried her timidest, most encouraging smile. Twice Yuri went to the sitting room to smoke a *papyroesa*. At seven Jenny went below to the dining room to get them both something to eat, and more broth and tea for Rachel.

They ate with the bedroom door ajar so they could hear Rachel; they talked in low voices, Yuri in his broken English, which by now rather charmed Jenny. She told him about Rachel's performance at the Moun-

taintop Country Club, and about the outpouring of money from rich American Jews. Yuri could not imagine such a place, but at Baryshin's seminars he had heard of the generosity of American Jews. As Jenny told it, Baryshin's bloodless statements came alive. Amazing! Another amazing fact: that so few people together *had* a hundred million dollars. Simply to *give* it away to people they had never met! No matter how moving the speech. What exactly moved them? There are no altruists, he told Jenny. He had learned that as a child.

Jenny spoke roughly, raising her voice: "Oh, yeah? Well, *I'm* here, aren't I? What's in it for *me*? You amaze me, you fucking skeptic!"

Her rough language made him giggle with embarrassment. He quickly changed the subject. Would she please tell him more about herself and Martin? He was filled with curiosity.

She began to tell him about Martin—impersonal things, of course. She described the store, the marvelous place that sold everything from Pampers to airplanes. Designer clothes, cosmetics, furs, the most marvelous furniture—the legacy of Moishe of Minsk—gems, and costume jewelry. You want books? We got 'em. We got carpets and luggage, linens and laces—just name it! Yes, all started by Moishe the furniture genius. The once-and-sometime revolutionary had turned out a leading capitalist, see? Oh, the store was *much* nicer than GUM in Moscow. The place was a fairyland, Jenny said, a palace, because it was put together with love. Martin's *soul* was in that store. It sparkled, and the men and women who waited on customers were gentlemen and ladies. None of your sullen-faced GUM counter-women. Well, he'd see for himself in a few days, wouldn't he? Yuri tried to imagine the place, but all he could picture were the fountains of GUM and the statues of Peter's summer palace in Leningrad.

"He *owns* soch store? Better than GUM?"

"Sure. Singer's. It's on Fifth Avenue. You've heard of Fifth Avenue?"

"For sure!" What did she take him for? "Also Vall Stritt," he added modestly, "and Brodevay."

"Terrific. You're a real cosmopolitan, Yuri."

"To own somet'ing so big, vun porson can still do? Dot vaht I khirr."

"You bet. One family. But Marty's selling it now. They're signing papers this week."

Yuri's mind reeled. "So tell me, Zhenny, khow moch he reciff for soch store?"

She was intrigued by his naïve curiosity. No one at Golden Oaks would dream of asking such a question. But, of course, they'd all *know*.

"I hope you won't hold this against me, Yuri. Or against Marty. Thirty-five million dollars. Don't pin me to exact figures, but about that."

Yuri was cowed into silence. He knew about millionaires; he knew about the limitless wealth of the tsars. But in this day! The Voice of America said inequality was less these days. Taxes, controls, limited wealth. Lies! Still, he would not admit it—not to himself, much less to her—but Jenny had just taken on a new dimension of bewitchment. She was a queen of sorts. That sable coat of hers was simply a glamorous symptom of untold possibilities. He wondered what kind of house she lived in, but was afraid to ask. Yes, it came back to him now—she had *three* homes—in New York, Florida, and Maine. It had meant nothing to him when Baryshin had first told him that. How could he be so impressed by such a tawdry matter as personal wealth? But he *was,* and he despised himself for it. He had been seduced by the Zhiguli, and now here was this woman. How contemptuous she'd be of the Zhiguli! He must fight this temptation! Was this the weakness that had turned Moishe from revolutionary to capitalist?

And what was the problem with Martin's health? Surely he had special doctors, went to a special hospital for the big shots. What exactly had prevented him from making the trip with Jenny?

"Oh, it's nothing. Gall bladder. Nothing, right? But we were worried to death. We thought it might be a cancer recurrence—a metastasis. It would have been the end."

As a physician he was curious. Where was the original growth? Did he have radiation? Chemotherapy? How long ago? She said she hated to talk about it and did not tell him anything more.

Talking of him, however, she suddenly felt the urge to talk again to Marty, see how he was doing, whether Clara was taking proper care of him. It had been nearly five days since they last spoke. She reached impulsively for the phone and placed the call. "If I'm not in this room, operator, I'll be in six forty-five—that's our room, isn't it?" Yuri nodded. The operator replied in her fractured English. There'd be a delay.

She was aware that Yuri was watching her as she placed the call; his expression was strange, a mixture of envy, gentleness, longing. Suddenly she wanted to tell him all about Marty. When pressed some day to tell why—by Adelsheim—she would never be able to say. That old psyche of hers was full of mysteries, frequently to itself. Thank God Adelsheim wasn't here now, with those terrible turtle eyes.

"I wanna tell you something, Yuri. A deep, dark secret. You know what that means? Can't tell a soul. Ever. Promise? Not even your wife."

"In Soviet Union is everything sicrit."

She laughed. "No, no, not that kind." In a low voice, almost a monotone, unnatural for her, she traced Martin's bout with cancer, what the surgeon had done to him. He was wordless, letting her talk. "Up to now we haven't wanted anyone to know. But you're a doctor, right? Medical secret. People might feel differently about Marty if they knew. He's so male, so virile. Everyone loves him for being such a—well, such a *man*. You know what I mean?"

Yuri nodded solemnly. She stopped talking, and they both sat silent for a long time, without embarrassment, taking each other's measure. Yuri was trying to absorb fully what she had just told him. It was not your everyday problem. Terrible for Martin, he supposed, but he didn't know Martin at all. What must it have meant for Jenny? Two years! A healthy, boisterous, flamboyant woman.

"I've told my psychiatrist, of course. It's privileged, so natch. I *hadda* tell someone."

"You khov psychiatrist? For vy you nidd? You not lunatic."

"Well, I'm tense. You know what I mean? It's really difficult. I'm crazy about Marty, but . . ." She took a long, slow sip of gin, as if it were wine. Her head, already a bit light, was shaking slowly.

"Tense," he echoed. "Bot is natural! Is amazing. You simm to me vonderful voman, Zhenny. You know dot? To khov soch problem! But to go to psychiatrist? For vy? Yes, you see, up to now I'm filling sorry for myself. Selfish man! I'm t'inking: for *kher* is everyt'ing perfect, bot for me is terrible. Is not so simple, no. Vould Yuri Karpeyko go eight t'ousand kilometer, to strange country, to some cousin I never mitt, never khirr about? I dun't biliff. Zhenny, Zhenny, you so naht'ing khow you simm! Big voman, funny, talk rough like man, drink like man, but inside!" He whistled. "Is gentle lady vid great kheart." He had become rather excited and his English was deteriorating. "Up to now, I am—khow you say—abandon? Cleo, Yelena, vee all demanded to give up everything! Medical practice, beautiful apartment, Academy of Science, Institute, new car, special shops—all vaht vee vork! Vee living okay! Not bad! Is not like lies in capitalist press! Bot all dot, finish! Finish! See khow I'm filling sorry for myself? So khow is it, voman vid such kheart, she has problem also? Is also serious! You still young voman!"

"Oh, I manage. Why make such a big thing of it?"

"So you khov maybe other men?"

"Not so far. Don't think I haven't thought of it, though. But, oh boy, how could I ever do that to Marty? There's no way you can keep a thing

like that secret in New York, not in our crowd. Everybody knows *every-thing*. Marty would be destroyed. I'm not sure *I'd* like it myself."

"I am same. I am never vid voman, only Cleo. Since thirty-vun yirrs. Oh, I have moch opportunity! Many voman doctor. And mothers, filling —khow you say—so gratefool? 'Vhat I can do for you, Professor? Khow I can pay you bock?' Temptation, yes, bot I don't." He wanted to touch her, but he held back. "Zhenny, you t'ink I get out? You t'ink KGB and costom pipple blind? You t'ink Yelena will get also? You t'ink is possible?"

"You bet. Sure as shootin'."

"I not."

"Now, don't sell the Israelis short. Gideon's no dope. You can see. He's been trained." She wondered what she was doing, reassuring *him*. She hadn't the faintest idea of what she was talking about. Still, why should *everybody* worry?

"Gideon khov big doubt himself. He vorn me. D'old voman, maybe she biliff is possible. Bot she naïve, dunt know KGB."

"You mustn't *talk* that way, Yuri! Or *think* that way. Everything's worked so far, hasn't it?"

He leaned toward her and touched her shoulder apologetically. "Plizz to call me not Yuri, okay? Is too formal. Vould be I'm calling you alvay Zhennifer. For more friendly, you call me Yurka. Better, Yurochka. Is more—khow you say—intimate?"

"Yurochka." She tried it out. "Cute. You're a pretty cute guy altogether, you know that, Yurochka?"

"Nearly forty-six yirrs, can still be 'cute'?"

"Why not? Look at me. I'm pretty cute, ain't I? In a gorgeous, corrupt, torchy kinda way." She giggled and he laughed.

"Better I go look on patient," he said rising. She followed him into the bedroom. Rachel was still sleeping. He felt her forehead. She was hotter and her breathing more labored. "She vorse now, bot take few hours for medicine to vork. I t'ink she be all right."

"That's what she's been saying all along."

Rachel stirred, and Jenny went to fetch her the bottled water to sip. It was time for her next shot. Yuri told Rachel he was sure her fever would subside by tomorrow. One more injection and she could begin to take the sulfa by mouth again. She rolled half over, exposed a buttock, and he gave her the shot. Before she could quite cover herself, she began to tremble as a chill racked her body. Yuri covered her quickly; Jenny took the blankets off the other bed, fetched Yuri's camel-hair coat and her own sable, and together they smothered her in warmth until, in a few minutes, the chill subsided.

"Always good to have a doctor in the family," Rachel chattered, drawing the sable tightly about her neck.

"You said it, *Baba*," Yuri said with new spirit; all three of them laughed. But Rachel had another coughing spell, and the laughter stopped as suddenly as it had started.

11

AT TEN, JOSH RETURNED, and an hour later Gideon came back. Both missions accomplished, after a fashion.

Yuri was taken aback by the news of Baryshin's arrest, and began to brood. Something had changed. The colonel had always been untouchable. Baryshin was the only person outside this room who knew where Yuri was and the entire scheme for the Karpeyko escape. On the other hand, Baryshin had been interrogated three times before and invariably released before the end of the day. They had simply been afraid to touch him. What had changed?

Jenny understood next to nothing about his concerns, which for the moment he kept to himself. "C'mon, Yuri, cheer up. I know it must be terrible when a friend's arrested, but you gotta look on the bright side. It could have been you!"

Yuri was not amused. "Chankov clever anti-Semite. Chief Security organs in Minsk. Play on pipple like instruments in orchestra. Baryshin vahnt to see khis daughter again, yes? Khis vife. Maybe vahnt exit visa. Vaht khee can offer? Khee khov somet'ing Chankov vahnt now—Yuri Karpeyko. You dun't see?"

"Would he do *that*? Your friend Baryshin? Who did so much for you?"

"Vy not? After KGB khov khim t'ree, four days. I only mitt him few vicks first time."

It could be a close thing. In little more than thirty-six hours they'd be back at Sheremetyevo, boarding Pan American flight 102, bound for Copenhagen and New York. Surely Baryshin would hold fast for two days. Yelena now had physical possession of the American passport and Soviet visitor's visa of a person named Honey Wright. Cleo was preparing to leave legally, with official permission, for Warsaw and Vienna at four

tomorrow afternoon. As the bureaucrats would put it, everything was in order. Might it not just work? It might just.

The young men finished discussing their activities of the evening in hushed tones. Jenny was amazed at her son's coolness. It was as if Josh went every day to the homes of men who had just been arrested, as if for years he had been disposing of hot money. Well, why not? He'd coped with Mexican cops and Cambridge cops; she mustn't underestimate him. A chip off old Marty, she thought. And old Jake-o. And old Moish. And her, too, damnit. Yes, her, too.

When he'd told all he had to tell and heard Gideon out, Josh kissed his mother good night, waved to the others, and went down to his room to call Tammy and see how her show had gone tonight in Moscow. Her second performance there had ended half an hour ago. He'd catch her when she got back to the Intourist. Then he'd try for a decent night's sleep. He was bushed.

At twelve-thirty Rachel's fever broke. She perspired profusely and after a bit her breathing became easier, her skin no longer burned, her coughing was less frequent. "I'm much better," she announced calmly at one o'clock. By now Yuri was out of his tie; he'd rolled his shirtsleeves up exactly the way Marty did. Jenny had kicked her shoes off and slumped in her chair. She was sure her hair was a mop and her makeup worn off—she must look like a Charles Addams witch, but she was too tired to give a damn.

Yuri plunged the last shot into Rachel's lean buttock with professional assurance, while Jenny looked on wearily and Gideon sat primly in the sitting room.

"I t'ink Zhenny and I go now, Rachel," Yuri said. "You try slipp. You be all right in morning." He had no idea what possessed him—perhaps it was the late hour—but he bent and kissed the old lady's pale, weather-beaten, worn cheek. "You great lady."

Rachel smiled sleepily. "You're okay yourself, Doctor. Go get some sleep."

They bade Gideon goodnight and started down the silent, dimly lit hotel corridor, Jenny wearily carrying her shoes in two fingers of her left hand, sable over left arm, while Yuri carried his jacket, tie, and camel-hair coat in his right. Their free hands clasped, and they held each other like strolling, playful, tired kids. When they reached their suite, she watched admiringly as he stood on a chair as Gideon had done and deactivated the mike and mini-recorder over the door between the rooms. The sight of him there, brow knitted seriously, unscrewing those tiny screws, gave her a kick.

She could feel herself blush like a teenager as she put on the same pale blue shorty nightgown—a Singer exquisite special she'd worn every night without a thought. Tonight she didn't bother to wear anything underneath. Too much bother, and why should she? He was a doctor. They'd been looking at Rachel's ass all night. She might as well sleep free and unfettered for a change. Couldn't hurt.

"Okay, Yuri, the bathroom's all yours," she called. Soon she was lying in bed, covers pulled primly to her chin as she'd drawn them up every other night. When Yuri came into the bedroom, he turned out the dim light on the night table and clambered into his own bed. They lay motionless in the dark as they had for four nights, neither saying anything until she broke the silence. "You think Rachel's gonna be okay, then?" she said in a small voice.

"Vy not? Strong voman."

"Was your mother a strong woman, Yuri?"

"Stronger as Rachel some vay. Also veeker. Like mercury. Up, down, up, down."

"I saw that terrible picture you told us about. What a horrible thing to preserve!"

He did not respond. She turned and, her eyes now accustomed to the dark, saw him dimly, staring at the ceiling. "You don't like to talk about your mother, do you?"

His voice was barely audible. "Is impossible."

"Why? Didn't you like her?"

He got out of bed and pattered into the small sitting room, where he lit a *papyroesa*, picked up an ashtray, and returned to bed with it. The *papyroesa* glowed in the dark as he drew on it.

"You von't mind?" he asked apologetically. "Cleo don't vahnt I smoke in bed."

"Why should I mind? Tell me about your mother."

"Vy you vahnt to know?"

"I wanna know everything there is about you," she said artlessly. "I can't decide where you're coming from."

"Minsk," he said, and she chortled. "Oh, Yuri, you dope. Go ahead, tell me."

"Better not." He tapped the ash off the *papyroesa*. She could see he was propped up now, distressed, both pillows behind his back.

"Some kind of secret?" He was unresponsive. "I told you mine, didn't I?"

"You vonderful voman, Zhenny. I vish I can do, but . . ." He inhaled,

and she saw the glow of the cigarette still in his lips describe horizontal arcs as he shook his head slowly.

"You know you meck me to remember. Yes. She somet'ing like you. Must have own vay. Stobborn. She vos tall voman, thin—bot full lively. Like you, make big fun. Dot vy I like fun myself. Laugh, but inside—stiff like rock. Cook very good also. You cooking good?"

"I can't boil an egg. Hey, you think maybe I'm *too* big? I've always been pretty sensitive about that."

"No, no! You see photographs my Cleo? Not little also, anh? Plenty body, eh? I like."

They remained silent while he smoked; she stirred, restless, sat up and waited. When she could tolerate the silence no longer, she said, "Nu?"

He drew the smoke into his lungs sharply as if he had made a decision. "I vos t'irteen," he said. "And engry vid Mama. Father gone to army. Vee only two. Is not so special for t'irteen-year boy can be engry vid mother, ordinary times. But vos not ordinary times. Nazis in streets. Everywhere. Automatic guns, tanks. Mama t'row me out from khouse. She go move in vid Bonov and Orlovsky, and send me to live vid Markovs. *Dot* vaht she vahnt. She say is better, live vid family not Jews, is too dangerous live vid Jews, bot I t'ink better to be vid kher. Okay? So I'm engry."

Jenny just then would have liked a shot of gin, to have *something*, feel some physical sensation, to inhale a cigarette, anything. Pure nervous reaction.

"Mama vos Party big shot—dot khow you say? Vork in agitprop depottment central committee, before Nazis come. Is big job, but ven Nazis come, is finish. Everybody in panic. Vee see Jews, Party members, dead in stritt. Vee see alvays new bodies. So I dun't know khow I find out, but Bonov and Orlovsky and Mama kipp in Bonov's cellar machine for printing. Vaht you call?"

"Mimeograph?"

"*Tochno!* Is light to move. Dey plan to meck resistance propaganda." He had overheard Orlovsky and Bonov. They must rally the people to help partisans, who were disappearing into the forests. Mama's job was to write the slogans—she had a pen of fire. The two men were to see that her messages were duplicated and distributed.

Jenny, her knees now drawn to her chin, turned to him. "You have another one of those things you're smoking?"

"*Papyroesa?*" He turned on the small lamp between the beds, reached for the pack on the night table between them, pulled one out, lit it from his own, and passed it to her. With one hand she pulled the covers tight

to her throat—propriety despite all—and inhaled, feeling soothed and strangely depraved as smoke irritated her throat and lungs. She hadn't touched a cigarette in fifteen years, but she needed this one; she needed to feel that irritation, which radiated through her, sensation of *some* kind— to *be* with this man, somehow. He turned the light out again.

He'd found much to quarrel with Father about, but never with Mama. But he was thirteen now, the only man in the house. A happy feeling, Father gone into service. Mama all to himself! Well, such foolish happiness ended abruptly enough when the first bombs smashed into Minsk. After bombers had gutted the central city Panzers rumbled into what was left, right up Leninsky Prospekt between the shattered ruins. From their flat Mama and he could hear the cleats clanking on cobblestones, the roar of their engines. While they were waiting for Comrade Markov to collect him, to take him away, Mama spoke her words of hard truth—the crack in her façade: "Never tell anyone your mother is Jewish. You understand me, Yurochka? Never! They'll kill you. Do what the Markovs tell you. Be a good boy." He understood why, but understanding does not necessarily help; he had never felt such bitterness. They had been so close! Whatever risks she ran he wanted to share.

No, she was going to live with the Bonovs. Bonov's wife had invited her. Too many people where they now lived knew she was Jewish; it would be unsafe. The Bonovs and the Orlovskys, who lived in the same building off the Svisloch, would protect her, that she was sure of. They were old comrades. Could he at least come to visit her? They'd see. Perhaps, if they were extremely careful. He must never tell anyone she was his mother. Why did this make him so furious? Because she *was* a Jew? For making him live away from her? For her dangerous work? What right had she to put herself in such danger? Didn't she owe herself to *him*?

The Markovs lived half a kilometer from the Yubeleinaya market, which the Nazis had turned into a ghetto. Tolya was then only nine, but he, too, had to go daily with his father and with Yuri to the work brigade. Minsk was not much more than a large town then, and the Nazis put the conscripted brigade to work repaving Railroad Station Square with cobblestones. No machines, no wheelbarrows; each stone had to be carried by hand long distances. Today the square was paved with the cobbles Yuri, Tolya, and thousands of others had placed there personally.

While they were working, Yuri sometimes saw local people, older men, but more often woman, accompanying two- or three-man Nazi detachments. The pattern was always the same: the collaborator would point out someone working, and nod. Sometimes as the victim was pulled away roughly the collaborator would spit out or mutter, *"Zhid!"* Usually the

victim was hustled away—to the ghetto, Tolya Markov's father said. But on two occasions one of the Nazis simply raised his weapon and shot the victim where he stood, pumping additional rounds into the fallen heap.

The victims were left to bleed to death; overseers barked, "Get a move on. Continue with the work." Several times a dozen or more in his work gang would be rounded up and driven off in an open truck. In the evening of such days, from the Markovs' flat, one could hear the spitting machine guns from the ghetto.

Working in Railway Station Square one day, Yuri saw truckloads of people laden with bundles and packages. Their clothes bore the yellow Star of David. These people, he heard, were being moved into the apartments of Minsk Jews who had run away, been shot, or been expelled to the ghetto. No doubt into the flat he and Mama had abandoned.

Local Jews wore no such insignia. The new people had been brought from Paris, Amsterdam, Berlin, Vienna, Brussels, Marseilles. Were the Nazis killing Soviet Jews to provide homes for Jews from the West? Were western Jews favored over eastern? Eventually he learned the truth, but for months it was one of the bitter mysteries of Minsk.

For a short time he was so furious with Mama he vowed never to see her again, but the feeling faded, and after a week of brooding, he decided that in the hour between work and curfew, he would visit her, danger or no. He thought about her constantly. When he arrived, he found her in Bonov's kitchen with Bonov's wife. Mama was not demonstrative when she saw him, but invited him to help with the meal, such as it was. This set the pattern for subsequent visits. The food was terrible—nothing but roots, many unrecognizable, which for lack of power or fuel had to be eaten raw. Still, there was dark bread, and Mama could do better with whatever was at hand than most. Bonov was a big bluff man, who often insisted on wrestling with Yuri like an overgrown, playful dog, while the small, thin Orlovsky sat bug-eyed, glued to his small secret radio, the dial set to one station, endlessly in search of good news, which was scarcer than meat.

Once when he came, he found Bonov, Orlovsky, and Mama studying with satisfaction a single, still-damp mimeographed leaflet. Yuri could read the first words in large capital letters: COUNTRYMEN RESIST! FIGHT TO THE DEATH! Yuri looked about the room. In the corner was a pile of such leaflets.

"But who else can do it?" Bonov asked.

"Since they took Melnikov, who is there?" Orlovsky said, turning to Yuri. He realized they were talking for his benefit.

"No, no," Mama shouted. "I won't have it. He's only a kid."

"So why don't we ask *him?*" Orlovsky said very quietly.

"I don't care what he says!" Mama cried, her short hair flying as she shook her head in despair, defeat in every gesture. The world was closing in on Mama. They were asking too much of her.

"Listen, Yurka," Bonov said, "someone has to take this little package to Markov's house. You live in Markov's house."

It was the first time Yuri realized that Tolya Markov's father, too, was involved in the Resistance.

"You can't do this!" Mama snapped. She tugged at a lock of her tousled hair. "Not my kid, goddamn you both!" She hugged Yuri, appealing to him with her entire body. "Yurochka, don't listen to these fools. Please!" But he could feel her weakening, could feel the desperation seize her. She said one thing and meant another.

A thirteen-year-old in those days was no mere boy, and Yuri was no fool. Bonov, the bear, put his enormous arms around Yuri's thin, half-wasted body. "Yurka, you want to be a slave? You want our people to be slaves? Your father is doing his duty in Stalingrad. You want your father to be ashamed of you? You see what these animals are doing to us? Especially to Jews? They shoot us in the streets like mad dogs. Blood is all we see. Your mother writes stirring messages to rouse the people, but your mother has no gun. She *can* rouse the people, but only if you bring her words to Markov and he gets them to the people with guns. *Our* people. You understand?"

Orlovsky, too, launched into a similar polemic. Mama's head was in her hands.

When Orlovsky finished, Yuri put a hand on Mama's shoulder, lifted her face. "I'm clever enough, Mama. They'll never catch me." A touch of bravado.

Bonov took him aside afterward. "No matter what, Yurka, never, never give us away. No matter what they do to you. Okay?" It was enough to nod and repeat, "Okay."

And so it began. He brought the packages to Markov's, and though he never knew how, by next morning he would see the leaflets littering Lenin Square. They were posted on doorways, were left on the seats of trams and buses. People read them quickly, crumpled them, and threw them away.

One gray October day he arrived at Bonov's building to visit Mama and to pick up his weekly package of pamphlets. This time he could not go in, because drawn up and parked on the sidewalk before the building entrance were three Nazi vehicles with a dozen SS troopers crowding the

entryway. Yuri remained frozen. He dared not run. Instead he sauntered forward, joining the SS men. They did not understand his question, but motioned him vaguely away—they were busy.

He vacillated, afraid to make any sudden move, and suddenly Mama emerged between two SS men, one holding each arm. Her cheek was a bruised ugly blotch of blood, her hair in terrible disarray, her eyes wide with fright, but her posture was erect, a heroine for the masses. Except there were no masses—only Yuri, a dozen uniformed men of the Liebstandarte division behind him, and a few onlookers across the street from the entrance, too alarmed to come any closer. The tableau Mama saw as she emerged was what he had suppressed for more than thirty years: her son, the betrayer, with the enemy. Who but he could have led them here? Behind her now came Bonov, slouching from his great height, one eye closed, bleeding from his nose and mouth, and skinny Orlovsky, head bowed, curly black hair flying. Two SS men accompanied each of them, and a seventh SS man, jabbing first one, then the other, with a handgun, muttered, "*Schwein! Geh, geh!*"

Bonov raised his head, and the sight of Yuri seemed to stagger him. Mama's eyes, when she looked at him, glazed over; she went past him without sign of recognition, a stranger. Orlovsky never looked up, did not see him at all.

He wanted to cry out, "It's not what you think, Mama! Not I! I don't know how they discovered you!" But of course he did not dare. Mama turned then, her eyes unfocused, as if she were staring at the Nazis behind him, but he knew the look was for him. He could scarcely believe it was the woman he knew. Those harrowed eyes were of a woman crucified. She was staring at the horror of her own inferno.

The three of them were jostled into three separate vehicles, and they careened off. The episode had taken only a few moments.

What would they do to her? He asked a man in the small knot of curiosity-seekers across the street, but the man turned away without answering. It took all his willpower to keep from chasing after, from calling her name. But the urge to survive was a ruthless master.

No way could be found, no way in the world, ever to tell her it was not he. Within a few days she had died—died in torment, tortured not only by mechanical beasts, operators of a slaughterhouse, but perhaps more by the knowledge that her son, her Yurochka, the assistant in her kitchen, her singing partner, had, for reasons she could only guess at, given away her life.

There was a man, Myzelov, who had served during the occupation as an interpreter at Nazi interrogations; he had sought Yuri out after the war

to tell him this: The interrogators tried to learn from Mama, as well as from Bonov and Orlovsky, where the pamphlets were taken, how they were distributed.

To loosen tongues, devices of various kinds were used, the last of which was the metal garrote. Nothing worked on Mama. The executioner would flip the screw a turn or two—Mama's screams were indescribable—and the interrogator would ask him to reverse the pressure, and would talk with extreme politeness to her, telling her if she answered, he could spare her life, asking if she cared to answer the questions now.

Finally, after one terrible session, she said to her interrogator, "I cannot help you unless you kill both my colleagues. When you show me their bodies, I will feel safe enough to tell you."

Soon afterward she was shown the wasted, distorted bodies of her two friends. "Then you know what she said?" Myzelov had told Yuri. "Not much left of her, you know, by this time; they'd pulled out almost all her hair, but she said, 'So now you must kill me, too, because I will never tell you.'"

This infuriated the interrogator. For three days they worked on her, until the interrogator shrugged and gave up, signaling the executioner to give the final turns of the screw. What they had written on her body was no exaggeration.

The day after Mama was arrested, Yuri and Andrei Khess, now working in the outskirts, made their move, and a week later Pyotr Feodorovich and Yuri were back at the station, hiding in the public toilet; from there he saw all three of them hanging in the Square—Bonov, his head almost severed, Orlovsky an unrecognizable side of beef, and Mama, her head bald, twisted crazily, tongue out, eyes bulging. KIKE BANDIT. STRANGLED . . .

"So I, also," Yuri was saying barely audibly, "I strangle slowly. Khow many yirrs? Most be now t'irty-two."

Jenny was too shaken to say anything.

"I'm t'ink every day, bot trying *not*. Khow can I tell kher? Vaht I vahnt to say? Vasn't *me*. No vay to tell kher! So she endure agony and belivv I give kher to Nazis! How do you like dot?"

His voice had become a keening, and he rocked back and forth as he sat up in bed, a tall, good-looking old Jew, Jenny was thinking, saying his goddamn kaddish in the high pitch of a Hassid. The tears were in his voice if not in his eyes.

She pushed her way out of her bed abruptly and moved to his.

"Yurochka." The unfamiliar name. "Listen to me." She drew his head to her breast, felt the force of his keening through the sheer gown. The keening became a low moan, sigh, as he rocked on, finally in silence.

"Yurochka," she said, her voice firm as a teacher's to a wayward child, "Why do you torture yourself? You're absolutely wrong. If she refused to tell them about *you*, how could she think it *was* you? Don't you see? It can't be both ways. Why would they be asking about you, if it was you that brought them to her? Even I can figure that much out."

He shook his head. "You don't see khow she look on me. Khorrible. Vaht Myzelov tell me, I don't know if true. Pipple who vork vid Nazis . . . such liars . . ."

He was quieting now slowly, laboriously lifting the sharp stones of pain under which he was buried as he rationalized, but he made no move to remove himself from her arms, nor did she withdraw. They sat together, his head in her embrace, and she whispered, soothing and reassuring, as to an injured child, "Shhh, Shhh. It's all right, it's all right."

He turned toward her and she kissed his forehead, then softly his eyes, his cheeks—gently, a mother's kisses, but suddenly he found her mouth, and he was kissing her. *At last,* she thought in spite of herself. A different signal was given with that kiss, and in that flick of tenderness, unmistakably moist, something that took less than a second, everything changed. At first Yuri was too overwrought to be surprised, and Jenny too sympathetic. She clasped him to herself as if she had just rescued him from some danger, as if he were physically injured, still suffering, but he was not.

Her gown had slipped from one shoulder, and she hesitated. Then she shrugged the other loose and let it fall. She felt his eager lips at her breast, and she felt herself melting elsewhere. Her insides felt the old tenseness, expectation, too, and she tried to persuade herself to resist. His lust it was, the impulse of man, that stirred her own, so long withered. How long? Christ, two years. Fair is fair. After an interminable silence, his hands, deft hands of a master magician, too, she thought, were upon her in ways familiar, yet not entirely. There was a careful unhurriedness. "Zhenny, Zhenny," he murmured apologetically, "vaht vee do? Vaht vee vahnt? Vee doing impossible!"

But it was not; he didn't stop, and neither did she. Could guilt take a holiday? Why not, she thought, why not? And whispered, "Yurochka, you beautiful, beautiful man." Words not of sympathy, but of encouragement.

The shrill clang of the telephone startled them. For a moment neither

of them could decide what it was. To Jenny it sounded like the accusing fire alarm at P.S. 70 in the Bronx. Yuri stirred, switched on the lamp, and as the clang persisted unrelenting, he walked to the bureau desk and picked up the instrument. She could not help seeing his erection wilt. He was almost too unnerved to remember to speak English, but caught himself in time. He listened, then turned to Jenny, who had restored her gown but made no attempt to cover its transparency, and had drawn her knees to her chin, pouting like a spoiled child.

"Is for you."

"Oh, my God." The call she had placed earlier. How could she have forgotten? She took the phone. Yuri stood beside her.

"Yeah, Marty?" Mentally she shook herself like a rag doll. Come back, little Sheba. "Can you hear me okay? How the hell are you, Marty?" Her voice, echoing, sounded stagey and strange to herself. Could he tell? Oh, boy! "I just felt I hadda hear your crazy voice. I've been missing you, but madly."

"Who's the guy?" Marty asked.

"Oh, wait'll I tell you! It's a long story, but not to worry, bubbala, and not on the phone. He's just here for a drink. So tell me, how's the old gut? You feeling okay?"

"Much better. By next week Sam says I'll be entirely out of the woods. Mother's been at me, of course, not to try to do too much too fast. You know her."

"It's good advice, Marty. Is the store thing settled?"

"Still haven't got the money, but the closing's next week."

"Oh, terrific! So look, Tammy's tour's going gangbusters. Josh is here in Minsk and told us all about it. They carried Tammy through the streets of Moscow as if she were Charlie Lindbergh. So help me! Yeah, honestly."

"Have you met our cousins yet?" Martin's voice sounded funny, as if he were a stranger . . . talking to a stranger.

She reached for Yuri's hand and held it. "Have I! You bet! This isn't a good time to tell you about it, Marty—know what I mean? Tomorrow we're all gonna meet in Moscow—Tammy and the rest of us, and on Thursday we'll be home. *Gott sei dank!* Then you won't be able to shut me up. I'll tell it all. Oh, how you'd've hated it this time, Marty! Oh, worse—much worse. We were practically arrested in Vilna."

"Now, listen, Jen," Martin said sternly. "Did you see Bill Cole?"

"Sure did."

"If you have any more trouble, *any* at all, remember to call him, okay?"

"Sure. Listen, Marty, it's getting pretty late here. Lemme put this guy

on the road, so I can get some sleep. I'll see ya Thursday. Miss you—God, how I miss you!"

"Not as much as I miss you. This is a very empty house."

She put the phone back on its cradle. Oh, what a liar she was! She peered at Yuri, standing beside her and watching her like an imp. Had they been saved by the bell from utter foolishness? Was the phone call a piece of good luck?

She started back to her bed, Yuri trailing behind her, and as she reached it, he took her in his arms. Oh, Lord! Her own arms went about him, and they sank to her bed.

The interruption had given them an instant to reconsider, a moment of grace, of sobriety—to weigh consequences. What might have been the mere stirring toward instinctive coupling in their overwrought states, in this cooler moment needed justifications in two teetering minds coming from quite different directions. But minds furnish rationalizations needed by desperate souls; in harmony they moved swiftly toward the forbidden goal they had been avoiding. They were alternately as awkward as teen-agers and as exploratory as Magellan.

"Yurochka, can you love Cleo *and* me?"

"Zhenny, so lovely Zhenny! You like movie star! Is for me drimm, is meckbiliff, voman from faravay planet, come to save me." Spoken as he kissed her in a whisper kiss.

They did reach their peaks, but the climb was hard, uncertain, and their breath came short. She could feel her Yurochka, a dear, hurt, desperate man, clinging to her like soft strands of cobweb, and at the same time thrusting slowly, gently, into her; her body trembled; she almost felt herself disembodied, floating, then rocketing, fire in her wake, until she was zooming, zooming upward. At last! At last! Ah, yes!

Yuri fell asleep, she still at first wide awake, until his even, steady breathing became contagious and she dozed; they curled into each other with a kind of desperation. At a quarter of seven Yuri awoke first, and before Jenny knew what was happening, before she had completely thrown off her slumber, he had started again—slowly, sweetly—a confident man now, not to be trifled with, seducing her awake. She was glad they were not children then. At least they could take their time and enjoy.

12

AT FOUR O'CLOCK NEXT AFTERNOON Cleo Karpeyko boarded the Warsaw train. In Warsaw she would have to change for a train to Vienna, overcoming all the hurdles and humiliations a hostile, anti-Semitic Polish bureaucracy had been able to invent for transiting Jews and their mates—Jewish or not—and their children. She had been warned. She was prepared to pay bribes for tickets she had already paid for, to be submissive when insults were hurled, and in Brest, before she passed from the Soviet Union forever, to have her body intimately searched. It would not be easy for Cleo, but it was once in a lifetime.

Yelena accompanied her mother to the station and saw her to the train. She would have liked to go as far as Brest with her, but Gideon had warned her not to. She'd be pulled off the train on some pretext. In any case the man was following her everywhere. Yelena's mood had improved a bit in recent days, and she'd been given a spectacular boost by last night's meeting with Gideon Aron, her Israeli cousin, who had promised her the world—she would complete her studies at the Hadassah Medical School of Hebrew University, and could have a position of responsibility in the research labs of the hospital.

She now carried in her large purse the American passport, the Soviet visitor's visa, the currency declaration, and the airline ticket Gideon had given her last night. He had also given her a first-class railway ticket from Minsk to Moscow departing tonight at eight. Under her thin raincoat she was wearing Honey Wright's gray, smartly tailored overcoat from Lazarus, but not the matching hat, which was in her purse. The challenge of her life now was to shake her tail after Cleo's train left, and to get on that Moscow train unobserved, like any other passenger. If her tail saw her board that train, she would be removed by the police on any trumped-up charge—having picked someone's pocket, anything. Later the militia

would concede its "mistake" and she would be released. Legalities, she now knew, meant nothing to the KGB. Yelena had therefore been carefully instructed by Gideon.

Her farewell to Cleo was tense, watchful, and, for Cleo, desperate. Both understood the hazards, but the mother, ordinarily an optimist, feared them more. She was going because Yuri had asked her to—an act of faith. Everything that boy Gideon had told her last night filled her with misgivings, but how dared she doubt those trying to help her? Yurochka had always come through; why not now? Still, the possibilities . . . she was not behaving well at all. She should be ashamed of these tears. Yelena, Yelena! How can I lose her? What if something goes wrong? How can I get through the next two days until I *know*? She forced herself to stop crying, and embraced Yelena. Day after tomorrow, then.

Think of something else: How would she and Yuri fare in America? How will Yelena do in Israel? Nice that Gideon and his grandmother would be there to look after her. If only Yelena and Yuri would simply get through the net! How wonderful that would be, Cleo thought.

As she watched her mother's train move along the platform, Cleo waving to her and trying to smile, on her way to the West at last, Yelena became for a moment completely disoriented. What was it Zhitnikov had said to her, after telling her she was "severed," in that muttered undertone? "You might find yourself a place abroad." Her only hope, and she was now on her own. She had to concentrate as never before on every move. The next four hours.

Her tail followed her into the small restaurant in the station and sat at an adjacent table. She nodded to him, he nodded in reply. She did exactly as Gideon had instructed. "My mother is gone," she said.

"She's a fool," the man sneered.

She smiled sweetly. "Can I get you a glass of tea? I would like to celebrate for my mother. Why don't you come and sit with me? It's silly for us to be at separate tables." He shook his head, remained at his table, and Yelena, with her back to him, ordered tea and bread for herself. She was amazed at how bold she could be if there was purpose. Normally she would be too frightened to speak to any stranger, much less the KGB man who was following her. Still, though refusing to join her, he was not unpleasant. His task was simple: to keep her always in view, or at least to know where she was, and at the same time to keep a sharp eye out for her father, the professor, the prey of this game. Everyone at headquarters was certain the professor would show up sooner or later. He personally was not so sure.

"What have you heard from your father?" he asked across the empty space in the clumsy way that foot soldiers have of stepping on their own toes.

"Nothing," she said over her shoulder. "Mama and I are terribly worried about him. I don't believe the KGB has let him go yet." The waiter brought the tea.

"Oh, they have."

"I don't believe it. Since when do they let anyone go?" She drank her tea.

"That is a slander. The organs are fair. They bend over backward to be fair these days. Only the guilty suffer."

"Well, then, what do they want with my father? He's guilty of nothing." She saw Gideon entering the restaurant. Gideon nodded to her. Now. Gideon sat at a table with two strange women on the other side of the room.

"Then he will have nothing to fear," the tail said. She sipped more tea, nibbled the bread, dawdled over it. After she had drunk the full glass, she rose. "Please excuse me." She went to the W.C., her purse carelessly over her wrist, and saw Gideon rise and start toward the table where the tail sat, now alone, his eyes glued to the women's-toilet door she was entering. In the booth she removed the raincoat from over Honey's coat and put on the matching gray tam; her costume was transformed. She waited several minutes until she heard the commotion. When she came out, there was a crowd around her tail's table, and people, including her tail, were shouting and gesticulating.

Gideon had taken the tail by his lapels and was shaking a finger in his face and screaming. She pulled the tam-o'-shanter forward and left the room quickly, walked swiftly out of the station into the busy square, and boarded the first trolley bus she came to, heading for the Minsk Hotel on Lenin Square. There she disembarked and went directly into the hotel entrance.

The doorman tried to stop her. "I am an American," she said, speaking the sentences carefully in English, part of a short speech she had practiced for two hours. She showed him Honey's passport, now graced with her own photo. "I'm staying at the Yubeleinaya. I've come to visit American friends." He studied the passport a moment, nodded, and let her pass. She headed directly for the women's restroom. There was no attendant at this hour. Her own American jeans, the overcoat, and the hat had all helped, but now she had to dress from head to toe as Honey Wright. She could take no chances. Suspected persons were occasionally stripped at the airport.

Gideon had told her these were all things given to him by Honey herself. Pantyhose by Burlington with a Shillito's label, a shirt by Hathaway, and Weejuns. As Gideon had suggested, Yelena spent the next forty-five minutes in a toilet booth, cutting up her own underwear and blouse with the scissors she had brought in her purse, and flushing them away, bit by bit. She did the same with her Soviet passport. Her own shoes she put in her purse.

Once her clothes were disposed of, she moved carefully about the city on buses and trolleys and at seven forty-five returned to the long-distance station. The tail was long gone in search of her. She felt almost sorry for the man. The argument Gideon had started, accusing the man of deliberately tripping, attacking, and robbing him, was an old KGB tactic. As soon as the altercation was settled and Gideon had identified himself as American and apologized, he quickly disappeared; the KGB agent sent a waitress into the women's toilet, but his pigeon had escaped, and the man knew he was in serious trouble. Minsk was a city of a million people. He'd better go back to her apartment and wait for her to return. If he was lucky, she'd return there, and he could pretend that nothing had happened. If she did not return . . . he preferred not to think about that possibility.

The train to Moscow had three deluxe sleeping cars. Rachel, now somewhat improved, but her face still drawn, along with Yuri, Jenny, Gideon, and Josh, stood on the platform with their Intourist guide, a young man who, after seeing that their baggage was safely aboard, shook hands with each of them efficiently, wished them a pleasant journey, and departed.

Josh had a compartment to himself. Gideon shared one with his grandmother, and Yuri and Jenny shared one. Yelena, who boarded separately, had a single compartment in the forward adjacent car. She carried only her purse and boarded immediately after they did.

After the train had left Minsk and began to move eastward into the empty night, Gideon went forward to fetch Yelena, and the six of them gathered in Gideon's compartment. In this cramped space, surrounded by their cousins from Israel and America, Yuri stood to embrace his daughter in silence. She seemed to him so young and frail, despite the faintest swelling of her midriff. But something had happened to Yelena since Yuri saw her last. She had met Gideon. He had brought word that her peers *wanted* her in Israel. Life beckoned. She liked her Israeli cousin. Dutifully, like a child, as she was introduced she kissed first Jenny, then Rachel, on both cheeks, then shook hands solemnly with Josh. "Mama got off all right, Daddy," she told him in Russian. "She will be in Vienna to-

morrow morning. She was quite excited before she left. She's been afraid to believe before now, and she's been upset about you."

Yuri shook his head. "Hard to believe, isn't it? So much trouble to leave a country!"

"Everybody insulted her, of course," Yelena said, "but luckily Dr. Shtainberg warned her. In Brest they'll search her. She's ready for that. They say they're looking for diamonds, for gold—can you imagine? Doctor Shtainberg says they're quite horrible. She didn't care. In the end she was happy to be getting away. She's missed you, Daddy. You have no idea! So did I."

A blue-uniformed woman attendant brought them six glasses of tea and six small packages of sweet crackers, uttering not a word. Yuri remarked that there was no problem talking on trains; Androprov's security machine seemed to have neglected enlisting the train attendants, who seemed anxious only to be by themselves and to provide as little service as possible.

Both Yuri and Rachel noticed how attentive Gideon was to Yelena, how eagerly she responded. Had the long night of her despair come to an end? Her listlessness had troubled Yuri as much as it had Cleo. In his labored Russian, Gideon asked Yelena more about her work. She said modestly that while it fascinated her, it made poor telling. He asked if she had thought further about the offer from Israel. Yes, she said, she wanted to accept it. She was tired of having to stew and look over her shoulder constantly because Daddy was partly Jewish. If all her coworkers were Jews, how could they mind?

Gideon laughed. "If you only knew. Your problem now will be your mother. Because of her, you know that in Israel you are no Jew at all?"

"True?"

Rachel shook her head sadly. "The rabbis," she said. "But it can be arranged. You'll be a citizen. You'll convert. So don't worry about it."

"And, of course, when you marry, you'll say you're a Jew, and that can be the end of the problem," Gideon said airily.

"I maybe should marry soon, then," Yelena said, smiling naïvely, "or what will my baby do for a father?"

Her sally brought abrupt, sudden silence. Yuri and Rachel glanced uneasily at each other with troubled eyes.

Yelena stammered, "I shouldn't have said that?"

Gideon translated her words into English.

Josh laughed and said, "That's not the only thing you shouldn't have done."

Yelena, who understood him, flushed and put her hand over her

mouth, and Gideon laughed and took her hand. "Don't worry, Yelena, it happens in the best of families."

Yelena, encouraged, told them about Kozhinskaya's plan for her to continue working in the lab while the students would keep an eye on the baby. Could that be done at Hadassah? Why not? They talked of the problems Cleo and Yuri would have in New York getting licenses to practice, finding hospital affiliations. They talked of learning English and Hebrew, of *ulpans* and cram courses. They talked of this and that, their eyes unrealistically on the future. Several things were clear: Cleo was absolutely determined to go to America, and Yuri would go with her. They could visit Yelena in Jerusalem, and Yelena could visit New York. To Yelena, and to a lesser degree even to Yuri, what they were saying had the ring of another world—flying, visiting, flitting back and forth across a world so small that everything was possible.

But Rachel's face was drawn into a tight, unhappy little smile. She would not give up. "Yurka, you got your *vyzov*, your invitation, from *me*. So listen, why do you want to go to America? They don't need you. *We* need you. We need Cleo, too. What did I say at that dinner in California? Tell him, Jenny. I said *I'm* going to the Soviet Union to *get* my cousin. I said *I* would be responsible for you. Come to us. Please. Before long, your friend Shtainberg will be coming, too, you'll see. We need you all."

Yuri listened as if possibly his mind could be changed, but he was merely being polite.

They talked in this fashion, courteously, about the future and pretended that decisions which had been irrevocably made could be changed. But of course they could not. And at midnight they agreed to retire.

Yelena said nothing to her father as he lurched off down the corridor with Jenny to their compartment, nor did Josh say anything to his mother. Everyone, including Rachel, simply pretended that Yuri and Jenny were only posing as a married couple, when indeed there was no longer any need for them to do so. Yelena could easily have shared her compartment with her father, and Josh could have shared his with his mother. But there was a small, reluctant conspiracy of silence. What, indeed, could be said? As a result, everyone, including Jenny and Yuri, felt uncomfortable; but not so uncomfortable that the principals would do anything to change it. By now they had needs, appetites of their own.

13

IN MOSCOW THE REUNION of the Americans that morning at the Hotel Intourist verged on the tumultuous. As their bags were being carried in from Gorky Street, where snow was falling lightly, Jenny saw their crowd in the plaza outside the lobby; and in the center of it all was Tammy, a waif trying to hold her own against reporters and fans, everyone firing questions or trying to get her to write her autograph on American jeans. Surrounded by her manager and his wife, the boys in the band, and their women, she was doing her best. Of the original sixteen in the troupe, two were missing—Josh and Honey Wright.

Just then Tammy spied Josh coming toward the entrance, uttered a cry of delight, pushed her way through the crowd of admirers, and curled into Josh's hug. He licked a snowflake from her nose.

Tammy left Josh's embrace to greet Jenny with a daughterly hug and kiss, shook Gideon's hand, pecked Rachel on the cheek, and greeted Yuri, a man she'd never seen, with a hug and called him Marty, as if he *were* her father-in-law. The kid, Jenny observed to herself, hadn't been exposed to the stage for a lifetime for nothing. Ten KGB guys watching carefully would've found every nuance perfect.

While Jenny, Yuri, Rachel, and Gideon went inside and sauntered up the broad flight of stairs to one of the dining rooms in search of breakfast, Josh, Tammy, and Yelena rejoined the band. Yuri was troubled to see his daughter disappear into the group of musicians. Each time they separated now he suffered a small death. By the merest flick of Tammy's eyebrows the signal was given that this was the one. The kids in the band, all in the know, were keyed up. If it worked, this would be their pleasure, and their quick glances of admiration indicated they thought this was a Russian worth rescuing. It would give them a special joy to put it over on Volodya, who, as their official shepherd both in Kiev and Moscow, had

been a terrific pain in the ass, limiting their movement like an old school-marm, treating them like juvenile delinquents.

The men in the band grinned their greeting to Yelena; the groupies called out to her, "Hi, Honey. Find the john? Feelin' better, kid?" as if they'd seen her a few minutes ago. This for the benefit of Volodya, who was just returning from making taxi arrangements. They all carefully positioned themselves so that Volodya wouldn't quite see Yelena's face. And Tammy went back to signing jeans and answering questions in her tremulous little voice, apologizing for the interruption. Volodya was relieved; yes, there was the singer's husband—the one they called Josh—and he could see the back of Yelena's head. The one they called Honey. American women were always redoing their hair. Well, another half hour and they'd be out of his hands. They made him very nervous.

At the entrance to the upstairs restaurant, Jenny found a phone; Yuri gave her two kopeks and she called the embassy. Bill Cole was kind enough to get on promptly.

"How's it going at your end?" Bill inquired mildly.

"Okay, I guess. Our plane leaves in a couple of hours. Oh, by the way, Bill, there's an American girl with my daughter-in-law's troupe who's had a problem. All her stuff was stolen. She's coming in to see the consul; she's gonna need a new passport and everything, but if the consul gives her a hard time, I told her to ask for you. She knows what a marvelous guy you are. Was that okay?"

"Sure, Jenny. But your son's already told me about this little tragedy."

"He *did*? I could've saved my two kopeks."

"Not to worry. Have a nice flight home. Tell Martin I was asking for him."

"Thanks for everything, Billy. Knowing you were there made all the difference."

She hung up, reassured and optimistic. By the time they left the hotel the snow was coming down heavily. They crowded into five taxis, black Volgas, with Volodya accompanying Tammy, her manager, his wife, and Josh in the first. Jenny, Yuri, Rachel, and Gideon brought up the rear; they were accompanied by Anya, their deluxe Intourist godmother, to see to things deluxely. As the five black cars snaked slowly through the light Moscow traffic, all they lacked, Jenny observed, was the hearse and flower car up front. Once they were out of the city, the procession became less funereal; they picked up speed and raced through the countryside, until Jenny was terrified by the wild ride in the blinding snow; but they made it.

If anything, Sheremetyevo was more bustling and disorderly than the day they had arrived. As they disembarked from the five cabs, drawn up in single file, the young people, all in high spirits, laughed, argued, horsed about—still the despair of Volodya, who by now could barely wait to get them to their plane. By the time all of them had claimed their luggage and had begun to stroll in disorderly fashion through the great departure and arrival hall, Volodya had about had it. Never again. Give him symphony orchestras any time. He would make that much clear to his boss.

The troupe wanted to thank him, Tammy's manager came up to him and told him, for all his help. Tammy came to shake his hand shyly and smiled her appreciation endearingly. "Everyone here was just wonderful, Volodya," she cooed. "The kids were marvelous." She had one crafty eye on Yelena, who remained hidden from Volodya by three of the boys in the band, huddling among the groupies. "And you were, too. What would we have done without you?" Then Tammy stood back from Volodya and formally clapped her hands together in personal, admiring applause for him; he smiled for the first time during the tour, his fears of American God-knows-what almost overcome. They hadn't really been that bad. The others in the troupe joined in the applause, calling "Bravo, Volodya," and "Da svidanya, Volodya." Tammy kissed him on each cheek, murmuring "Bolshoi spasiba," and then two other members of the band came to shake his hand. He hurried over to the customs tables and spoke officially and quietly to an inspector, waving a last farewell toward the troupe, then raised both hands and clasped them overhead American style to signify he had taken care of everything, formalities and all. There'd be no difficulty or delay. He had done his duty perfectly. He thought his boss would be pleased. An elitist to the core, he was proud that he had gained the approval of Tammy herself, the only one he really gave a damn about. She'd kissed and thanked him profusely. What more could a man expect?

Anya, the Intourist godmother from the hotel, went from Jenny's taxi into the great hall and fetched them a baggage man. At the taxi she shook hands with each of her four deluxe charges, wishing them, as she customarily did every departing American deluxe party, bon voyage. She ducked back into the Volga and before they realized they had been abandoned by their godmother, her cab was squealing its way back toward the seven spires of Moscow.

For half an hour everyone in both parties worked on currency declarations, finding the proper forms, going to bank windows to change excess rubles back into dollars (rubles could not be taken out), digging out air tickets, visas, and passports. Several troupe members who had climbed to the observation gallery returned to report they could see bulldozers and

tractors on the tarmac sweeping snow back and clearing the runways. They weren't quite socked in.

Huddled under the stairs, only a few yards from the customs area, Jenny and Yuri saw a dozen figures sitting dejectedly on their luggage, somber and quiet. From time to time one or another of them would look, as if for succor, in the direction of the customs inspectors. "Who are those people?" Jenny asked, but Yuri shrugged. Gideon went to inquire.

"Our people," he said when he returned. "Lucky ones. They hov exit visas to Israel. Waiting here already t'ree days to have baggage inspected. Sleep here. Everyt'ing confiscate. Will hov body searches." He shrugged. "Next year in Yerushalayam. That what they dreaming." He looked back toward the strangers and waved. Two men waved back.

Tammy's manager had come back from talking with the customs inspector. "Okay, kids. We're up. Let's go." They meandered to the customs area and lined up, almost orderly for the first time. The troupe headed the line, followed by Yuri, Jenny, Rachel, and Gideon, in that order. A group of onlookers, fans of Tammy's, assembled to watch, called to her. As those upfront reached the inspector they placed their bags on the long table. Those behind moved their luggage along as the inspection progressed.

Yelena stood third, behind Max the sound man, and in front of Si Goulder. Looking more middle-American than any of the others in her Lazarus coat and hat, she carried Honey Wright's tan leather suitcase with its bullseye label: CANTON, OHIO. In her free hand she held her currency declaration, passport, visa, and Honey's New York-Helsinki-Kiev-Moscow-New York air ticket. Yuri thought she was beginning to look pregnant; she also had high color and her pulse was fast. She was wondering how she would fare if it came to a body search. Did they ever do that to Americans? Two customs men were examining Max's acoustical equipment—his mikes, speakers, vibeboxes, amplifier. They were fascinated, but satisfied. Ah, a hand was reaching toward Yelena. "Ticket, please?" She gave the hand her ticket and documents. "Open, please." She opened Honey's bag; nothing extraordinary. A face. Passport flipped open, closed. Currency declaration studied. Stamped, taken away. Visa examined, taken. A small, almost invisible chin motion. In there, please, the booth. A matron in the cubicle patted her perfunctorily. Okay. That way out. She walked toward the transit lounge, not daring to look around to see Daddy. Her heart slowed. Could it be this easy? Yuri watched her go through and he, too, was amazed. It *was* that easy.

Volodya had told the young customs man that Tammy was to get special treatment. He smiled, waved her in. No need to open luggage, no, no,

glad to be of help to the brave little singer who was not afraid to tell America the truth about Vietnam. As she moved into the cubicle the crowd applauded and called to her with love, reluctant to disperse.

After the troupe had been processed, Yuri presented his passport to the hand. But the hand did not accept it. Instead it reached for Jenny's. "Ladies first, sir," the voice said. Everything was done with extraordinary swiftness. No baggage examination. "Thank you, madam." The hand reached toward Rachel. Yuri stood there, unable and unwilling to protest, immobilized. Jenny waited for him.

The hand reached toward Gideon. "Passport, sir." The inspector, as he examined Gideon's papers, eyed Jenny's sable admiringly, but motioned her impatiently toward one of the personal inspection cubicles.

Still she hesitated. "In there, madam. Please." He handed Gideon's passport back, took his other documents, and signaled him toward another of the cubicles. "For you, sir. In there." Gideon went.

Jenny, ignoring the directions of the inspector, continued to wait. But something was happening. The customs inspector now held up his hand, as if he were a policeman stopping traffic. In Russian and English he spoke to the departing passengers behind Yuri: "Go to another line. This line is closed." And turning to Yuri, still in Russian, "Passport." Yuri held his passport out, hand unsteady; the inspector took it.

Three other men in plainclothes moved suddenly from among the onlookers to within inches of him. "You are planning to leave, citizen?" The shortest of them took Yuri's elbow, and the others closed in on him, blocking his movement. "There has been a change in plans, Doctor Karpeyko." The small man spoke with heavy irony. "Come." They moved in a phalanx away from the customs tables. There was curiosity among the onlookers.

It happened so swiftly, Jenny had no time to think. "What are you *doing?*" she cried after the now swiftly moving men. "That's my *husband*, you crazy bastards! We're trying to make a plane!"

But before she was able to take more than two steps toward the men hurrying Yuri through the crowd, she felt talonlike fingers holding her arm: Gideon's.

"Come." Rachel muttered the command. "Come!" Gideon shoved her toward the inspection cubicle toward which she had been heading when Yuri was seized. She looked back, and for a moment she could see his face, pale, filled with wild despair, hopeless, wide-eyed, but still defiant— a face so distorted, it would come to haunt her. She thought his lips formed "Zhenny!" but he was too far away to hear. Her two Israeli cousins kept moving her toward the booth. The customs inspector made

no attempt to interfere with their progress. In the booth, a stony-faced blond matron reached under her sable, felt her clothes perfunctorily. "This way out." As she emerged, Rachel took hold of one of her arms and Gideon the other; they had her pinioned and raced her along the great wide-windowed hall toward the Pan Am gate.

14

As often happened in those days, at the moment the plane's wheels left the ground at Sheremetyevo, the passengers applauded, Americans rejoicing over their departure from suffocation; they could breathe again, this was the moment of their return to their known world, too long unappreciated. The shopworn word was freedom, but Jenny, weeping through the applause, thought she might now understand it, at least faintly. She was right, and so was Martin, she thought bitterly, holding one consoling, motherly arm about a now weeping Yelena, her own tears still at full stream. It was a *shitty* country.

Gideon and Rachel were silent, pale, sitting together, withdrawn. They had had a close call. At last Rachel, looking like walking death, came to join Jenny and Yelena and bent over them. "I want to apologize for dragging you off like that, Jenny. But one must know when to withdraw. Don't weep, don't weep. Yelena, you must be brave. We'll keep trying. We must. At least you and your mother are both free." She patted Jenny's hand like a grandmother, as though she understood everything, and kissed Yelena's cheek, as the pilot's voice crackled in perfect English over the intercom: "Ladies and Gentlemen, welcome aboard Pan American flight 102 . . . Our flying time to Copenhagen will be three hours and fifteen minutes and we'll be flying at an altitude . . ."

Tammy and her troupe were continuing on to New York, but Jenny, the Israelis, and Yelena deplaned in Copenhagen. Gideon bought them tickets on the next plane to Vienna; they were obliged to wait almost four hours for that plane.

After a bit Jenny headed for the phones. She hoped she could handle it coolly, be in complete control of herself. "Marty," she planned to say efficiently, "it's been a day of ups and downs. We got Cleo. We got

Yelena. The only one we didn't get was Yuri. Two out of three. Not bad. Getting the women was a coup, wasn't it?" Marty must never suspect a thing.

The phone in her booth rang. "Ready with New York."

"Marty? Marty? How the hell are you?"

"Fine. Never better. I'm actually up and around. What are you doing in Copenhagen? I was coming out to Kennedy in a few hours to meet you."

"No, no. Not yet. I have to go to Vienna."

"What for?"

"Oh, Jesus, Marty, what can I tell you? I can't—I can't—It's been murder, Marty, just murder—" Her words dissolved into a wail, the wail to tears, tears flooding her eyes, keeping her from words. She tried to talk, tried to form Marty's name, as if that would save her somehow—a child badly hurt, reaching for solace, not finding it. "Marty, I can't talk about it. I can't. Stay where you are, I'll call in a little while." Sobbing, she hung up.

An hour later she composed herself and called again, and this time did better. She told him what she had rehearsed. They were going to Vienna to bring Yelena to her mother. To tell Cleo what had happened.

Martin was no fool. Her tears, her jumbled words, and the memory of that man's voice in the hotel in Minsk fell together. He knew everything she intended not to tell him. He had plenty of time to ponder, to separate the threads of the braid, to feel the pain, and, yes, the sympathy. For Martin Singer was an extraordinary man, and since his prostate surgery he had faced extraordinary challenges. He understood Jenny's needs and nature. He loved her and needed her; as long as he had the gift of life, there would have to be compromises, something he had avoided facing. A man entering his sixth decade had to learn to make peace however he could. Fair was fair. He'd had his share of women. He'd had Jenny as no other man would or ever could. He still had her in his way. Who could tell how many years he had left? The threat of metastasis, goddamn cells running wild, hung like the sword of Damocles. Whatever had happened to her on this rescue mission, he would have to manage it, absorb it somehow. He'd have to. It was not a matter of forgiving her trespasses. Jenny was not an entirely tame creature, and there'd be other trespasses. No question. He would manage. Yes, you have to know when to settle. Thirty-eight million dollars and this. There'd be great pain, there *was*

pain now, but he had handled pain before. For him, Jenny was all of it. He could not conceive of living without her.

The bedraggled and exhausted quartet looking for Cleo arrived at Dreher-strasse, on Vienna's outskirts. Jenny saw first the huge red cross embla-zoned on the dining hall roof. High-rise apartments and open fields sur-rounding the place gave it an air of hostility and inconsequentiality; stiff Austrian police huddled in their tiny booths; the wire enclosure about the huge establishment to keep strangers out made it look like a prison rather than a place of refuge. At the video-controlled gate with its ominous jag-ged spikes, they heard only the taxi motor, the cackling of chickens, and the baaing of sheep from the nearby fields.

Gideon had half an hour's frustrating argument with disembodied elec-tronic voices booming challenges. At last he was invited in.

"You alone," the voice droned in German. The gate hummed to the side electronically.

Dovid, the chubby camp director, told the Austrian guards the moment he set eyes on Gideon that, yes, they must let them all in; that was Rachel Aron out there. Herself. A great woman. Hurry, thank you.

Dovid watched as they entered his small office. "*Shalom*. Please sit down." He shook Yelena's hand first, apologizing to Rachel. "The client comes first, Mrs. Aron. Let me see, now." He looked through sheets of paper on his desk. "From Minsk. Mmmm. Yes, here. Karpeyko, Cleo. She wants to go to America. She's expecting her daughter *and* her husband. So where's the husband?"

They told him. He sent for the camp doctor, a muscular, gruff, wiry Is-raeli with dark, sunken eyes and a shock of black hair, who arrived with a medical bag. When Dovid told him what had happened, he took a seat and waited. Dovid then asked that Cleo be sent to them.

Cleo came eagerly. She saw Yelena first and, uttering a cry of joy, em-braced her without speaking. Turning then, with growing uncertainty, "Yurochka . . . ?" But Yelena was weeping, and from the faces of the others Cleo knew it all. She looked from face to face, seeking some kind of miracle, a reprieve.

The doctor asked, "Would you like a tranquilizer, madam?"

She regarded the doctor with surprise. "I'm a physician, too, Doctor," she said. "I'll be all right. It's only . . ." And before their eyes she fell apart; she could not help herself. Furious sounds of woe and anger choked from her throat, her head was bowed, her hands loose at her sides. Jenny hastened to her, wrapped her arms about her, offered herself to weep

upon, curled a hand behind her shoulder, and murmured words Cleo could not understand.

"They are such *shits*, Cleo. I know how you feel. He's such a nice, wonderful man. Go ahead, honey, cry. I've done my crying already."

Holding her, Jenny felt herself to be Cleo, a kinship not of blood but of sheer identity. They were feeling the same thing. Almost.

The doctor gave Cleo the tranquilizer and a glass of water.

On the second day, though still dazed, Cleo was a bit more composed and seemed willing to talk of the future. If Yelena wanted so much to go to Jerusalem to work and study, all right. She would go with her to see her settled, and after she was sure, absolutely sure . . . well, she'd see. She still thought that for herself—yes, New York. In America she could help Yuri most.

From Vienna an El Al 727 took off to Ben Gurion Airport, with ninety-four Russian Jews aboard, people planning, each with his own misgivings, to make a new life in Israel. Cleo went along to look after Yelena, and Jenny went because Nettie was in Haifa and this was a terrific chance to see her daughter.

The pilot on that flight, by his own request, was Avram Yevorakh, alerted from Vienna by his old war-buddy Gideon. After takeoff, he sauntered back from the cockpit, hugged Gideon, and bowed to Jenny, who at first didn't realize who he was. He kidded her. "You hov to get used to me, Tchenny." He bent and kissed her. "You must learn to recognize me. You're going to be my Mama. The wedding is Saturday night."

"Oy," Jenny said laconically. "That Nettie! My God, a wedding! Without telling her own mother! Not a word, how do you like that? I've got nothing to wear! Can't we get Marty over? Somehow? Why couldn't you two get married in New York, like civilized people? I'm the bride's mother. *We're* supposed to give . . ."

"Too late," Avram said. "Everything's arranged. It will be, how you say, 'big time.' "

"Marty's mother'll want to come, too, old Debbie, bet you anything. And how about Roger and Josh and Tammy and—Can we get enough hotel rooms in Haifa? Well, what the hell, we'll tell 'em we're UJA."

Gideon introduced Avram to Cleo and Yelena. "It turns out we all related, Avram. You now included, by marriage. One way and another."

"So. Is Jewish geography," Avram said drily. He turned to Yelena and spoke with enthusiasm. "So, Minsk cousin, you will come also to the wedding?" To Cleo: "And you? Next Saturday night—after *shabbat*. Rachel? You, too? Please?" Rachel nodded, delighting Avram.

On the tarmac at Ben Gurion the prime minister herself was there to greet the Russian newcomers on this special occasion. She had come primarily to meet her old friend Rachel Aron, who, she had been informed, was on this plane, but it was always good politics to meet a Russian planeload. Rachel, she'd heard, had been up to her usual tricks. The prime minister had come intending to tell her old friend how furious she was with her, but when she saw Rachel, she could not, and instead hugged her and thanked her for what she had done in America with UJA.

15

My dear Jenny,

Five years today—five *years!* I still see your face, I will always see it—frozen in a silent scream as if for all time. I see you in other ways, too. That helps keep me alive.

As I write, I am reminded of the old letters you told me about, from Martin's grandparents, from Rachel's mother, from my grandmother. One should carry on the tradition, don't you agree? But what a price! This letter, however, I send to your place of work, not home.

In all this time I have never received a letter from you. Like everything else here—not allowed. Cleo's two monthly letters are, for which I am grateful. I tell myself her letters come also from you. She tells me all about you and your incredible kindnesses. How can I thank you and Martin for taking her into your house, for using your influence to find her a place on the staff of such a fine hospital? This is far beyond ordinary human kindness! Since she has her license and has gone to work, her letters are shorter, more cheerful, more like my old Cleo. Of course our separation still destroys everything, but we both force ourselves against odds to hope and look to the future.

As you know, I'm allowed to write letters only twice a month and to Cleo alone, but I know she shows them to you and sends them to Yelena. This extra, forbidden letter is to *you*. It will be mailed in Moscow by someone leaving here soon. I will add a bit each day, but when this *zek* leaves, the letter must end.

You may imagine things are worse for me than they are. This is no sanatorium, the guards are not nursemaids, they are stupid and bastards and bored and cruel, but Stalin, thank God, is no more,

this is not 1948, and although I must have lost forty pounds, I am not Ivan Denisovich.

Although here we sit on three meters of permafrost, I find it not so bad for me. The five months I spent in the KGB building in Minsk were much worse. Then six months in a prison. There's no way to describe that. By the end I prayed to die. Why were they so long coming to trial? I was ready to confess to anything—anything! Of course, the trial went exactly as Pyotr Feodorovich predicted, with one element added. I had tried to leave the country illegally. No doubt about that. My fables were judged viciously anti-Soviet. Two mothers testified they had given me gifts. Perhaps they did. Cleo and I wanted the soft life. What a grim joke! No question I had a firearm on the wall of my apartment. The pharmacist at the hospital where I had been director testified that I took unnecessary amounts of morphine. I confessed it was for Father. By the time of the trial Father was dead by his own hand—Chankov's final revenge. Throughout the trial I kept thinking: why did Baryshin suddenly get permission to go to Israel, after almost four years of being refused? By the time of my trial he was gone! There could be only one answer. I was bitter at him, but I asked myself, if positions were reversed, and I could *today* assure myself that I would be reunited with my wife and daughter, would I do the same? Why not? What's Baryshin to me? What could I have been to him?

Here I practice my profession—I am the camp doctor. I have unwanted power and influence. Also I must do all the autopsies. That is not my favorite activity, since my subjects are often old friends who have been for some time in my "hospital," and as I work I'm forced to wonder whether I may one day be the cadaver. Autopsies here have strict rules. Certain causes of death are forbidden—overexposure, malnutrition, torture. Not to humiliate my friends, I head straight for the liver to find the "cause" of death. Last month we had nineteen cirrhosis and three hepatitis victims, while one poor *zek* died of overeating. Amazingly he weighed only forty kilos (eighty-eight pounds)! The camp commander is well satisfied, however, since everyone dies of causes which are permitted under the regulations. As for the living, I alone decide who is too sick to work, who is not, etc. My own food, though almost inedible, is not quite as abominable as the other *zeks* get. I'm not forced to do hard labor out in the cold; I must remain here to look after the sick and dying —mostly the latter. We have no drugs, no facilities. Nevertheless, while practicing tenth-century medicine, I'm usually able to keep warm. This is something of a triumph. Have you ever been cold in your bones for months at a time with no relief? For a while I received packages of food irregularly from "friends," who, I suspect,

were helped to send them by the Helsinki Watch committee in Moscow. Because of my sentence, they considered me an "activist," a hero of sorts. I'm not. Most of the committee men are themselves in prison or camp now, real heros. Is it worth it?

What does one do with five years? My mind first: it was impossible to keep up in pediatric hematology. My doctor "friends" were afraid to send literature, or to be connected with me in any way. So I've learned English by studying endlessly. I believe you will find this grammatical. My speaking is still not so good because I have no one to listen to, although I practice as best I can. I am slower with Hebrew because it is more difficult to get Hebrew books; they're strictly forbidden. But I have seen a few. I want to be able to speak with my Israeli granddaughter Tamar and the new baby, I hope a boy, in Jerusalem, and fluently to my cousins in New York.

More important than the mind, I have reached down into myself and have discovered my buried Jewishness. I have dug deep and learned to feel—to open myself up, to let the feeling flow, to laugh —not a controlled, intellectual laugh which I have always done, but from emotion—and, equally important, to cry. This was a difficult transformation. I had to be my own—as you say—"shrink." I think Sigmund Freud would be satisfied with my progress. Most *zeks* here, especially politicals, are the opposite. They've erected steel shells around themselves. What a field day Freud would have with them! Sometimes I wonder if my own "coming out" is merely malnutrition. Nevertheless, the fact is, between my days in the forest until a certain night in the Yubeleinaya Hotel—for thirty years—I never cried. I had forgotten how. There was plenty to cry about, but I forced it away, buried it. I, my feelings, were imprisoned in a bottle. My mind was the cork.

All across the world, I discover, are people who are mine. Amazing! They are of me, and I of them. We are mirrors for each other. We recognize each other wherever we are, although we are all different and have had different cultures grafted to us.

They sent me here to be "re-educated." In a way, yes, I have been de-mythologized, de-intellectualized, de-programmed. I cry over simple things, not necessarily sad. I read, one day, in a forbidden American *Newsweek* article smuggled to us, that there was a mass gathering in New York, a demonstration at the Soviet U.N. headquarters—ten thousand kilometers from where I write these words. I saw this photograph of thousands of complete strangers carrying a huge portrait of *me* under a large sign: FREE YURI KARPEYKO! I read that each mention of my name was cheered by strangers. Martin Singer himself made a moving speech. He introduced Cleo, who said quietly to the crowd in her newly-learned En-

glish, "Help me, America. Please. Help me get my husband back."
Yelena, visiting New York for this occasion with her husband
Gideon, my little Yelena stood also to tell the people—and now me
—she has faith, faith that her dear, beloved father will come soon. I
read on. A tall woman, Jenny Singer, daughter-in-law of the late
Supreme Court justice, stylishly cloaked in sable, held the microphone and tried to talk, but could not, for weeping; it took some
time for her to compose herself. When she did, she cried out, "They
took a good man and locked him up! For being a Jew! They
trumped up a case because he was a Jew, and they call it justice. It's
a crime against me; it's a crime against you! It's a crime!" Then I
cried. I was not sad or unhappy. The opposite. My feelings tumbled. I was so moved. I still am. Can I name what I feel? How can
I? I am loved. I am missed. I am remembered! My spirit soars, although tears flow.

Christians tell us Jesus suffered and died for mankind. One Jew
of millions, but what makes Jesus special? Don't we all suffer from
time to time for mankind? Recently six million of us were put to
death—in Minsk alone, many tens of thousands, including my
mother. Whenever Man loses patience with himself, he kills Jews—
one or six million. He sends them to gulags, burns them in public
squares, calls them traitors or heretics or worse. If they were to run
out of Jews, whom would they have to crucify and burn and gas but
each other? Thus we save them! And Jesus gets all the credit!

I have five months to go in this sumptuous Siberian sanatorium.
My job is to live through them. My five-year, state-paid vacation
draws at last to a close. I am of no further use to the authorities, so
perhaps they'll let me go. With Father's suicide, Chankov must be
satisfied. I hope so. It has been hinted to me that once I am
released, it's not impossible I'll receive an exit visa. Better late than
never. Will we ever see each other again? Will I see Cleo, Yelena?

This may seem strange: you once said you did not like my country. Would I like yours? I hear of many Soviet citizens who settled
there but are miserable in the U.S.A. Don't most of us like the injustices we are used to? Or willingly put up with them? You put up
with racism, poverty, fight unjust wars; you accept exploitation, unemployment, recessions. We put up with other things. The Israelis
put up with their terrible insecurity—Arabs all around them, among
them—opposition, even hatred, from most of the world, a life full of
uncertainty, bureaucracy—yes, and also racism. So we each cherish
our faults, understand them, while the faults of others are the work
of some foreign devil. Here in this camp I no longer have palpitations—but when I begin to think about my life in America, they
come again! It makes no sense. *Feeling,* fear of the unknown.

I am not likely to be delighted, if ever I get there, except to see Cleo. Cleo, I believe, is not "happy" in America and never will be. So what to do? What choice? To start again in America at the age of fifty-one! Can you imagine if you and Martin had to move to Moscow? I hear those who have gone to Israel have similar stories.

Our children, that's something different. Yelena accepts her new life; she embraces it. She has an Israeli husband she adores, a baby girl who's a *sabra*, and the work she loves. But Cleo and I—Cleo has written me this, too—we are so deeply Soviet, so much part of our own place, our own city, that all we can hope for in our exile is some relief from pain—narcotics: a favorable job; money, which Cleo now has; even pleasant new associates. But until we die, deep within us we will be the lost souls of our generation. It's no tragedy. We'll be gone in twenty or thirty years. You hate my country. If ever I am so lucky as to leave it, I will miss it more than you can understand. My passion is here, my soul is here. Still, I will leave if I can.

Don't think me ungracious, I beg. You are the only person in the world to whom I dare to tell the entire truth of my feelings, feelings I dare not share with Cleo—why make things harder for her by reinforcing her complaints? I do the opposite.

Greetings to Martin, whom I'm sorry I never met, and to your delightful son, whom I met only too briefly. Perhaps we'll be lucky. I hope. I hope to come to America. We are not simple, are we? I am a mass of contradictions. Aren't most of us? In spite of all my misgivings, I am not ashamed to hope. It keeps me going. The *zek* is leaving today—March 16, 1979.

Yurochka

16

ON SEPTEMBER 29, 1980, Yuri Ivanovich Karpeyko, a nonperson camping in the Markov flat, received a call that he had been granted permission to emigrate, even though many fewer permits were being given now in the new atmosphere since Afghanistan and the Olympics in Moscow. After satisfying all the requirements of OVIR, on the day before his fifty-second birthday, he, together with three others leaving Minsk that day, boarded the train to Warsaw, where they were to change trains. The following morning he arrived at South Station, Vienna, a gaunt, tall man, hatless despite the cool autumn weather, wearing only the cast-off suit of his friend Tolya Markov, which hung comically loose on his bony frame. All his hair was gone.

After the Austrian security police, he was the first to step uncertainly from the train to the platform, looking about, expecting to be met by the Israeli from the Jewish Agency, who came to pick up emigrants. There, gathered to meet him, running to meet him as soon as they saw him, were his radiant wife Cleo, looking her most stunning, dressed like an American woman for the occasion by her cousin Jenny; his daughter Yelena and son-in-law Gideon, who had come with their six-year-old daughter Tamar, and a four-month-old baby boy in blue bunting, in Yelena's arms—from Jerusalem; and three cousins—Martin and Jenny Singer from New York, and Rachel Aron, who in her eighty-first year had traveled from Savyon. The strange man they had come to greet was smiling and weeping at the same time, swept by what he felt. In addition to tears and laughter there were cries of "Happy Birthday" in three languages, and "Yurochka," and kisses and hugs, and everyone trying to speak at once. *Daddy! Yurochka! Doctor Karpeyko!*

Yelena said in a small voice, "Daddy, meet your new grandson. He is

called Uri. I hope you don't mind." Yuri touched the new face with one waggling finger, his eyes gleaming with pleasure.

In the lull, one of those sudden silences that cannot be explained, six-year-old Tamar Aron, who had been staring wide-eyed at him, tugged her mother's skirt, whispering in Hebrew, "Mama, mama, is that Grandpa? Why is he crying?"

Yelena watched her father in amazement; he made no attempt to conceal what he felt. It was not like Daddy at all. She had never seen him cry.

Gideon, the child's father, lifted the blond little girl, whose features and coloring were more German than Israeli, and said, "Yes, Tamar. Yes. Why don't you give Grandpa a kiss?"